THE WESTERN STORY

THE
WESTERN
STORY

A Chronological Treasury

Edited and Introduced

BY

JON TUSKA

University of Nebraska Press
Lincoln and London

Acknowledgments for previously
published work appear on pages vii–viii.

Published by arrangement with
the Golden West Literary Agency.

Library of Congress
Cataloging-in-Publication Data

The western story : a chronological
treasury / edited and
introduced by Jon Tuska.
p.   cm.
ISBN 0-8032-4428-2 (cl : alk. paper)
1. Western stories.   2. West (U.S.)—Social
life and customs—Fiction.
I. Tuska, Jon.
PS648.W4W46   1995
813′.087408—dc20
94–46857
CIP

The texts of the stories contained in this work,
as well as all the editorial matter,
adhere as closely as possible to the
original manuscripts of all the authors included.

For Willis G. Regier,
to whom this new book
owes its life.

Contents

ACKNOWLEDGMENTS

BRAND, Max. "Werewolf" first appeared in *Western Story Magazine*. Copyright ©
1926 by Street & Smith Publications, Inc. Copyright © renewed 1954 by Dorothy
Faust. Acknowledgment is made to Condé Nast Publications, Inc., successors-in-
interest to Street & Smith Corporation. Reprinted by arrangement with the Golden
West Literary Agency. All rights reserved.

BOWER, B. M. "Bad Penny" first appeared in *Argosy*. Copyright © 1933 by Frank A.
Munsey Publications, Inc. Copyright © renewed 1961 by Dele Newman Doke. Reprinted by arrangement with the Golden West Literary Agency. All rights reserved.

HAYCOX, Ernest. "Blizzard" first appeared in *Collier's*. Copyright © 1939 by the
Crowell Collier Corporation. Copyright © renewed 1967 by Jill Marie Haycox. Reprinted by arrangement with the Golden West Literary Agency. All rights reserved.

DAWSON, Peter. "Retirement Day" first appeared in *Western Tales*. Copyright © 1942
by Popular Publications, Inc. Copyright © renewed 1970 by Dorothy S. Ewing. Reprinted by arrangement with the Golden West Literary Agency. All rights reserved.

FLYNN, T. T. "'What Color Is Heaven?'" first appeared under the title "Those Fighting Gringo Devils" in *Dime Western*. Copyright © 1942 by Popular Publications,
Inc. Copyright © renewed 1970 by T.T. Flynn. Copyright © 1995 by Thomas B.
Flynn, M.D. Reprinted by arrangement with the Golden West Literary Agency. All
rights reserved.

CLARK, Walter Van Tilburg. "The Wind and the Snow of Winter" first appeared in *Yale
Review*. Copyright © 1944 by the Trustees of Yale University. Copyright © renewed
1972 by Robert M. Clark. Reprinted by arrangement with International Creative
Management in association with the Golden West Literary Agency. All rights reserved.

JOHNSON, Dorothy M. "A Man Called Horse" first appeared in *Collier's*. Copyright ©
1949 by the Crowell Collier Corporation. Copyright © renewed 1977 by Dorothy M.
Johnson. Reprinted by arrangement with McIntosh and Otis, Inc., in association
with the Golden West Literary Agency. All rights reserved.

SAVAGE, Les, Jr. "The Shadow in Renegade Basin" first appeared under the title
"Tombstones for Gringos" in *Frontier Stories*. Copyright © 1950 by Fiction House.
Copyright © renewed 1978 by Marian R. Savage. Copyright © 1995 by Marian R.
Savage. Reprinted by arrangement with the Golden West Literary Agency. All rights
reserved.

L'AMOUR, Louis. "War Party" first appeared in *The Saturday Evening Post*. Copyright © 1959 by the Curtis Publishing Company. Copyright © renewed 1987 by the Curtis Publishing Company. Reprinted by permission of the Curtis Publishing Company and arrangement with the Golden West Literary Agency. All rights reserved.

HENRY, Will. "The Tallest Indian in Toltepec" first appeared in SONS OF THE WESTERN FRONTIER. Copyright © 1966 by Henry Wilson Allen. Copyright © renewed 1994 by Dorothy H. Allen. Reprinted by arrangement with the Golden West Literary Agency. All rights reserved.

KELTON, Elmer. "Desert Command" was adapted by Jon Tuska from sections of THE WOLF AND THE BUFFALO and first appeared in the first edition of this book. Copyright © 1980 by Elmer Kelton. Reprinted by permission of Doubleday & Company and Elmer Kelton and by arrangement with the Golden West Literary Agency. All rights reserved.

OLSEN, T. V. "Jacob's Journal" first appeared in *Louis L'Amour's Western Magazine*. Copyright © 1994 by T. V. Olsen. Acknowledgment is made to the Dell Magazines division of Bantam Doubleday Dell. Reprinted by arrangement with the Golden West Literary Agency. All rights reserved.

HASELOFF, Cynthia. "Redemption at Dry Creek" appears here for the first time. Copyright © 1995 by Cynthia Haseloff. Published by arrangement with the Golden West Literary Agency. All rights reserved.

Introduction

I

The most fundamental observation I can make about the Western story, whether in film or in fiction, is that it is impossible — absolutely impossible — to *generalize* on the subject. It is quite simply too vast and too varied a domain of human endeavor. Most of the critical works written on the Western story, because of this vastness, have tended to confine themselves to a few representative works or authors and on this basis to draw all manner of conclusions by inductive reasoning. This is fashionable, I supposed, because it is easy; but it is scarcely reliable. The blocks of quotations on which Christine Bold in SELLING THE WILD WEST: POPULAR WESTERN FICTION 1860–1960 (Indiana University Press, 1987) based her critique of Zane Grey's view of the American West come mostly from books he did not write. My favorite novel by Zane Grey which was not entirely his work — first published in serial form in 1925 as "Desert Bound" and much later in book form as CAPTIVES OF THE DESERT (Harper, 1952) — was written in rough draft by Grey's secretary/companion in the mid 1920s, Millicent Smith, and only polished for publication by Grey! This is one example, but one among thousands, that the deeper you probe into questions of authorship the more complex the issue becomes. Above all, in the history of the development of the Western story in the 20th Century, most often authors merely proposed while editors and publishers instructed them in what was permitted, what was wanted, what was forbidden, what was unacceptable, and in some cases even substantially edited, abridged, or even rewrote what had been submitted prior to publication.

The second observation I would make about the Western story is that there have been as many views of the American West in the last two and a half centuries as there have been authors, screenwriters, and film directors to project them, with the usual interference from the representatives of the money men: the editors and marketing departments in publishing, the front office and film producers in motion pictures.

Beyond all this — and the one conclusion of which I am certain in a very uncertain terrain — would be that the Western story constitutes the single most important literary movement in the history of the United States and the only unique body of literature which this country has contributed to the wealth of world culture. The Western story is unique to this country because of where it is set: in the American West. There was no place in all history quite like it before and there is no place quite like it now. But this does not mean that the origins of the Western story are easy to trace. They are not. It is so because in its way the Western story grew up with our nation and passed through all those painful periods of internal or external conflict which have shocked, torn, and divided, as well as united and made bold and visionary, the people of our land. How else could it have been for a nation of so many nations?

The West of the Western story is an imaginary West. It draws its life blood from the belief — even now — that there can be a better way and that, if we have the grit of character and the fortitude needed to endure the ordeal, we shall find it. Conventions in the Western story have changed, what marketing departments say is wanted, what editors claim is allowable have changed in the past as they will in the future, but not this. This can never change because if once a people lose faith in themselves the result is no different than when an individual does. Having spent the better part of my life concerned in one way or another with the Western story, that is the conclusion to which I have come. It is why the Vietnam War years so hurt the Western story — we could see only the tragedy of our nation's past, the toll in human lives, the suffering, and not the other side, the fact that what the American frontier experience offered from its beginning, and still offers today, is a second chance — indeed, a third, and a fourth, and a fifth chance. Nor has the frontier really closed. The Western story has kept it open and real and available to us and the hope that it holds out.

The Western story at base is a story of renewal and that is what has made it so very different from any other form of literary enterprise. It is refreshing, even revitalizing, in these days of a medically over-educated culture obsessed with health and terrified of old age and dying to behold once again generations of Americans to which such obsessions and terrors meant nothing. It is spiritually encouraging in these days of political correctness, timidity, and herd-notions such as one-settlement culture which wants everyone to believe in a lock-step approach to life to contemplate those generations where individual, cultural, and ethnic differences were abundant, where not one culture but many co-existed even if warfare between them was unceasing. We have benefited from that time. There is no one idea and no one cause that can possibly ever win endorsement from everybody. We still live now with that reality of the frontier as part of our social existence.

Above all, the greatest lesson the pioneers learned from the Indians is with us still: that it is each man's and each woman's *inalienable* right to find his own path in life, to follow his own vision, to achieve his own destiny — even should one fail in the process. There is no principle so singularly revolutionary as this one in the entire intellectual history of the Occident and the Orient before the American frontier experience, and it grew from the very soil of this land and the peoples who came to live on it. It is this principle which has always been the very cornerstone of the Western story. Perhaps for this reason critics have been wont to dismiss it as subversive and inconsequential because this principle reduces their voices to only one among many. Surely it is why the Western story has been consistently banned by totalitarian governments. Such a principle undermines the very foundations of totalitarianism and collectivism because it cannot be accommodated by the political correctness of those who would seek to exert power over others and replace all options with a single, all-encompassing, monolithic pattern for living.

The Western story is — as Frederick D. Glidden who wrote as Luke Short — once put it: an honorable entertainment. There is no other kind of literary endeavor which has so repeatedly posed the eternal questions — how do I wish to live, in what do I believe, what do I want from life, what have I to give to life? — as has this form of honorable entertainment, the *Western* story. There is no other kind of literary enterprise since Greek drama which has so invariably posed ethical and moral questions about life as a fundamental of its narrative structure, that has taken a stand and said: this is wrong, this is right. Individual authors, as individual filmmakers, may present us with notions with which we do not agree, but in so doing they have made us think again about things which the herd has always been only too anxious to view as settled and outside the realm of questioning. The Western story is the product of our frontier heritage and, if today we fall short of those who went before us in basic virtues such as courage and the hope for a second chance, it is there to remind us that those are still human possibilities.

Only when courage and hope are gone will the Western story cease to be relevant to all of us.

II

On a trip I made many years ago to Mexico, one of the books I took along for the journey was John R. Milton's THE NOVEL OF THE AMERICAN WEST (University of Nebraska Press, 1980). Now I must confess to the reader, as I did to Professor Milton in letters we exchanged, that I found his definition of what constitutes legitimate Western American fiction too narrow and exclusive. Having surveyed the entire field of fiction set in the American West, he excluded many who I would insist have made a definite and genuine artistic contribution; indeed, with the exception of Walter Van Tilburg Clark, he excluded every author whose work appears in this collection.

Notwithstanding, I enjoyed Professor Milton's book, primarily for what it does have to say about authors who I agree have enriched our American literature. Moreover, he raises a point which I feel is essential to any understanding of the nature and intention of the Western story. "To continue reviving the past in order to maintain a belief that 'those were the good old days' is an act of nos-

talgia which is eventually self-defeating,'' he wrote in the chapter he titled
"The Writer's West." "However, if we consider memory of the past to be spiritual as it conquers historical time, we then think not of a conserving memory,
not of nostalgia, but of a creatively transfiguring memory, not static but dy-
namic, its purpose to keep what is alive for future generations.'' To this I would
add my own belief that there has to be a reason for setting a story or a novel in
the American West. The land must be a character and, beyond that, the land
must be seen to influence the other characters, physically and spiritually.

For centuries the European knew what Professor Milton called "the power
of a creatively transfiguring memory.'' Just how much was brought home to me
by another book I had taken along and which I read next, Heinrich Heine's DIE
GÖTTER IM EXIL [THE GODS IN EXILE], a book which Heine first published in 1836 and then had reissued in a new edition during the years of his own
exile in Paris. There is a passage at the beginning of his book which portrays a
German knight, a hero from the Northland on a pilgrimage to Italy, espying a
statue from Classical Antiquity. I would translate it:

> It is perhaps the Goddess of Beauty, and he stands face to face across
> from her, and the heart of the young barbarian becomes secretly seized by
> the old magic. What is it? Such tapering limbs he has never seen before
> and in this marble he senses a vitalizing life, as he had found formerly in
> the red cheeks and lips and in the consummate physical sensuality of the
> peasant women in his own region. These white eyes regard him, seeming
> so filled with delight and yet at the same time so possessed by sadness that
> his breast fills with both love and compassion, compassion and love.

For Heine. as for a number of other Europeans, the gods and goddesses of
Antiquity, or at least their spirits, have never really died; they have only gone
into hiding. Just how and where and what they were doing in 1836 is the subject
of DIE GÖTTER IM EXIL. Heine rejected the traditional Judaism of his family
and he could never embrace Christianity, but his soul found sustenance in the
creatively transfiguring memory of Antiquity. The last time he was still able to
walk under his own motion, he went to the Louvre and he broke down weeping
before the feet of *Venus de Milo*. The spirit of Venus had a special meaning, a
reality of her own, for Heine.

If a contemporary European is inclined to seek an alternative culture, he has
the varied heritage of century upon century from which to draw. If he does not
like one culture, he can choose another. The contemporary American, however, is even more fortunate. He has the combined experiences of dozens of cultures transposed to the New World as well as the cultures of hundreds of Indian
nations who had ventured to this land millennia earlier. Yet, despite this embar-
rassment of riches, there are many Americans who are only able to look back
toward Europe with love and yearning. In the words of our editor on the first
edition of the ENCYCLOPEDIA OF FRONTIER AND WESTERN FICTION

(McGraw-Hill, 1983) edited by Jon Tuska and Vicki Piekarski when he learned we lived in Oregon: "But doesn't civilization end at the Jersey border?" However, for me, culture like civilization is a nebulous word and should never be associated with a place, *any* place. It is, to the contrary, descriptive of an inner state.

The European was very early shaped by an urban culture. Elysium, the Islands of the Blest in the Western Ocean, along with the Garden of Eden of the Semites were replaced quickly enough by the city state, the grandeur of Rome in the Augustan age, St. John's New Jerusalem, and St. Augustine's City of God. Living in Portland I can look out the wrap-around windows of the sun room which adjoins the Golden West room and see little other than trees and the garden below; but it is only a short distance to the cold beaches on the Pacific Ocean, or snow-topped Mount Hood, or the high desert. The American West has made for an unique kind of love affair, one Willa Cather evoked in the section I took from O PIONEERS! (Houghton Mifflin, 1913) and titled "The Wild Land" when she wrote of Alexandra that . . .

> For the first time, perhaps, since that land emerged from the waters of geologic ages, a human face was set toward it with love and yearning. It seemed beautiful to her, rich and strong and glorious. Her eyes drank in the breath of it, until her tears blinded her. Then the Genius of the Divide, the great, free spirit which breathes across it, must have bent lower than it ever bent to a human will before. The history of every country begins in the heart of a man or a woman.

And so, too, the history of a culture.

However divergent from each other they may have been or may continue to be, the multitudinous American cultures underwent a common fate, what historians call the American frontier experience. It did, of course, mean something different to almost every person who underwent it, as it has to virtually everyone who has come to write about it; but it is this unifying notion — the American frontier experience — which is at the heart of all the fiction I have assembled for this collection, the American frontier experience as it was historically and as it will always be in our hearts and our souls.

III

Comparing the contents of this second edition with the first, it will be noted that precisely one half of the stories are different. In part this reflects the variety and advanced scope of my reading as well as rectifying serious omissions in the first edition. With over 100,000 copies in print of that edition, it should be easy enough to find, and it is also available from Dove Audio.

One thing I have found is that with deepened experience and reading, selecting stories becomes not easier but more difficult. It is very much akin to when I set out to acquire all the issues of the periodical which began as *The Lariat Story*

Magazine (8/25) and ceased as *Lariat Story Magazine* (Spring, 50). In the beginning issues were swiftly added as I encountered them because I had so few. But when I got down to the last ten, and then five, issues to make a complete run, the quest became far more arduous.

Different stories by some of the same authors have been substituted. One of the reasons for doing this is that I have decided to limit this survey to stories which appeared between the years 1892 and 1994, a little over a hundred years. The categories for the narrative structures found in the Western story in the first edition reflected the three we had devised for the first edition of the ENCYCLOPEDIA: the formulary Western, the romantic historical reconstruction, and the historical reconstruction. For the second edition of the ENCYCLOPEDIA we have refined these categories to only two: the traditional Western story and the historical Western story. So, accordingly, those are the distinctions used in the second edition of this collection.

The traditional Western story does not begin with one particular book or story, but for the sake of convenience I prefer to regard it for the present purpose as ideally embodied in Owen Wister's THE VIRGINIAN (Macmillan, 1902). In the previous edition, Wister's first story to feature the Virginian was dated 1900 and this date derived from the appearance of "Hank's Woman" in his collection, THE JIMMYJOHN BOSS AND OTHER STORIES (Harper, 1900). For the present edition "Hank's Woman" has been restored to the way it appeared in *Harper's Weekly* in the issue for August 27, 1892. In it Lin McLean, the subject of Wister's first novel, is the narrator of the events surrounding the marriage of Hank and Willomene. In the revised version, this role of narrator is given instead to the Virginian who was, by then, the character Wister favored and whose story after it appeared in book form won him a Pulitzer Prize and has never been out of print since.

Rather than the excerpt from Mark Twain's ROUGHING IT (American Publishing Company, 1872) which I titled "Jack Slade, Desperado," I have substituted "The Californian," a story from 1893 which subsequently was published in *Harper's Monthly*. It makes an interesting contrast with the Bret Harte story I have chosen for this second edition, "Three Vagabonds of Trinidad," in which the central characters are three social outcasts. Harte noted on this story which he prepared to appear in a *Punch* supplement that he had begun it on February 1, 1900 in London and completed it February 14, 1900 at Camberley. In "Salomy Jane's Kiss," a similarly late story from 1897 and the one included in the first edition, Harte might be accused of the slightest hint of romantic sentimentality. That is not the case here where it is with a far more critical, albeit still humorous, eye that he portrays Californian society in the days following the Gold Rush. I have retained Frederic Remington's "A Sergeant of the Orphan Troop" which first appeared in *Harper's Monthly* in August, 1897, for the reasons cited in the Preface to that story. However, the year in the first edition was given as the succeeding year because that was the year it appeared in book form in CROOKED TRAILS (Harper, 1898).

Until recently, authors had three markets for a Western story and of these three — magazine or newspaper publication, book publication, and low-price reprint book editions — magazines usually paid them best. But this also meant that an author's story would be submitted to the possible intervention of at least two editors, neither of whom would necessarily have the same notion of what was or was not acceptable to the market which he or she served. That is why, in some cases, such as "'What Color Is Heaven?'" by T.T. Flynn and "The Shadow in Renegade Basin" by Les Savage, Jr., I have had to restore the stories to the original manuscript versions to publish them as their authors wrote them. Just why this has so often been the case is something I intend to address presently.

When W.H. Hutchinson first published what would become the introduction to his collection of short stories by Eugene Manlove Rhodes under the title "Virgins, Villains and Varmints" in the *Huntington Library Quarterly* in August, 1953, shortly thereafter Bernard DeVoto in his "The Easy Chair" column subtitled "Phaëton on Gunsmoke Trail" in *Harper's* in December, 1954, commented that "back in 1938 I pointed out that only Gene Rhodes had succeeded in making first-rate fiction out of the cattle business. The statement still stands." The prior occasion was DeVoto's Introduction to THE HIRED MAN ON HORSEBACK: MY STORY OF EUGENE MANLOVE RHODES (Houghton Mifflin, 1938) by Rhodes's widow, May Davison Rhodes. Rhodes has always had his advocates, and I imagine always will. Hutchinson, following publication of his A BAR CROSS MAN: THE LIFE AND PERSONAL WRITINGS OF EUGENE MANLOVE RHODES (University of Oklahoma Press, 1956), was able to convince Oklahoma to reissue mostly in hard cover reprint editions the major novels Rhodes had first written as magazine serials, principally for *The Saturday Evening Post*.

The first edition of this book has been used widely in the school adoption market, primarily for undergraduate and graduate courses in Western American fiction. Just how widely was brought home to me during the brief hiatus between the original Mentor Books edition from New American Library and the trade paperback edition from the University of Nebraska Press when I received numerous urgent telephone calls from enterprising professors who had been able to locate me to ask about a new edition. I used it myself more than a decade ago in my class "Images of the American West" at various colleges and universities when I had the luxury to devote some of my time to teaching. However, my students invariably would complain about the archaic style and ponderous literary allusions in the story by Rhodes included in the first edition, "The Bird in the Bush," which first appeared in *Red Book* in April, 1917; and these complaints were echoed and reechoed in letters I received from readers and professors. Therefore, while it has been done with regret, I have omitted Rhodes from the second edition. I agree with Robert Easton, whose THE HAPPY MAN (Viking, 1943) is one of the imperishable literary efforts depicting 20th-Century ranch life in California, that Rhodes is in his way utterly authentic. However, I also suspect enjoyment of his work since the early 1930s has been an acquired taste — perhaps it always was.

Because this time around I have designed the contents of this book to present the Western story in a chronological fashion, the order of some of the stories which have been retained has been changed. "The Last Thunder Song" by John G. Neihardt, first published in *The Overland Monthly* in the October, 1904 issue and included in Neihardt's story collection, THE LONESOME TRAIL (Lane, 1907), and again in his INDIAN TALES AND OTHERS (Macmillan, 1925), was first brought to my attention by Jack Schaefer who included it in his anthology, OUT WEST (Houghton Mifflin, 1955). It is now where it belongs chronologically with the earlier stories; but it is also a transitional story leading to the much different tone to be found in Western fiction by Willa Cather, Zane Grey, and Max Brand's Indian novels. Neihardt, as is pointed out in the Preface to his story, did not include some of his finest early stories in either of the two collections he published, but even before the first decade of the 20th Century was over he was already promulgating a vision of the American Indian that would still seem iconoclastic more than fifty years later when Will Henry published FROM WHERE THE SUN NOW STANDS (Random House, 1959).

The first edition concluded with "Candles in the Bottom of the Pool" by Max Evans which first appeared in *South Dakota Review* (Autumn, 1973). Little that Max has written since that story has approached the sad and haunting novel of modern range life he produced in THE HI-LO COUNTRY (Macmillan, 1961), whereas Louis L'Amour, Will Henry, Elmer Kelton, T.V. Olsen, and Cynthia Haseloff have all brought greater visibility to the narrative power and relevance of the Western story. Marc Jaffe, who succeeded Saul David as L'Amour's editor at Bantam Books, also brought Henry Wilson Allen who wrote as Will Henry and Clay Fisher to the Bantam imprint for paperback reprints of hard cover novels he had written for Harry E. Maule at Random House and Austin Olney at Houghton Mifflin. Once when Hank wrote to me in a disgruntled mood about his sales of 15 million copies compared to L'Amour's then 100 million, he mentioned that Marc, in an effort to cheer him up, had reminded Hank that at Bantam L'Amour was the mass, Will Henry the class. However, as Marc observed "about the miracle of L'Amour" in his Introduction to FOUR GREAT NOVELS OF THE WEST (Random House, 1994), "the ingredients of the miracle are not mysterious. They include a writer with great innate storytelling ability and a powerful ego to go with a powerful presence and physique; a writer with an honest drive to communicate a passion for a land and history he knew and loved. Combine this writer with a publisher whose sense of what the total marketing of paperback books — publicity, promotion, distribution —

was all about in the 1970s and '80s. The result is a publishing phenomenon, the making of a celebrity author, the sale of millions of books in paperback and hard covers, in stores and through the mails, not to speak of audio tapes, films. and TV series. This is a business phenomenon worth study. . . .''

Even in the 1990s and with the author now deceased, his titles continue to sell 5 million copies a year. I do not intend to take away from L'Amour anything of his tremendous accomplishment. He believed in himself and his work. He once told me in all seriousness that just as we were sitting there that day in his study at his home off Sunset Boulevard in Los Angeles, twenty-five years from then he would be the only Western writer presently at work who would still be read. It was perhaps not a very gracious comment, if notwithstanding a wholly characteristic one, for him to have made. The irony is that for the kind of Western story L'Amour wrote there have been dozens of more capable and more artistically talented authors of the Western story whose works may be overlooked, and the joy and satisfaction those books can bring will never be experienced, because of L'Amour's singular product identification among the reading public. As too often is the case, this product identification does not encourage readers to try other authors, but rather to remain ''loyal'' to the one brand they know and love.

If readers of this collection find new directions to pursue in their reading of the Western story because of the stories I have included, then part of my overall purpose and design will have been accomplished. I have also added two more women authors of Western fiction to Willa Cather and Dorothy M. Johnson whose stories remain from the first edition. They are B.M. Bower, one of the most popular Western writers in her time but whose life is almost more interesting than any story she ever told; and Cynthia Haseloff who, for a time, was promoted by Bantam Books as a striking new presence in the world of the Western story certain to be warmly received by anyone who enjoyed Louis L'Amour's books. Beyond this I did not want to go because Vicki Piekarski's collection, WESTWARD THE WOMEN (Doubleday, 1983), is still in print from the University of New Mexico Press and features only women authors of Western fiction and she is now at work assembling a second collection bringing together more stories by yet other women authors of the Western story from Elsa Barker and Eli(za) Colter to Janice Holt Giles and Jeanne Williams.

Of course, the literally hundreds of authors I have had to exclude for reasons of space is also a matter of profound regret, partially compensated by a revised and expanded final section on Suggested Further Reading. There are as well other anthologies and collections I have done, or which are in the planning stages, which may allow me to include many of these authors. Moreover, by devoting what time remains to an overview of the development of the Western story in this century, I am in a position at least to mention a number of other authors who have made substantial and rewarding contributions to the Western story even if I have not been able to include one of their stories. Let me also stress that it is by no means accidental that virtually every author whose work is included in this collection, with the exception of Cynthia Haseloff who came too late onto the scene, began writing for the magazine market during the Golden Age of American magazine fiction. They had to master the form of the short story in order to be published. Some of them, from Bret Harte, Owen Wister, and Frederic Remington to B.M. Bower, John G. Neihardt, and Dorothy M. Johnson, would never produce novels as fine as their short stories. Others, such as Zane Grey, Willa Cather, Elmer Kelton, and Walter Van Tilburg Clark, rarely wrote short stories as fine as their best novels. And still others, such as Max Brand, Ernest Haycox, T.T. Flynn, Peter Dawson, Les Savage, Jr., and T.V. Olsen excelled equally in both the long and short forms of the Western story.

Finally, those authors whose stories I have selected all have reputations that are secure and all of them — regardless of when they began to write — are still variously available in print at the time this second edition is published. There are numerous authors who might have a peripheral attraction for some readers of this book, just as some are perhaps more interested in the plays of John Ford than in those of William Shakespeare when it comes to the history of the British stage drama, but I have resisted all deviant impulses in arcane directions. Douglas C. Jones, in my opinion, is the finest author of historical fiction set in the American West I have ever read, but I could find no short story by him that could match the complex tapestry and magnificent artistry of SEASON OF YELLOW LEAF (Holt, Rinehart, and Winston, 1983) or GONE THE DREAMS AND DANCING (Holt, Rinehart, and Winston, 1984). But I have been able to pay tribute to him and his magnificent achievement by naming the final section of these stories after one of his most beautiful and memorable novels. For still others, whose stories are frequently found in less mainstream collections than this one, or the very new voices from the West, I can only evoke a literary historian's prerogative.

I recall once at a concert of new American music in New York City, Leopold Stokowski came out on stage, turned on a tape recorder connected to several loud speakers, and then retired to listen with the audience of assembled music critics to a recent composition for prepared tape recorder by Vladimir Ussachevsky. After all the strange electronic sounds of this piece of music had concluded and Mr. Stokowski again returned to the stage to shut off the tape recorder, one of the critics in the audience asked him if he believed what we had just heard was truly great music. "I honestly do not know," Mr. Stokowski replied, ". . . but it should be heard." When it comes to the new voices and this collection, as with the second edition of the ENCYCLOPEDIA OF FRONTIER AND WESTERN FICTION, it is perhaps best to wait until the stature and direction and talent of a particular author have had time to solidify, until his or her work has been in print long enough to give some indication of its final form, and until his or her contribution to the growing body of Western fiction has become somewhat clarified before venturing to make any critical judgment. Many of these new voices deserve to be read, but their place is not yet in "a chronological treasury" of the Western story.

IV

For the purpose of this collection, the Western story begins with the appearance in 1892 of a brace of short stories in *Harper's Weekly* by Owen Wister. These stories were set in Wyoming and, for readers, held much the same freshness and excitement as once had the stories of Bret Harte in *The Overland Monthly* or Mark Twain's books of anecdotes and reminiscences like ROUGHING IT. Frederic Remington began illustrating Wister's stories and then turned to writing and illustrating his own. It is interesting to reflect that Bret Harte was resident in England by this time, writing his stories of the American West for British readers, while John G. Neihardt was beginning to publish his own short stories in *The Overland Monthly* in which Bret Harte had first come to national attention in the 1860s. Mark Twain himself was writing for *Harper's* at the same time Wister and Remington were.

Even at this point in its history the Western story was cyclical. Prior to Wister's and Remington's emergence it had been at one of its lower ebbs. The great impetus, though, which again brought the Western story into national prominence was the publication of THE VIRGINIAN in 1902. The Virginian was a cowboy in a story without any cows, but his story was a ranch romance and its popularity established the cowboy as a worthy embodiment of the American hero. Two years later B.M. Bower's "Chip of the Flying U" was serialized in Street & Smith's *The Popular Magazine* and caused a similar literary sensation. Bower was a Westerner from Montana and, if Chip was a cowpoke with artistic proclivities and an interest in literary classics, those around him, whom Bower came to refer to as "The Happy Family," offered a wide and attractive variety of typical men of the range. Clarence E. Mulford began his series of inter-related stories about the Bar-20 crew, including Hopalong Cassidy, in 1907 in *The Outing Magazine*.

If the image of the Western hero as a loner was given much of its initial impetus by Wister in his tales about Lin McLean, the Virginian, and Scipio LeMoyne, he was no less a generative influence in creating the notion of the extended family in the traditional Western. Indeed, Wister called one of his story collections MEMBERS OF THE FAMILY (Macmillan, 1911). B.M. Bower only further solidified this direction with The Happy Family and, periodically, over the next four decades Chip Bennett and the other family members would return for yet another adventure. Hopalong Cassidy, Red Connors, Johnny Nelson, Tex Ewalt, and, later, Mesquite Jenkins in Mulford's Bar-20 saga would continue in a long series of novels and stories. Because the Bar-20 had proved so consistently popular, Mulford created a second saga with a different set of characters beginning with CORSON OF THE J.C. (Doubleday, Page, 1927).

The groundwork was thus well laid for Janice Holt Giles when she began her own saga with THE KENTUCKIANS (Houghton Mifflin, 1953), tracing the settlement of the American frontier through four generations of a Kentucky family that eventually moves West. Although scarcely in a class with Giles, Louis L'Amour subsequently created three separate series of sagas having to do with large families who migrate West. What Giles and L'Amour and myriad other authors of series of sagas having to do with large families have most in common is that they unite the formerly loose conclaves of individuals in Wister, Bower, and Mulford into actual family units bound by blood ties. If in BAR-20 THREE (A.C. McClurg, 1921), Mulford has Cassidy and Conners come to the aid of Johnny Nelson, now a rancher in his own right but still a member of their extended family, at the conclusion of MOJAVE CROSSING (Bantam, 1964) L'Amour has Tell Sackett saved from torture and death by Nolan Sackett, a distant relative and up until this point in the employ of the villains.

The unifying spirit behind these family-oriented traditional Westerns, as well as in some historical Westerns such as Giles's Kentuckian saga, is quite the same as Ralph Brauer observed in THE HORSE, THE GUN, AND THE PIECE OF PROPERTY: CHANGING IMAGES OF THE TV WESTERN (Bowling Green Popular Press, 1975) in the plethora of family and community Westerns which were featured so prominently on television in the 1960s and 1970s. "Seth Adams [of "Wagon Train"]," Brauer wrote, "and Gil Favor [of "Rawhide"] and John Kennedy ask not what you can do for truth, justice, and morality...but rather ask what you can do for the trail crew, the wagon train, the organization, the country" — or, in a word, the family. Although there is a degree of individual initiative permitted in the family-oriented Westerns, the fact remains that their major significance in the history of the Western story is the emphasis they place on collectivism as opposed to isolated individuals, their repudiation of individual freedom for co-operation within a community, their rejection of the American Indian notion that each man must seek his own vision and follow his own destiny, for which they substitute the overwhelming desire for social conformity, the search for that feeling of consensus which has so long preoccupied and eluded Americans in all generations. At the same time, this pattern in narrative structures co-exists with an ever greater feeling Americans have had of social isolation, even in urban areas. La Rochefoucauld's observation in his RE-FLECTIONS MORALES (1678) is no less trenchant today then when he wrote it: *"Nos vertus ne sont, le plus souvent, que des vices déguisés"* [Our virtues are most often nothing but our vices disguised.]

Frederick D. Glidden was an accomplished craftsman who wrote a number of monochromatic traditional Westerns. He persuaded his older brother, Jonathan H. Glidden, to try his hand at writing Western fiction, and Jonathan did so quite successfully in over 120 short stories and novelettes and fifteen book-length Western serials under the byline Peter Dawson. Fred always remained open and helpful to other writers just beginning, until in his later years physical maladies began to plague him. He was enough of a realist to joke once that, if there was so much money to be made from writing Western fiction, why then was he not a rich man? He confided to Brian Garfield, when Garfield was first starting out, that a good Western is first of all a good story and should be able to stand on its own merits no matter where it is set. Glidden warned Garfield that a Western story isn't only gunplay and horsemanship.

As an adviser Fred was never as consistent as he was as a craftsman. One day when Jonathan and his wife, Moe, were living across the road in Pojoaque, New Mexico, and Fred's wife, Butch, was also writing Western stories for Street & Smith's *Romantic Range* and Standard Magazines' *Thrilling Ranch Stories,* Butch found herself at an impasse in a story. Now, if this happened to Jon, he would come across the road and talk it over with Fred. Butch who wrote at a desk on the other side of the living room from Fred's desk posed a similar question to her husband. Even though a ranch romance was a very different kind of Western story than the kind Fred was writing, his answer to her was the same as it was often to Jon: "Just throw in some action."

The importance of these comments is that in the Western story, as Fred Glidden wrote it, the Western setting is not particularly relevant. This is again borne out in a posthumous tribute he paid Ernest Haycox in *The Call Number* (Fall, 1963-Spring, 1964). "...My favorite Haycox yarns don't lean on a known time or place," Glidden wrote. "In these stories, I suspect Haycox made his own geography, named his own towns and mountains and rivers; he peopled them with tough and abrasive characters whose only law was their self-will." The world of the traditional Western, according to this perspective, is a world of total make-believe; what charm it has is derived from the fact that it can never intersect with the real world.

It may seem a great leap from the romantic view of range life in Wyoming projected by Owen Wister in his early stories to this never-never land, but as with most literary developments it was in large part a consequence of how the Western story was marketed. By the time Zane Grey's first Western novel, THE HERITAGE OF THE DESERT (Harper, 1910), began appearing in serial installments in *The Popular Magazine* with the issue dated May 25, 1910, magazines had already been the mainstay for popular fiction of all kinds in the United States for nearly a hundred years. Ann S. Stephens had worked variously as an associate editor for *Ladies Companion,* beginning in 1837, and had joined the staff for *Peterson's Magazine* in 1841 at the time when Edgar Allan Poe was its editor. She was well known by 1850 for her magazine serials. In 1860 Irwin P.

Beadle paid Stephens $250 for the rights to reprint one of these early serials in paperback book form. This serial, MALAESKA: THE INDIAN WIFE OF THE WHITE HUNTER, became the first Beadle dime novel upon publication in June as well as a best-seller. For the next thirty years thousands of these dime novels were published, with at least thirty distinct series about various frontier heroes, including the totally fictional Deadwood Dick as well as Buffalo Bill Cody in a series based on the former buffalo hunter and showman written by a number of different authors.

As more and more publishers entered the dime novel arena, Orville J. Victor, the editor for the dime novels published by Beadle & Adams, told his writers that to stave off the competition they would have to kill off a few more Indians. "Killing a few more Indians meant, in practice, exaggerating violence and bloodshed for their own sakes to the point of an overt sadism," Henry Nash Smith observed in VIRGIN LAND: THE AMERICAN WEST AS SYMBOL AND MYTH (Harvard University Press, 1950). "By the 1890s the Western dime novel had come to hinge almost entirely upon conflicts between detectives and bands of robbers that had little to do with the ostensibly Western locales." A schoolmate of Clarence E. Mulford's recalled how as a youth Mulford would keep dime novels hidden in his desk and read them at every available opportunity. When Mulford was living in Maine and writing historical articles for *The Frontier* in the mid 1920s, Harry E. Maule, that magazine's editor, might justifiably claim that Mulford had one of the most imposing personal libraries of Western Americana in the country, and the backgrounds of his Western novels and stories might be authentic in many respects, but his plots of shoot-outs and violence came not so much from frontier history as from the tradition of the dime novel. In the novels and stories featuring Hopalong Cassidy from BAR-20 (Outing, 1907) to HOPALONG CASSIDY SERVES A WRIT (Doubleday, Doran, 1941), this character whom Mulford once described as "a cowpuncher who lived and worked in the days when the West was wild and rough and lawless; and who, like others, through the medium of the only court at hand, Judge Colt, enforced justice as he believed it should be enforced," in the course of the saga would lethally discharge Judge Colt's justice at 200 men.

By the second decade of the 20th Century, dime novel publishers were running at a loss. Production costs had kept rising. Street & Smith, in an effort to economize, revamped *Buffalo Bill Stories* into the *New Buffalo Bill Weekly* which had much shorter stories and sold for a nickel. In an alternative strategy, publishers also introduced the double-dimer. Dime novel writers were told to increase their production, i.e., "kill a few more Indians," to one and a half times the average 45,000-word length of a dime novel. These double-dimers, as the name implies, sold for 20¢. Only they didn't sell. The reading public which for over forty years had been accustomed to paying a nickel or a dime for a paperback book balked at twice the price.

In 1919, just before leaving on a trip to France, Ormond G. Smith, president of Street & Smith, told Henry Ralston to sell the *New Buffalo Bill Weekly* for whatever he could get. The real Buffalo Bill Cody had died in Denver, Colorado, on January 10, 1917 and, with his passing, interest in his ongoing adventures had waned. When Ralston found no takers, he came up with another idea which he presented to George Smith, vice-president of Street & Smith. Why not revamp the magazine into one devoted to general Western fiction and call it *Western Story Magazine*? George Smith liked the idea and gave Ralston a free hand to do just that. On July 12, 1919 the first issue of *Western Story Magazine,* dated September 5, 1919 and priced at 10¢, went on sale on newsstands.

Beneath the title was a notice that ran for the next eight weeks: "Formerly *New Buffalo Bill Weekly,*" and also a reminder that its contents were "Big Clean Stories of Western Life." Already in the first issue there was established an editor's page titled "The Roundup" and, among other things, readers were promised that "the best writers of Western adventure stories will entertain you." In large part, throughout its thirty-year history, this proved to be a truthful statement. Henry Ralston's name was still on the declaration of ownership when it was published for the last time in August, 1949.

Ralston had designed *Western Story Magazine* as a bi-weekly but by November, 1920, circulation had reached 300,000 copies per issue and George Smith decided that the time had come for the magazine to become a weekly. The first issue had featured two novelettes, two serials, five short stories, and eight feature items, which would remain more or less its basic format until it became a monthly in 1944. Among the contributors in that first issue were some of the best-known names writing Western fiction at the time, including William Mac-Leod Raine, Jackson Gregory, and Bertrand W. Sinclair. Sinclair had been the second husband of B.M. Bower. They had met when Sinclair was an untutored former cowboy presently tending bar at the old Exchange Saloon in Big Sandy, Montana. Sinclair was known locally as "Old Fiddleback." He taught Bower all he knew about cowboying, which she incorporated into her stories about Chip and the other Flying U ranch hands, and Bower in turn taught Sinclair how to write and for twenty years he went on to produce a number of Western serials and short stories for the magazine market.

As a marketing strategy, *Western Story Magazine* was a brilliant invention. Novels of 85,000 words that would not sell at 20¢ could be serialized over six issues and cost an interested reader 60¢!

Zane Grey's "Desert Gold" was serialized in *The Popular Magazine* in 1913 after which he began selling first serial rights to his Western novels to Bob Davis at Munsey Publications. "The Light of Western Stars" was serialized in *Munsey's Magazine* in 1913; "The Lone Star Rangers" appeared as a serial in *All-Story Cavalier Weekly* in 1914; and "The Last of the Duanes" was cut down to a novelette later that year for publication in *Argosy.* For book publication,

Grey rather clumsily fused this novelette with the serial to form THE LONE STAR RANGER (Harper, 1915). "The Desert Crucible," which became THE RAINBOW TRAIL (Harper, 1915), was serialized in *Argosy* as was "The Border Legion." Grey entered the slick magazine market with "Wildfire," serialized in *The Country Gentleman,* in 1916. Bob Davis needed someone to replace Zane Grey and he chose Frederick Faust, a California writer living in New York. He gave Faust the two *Argosy* serials by Grey to read, and asked him to write something just like them. The result was "Above the Law," a novelette featured in *All-Story Weekly* for the issue dated August 31, 1918, and now reprinted for the first time in THE COLLECTED STORIES OF MAX BRAND (University of Nebraska Press, 1994). With THE UNTAMED (Putnam, 1919) and other novels published in Munsey magazines, Faust under the pseudonym Max Brand experienced a meteoric rise in popularity.

Faust's first appearance in *Western Story Magazine* was with the serial titled "Jerry Peyton's Notched Inheritance" which began in the issue dated November 15, 1920. For *Western Story Magazine,* he created a new pseudonym, George Owen Baxter, and in succeeding years would add to this string eighteen other *noms de plume*. Faust was so prolific an author that during the 1920s he might have a serial by David Manning, a serial by George Owen Baxter, and a novelette by Max Brand all running in the same issue, and this remained the case as late as the issue dated April 2, 1932. "How did I get hold of Faust?" Frank Blackwell, the editor of *Western Story Magazine,* once recalled. "Bob Davis was over-bought. Munsey found it out, told Bob he'd have to shut off buying for as long as six months, and use up some of the stuff in the safe. Faust, always in need of money, no matter how much he made, came to me with a story. I bought it. He was mine, and mine only from there on." Thanks largely to Faust's tremendously prodigious contributions, circulation of *Western Story Magazine* increased to 2 million by 1922. The cover price was also increased to 15¢. On an average issue, Street & Smith showed a profit of $400,000. Blackwell could afford to pay Faust's rate of a nickel a word.

Faust's stories, like Grey's early Western fiction, are more archetypal psycho-dramas than realistic fiction. What events mean to the protagonists and how they affect their souls are what his stories are really about and, while he had a natural sense of fast pacing, there is little violence in his Western fiction. Much of this pacing, however, has to do with the fact that virtually all Faust's fiction is character-driven, not plot-driven, which goes a long way in explaining why he has retained his popularity over the years whereas many of his contemporaries are now all but forgotten. The violence true of the dime novels is to be found, rather, in the competitors of *Western Story Magazine,* in Fiction House's *Action Stories,* begun in 1922, in *Lariat Story Magazine,* in *Argosy,* and in *The Frontier* and *West* and *Short Stories,* the last three published by Doubleday, Page & Company. Then, as later, the better authors of the Western story, from

Max Brand, William MacLeod Raine, and Jackson Gregory to B.M. Bower, Dane Coolidge, and Ernest Haycox (who began writing for *Western Story Magazine, West,* and *The Frontier* but by 1931 had moved on into the pages of *Collier's*) eschewed violence in their stories.

Yet, before saying more on this subject, it is worth noting that violence in dime novels was never confined just to Western stories. It was a characteristic of most fiction published by dime novel publishers. The same was no less true for the pulp magazines which succeeded the dime novels on the newsstands. Violence was indigenous to all kinds of action stories. In Dashiell Hammett's RED HARVEST (Knopf, 1929), which appeared serially in *The Black Mask Magazine,* the setting is contemporary and there is so much killing that the characters, in the words of Hammett's nameless narrator, have become "blood simple." The tradition of the Western story as an occasion for violence of all kinds was carried forward in Western pulp magazines by such authors as William Colt MacDonald, James P. Olsen, T.W. Ford (pseudonym for Ford Roper), and Eugene Cunningham. MacDonald's "The Red Raider" is a four-part serial which began in the very first issue of *The Lariat Story Magazine* (the magazine soon dropped *"The"* from its name because there was a Western poetry magazine at the time titled *The Lariat*).

Eugene Cunningham became a featured author at *Lariat Story Magazine* as early as 1926 in which year appeared the first installment of a five-part serial titled "Burned Brands." This fictional treatment of the Lincoln County War would be published eight years later in book form as DIAMOND RIVER MAN (Houghton Mifflin, 1934). "Buck from the Border" appeared in five installments between December, 1927, and April, 1928, and was first published in book form as BORDER GUNS (Covici, Friede, 1935) under the pseudonym Leigh Carder. The reason for alternative pseudonyms in the pulp magazines was that no editor wanted two stories by the same author in a single issue if it could be avoided. Among book publishers, each house regarded an author's name as their property and so, if an author had more than one publisher, he also had to adopt the anonymity of pseudonyms. "The Trackless Bunch" by Cunningham appeared in *Lariat* in five installments in 1927 and was published as TEXAS SHERIFF (Houghton Mifflin, 1934). RIDERS OF THE NIGHT (Houghton Mifflin, 1932) first appeared as a five-part serial titled "The Mesquite Raiders" in *Lariat* from September, 1928, through the January, 1929, issue and was later reprinted in one installment in the March, 1936, issue of *Western Novel and Short Stories.* Since Jack Kelly, fiction editor at Fiction House, had been Cunningham's mentor, it is not surprising that RIDERS OF THE NIGHT is dedicated to "J.B. Kelly Editor, Publisher, Friend." In the course of this novel thirty-five men are killed and another thirty-five are known to be killed *en camera.* In the same issue of *Lariat* in which "The Mesquite Raiders" concluded a new Cunningham serial titled "Buckaroo" began. It was subsequently published as BUCKAROO (Houghton Mifflin, 1933). In this story the number of villains in need of killing is expanded to 300, taken on by three Texas Rangers who form a trio of heroes.

There is also a trio of gunfighting heroes in RIDERS OF THE NIGHT, Sandrock Tom, Three Rivers, and Happy Jack, to whom Cunningham gave the sobriquet the Three Mesquiteers. William Colt MacDonald picked up on this idea and in LAW OF THE FORTY-FIVES (Covici, Friede, 1933) added Lullaby Joslin as the third hero to the duo he had first introduced in RESTLESS GUNS (Chelsea House, 1929) of Tucson Smith and Stony Brooke. MacDonald's trio went on to appear in a long series of novels and some fifty-two "B" Western films (John Wayne starring in eight of them as Stony Brooke). MacDonald's pattern in these novels is identical with Cunningham's and he invariably has his trio riding into a community intimidated by a master villain and his minions, a situation which in Tucson Smith's words in LAW OF THE FORTY-FIVES calls for "the only law effective in this sort of case — gun law."

The West in these stories is another variation of the make-believe world to which Fred Glidden referred. Once you accept this premise, it is possible to approach critically each author of this kind of traditional Western story and to reconstruct and compare the various make-believe worlds true for each one of them, like indexing the different kinds of Martians featured in various science fiction stories in *Astounding Science Fiction* and similar pulp magazines of the period. One is free to speculate about innovations and who influenced whom, never forgetting that while the terrain may have a Western appearance the topography is imaginary and the characters components of a ritualized, conventionalized, and collective fantasy the sole function of which is to divert us from our lives and never to touch in any way the depths of the soul. As Hoot Gibson, a movie cowboy who played Stony Brooke in POWDERSMOKE RANGE (RKO, 1935), once put it to me, "People like Westerns because they always know who's gonna win." Then he smiled, a bit sadly because he had had a bitter and hard time of it. "But," he added, "it ain't that way in life." This kind of traditional Western has always been popular with a certain kind of reader, the one who prefers to know beforehand how the story must come out.

C.G. Jung in ZWEI SCHRIFTEN ÜBER ANALYTISCHE PSYCHOLOGIE [TWO ESSAYS ON ANALYTICAL PSYCHOLOGY] (Rascher Verlag, 1967) developed a concept which I believe to be helpful in understanding the meaning of stories which depend upon killing and violence as the basic plotline and even their sole reason for existence. The concept is that of the *mana-personality,* an archetype of the collective unconscious, "a being filled with an occult, conjuring capacity, or *mana,* and endowed with magical skills and powers." Jung felt compelled to warn:

One can only alter his attitude in an effort to impede being naïvely possessed by an archetype that forces him to play a role at the cost of his humanity. Possession by an archetype makes a man into a purely collective figure, after the fashion of a mask, behind which his humanity can no longer develop, but rather increasingly atrophies. One must remain conscious of the danger of falling beneath the dominant of the *mana-personality*. The danger consists not merely in the fact that one person assumes the mask of a father figure but that that person can fall victim to the same mask when it's worn by another person. In this sense, master and pupil are one and the same.

Expressed in other words and applied to the subject at hand: if we allow ourselves to believe in the existence of an avenging, killing hero, we will frequently attempt to emulate in ourselves the values we have projected onto him; and, when we do this, we become, as such a hero is, a purely collective figure, and our humanity atrophies. One strain of the *mana-personality* can certainly be traced through the kind of Western story best described in that laconic slang term: a "shoot-'em-up."

The *mana* of such a hero has already been described in Glidden's encomium for Haycox (albeit I am *not* willing to concede that he was correct in attributing this to Haycox). It is the hero's virtuous and triumphantly superior self-will. In the unfolding of the ritualized, violent competitiveness between degrees of self-willedness from Wister's THE VIRGINIAN to the ultra-violent dime novels of the 1880s and the ultra-violent paperback novels of the 1980s, the heroine must become as dehumanized and as convinced of the efficacy of violence as the only solution to social frustration as is the hero. Accepting the Virginian as a hero requires of heroine Molly Stark Wood that she condone the Virginian's placing property before friendship in the execution of his friend Steve and that, in order for the Virginian to maintain his status as a hero in the community, he must shoot and kill Trampas. The Virginian set the tone for a new generation of violent Western heroes.

In THE RANGE BOSS (A.C. McClurg, 1917) Charles Alden Seltzer, whose Western serials such as this one remained a fixture at *Argosy,* has his hero inform the heroine, an Easterner who inherits a ranch in the West, "'You'll shape up real Western — give you time.... You'll be ready to take your part, without depending on laws to do it for you — laws that don't reach far enough.'" Such a hero has to have some kind of motivation and in a later novel, SQUARE DEAL SANDERSON (A.C. McClurg, 1922), Seltzer spelled it out rather succinctly when the reader learns that Sanderson "was deliberately and unwarrantedly going to the Double A to interfere, to throw himself into a fight with persons with whom he had no previous acquaintance, for no other reason than that his chivalrous instincts had prompted him." Engaging in such a contest means that Sanderson must and will vanquish the villain.

Seltzer drew Western heroes who were grim, quiet, powerful men and this, too, became a convention in traditional Western stories. But at the same time, there were other authors with yet other views of the meaning of the West and who projected different kinds of heroes. Walt Coburn, a former cowboy raised on the Circle C Ranch in Montana, was hailed as the "cowboy author" at Fiction House in *Action Stories* and *Lariat Story Magazine*. There is an authenticity to his early stories that shows them to be cut from the same whole cloth as earlier the cowboy fiction of Andy Adams or, contemporary with Coburn, by Will James who illustrated Coburn's novelette "Riders of the Purple" in the first issue of *Lariat*.

However, if this is where matters stood in the 1920s, few aspects of the Western story failed to be affected by the onset of the Great Depression in 1930. If the 1920s proved the beginning of a Golden Age in book publishing (with some of the finest book jacket illustrations we have ever had) and in magazines, even this brightness dimmed during those dark years. To compete with *Western Story Magazine,* which was considered old-fashioned with its good, clean stories of outdoor life, Popular Publications launched *Dime Western* in late 1932 with the December issue. Walt Coburn, Gene Cunningham, Cliff Farrell, and Harry F. Olmsted, all well-established Western writers, had stories in that first issue, but so did T.T. Flynn who had been writing fiction for magazines since the mid 1920s but never until now a Western story. "The Last of the Black Tantralls" by T.T. Flynn propounded a totally unique situation for its Western protagonist: he is outlawed, surrounded on all sides by armed and hostile forces. His story is set against a fearsome country with the promise of cruelty in its harshness and darkness, an unfriendly terrain peopled by men with a grim past heading into a future made even more grim.

It is difficult today to realize how electrifying this new perspective on the Western story was at that time. *Dime Western* became sensationally successful when other Western pulp magazines were forced to cease publication. Rogers Terrill, who edited *Dime Western,* had had his early training as a writer contributing to *Action Stories*. He combined the dark vision of the isolated protagonist with violence of wholesale killing as a guideline for contributors. By the April, 1933 issue of *Dime Western* the lead novelette was "Valley of Flaming Guns" by Harry F. Olmsted, and featured stories included "Death for One" by Gunnison Steele (pseudonym for Benny Wilson Gardner), "Bullet Tally" by Walt Coburn, and "The Death Whistler," one of E.B. Mann's "Whistler" stories with the characteristic caption: "Death to the stranger who wears two guns — and whistles the Devil's requiem for those he kills!" Coburn and the others were not writing this kind of story because it was the kind of story they preferred. In fact, the titles were most often supplied by Rogers Terrill and promised blood-letting the stories didn't always deliver.

Following upon this success, *Star Western* was launched by Popular Publications with the November, 1933, issue, again with a T.T. Flynn story in it. *Western Story Magazine* had to cut its price from 15¢ to 10¢ but it stayed at 128 pages. *Star Western* cost 15¢ but it offered 160 pages. "Hell's Half Acre" by T.T. Flynn was joined with stories such as "Lawless Range" by Eugene Cunningham, "Nester Luck" by Walt Coburn, and "Brave Men Can Die!" by Gunnison Steele.

It cannot be emphasized too much that from the time of Orville J. Victor at Beadle & Adams to the present day, authors of Western fiction most often have had to write the kinds of stories editors and publishers tell them to write. Fred Glidden, recently married and living in Santa Fe, perused *Dime Western* and *Star Western* and was convinced he could write a story as well as any he had read. Since he had had first-hand experience living and working in the arctic, he tried his hand at North-Westerns. They were met by rejection. Fred and Butch were renting two adjacent adobe houses which they used as a combined unit from Brian Boru Dunne. Fred asked Dunne if he knew of an agent. Dunne didn't, but he had another tenant who was a writer and who had a good one and he would ask him. That writer was T.T. Flynn. Marguerite E. Harper was the agent. She told Fred to redraft his North-Westerns as Westerns. In October, 1934 Fred sent Harper a story titled "Six-Gun Lawyer" and signed it F.D. Glidden. On April 17, 1935 Harper sold that story to *Cowboy Stories,* a pulp magazine Street & Smith had acquired from the bankrupt Clayton House for the princely sum of $100. It appeared in the August, 1935, issue.

Harper told Fred she was concerned about his name. F. Orlin Tremaine, who had come to Street & Smith with *Cowboy Stories,* complained that it didn't sound very "Western." At first Fred thought of Lew Short — he wanted something "short" and memorable like Max Brand — and finally settled on Luke Short without realizing that this was the name of an actual gunman and gambler in the Old West. When Butch started writing Western romances, Harper named her Vic Elder (her maiden name was Florence Elder); and, when Jonathan started writing stories and she sold his first one to Street & Smith's *Complete Stories,* she named him Peter Dawson after an actual brand of Scotch whiskey she liked to drink.

This, then, was the climate in which violence in the Western story reigned supreme. While there had been violence prior to Cunningham and MacDonald in the dime novels, it was again present in ever greater abundance and the death of a human being in these stories was treated with a casual indifference. MacDonald's Mesquiteer novels consist of one chapter after another of blood-letting until the final chapter in which the master villain himself is destroyed. Because it is all make-believe anyway, such violence is possibly no more meaningful than it is in theatrical cartoons. But the impact it had on many Western writers was far from salutary. In Norman A. Fox's SILENT IN THE SADDLE (Dodd, Mead, 1945), Fox's hero Brad Seldon reflects after a shoot-out that he will never know "a moment's regret for that killing" and in Louis L'Amour's TO TAME A LAND (Fawcett, 1955) L'Amour's hero, Rye Tyler, observes that "for once I didn't feel bad about a shooting."

To echo a character from SMOKE OF THE GUN (Signet, 1958) by John S. Daniels (pseudonym for Wayne D. Overholser), "Murder was a treadmill. Once you started it, you couldn't stop it, and you couldn't get off." It would seem to be a law of group psychology that what was at first sensational upon repetition becomes routine and even boring. In Standard Magazines' line of superhero Western pulps, from *Texas Rangers* which was launched in 1936 and featured stories about Texas Ranger Jim Hatfield, to *Range Riders Western, Masked Rider Western,* and *Rio Kid Western,* the general plotline was always the same: a superhero dispatching gang after villainous gang. Leslie Scott, who created Jim Hatfield and wrote many of the Hatfield stories, also created Walt Slade, Texas Ranger for Standard Magazines' *Thrilling Western Stories* and began a second series of stories with this plotline. Gene Cunningham's Texas Ranger heroes had spawned a host of imitators.

Under the Bradford Scott byline, Scott wrote an additional 125 entries in the Walt Slade series for Pyramid Books in the 1950s. Although he did expand some of his pulp novelettes for this book series, the plotline remained the same. Slade is joined by two friends, Estevan (a Mexican knife-man whose dialogue is generally confined to "my blade thirsts") and Sheriff Gene Putnam. The tradition was further enhanced by a number of British writers, among them J.T. Edson, whose American publishers guaranteed readers at least twelve major killings per book, and Terry Harknett. Harknett's career began with his novelization of Sergio Leone's A FISTFUL OF DOLLARS (United Artists, 1967) after which, under the pseudonym George G. Gilman, he created the Edge series of *Blut und Boden* Western fiction as well as co-authoring the Apache series with Laurence James under the *nom de plume* William M. James.

When Lauran Paine and Gordon D. Shirreffs were both writing for editor Robert W. Lowndes at Columbia Publishing for such pulp magazines as *Real Western,* Paine started counting and usually a Shirreffs story had three dead bodies already on the first page. Paine wanted to write character-driven Western stories, but his publishers, even in the 1990s, would pare back his novels, cutting out all the character and leaving just the action, as happened as recently as THE GUNS OF PERALTA (Walker, 1994). Shirreffs apparently experienced no such editorial interference because of the kind of story he wrote. In his Lee Kershaw saga for Fawcett Gold Medal, the end of a story usually finds Kershaw alone because everyone else is dead.

All of which brings me to a further observation about the *mana-personality.* The stronger the hero's *mana* — and we can now expand this idea to encompass the hero's self-willedness, his ability to kill better than anyone else, his inhumanity reflected in his indifference to human life — the greater the dehumanization of the heroine. Once killing becomes wholesale, the traditional heroine must either vanish completely or be transformed herself into a blood-letter.

Dane Coolidge's HIDDEN WATER (A.C. McClurg, 1910) was in the vanguard of a Western story that employs the theme of the two heroines, although James Fenimore Cooper and Sir Walter Scott had both employed it in the previous century. When it comes to fiction, as with much human endeavor, the *koheleth* in Ecclesiastes whom St. Jerome translated into Latin as having said *nihil sub sole novum* [there is nothing new under the sun] seems to have made a particularly cogent observation. In this plot the hero must choose between the two heroines by the end of the story. Ernest Haycox frequently used this theme; but no matter where you find it in this author's fiction, the reason behind the selection is nearly always identical. "'We're exactly the same kind of people,'" Diana Castle tells Jeff Pierce in Haycox's ALDER GULCH (Little, Brown, 1941). "'It is all or nothing with each of us.'"

In Luke Short's first published Western novel, THE FEUD AT SINGLESHOT (Farrar and Rinehart, 1936), Dave Turner tells Dorsey Hammond that the only way the world gives a man what belongs to him is if he is willing to fight and die for it. By the end of this story, after Turner has dispatched a number of villains, he remarks to Dorsey: "'It was pretty bloody.'" Dorsey, however, has no compunction about admitting, "'But if a man doesn't fight for what he has and loves, people will take them away from him.'" This same thralldom with property and violence are combined in other Luke Short novels with the theme of the two heroines, such as in RIDE THE MAN DOWN (Doubleday, Doran, 1942). Celia Evarts is drawn to Will Ballard because she, as opposed to Lottie Priest, admires Ballard for the violence by which he must live to protect her property; she doesn't even object when Ballard must shoot and kill her fiancé. In contrast to Ballard and his ascendant *mana,* there is a weak man named Kennedy with virtually no *mana* at all and a corresponding difference in the kind of woman drawn to him: "She was a plain drudge of a girl, Will saw, probably the only kind of woman Kennedy could attract." Both T.T. Flynn and Peter Dawson wrote Western stories which resonate with a sense of humanity and compassion for the sufferings of their characters. Luke Short, on the other hand, was not capable of rising above the severe Calvinistic moral universe in which rigid judgments such as Ballard's view of Kennedy and his woman are inevitable. For this reason, while he enjoyed greater commercial success than either T.T. Flynn and Peter Dawson when alive, their contributions to the Western story have been more lasting; and, rather than including a story by Luke Short as I did in the first edition, I have now included instead one by Flynn and one by Dawson.

The September, 1946, issue of *Star Western* went on sale at newsstands with the price raised to a quarter. Readers were offered thirty-two more pages but the magazine had shrunk over the years to less than 100 pages and this expansion now had it at 128 pages. The reading public resisted this price change just as an earlier generation had resisted the double-dimer. In a desperate effort to increase circulation after going bi-monthly, editor Mike Tilden changed the contents of the magazine to emphasize sexuality and brutality. In the May, 1949 issue there are stories such as "Señorita Spitfire Runs Her Guns!" by Bob Obets, "The Rose of Dead Man's Range" by John Jo Carpenter, "Hellcat of Hopateh" by Norman B. Wolfe. and "A Woman and A Knife!" by Thomas Thompson. Thompson had become so disgusted with the way Tilden kept changing his titles into something garish and spectacular, he stopped titling his stories altogether and merely numbered them, expecting Tilden to supply the title. Thompson's first hard cover Western novel, RANGE DRIFTER (Doubleday, 1949), was featured in condensed magazine form in *Lariat Story Magazine* in the January, 1949, issue under the characteristic pulp title "Gun-Mistress of the Smoke-Pole Pack."

Titles, contents, blurbs, none of this could save the pulp magazines. *Dime Western* now cost a quarter and right near it on newsstands were paperback books for the same price, printed on better paper, more compact, and a bargain since they were often reprints of hard cover novels which had sold for $2.00. In 1950 Street & Smith announced in *The New York Times* that the pulp magazine era had ended. Scott and Shirreffs and dozens of other pulp writers moved right on to the original paperback Western. And the violence and the blood-letting in stories in Western paperbacks continued to escalate as the years passed. Although Shirreffs's Lew Kershaw has a different female companion in each adventure, the woman is able to engage in cold-blooded killing right along with Kershaw. When in Shirreffs's THE MARAUDERS (Fawcett, 1977) the woman is smashed in the face with a rifle butt by the master villain and has had her thigh ripped into by a shark — when, in short, she is dying — all she can think of is having sexual intercourse with Kershaw one last time and all Kershaw can feel about her after he humps her and after she dies is that "she was only a woman and a half-breed Yaqui at that."

Now, obviously, series such as these have done little to promote the literary reputation of the Western story and there are perhaps many who think that when you refer to a Western this is what is meant! Yet, there was an inevitable progression from these ultra-violent Westerns in paperback editions similar to what happened to *Star Western,* only by the 1970s publishers could actually include openly pornographic passages in these sexually explicit Westerns which in earlier decades had run into problems with censorship laws and the U.S. Postal Service. By 1979 nearly every major paperback publishing house had a sexually explicit Western series, or was preparing one. In these series women are stripped of their clothing and their souls; they are reduced to nothing but physical objects capable of producing temporary detumescence in the heroes following the heroes' bouts of incredible carnage and slaughter. Just as the Jim Hatfield stories for *Texas Rangers* were written by numerous authors under a house name, so Jake Logan and Tabor Evans and numerous other house names were selected for marketing these series.

To take but a single instance, in SLOCUM'S REVENGE (Playboy, 1979) by Jake Logan, Slocum (a play on words!) asks as his price for returning a property deed to a beautiful young Spanish virgin that they spend a night together. The ecstasy and repeated orgasms she experiences are recounted in explicit and graphic detail. Jake Logan was being billed as "the hottest best-selling Western author since Louis L'Amour," but there is nothing particularly "Western" about this and other series like it except the manner of dress and the geographic setting. What these sexually explicit Westerns do illustrate is a story completely under the dominant of the *mana-personality*. Men and women alike are denied all possibility of humanity. They are purely collective figures, indulging in orgies of sexuality and violence. Slocum and his brethren use women insensately and sometimes brutally before casually moving on to their next conquest. It would do us well in this connection to recall the scene from Leo Tolstoy's WAR AND PEACE (1862–1869) where Napoleon surveys the battlefield at Borodino. To describe this scene Tolstoy resorted to a fragment from Euripides translated into Latin by Plutarch: *Quos Deus vult perdere, prius dementat* [Whoso a god desires utterly to destroy is broken beforehand in spirit.]

When I stated that the West of the Western story is an imaginary West, I was speaking in spiritual terms. In the ultra-violent and sexually explicit stories from the days of the dime novels until the mass merchandise paperbacks of the 1980s and early 1990s, we are dealing with an imaginary West that has been created in such a way as to destroy all of the humanity possible in a human soul. If it is true that many young people enjoy reading the Western story, as they really always have, I shudder to think what would be their impression of the roles of men and women in the West after reading these books or what impression they might have of the value of human life.

V

If the apparatus by which the Western story has been marketed over the years has not been more than amply filled with pitfalls for the author, there has been yet another kind of interference. To sum it up in a sentence it has been the postures of political correctness which are expected to prevail even if this means suppressing historical accuracy. Zane Grey's THE VANISHING AMERICAN (Harper, 1925) appeared in serial form first in *Ladies Home Journal* in 1922, then a Curtis Publication as were *The Saturday Evening Post* and *The Country Gentleman*. The story tells of Nophaie, a full-blood Navajo brave, kidnapped when a child and educated by whites, returning to his reservation as a young man only to find it dominated by an unscrupulous missionary who uses his dogmatic creed to get his way. As such, this is an historical Western, which is to say that characters have greater depth, events are more complicated. But, as the traditional Western, the historical Western is also a variety of romance. Now, in the abstract, a romance is a narrative form that can arrange events so as to support an ideological conviction on the part of the author.

Grey's ideological orientation, as that of William MacLeod Raine and a number of other authors of Western fiction in the early decades of this century, was profoundly influenced by the postulates of Herbert Spencer's social Darwinism. Grey seems to have believed that human existence and the survival of the races are guided by inflexible laws of an evolutionary scheme which endorses industrial progress and technology and therefore endows European and Anglo-American civilization with a self-evident and wholly natural superiority provided, however, that what Grey meant by the "heritage of the desert" — the character developed as a result of subduing the elements of nature and the need for everyone to develop such a character — is always taken into account. In one of Grey's Indian stories, "Blue Feather," unpublished until long after his death when it appeared in the collection, BLUE FEATHER AND OTHER STORIES (Harper, 1961), Grey articulated his ideology of evolutionary social history, highest to the lowest: "Human being, man, Indian, savage, primitive beast."

In THE VANISHING AMERICAN, Grey has Nophaie reject his Nopah religion but he is also unwilling to accept the missionary's Christianity. Instead, Nophaie arrives at some nebulous pantheism in which the white Christ and nature become dual manifestations of God. "Indians," Grey summed up his view of the Stone Age culture of the indigenous American nations, "were merely closer to the original animal progenitor of human beings!" Nophaie falls in love with the blonde-haired, blue-eyed schoolteacher and, so inspired by this love does he become, that he is prompted to enforce among his own people Grey's public prejudice regarding the supreme importance of sexual virginity prior to marriage. I describe this as a "public" prejudice because in his private life Grey was notorious for womanizing among his secretaries. Morgan, the missionary, likes to seduce young Indian maidens at his mission school. One of them, Gekin Yasha, is taught by Nophaie that "'when a white woman loves she holds herself sacred for the man who has won her.'" "'This moral exhortation doesn't do Gekin Yasha much good. She is seduced by Morgan, becomes pregnant, returns to the reservation, and marries an Indian, only to pay the price frequently paid in Grey's stories by those who indulge in sexual intercourse outside a single monogamous relationship: she dies.

"'Let the Indians marry white women and Indian girls marry white men,'" Nophaie comments in the magazine version. "'It would make for a more virile race...absorbed by the race that has destroyed him. Red blood into white! It means the white race will gain and the Indian vanish....'" Grey's portrait of Nophaie added an additional termination to the dichotomy set forth by James Fenimore Cooper for whom Indians were either villains or noble savages. He is a *romantic* savage who wants to vanish for the betterment of the white race. "'Example of the white man's better ways,'" he says, "'would inevitably follow association.'" The magazine version originally concluded with Nophaie and the yellow hair in each other's arms, about to achieve Grey's synthesis of "red blood into white." But this ending — not to mention Grey's somewhat accurate portrait of reservation missionaries' fallibilities — caused such a furor at the editorial office of *Ladies Home Journal* that he was compelled to rewrite the conclusion. In the first published version, Nophaie dies but, when he does, a miracle occurs, and he turns white.

Paramount Pictures was anxious to bring this story to the screen with Richard Dix as Nophaie and Lois Wilson, albeit with dark hair, as the schoolteacher. However, even this compromise ending was not regarded as politically correct. So Grey rewrote the ending again, this time having Nophaie die in a shoot-out at the reservation. Harper & Bros. were willing to allow this new ending to stand, but they objected to the portrait of the missionary and called Grey's attention to the number of protesting letters from religious people objecting to *Ladies Home Journal* for publishing such a damning portrayal. Grey defended his view and the fight went back and forth until he finally agreed to some modifications. Now, in the first book version, Nophaie, shot fatally, succumbs while murmuring, "'Vanishing…vanishing…vanishing.'"

For the motion picture version, THE VANISHING AMERICAN (Paramount, 1925), Lucien Hubbard, who did the adaptation, borrowed a portion of the first chapter of THE THUNDERING HERD (Harper, 1925), some of the text from the unpublished "Blue Feather," and from these two fashioned a prologue in which it was shown how the Indians had preyed upon each other, one tribe wiping out another, albeit weaker, tribe, until at last the culmination of the evolutionary scheme had been attained with the arrival of the white man, signaling to all the remaining Indians who had survived the struggle for existence this far that now the time had come for them to vanish. This was what was considered politically correct in 1925. In 1995, the casting of the film with a white actor playing an Indian would be the sorest bone of contention and, if there were to be any villains at all, they would now have to be white men. This is to say, ninety years later there would have been no objection at all to an unscrupulous missionary or a crooked Indian agent! On the other hand, because it was now considered more politically correct than in 1922, Dr. Loren Grey, Zane Grey's younger son, could have the book finally published just as Grey wrote it in THE VANISHING AMERICAN (Pocket Books, 1982).

However, in 1922, as the furor died down at *Ladies Home Journal,* it was decided that henceforth Curtis Publications would no longer buy Western stories in which Indians were characterized at all. Indian characters might be present but, if they were, they must be portrayed as renegades or fill only minor roles. The far-reaching effects of this editorial policy can be seen in a number of the serials which ran in *The Saturday Evening Post* and which were subsequently made into films: Ernest Haycox's "Bugles in the Afternoon" in 1943 and his "Canyon Passage" in 1945; Luke Short's "Ambush" in 1948; Alan LeMay's "The Seachers" in 1954 and "The Unforgiven" in 1957; James Warner

Bellah's stories about Fort Starke (four of which comprise film director John Ford's cavalry trilogy); and Will Cook's "Comanche Captives" in 1959 which was also filmed by John Ford under the title TWO RODE TOGETHER (Columbia, 1961). I could go on, but the point is it would be absurd to expect, when the Indians were not characterized in the original stories, that they should somehow come to be characterized in films based on those stories. Editors were exhorting Western writers to follow an agenda of political correctness if they wished to be published, and so they followed it. Peter Dawson, who wrote serials for *The Saturday Evening Post* in this period, refused to deal with Indian stories at all, commenting that there were two sides to the issue and he would rather avoid it altogether than to show only one side.

George Orwell provided what is probably the most succinct definition of political correctness to be found anywhere in NINETEEN EIGHTY-FOUR (Harcourt, Brace, 1949):

> Day by day and almost minute by minute the past was brought up to date. In this way every prediction made by the Party could be shown by documentary evidence to have been correct; nor was any item of news, or any expression of opinion, which conflicted with the needs of the moment, ever allowed to remain on record. All history was a palimpsest, scraped clean and reinscribed exactly as often as was necessary.

Count Joseph de Maistre wrote in the 19th Century: "...le véritable vainqueur, come le véritable vaincu, c'est celui qui croit l'être" [the true conqueror, like the truly vanquished, is whoever believes himself to be the conqueror]. It is the same with historical personalities and the events of history when subjected to an ideological purpose, be it to prove something from history or to be politically correct at a particular moment in time: they are what we wish them to have been. As Oakley Hall put it in his Prefatory Note to WARLOCK (Viking, 1958), "by combining what did happen with what might have happened, I have tried to show what should have happened." There is no ultimate historical reality. It is argued instead that we can never know the truth. All we can have is an interpretation of what happened.

"You look at me," Sandoval [Old Man Buffalo Grass] told Aileen O'Bryan in November, 1928, when she was acting as the Navajo chief's amanuensis recording his stories and myths about his people, "you look at me, and you see only an old ugly man, but within I am filled with great beauty. I sit as on a mountain top and I look into the future. I see my people and your people living together. In time to come my people will have forgotten their early way of life unless they learn it from white men's books. So you must write down what I tell you; and you must have it made into a book that coming generations may know this truth."

For the white man, too, it is necessary to go to the "white man's books" to learn what happened in the past. But the truth isn't always concerned with purely physical events; sometimes, maybe even most of the time, it has to do with spiritual events. To reclaim this past, the spiritual past, to know what happened and why it happened, is the objective of sound historical fiction. The finest examples of the Western story are set in the American West because they have everything to do with the American West and could not really have happened elsewhere in quite the same way. This is the distance we have traveled from the advice Luke Short once gave to Brian Garfield.

In the 1990s "historical" Westerns have proliferated in paperback books on newsstands. This phenomenon has nothing at all to do with what the reading public wants to read in the way of a Western story. Rather it has to do with the fact that we have again arrived at the same sticking point in publishing that dime novel publishers had encountered in the early years of this century. In June, 1993, at the annual meeting of the Western Writers of America held that year in Springdale, Arkansas, I announced the end of the mass merchandise paperback era as a means for marketing original Western fiction.

What was killing the paperback book was the same thing that killed the dime novel: rising production costs were forcing price increases on the publishers, price increases that the reading public was resisting. From the close of the Civil War until 1957, most magazines and, later, paperback books were distributed to newsstands by the American News Company. In 1957, with the declining magazine market, American News collapsed. Paperback publishers could have taken this opportunity to set up their own distribution system as Street & Smith had already done in 1925 when it pulled out of American News, but they opted not to spend the money. Instead, they promoted the small regional distributors into an independent distribution system. By 1990 the power of these independent distributors had become so great, it was their drivers who stocked newsstands and paperback racks and who decided which titles were to be racked where, in what position on the racks, and they treated paperback books the same as magazines: no title remained on any one rack for longer than four weeks at which time, as far as that rack was concerned, it was regarded as a back issue. If a paperback title sold out, it was replaced by a new title just off the truck, rather than having the sold-out title racked a second time.

Pocket Books which in the late 1940s kept its paperback books continuously on racks had sales figures for many Western titles between 500,000 to 1 million copies. Max Brand's SINGING GUNS (Dodd, Mead, 1939) in paperback reprint was awarded a Gertude by Pocket Books for having sold a million copies. The Pocket Book edition of RED RANGE (Houghton Mifflin, 1939) by Eugene Cunningham also was awarded a Gertrude. By 1990 Pocket Books was lucky to sell 18,000 copies of a paperback Western in the four months of rack exposure allowed to it by the independent distributors.

If the reading public was resisting buying a 200-page Western novel for anywhere between $3.95 and $4.50, then there seemed only one solution — right out of Ecclesiastes — and that was the 1990s equivalent of a double dimer, an "historical" Western at between 90,000 and 120,000 words that could be listed at $4.95, or even $5.95. It might have worked, if the reading public had wanted longer Western stories. But that does not appear to have been the case. So once again, as when *Western Story Magazine* was born, the marketing of the Western story is entering a new era in a new package — or, better said, new packages. They are being bought in large numbers in full-length audio versions, in trade paperback editions, and the hard cover Western is having a resurgence, only this time they are being published by smaller publishing houses. The seven conglomerates which dominated American publishing in the early 1990s had forsaken all others to go in pursuit of only the best-seller. Any title that would sell under 75,000 copies was not to be considered commercially viable.

Mircea Eliade reflected in his book, MYTH AND REALITY (Harper's, 1963):

This is one of the few encouraging syndromes of the modern world. Western cultural provincialism — which began history with Egypt, literature with Homer, and philosophy with Thales — is being rapidly outmoded. But this is not all: through this historiographic *anamnesis* man enters deep into himself. If we succeed in understanding a contemporary Australian, or his homologue, a paleolithic hunter, we have succeeded in "awakening" in the depths of our being the existential situation and the resultant behavior of a prehistoric humanity. It is not a matter of a mere "external" knowledge, as when we learn the name of the capital of a country or the date of the fall of Constantinople. A true historiographic *anamnesis* finds expression in the discovery of our solidarity with these vanished or peripheral peoples.

If for "vanished and peripheral peoples" we substitute the many nations in the American West, this is what we experience by means of the Western story. We come to recognize our solidarity with those from the past; we relive their lives, face the issues which confronted them, and, it is to be hoped, come to some deeper understanding of ourselves. The best in the Western story demonstrates that it is possible to write fiction that is stirring and entertaining and still be historically accurate, truthful to the time, the place, the people.

"I have to locate those little details, those fine points that can make a book seem real," Cynthia Haseloff once described her method of research. These details provide a reader with a window into the times about which she was writing and a better understanding of past events and the people who lived through them. This may be nowhere better illustrated than in Haseloff's MARAUDER (Bantam, 1982) when the corpses of two of Crysop's guerrillas are photographed:

Darwood's picture became famous and was printed in a number of books later. Every time I see it, I'm caught by the barbarism of that time of quick death. I do not think I am ever sorry the two men are dead. They had earned their wages, but I think it strange now how callous we were to their death's privacy. We took all death seriously, grimly, intimately, but not privately. Somehow privacy was not much thought of in our small towns. We all knew each other too well, like a family without secrets among members. There was a sense, too, that these men had forfeited something by their actions. Perhaps it was our sympathy or respect. In our naïveté we photographed death to hold a moment in time close. We did not, of course, anticipate our own mortality in the face of the picture's immortality. All that remains for the casual viewer today is a grisly portrait of two lifeless men and the sleeves and arms and hat brims of those leaning against the wagon. ...Sometimes the captions are cute or witty, 'Swift Justice' or 'Arkansas trial methods.' ...The casual viewer turns the page quickly to avoid the detail or lingers in morbid fascination. ...The viewer clicks his teeth and shakes his head and wonders how we could have killed these men and taken the picture. It is not Blackie Foard or Sweet William who are indicted, then, but our time. And we are envied for swift justice or shunned for our cruelty and unenlightened humanity. And the casual viewer does not know our conflict, our choice, our questions, or our reality as he looks at the flat grey picture in the lifeless books.

I began this introductory essay with a reference to classical mythology. Historiography, too, began in Classical Antiquity. Herodotus said that he wrote his HISTORIES so that the deeds of men should not be lost to the passage of time. Other historians of Antiquity had different reasons for writing history. Thucydides wanted to show the effects of the struggle for power, a drive he felt indigenous to human nature; Polybius began writing history with the intention of demonstrating that the Roman Empire was the logical culmination of the forces of world history before his time, but he had second thoughts which only further reinforced his conviction that the experience one has while studying history is the best kind of education to be found in life; Livy, as Plutarch, studied history to find "models for ourselves and for our country." Tacitus went so far as to see all history as peopled by heroes and villains.

Unlike the characters in Orwell's NINETEEN EIGHTY-FOUR we cannot persist in constantly rewriting our history to suit the fashion of the moment, as if political correctness could ever be a substitute for historical reality. Conversely, to fall victim to the dominant of the *mana-personality,* to dehumanize ourselves in an orgy of carnality and violence, is not healthy in any form of fictional entertainment. The Western story, in an ideal sense, may help us to understand ourselves better and enable us better to confront the spiritual state that today seems so perplexing to us in our contemporary society. I believe that the literary purpose of the Western story as of all artistic endeavor is — to paraphrase Dr. Samuel Johnson — to prepare us better to understand life or, when that proves impossible, at least better able to endure it.

There are authors of the Western story — some of whom I have been able to include in this anthology — who have recognized in the depths of their being that the past does have something to teach us, if we are willing to learn from it. They have believed that the Western story is the ideal literary form through which our American past can be evoked vividly and painfully — painfully, because often it was painful. The story of the American West is not so much romance, nor is it necessarily tragedy, although it can be both. It is most often, even when the circumstances are tragic, as Æschylus understood so well, a celebration of human nobility. Most of all the Western story is about human beings in nature, not the denatured, mechanical, sterile world that increasingly has come to serve as a backdrop for human activity in other kinds of fiction. In this sense, the American West is just what the Indians always believed it to be, the land *just before* the land beyond the sun, the Spiritland, and it can still enthrall us when an author is able to conjure its magic.

PART ONE

THE EAST GOES WEST

OWEN WISTER

OWEN WISTER (1860–1938) was born in Philadelphia, Pennsylvania. He was graduated from Harvard in 1882 with honors, having majored in music. In 1885, after suffering a nervous breakdown, Wister went to Wyoming for the first time. It was to be only one of many such trips he would make to the West over the next several years, initially for his health and then to find more material for his fiction. Returning to the East later in 1885, he attended Harvard Law School from which he was graduated in 1888, and went to work in a Philadelphia law office.

In 1892, following his fifth trip to Wyoming, Wister published his first Western stories, "Hank's Woman" in *Harper's Weekly* (8/27/92) and "How Lin McLean Went East" in *Harper's New Monthly Magazine* (12/92). These stories proved so popular with readers that in time the publisher financed Wister on a trip throughout the West and hired Frederic Remington to illustrate the stories Wister wrote as a result of his experiences. It was through this collaboration that a friendship developed between the two men that is narrated in some detail in Ben Merchant Vorpahl's MY DEAR WISTER: THE FREDERIC REMINGTON–OWEN WISTER LETTERS (American West Publishing, 1973). Wister's impressions and reflections from the years 1885 to 1895, written while he was on these various sojourns, are to be found in OWEN WISTER OUT WEST: HIS JOURNALS AND LETTERS (University of Chicago Press, 1958) edited by Fanny Kemble Wister. On the title page of this book four lines by Wister are reproduced that are worth citing:

> Would I might prison in my words
> And so hold by me all the year
> Some portion of the Wilderness
> Of freedom that I walk in here.

Near the end of the period recounted in his journals, Wister published his essay, "The Evolution of the Cow-Puncher" in *Harper's New Monthly Magazine* (9/95). It articulated his vision of the cowboy as the modern incarnation of the medieval knight of romance. In retrospect, it would seem that Wister's personal values constantly interfered with his objective to describe the West and its peoples as they really were. Romance and marriage in his novels, as in some of his stories, serve only to emasculate his cowboys, to make them docile Easterners concerned more with personal ambition, accumulation of wealth, and achieving what by Eastern standards could only be considered social standing, rather than luxuriating in their freedom, the openness and emptiness of the land, and the West's utter disregard for family background. To make his cowboys acceptable heroes to *himself,* as well as to his Eastern readers, Wister felt compelled to imbue them with his own distinctly patrician values. For this reason his stories cannot be said to depict truthfully the contrasts and real conflicts between the East and West of his time and Western readers of his stories have always tended to scoff at what he was presenting as the reality of Western life.

Wister in his political philosophy was a progressive and what has come to be termed a social Darwinist (note, it is the *evolution* of the cow-puncher). He believed in a natural aristocracy, a survival of the fittest — the fittest being those who measured up best to the elective affinities of his own value system. He put this philosophy into the mouth of the Virginian when he remarks, "'Now back East you can be middling and get along. But if you go to try a thing in this Western country, you've got to do it *well!*'" Yet, privately (and this is why his journals are so illuminating), he lamented the sloth which he felt the West induced in people, and it was his ultimate rejection of the real West that brought about his disillusionment with it and his refusal, after 1911, ever to return there.

Wister's best defense against his dislike of the West came through exalting his heroes but, as the late Mody C. Boatright observed in "The American Myth Rides the Range: Owen Wister's Man on Horseback" in *Southwest Review* (Summer, 51), "Wister's pathetic search for a leader brought him to the conclusion that Theodore Roosevelt was 'the greatest benefactor we people have known since Lincoln.'" Wister published an earlier version of a chapter from THE VIRGINIAN titled "Balaam and Pedro" in *Harper's New Monthly Magazine* (1/94) and told somewhat explicitly how Balaam gouged out the eye of a horse. Roosevelt chided Wister for what he felt was a slip in good taste. Wister deleted the offending passage from the version which appears in the novel, dedicated the novel to Roosevelt, and therefore it should come as little surprise that his last book should have been ROOSEVELT: THE STORY OF A FRIENDSHIP 1880–1919 (Macmillan, 1930).

In "At the Sign of the Last Chance" published in *Cosmopolitan* (2/28), a group of old-time cowboys realize that their once prosperous lives and wondrous times are over. In accordance with an old English custom, they remove the sign from in front of their saloon and give it a proper burial. In Wister's bitter words: "Yes, now we could go home. The requiem of the golden beards, their romance, their departed West, too good to live forever, was finished." Wister included this as the final story in his last Western story collection, WHEN WEST WAS WEST (Macmillan, 1928). The publisher apparently was not of the same disposition. The illustration for the dust jacket of the first edition was a reproduction of Frederic Remington's famous bronze sculpture, "Bronco Buster."

Both a representative selection of Wister's short stories and a modern edition of THE VIRGINIAN are now available from the University of Nebraska Press and a reference to Wister's first story, which follows, is to be found in THE VIRGINIAN in the chapter titled "Through Two Snows." "Hank's Woman" has nothing of Wister's subsequent *fin de siècle* mood, but rather much of the startlement and wonder Wister himself must have felt when he first ventured to that corner of Yellowstone Park, near Pitchstone Cañon, where Lin McLean and others reputedly were witnesses to — in Wister's words in THE VIRGIN-IAN — "a sad and terrible drama that has been elsewhere chronicled." This is that chronicle.

HANK'S WOMAN
1892

"He decided second thoughts were best, too," I said. This was because a very large trout who had been flirting with my brown hackle for some five minutes, suddenly saw through the whole thing, and whipped into the deep water that wedged its calm into the riffle from below.

"Try a grasshopper on him." And Lin McLean, whom among all cowpunchers I love most, handed me one from the seat pocket of his overalls.

An antelope earlier that day had given us his attention, as, huddled down in some sagebrush under the burning cloudless sun, I waved a red handkerchief while Lin lay on his back and shook his boots in the air. But the antelope, after considering these things from the point of view of some hundred yards away, had irrelevantly taken off to the foothills. We fired the six-shooter, and watched his exasperating white tailless rear twinkle out of sight across the flats.

"If you hadn't gone so crazy with your boots," I said, "he'd have come up close."

"And if yu'd brought yer rifle along, as I said yu'd ought to," responded Lin, "we'd have had some fresh meat to pack into camp."

Of fish, however, we certainly had enough for lunch now and enough to take back for supper and breakfast. We had ridden down Snake River from camp on Pacific Creek to where Buffalo Fork comes sweeping in; and there on the single point and on a log half sunk in the swimming stream, we had persuaded out of the depths some dozen of that silver-sided, many-speckled sort that does fight. None was shorter than twelve inches; one measured twenty. Therefore, in satisfaction, Lin and I hauled our boots off, tore open shirts and breeches so they dropped where we stood, and regardless of how many trout we might now disturb, splashed into the cool slow breadth of backwater the bend makes just there. Then I set about cleaning a couple of fish, and Lin made the fire, and got the lunch from our saddles, setting the teapot to boil, and slicing bacon into the pan.

"As fer second thoughts," said Lin, "animals in this country has 'em more'n men do."

I thought so too, and said nothing.

"Yu' take the way they run the Bar-Circle-Zee. Do yu' figure Judge Henry knows his foreman's standin' in with rustlers like Ed Rogers is? If he'd taken time to inquire why that foreman left Montana, he'd not be gettin' stole from right along, you bet! And Ed Rogers'll be dealt with one of these days. He's a-growin' bold, the way he takes calves this year. He's forgettin' about second thoughts, I expect.''

We were silent, and ate some fish and drank some tea — you cannot make good coffee out-of-doors. But Mr. McLean's mind was for the moment running in a channel of prudence. You would have supposed he had never acted hastily in the whole of his twenty-eight years.

"Folks is poor in Wyoming through bein' too quick,'' he resumed. "Look at the way them fellers in Douglas got cinched.''

"Who, and how?'' I inquired.

"Bankers and stockmen. They figured on Douglas bein' a big town, and all because the railroad come there on its way somewheres else that ain't nowheres its own self. I've been in this country since '77, and that's eleven years, and I say yu' can't never make a good town out o' sagebrush.''

Lin paused, looking southward across the great yellow-gray plain of the Teton Basin. The Continental Divide rose to the left of us; to the right were the Tetons, shutting us in from Idaho, with their huge magical peaks of blue cutting sharp and sudden into the sky.

"Take marriage,'' continued the cowpuncher, stretching himself till he sank flat backward on the ground, with his long legs spread wide. "Sometimes there ain't so much as first thoughts before a man's been and done it.''

"Wyoming is not peculiar in that respect,'' I said.

"We come over this trail,'' said Lin, not listening to me, "the year after the President and Sheridan did. Me and Hank and Honey Wiggin. I'd quit workin' fer the old '76 outfit, and come to Lander after a while and met up with them two fellers, and we figured we'd take a trip through the Park. Now, there was Hank. Yu' never knowed Hank?''

I never had.

"Well, yu' didn't lose much.'' Lin now rolled comfortably over on his stomach. "Hank, he married a woman. He was small and she was big — awful big; and neither him nor her was any account — him 'specially.''

"Probably they would not agree with you,'' I said.

"She would now, you bet!'' said Lin, sitting up and laying his hand on my knee. "They got married on one week's acquaintance, which ain't enough.''

"That's true, I think.''

"Folks try it in this Western country,'' Lin pursued, "where a woman's a scarce thing anyhow, and men unparticular and hasty, but it ain't sufficient in nine times out o'ten. Hank, yu' see, he staid sober that one week, provin' she ought to seen him fer two anyways; and if I was a woman, knowin' what I know about me, it wouldn't be two weeks nor two months neither.'' The cowpuncher paused and regarded me with his wide-open, jocular eyes. "When are you goin' to tie up with a woman?'' he inquired. "I'm comin' that day.''

"Was Hank married when you went to the Park?" said I.

"Of course he weren't. Ain't I tryin' to tell yu'? Him and me and Honey joined a prospectin' outfit when we was through seein' the Park, and Hank and me come into the Springs after grub from Galena Creek, where camp was. We lay around the Springs and Gardner fer three days, playin' cards with friends; and one noon he was settin' in the hotel at the Mammoth Springs waitin' fer to see the stage come in, though that wasn't nuthin' he hadn't seen, nor nuthin' was on it fer him. But that was Hank. He'd set around waitin' fer nuthin' like that till somebody said whiskey, and he'd drink and wait some more. Well, the hotel kid yells out, 'Stage!' after a while, soon as he seen the dust comin' up the hill. Ever notice that hotel at Hot Springs before and after the kid says, 'Stage?'"

I shook my head.

"Well, sir," said Lin, "yu' wouldn't never suppose the place was any relation to itself. Yu' see, all them guests and Raymonds clear out for the Norris Basin right after breakfast, and none comes in new from anywheres till 'round noon, and you bet the hotel folks has a vacation! Yes, sir, a regular good lay-off. Yu'd ought to see the Syndicate manager a-sleepin' behind the hotel counter, and nobody makin' no noise high nor low, but all plumb quiet and empty like — maybe a porter foolin' around the ice cooler, and the flies buzzin'. Then that kid — he's been on the watch-out; he likes it, you bet! — he sings out, 'Stage!' sudden like, and shoo! the entire outfit stampedes, startin' with them electric bells ring-jinglin' all over. The Syndicate manager flops his hair down quick front of a lookin'-glass he keeps handy fer his private satisfaction, and he organizes himself behind the hotel register book; and the young photograph chap comes out of his door and puts his views out for sale right acrosst from where the cigar-seller's a-clawin' his goods into shape. Them girls quits leanin' over the rail upstairs and skips, and the porters they line up on the front steps, and the piano man he digs his fingers into the keys, and him and the fiddlers starts raisin' railroad accidents. Yes, sir. That hotel gets that joyous I expect them arrivin' Raymonds judge they've struck ice cream and balance partners right on the surface.

"Well, Hank, now, he watched 'em that day same as every day, and the guests they clumb down off the stage like they always do — young ladies hoppin' spry and squealin' onced in a while, and dusty old girls in goggles clutchin' the porters, and snufflin', and sayin', 'Oh dear!'

"Then out gets a big wide-faced woman, thick all through any side yu' looked at her, and she was kind o' dumb-eyed, but fine appearin', with lots of yaller hair. Yu' could tell she were raised in one of them German countries like Sweden, for she acted slow, and stared at the folks hustlin', and things noisy, and waltzes playin' inside. Hank seen her, and I expect he got interested on sight, for he was a small man, and she was big, and twiced as big as him. Did yu' ever notice that about small fellers? She was a lady's maid, like they have in the States."

Lin stopped and laughed.

"If any woman in this country was to have to hire another one to help her clothes off her, I guess she'd be told she'd ought to go to bed soberer," he remarked. "But this one was sure a lady's maid, and out comes her lady right there. And my! 'Where have you put the keys, Willomene?'"

Lin gave a scornful imitation of the lady's voice.

"Well, Willomene fussed around her pockets, and them keys wasn't there, so she started explainin' in tanglefoot English to her lady how her lady must have took them from her in the 'drain,' as she said, meaning the cars. But the lady was gettin' madder, tappin' her shoe on the floor, like Emma Yoosh does in the opera — *Carmen,* or somethin' I seen onced in Cheyenne.

"Them ladies," said Lin, after a silence during which I deplored his commentative propensity, "seems to enjoy hustlin' themselves into a rage. This one she got a-goin', and she rounded up Willomene with words yu' seldom see outside a book. 'Such carelessness,' says she, 'is too exasperatin'. . .'; and a lot more she said, and it were all up to that standard, you bet! Then she says, 'You are discharged,' and off she struts. A man come out soon (her husband, most likely), and he paid the lady's maid some cash (a good sum it was, I expect), and she stood right there for a spell; then all of a sudden she says, 'Ok yayzoo!' and sits down and starts cryin'.

"When yu' see that, yu' feel sorry, but yu' can't say nuthin'; so we was all standin' round on the piazza, kind o' shiftless. Then the baggage-wagon come in, and they picked the keys up on the road from Gardner; so the lady was all right, but that didn't do no good to Willomene. They stood her trunk down with the rest — a brass-nailed concern it was, I remember, same as an Oswego starch box in six — and there was Willomene out of a job and afoot a long ways from anywheres, settin' in the chair, and onced in a while she'd cry some more. We got her a room in a cheap hotel where the Park drivers sleeps when they're in at the Springs, and she acted grateful like, thankin' everybody in her tanglefoot English. And she was a very nice-speakin' woman. Her folks druv off to the Fountain next mornin', and she seemed dazed like; fer I questioned her where she'd like to go, and she was told about how to get to the railroad, and she couldn't say if she wanted to travel east or west. There's where she weren't no account, yu' see.

"Over acrosst at the post-office I told the postmistress about Willomene, and she had a spare bed, an' bein' a big-hearted woman, she had her to stay and help wait on the store. That store's popular with the soldiers. The postmistress is a little beauty, and they come settin' round there, privates and sergeants, too, expectin' some day she'll look at 'em twiced. But she just stays good-natured to all, and minds her business, you bet! So Hank come round, settin' like the soldiers, and he'd buy a pair of gloves, maybe, or cigars, and Willomene she'd wait on him. I says to Hank we'd ought to pull out for camp, but he wanted to wait. So I played cards, and had a pretty fair time with the boys, layin' round the Springs and over to Gardner.

"One night I come on 'em — Hank and Willomene — walkin' among the pines where the road goes down. Yu'd ought to have seen that pair! Her big shape was plain and kind of steadfast in the moon, and alongside of her little black Hank. And there it was. He'd got stuck on her all out of her standin' up so tall and round above his head. I passed close, and nobody said nuthin', only next day, when I remarked to Hank he appeared to be catchin' on. And he says, 'That's my business, I guess'; and I says, 'Why, Hanky, I'm sure pleased to notice your earnest way.' It wasn't my business if he wanted to be a fool, and take a slow-understandin' woman like she was up to the mines.

"Well, that night I caught 'em again, near the formation, and she says to me 'how beautifool was de wasser streamin' and tricklin' over them white rocks!' And I laffed.

"'Hank,' says I (not then, but in the mornin'), 'before you've made yer mind up right changeless, if I was you, I'd take Miss Willomene over to the Syndicate store and get her weighed.'

"And he says, 'What do yu' mean?'

"So I gave my opinion that if the day was to come when him and her didn't want to travel the same road, why, he'd travel hern, and not his'n. 'Fer she could pack yu' on her back and lift yu' down nice anywheres she pleased,' says I to Hank.

"And I tell yu' it's a queer thing I come to say that."

Lin stopped and jerked his overalls into a more comfortable fit. "They was married the Toosday after, at Livingston," he went on; "and Hank was that pleased with himself he gave Willomene a weddin' present with the balance of his cash, spendin' his last nickel on buyin' her a red-tailed parrot they had for sale at the First National Bank. The feller hollered so at the bank, the president told the cashier he must get rid of it.

"Hank and Willomene staid a week up in Livingston on her money, and then he brought her back to Gardner, and bought their grub and come up to the camp we had on Galena Creek. She'd never slep' out before, and she'd never been on a horse, neither, and near rolled off down into Little Death Cañon comin' up by the cut-off trail. Now just see that foolishness — to fetch that woman and pack horses heavy loaded along such a turrable bad place like that cut-off trail is, where a man wants to lead his own horse 'fear of goin' down. You know them big tall grass-topped mountains over in the Hoodoo country, and how they comes clam down through the cross timber yu' can't go through hardly on foot, till they pitches over into lots and lots of little cañons, with maybe two inches of water runnin' in the bottom? All that's East Fork water, and over the divide's Clark's Fork, or Stinkin' Water if yu' take the country further southeast. But anywheres yu' go is them turrable steep slopes, and the cut-off trail takes along about the worst in the business.

"Well, Hank got his bride over it somehow, and yu'd ought to have seen them two pull into our camp. Yu'd sure never figured it were a weddin' trip. He was leadin' but skewed around in his saddle to jaw back at Willomene fer ridin' so poorly. And what kind of a man's that, I'd like to know, jawin' at her in the hearin' of the whole outfit of us fellers, and them not married two weeks? She was settin' straddleways like a mountain, and between him and her went the three pack animals, plumb played out, and the flour — they had two hundred pounds — tilted over downwards, with the red-tailed parrot a-hollerin' landslides in his cage tied on top.

"Hank, he'd had a scare over Willomene comin' so near fallin', and it turned him sour, so he'd hardly speak, but just said, 'How!' kind of gruff, when we come up to congratulate him. But Willomene, she says when she seen me, 'Oh, I am so glad to see you!' and we shook hands right friendly; fer I'd talked to her down at the Springs, yu' know. And she told me how near she come to gettin' killed. Yu' ain't been over that there trail?" inquired Lin of me. "Yu'd ought to see that cañon."

"No," said I; "I've seen enough of the Park, and the Grand Cañon satisfies me."

"Taint's the same thing. That Grand Cañon's pretty, but Little Death Cañon ain't; it's one of them queer places, somethin' the same style as a geyser is, surprisin' a feller. If Willomene had went down there that afternoon — well, I'll tell yu', so yu' can judge. She seen the trail gettin' nearer and nearer the edge, between the timber and the jumpin'-off place, and she seen how them little loose stones and the crumble stuff kep' a-slidin' away under the horse's feet, and rattlin' down out of sight she didn't know where to, so she tried to git off and walk without sayin' nuthin' to Hank. He kep' a-goin', and Willomene's horse she had pulled up, started to follow as she was half off, and that gave her a tumble, but she got her arm hitched around a rock just as the stones started to slide over her. But that's only the beginning of what fallin' into that hole is. A man sometimes falls down a place all right and crawls out after a while. There ain't no crawlin' out in Little Death Cañon, you bet! Down in there, where yu' can't see, is sulfur caves. Yu' can smell 'em a mile away. That cañon's so narrer where they open out and puff steam that there's no breathin' to be done, for no wind gets in to clean out the smell. If yu' lean pretty far over yu' can see the bottom, and a little green water tricklin' over cream-colored stuff like pie. Bears and elk climbin' round the sides onced in a while gets choked by the risin' air, and tumbles and stays fer good. Why, us fellers looked in one time and seen two big silver-tipped carcasses, and didn't dare go in after the hides, though I don't say yu' couldn't never make the trip. Some days the steam comes out scantier; but how's a man to know if them caves ain't a-goin' to start up again sudden like a cough? I have seen it come in two seconds. And when it comes that way after sundown, risin' out of the cañon with a fluffy kind of a sigh — yes, sir, I tell yu' that's a sick noise it makes! Why, I don't like to be passin' that way myself, though knowin' so well it's only them sulfur caves down in there. Willomene was in luck when she come out safe.

"Anyway, there they was, come to camp without any accident. She looked surprised when she seen Hank's tent him and her was to sleep in. And Hank he looked surprised at the bread she cooked.

"'What kind of a Dutch woman are yu',' says he, half jokin', 'if yu' can't use a Dutch oven?'

"'You said to me you have a house to live in,' says Willomene. 'Where is that house?'

"'I didn't figure on gettin' a woman when I left camp,' says Hank, grinnin', but not pleasant, 'or I'd have hurried up with the shack I'm a-buildin'.'

"He was buildin' one. Well, that's the way they started into matrimony, and in three weeks they quit havin' much to say to each other. The only steady talkin' done in that home was done by the parrot, and he was a rattlin' talker. Willomene she used to talk with me at first, but she gave it up soon; I don't know why. I liked her mighty well, and so we all did. She done her best, but I guess she hadn't never seen this style of life, and kindness such as we could show her, I suppose, didn't show up fer as well as it was intended.

"There was six of us workin' claims. Some days the gold washed out good in the pan, but mostly it was that fine it floated off without ever settlin' at all. But we had a good crowd, and things was pleasant, and not too lively nor yet too slow. Willomene used to come round the ditch silent like and watch us workin', and then she'd be apt to move off into the woods, singin' German songs, not very loud. I knowed well enough she felt lonesome, but what can yu' do? As fer her, she done her best; only it ain't the sensible way fer a wife to cry at her husband gettin' full, as of course Hank done, same as always since I'd knowed him, bar one week at the Mammoth. A native American woman could have managed Hank so he'd treat her good and been sorry instead of glad every time he'd been drunk. But we liked Willomene because she'd do anything she could for us, cookin' up an extra meal if we come back from a hunt, and patchin' our clothes. Nor she wouldn't take pay. She was a good woman, but no account in a country like Galena Creek was. Honey Wiggin and me helped her finish the shack, so she and Hank could move in there, and then she fixed up one of them crucifixes she had in the little trunk, and used to squat down at it night and morning, makin' Hank crazy.

"There it was again! Yu' see he couldn't make no allowances fer her bein' Dutch and different. Not because he was bad — there weren't enough of Hank to be bad — but because he had no thoughts. I kind of laffed myself first time I seen Willomene at it. Hank says to me, soft, 'Come here, Lin,' and I peeped in where she was a-prayin' to that crucifix. She seen us, too, but she didn't quit. Them are things yu' don't know about. I figured it this way — that she couldn't make no friends with Hank, and couldn't with us neither, and bein' far away from all she was used to, why, that crucifix was somethin' that staid by her, remindin' her of home, I expect, and anyway keepin' her sort of company when she felt lonesome. And of course, over in Europe, I guess, she'd been accustomed to believin' in God and a hereafter, and hearin' a lot of singin' in them Catholic churches. So yu' see what she must have thought about Galena Creek.

"One day Hank told her he was goin' to take his dust to town, and when he come back if he found that thing in the house he'd do it up fer her. 'So yu'd better pack off yer wooden dummy somewheres,' says he.

"I tell you," said Lin, fixing his eyes on mine, "a man don't always know how what he speaks is a-goin' to act on others. She said nuthin', and I guess Hank forgot all about it. But I can see the way she looked right now — kind o' stone like and solemn. And I happened to go into the shack around noon to get some matches, and there she was prayin', and *that* time she jumped.

"The night before Hank was to start fer town, a young chap they called Chalkeye come into camp. He'd been drivin' a bunch of horses to sell 'round Helena and Bozeman, and he'd lost the trail over to Stinkin' Water where he was goin' back to Meeteetsee. Chalkeye had cigars and good whiskey, and he set up royal fer the gang. That night was the first time I ever knowed him, but him and me has knowed each other pretty well since. He was a surprisin' hand at gettin' on the right side of women without doin' nuthin' special. I've been there some myself first and last, but there's no use tryin if Chalkeye happens to be on the same trail. Willomene she h'arkened to his talk, and I noticed her, and I concluded she was comparin' him with Hank. After a while we started a game of stud poker, and Chalkeye cleaned Hank out, who couldn't play cards good. He played horses against Hank's gold dust, and by midnight he'd got away with the dust. And Willomene took to his eye, which was jovial like, and I guess she may have been figurin' that if she was a-goin' to marry over again she'd 'a liked to have been acquainted with Chalkeye before the ceremony with Hank. I think she had them thoughts goin' through her mind in a mixed sort of a way.

"There was one occurrence as to the crucifix which Hank's eye lit on during the game, and he said something nasty. And Chalkeye claimed such things must be a god-send to them as took stock in 'em. He spoke serious all the while he was dealin' the cards; nor it wasn't through desirin' to get in his work with Willomene, but because of feelin's on his part that ain't common in this country, and do a man credit, no matter what his acts may sometimes be. Next day he pulled out for Stinkin' Water, havin' treated Willomene with respect, and Hank not havin' any dust left, went to town all the same, leavin' Willomene at the camp. She come down after a while, and watched us as usual, walkin' around slow, and singin' her German songs that hadn't no tune to 'em. And so it was fer about a week. She'd have us all in to supper up at the shack, and look at us eatin' while she'd walk around puttin' grub on your plate. Mighty pleasant she acted always, but she'd not say nuthin' hardly at all.

"Hank come back, and he was used up, you bet! His little winkin' eyes was sweatin' from drink, and Willomene she took no notice of him, nor she didn't cry, neither, for she didn't care no more.

"Hank seen the crucifix same as always, and he says, 'Didn't I tell yu' to take that down?'

"'You did,' says Willomene, very quiet; and she looked at him, and he quit talkin'.

"We was out of meat, and figured we'd go on a hunt before snow came. Yu' see, October was gettin' along, and though we was havin' good weather, all the same, when yu' find them quakin'-asps all turned yaller, and the leaves keeps a-fallin' without no wind to blow 'em down, you're liable to get snowed in on short notice. Hank staid in camp, and before we started up the mountain, I says to him: 'Hank, yu'd ought to leave Willomene do what she wants about prayin'. It don't hurt neither of yu'.'

"And Hank, bein' all trembly from spreein' in town, he says, 'You're all agin me,' like as if he was a baby.

"We was away three days, and awful cold it got to be, with the wind never stoppin' all night roarin' through the timber down the big mountain below where we was camped. We come back to Galena Creek one noon with a good load of elk meat, and looked around. It was plain nobody was there, fer always Willomene come to the door when we'd been out fer a hunt, and, anyway, it was dinner-time, but no smoke was comin' from their chimney.

"'They've quit,' says Honey to me.

"'Well,' I says, 'then they've left word somewheres.'

"'Why, the door's wide open,' says Honey, as we come round that corner of the shack. So we all hollered. Well, it was beginnin' to be strange, and I stepped inside, after waitin' to hear if anybody'd answer. The first thing I seen was that crucifix and a big hole plumb through the middle of it. I don't know why we took the concern down, but we did, and there was the bullet in the log. Things was kind of tossed around in that shack, and Honey says, 'He's shot her too.'

"While we was a-wonderin', something made a noise, and us fellows jumped. It was that parrot, and he was a-crouchin' flat on the floor of the cage, a-swingin' his head sideways, and when we come up he commenced talkin' and croakin' fast, but awful low, and never screechin' oncet, but lookin' at us with his cussed eye. And would yu' believe it, us fellers come and stood around that cage like fools, watchin' the bird and Honey whispers to me, 'You bet he knows!' And then his foot trod on somethin', and he gets down and pulls out an ax. I was along that time, and Hank skinned that bear with his knife, and didn't use an ax. We found nuthin' further till I stepped outside the shack and seen Willomene's trail heavy like in the gravel.

"That set me on trails, and I seen Hank's leadin' into the shack, but not out. So we hunted some more, but gave up, and then I says, 'We must follow up Willomene.' And them big marks took us right by the ditch, where they sunk kind of deep in the soil that was kind of soggy, and then down the cut-off trail. Mighty clear them marks were, and like as they had been made by a person movin' slow. We come along to Little Death Cañon, and just gettin' out of the timber to where the trail takes on to that ledge of little slidin' stones, Honey Wiggin says, 'Look a-there!'

"We stopped, and all seen a black thing ahead. 'Can yu' make it out?' says Honey, and we starts runnin'.

" 'It's a man,' somebody says.

" 'What's he pointin' that way for?' says Honey, and we kep' a-runnin', and come closer, and my God! it was Hank. He was kind of leanin' queer over the edge of the cañon, and we run up to him. He was stiff and stark, and caught in the roots of a dead tree, and the one arm wheeled around like a scarecrow, pointin', and a big cut in his skull. The slide was awful steep where he was, and we crawled and looked over the edge of them brown rock walls. Well, sir, it's a wonder Honey didn't go over that place; and he would, but I seen him stagger and I gripped his arm. Down there, in the bottom, tumbled all in a heap, was Willomene, and Hank's finger was a-pointin' straight at her. She was just a bumped-up brown bundle, and one leg was twisted up like it was stuffed with bran. If fallin' didn't kill her, she must have got choked soon. And we figured out what them two had done, and how she come to fall. Yu' see, Hank must have shot the crucifix when they was havin' hot words, and likely he said she'd be the next thing he'd pump lead into, and she just settled him right there, and I guess more on account of what he done to the crucifix than out of bein' scared for herself. So she packed him on her back when she got cool, figurin' she'd tip him over into the cañon where nobody would suspicion he hadn't fell through accident or bein' drunk. But heftin' him all that ways on her back, she got played out, and when she was on that crumble stuff she'd slipped. Hank got hooked in the tree root, and she'd gone down 'stead of him, with him stuck on top pointin' at her exactly like if he'd been sayin', 'I have yu' beat after all.'

"While we was a-starin', puff! up comes the steam from them sulfur caves, makin' that fluffy sigh. And Honey says, 'Let's get out of here.'

"So we took Hank and buried him on top of a little hill near camp, but Willomene had to stay where she'd fell down in there. We felt kind of bad at havin' to leave her that way, but there was no goin' into that place, and wouldn't be to rescue the livin', let alone to get the dead." Lin paused.

"I think," said I, "you'd have made a try for Willomene if she had been alive, Lin."

The cowpuncher laughed indifferently, as his way is if you discuss his character. "I guess not," he said. "Anyway, what's a life? Why, when yu' remember we're all no better than coyotes, yu' don't seem to set much store by it."

But though Lin occasionally will moralize in this strain, and justify vice and a number of things, I don't think he means it.

MARK TWAIN

SAMUEL LANGHORNE CLEMENS (1835–1910) was born in Florida, Missouri. When he was five, his family, which was always on the move, settled in Hannibal. There, in 1847, Clemens's father died. This brought to an end the young Clemens's limited schooling as he was at once apprenticed to his brother, Orion, who ran a country newspaper, *The Missouri Courier*. In 1853 Clemens decided to head East as a journeyman printer but, presently, he was back again with Orion who was by this time publishing a newspaper in Keokuk, Iowa. After attempting and failing to get to South America in 1857, Clemens forsook printing to become an apprentice pilot on a Mississippi riverboat.

Clemens first went West after serving about two weeks as a second lieutenant in the Confederate Army. He tried his hand at prospecting in the Nevada Territory but without success. He eventually found employment as a reporter for a newspaper in Carson City. By 1862 he was city editor of *The Enterprise* in Virginia City and it was at this time that he officially adopted Mark Twain as his pseudonym, after a depth call made by Mississippi riverboat pilots. A ridiculous duel was the immediate cause of his sudden departure from Nevada and for his landing in San Francisco where he met Bret Harte. In 1865 Twain published his famous short story, "The Celebrated Jumping Frog of Calaveras County," in a New York newspaper and was on his way to becoming a nationally known frontier humorist. For Harte, fame would come nearer to the end of the decade once he had become editor of *The Overland Monthly*.

Twain's contribution to the Western story is varied, but a substantial part of it is as a result of such non-fiction books as ROUGHING IT and LIFE ON THE MISSISSIPPI (J.R. Osgood, 1883). Both are more contemporary in tone and more perceptive of frontier conditions than much of the Western fiction which appeared after them, and yet both are written in a style that makes them seem almost like fiction (and, in truth, much that is in them is certainly imaginatively enhanced). All of Twain's stories with a Western setting are to be found in THE COMPLETE SHORT STORIES OF MARK TWAIN (Doubleday, 1957) edited by Charles Neider. The best biography about him remains MR. CLEMENS AND MARK TWAIN (Simon and Schuster, 1966) by Justin Kaplan. THE AUTOBIOGRAPHY OF MARK TWAIN (Harper, 1959) edited by Charles Neider has many glimpses of the American West in its pages as well as a lengthy diatribe on Bret Harte. A balanced view of these two authors is to be found in Margaret Duckett's MARK TWAIN AND BRET HARTE (University of Oklahoma Press, 1964). Duckett compared Mark Twain's episode of "Buck Fanshaw's Funeral" in ROUGHING IT with Harte's story, "Tennessee's Partner" (1869). She found Twain's story to be "a perfect example of the 'heart-of-gold formula' associated with Harte's best known works," but could not decide "whether Mark Twain was imitating or mocking the sentimental endings which are, perhaps, the weakest parts of Bret Harte's stories." The truth may be that there was little room in Twain's caustic and disillusioned soul for the sentimentality Harte felt in his own halcyon years because of the uninterrupted streak of luck he was then enjoying. Duckett also suggested that it was Harte's basic technique in his poem, "Plain Language from Truthful James" (1870), of "communicating in the words of an unsophisticated narrator social criticism and comedy of which he himself is totally unconscious" that Twain exploited, in what remains his finest novel, "to convey fairly sophisticated social commentary and humor in the words of the humorless Huck Finn."

In 1877 Twain and Harte collaborated on a stage play they titled "Ah Sin." While it is evident to us now that Twain's concern for the Chinese population in San Francisco was but a passing interest, for Harte sympathy for the disenfranchised remained a lifelong passion and, indeed, is the keystone of his fictional world. Twain remarked in his curtain speech on the opening night of "Ah Sin" in New York that "the Chinaman is going to become a very frequent spectacle all over America, by and by, and a difficult political problem, too. Therefore it seems well enough to let the public study him a little on the stage beforehand."

The subsequent rupture in their friendship has been variously attributed to the fact that Twain had loaned Harte large sums of money which he never repaid; that reversals in life had made Harte exacting, critical, and sarcastic; that ill-health, debt, and professional failures had transformed Harte's once jovial disposition into mean-spirited irritability. All this may be true and yet it does not address the most essential difference that had arisen between the two men: they were in 1877 at opposite poles politically and philosophically from where they had been a decade earlier when their friendship began. Indeed, Twain retained many of the racial prejudices Harte customarily attacked.

When Charles Dickens died, Harte wrote of him in *The Overland Monthly:* "No one before him wrote so tenderly of childhood, for no one before him carried into the wisdom of maturity an enthusiasm so youthful — a faith so boylike." Since in Harte's short novel, M'LISS: AN IDYL OF RED MOUNTAIN (1860 and 1863), children are the central characters — M'Liss, the orphan of Smith's Pocket, and the young boy, Risty — Duckett may be justified in her hypothesis "that the shabby little M'Liss with her friend Risty stood, recognized or unrecognized, in the shadowy backgrounds of Mark Twain's mind when he was writing [THE ADVENTURES OF] TOM SAWYER [American Publishing, 1876] and [THE ADVENTURES OF] HUCKLEBERRY FINN [Webster, 1884]" and that this "is altogether compatible with Bernard DeVoto's conclusion in MARK TWAIN'S AMERICA [Little, Brown, 1935] that with Tom Sawyer, Mark Twain found the theme best suited to his interest, his experiences, and his talents. And it does not dim in any way any appreciation of Mark Twain's artistic achievements in writing his two most famous books." However, it is no less worth stressing that, as they aged, Mark Twain's fictional persona began increasingly to form a dichotomy with his inner convictions while Harte's displayed an extraordinary consistency and unity even after the personal disasters of the 1870s. Harte, as he aged, grew increasingly mellow, Twain increasingly irascible. Harte continued to speak with admiration of Twain, whereas Twain's bitterness toward Harte could not be assuaged by time. When news of Harte's death was brought to Twain, he entered upon a long diatribe about someone named "Frank" and only later did it occur to his auditors that he had been referring to Harte by the name by which he had first known him.

Duckett, of course, was scarcely the first to see parallels between Twain's best work and Harte's. It happened so much when both men were alive that, after their friendship ended, even a hint of it could send Twain into a tantrum of vituperation. When a reporter from the Sydney *Argus* interviewed Twain in 1895 while he was in Australia on a lecture tour, the reporter made the mistake of mentioning Harte's name. "I detest him," Twain said, "because I think his work is 'shoddy.' His forte is pathos, but there should be no pathos which does not come out of a man's heart. He has no heart, except his name, and I consider he has produced nothing that is genuine. He is artificial." Surely it did not endear Harte to Twain when the former warned him that he was in danger of letting the showman overshadow his true self. Twain, of course, did not listen and succeeded so well that his projection of himself as a folk personality has been kept alive to this day by various actors who still portray him in stage and television shows.

Twain was ambivalent about frontier freedom, feeling when in the midst of it — as he was during the days he describes in ROUGHING IT — that one could only be appalled by it. Yet, when living in the East in the Gilded Age, he dreamed with Huck of heading out to the territories. "The Californian's Tale" was first published in October, 1893, when it was included as one of 104 stories by various authors in the first book to be issued privately by The Author's Club in New York City. It appeared for the first time in magazine form in the March, 1902 issue of *Harper's Monthly*. In it Twain is dealing with materials familiar from Bret Harte's tales about the aftermath of the Gold Rush days; and, if it makes for an interesting contrast with the story by Harte which I have included, there is also about it an uncanniness reminiscent in the gentler tones of daylight of that dark, nightmarish period in Twain's life when he began sleepwalking following the shock he experienced when as a youth he witnessed a *post-mortem* performed on his father's cadaver.

THE CALIFORNIAN'S TALE
1893

Thirty-five years ago I was out prospecting on the Stanislaus, tramping all day long with pick and pan and horn, and washing a hatful of dirt here and there, always expecting to make a rich strike, and never doing it. It was a lovely region, woodsy, balmy, delicious, and had once been populous, long years before, but now the people had vanished and the charming paradise was a solitude. They went away when the surface diggings gave out. In one place, where a busy little city with banks and newspapers and fire companies and a mayor and aldermen had been, was nothing but a wide expanse of emerald turf, with not even the faintest sign that human life had ever been present there. This was down toward Tuttletown. In the country neighborhood thereabouts, along the dusty roads, one found at intervals the prettiest little cottage homes, snug and cozy, and so cobwebbed with vines snowed thick with roses that the doors and windows were wholly hidden from sight — sign that these were deserted homes, forsaken years ago by defeated and disappointed families who could neither sell them nor give them away. Now and then, half an hour apart, one came across solitary log cabins of the earliest mining days, built by the first gold-miners, the predecessors of the cottage-builders. In some few cases these cabins were still occupied; and when this was so, you could depend upon it that the occupant was the very pioneer who had built the cabin; and you could depend on another thing, too — that he was there because he had once had his opportunity to go home to the States rich, and had not done it; had rather lost his wealth, and had then in his humiliation resolved to sever all communication with his home relatives and friends, and be to them thenceforth as one dead. 'Round about California in that day were scattered a host of these living dead men — pride-smitten poor fellows, grizzled and old at forty, whose secret thoughts were made all of regrets and longings — regrets for their wasted lives, and longings to be out of the struggle and done with it all.

It was a lonesome land! Not a sound in all those peaceful expanses of grass and woods but the drowsy hum of insects; no glimpse of man or beast; nothing to keep up your spirits and make you glad to be alive. And so, at last, in the early part of the afternoon, when I caught sight of a human creature, I felt a most grateful uplift. This person was a man about forty-five years old, and he was standing at the gate of one of those cozy little rose-clad cottages of the sort al-

ready referred to. However, this one hadn't a deserted look; it had the look of
being lived in and petted and cared for and looked after; and so had its front
yard, which was a garden of flowers, abundant, gay, and flourishing. I was invited in, of course, and required to make myself at home — it was the custom of
the country.

It was delightful to be in such a place, after long weeks of daily and nightly
familiarity with miners' cabins — with all which this implies of dirt floor,
never-made beds, tin plates and cups, bacon and beans and black coffee, and
nothing of ornament but war pictures from the Eastern illustrated papers tacked
to the log walls. That was all hard, cheerless, materialistic desolation, but here
was a nest which had aspects to rest the tired eye and refresh that something in
one's nature which, after long fasting, recognizes, when confronted by the belongings of art, howsoever cheap and modest they may be, that it has unconsciously been famishing and now has found nourishment. I could not have believed that a rag carpet could feast me so, and so content me; or that there could
be such solace to the soul in wall-paper and framed lithographs, and bright-
colored tidies and lamp-mats, and Windsor chairs, and varnished what-nots,
with sea-shells and books and china vases on them, and the score of little un-
classifiable tricks and touches that a woman's hand distributes about a home,
which one sees without knowing he sees them, yet would miss in a moment if
they were taken away. The delight that was in my heart showed in my face, and
the man saw it and was pleased; saw it so plainly that he answered it as if it had
been spoken.

"All her work," he said, caressingly; "she did it all herself — every bit,"
and he took the room in with a glance which was full of affectionate worship.
One of those soft Japanese fabrics with which women drape with careful negli-
gence the upper part of a picture-frame was out of adjustment. He noticed it,
and rearranged it with cautious pains, stepping back several times to gauge the
effect before he got it to suit him. Then he gave it a light finishing pat or two
with his hand, and said: "She always does that. You can't tell just what it lacks,
but it does lack something until you've done that — you can see it yourself after
it's done, but that is all you know; you can't find out the law of it. It's like the
finishing pats a mother gives the child's hair after she's got it combed and
brushed, I reckon. I've seen her fix all these things so much that I can do them
all just her way, though I don't know the law of any of them. But she knows the
law. She knows the why and the how both; but I don't know the why; I only
know the how."

He took me into a bedroom so that I might wash my hands; such a bedroom
as I had not seen for years: white counterpane, white pillows, carpeted floor,
papered walls, pictures, dressing-table, with mirror and pin-cushion and dainty
toilet things; and in the corner a wash-stand, with real china-ware bowl and
pitcher, and with soap in a china dish, and on a rack more than a dozen towels,

towels too clean and white for one out of practice to use without some vague sense of profanation. So my face spoke again, and he answered with gratified words:

"All her work; she did it all — herself every bit. Nothing here that hasn't felt the touch of her hand. Now you would think.... But I mustn't talk so much."

By this time I was wiping my hands and glancing from detail to detail of the room's belongings, as one is apt to do when he is in a new place, where everything he sees is a comfort to his eye and his spirit; and I became conscious, in one of those unaccountable ways, you know, that there was something there somewhere that the man wanted me to discover for myself. I knew it perfectly, and I knew he was trying to help me by furtive indications with his eye, so I tried hard to get on the right track, being eager to gratify him. I failed several times, as I could see out of the corner of my eye without being told; but at last I knew I must be looking straight at the thing — knew it from the pleasure issuing in invisible waves from him. He broke into a happy laugh, and rubbed his hands together, and cried out:

"That's it! You've found it. I knew you would. It's her picture."

I went to the little black-walnut bracket on the farther wall, and did find there what I had not yet noticed — a daguerreotype-case. It contained the sweetest girlish face, and the most beautiful, as it seemed to me, that I had ever seen. The man drank the admiration from my face, and was fully satisfied.

"Nineteen her last birthday," he said, as he put the picture back; "and that was the day we were married. When you see her... ah, just wait till you see her!"

"Where is she? When will she be in?"

"Oh, she's away now. She's gone to see her people. They live forty or fifty miles from here. She's been gone two weeks today."

"When do you expect her back?"

"This is Wednesday. She'll be back Saturday, in the evening...about nine o'clock, likely."

I felt a sharp sense of disappointment.

"I'm sorry, because I'll be gone then," I said, regretfully.

"Gone? No...why should you go? Don't go. She'll be so disappointed."

She would be disappointed — that beautiful creature! If she had said the words herself they could hardly have blessed me more. I was feeling a deep, strong longing to see her — a longing so supplicating, so insistent, that it made me afraid. I said to myself: "I will go straight away from this place, for my peace of mind's sake."

"You see, she likes to have people come and stop with us...people who know things, and can talk...people like you. She delights in it; for she knows...oh, she knows nearly everything herself, and can talk, oh, like a bird...and the books she reads, why, you would be astonished. Don't go; it's only a little while, you know, and she'll be so disappointed."

I heard the words, but hardly noticed them, I was so deep in my thinkings and strugglings. He left me, but I didn't know. Presently he was back, with the picture-case in his hand, and he held it open before me and said:

"There, now, tell her to her face you could have stayed to see her, and you wouldn't."

That second glimpse broke down my good resolution. I would stay and take the risk. That night we smoked the tranquil pipe, and talked till late about various things, but mainly about her; and certainly I had had no such pleasant and restful time for many a day. The Thursday followed and slipped comfortably away. Toward twilight a big miner from three miles away came — one of the grizzled, stranded pioneers — and gave us warm salutation, clothed in grave and sober speech. Then he said:

"I only just dropped over to ask about the little madam, and when is she coming home. Any news from her?"

"Oh yes, a letter. Would you like to hear it, Tom?"

"Well, I should think I would, if you don't mind, Henry!"

Henry got the letter out of his wallet, and said he would skip some of the private phrases, if we were willing; then he went on and read the bulk of it — a loving, sedate, and altogether charming and gracious piece of handiwork, with a postscript full of affectionate regards and messages to Tom, and Joe, and Charley, and other close friends and neighbors.

As the reader finished, he glanced at Tom, and cried out:

"Oho, you're at it again! Take your hands away, and let me see your eyes. You always do that when I read a letter from her. I will write and tell her."

"Oh no, you mustn't, Henry. I'm getting old, you know, and any little disappointment makes me want to cry. I thought she'd be here herself, and now you've got only a letter."

"Well, now, what put that in your head? I thought everybody knew she wasn't coming till Saturday."

"Saturday! Why, come to think, I did know it. I wonder what's the matter with me lately? Certainly I knew it. Ain't we all getting ready for her? Well, I must be going now. But I'll be on hand when she comes, old man!"

Late Friday afternoon another gray veteran tramped over from his cabin a mile or so away, and said the boys wanted to have a little gaiety and a good time Saturday night, if Henry thought she wouldn't be too tired after her journey to be kept up.

"Tired? She tired! Oh, hear the man! Joe, *you* know she'd sit up six weeks to please any one of you!"

When Joe heard that there was a letter, he asked to have it read, and the loving messages in it for him broke the old fellow all up; but he said he was such an old wreck that *that* would happen to him if she only just mentioned his name. "Lord, we miss her so!" he said.

Saturday afternoon I found I was taking out my watch pretty often. Henry noticed it, and said, with a startled look:

"You don't think she ought to be here so soon, do you?"

I felt caught, and a little embarrassed; but I laughed, and said it was a habit of mine when I was in a state of expectancy. But he didn't seem quite satisfied; and from that time on he began to show uneasiness. Four times he walked me up the road to a point whence we could see a long distance; and there he would stand, shading his eyes with his hand, and looking. Several times he said:

"I'm getting worried, I'm getting right down worried. I know she's not due till about nine o'clock, and yet something seems to be trying to warn me that something's happened. You don't think anything has happened, do you?"

I began to get pretty thoroughly ashamed of him for his childishness; and at last, when he repeated that imploring question still another time, I lost my patience for the moment, and spoke pretty brutally to him. It seemed to shrivel him up and cow him; and he looked so wounded and so humble after that, that I detested myself for having done the cruel and unnecessary thing. And so I was glad when Charley, another veteran, arrived toward the edge of the evening, and nestled up to Henry to hear the letter read, and talked over the preparations for the welcome. Charley fetched out one hearty speech after another, and did his best to drive away his friend's bodings and apprehensions.

"Anything *happened* to her? Henry, that's pure nonsense. There isn't anything going to happen to her; just make your mind easy as to that. What did the letter say? Said she was well, didn't it? And said she'd be here by nine o'clock, didn't it? Did you ever know her to fail of her word? Why, you know you never did. Well, then, don't you fret; she'll be here, and that's absolutely certain, and as sure as you are born. Come, now, let's get to decorating...not much time left."

Pretty soon Tom and Joe arrived, and then all hands set about adorning the house with flowers. Toward nine the three miners said that as they had brought their instruments they might as well tune up, for the boys and girls would soon be arriving now, and hungry for a good, old-fashioned break-down. A fiddle, a banjo, and a clarinet these were the instruments. The trio took their places side by side, and began to play some rattling dance-music, and beat time with their big boots.

It was getting very close to nine. Henry was standing in the door with his eyes directed up the road, his body swaying to the torture of his mental distress. He had been made to drink his wife's health and safety several times, and now Tom shouted:

"All hands stand by! One more drink and she's here!"

Joe brought the glasses on a waiter, and served the party. I reached for one of the two remaining glasses, but Joe growled, under his breath:

"Drop that! Take the other."

Which I did. Henry was served last. He had hardly swallowed his drink when the clock began to strike. He listened till it finished, his face growing pale and paler; then he said:

"Boys, I'm sick with fear. Help me...I want to lie down!"

They helped him to the sofa. He began to nestle and drowse, but presently spoke like one talking in his sleep, and said: "Did I hear horses' feet? Have they come?"

One of the veterans answered, close to his ear: "It was Jimmy Parrish come to say the party got delayed, but they're right up the road a piece, and coming along. Her horse is lame, but she'll be here in half an hour."

"Oh, I'm so thankful nothing has happened!"

He was asleep almost before the words were out of his mouth. In a moment those handy men had his clothes off, and had tucked him into his bed in the chamber where I had washed my hands. They closed the door and came back. Then they seemed preparing to leave; but I said: "Please don't go, gentlemen. She won't know me; I am a stranger."

They glanced at each other. Then Joe said:

"She? Poor thing, she's been dead nineteen years!"

"Dead?"

"That or worse. She went to see her folks half a year after she was married and, on her way back, on a Saturday evening, the Indians captured her within five miles of this place, and she's never been heard of since."

"And he lost his mind in consequence?"

"Never has been sane an hour since. But he only gets bad when that time of the year comes 'round. Then we begin to drop in here, three days before she's due, to encourage him up, and ask if he's heard from her, and Saturday we all come and fix up the house with flowers, and get everything ready for a dance. We've done it every year for nineteen years. The first Saturday there was twenty-seven of us, without counting the girls; there's only three of us now, and the girls are all gone. We drug him to sleep, or he would go wild; then he's all right for another year...thinks she's with him till the last three or four days come round; then he begins to look for her, and gets out his poor old letter, and we come and ask him to read it to us. Lord, she was a darling!"

FREDERIC REMINGTON

FREDERIC SACKRIDER REMINGTON (1861–1909) was born in Canton, New York. He attended the Yale School of Fine Arts from 1878 to 1880 before he went to Kansas to take up sheep ranching. In the spring of 1884 he decided to sell his ranch and become a wanderer. He went first to Kansas City and then proceeded southwest through the Nations and into Arizona Territory. He returned in late summer of that year and went into partnership in a saloon. When his partners cheated him out of his interest, he took up a pistol and wanted to use a little "frontier justice" on them before he was talked out of it. In the summer of 1885, his marriage to Eva Adele Caten failed, because of her distrust of the time he devoted to art, because of the riff-raff who were his business associates, and because of the instability of his income. Determined to find wealth elsewhere prompted Remington again to enter Arizona Territory where by chance he was prospecting in the Pinal Range when Geronimo coincidentally broke loose from reservation captivity. The 3rd U.S. Cavalry under General George Crook took to the field. Remington used this situation to his advantage by sketching several Apache Indians on the San Carlos reserve and three renegades who paid a hungry visit one night to his camp.

I will grant that originally it had been Remington's intention to join in the pursuit of Geronimo and to sketch the military campaign. He had second thoughts, though, and instead made the theme of these sketches "Soldiering in the Southwest." Remington's portfolio of sketches caused a sensation once they were published. If he hadn't come within two hundred miles of Geronimo, this didn't faze anyone in the East. General Miles replaced General Crook and Remington had occasion to meet Miles once Geronimo had surrendered. Miles could see the usefulness of having a champion of the U.S. Cavalry associated with *Harper's Weekly* and so he proposed to assist Remington in preparing a report on the positive aspects of the campaign. Later the general would provide Remington with the opportunity of illustrating the pursuit of Geronimo for his book, PERSONAL REMINISCENCES AND OBSERVATIONS OF GENERAL NELSON A. MILES (Werner, 1897).

"The depth of Remington's understanding of the West and the degree to which his impressions of it approximate reality are certainly debatable issues," G. Edward White wrote in THE EASTERN ESTABLISHMENT AND THE

WESTERN EXPERIENCE (Yale University Press, 1968). "...Remington's image of the West had both its complex and superficial, its 'realistic' and 'romantic' aspects and his understanding of Indian nature exhibited for the most part a considerable bias." Notwithstanding, commencing in 1886 and for the next decade and a half, Remington was widely hailed as an expert on the West.

Theodore Roosevelt, who had just begun publishing the sketches that would eventually comprise his book, RANCH LIFE AND THE HUNTING TRAIL (Century Company, 1888), asked his publisher for Remington to illustrate his text while it was appearing serially in *The Century Magazine*. Remington complied and he was commercially cynical enough, years later, to paint on a commission directly from Roosevelt the fantasy portrait of T.R. boldly leading the Rough Riders in a charge up San Juan Hill. The phenomenon of American politicians using the media to project a highly favorable image of their activities is scarcely a recent development and it does us well to recall that hard on a century ago Mark Twain remarked that the only native American criminal class sits in Congress.

Along with his work as an illustrator, Remington himself turned to writing, often illustrating his own material, and in the 1890s he collected some of his stories and sketches into a brace of volumes, PONY TRACKS (Harper, 1895) and CROOKED TRAILS (Harper, 1898). Peggy and Harold Samuels, private art dealers specializing in art of the American West, far more recently assembled everything that Remington ever wrote about the West in THE COLLECTED WRITINGS OF FREDERIC REMINGTON (Doubleday, 1979) which also reproduces all of Remington's illustrations for his stories. This collection includes Remington's one novel, JOHN ERMINE OF THE YELLOWSTONE (Macmillan, 1902), published the same year as Owen Wister's THE VIRGINIAN, and yet so very different in tone and perspective. FREDERIC REMINGTON: A BIOGRAPHY (Doubleday, 1982) by Peggy and Harold Samuels followed, an absolutely definitive study of the man, his life, his associations, his literary efforts, his sketches, paintings, and sculptures.

The impression might be gained from what I have described so far of Remington's formative years that his paintings and sculptures were as widely embraced as his illustrations were in demand among publishers. Nothing could be further from the truth. The acceptance of Remington's paintings and sculptures did not really begin until the year he died. "In 1902, he was able to return to his original mission to present the West to America, on canvas and in bronze, choosing the absolute essence of the West in a manner that was vastly significant to the nation," Peggy and Harold Samuels wrote in their biography. "Monet was his one influence, in the theory of light in relation to art, where paint was merely the means of bringing light to the picture. In Remington's paintings, Monet was present in the silver radiance, the harsh bronze effects, the gray-green early night, and the glow of the camp fire. This was vibration, the mysterious suggestion of sentient life. The complete acceptance of Remington's work in 1909 was both the American nation awakening to its own art possibilities and the passage of time overcoming a 'national stupidity' concerning Remington."

For Remington the author, the meaning of the American West was confrontation, between men with each other and with a hostile environment. He was quite definitely not romantic in the same way Wister was, nor was he a believer, as was Roosevelt, in the rugged life for its own sake. In 1898 he purchased an island off Chippewa Bay and, in 1908, he retired to a fifty-acre farm in Ridgefield, Connecticut, where he literally ate and drank himself to death. His disillusionment, while different in character from Wister's and arising from different sources, was for all that even more trenchant. "I knew the railroad was coming," he wrote in 1905. "I saw men already swarming into the land. I knew the derby hat, the smoking chimneys, the cord-binder, and the thirty-day note were upon us in a restless surge. I knew the wild riders and vacant land were about to vanish forever, and the more I considered the subject, the bigger the forever loomed." In 1907 he burned seventy-five of his Western canvases, retaining only his landscape studies; in 1908 he burned twenty-seven more of his best-known Western paintings.

"A Sergeant of the Orphan Troop" was published in the August, 1897 issue of *Harper's Monthly*. In the words of Ben Merchant Vorpahl in FREDERIC REMINGTON AND THE WEST (University of Texas Press, 1978), "because of his preference for military subjects, his desire for war, and his wish to somehow formulate a scheme of things in which the present did not exist," Remington conceived of this story and set it during the Cheyenne ordeal of 1879 at Fort Robinson. Carter Johnson was a real person, a lieutenant in the 10th U.S. Cavalry whom General Miles once called "one of the most skilful and persistent cavalrymen of the young men in the army." Remington first met Johnson in the summer of 1896 and made him his hero; and, like that other hero whom he illustrated for his friend, Wister, he referred to Johnson more often as the "Virginian" than by his rightful name.

Remington believed in heroes, be they cowboys or soldiers. "Cowboys!" he cried when near death. "There are no cowboys any more." Yet he, along with Wister and Roosevelt, helped create such a fantasy around the figure of the cowboy, and because what they created had such a powerful impact on our nation's collective psyche, others experienced their same feelings of loss. What was there left to fill this void? I do not think it accidental that the years shortly before Remington's death saw the emergence on screen of "Broncho Billy" Anderson, and he would be followed by generations of what we came to call "movie cowboys," Tom Mix, Ken Maynard, Gene Autry, John Wayne among them.

John Henley in his article, "Illustrating the West," in *Firsts Magazine*

(5/93) traced the influence of only one Remington image, but this example could be multiplied a hundred-fold and still not exhaust the subject.

A young illustrator by the name of Nick Eggenhofer produced an illustration which was used on a cover for *Western Story Magazine* (4/5/20). To anyone familiar with Western art, this illustration bore a striking resemblance to Frederic Remington's painting, "Drawing Down the Nigh Leader." Some years later, someone enjoying the movie STAGECOACH (United Artists, 1939) might have smirked just a little at a scene which resembled both Eggenhofer's and Remington's image. From this particular instance, one could infer that Western artists, illustrators, and film directors all copied one another. Yet, if that is grounds for holding these art forms in disdain, one might as equally hold all artists everywhere in contempt for continually painting nude women — a fact which oddly enough doesn't seem to bother anyone. It is important, however, to understand that Western art, illustration, and films all share as their subject a particular landscape and history that occurred in a period that covered perhaps seventy-five years, tops. It would be difficult, indeed, to imagine the Old West without horses, stagecoaches, wagon trains, Indians, cavalry charges, and blazing guns. In the case mentioned, wherein we have the image of an American Indian trying to stop a stage by downing the lead horse, the painting came first, followed by the illustration, then followed by the motion picture. But in other cases, an illustration for a book or its cover may have preceded a painting or sculpture.

I realize I am in the same danger, with the analogy I have in mind, as that friend of mine who took a visitor from Italy on a tour of old churches from the turn of the century in Portland, Oregon, and could not understand why she wasn't more impressed by their antiquity. However, when it comes to our images of the Old West, Remington as Homer before him in creating the epic poem had the considerable advantage of having been there first.

A SERGEANT OF THE ORPHAN TROOP
1897

While it is undisputed that Captain Dodd's troop of the Third Cavalry is not an orphan, and is, moreover, quite as far from it as any troop of cavalry in the world, all this occurred many years ago, when it was, at any rate, so called. There was nothing so very unfortunate about it, from what I gather, since it seems to have fought well on its own hook, quite up to all expectations, if not beyond. No officer at that time seemed to care to connect his name with such a rioting, nose-breaking band of desperado cavalrymen, unless it was temporarily, and that was always in the field, and never in garrison. However, in this case it did not have even an officer in the field. But let me go on to my sergeant.

This one was a Southern gentleman, or rather a boy, when he refugeed out of Fredericksburg with his family, before the Federal advance, in a wagon belonging to a Mississippi rifle regiment; but nevertheless some years later he got to be a gentleman, and passed through the Virginia Military Institute with honor. The desire to be a soldier consumed him, but the vicissitudes of the times compelled him, if he wanted to be a soldier, to be a private one, which he became by duly enlisting in the Third Cavalry. He struck the Orphan Troop.

Physically, Nature had slobbered all over Carter Johnson; she had lavished on him her very last charm. His skin was pink, albeit the years of Arizona sun had heightened it to a dangerous red; his mustache was yellow and ideally military; while his pure Virginia accent, fired in terse and jerky form at friend and enemy alike, relieved his natural force of character by a shade of humor. He was thumped and bucked and pounded into what was in the seventies considered a proper frontier soldier, for in those days the nursery idea had not been lugged into the army. If a sergeant bade a soldier "go" or "do," he instantly "went" and "did" — otherwise the sergeant belted him over the head with his six-shooter, and had him taken off in a cart. On pay-days, too, when men who did not care to get drunk went to bed in barracks, they slept under their bunks and not in them, which was conducive to longevity and a good night's rest. When buffalo were scarce they ate the army rations in those wild days; they had a fight often enough to earn thirteen dollars, and at times a good deal more. This was the way with all men at that time, but it was rough on recruits.

So my friend Carter Johnson wore through some years, rose to be a corporal, finally a sergeant, and did many daring deeds. An atavism from "the old border riders" of Scotland shone through the boy, and he took on quickly. He could act the others off the stage and sing them out of the theatre in his chosen profession.

There was fighting all day long around Fort Robinson, Nebraska — a bushwhacking with Dull-Knife's band of the Northern Cheyennes, the Spartans of the plains. It was January; the snow lay deep on the ground, and the cold was knifelike as it thrust at the fingers and toes of the Orphan Troop. Sergeant Johnson with a squad of twenty men, after having been in the saddle all night, was in at the post drawing rations for the troop. As they were packing them up for transport, a detachment of F Troop came galloping by, led by the sergeant's friend, Corporal Thornton. They pulled up.

"Come on, Carter...go with us. I have just heard that some troops have got a bunch of Injuns corralled out in the hills. They can't get 'em down. Let's go help 'em. It's a chance for the fight of your life. Come on."

Carter hesitated for a moment. He had drawn the rations for his troop, which was in sore need of them. It might mean a court-martial and the loss of his chevrons — but a fight! Carter struck his spurred heels, saying, "Come on, boys; get your horses; we will go."

The line of cavalry was half lost in the flying snow as it cantered away over the white flats. The dry powder crunched under the thudding hoofs, the carbines banged about, the overcoat capes blew and twisted in the rushing air, the horses grunted and threw up their heads as the spurs went into their bellies, while the men's faces were serious with the interest in store. Mile after mile rushed the little column, until it came to some bluffs, where it drew rein and stood gazing across the valley to the other hills.

Down in the bottoms they espied an officer and two men sitting quietly on their horses, and on riding up found a lieutenant gazing at the opposite bluffs through a glass. Far away behind the bluffs a sharp ear could detect the reports of guns.

"We have been fighting the Indians all day here," said the officer, putting down his glass and turning to the two "non-coms." "The command has gone around the bluffs. I have just seen Indians up there on the rimrocks. I have sent for troops, in the hope that we might get up there. Sergeant, deploy as skirmishers, and we will try."

At a gallop the men fanned out, then forward at a sharp trot across the flats, over the little hills, and into the scrub pine. The valley gradually narrowed until it forced the skirmishers into a solid body, when the lieutenant took the lead, with the command tailing out in single file. The signs of the Indians grew thicker and thicker — a skirmisher's nest here behind a scrub-pine bush, and there by the side of a rock. Kettles and robes lay about in the snow, with three "bucks" and some women and children sprawling about, frozen as they had died; but all was silent except the crunch of the snow and the low whispers of the men as they pointed to the telltales of the morning's battle.

As the column approached the precipitous rimrock the officer halted, had the horses assembled in a side cañon, putting Corporal Thornton in charge. He ordered Sergeant Johnson to again advance his skirmish-line, in which formation the men moved forward, taking cover behind the pine scrub and rocks, until they came to an open space of about sixty paces, while above it towered the cliff for twenty feet in the sheer. There the Indians had been last seen. The soldiers lay tight in the snow, and no man's valor impelled him on. To the casual glance the rimrock was impassable. The men were discouraged and the officer nonplused. A hundred rifles might be covering the rock fort for all they knew. On closer examination a cutting was found in the face of the rock which was a rude attempt at steps, doubtless made long ago by the Indians. Caught on a bush above, hanging down the steps, was a lariat, which, at the bottom, was twisted around the shoulders of a dead warrior. They had evidently tried to take him up while wounded, but he had died and had been abandoned.

After cogitating, the officer concluded not to order his men forward, but he himself stepped boldly out into the open and climbed up. Sergeant Johnson immediately followed, while an old Swedish soldier by the name of Otto Bordeson fell in behind them. They walked briskly up the hill, and placing their backs against the wall of rock, stood gazing at the Indian.

With a grin the officer directed the men to advance. The sergeant, seeing that he realized their serious predicament, said:

"I think, Lieutenant, you had better leave them where they are; we are holding this rock up pretty hard."

They stood there and looked at each other. "We's in a fix," said Otto.

"I want volunteers to climb this rock," finally demanded the officer.

The sergeant looked up the steps, pulled at the lariat, and commented: "Only one man can go at a time; if there are Indians up there, an old squaw can kill this command with a hatchet; and if there are no Indians, we can all go up."

The impatient officer started up, but the sergeant grabbed him by the belt. He turned, saying, "If I haven't got men to go, I will climb myself."

"Stop, Lieutenant. It wouldn't look right for the officer to go. I have noticed a pine-tree, the branches of which spread over the top of the rock," and the sergeant pointed to it. "If you will make the men cover the top of the rimrock with their rifles, Bordeson and I will go up"; and turning to the Swede, "Will you go, Otto?"

"I will go anywhere the sergeant does," came his gallant reply.

"Take your choice, then, of the steps or the pine-tree," continued the Virginian; and after a rather short but sharp calculation the Swede declared for the tree, although both were death if the Indians were on the rimrock. He immediately began sidling along the rock to the tree, and slowly commenced the ascent. The sergeant took a few steps up the cutting, holding on by the rope. The officer stood out and smiled quizzically. Jeers came from behind the soldiers' bushes — "Go it, Otto! Go it, Johnson! Your feet are loaded! If a snow-bird flies, you will drop dead! Do you need any help? You'll make a hell of a sailor!" and other gibes.

The gray clouds stretched away monotonously over the waste of snow, and it was cold. The two men climbed slowly, anon stopping to look at each other and smile. They were monkeying with death.

At last the sergeant drew himself up, slowly raised his head, and saw snow and broken rock. Otto lifted himself likewise, and he too saw nothing. Rifle shots came clearly to their ears from far in front — many at one time, and scattering at others. Now the soldiers came briskly forward, dragging up the cliff in single file. The dull noises of the fight came through the wilderness. The skirmish-line drew quickly forward and passed into the pine woods, but the Indian trails scattered. Dividing into sets of four, they followed on the tracks of small parties, wandering on until night threatened. At length the main trail of the fugitive band ran across their front, bringing the command together. It was too late for the officer to get his horses before dark, nor could he follow with his exhausted men, so he turned to the sergeant and asked him to pick some men and follow on the trail. The sergeant picked Otto Bordeson, who still affirmed that he would go anywhere that Johnson went, and they started. They were old hunting companions, having confidence in each other's sense and shooting. They ploughed through the snow, deeper and deeper into the pines, then on down a cañon where the light was failing. The sergeant was sweating freely; he raised his hand to press his fur cap backward from his forehead. He drew it quickly away; he stopped and started, caught Otto by the sleeve, and drew a long breath. Still holding his companion, he put his glove again to his nose, sniffed at it again, and with a mighty tug brought the startled Swede to his knees, whispering, "I smell Indians; I can sure smell 'em, Otto...can you?"

Otto sniffed, and whispered back, "Yes, plain!"

"We are ambushed! Drop!" and the two soldiers sunk in the snow. A few feet in front of them lay a dark thing; crawling to it, they found a large calico rag, covered with blood.

"Let's do something, Carter; we's in a fix."

"If we go down, Otto, we are gone; if we go back, we are gone; let's go forward," hissed the sergeant.

Slowly they crawled from tree to tree.

"Don't you see the Injuns?" said the Swede, as he pointed to the rocks in front, where lay their dark forms. The still air gave no sound. The cathedral of nature, with its dark pine trunks starting from gray snow to support gray sky, was dead. Only human hearts raged, for the forms which held them lay like black boulders.

"*Egah...lelah washatah,*" yelled the sergeant.

Two rifle-shots rang and reverberated down the cañon; two more replied instantly from the soldiers. One Indian sunk, and his carbine went clanging down the rocks, burying itself in the snow. Another warrior rose slightly, took aim, but Johnson's six-shooter cracked again, and the Indian settled slowly down without firing. A squaw moved slowly in the half-light to where the buck lay. Bordeson drew a bead with his carbine.

"Don't shoot the woman, Otto. Keep that hole covered; the place is alive with Indians"; and both lay still.

A buck rose quickly, looked at the sergeant, and dropped back. The latter could see that he had him located, for he slowly poked his rifle up without showing his head. Johnson rolled swiftly to one side, aiming with his deadly revolver. Up popped the Indian's head, crack went the six-shooter; the head turned slowly, leaving the top exposed. Crack again went the alert gun of the soldier, the ball striking the head just below the scalp-lock and instantly jerking the body into a kneeling position.

Then all was quiet in the gloomy woods.

After a time the sergeant addressed his voice to the lonely place in Sioux, telling the women to come out and surrender — to leave the bucks, etc.

An old squaw rose sharply to her feet, slapped her breast, shouted "*Lelah washatah,*" and gathering up a little girl and a bundle, she strode forward to the soldiers. Three other women followed, two of them in the same blanket.

"Are there any more bucks?" roared the sergeant, in Sioux.

"No more alive," said the old squaw, in the same tongue.

"Keep your rifle on the hole between the rocks; watch these people; I will go up," directed the sergeant, as he slowly mounted to the ledge, and with leveled six-shooter peered slowly over. He stepped in and stood looking down on the dead warriors.

A yelling in broken English smote the startled sergeant. "Tro up your hands, you d — Injun! I'll blow the top off you!" came through the quiet. The sergeant sprang down to see the Swede standing with carbine leveled at a young buck confronting him with a drawn knife in his hands, while his blanket lay back on the snow.

"He's a buck...he ain't no squaw; he tried to creep on me with a knife. I'm going to kill him," shouted the excited Bordeson.

"No, no, don't kill him. Otto, don't you kill him," expostulated Johnson, as the Swede's finger clutched nervously at the trigger, and turning, he roared, "Throw away that knife, you d — Indian!"

The detachment now came charging in through the snow, and gathered around excitedly. A late arrival came up, breathing heavily, dropped his gun, and springing up and down, yelled, "Be jabbers, I have got among om at last!" A general laugh went up, and the circle of men broke into a straggling line for the return. The sergeant took the little girl up in his arms. She grabbed him fiercely by the throat like a wild-cat, screaming. While nearly choking, he yet tried to mollify her, while her mother, seeing no harm was intended, pacified her in the soft gutturals of the race. She relaxed her grip, and the brave Virginian packed her down the mountain, wrapped in his soldier cloak. The horses were reached in time, and the prisoners put on double behind the soldiers, who fed them crackers as they marched. At two o'clock in the morning the little command rode into Fort Robinson and dismounted at the guard-house. The little girl, who was asleep and half frozen in Johnson's overcoat, would not go to her mother: poor little cat, she had found a nest. The sergeant took her into the guard-house, where it was warm. She soon fell asleep, and slowly he undid her, delivering her to her mother.

On the following morning he came early to the guard-house, loaded with trifles for his little Indian girl. He had expended all his credit at the post-trader's, but he could carry sentiment no further, for "To horse!" was sounding, and he joined the Orphan Troop to again ride on the Dull-Knife trail. The brave Cheyennes were running through the frosty hills, and the cavalry horses pressed hotly after. For ten days the troops surrounded the Indians by day, and stood guard in the snow by night, but coming day found the ghostly warriors gone and their rifle-pits empty. They were cut off and slaughtered daily, but the gallant warriors were fighting to their last nerve. Towards the end they were cooped in a gully on War-Bonnet Creek, where they fortified; but two six-pounders had been hauled out, and were turned on their works. The four troops of cavalry stood to horse on the plains all day, waiting for the poor wretches to come out, while the guns roared, ploughing the frozen dirt and snow over their little stronghold; but they did not come out. It was known that all the provisions they had was the dead horse of a corporal of E Troop, which had been shot within twenty paces of their rifle-pits.

So, too, the soldiers were starving, and the poor Orphans had only crackers to eat. They were freezing also, and murmuring to be led to "the charge," that they might end it there, but they were an orphan troop, and must wait for others to say. The sergeant even asked an officer to let them go, but was peremptorily told to get back in the ranks.

The guns ceased at night, while the troops drew off to build fires, warm their rigid fingers, thaw out their buffalo moccasins, and munch crackers, leaving a strong guard around the Cheyennes. In the night there was a shooting — the Indians had charged through and had gone.

The day following they were again surrounded on some bluffs, and the battle waged until night. Next day there was a weak fire from the Indian position on the impregnable bluffs, and presently it ceased entirely. The place was approached with care and trepidation, but was empty. Two Indian boys, with their feet frozen, had been left as decoys, and after standing off four troops of cavalry for hours, they too had in some mysterious way departed.

But the pursuit was relentless; on, on over the rolling hills swept the famishing troopers, and again the Spartan band turned at bay, firmly entrenched on a bluff as before. This was the last stand — nature was exhausted. The soldiers surrounded them, and Major Wessells turned the handle of the human vise. The command gathered closer about the doomed pits — they crawled on their bellies from one stack of sagebrush to the next. They were freezing. The order to charge came to the Orphan Troop, and yelling his command, Sergeant Johnson ran forward. Up from the sagebrush floundered the stiffened troopers, following on. They ran over three Indians, who lay sheltered in a little cut, and these killed three soldiers together with an old frontier sergeant who wore long hair, but they were destroyed in turn. While the Orphans swarmed under the hill, a rattling discharge poured from the rifle-pits; but the troop had gotten under the fire, and it all passed over their heads. On they pressed, their blood now quickened by excitement, crawling up the steep incline, while volley on volley poured over them. Within nine feet of the pits was a rimrock ledge over which the Indian bullets swept, and here the charge was stopped. It now became a duel. Every time a head showed on either side, it drew fire like a flue-hole. Suddenly our Virginian sprang on the ledge, and like a trill on a piano poured a six-shooter into the entrenchment, and dropped back.

Major Wessells, who was commanding the whole force, crawled to the position of the Orphan Troop, saying, "Doing fine work, boys. Sergeant, I would advise you to take off that red scarf" — when a bullet cut the major across the breast, whirling him around and throwing him. A soldier, one Lannon, sprang to him and pulled him down the bluff, the major protesting that he was not wounded, which proved to be true, the bullet having passed through his heavy clothes.

The troops had drawn up on the other sides, and a perfect storm of bullets whirled over the entrenchments. The powder blackened the faces of the men, and they took off their caps or had them shot off. To raise the head for more than a fraction of a second meant death.

Johnson had exchanged five shots with a fine-looking Cheyenne and, every time he raised his eye to a level with the rock, White Antelope's gun winked at him.

"You will get killed directly," yelled Lannon to Johnson; "they have you spotted."

The smoke blew and eddied over them; again Johnson rose, and again White Antelope's pistol cracked an accompaniment to his own; but with movement like lightning the sergeant sprang through the smoke, and fairly shoving his carbine to White Antelope's breast, he pulled the trigger. A .50 caliber gun boomed in Johnson's face, and a volley roared from the pits, but he fell backward into cover. His comrades set him up to see if any red stains came through the grime, but he was unhurt.

The firing grew; a blue haze hung over the hill. Johnson again looked across the glacis, but again his eye met the savage glare of White Antelope.

"I haven't got him yet, Lannon, but I will"; and Sergeant Johnson again slowly reloaded his pistol and carbine.

"Now, men, give them a volley!" ordered the enraged man, and as volley answered volley through the smoke sprang the daring soldier, and standing over White Antelope as the smoke swirled and almost hid him, he poured his six balls into his enemy, and thus died one brave man at the hands of another in fair battle. The sergeant leaped back and lay down among the men, stunned by the concussions. He said he would do no more. His mercurial temperament had undergone a change, or, to put it better, he conceived it to be outrageous to fight these poor people, five against one. He characterized it as "a d — infantry fight," and rising, talked in Sioux to the enemy — asked them to surrender, or they must otherwise die. A young girl answered him, and said they would like to. An old woman sprang on her and cut her throat with a dull knife, yelling meanwhile to the soldiers that "they would never surrender alive," and saying what she had done.

Many soldiers were being killed, and the fire from the pits grew weaker. The men were besides themselves with rage. "Charge!" rang through the now still air from some strong voice, and, with a volley, over the works poured the troops, with six-shooters going, and clubbed carbines. Yells, explosions, and amid a whirlwind of smoke the soldiers and Indians swayed about, now more slowly and quieter, until the smoke eddied away. Men stood still, peering about with wild open eyes through blackened faces. They held desperately to their weapons. An old bunch of buckskin rags rose slowly and fired a carbine aimlessly. Twenty bullets rolled and tumbled it along the ground, and again the smoke drifted off the mount. This time the air grew clear. Buffalo robes lay all about, blood-spotted everywhere. The dead bodies of thirty-two Cheyennes lay, writhed and twisted, on the packed snow, and among them many women and children, cut and furrowed with lead. In a corner was a pile of wounded squaws, half covered with dirt swept over them by the storm of bullets. One broken creature half raised herself from the bunch. A maddened trumpeter threw up his gun to shoot, but Sergeant Johnson leaped and kicked his gun out of his hands high into the air, saying, "This fight is over."

BRET HARTE

FRANCIS BRETT HARTE (1826–1902) was born in Albany, New York. He deserted the East at seventeen to go to California where he worked, variously, as a schoolteacher, a typesetter, and in a mint. Presently he began publishing short sketches and poems in magazines and in 1857 he contributed several sketches to *The Golden Era* under the byline Bret Harte. It was also here in 1863 that an early version of his short novel, M'LISS: AN IDYLL OF RED MOUNTAIN, appeared. It was based on his experiences as a schoolteacher in a mining district. M'LISS was Harte's longest, most sustained inspiration to this point, and it vividly captures the people who came West in pursuit of gold.

By 1868 Harte had achieved sufficient local fame as a writer to be hired to edit a new magazine, *The Overland Monthly*. It was in its pages that Harte's most famous short stories first saw publication. The first of these, "The Luck of Roaring Camp" (1868), incorporates the archetype of the divine child. However, the tale is also a parody of the sentimental Nativity in St. Luke's Gospel. The child is born to "Cherokee Sal," a prostitute and the only female in the mining camp. Among the bystanders is the gambler, John Oakhurst, who had "the melancholy air and intellectual abstraction of a Hamlet." It is Oakhurst who names the newborn. "'It's better,' said the philosophical Oakhurst, 'to take a fresh deal all round. Call him Luck, and start him fair.'" The advent of Tommy Luck transforms the camp, introducing a new element of human concern into an intensely selfish world, and his life is forfeit when one night "the North Fork suddenly leaped over its banks and swept up the triangular valley of Roaring Camp." This short story embodies both of those aspects which singularly characterized life on the frontier: a new incarnation of *rota Fortunæ* and the tenuousness of human existence in the face of the implacable forces of Nature. What shocked some, including the female typesetter who refused to set this story in type, was that Harte had made a gambler and a prostitute central characters and lauded unconventional aspects of American society that rubbed abrasively against the grain of social conformity.

These themes are even more poignantly developed in "The Outcasts of Poker Flat" (1869) in which a gambler, a prostitute, and a drunk are evicted from a mining camp as undesirables. John Oakhurst is the gambler with whom "life was at best an uncertain game, and he recognized the percentage in favor of the dealer.'' When catastrophe strikes in the form of a blizzard, these three joined now by a girl whose fiancé rides out for Poker Flat to get help are up against the imponderable. Uncle Billy, the drunk, makes off with the remaining horse. Oakhurst reflects ''on the folly of 'throwing up their hand before the game was played out.''' The analogy of life and a game of cards would come to be a dominant theme in Western fiction in the next century and figures prominently in short stories by Ernest Haycox and T.T. Flynn, among several other later authors. Harte, in his immediate future, would have been well advised to have heeded Oakhurst's observation that luck '''is a mighty queer thing. All you know about it for certain is that it's bound to change. And it's finding out when it's going to change that makes you.''' After Oakhurst takes his own life and his body is found by the rescue party, Harte concluded that ''beneath the snow lay he who was at once the strongest and yet the weakest of the outcasts of Poker Flat.''

Because of the national circulation of *The Overland Monthly,* Harte's tales, so filled with new characters, new experiences, and new ways of looking at things, caused a sensation in the East. Harte's literary West was not the black-and-white stereotype of virtue versus vice typical of so many later writers; rather it was an image of a harsh, hostile world where, quite literally, luck or even a change in the weather could mean the difference between life and death. His bad men were occasionally soft-hearted and his good men were often unjust and tyrannical. ''It *was* a very special world, that gold-rush world,'' Walter Van Tilburg Clark wrote in his Foreword to BRET HARTE: STORIES OF THE EARLY WEST (Platt & Munk, 1964), ''with ways of living, thinking, feeling, and acting so particularly its own that there has never been anything quite like it anywhere, before or since. Which is what the literary histories mean when they call Bret Harte a local-color writer.'' In SAN FRANCISCO'S LITERARY FRONTIER (Knopf, 1939), Franklin Walker gave credit where credit was due when he observed that ''with situations in which what was said was only less forceful than what was implied, Harte created the land of a million Westerns, a land in which gun-play was chronic, vigilante committees met before breakfast, and death was as common as a rich strike in the diggings.'' Walker stated correctly that Harte's stories ''succeeded in turning the gold-rush days into what he called 'an era replete with a certain heroic Greek poetry.' Roaring Camp, Poker Flat, Sandy Bar, Wingdam, and Red Gulch were mythical towns inhabited by a society grown in two decades almost as romantic as Camelot or Bagdad.'' What Walker did not point out, but well could have, is that the geography was nearly as mythical as the place-names themselves. Harte, who claimed to have worked briefly as an express rider on a stagecoach, once routed a character from Fiddletown to San Francisco by way of Hangtown, Dutch Flat, and Sacramento, an impossible route that would have ventured into impassable *cañadas* and was without an established stage road. Perhaps his most significant contribution, though, was not the uniqueness of his subject but the form in which he told of it: the short story. It is to Bret Harte that one must look for one of the early great masters of the short story form, and his skill in constructing them has been equaled but, when at his best, never surpassed.

In 1871, at the behest of Eastern editors, Harte went to New York City and, as it happened, never returned to the West. For a time he lived extravagantly and relished his stature as a literary idol, but soon he fell into financial difficulties, trying lecture tours and even collaborating with Mark Twain on "Ah Sin." In 1878 Harte accepted a position as U.S. consular agent in Krefeld, Germany. Two years later he was transferred to Glasgow, eventually settling in London where he continued to write short stories and was a welcome guest in literary circles.

Harte had always been a slow worker, never writing more than a thousand words a day, often less. A.P. Watt, who became his literary agent, organized his markets and his editors so he knew where virtually every story would be published, how much he was to be paid for it, what length it must be, and what must be the general nature of its themes. Some of his best fiction came about as a result of this collaboration and possibly "A *Protégée* of Jack Hamlin's" (1894) and "An Ingénue of the Sierras" (1895) surpass even his very early work for *The Overland Monthly*. He kept out of debt, although he generously continued to send $250 a month to his estranged wife, Anna, and made loans to others in need, including his sister, Eliza. Harte, who had once been notorious for borrowing money and not paying it back, even came in old age to complain to Anna that their son Frank's inability to repay a loan was the reason his full payment to her that month was coming late. As his health failed and the pain of neuralgia in his lower extremities increased until it was incessant, he produced some of his finest work, entitling him as surely as any medieval painter to write instead of *finis* the words *in doloribus pinxi* upon completion of each story. His esophageal carcinoma was long misdiagnosed as a sore throat but even once his condition was correctly identified he continued to write. He was writing on May 5, 1902, the day he collapsed at his writing-table with a thoracic hemorrhage. As Mr. John Oakhurst, whom he had once brought back from the dead, Bret Harte died resigned to abide by the fortune the cards dealt him at the last. He left an estate of £360 6s 9d. He had no debts.

Even if some of them appear only once in his saga, he created imperishable characters: Salomy Jane who saves an outlaw and makes a new life for herself; See Yup and Wan Lee among his Chinese characters; to say nothing of dogs and horses who take on a life of their own. It is also worth noting, as Henry Adams did, that "Bret Harte was the only writer of fiction for the 19th-Century magazines who, in the manner of the classics, insisted on the power of sex as a motivating force rather than a mere matter of sentiment." Henry Seidel Canby concluded that "waves of influence run from the man, and indeed the literary West may be said to have founded itself upon the imagination of Bret Harte."

Harte, of course, has always had his detractors, and they have been nearly legion compared to his admirers. Yet, conversely, Arthur Hobson Quinn in his A HISTORY OF THE AMERICAN DRAMA FROM THE CIVIL WAR UNTIL THE PRESENT DAY (Harper, 1927) felt Harte's "great contribution to modern literature, the portrayal of moral contrasts in human beings from an objective, unmoral point of view, is in itself essentially dramatic." If that is so, why were his attempts at writing stage plays not more successful? The answer, possibly, lies in the fact that Harte's fiction is not so much dramatic in the theatrical sense as cinematic, which explains the numerous successful and memorable motion picture versions based on his fiction in the century following his death.

Harte wrote with economy. He could generate mood, tone, and a visually distinctive sense of place in a matter of a few words. He mastered the art *de façon entendue,* as the French have termed it. At times he could be sentimental and he saw the West as a place for new beginnings; but it was just that for thousands, even millions of people. In THREE PARTNERS (Houghton Mifflin, 1897), perhaps Harte's most successful attempt at a book-length story, three partners have struck it rich and sell out their claim to pursue their individual lives after living and working together for years. Jack Hamlin, a gambler, is on hand to observe and, at times, to protect them. "'I believe in luck!'" he tells them. "'And it comes a mighty sight oftener than a fellow thinks its does. But it doesn't come to stay. So I'd advise you to keep your eyes skinned and hang on to it while it's with you, like grim death.'" When John Oakhurst had held forth on luck, the author had been a different man, with his future before him and all the promise it held. When Jack Hamlin made this statement, Harte had learned from experience that luck does not stay. There is nothing of the sentimental in this novel. The author had learned that "of all optimism that of love is the most convincing," but it does not end as one might expect or hope. When the youngest partner's wife decides to leave him for another man, Hamlin is inclined to interfere even though "personally he could not conceive why a man should ever try to prevent a woman from running away from him...but then Mr. Hamlin's personal experiences had been quite the other way" — a remark that rings back over the years all the way to "Brown of Calaveras" (1869).

Dick Hall, a drunkard better known to the camp as Alky Hall, makes his first appearance in the novelette, "Devil's Ford" (1884). In THREE PARTNERS he has reformed, "but with the accession of sobriety he had lost his good humor, and had the irritability and intolerance of virtuous restraint," a posture painfully familiar to generations of Americans subjected to prohibitionism against alcohol, tobacco, gambling, and sexual freedom. Harte's philosophy, in contrast, was best summed up in a remark to be found in "A Passage in the Life of Mr. John Oakhurst" (1875) when a young lady inquires about Oakhurst, "'But isn't he a gambler?'" "'He is,'" she is told, "'but I wish my dear young lady, that we all played as open and honest a game as our friend yonder, and were as willing as he is to abide by its fortunes.'" Such, too, proves to be the case in the lives of the three partners who come to be reunited at the end.

Harte's single greatest literary success was his off-trail poem in 1870, "Plain Language from Truthful James," which became better known by the title "The Heathen Chinee" and depicted a Chinaman as an unscrupulous adversary. No less than three popular songs were created with lyrics based on "The Heathen Chinee." The poem was on everyone's lips and oft-quoted. It would later disgust him that this one occasion, when he had indulged a xenophobic attempt at humor, retained its currency while many of his other, far more realistic and sympathetic portraits of the dilemmas and clashes between Oriental and Occidental culture in the West should be ignored. In "Three Vagabonds of Trinidad," one of his finest stories, he drew sympathetic portraits of an Indian, a Chinaman, and a mongrel dog, all ostracized from the community. When Indian Jim regards Li Tee, to his troubled mind occurs the notion that "equal vagabonds though they were, Li Tee had more claims upon civilization, through those of his own race who were permitted to live among the white men, and were not hunted to 'reservations' and confined there like Jim's people."

It may be that a reassessment of Bret Harte, although inevitable, will not occur until the 21st Century. Yet, when it does come, the words of Harte's first biographer, T. Edgar Pemberton, may well prove prophetic and from beginning to end his California stories will be recognized as the first important steps toward a "characteristic Western American literature." One thing is certain. His great legacy — as Homer's geography in ODYSSEY — is the "Bret Harte country" of the imagination, a world without boundaries in which the lure of gold will be recognized as a metaphor for an entire nation in search of a way of life that would prove somehow very different from all that had gone before it, in which the struggle for social justice and civil rights is combined uniquely with Harte's totally characteristic plea that the most significant achievement humanity can ever hope to attain is to show more mercy toward human beings.

THREE VAGABONDS OF TRINIDAD
1900

"Oh! It's you, is it?" said the Editor.

The Chinese boy to whom the colloquialism was addressed answered literally, after his habit:

"Allee same Li Tee; me no changee. Me no ollee China boy."

"That's so," said the Editor with an air of conviction. "I don't suppose there's another imp like you in all Trinidad County. Well, next time don't scratch outside there like a gopher, but come in."

"Lass time,"·suggested Li Tee blandly, "me tap tappee. You no like tap tappee. You say, allee same dam wood-peckel."

It was quite true — the highly sylvan surroundings of the Trinidad *Sentinel* office — a little clearing in a pine forest — and its attendant fauna, made these signals confusing. An accurate imitation of a woodpecker was also one of Li Tee's accomplishments.

The Editor without replying finished the note he was writing; at which Li Tee, as if struck by some coincident recollection, lifted up his long sleeve, which served him as a pocket, and carelessly shook out a letter on the table like a conjuring trick. The Editor, with a reproachful glance at him, opened it. It was only the ordinary request of an agricultural subscriber — one Johnson — that the Editor would "notice" a giant radish grown by the subscriber and sent by the bearer.

"Where's the radish, Li Tee?" said the Editor suspiciously.

"No hab got. Ask Mellikan boy."

Here Li Tee condescended to explain that on passing the schoolhouse he had been set upon by the schoolboys, and that in the struggle the big radish — being, like most such monstrosities of the quick Californian soil, merely a mass of organized water — was "mashed" over the head of some of his assailants. The Editor, painfully aware of these regular persecutions of his errand boy, and perhaps realizing that a radish which could not be used as a bludgeon was not of a sustaining nature, forbore any reproof.

"But I cannot notice what I haven't seen, Li Tee," he said good-humoredly.

"S'pose you lie — allee same as Johnson," suggested Li with equal cheerfulness. "He foolee you with lotten stuff — you foolee Mellikan man, allee same."

The Editor preserved a dignified silence until he had addressed his letter. "Take this to Mrs. Martin," he said, handing it to the boy; "and mind you keep clear of the schoolhouse. Don't go by the Flat either if the men are at work, and don't, if you value your skin, pass Flanigan's shanty, where you set off those firecrackers and nearly burnt him out the other day. Look out for Barker's dog at the crossing, and keep off the main road if the tunnel men are coming over the hill." Then remembering that he had virtually closed all the ordinary approaches to Mrs. Martin's house, he added, "Better go round by the woods, where you won't meet *any one.*"

The boy darted off through the open door, and the Editor stood for a moment looking regretfully after him. He liked his little *protégé* ever since that unfortunate child — a waif from a Chinese wash-house—was impounded by some indignant miners for bringing home a highly imperfect and insufficient washing, and kept as hostage for a more proper return of the garments. Unfortunately, another gang of miners, equally aggrieved, had at the same time looted the wash-house and driven off the occupants, so that Li Tee remained unclaimed. For a few weeks he became a sporting appendage of the miners' camp; the stolid butt of good-humored practical jokes, the victim alternately of careless indifference or of extravagant generosity. He received kicks and half-dollars intermittently, and pocketed both with stoical fortitude. But under this treatment he presently lost the docility and frugality which was part of his inheritance, and began to put his small wits against his tormentors, until they grew tired of their own mischief and his. But they knew not what to do with him. His pretty nankeen-yellow skin debarred him from the white "public school," while, although as a heathen he might have reasonably claimed attention from the Sabbath school, the parents who cheerfully gave their contributions to the heathen abroad objected to him as a companion of their children in the church at home. At this juncture the Editor offered to take him into his printing office as a "devil." For a while he seemed to be endeavoring, in his old literal way, to act up to that title. He inked everything but the press. He scratched Chinese characters of an abusive import on "leads," printed them, and stuck them about the office; he put "punk" in the foreman's pipe, and had been seen to swallow small type merely as a diabolical recreation. As a messenger he was fleet of foot, but uncertain of delivery. Some time previously the Editor had enlisted the sympathies of Mrs. Martin, the good-natured wife of a farmer, to take him in her household on trial, but on the third day Li Tee had run away. Yet the Editor had not despaired, and it was to urge her to a second attempt that he dispatched that letter.

He was still gazing abstractedly into the depths of the wood when he was conscious of a slight movement — but no sound — in a clump of hazel near him, and a stealthy figure glided from it. He at once recognized it as "Jim," a well-known drunken Indian vagrant of the settlement — tied to its civilization by the single link of "fire water," for which he forsook equally the reservation, where it was forbidden, and his own camps, where it was unknown. Unconscious of his silent observer, he dropped upon all fours, with his ear and nose alternately to the ground like some tracking animal. Then, having satisfied himself, he rose, and bending forward in a dogged trot, made a straight line for the woods. He was followed a few seconds later by his dog — a slinking, rough, wolf-like brute, whose superior instinct, however, made him detect the silent presence of some alien humanity in the person of the Editor, and to recognize it with a yelp of habit, anticipatory of the stone that he knew was always thrown at him.

"That's cute," said a voice, "but it's just what I expected all along."

The Editor turned quickly. His foreman was standing behind him, and had evidently noticed the whole incident.

"It's what I allus said," continued the man. "That boy and that Injin are thick as thieves. Ye can't see one without the other — and they've got their little tricks and signals by which they follow each other. T'other day when you was kalkilatin' Li Tee was doin' your errands I tracked him out on the marsh, just by followin' that ornery, pizenous dog o' Jim's. There was the whole caboodle of 'em — including Jim — campin' out, and eatin' raw fish that Jim had ketched, and green stuff they had both sneaked outer Johnson's garden. Mrs. Martin may *take* him, but she won't keep him long while Jim's round. What makes Li foller that blamed old Injin soaker, and what makes Jim, who, at least, is a 'Merican, take up with a furrin' heathen, just gets me."

The Editor did not reply. He had heard something of this before. Yet, after all, why should not these equal outcasts of civilization cling together?

Li Tee's stay with Mrs. Martin was brief. His departure was hastened by an untoward event — apparently ushered in, as in the case of other great calamities, by a mysterious portent in the sky. One morning an extraordinary bird of enormous dimensions was seen approaching from the horizon, and eventually began to hover over the devoted town. Careful scrutiny of this ominous fowl, however, revealed the fact that it was a monstrous Chinese kite, in the shape of a flying dragon. The spectacle imparted considerable liveliness to the community which, however, presently changed to some concern and indignation. It appeared that the kite was secretly constructed by Li Tee in a secluded part of Mrs. Martin's clearing, but when it was first tried by him he found that through some error of design it required a tail of unusual proportions. This he hurriedly supplied by the first means he found — Mrs. Martin's clothes-line, with part of the weekly wash depending from it. This fact was not at first noticed by the ordinary sightseer, although the tail seemed peculiar — yet perhaps not more peculiar than a dragon's tail ought to be. But when the actual theft was discovered and reported through the town, a vivacious interest was created, and spyglasses were used to identify the various articles of apparel still hanging on that ravished clothes-line. These garments, in the course of their slow disengagement from the clothes-pins through the gyrations of the kite, impartially distributed themselves over the town — one of Mrs. Martin's stockings falling upon the verandah of the Polka Saloon, and the other being afterwards discovered on the belfry of the First Methodist Church — to the scandal of the congregation. It would have been well if the result of Li Tee's invention had ended here. Alas! the kite-flyer and his accomplice, "Injin Jim," were tracked by means of the kite's tell-tale cord to a lonely part of the marsh and rudely dispossessed of their charge by Deacon Hornblower and a constable. Unfortunately, the captors overlooked the fact that the kite-flyers had taken the precaution of making a "half-turn" of the stout cord around a log to ease the tremendous pull of the kite — whose power the captors had not reckoned upon — and the Deacon incautiously substituted his own body for the log. A singular spectacle is said to have then presented itself to the on-lookers. The Deacon was seen to be running wildly by leaps and bounds over the marsh after the kite, closely followed by the constable in equally wild efforts to restrain him by tugging at the end of the line. The extraordinary race continued to the town until the constable fell, losing his hold of the line. This seemed to impart a singular specific levity to the Deacon who, to the astonishment of everybody, incontinently sailed up into a tree! When he was succored and cut down from the demoniac kite, he was found to have sustained a dislocation of the shoulder, and the constable was severely shaken. By that one infelicitous stroke the two outcasts made an enemy of the Law and the Gospel as represented in Trinidad County. It is to be feared also that the ordinary emotional instinct of a frontier community, to which they were now simply abandoned, was as little to be trusted. In this dilemma they disappeared from the town the next day — no one knew where. A pale blue smoke rising from a lonely island in the bay for some days afterwards suggested their possible refuge. But nobody greatly cared. The sympathetic mediation of the Editor was characteristically opposed by Mr. Parkin Skinner, a prominent citizen:

"It's all very well for you to talk sentiment about niggers, Chinamen, and Injins, and you fellers can laugh about the Deacon being snatched up to heaven like Elijah in that blamed Chinese chariot of a kite...but I kin tell you, gentlemen, that this is a white man's country! Yes, sir, you can't get over it! The nigger of every description yeller, brown, or black, call him 'Chinese,' 'Injin,' or 'Kanaka,' or what you like — hez to clar off of God's footstool when the Anglo-Saxon gets started! It stands to reason that they can't live alongside o' printin' presses, M'Cormick's reapers, and the Bible! Yes, sir! the Bible; and Deacon Hornblower kin prove it to you. It's our manifest destiny to clar them out — that's what we was put here for — and it's just the work we've got to do!"

I have ventured to quote Mr. Skinner's stirring remarks to show that proba-

bly Jim and Li Tee ran away only in anticipation of a possible lynching, and to
prove that advanced sentiments of this high and ennobling nature really ob-
tained forty years ago in an ordinary American frontier town which did not then
dream of Expansion and Empire!

Howbeit, Mr. Skinner did not make allowance for mere human nature. One
morning Master Bob Skinner, his son, aged twelve, evaded the schoolhouse,
and started in an old Indian "dug-out" to invade the island of the miserable refugees. His purpose was not clearly defined to himself, but was to be modified
by circumstances. He would either capture Li Tee and Jim, or join them in their
lawless existence. He had prepared himself for either event by surreptitiously
borrowing his father's gun. He also carried victuals, having heard that Jim ate
grasshoppers and Li Tee rats, and misdoubting his own capacity for either diet.
He paddled slowly, well in shore, to be secure from observation at home, and
then struck out boldly in his leaky canoe for the island — a tufted, tussocky
shred of the marshy promontory torn off in some tidal storm. It was a lovely
day, the bay being barely ruffled by the afternoon "trades"; but as he neared the
island he came upon the swell from the bar and the thunders of the distant Pacific, and grew a little frightened. The canoe, losing way, fell into the trough of
the swell, shipping salt water, still more alarming to the prairie-bred boy. Forgetting his plan of a stealthy invasion, he shouted lustily as the helpless and wa-
ter-logged boat began to drift past the island; at which a lithe figure emerged
from the reeds, threw off a tattered blanket, and slipped noiselessly, like some
animal, into the water. It was Jim who, half wading, half swimming, brought
the canoe and boy ashore. Master Skinner at once gave up the idea of invasion,
and concluded to join the refugees.

This was easy in his defenseless state, and his manifest delight in their rude
encampment and gypsy life, although he had been one of Li Tee's oppressors in
the past. But that stolid pagan had a philosophical indifference which might
have passed for Christian forgiveness, and Jim's native reticence seemed like
assent. And, possibly, in the minds of these two vagabonds there might have
been a natural sympathy for this other truant from civilization, and some delicate flattery in the fact that Master Skinner was not driven out, but came of his
own accord. Howbeit, they fished together, gathered cranberries on the marsh,
shot a wild duck and two plovers and, when Master Skinner assisted in the
cooking of their fish in a conical basket sunk in the ground, filled with water,
heated by rolling red-hot stones from their drift-wood fire into the buried basket, the boy's felicity was supreme. And what an afternoon! To lie, after this
feast, on their bellies in the grass, replete like animals, hidden from everything
but the sunshine above them; so quiet that gray clouds of sandpipers settled fear-
lessly around them, and a shining brown muskrat slipped from the ooze within a
few feet of their faces — was to feel themselves a part of the wild life in earth
and sky. Not that their own predatory instincts were hushed by this divine

peace; that intermitting black spot upon the water, declared by the Indian to be a seal, the stealthy glide of a yellow fox in the ambush of a callow brood of mallards, the momentary straying of an elk from the upland upon the borders of the marsh, awoke their tingling nerves to the happy but fruitless chase. And when night came, too soon, and they pigged together around the warm ashes of their camp-fire, under the low lodge poles of their wigwam of dried mud, reeds, and driftwood, with the combined odors of fish, wood-smoke, and the warm salt breath of the marsh in their nostrils, they slept contentedly. The distant lights of the settlement went out one by one, the stars came out, very large and very silent, to take their places. The barking of a dog on the nearest point was followed by another farther inland. But Jim's dog, curled at the feet of his master, did not reply. What had he to do with civilization?

The morning brought some fear of consequences to Master Skinner, but no abatement of his resolve not to return. But here he was oddly combated by Li Tee. "S'pose you go back allee same. You tellee fam'lee canoe go topside down...you plentee swimee to bush. Allee night in bush. Housee big way off... how can get? *Sabe?*"

"And I'll leave the gun, and tell Dad that when the canoe upset the gun got drowned," said the boy eagerly.

Li Tee nodded.

"And come again Saturday and bring more powder and shot and a bottle for Jim," said Master Skinner excitedly.

"Good!" grunted the Indian.

Then they ferried the boy over to the peninsula, and set him on a trail across the marshes, known only to themselves, which would bring him home. And when the Editor the next morning chronicled among his news, "Adrift on the Bay — A Schoolboy's Miraculous Escape," he knew as little what part his missing Chinese errand boy had taken in it as the rest of his readers.

Meantime the two outcasts returned to their island camp. It may have occurred to them that a little of the sunlight had gone from it with Bob; for they were in a dull, stupid way fascinated by the little white tyrant who had broken bread with them. He had been delightfully selfish and frankly brutal to them, as only a schoolboy could be, with the addition of the consciousness of his superior race. Yet they each longed for his return, although he was seldom mentioned in their scanty conversation — carried on in monosyllables, each in his own language, or with some common English word, or more often restricted solely to signs. By a delicate flattery, when they did speak of him it was in what they considered to be his own language.

"Boston boy, plenty like catchee *him,*" Jim would say, pointing to a distant swan. Or Li Tee, hunting a striped water snake from the reeds, would utter stolidly, "Mellikan boy no likee snake." Yet the next two days brought some trouble and physical discomfort to them. Bob had consumed, or wasted, all their provisions — and, still more unfortunately, his righteous visit, his gun, and his superabundant animal spirits had frightened away the game, which their habitual quiet and taciturnity had beguiled into trustfulness. They were half starved, but they did not blame him. It would come all right when he returned. They counted the days, Jim with secret notches on the long pole, Li Tee with a string of copper "cash" he always kept with him. The eventful day came at last — a warm autumn day, patched with inland fog like blue smoke and smooth, tranquil, open surfaces of wood and sea; but to their waiting, confident eyes the boy came not out of either. They kept a stolid silence all that day until night fell, when Jim said, "Mebbe Boston boy go dead." Li Tee nodded. It did not seem possible to these two heathens that anything else could prevent the Christian child from keeping his word.

After that, by the aid of the canoe, they went much on the marsh, hunting apart, but often meeting on the trail which Bob had taken, with grunts of mutual surprise. These suppressed feelings, never made known by word or gesture, at last must have found vicarious outlet in the taciturn dog, who so far forgot his usual discretion as to once or twice seat himself on the water's edge and indulge in a fit of howling. It had been a custom of Jim's on certain days to retire to some secluded place where, folded in his blanket, with his back against a tree, he remained motionless for hours. In the settlement this had been usually referred to as the after-effects of drink, known as the "horrors," but Jim had explained it by saying it was "when his heart was bad." And now it seemed, by these gloomy abstractions, that "his heart was bad" very often. And then the long-withheld rains came one night on the wings of a fierce southwester, beating down their frail lodge and scattering it abroad, quenching their camp-fire, and rolling up the bay until it invaded their reedy island and hissed in their ears. It drove the game from Jim's gun; it tore the net and scattered the bait of Li Tee, the fisherman. Cold and half starved in heart and body, but more dogged and silent than ever, they crept out in their canoe into the storm-tossed bay, barely escaping with their miserable lives to the marshy peninsula. Here, on their enemy's ground, skulking in the rushes, or lying close behind tussocks, they at last reached the fringe of forest below the settlement. Here, too, sorely pressed by hunger, and doggedly reckless of consequences, they forgot their caution, and a flight of teal fell to Jim's gun on the very outskirts of the settlement.

It was a fatal shot, whose echoes awoke the forces of civilization against them. For it was heard by a logger in his hut near the marsh who, looking out, had seen Jim pass. A careless, good-natured frontiersman, he might have kept the outcasts' mere presence to himself; but there was that damning shot! An Indian with a gun! That weapon, contraband of law, with dire fines and penalties to whoso sold or gave it to him! A thing to be looked into — some one to be punished! An Indian with a weapon that made him the equal of the white! Who was safe? He hurried to town to lay his information before the constable but, meeting Mr. Skinner, imparted the news to him. The latter pooh-poohed the constable, who he alleged had not yet discovered the whereabouts of Jim, and suggested that a few armed citizens should make the chase themselves. The fact was that Mr. Skinner, never quite satisfied in his mind with his son's account of the loss of the gun, had put two and two together and was by no means inclined to have his own gun possibly identified by the legal authority. Moreover, he went home and at once attacked Master Bob with such vigor and so highly colored a description of the crime he had committed, and the penalties attached to it, that Bob confessed. More than that, I grieve to say that Bob lied. The Indian had "stoled his gun," and threatened his life if he divulged the theft. He told how he was ruthlessly put ashore, and compelled to take a trail only known to them to reach his home. In two hours it was reported throughout the settlement that the infamous Jim had added robbery with violence to his illegal possession of the weapon. The secret of the island and the trail over the marsh was told only to a few.

Meantime it had fared hard with the fugitives. Their nearness to the settlement prevented them from lighting a fire, which might have revealed their hiding-place, and they crept together, shivering all night in a clump of hazel. Scared thence by passing but unsuspecting wayfarers wandering off the trail, they lay part of the next day and night amid some tussocks of salt grass, blown on by the cold sea breeze; chilled, but securely hidden from sight. Indeed, thanks to some mysterious power they had of utter immobility, it was wonderful how they could efface themselves, through quiet and the simplest environment. The lee side of a straggling vine in the meadow, or even the thin ridge of cast-up drift on the shore, behind which they would lie for hours motionless, was a sufficient barrier against prying eyes. In this occupation they no longer talked together, but followed each other with the blind instinct of animals — yet always unerringly, as if conscious of each other's plans. Strangely enough, it was the real animal alone — their nameless dog — who now betrayed impatience and a certain human infirmity of temper. The concealment they were resigned to, the sufferings they mutely accepted, he alone resented! When certain scents or sounds, imperceptible to their senses, were blown across their path, he would, with bristling back, snarl himself into guttural and strangulated fury. Yet, in their apathy, even this would have passed them unnoticed, but that on the second night he disappeared suddenly, returning after two hours' absence with bloody jaws — replete, but still slinking and snappish. It was only in the morning that, creeping on their hands and knees through the stubble, they came upon the torn and mangled carcass of a sheep. The two men looked at each other without speaking — they knew what this act of rapine meant to themselves. It meant a fresh hue and cry after them — it meant that their starving companion had helped to draw the net closer round them. The Indian grunted, Li Tee smiled vacantly; but with their knives and fingers they finished what the dog had begun, and became equally culpable. But that they were heathens, they could not have achieved a delicate ethical responsibility in a more Christian-like way.

Yet the rice-fed Li Tee suffered most in their privations. His habitual apathy increased with a certain physical lethargy which Jim could not understand. When they were apart he sometimes found Li Tee stretched on his back with an odd stare in his eyes, and once, at a distance, he thought he saw a vague thin vapor drift from where the Chinese boy was lying and vanish as he approached. When he tried to arouse him there was a weak drawl in his voice and a drug-like odor in his breath. Jim dragged him to a more substantial shelter, a thicket of alder. It was dangerously near the frequented road, but a vague idea had sprung up in Jim's now troubled mind that, equal vagabonds though they were, Li Tee had more claims upon civilization, through those of his own race who were permitted to live among the white men, and were not hunted to "reservations" and confined there like Jim's people. If Li Tee was "heap sick," other Chinamen might find and nurse him. As for Li Tee, he had lately said, in a more lucid interval: "Me go dead...allee samee Mellikan boy. You go dead too...allee samee," and then lay down again with a glassy stare in his eyes. Far from being frightened at this, Jim attributed his condition to some enchantment that Li Tee had evoked from one of his gods — just as he himself had seen "medicine-men" of his own tribe fall into strange trances, and was glad that the boy no longer suffered. The day advanced, and Li Tee still slept. Jim could hear the church bells ringing; he knew it was Sunday — the day on which he was hustled from the main street by the constable; the day on which the shops were closed, and the drinking saloons open only at the back door; the day whereon no man worked — and for that reason, though he knew it not, the day selected by the ingenious Mr. Skinner and a few friends as especially fitting and convenient for a chase of the fugitives. The bell brought no suggestion of this — though the dog snapped under his breath and stiffened his spine. And then he heard another sound, far off and vague, yet one that brought a flash into his murky eye, that lit up the heaviness of his Hebraic face, and even showed a slight color in his high cheekbones. He lay down on the ground, and listened with suspended breath. He heard it now distinctly. It was the Boston boy calling, and the word he was calling was "Jim."

Then the fire dropped out of his eyes as he turned with his usual stolidity to where Li Tee was lying. Him he shook, saying briefly: "Boston boy come back!" But there was no reply, the dead body rolled over inertly under his hand; the head fell back, and the jaw dropped under the pinched yellow face. The Indian gazed at him slowly, and then gravely turned again in the direction of the voice. Yet his dull mind was perplexed for, blended with that voice, were other sounds like the tread of clumsily stealthy feet. But again the voice called "Jim!" and, raising his hands to his lips, he gave a low whoop in reply. This was followed by silence, when suddenly he heard the voice — the boy's voice — once again, this time very near him, saying eagerly:

"There he is!"

Then the Indian knew all. His face, however, did not change as he took up his gun, and a man stepped out of the thicket into the trail.

"Drop that gun, you d—d Injin!"

The Indian did not move.

"Drop it, I say!"

The Indian remained erect and motionless.

A rifle shot broke from the thicket. At first it seemed to have missed the Indian, and the man who had spoken cocked his own rifle. But the next moment the tall figure of Jim collapsed where he stood into a mere blanketed heap.

The man who had fired the shot walked towards the heap with the easy air of a conqueror. But suddenly there arose before him an awful phantom, the incarnation of savagery — a creature of blazing eyeballs, flashing tusks, and hot carnivorous breath. He had barely time to cry out "A wolf!" before its jaws met in his throat, and they rolled together on the ground.

But it was no wolf— as a second shot proved — only Jim's slinking dog; the only one of the outcasts who at that supreme moment had gone back to his original nature.

JOHN G. NEIHARDT

JOHN GNEISENAU NEIHARDT (1881–1973) was born near Sharpsburg, Illinois. In 1886 he went with his family to live in his pioneer grandparents' sod house on the upper Solomon River in Kansas. In 1891 the family moved again, this time to Wayne, Nebraska, and it was here that Neihardt was graduated with a Bachelor's degree at the age of sixteen from Nebraska Normal College. Neihardt's first published book was a volume of poetry, THE DIVINE ENCHANTMENT (James T. White, 1900).

In 1901 he became assistant to a trader working among the Omaha Indians on their reservation. For a time he edited a country weekly newspaper and in 1908 he married Mona Martinsen. She was a sculptress and a former student of Auguste Rodin. Although his wife came from a family of comfortable wealth, she willingly committed herself to sharing Neihardt's frugal existence as a poet while he worked on what he felt would be his masterpiece, the five American epic poems which began with THE SONG OF HUGH GLASS (Macmillan, 1915) and which were finally collected together in a single volume titled A CYCLE OF THE WEST (Macmillan, 1949). In old age, no longer able to read print, busloads of students would regularly visit Neihardt and sit around his wheelchair as he would recite his poetry from memory.

For me, Neihardt's finest contributions to the Western story consist of the many short stories he wrote for the magazine market in the first decade of the 20th Century, only some of which he collected in book form, THE LONESOME TRAIL and INDIAN TALES AND OTHERS; his only novel, WHEN THE TREE FLOWERED: AN AUTHENTIC TALE OF THE OLD SIOUX WORLD (Macmillan, 1951); and his work as amanuensis for the aged Sioux medicine man, Black Elk. This last is now available in a trade paperback edition from the University of Nebraska Press. If you are not familiar with it, I cannot recommend this book highly enough. Also, Lucile F. Aly has written an interesting, if brief, literary appraisal of Neihardt's poetry and fiction in her chapbook, JOHN G. NEIHARDT (Boise State University Press, 1976). It may prompt you, as it did me, to seek out Neihardt's many uncollected stories in various magazine issues.

Black Elk himself felt that his spirit vision, imparted to him when he was but nine years of age, failed; but neither Neihardt nor many modern readers — myself among them — are so sure of this, since this spirit vision was not necessarily limited to the present time. Neihardt recognized that the fulfillment of both the cultural and spiritual ideals of Americans could not be separated from the vision of man's role as a part of Nature; that not until all subsequent Americans came to love and respect the land equally would a truly spiritual and epochal period be possible. This may strike some readers as ridiculous idealism. But it was endorsed by the Sioux nation which, at Neihardt's funeral service in 1973, held their own sacred ceremony.

I recall when I was young and in college I read André Malraux's LA TENTATION DE L'OCCIDENT [THE TEMPTATION OF THE WEST] first published in Paris in 1926. It is structured in the form of letters exchanged between A.D., a Frenchman living in the Far East, and Ling, a Chinese traveling in Europe. I was extremely moved by Ling's observation in one of his letters that Christians, in attempting to picture their God and Redeemer, do not show the stone thrust back at His grave, but rather most of the time prefer to depict His bleeding, lacerated body hanging from a crucifix. I was reminded of this observation again, years later, when I read an essay C.G. Jung wrote in 1928 titled *"Das Seelenproblem des modernen Menschen"* ["The Spiritual Problem of Modern Humanity"]. Jung concluded it with the reflection that a new tempo had been introduced into the world, the American tempo, and that perhaps it is "a healthier or a more desperate attempt to escape from the dark laws of nature and to effect an even greater, even more heroic victory for the state of vigilance over the sleep of the ages." Jung felt this was "a question which history would answer." It was in this same essay that he told the following story.

I have an Indian friend who is a Pueblo chieftain. We spoke once confidentially about the white man and he said: "We do not understand the white men. They always want something; they are always restless; they are always searching for something. What are they searching for? We don't know. We cannot understand them. They have such sharp noses, such thin, gruesome lips, such lines in their faces. We believe they are all crazy." My friend, without being able to find a name for him, had readily recognized the Aryan bird of prey and his insatiable eagerness for plunder which has led him into lands that otherwise would not concern him in the least and once there to foster our greatest delusion, that Christianity is the only truth, the white Christ the only Redeemer.

I could not help but be reminded of these observations when I read for the first time the story which follows. Many, many Indian nations at the time of first contact with the emigrant Europeans possessed systems of religious beliefs far more profound than were ever true for most Europeans. Yet the first thing the Europeans set about doing, beyond physical exploitation of the natural resources of the New World, was to attempt to destroy native religions and replace them with one or another Christian sect. Nor has this "missionary" impulse completely vanished today. It is, I believe, an unpardonable sin for one people to commit against another. Neihardt obviously felt the same way. It is apparent in this story. And in those cases where the European missionaries and, later, the Anglo-American apostles of Christianity were successful, when belief in the Great Spirit and in a whole world of spirits was vanquished and replaced by the cross, what, then, was left to these peoples? Neihardt's experiences on the Omaha reserve suggested an answer to him and he framed it dramatically in a form of fiction approaching parable.

THE LAST THUNDER SONG
1904

It is an ancient custom to paint tragedy in blood tints. This is because men were once merely animals, and have not as yet been able to live down their ancestry. Yet the stroke of a dagger is a caress beside the throb of hopeless days.

Life can ache; the living will tell you this. But the dead make no complaint.

There is no greater tragedy than the fall of a dream! Napoleon dreamed; so did a savage. It is the same. I know of the scene of a great tragedy. Very few have recognized it as such; there was so little noise along with it. It happened at the Omaha Agency, which is situated on the Missouri River some seventy miles above Omaha.

The summer of 1900 debilitated all thermal adjectives. It was not hot; it was *Saharical!* It would hardly have been hyperbole to have said that the Old Century lay dying of a fever. The untilled hills of the reservation thrust themselves up in the August sunshine like the emaciated joints of one bedridden. The land lay as yellow as the skin of a fever patient, except in those rare spots where the melancholy corn struggled heartlessly up a hillside, making a blotch like a bedsore!

The blood of the prairie was impoverished, and the sky would give no drink with which to fill the dwindling veins. When one wished to search the horizon for the cloud that was not there, he did it from beneath an arched hand. The small whirlwinds that awoke like sudden fits of madness in the sultry air, rearing yellow columns of dust into the sky — these alone relieved the monotony of dazzle.

Every evening the clouds rolled flashing about the horizon and thundered back into the night. They were merely taunts, like the holding of a cool cup just out of reach of a fevered mouth; and the clear nights passed, bringing dewless dawns, until the ground cracked like a parched lip!

The annual Indian powwow was to be ended prematurely that year, for the sun beat uninvitingly upon the flat bottom where the dances were held, and the Indians found much comfort in the shade of their summer teepees. But when it was noised about that, upon the next day, the old medicine-man, Mahowari (Passing Cloud), would dance potent dances and sing a thunder song with which to awaken the lazy thunder spirits to their neglected duty of rain-making, then the argument of the heat became feeble.

So the next morning, the bronze head of every Indian teepeehold took his pony, his dogs, his squaw, and his papooses of indefinite number to the powwow ground. In addition to these, the old men carried with them long memories and an implicit faith. The young men, who had been away to Indian school, and had succeeded to some extent in stuffing their brown skins with white souls, carried with them curiosity and doubt, which, if properly united, beget derision.

The old men went to a shrine; the young men went to a show. When a shrine becomes a show, the world advances a step. And *that* is the benevolence of Natural Law!

About the open spaces in which the dances were held, an oval covering had been built with willow boughs, beneath which the Indians lounged in sweating groups. Slowly about the various small circles went the cumbersome stone pipes.

To one listening, drowsed with the intense sunlight, the buzzle and mutter and snarl of the gossiping Omahas seemed the grotesque echoes from a vanished age. Between the dazzle of the sun and the sharply contrasting blue shade, there was but a line of division; yet a thousand years lay between one gazing into the sun and those dozing in the shadow. It was as if God had flung down a bit of the Young World's twilight into the midst of the Old World's noon. Here lounged the masterpiece of the toiling centuries — a Yankee. There sat the remnant of a race as primitive as Israel. Yet the white man looked on with the contempt of superiority.

Before ten o'clock everybody had arrived and his family with him. A little group, composed of the Indian Agent, the Agency physician, the mission preacher, and a newspaper man, down from the city for reportorial purposes, waited and chatted, sitting upon a ragged patch of available shadow.

"These Omahas are an exceptional race," the preacher was saying in his ministerial tone of voice; "an exceptional race!"

The newspaper man mopped his face, lit a cigarette and nodded assent with a hidden meaning twinkling in his eye.

"Quite exceptional!" he said, tossing his head in the direction of an unusually corpulent bunch of steaming, sweating, bronze men and women. "God, like some lesser master-musicians, has not confined himself to grand opera, it seems!"

He took a long pull at his cigarette, and his next words came out in a cloud of smoke.

"This particular creation savors somewhat of opera bouffe!"

With severe unconcern the preacher mended the broken thread of his discourse. "Quite an exceptional race in many ways. The Omaha is quite as honest as the white man."

"That is a truism!" The pencil-pusher drove this observation between the minister's words like a wedge.

"In his natural state he was much more so," uninterruptedly continued the preacher; he was used to continuous discourse. "I have been told by many of the old men that in the olden times an Indian could leave his teepee for months at a time, and on his return would find his most valuable possessions untouched. I tell you, gentlemen, the Indian is like a prairie flower that has been transplanted from the blue sky and the summer sun and the pure winds into the steaming, artificial atmosphere of the hothouse! A glass roof is not the blue sky! Man's talent is not God's genius! That is why you are looking at a perverted growth.

"Look into an Indian's face and observe the ruins of what was once manly dignity, indomitable energy, masterful prowess! When I look upon one of these faces, I have the same thought as, when traveling in Europe, I looked upon the ruins of Rome.

"Everywhere broken arches, fallen columns, tumbled walls! Yet through these as through a mist one can discern the magnificence of the living city. So in looking upon one of these faces, which are merely ruins in another sense. They were once as noble, as beautiful as...."

In his momentary search for an eloquent simile, the minister paused.

"As pumpkin pies!" added the newspaper man with a chuckle; and he whipped out his notebook and pencil to jot down his brilliant thought, for he had conceived a very witty "story" which he would pound out for the Sunday edition.

"Well," said the Agency Physician, finally sucked into the whirlpool of discussion, "it seems to me that there is no room for crowding on either side. Indians are pretty much like white men; liver and kidneys and lungs, and that sort of thing; slight difference in the pigment under the skin. I've looked into the machinery of both species and find just as much room in one as the other for a soul!"

"And both will go upward," added the minister.

"Like different grades of tobacco," observed the Indian Agent, "the smoke of each goes up in the same way."

"Just so," said the reporter; "but let us cut out the metaphysics. I wonder when this magical *cuggie* is going to begin his humid evolutions. Lamentable, isn't it, that such institutions as rain prayers should exist on the very threshold of the 20th Century?"

"I think," returned the minister, "that the 20th Century has no intention of eliminating God! This medicine-man's prayer, in my belief, is as sacred as the prayer of any churchman. The difference between Wakunda and God is merely orthographical."

"But," insisted the cynical young man from the city, "I had not been taught to think of God as of one who forgets! Do you know what I would do if I had no confidence in the executive ability of my God?"

Taking the subsequent silence as a question, the young man answered: "Why, I would take a day off and whittle one out of wood!"

"A youth's way is the wind's way," quoted the preacher, with a paternal air.

"And the thoughts of youth are long, long thoughts; but what is all this noise about?" returned the reporter.

A buzz of expectant voices had grown at one end of the oval, and had spread contagiously throughout the elliptical strip of shade. For with slow, majestic steps the medicine-man, Mahowari, entered the enclosure and walked towards the center. The fierce sun emphasized the brilliancy of the old man's garments and glittered upon the profusion of trinkets, the magic heirlooms of the medicine-man. It was not the robe nor the dazzling trinkets that caught the eye of one acquainted with Mahowari. It was the erectness of his figure, for he had been bowed with years, and many vertical suns had shone upon the old man's back since his face had been turned toward the ground. But now with firm step and form rigidly erect he walked.

Any sympathetic eye could easily read the thoughts that passed through the old man's being like an elixir infusing youth. Now in his feeble years would come his greatest triumph! Today he would sing with greater power than ever he had sung. Wakunda would hear the cry. The rains would come! Then the white men would be stricken with belief!

Already his heart sang before his lips. In spite of the hideous painting of his face, the light of triumph shone there like the reflection of a great fire.

Slowly he approached the circle of drummers who sat in the glaring center of the ellipse of sunlight. It was all as though the 1st Century had awakened like a ghost and stood in the very doorway of the 20th!

When Mahowari had approached within a yard of the drums, he stopped and, raising his arms and his eyes to the cloudless sky, uttered a low cry like a wail of supplication. Then the drums began to throb with that barbaric music as old as the world; a sound like the pounding of a fever temple, with a recurring snarl like the warning of a rattlesnake.

Every sound of the rejoicing and suffering prairie echoes in the Indian's drum.

With a slow, majestic bending of the knees and an alternate lifting of his feet, the medicine-man danced in a circle about the snarling drums. Then like a faint wail of winds toiling up a wooded bluff, his thunder song began.

The drone and whine of the mysterious, untranslatable words pierced the drowse of the day, lived for a moment with the echoes of the drums among the surrounding hills, and languished from a whisper into silence. At intervals the old man raised his face, radiant with fanatic ecstasy, to the meridian glare of the sun, and the song swelled to a supplicating shout.

Faster and faster the old man moved about the circle; louder and wilder grew the song. Those who watched from the shade were absorbed in an intense silence, which, with the drowse of the sultry day, made every sound a paradox! The old men forgot their pipes and sat motionless.

Suddenly, at one end of the covering, came the sound of laughter! At first an indefinite sound like the spirit of merriment entering a capricious dream of sacred things; then it grew and spread until it was no longer merriment, but a loud jeer of derision! It startled the old men from the intenseness of their watching. They looked up and were stricken with awe. The young men were jeering this, the holiest rite of their fathers!

Slower and slower the medicine-man danced; fainter and fainter grew the song and ceased abruptly. With one quick glance, Mahowari saw the shattering of his hopes. He glanced at the sky, but saw no swarm of black spirits to avenge such sacrilege. Only the blaze of the sun, the glitter of the arid zenith!

In that one moment, the temporary youth of the old man died out. His shoulders drooped to their wonted position. His limbs tottered. He was old again.

It was the Night stricken heart-sick with the laughter of the Dawn. It was the audacious Present jeering at the Past, tottering with years. At that moment, the impudent, cruel, brilliant youth called Civilization snatched the halo from the gray hairs of patriarchal Ignorance. Light flouted the rags of Night. A clarion challenge shrilled across the years.

Never before in all the myriad moons had such a thing occurred. It was too great a cause to produce an effect of grief or anger. It stupefied. The old men and women sat motionless. They could not understand.

With uneven step and with eyes that saw nothing, Mahowari passed from among his kinsmen and tottered up the valley toward his lonesome shack and teepee upon the hillside. It was far past noon when the last of the older Omahas left the scene of the dance.

The greatest number of the white men who had witnessed the last thunder dance of the Omahas went homeward much pleased. The show had turned out quite funny indeed. "Ha, ha, ha! Did you see how surprised the old *cuggie* looked? He, he, he!" Life, being necessarily selfish, argues from its own standpoint.

But as the minister rode slowly toward his home there was no laughter in his heart. He was saying to himself: "If the whole fabric of my belief should suddenly be wrenched from me, what then?" Even this question was born of selfishness, but it brought pity.

In the cool of the evening the minister mounted his horse and rode to the home of Mahowari, which was a shack in the winter and a teepee in the summer. Dismounting, he threw the bridle reins upon the ground and raised the door flap of the teepee. Mahowari sat cross-legged upon the ground, staring steadily before him with unseeing eyes.

"How!" said the minister.

The old Indian did not answer. There was no expression of grief or anger or despair upon his face. He sat like a statue. Yet, the irregularity of his breathing showed where the pain lay. An Indian suffers in his breast. His face is a mask.

The minister sat down in front of the silent old man and, after the immemorial manner of ministers, talked of a better world, of a pitying Christ, and of God, the Great Father. For the first time the Indian raised his face and spoke briefly in English:

"God? He dead, guess!"

Then he was silent again for some time.

Suddenly his eyes lit up with a light that was not the light of age. The heart of his youth had awakened. The old memories came back and he spoke fluently in his own tongue, which the minister understood.

"These times are not like the old times. The young men have caught some of the wisdom of the white man. Nothing is sure. It is not good. I cannot understand. Everything is young and new. All old things are dead. Many moons ago, the wisdom of Mahowari was great. I can remember how my father said to me one day when I was yet young and all new before me: 'Let my son go to a high hill and dream a great dream'; and I went up in the evening and cried out to Wakunda and I slept and dreamed.

"I saw a great cloud sweeping up from under the horizon, and it was terrible with lightning and loud thunder. Then it passed over me and rumbled down the sky and disappeared. And when I awoke and told my people of my dream, they rejoiced and said: 'Great things are in store for this youth. We shall call him the Passing Cloud, and he shall be a thunder man, keen and quick of thought, with the keenness and quickness of the lightning; and his name shall be as thunder in the ears of men.' And I grew and believed in these sayings and I was strong. But now I can see the meaning of the dream — a great light and a great noise and a passing."

The old man sighed, and the light passed out of his eyes. Then he looked searchingly into the face of the minister and said, speaking in English:

"You white medicine-man. You pray?"

The minister nodded.

Mahowari turned his gaze to the ground and said wearily:

"White God dead too, guess."

PART TWO

FOUNDERS OF THE GOLDEN AGE

WILLA CATHER

WILLA CATHER (1873–1947) was born Wilella near Winchester, Virginia; she herself changed her *prænomen,* abbreviating it to Willa. In 1883 her family moved to Nebraska and the young Willa, curious about her new and strange environment, spent many hours wandering about on the prairies. I do not doubt that she often felt as Alexandra does in "The Wild Land" when walking alone. Cather visited with foreign-born and second-generation settlers, many of whom she would someday use as models for characters in her pioneer stories.

She was educated at home, by family and friends, studying English and the Greek and Latin classics, until her family settled permanently in Red Cloud, Nebraska. Red Cloud was then a small railroad town — named after the great Sioux chieftain earlier removed from the area by the War Department — and Cather used it as a setting, although somewhat disguised, for several short stories and six of her thirteen novels.

Cather was very boyish as a youth and had plans to enter medicine. However, while attending the University of Nebraska, her ability to write became manifest and she decided instead to pursue a literary career. Shortly after she was graduated, she went to Pittsburgh where she worked as a professional journalist until 1901, the year she began teaching. In 1906 she was invited to New York City to join the staff of *McClure's* magazine, and she remained in that city the rest of her life.

With the publication of her first novel, ALEXANDER'S BRIDGE (Houghton Mifflin, 1912), Cather both established herself in the literary world of the day and felt in herself a need to change her course which, until that time had been greatly influenced in theme and style by Henry James. Sarah Orne Jewett, an author whom Cather particularly admired, told her in a letter that "...you must find your own quiet centre of life, and write from that to the world...in short, you must write to the human heart...." Cather, who had previously been ambivalent about small-town life and the years spent in Nebraska, finally found her "quiet centre" when she went back to her past and wrote about her childhood experiences and the people she had come to love on the Nebraska prairies.

O PIONEERS! (Houghton Mifflin, 1913) heralded Cather's literary transition, followed by MY ÁNTONIA (Houghton Mifflin, 1918) and the stories collected in OBSCURE DESTINIES (Knopf, 1932). These are her finest works about pioneers and pioneering, written in a nostalgic, elegiac tone, but filled with warmth, humanity, and the richness of life. Later authors like A.B. Guthrie, Jr., were to criticize Cather for dealing with only the positive aspects of pioneer life and omitting the brutality, the hardship, and the savagery. Of course, there is some justification for such a charge, but I do not believe it was ever Willa Cather's intention to present a complete portrait, but rather a series of impressions, of moods, moments of brightness in lives usually surrounded by shadows.

Among her books I particularly favor THE PROFESSOR'S HOUSE (Knopf, 1925) and DEATH COMES FOR THE ARCHBISHOP (Knopf, 1927). The latter is set in New Mexico and has all the ingredients of a romantic fantasy; but it also has something else, something which makes it especially endearing, and that is its evocation of a lasting and meaningful friendship.

The final chapter in one of the best books about her — James Woodress's WILLA CATHER: HER LIFE AND ART (Western Publishing, 1970) — is titled "The Rest Is Silence: 1933–1947." It is apt, because Cather quit writing. She felt out of joint with the changing world around her. Perhaps to a degree she had always been that way. During her last days, she listened over and over to recordings of Beethoven's Late Quartets. In her own best work she had found the profound harmony, the "quiet centre" of those quartets, and I suspect she found it, too, in the solitude of her own soul.

"The Wild Land" is from O PIONEERS! It is set in Nebraska and it is an intimate glimpse into the lives of the Bergson family, Alexandra, her mother, and her brothers, Oscar, Lou, and young Emil, who is like a son to his sister. When Alexandra's father dies, she becomes the head of the family. For women like Alexandra — and in the actual history of the American frontier there were many like her — the West was not just a *masculine* experience.

THE WILD LAND
1913

For the first three years after John Bergson's death, the affairs of his family prospered. Then came the hard times that brought every one on the Divide to the brink of despair; three years of drought and failure, the last struggle of a wild soil against the encroaching plowshare. The first of these fruitless summers the Bergson boys bore courageously. The failure of the corn crop made labor cheap. Lou and Oscar hired two men and put in bigger crops than ever before. They lost everything they spent. The whole country was discouraged. Farmers who were already in debt had to give up their land. A few foreclosures demoralized the county. The settlers sat about on the wooden sidewalks in the little town and told each other that the country was never meant for men to live in; the thing to do was to get back to Iowa, to Illinois, to any place that had been proved habitable. The Bergson boys, certainly, would have been happier with their Uncle Otto, in the bakery shop in Chicago. Like most of their neighbors, they were meant to follow in paths already marked out for them, not to break trails in a new country. A steady job, a few holidays, nothing to think about, and they would have been very happy. It was no fault of theirs that they had been dragged into the wilderness when they were little boys. A pioneer should have imagination, should be able to enjoy the idea of things more than the things themselves.

The second of these barren summers was passing. One September afternoon Alexandra had gone over to the garden across the draw to dig sweet potatoes — they had been thriving upon the weather that was fatal to everything else. But when Carl Linstrum came up the garden rows to find her, she was not working. She was standing lost in thought, leaning upon her pitchfork, her sunbonnet lying beside her on the ground. The dry garden patch smelled of drying vines and was strewn with yellow seed-cucumbers and pumpkins and citrons. At one end, next the rhubarb, grew feathery asparagus, with red berries. Down the middle of the garden was a row of gooseberry and currant bushes. A few tough zenias and marigolds and a row of scarlet sage bore witness to the buckets of water that Mrs. Bergson had carried there after sundown, against the prohibition of her sons. Carl came quietly and slowly up the garden path, looking intently at Alexandra. She did not hear him. She was standing perfectly still, with that serious ease so characteristic of her. Her thick, reddish braids, twisted about her head, fairly burned in the sunlight. The air was cool enough to make the warm sun pleasant on one's back and shoulders, and so clear that the eye could follow a hawk up and up, into the blazing blue depths of the sky. Even Carl, never a very cheerful boy, and considerably darkened by these last two bitter years, loved the country on days like this, felt something strong and young and wild come out of it, that laughed at care.

"Alexandra," he said as he approached her, "I want to talk to you. Let's sit down by the gooseberry bushes." He picked up her sack of potatoes and they crossed the garden. "Boys gone to town?" he asked as he sank down on the warm, sunbaked earth. "Well, we have made up our minds at last, Alexandra. We are really going away."

She looked at him as if she were a little frightened. "Really, Carl? Is it settled?"

"Yes, Father has heard from St. Louis, and they will give him back his old job in the cigar factory. He must be there by the first of November. They are taking on new men then. We will sell the place for whatever we can get, and auction the stock. We haven't enough to ship. I am going to learn engraving with a German engraver there, and then try to get work in Chicago."

Alexandra's hands dropped in her lap. Her eyes became dreamy and filled with tears.

Carl's sensitive lower lip trembled. He scratched in the soft earth beside him with a stick. "That's all I hate about it, Alexandra," he said slowly. "You've stood by us through so much and helped Father out so many times, and now it seems as if we were running off and leaving you to face the worst of it. But it isn't as if we could really ever be of any help to you. We are only one more drag, one more thing you look out for and feel responsible for. Father was never meant for a farmer, you know that. And I hate it. We'd only get in deeper and deeper."

"Yes, yes, Carl, I know. You are wasting your life here. You are able to do much better things. You are nearly nineteen now, and I wouldn't have you stay. I've always hoped you would get away. But I can't help feeling scared when I think how I will miss you — more than you will ever know." She brushed the tears from her cheeks, not trying to hide them.

"But, Alexandra," he said sadly and wistfully, "I've never been any real help to you beyond sometimes trying to keep the boys in a good humor."

Alexandra smiled and shook her head. "Oh, it's not that. Nothing like that. It's by understanding me, and the boys, and mother, that you've helped me. I expect that is the only way one person ever really can help another. I think you are about the only one that ever helped me. Somehow it will take more courage to bear your going than everything that has happened before."

Carl looked at the ground. "You see, we've all depended so on you," he said, "even Father. He makes me laugh. When anything comes up he always says, 'I wonder what the Bergsons are going to do about that? I guess I'll go and ask her.' I'll never forget that time, when we first came here, and our horse had the colic, and I ran over to your place — your father was away, and you came home with me and showed Father how to let the wind out of the horse. You were only a little girl then, but you knew ever so much more about farm work than poor Father. You remember how homesick I used to get, and what long talks we used to have coming from school? We've someway always felt alike about things."

"Yes, that's it; we've liked the same things and we've liked them together, without anybody else knowing. And we've had good times, hunting for Christmas trees and going for ducks and making our plum wine together every year. We've never either of us had any other close friend. And now...," Alexandra wiped her eyes with the corner of her apron, "and now I must remember that you are going where you will have many friends, and will find the work you were meant to do. But you'll write to me, Carl? That will mean a great deal to me here."

"I'll write as long as I live," cried the boy impetuously. "And I'll be working for you as much as for myself, Alexandra. I want to do something you'll like and be proud of. I'm a fool here, but I know I can do something!" He sat up and frowned at the red grass.

Alexandra sighed. "How discouraged the boys will be when they hear. They always come home from town discouraged, anyway. So many people are trying to leave the country, and they talk to our boys and make them low-spirited. I'm afraid they are beginning to feel hard toward me because I won't listen to any talk about going. Sometimes I feel like I'm getting tired of standing up for this country."

"I won't tell the boys yet, if you'd rather not."

"Oh, I'll tell them myself, tonight, when they come home. They'll be talking wild, anyway, and no good comes of keeping bad news. It's all harder on them than it is on me. Lou wants to get married, poor boy, and he can't until times are better. See, there goes the sun, Carl. I must be getting back. Mother will want her potatoes. It's chilly already, the moment the light goes."

Alexandra rose and looked about. A golden afterglow throbbed in the west, but the country already looked empty and mournful. A dark moving mass came over the western hill, the Lee boy was bringing in the herd from the other half-section. Emil ran from the windmill to open the corral gate. From the log house, on the little rise across the draw, the smoke was curling. The cattle lowed and bellowed. In the sky the pale half-moon was slowly silvering. Alexandra and Carl walked together down the potato rows. "I have to keep telling myself what is going to happen," she said softly. "Since you have been here, ten years now, I have never really been lonely. But I can remember what it was like before. Now I shall have nobody but Emil. But he is my boy, and he is tender-hearted."

That night, when the boys were called to supper, they sat down moodily. They had worn their coats to town, but they ate in their striped shirts and suspenders. They were grown men now, and, as Alexandra said, for the last few years they had been growing more and more like themselves. Lou was still the slighter of the two, the quicker and more intelligent, but apt to go off at half-cock. He had a lively blue eye, a thin, fair skin (always burned red to the neck-band of his shirt in summer), stiff, yellow hair that would not lie down on his head, and a bristly little yellow mustache, of which he was very proud. Oscar could not grow a mustache; his pale face was as bare as an egg, and his white eyebrows gave it an empty look. He was a man of powerful body and unusual endurance; the sort of man you could attach to a corn-sheller as you would an engine. He would turn it all day, without hurrying, without slowing down. But he was as indolent of mind as he was unsparing of his body. His love of routine amounted to a vice. He worked like an insect, always doing the same thing over in the same way, regardless of whether it was best or no. He felt that there was a sovereign virtue in mere bodily toil, and he rather liked to do things in the hardest way. If a field had once been in corn, he couldn't bear to put it into wheat. He liked to begin his corn-planting at the same time every year, whether the season were backward or forward. He seemed to feel that by his own irreproachable regularity he would clear himself of blame and reprove the weather. When the wheat crop failed, he threshed the straw at a dead loss to demonstrate how little grain there was, and thus prove his case against Providence.

Lou, on the other hand, was funny and flighty; always planned to get through two days' work in one, and often got only the least important things done. He liked to keep the place up, but he never got round to doing odd jobs until he had to neglect more pressing work to attend to them. In the middle of the wheat harvest, when the grain was over-ripe and every hand was needed, he would stop to mend fences or to patch the harness; then dash down to the field and overwork and be laid up in bed for a week. The two boys balanced each other, and they pulled well together. They had been good friends since they were children. One seldom went anywhere, even to town, without the other.

Tonight, after they sat down to supper, Oscar kept looking at Lou as if he expected him to say something, and Lou blinked his eyes and frowned at his plate. It was Alexandra herself who at last opened the discussion.

"The Linstrums," she said calmly, as she put another plate of hot biscuits on the table, "are going back to St. Louis. The old man is going to work in the cigar factory again."

At this Lou plunged in. "You see, Alexandra, everybody who can crawl out is going away. There's no use of us trying to stick it out, just to be stubborn. There's something in knowing when to quit."

"Where do you want to go, Lou?"

"Any place where things will grow," said Oscar grimly.

Lou reached for a potato. "Chris Arnson has traded his half-section for a place down on the river."

"Who did he trade with?"

"Charley Fuller, in town."

"Fuller the real estate man? You see, Lou, that Fuller has a head on him. He's buying and trading for every bit of land he can get up here. It'll make him a rich man, some day."

"He's rich now, that's why he can take a chance."

"Why can't we? We'll live longer than he will. Some day the land itself will be worth more than all we can ever raise on it."

Lou laughed. "It could be worth that, and still not be worth much. Why, Alexandra, you don't know what you're talking about. Our place wouldn't bring now what it would six years ago. The fellows that settled up here just made a mistake. Now they're beginning to see this high land wasn't never meant to grow nothing on, and everybody who ain't fixed to graze cattle is trying to crawl out. It's too high to farm up here. All the Americans are skinning out. That man Percy Adams, north of town, told me that he was going to let Fuller take his land and stuff for four hundred dollars and a ticket to Chicago."

"There's Fuller again!" Alexandra exclaimed. "I wish that man would take me for a partner. He's feathering his nest! If only poor people could learn a little from rich people! But all these fellows who are running off are bad farmers, like poor Mr. Linstrum. They couldn't get ahead even in good years, and they all got into debt while Father was getting out. I think we ought to hold on as long as we can on Father's account. He was so set on keeping this land. He must have seen harder times than this, here. How was it in the early days, Mother?"

Mrs. Bergson was weeping quietly. These family discussions always depressed her, and made her remember all that she had been torn away from. "I don't see why the boys are always taking on about going away," she said, wiping her eyes. "I don't want to move again; out to some raw place, maybe, where we'd be worse off than we are here, and all to do over again. I won't move! If the rest of you go, I will ask some of the neighbors to take me in, and stay and be buried by Father. I'm not going to leave him by himself on the prairie, for cattle to run over." She began to cry more bitterly.

The boys looked angry. Alexandra put a soothing hand on her mother's shoulder. "There's no question of that, Mother. You don't have to go if you don't want to. A third of the place belongs to you by American law, and we can't sell without your consent. We only want you to advise us. How did it use to be when you and Father first came? Was it really as bad as this, or not?"

"Oh, worse! Much worse," moaned Mrs. Bergson. "Drought, chince-bugs, hail, everything! My garden all cut to pieces like sauerkraut. No grapes on the creek, no nothing. The people all lived just like coyotes."

Oscar got up and tramped out of the kitchen. Lou followed him. They felt that Alexandra had taken an unfair advantage in turning their mother loose on them. The next morning they were silent and reserved. They did not offer to take the women to church, but went down to the barn immediately after breakfast and stayed there all day. When Carl Linstrum came over in the afternoon, Alexandra winked to him and pointed toward the barn. He understood her and went down to play cards with the boys. They believed that a very wicked thing to do on Sunday, and it relieved their feelings.

Alexandra stayed in the house. On Sunday afternoon Mrs. Bergson always took a nap, and Alexandra read. During the week she read only the newspaper, but on Sunday, and in the long evenings of winter, she read a good deal; read a few things over a great many times. She knew long portions of the "Frithjof Saga" by heart, and, like most Swedes who read at all, she was fond of Longfellow's verse — the ballads and the "Golden Legend" and "The Spanish Student." Today she sat in the wooden rocking-chair with the Swedish Bible open on her knees, but she was not reading. She was looking thoughtfully away at the point where the upland road disappeared over the rim of the prairie. Her body was in an attitude of perfect repose, such as it was apt to take when she was thinking earnestly. Her mind was slow, truthful, steadfast. She had not the least spark of cleverness.

All afternoon the sitting-room was full of quiet and sunlight. Emil was making rabbit traps in the kitchen shed. The hens were clucking and scratching brown holes in the flower beds, and the wind was teasing the prince's feather by the door.

That evening Carl came in with the boys to supper.

"Emil," said Alexandra, when they were all seated at the table, "how would you like to go traveling? Because I am going to take a trip, and you can go with me if you want to."

The boys looked up in amazement; they were always afraid of Alexandra's schemes. Carl was interested.

"I've been thinking, boys," she went on, "that maybe I am too set against making a change. I'm going to take Brigham and the buckboard tomorrow and drive down to the river country and spend a few days looking over what they've got down there. If I find anything good, you boys can go down and make a trade."

"Nobody down there will trade for anything up here," said Oscar gloomily.

"That's just what I want to find out. Maybe they are just as discontented down there as we are up here. Things away from home often look better than they are. You know what your Hans Andersen book says, Carl, about the Swedes liking to buy Danish bread and the Danes liking to buy Swedish bread, because people always think the bread of another country is better than their own. Anyway, I've heard so much about the river farms, I won't be satisfied till I've seen for myself."

Lou fidgeted. "Look out! Don't agree to anything. Don't let them fool you."

Lou was apt to be fooled himself. He had not yet learned to keep away from the shell-game wagons that followed the circus.

After supper Lou put on a necktie and went across the fields to court Annie Lee, and Carl and Oscar sat down to a game of checkers, while Alexandra read THE SWISS FAMILY ROBINSON aloud to her mother and Emil. It was not long before the two boys at the table neglected their game to listen. They were all big children together, and they found the adventures of the family in the tree house so absorbing that they gave them their undivided attention.

Alexandra and Emil spent five days down among the river farms, driving up and down the valley. Alexandra talked to the men about their crops and to the women about their poultry. She spent a whole day with one young farmer who had been away at school, and who was experimenting with a new kind of clover hay. She learned a great deal. As they drove along, she and Emil talked and planned. At last, on the sixth day, Alexandra turned Brigham's head northward and left the river behind.

"There's nothing in it for us down there, Emil. There are a few fine farms, but they are owned by the rich men in town, and couldn't be bought. Most of the land is rough and hilly. They can always scrape along down there, but they can never do anything big. Down there they have a little certainty, but up with us there is a big chance. We must have faith in the high land, Emil. I want to hold on harder than ever, and when you're a man you'll thank me." She urged Brigham forward.

When the road began to climb the first long swells of the Divide, Alexandra hummed an old Swedish hymn, and Emil wondered why his sister looked so happy. Her face was so radiant that he felt shy about asking her. For the first time, perhaps, since that land emerged from the waters of geologic ages, a human face was set toward it with love and yearning. It seemed beautiful to her, rich and strong and glorious. Her eyes drank in the breadth of it, until her tears blinded her. Then the Genius of the Divide, the great, free spirit which breathes across it, must have bent lower than it ever bent to a human will before. The history of every country begins in the heart of a man or a woman.

Alexandra reached home in the afternoon. That evening she held a family council and told her brothers all that she had seen and heard.

"I want you boys to go down yourselves and look it over. Nothing will convince you like seeing with your own eyes. The river land was settled before this, and so they are a few years ahead of us, and have learned more about farming. The land sells for three times as much as this, but in five years we will double it. The rich men down there own all the best land, and they are buying all they can get. The thing to do is to sell our cattle and what little old corn we have, and buy the Linstrum place. Then the next thing to do is to take out two loans on our half-sections, and buy Peter Crow's place; raise every dollar we can, and buy every acre we can."

"Mortgage the homestead again?" Lou cried. He sprang up and began to wind the clock furiously. "I won't slave to pay off another mortgage. I'll never do it. You'd just as soon kill us all, Alexandra, to carry out some scheme!"

Oscar rubbed his high, pale forehead. "How do you propose to pay off your mortgages?"

Alexandra looked from one to the other and bit her lip. They had never seen her so nervous. "See here," she brought out at last. "We borrow the money for six years. Well, with the money we buy a half-section from Linstrum and a half from Crow, and a quarter from Struble, maybe. That will give us upwards of fourteen hundred acres, won't it? You won't have to pay off your mortgages for six years. By that time, any of this land will be worth thirty dollars an acre...it will be worth fifty, but we'll say thirty; then you can sell a garden patch anywhere, and pay off a debt of sixteen hundred dollars. It's not the principal I'm worried about, it's the interest and taxes. We'll have to strain to meet the payments. But as sure as we are sitting here to-night, we can sit down here ten years from now independent landowners, not struggling farmers any longer. The chance that Father was always looking for has come."

Lou was pacing the floor. "But how do you know that land is going to go up enough to pay the mortgages and...."

"And make us rich besides?" Alexandra put in firmly. "I can't explain that, Lou. You'll have to take my word for it. I *know,* that's all. When you drive about over the country you can feel it coming."

Oscar had been sitting with his head lowered, his hands hanging between his knees. "But we can't work so much land," he said dully, as if he were talking to himself. "We can't even try. It would just lie there and we'd work ourselves to death." He sighed, and laid his callused fist on the table.

Alexandra's eyes filled with tears. She put her hand on his shoulder. "You poor boy, you won't have to work it. The men in town who are buying up other people's land don't try to farm it. They are the men to watch, in a new country. Let's try to do like the shrewd ones, and not like these stupid fellows. I don't want you boys always to have to work like this. I want you to be independent, and Emil to go to school."

Lou held his head as if it were splitting. "Everybody will say we are crazy. It must be crazy, or everybody would be doing it."

"If they were, we wouldn't have much chance. No, Lou, I was talking about that with the smart young man who is raising the new kind of clover. He says the right thing is usually just what everybody don't do. Why are we better fixed than any of our neighbors? Because Father had more brains. Our people were better people than these in the old country. We ought to do more than they do, and see further ahead. Yes, Mother, I'm going to clear the table now."

Alexandra rose. The boys went to the stable to see to the stock, and they were gone a long while. When they came back Lou played on his *dragharmonika* and Oscar sat figuring at his father's secretary all evening. They said nothing more about Alexandra's project, but she felt sure now that they would consent to it. Just before bedtime Oscar went out for a pail of water. When he did not come back, Alexandra threw a shawl over her head and ran down the path to the windmill. She found him sitting there with his head in his hands, and she sat down beside him.

"Don't do anything you don't want to do, Oscar," she whispered. She waited a moment, but he did not stir. "I won't say any more about it, if you'd rather not. What makes you so discouraged?"

"I dread signing my name to them pieces of paper," he said slowly. "All the time I was a boy we had a mortgage hanging over us."

"Then don't sign one. I don't want you to, if you feel that way."

Oscar shook his head. "No, I can see there's a chance that way. I've thought a good while there might be. We're in so deep now, we might as well go deeper. But it's hard work pulling out of debt. Like pulling a threshing-machine out of the mud; breaks your back. Me and Lou's worked hard, and I can't see it's got us ahead much."

"Nobody knows about that as well as I do, Oscar. That's why I want to try an easier way. I don't want you to have to grub for every dollar."

"Yes, I know what you mean. Maybe it'll come out right. But signing papers is signing papers. There ain't no maybe about that." He took his pail and trudged up the path to the house.

Alexandra drew her shawl closer about her and stood leaning against the frame of the mill, looking at the stars which glittered so keenly through the frosty autumn air. She always loved to watch them, to think of their vastness and distance, and of their ordered march. It fortified her to reflect upon the great operations of Nature, and when she thought of the law that lay behind them, she felt a sense of personal security. That night she had a new consciousness of the country, felt almost a new relation to it. Even her talk with the boys had not taken away the feeling that had overwhelmed her when she drove back to the Divide that afternoon. She had never known before how much the country meant to her. The chirping of the insects down in the long grass had been like the sweetest music. She had felt as if her heart were hiding down there, somewhere, with the quail and the plover and all the little wild things that crooned or buzzed in the sun. Under the long shaggy ridges, she felt the future stirring.

ZANE GREY

ZANE GREY (1872–1939) was born Pearl Zane Gray in Zanesville, Ohio. He
was graduated from the University of Pennsylvania in 1896 with a degree in
dentistry. He conducted a practice in New York City from 1898 to 1904, meanwhile striving to make a living by writing. He met Lina Elise Roth in 1900 and
always called her Dolly. In 1905 they were married. With Dolly's help, Grey
published his first novel himself, BETTY ZANE (Charles Francis Press, 1903),
a story based on certain of his frontier ancestors. Closing his dental office
shortly after his marriage, Grey moved with Dolly into a cottage on the Dela-
ware River, near Lackawaxen, Pennsylvania. It is now a national landmark.

Although it took most of her savings, it was Dolly Grey who insisted that her
husband take his first trip to Arizona in 1907 with C.J. "Buffalo" Jones, a retired buffalo hunter who had come up with a scheme for crossing the remaining
bison population with cattle. In the event, Grey could not have been more fortunate in his choice of a mate. Dolly Grey assisted him in every way he desired
and yet left him alone when he demanded solitude; trained in English at Hunter
College, she proof-read every manuscript he wrote and polished his prose; she
managed all financial affairs and permitted Grey, once he began earning a good
income, to indulge himself at will in his favorite occupations, hunting, fishing,
sailing, and exploring the Western regions.

After his return from that first trip to the West, Grey wrote a memoir of his
experiences titled THE LAST OF THE PLAINSMEN (Outing, 1908) and followed it with his first Western romance, THE HERITAGE OF THE DESERT
(Harper, 1910). It remains one of his finest novels. The profound effect that the
desert had had on him was vibrantly captured so that, after all of these years, it
still comes alive for a reader. In a way, too, it established the basic pattern Grey
would use in much of his subsequent Western fiction. The hero, Jack Hare, is an
Easterner who comes West because he is suffering from tuberculosis. He is reju-
venated by the arid land. The heroine is Mescal, desired by all men but pledged
by the Mormon church to a man unworthy of her. Mescal and Jack fall in love
and this causes her to flee from Snap Naab, for whom she will be a second wife.
Snap turns to drink, as will many another man rejected by heroines in other
Grey romances, and finally kidnaps her. The most memorable characters in this
novel, however, are August Naab, the Mormon patriarch who takes Hare in at

his ranch, and Eschtah, Mescal's grandfather, a Navajo chieftain of great dignity and no less admirable than Naab. The principal villain — a type not too frequently encountered in Grey's Western stories with notable exceptions such as DESERT GOLD (Harper, 1913) — is Holderness, a Gentile and the embodiment of the Yankee business spirit that will stop at nothing to exploit the land and its inhabitants for his own profit. Almost a century later, he is still a familiar figure in the American West, with numerous bureaucratic counterparts in various federal agencies. In the end Holderness is killed by Hare; but then, Hare is also capable of pardoning a man who has done wrong if there is a chance for his reclamation, a theme Grey shared with Max Brand.

Grey had trouble finding a publisher for his early work and it came as a considerable shock to him when his next novel, RIDERS OF THE PURPLE SAGE (Harper, 1912), arguably the greatest Western story ever published, was rejected by the same editor who had bought THE HERITAGE OF THE DESERT. Grey asked the vice president at Harper & Bros. to read the new novel. Once he did, and his wife did, it was accepted for publication. It has never been out of print since that first edition, most recently reprinted in an "Authorized Edition" by the University of Nebraska Press with a Foreword by Dr. Loren Grey, Grey's younger son. RIDERS OF THE PURPLE SAGE may be Grey's best-known Western romance, but I do not regard it as his masterpiece. That distinction, I believe, should be reserved for its sequel, THE RAINBOW TRAIL (Harper, 1915), also reprinted in an "Authorized Edition" by the University of Nebraska Press.

RIDERS OF THE PURPLE SAGE is dominated by dream imagery and nearly all of the characters, at one time or another, are preoccupied with their dreams. For its hero Grey created the gunfighter, Lassiter, another enduring prototype, the experienced Westerner to be contrasted with the Eastern neophyte, Lassiter with his "leanness, the red burn of the sun, and the set changelessness that came from years of silence and solitude...the intensity of his gaze, a strained weariness, a piercing wistfulness of keen, gray sight, as if the man was forever looking for that which he never found." In this, as well, Lassiter is the prototype for all those searchers and wanderers found in Grey's later stories, above all John Shefford in THE RAINBOW TRAIL and Adam Larey in WANDERER OF THE WASTELAND (Harper, 1923).

Hermann Hesse went East for inspiration in his dreaming; Zane Grey went West. "Yes," Hesse wrote in DEMIAN (S. Fischer, 1919), "one must find his dream, for then the way is easy. However, there is no forever-enduring dream. Each dream surrenders to a new one, and one is able to hold fast to none of them." In RIDERS OF THE PURPLE SAGE, life itself, the outer world, and human evil do not permit dreams to last indefinitely. Bishop Dyer dreams. Jane Withersteen dreams. Venters and Bess dream. Lassiter lives in a dream of vengeance. Lassiter in his relationship with Jane and Fay fulfills Milly's ancient dream of a family and, through his actions, fulfills his own dream by destroying Bishop Dyer. Lassiter gives Bess the locket with pictures in it of her real mother and father. At the close, Lassiter, Jane, and Fay are alone, sealed in Surprise Valley. Hermann Hesse and Frederick Faust who wrote as Max Brand became familiar with Jungian ideas and each for a time consulted with Jung. Grey could know nothing of the process of individuation in 1912 but what he grasped intuitively. For him, personal rebirth into a state of wholeness, the restoration of the Garden of Eden and a state of innocence, came after the expenditure of passion and the vanquishment of evil. This would remain the psycho-drama underlying many of Zane Grey's finest Western stories.

Grey's success for a time exceeded even his wildest dreams. The magazine serials, the books, the motion pictures — and Grey at 108 films still holds the world's record for cinematic derivations based on the works of a single author — brought in a fortune. He had homes on Catalina Island, in Altadena, California, a hunting lodge in Arizona, a fishing lodge in the Rogue River area in Oregon.

Whatever his material prosperity, Grey continued to believe in the strenuous life. His greatest personal fear was that of growing old and dying. It was while fishing the North Umpqua River in Oregon in the summer of 1937 that Grey collapsed from an apparent stroke. It took him a long time to recover use of his faculties and his speech. Cardiovascular disease was congenital on Grey's side of the family. Despite medical advice to the contrary, Grey refused to live a sedentary life. He was convinced that the heart was a muscle and the only way to keep it strong was to exercise it vigorously. Early in the morning on October 23, 1939, Dolly was awakened by a call from her husband. Rushing to his room, she found Grey clutching his chest. "Don't ever leave me, Dolly!" he pleaded. He lived until the next morning when, after rising and dressing, he sat down on his bed, cried out suddenly, and fell over dead.

Even more than with Bret Harte, there has always been a tendency among literary critics to dismiss Zane Grey; and, unlike Harte, Grey at no point enjoyed any great favor with them. Part of this attitude may have come about because he was never a realistic writer. This he could not be, since he was one who charted the interiors of the soul through encounters with the wilderness. If he provided us with characters no more realistic than are to be found in Balzac, Dickens, or Thomas Mann, they nonetheless have a vital story to tell. "There was so much unexpressed feeling that could not be entirely portrayed," Loren Grey once commented about his father, "that, in later years, he would weep when re-reading one of his own books." Zane Grey's Western romances, particularly those from 1910 through 1930, are not the kind of Western fare of gunfights and confrontations that his paperback publishers perversely have always tried to market them as being. They are psycho-dramas about the spiritual odysseys of the human soul. They may not be the stuff of the real world, but without such odysseys the real world has no meaning.

Nas Ta Bega, a Navajo, as a character overshadows THE RAINBOW TRAIL and I think you are more likely to remember him after you have closed the book than any one else in the story. Grey drew him from life. His model was Nasjha Be Gay, and he was the Piute Indian guide who led the first white men — the Cummings Weatherill expedition — to the Rainbow Bridge in 1908; and he led Zane Grey there in 1913. Loren Grey has included photographs of the Rainbow Bridge taken on that journey in ZANE GREY: A PHOTOGRAPHIC ODYSSEY (Taylor Publishing, 1985).

Nasjha Be Gay died in the influenza epidemic which hit the Navajo reservation in 1918, but his spirit has been perpetuated in the novel Grey wrote. THE RAINBOW TRAIL was serialized in *The Argosy* in 1915 under the title "The Desert Crucible" and I have retained that title for this story which narrates the beginning of John Shefford's friendship with Nas Ta Bega.

THE DESERT CRUCIBLE
1915

Shefford at first saw nothing except the monotonous gray valley reaching far to the strange, grotesque monuments of yellow cliff. Then, close under the foot of the slope, he espied two squat stone houses with red roofs, and a corral with a pool of water shining in the sun.

The trail leading down was steep and sandy, but it was not long. Shefford's sweeping eyes appeared to take in everything at once — the crude stone structures with their earthen roofs, the piles of dirty wool, the Indians lolling around, the tents, and wagons, and horses, little lazy burrows and dogs, and scattered everywhere, saddles, blankets, guns, and packs.

Then a white man came out of the door. He waved a hand and shouted. Dust and wool and flour were thick upon him. He was muscular and weather-beaten, and appeared young in activity rather than face. A gun swung at his hip and a row of brass-tipped cartridges showed in his belt. Shefford looked into a face that he thought he had seen before, until he realized the similarity was only the bronze and hard line and rugged cast common to desert men. The gray searching eyes went right through him.

"Glad to see you. Get down and come in. I'm the trader Withers," he said to Shefford. His voice was welcoming and the grip of his hand made Shefford's ache.

Shefford told his name and said he was as glad as he was lucky to arrive at Kayenta.

Withers led Shefford by the first stone house, which evidently was the trading-store, into the second. The room Shefford entered was large, with logs smoldering in a huge open fireplace, blankets covering every foot of floor space, Indian baskets and silver ornaments everywhere, and strange Indian designs painted upon the whitewashed walls. Withers called his wife and made her acquainted with Shefford. She was a slight, comely little woman, with keen, earnest, dark eyes. She seemed to be serious and quiet, but she made Shefford feel at home immediately. He refused, however, to accept the room offered him, saying that he meant to sleep out under the open sky. Withers laughed at this and said he understood.

"Sure am glad you rode in," said Withers, for the fourth time. "Now you make yourself at home. Stay here...come over to the store...do what you like. I've got to work. Tonight we'll talk."

That night after supper, when Withers and Shefford sat alone before the blazing logs in the huge fireplace, the trader laid his hand on Shefford's and said, with directness and force:

"I've lived my life in the desert. I've met many men and have been a friend to most.... You're no prospector or trader or missionary?"

"No," replied Shefford.

"You've had trouble?"

"Perhaps I wronged myself, but no one else," replied Shefford, steadily.

"I reckoned so. Well, tell me, or keep your secret...it's all one to me."

Shefford felt a desire to unburden himself. This man was strong, persuasive, kindly. He drew Shefford.

"You're welcome in Kayenta," went on Withers. "Stay as long as you like. I take no pay from a white man. If you want work I have it plenty."

"Thank you. That is good. I need to work. We'll talk of it later.... But just yet I can't tell you why I came to Kayenta, what I want to do, how long I shall stay. My thoughts put in words would seem so like dreams. Maybe they are dreams. Perhaps I'm only chasing a phantom...perhaps I'm only hunting the treasure at the foot of the rainbow."

"Well, this is the country for rainbows," laughed Withers. "In summer from June to August when it storms we have rainbows that'll make you think you're in another world. The Navajos have rainbow mountains, rainbow cañons, rainbow bridges of stone, rainbow trails. It sure is rainbow country."

That deep and mystic chord in Shefford thrilled. Here it was again — something tangible at the bottom of his dream.

Withers did not wait for Shefford to say any more, and almost as if he read his visitor's mind he began to talk about the wild country he called home.

He had lived at Kayenta for several years — hard and profitless years by reason of marauding outlaws. He could not have lived there at all but for the protection of the Indians. His father-in-law had been friendly with the Navajos and Piutes for many years, and his wife had been brought up among them. She was held in peculiar reverence and affection by both tribes in that part of the country. Probably she knew more of the Indians' habits, religion, and life than any white person in the West. Both tribes were friendly and peaceable, but there were bad Indians, half-breeds, and outlaws that made the trading-post a venture Withers had long considered precarious, and he wanted to move and intended to some day. His nearest white neighbors in New Mexico and Colorado were a hundred miles distant and at some seasons the roads were impassable. To the north, however, twenty miles or so, was situated a Mormon village named Stonebridge. It lay across the Utah line. Withers did some business with this village, but scarcely enough to warrant the risks he had to run. During the last year he had lost several pack trains, one of which he had never heard of after it left Stonebridge.

"Stonebridge!" exclaimed Shefford, and he trembled. He had heard that name. In his memory it had a place beside the name of another village Shefford longed to speak of to this trader.

"Yes...Stonebridge," replied Withers. "Ever heard the name?"

"I think so. Are there other villages in...in that part of the country?"

"A few, but not close. Glaze is now only a water-hole. Bluff and Monticello are far north across the San Juan.... There used to be another village...but that wouldn't interest you."

"Withers, pardon an impertinence...I am deeply serious.... Are you a Mormon?"

"Indeed I'm not," replied the trader, instantly.

"Are you for the Mormons or against them?"

"Neither. I get along with them. I know them. I believe they are a misunderstood people."

"That's *for* them."

"No. I'm only fair-minded."

Shefford paused, trying to curb his thrilling impulse, but it was too strong.

"You said there used to be another village.... Was the name of it...Cottonwoods?"

Withers gave a start and faced 'round to stare at Shefford in blank astonishment.

"You're no spy on the lookout for sealed wives?"

"Absolutely not. I don't even know what you mean by sealed wives."

"Well, it's damn strange that you'd know the name Cottonwoods.... Yes, that's the name of the village I meant...the one that used to be. It's gone now, all except a few stone walls."

"What became of it?"

"Torn down by Mormons years ago. They destroyed it and moved away. I've heard Indians talk about a grand spring that was there once. It's gone, too. Its name was...let me see...."

"Amber Spring," interrupted Shefford.

"By George, you're right!" rejoined the trader, again amazed. "Shefford, this beats me. I haven't heard that name for ten years. I can't help seeing what a tenderfoot...stranger...you are to the desert. Yet, here you are...speaking of what you should know nothing of.... And there's more behind this."

Shefford rose, unable to conceal his agitation.

"Did you ever hear of a rider named Venters?"

"Rider? You mean a cowboy? Venters. No, I never heard that name."

"Did you ever hear of a gunman named Lassiter?" queried Shefford, with increasing emotion.

"No."

"Did you ever hear of a Mormon woman named...Jane Withersteen?"

"No."

Shefford drew his breath sharply. He had followed a gleam…he had caught a fleeting glimpse of it.

"Did you ever hear of a child…a girl…a woman…called Fay Larkin?"

Withers rose slowly with a paling face.

"If you're a spy it'll go hard with you…though I'm no Mormon," he said, grimly.

Shefford lifted a shaking hand.

"I was a clergyman. Now I'm nothing…a wanderer…least of all a spy."

Withers leaned closer to see into the other man's eyes; he looked long and then appeared satisfied.

"I've heard the name Fay Larkin," he said slowly. "I reckon that's all I'll say till you tell your story."

Shefford stood with his back to the fire and he turned the palms of his hands to catch the warmth. He felt cold. Withers had affected him strangely. What was the meaning of the trader's somber gravity? Why was the very mention of Mormons attended by something austere and secret?

"My name is John Shefford. I am twenty-four," began Shefford. "My family.…"

Here a knock on the door interrupted Shefford.

"Come in," called Withers.

The door opened and like a shadow Nas Ta Bega slipped in. He said something in Navajo to the trader.

"How," he said to Shefford, and extended his hand. He was stately, but there was no mistaking his friendliness. Then he sat down before the fire, doubled his legs under him after the Indian fashion, and with dark eyes on the blazing logs seemed to lose himself in meditation.

"He likes the fire," explained Withers. "Whenever he comes to Kayenta he always visits me like this.… Don't mind him. Go on with your story."

"My family were plain people, well-to-do, and very religious," went on Shefford. "When I was a boy we moved from the country to a town called Beaumont, Illinois. There was a college in Beaumont and eventually I was sent to it to study for the ministry. I wanted to be…but never mind that. By the time I was twenty-two I was ready for my career as a clergyman. I preached for a year around at different places and then got a church in my home town of Beaumont. I became exceedingly good friends of a man named Venters, who had recently come to Beaumont. He was a singular man. His wife was a strange, beautiful woman, very reserved, and she had wonderful dark eyes. They had money and were devoted to each other, and perfectly happy. They owned the finest horses ever seen in Illinois, and their particular enjoyment seemed to be riding. They were always taking long rides. It was something worth going far for to see Mrs. Venters on a horse.

"It was through my own love of horses that I became friendly with Venters. He and his wife attended my church and as I got to see more of them, gradually we grew intimate. And it was not until I did get intimate with them that I realized that both seemed to be haunted by the past. They were sometimes sad even in their happiness. They drifted off into dreams. They lived back in another world. They seemed to be listening. Indeed, they were a singularly interesting couple, and I grew genuinely fond of them. By and by they had a little girl whom they named Jane. The coming of the baby made a change in my friends. They were happier, and I observed that the haunting shadow did not so often return.

"Venters had spoken of a journey West that he and his wife meant to take some time. But after the baby came he never mentioned his wife in connection with the trip. I gathered that he felt compelled to go to clear up a mystery or to find something...I did not make out just what. But eventually, and it was about a year ago, he told me his story...the strangest, wildest, and most tragic I ever heard.

"I can't tell it all now. It is enough to say that fifteen years before he had been a rider for a rich Mormon woman named Jane Withersteen, of this village Cottonwoods. She had adopted a beautiful Gentile child named Fay Larkin. Her interest in Gentiles earned the displeasure of her churchmen, and as she was proud there came a breach. Venters and a gunman named Lassiter became involved in her quarrel. Finally Venters took to the cañons. Here in the wilds he found the strange girl he eventually married. For a long time they lived in a wonderful hidden valley, the entrance to which was guarded by a huge balancing rock. Venters got away with the girl. But Lassiter and Jane Withersteen and the child Fay Larkin were driven into the cañon. They escaped to the valley where Venters had lived. Lassiter rolled the balancing rock, and, crashing down the narrow trail, it loosened the weathered walls and closed the narrow outlet forever."

Shefford ended his narrative out of breath, pale and dripping with sweat. Withers sat leaning forward with an expression of intense interest. Nas Ta Bega's easy, graceful pose had succeeded to one of strained rigidity. He seemed a statue of bronze. Could a few intelligible words, Shefford wondered, have created that strange, listening posture?

"Venters got out of Utah, of course, as you know," went on Shefford. "He got out, knowing...as I feel I would have known...that Jane, Lassiter, and little Fay Larkin were shut up, walled up in Surprise Valley. For years Venters considered it would not have been safe for him to venture to rescue them. He had no fears for their lives. They could live in Surprise Valley. But Venters always intended to come back with Bess and find the valley and his friends. No wonder he and Bess were haunted. However, when his wife had the baby that made a difference. It meant he had to go alone. And he was thinking seriously of starting when I...when there were developments that made it desirable for me to leave Beaumont. Venters's story haunted me as he had been haunted. I dreamed of that wild valley...of little Fay Larkin grown to womanhood...such a woman as Bess Venters was. And the longing to come was great.... And, Withers... here I am."

The trader reached out and gave Shefford the grip of a man in whom emotion was powerful, but deep and difficult to express.

"Listen to this...I wish I could help you. Life is a queer deal...Shefford, I've got to trust you. Over here in the wild cañon country there's a village of Mormons' sealed wives. It's in Arizona, perhaps twenty miles from here, and near the Utah line. When the United States government began to persecute, or prosecute, the Mormons for polygamy, the Mormons over in Stonebridge took their sealed wives and moved them out of Utah, just across the line. They built houses, established a village there. I'm the only Gentile who knows about it. And I pack supplies every few weeks in to these women. There are perhaps fifty women, mostly young...second or third or fourth wives of Mormons...sealed wives. And I want you to understand that sealed means sealed in all that religion or loyalty can get out of the word. There are also some old women and old men in the village, but they hardly count. And there's a flock of the finest children you ever saw in your life.

"The idea of the Mormons must have been to escape prosecution. The law of the government is one wife for each man...no more. All over Utah polygamists have been arrested. The Mormons are deeply concerned. I believe they are a good, law-abiding people. But this law is a direct blow at their religion. In my opinion they can't obey both. And therefore they have not altogether given up plural wives. Perhaps they will some day. I have no proof, but I believe the Mormons of Stonebridge pay secret night visits to their sealed wives across the line in the lonely, hidden village.

"Now once over in Stonebridge I overheard some Mormons talking about a girl who was named Fay Larkin. I never forgot the name. Later I heard the name in this sealed-wife village. But, as I told you, I never heard of Lassiter or Jane Withersteen. Still, if Mormons had found them I would never have heard of it...I'm not surprised at your rainbow-chasing adventure. It's a great story.... This Fay Larkin I've heard of might be your Fay Larkin...I almost believe so. Shefford, I'll help you find out."

"Yes, yes...I must know," replied Shefford. "Oh, I hope, I pray we can find her! But...I'd rather she was dead...if she's not still hidden in the valley."

"Naturally. You've dreamed yourself into rescuing this lost Fay Larkin.... But, Shefford, you're old enough to know life doesn't work out as you want it to. One way or another I fear you're in for a bitter disappointment."

"Withers, take me to the village."

"Shefford, you're liable to get in bad out here," said the trader gravely.

"I couldn't be any more ruined than I am now," replied Shefford, passionately.

"But there's risk in this...risk such as you never had," persisted Withers.

"I'll risk anything."

"Reckon this's a funny deal for a sheep-trader to have on his hands," continued Withers. "Shefford, I like you. I've a mind to see you through this. It's a damn strange story.... I'll tell you what...I will help you. I'll give you a job packing supplies into the village. I meant to turn that over to a Mormon cowboy...Joe Lake. The job shall be yours, and I'll go with you first trip. Here's my hand on it.... Now, Shefford, I'm more curious about you than I was before you told your story. What ruined you? As we're to be partners, you can tell me now. I'll keep your secret. Maybe I can do you good."

Shefford wanted to confess, yet it was hard. Perhaps, had he not been so agitated, he would not have answered to impulse. But this trader was a man...a man of the desert...he would understand.

"I told you I was a clergyman," said Shefford in low voice. "I didn't want to be one, but they made me one. I did my best. I failed.... I had doubts of religion...of the Bible...of God, as my church believed in them. As I grew older thought and study convinced me of the narrowness of religion as my congregation lived it. I preached what I believed. I alienated them. They put me out, took my calling from me, disgraced me, ruined me."

"So that's all!" exclaimed Withers, slowly. "You didn't believe in the God of the Bible.... Well, I've been in the desert long enough to know there is a God, but probably not the one your church worships.... Shefford, go to the Navajo for a faith!"

Shefford had forgotten the presence of Nas Ta Bega, and perhaps Withers had likewise. At this juncture the Indian rose to his full height, and he folded his arms to stand with the somber pride of a chieftain while his dark, inscrutable eyes were riveted upon Shefford. At that moment he seemed magnificent. The difference was obscure to Shefford. But he felt that it was there in the Navajo's mind. Nas Ta Bega's strange look was not to be interpreted. Presently he turned and passed from the room.

"By George!" cried Withers, suddenly, and he pounded his knee with his fist. "I'd forgotten."

"What?" ejaculated Shefford.

"Why, that Indian understood every word we said. He knows English. He's educated. Well, if this doesn't beat me.... Let me tell you about Nas Ta Bega."

Withers appeared to be recalling something half forgotten.

"Years ago, in fifty-seven, I think, Kit Carson with his soldiers chased the Navajo tribes and rounded them up to be put on reservations. But he failed to catch all the members of one tribe. They escaped up into wild cañons like the Sagi. The descendants of these fugitives live there now and are the finest In-

dians on earth…the finest because they're unspoiled by the white man. Well, as
I got the story, years after Carson's round-up one of his soldiers guided some
interested travelers in there. When they left they took an Indian boy with them
to educate. From what I know of Navajos I'm inclined to think the boy was
taken against his parents' wish. Anyway, he was taken. That boy was Nas Ta
Bega. The story goes that he was educated somewhere. Years afterward, and
perhaps not long before I came in here, he returned to his people. There have
been missionaries and other interested fools who have given Indians a white
man's education. In all the instances I know of, these educated Indians returned
to their tribes, repudiating the white man's knowledge, habits, life, and religion. I have heard that Nas Ta Bega came back, laid down the white man's
clothes along with the education, and never again showed that he had known
either.

"You have just seen how strangely he acted. It's almost certain he heard our
conversation. Well, it doesn't matter. He won't tell. He can hardly be made to
use an English word. Besides, he's a noble red man, if there ever was one. He
has been a friend in need to me. If you stay long out here you'll learn something
from the Indians."

Later Shefford went outdoors to walk and think. There was no moon, but the
stars made light enough to cast his shadow on the ground. The dark, illimitable
expanse of blue sky seemed to be glittering with numberless points of fire. The
air was cold and still. A dreaming silence lay over the land. Shefford saw and
felt all these things, and their effect was continuous and remained with him and
helped calm him. He was conscious of a burden removed from his mind. Con-
fession of his secret had been like tearing a thorn from his flesh, but, once done,
it afforded him relief and a singular realization that out here it did not matter
much. In a crowd of men all looking at him and judging him by their standards
he had been made to suffer. Here, if he were judged at all, it would be by what
he could do, how he sustained himself and helped others.

He walked far across the valley toward the low bluffs, but they did not seem
to get any closer. And, finally, he stopped beside a stone and looked around at
the strange horizon and up at the heavens. He did not feel utterly aloof from
them, nor alone in a waste, nor a useless atom amid incomprehensible forces.
Something like a loosened mantle fell from about him, dropping down at his
feet; and all at once he was conscious of freedom. He did not understand in the
least why abasement left him, but it was so. He had come a long way, in bitterness, in despair, believing himself to be what men had called him. The desert
and the stars and the wind, the silence of the night, the loneliness of this vast
country where there was room for a thousand cities…these somehow vaguely,
yet surely, bade him lift his head. They withheld their secret, but they made a
promise. The thing which he had been feeling every day and every night was a
strange enveloping comfort. And it was at this moment that Shefford, divining

whence his help was to come, embraced all that wild and speaking Nature around and above and surrendered himself utterly.

"I am young. I am free. I have my life to live," he said. "I'll be a man. I'll take what comes. Let me learn here!"

When he had spoken out, settled once and forever his attitude toward his future, he seemed to be born again, wonderfully alive to the influences around him, ready to trust what yet remained a mystery.

Then his thoughts reverted to Fay Larkin. Could this girl be known to the Mormons? It was possible. Fay Larkin was an unusual name. Deep into Shefford's heart had sunk the story Venters had told. Shefford found that he had unconsciously created a like romance…he had been loving a wild and strange and lonely girl, like beautiful Bess Venters. It was a shock to learn the truth, but, as it had been only a dream, it could hardly be vital.

Shefford retraced his steps toward the post. Half-way back he espied a tall, dark figure moving toward him, and presently the shape and the step seemed familiar. Then he recognized Nas Ta Bega. Soon they were face to face. Shefford felt that the Indian had been trailing him over the sand, and that this was to be a significant meeting. Remembering Withers's revelation about the Navajo, Shefford scarcely knew how to approach him now. There was no difference to be made out in Nas Ta Bega's dark face and inscrutable eyes, yet there was a difference to be felt in his presence. But the Indian did not speak, and turned to walk by Shefford's side. Shefford could not long be silent.

"Nas Ta Bega, were you looking for me?" he asked.

"You have no gun," replied the Indian.

But for his very low voice, his slow speaking of the words, Shefford would have thought him a white man. For Shefford there was indeed instinct in this meeting, and he turned to face the Navajo.

"Withers told me you had been educated, that you came back to the desert, that you never showed your training…. Nas Ta Bega, did you understand all I told Withers?"

"Yes," replied the Indian.

"You won't betray me?"

"I am a Navajo."

"Nas Ta Bega, you trail me…you say I have no gun." Shefford wanted to ask this Indian if he cared to be the white man's friend, but the question was not easy to put, and, besides, seemed unnecessary. "I am alone and strange in this wild country. I must learn."

"Nas Ta Bega will show you the trails and the water-holes."

"For money…for silver you will do this?" inquired Shefford.

Shefford felt that the Indian's silence was a rebuke. He remembered Withers's singular praise of this red man. He realized he must change his idea of Indians.

"Nas Ta Bega, I know nothing. I feel like a child in the wilderness. When I speak it is out of the mouths of those who have taught me. I must find a new voice and a new life.... You heard my story to Withers. I am an outcast from my own people. If you will be my friend...be so."

The Indian clasped Shefford's hand and held it in a response that was more beautiful for its silence. So they stood for a moment in the starlight.

"Nas Ta Bega, what did Withers mean when he said go to the Navajo for a faith?" asked Shefford.

"He meant the desert is my mother.... Will you go with Nas Ta Bega into the cañons and the mountains?"

"Indeed I will."

They unclasped hands and turned toward the trading-post.

"Nas Ta Bega, have you spoken my tongue to any other white man since you returned to your home?" asked Shefford.

"No."

"Why do you...why are you different for me?"

"*Bi Nai!* The Navajo will call his white friend *Bi Nai*...brother," said Nas Ta Bega, and he spoke haltingly, not as if words were hard to find, but strange to speak. "I was stolen from my mother's hogan and taken to California. They kept me ten years in a mission at San Bernardino and four years in a school. They said my color and my hair were all that was left of the Indian in me. But they could not see my heart. They took fourteen years of my life. They wanted to make me a missionary among my own people. But the white man's ways and his life and his God are not the Indian's. They never can be."

How strangely productive of thought for Shefford to hear the Indian talk! What fatality in this meeting and friendship! Upon Nas Ta Bega had been forced education, training, religion, and that had made him something more and something less than an Indian. It was something assimilated from the white man which made the Indian unhappy and alien in his own home — something meant to be good for him and his kind that had ruined him. For Shefford felt the passion and the tragedy of this Navajo.

"*Bi Nai,* the Indian is dying!" Nas Ta Bega's low voice was deep and wonderful with its intensity of feeling. "The white man robbed the Indian of lands and homes, drove him into the deserts, made him a gaunt and sleepless spiller of blood.... The blood is all spilled now, for the Indian is broken. But the white man sells him rum and seduces his daughters.... He will not leave the Indian in peace with his own God...! *Bi Nai,* the Indian is dying!"

The heat of midsummer came, when the blistering sun shone, and a hot blast blew across the sand, and the furious storms made floods in the washes. Day and night Shefford was always in the open, and any one who had ever known him in the past would have failed to recognize him now.

In the early fall, with Nas Ta Bega as companion, he set out to the south of

Kayenta upon long-neglected business of the trader. They visited Red Lake, Blue Cañon, Keams Cañon, Oribi, the Moki villages, Tuba, Moencopie, and Moen Ave. This trip took many weeks and gave Shefford all the opportunity he wanted to study the Indians, and the conditions near to the border of civilization. He learned the truth about the Indians and the missionaries. But he knew he must plunge on and on until he fulfilled his mission — to find Fay Larkin and make her his wife.

MAX BRAND™

FREDERICK SCHILLER FAUST (1892–1944) was born in Seattle, Washington. He wrote over 500 average-length books (300 of them Westerns) under nineteen different pseudonyms, but Max Brand — "the Jewish cowboy," as he once dubbed it — has become the most familiar and is now his trademark. Faust was convinced very early that to die in battle was the most heroic of deaths and so, when the Great War began, he tried to get overseas. All of his efforts came to nothing and in 1917, working at manual labor in New York City, he wrote a letter which was carried in *The New York Times* protesting this social injustice. Mark Twain's sister came to his rescue by arranging for Faust to meet Robert H. Davis, an editor at The Frank A. Munsey Company.

Faust wanted to write poetry. What happened instead was that Davis provided Faust with a brief plot idea, told him to go down the hall to a room where there was a typewriter, only to have Faust return some six hours later with a story suitable for publication. That was "Convalescence," a short story which appeared in *All-Story Weekly* (3/31/17) and which launched Faust's career as an author of fiction. Zane Grey had recently abandoned the Munsey publications, *All-Story Weekly* and *The Argosy,* as a market for his Western serials, selling them instead to the slick-paper *Country Gentleman.* The more fiction Faust wrote for Davis, the more convinced this editor became that Faust could equal Zane Grey at the Western story.

The one element that is the same in Zane Grey's early Western stories and Faust's from beginning to end is that they are psycho-dramas. What impact events have on the soul, the inner spiritual changes wrought by ordeal and adversity, the power of love as an emotion and a bond between a man and a woman, and above all the meaning of life and one's experiences in the world conspire to transfigure these stories and elevate them to a plane that shimmers with nuances both symbolic and mythical. In 1920 Faust expanded the market for his fiction to include Street & Smith's *Western Story Magazine* for which throughout the next decade he would contribute regularly a million and a half words a year at a rate of 5¢ a word. It was not unusual for him to have two serial installments and a short novel in a single issue under three different names nor to earn from just this one source $2,500 a week.

In 1921 Faust made the tragic discovery that he had an incurable heart condition from which he might die at any moment. This condition may have been in part emotional. At any rate, Faust became depressed about his work and consulted H.G. Baynes, a Jungian analyst in England, and finally even met with C.G. Jung himself who was visiting England at the time on his way to Africa. They had good talks although Jung did not take Faust as a patient. Jung did advise Faust that his best hope was to live a simple life. This advice Faust rejected. He went to Italy where he rented a villa in Florence, lived extravagantly, and was perpetually in debt. Faust needed his speed at writing merely to remain solvent. Yet what is most amazing about him is not that he wrote so much, but that he wrote so much so well!

By the early 1930s Faust was spending more and more time in the United States. Carl Brandt, his agent, persuaded him to write for the slick magazines since the pay was better and, toward the end of the decade, Faust moved his family to Hollywood where he found work as a screenwriter. He had missed one war; he refused to miss the Second World War. He pulled strings to become a war correspondent for *Harper's Magazine* and sailed to Europe and the Italian front. Faust hoped from this experience to write fiction about men at war and he lived in foxholes with American soldiers involved in some of the bloodiest fighting on any front. These men, including the machine-gunner beside whom Faust died, had grown up reading his stories with their fabulous heroes and their grand deeds, and that is where on a dark night in 1944, hit by shrapnel, Faust expired, having asked the medics to attend first to the younger men who had been wounded.

Faust's Western fiction has nothing intrinsically to do with the American West, although he had voluminous notes and research materials on virtually every aspect of the frontier. THE UNTAMED (Putnam, 1919) was his first Western novel and in Dan Barry, its protagonist, Faust created a man who is beyond morality in a Nietzschean sense, who is closer to the primitive and the wild in nature than other human beings, who is both frightening and sympathetic. His story continues, and his personality gains added depth, in the two sequels which complete his story, THE NIGHT HORSEMAN (Putnam, 1920) and THE SEVENTH MAN (Putnam, 1921). It is significant, I believe, that THE UNTAMED appeared in standard print in both a jacketed reprint edition and a trade paperback from the University of Nebraska Press as well as in full-length audio from Books on Tape in 1994, seventy-five years after it was first published.

Those who worked with Faust in Hollywood were amazed at his fecundity, his ability to plot stories. However, for all of his incessant talk about plot and plotting, Faust's Western fiction is uniformly character-driven. His plots emerge from the characters as they are confronted with conflicts and frustrations. Above all, there is his humor — the hilarity of the opening chapters of THE RETURN OF THE RANCHER (Dodd, Mead, 1933), to give only one instance, is sustained by the humorous contrast between irony and naïveté. And so many of Faust's characters are truly unforgettable, from the most familiar, like Dan Barry and Harry Destry, to such marvelous creations as José Ridal in BLACKIE AND RED (Chelsea House, 1926) or Gaspar Sental in THE RETURN OF THE RANCHER.

Too often, it may appear, Faust's plots are pursuit stories and his protagonists in quest of an illustrious father or victims of an Achilles' heel, but these are premises and conventions that are ultimately of little consequence. His characters are in essence psychic forces. In Faust's fiction, as Robert Sampson concluded in the first volume of YESTERDAY'S FACES (Bowling Green University Popular Press, 1983), "every action is motivated. Every character makes decisions and each must endure the consequences of his decisions. Each character is gnawed by the conflict between his wishes and the necessities of his experience. The story advances from the first interactions of the first characters. It continues, a fugue for full orchestra, ever more complex, modified by decisions of increasing desperation, to a climax whose savagery may involve no bloodshed at all. But there will be psychological tension screaming in harmonics almost beyond the ear's capacity."

Faust's finest fiction can be enjoyed on the level of adventure, or on the deeper level of psychic conflict. He knew in his heart that he had not resolved the psychic conflicts he projected into his fiction, but he held out hope to the last that the resolutions he had failed to find in life and in his stories might somehow, miraculously, be achieved on the higher plane of the poetry which he continued to write. Yet Faust is not the first writer, and will not be the last, who treasured least what others have come to treasure most. It may even be possible that a later generation, having read his many works as he wrote them (and they are now being restored after decades of inept abridgments and rewriting), will find Frederick Faust to have been, truly, one of the most significant American literary artists of the 20th Century. Much more about Faust's life, his work, and critical essays on various aspects of his fiction of all kinds will be found in THE MAX BRAND COMPANION (Greenwood Press, 1996).

"Werewolf" was written more than ten years after Zane Grey's "The Desert Crucible," and yet there comes a time in this story — when Christopher encounters the aged Indian, the old wise man — that the terrain is again, suddenly, familiar to us. It shimmers with the multiple affinities of meaning conjured by the unconscious, which Vergil once sought to capture within an image both awesome and sinister: *numina magna deum*. For Christopher, in fleeing, finds that he is become a wanderer, a searcher, and it is in the deep fastnesses of the wilderness that he is confronted with the terrors of his own soul and the meaning of his life. He has found love, as deep and abiding as it is ever given to human beings to know, but it is lost to him until his own spiritual odyssey shall have completed its course, until he has had his spirit vision, confronted the terrifying shadow within, with only the mournful howl of an ancient werewolf to accompany him on this lonely, and terrible, and anguished journey to the center of his soul.

WEREWOLF
1926

I
"The New Comer"

All day the storm had been gathering behind Chimney Mountain and, peering around the edges of that giant with a scowling brow, now and again; and all day there had been strainings of the wind and sounds of dim confusion in the upper air, but not until the evening did the storm break. A broad, yellow-cheeked moon was sailing up the eastern sky when ten thousand wild horses of darkness rushed out from behind Mount Chimney and covered the sky with darkness. Dashes and scatterings of rain and hail began to clang on the tin roofs in the valley, and the wind kept up a continual insane whining, now and then leaping against window or door and shaking them in an impatient frenzy.

On such a night as this, few men got as far as Yates's Saloon beyond the outskirts of the town of Royal, but nevertheless he was always glad to have this weather, for those who *did* come stayed long and opened their purses with as much freedom as though the morrow was to be doomsday, and as though their souls needed much warming with honest rye whisky against that great event.

Mr. Yates had two rooms. The bar was in one, with a round iron stove at one end where the guests might warm themselves, and a row of chairs against the walls, for one of the maxims of Yates had to do with the evils of drinking — while standing.

He was engaged in giving good advice at this moment to a youth who rested one elbow on the edge of the bar and poised the other fist upon his hip — a tall, strong, fierce young man who smiled down at the saloon keeper partly in contempt for the advice and partly in mild recognition of the privilege of white hairs.

"You give me another slug of the red-eye, old boy," said the cowpuncher.

Mr. Yates filled the glass with an unwilling shake of the head. As he pushed it back across the bar and gathered in the fifty-cent piece he said gloomily:

"You can't hurry liquor, my son. Whisky is something that can't be rushed. You got to go slow and easy, let it mellow you, treat it with caution...and then whisky will stand your friend."

"All right," said the cowpuncher, tossing off the drink and shoving back the glass. "Never mind the change. Gimme another, will you…and then you can talk some more."

Mr. Yates came to a pause.

"I dunno that I ought to let you drink another so quick," he said.

"You dunno?" said the young man. "I know, though. Fill up that glass!"

There were five men in the barroom, their chairs tilted against the wall, and now five chairs swung softly forward and five heads were raised.

"I tell you, lad," explained the saloon keeper, "that the whisky which will be a friend to the wise man can turn into a devil if it's treated carelessly. You can't crowd it into a corner. You can't treat it like a slave!"

"What'll it do?" asked the boy. And stretching out his arm with a movement of snaky speed, he wrenched the bottle from the hands of the saloon keeper, and filled his glass with such a careless violence that an extra quantity spilled upon the well-rubbed varnish of the bar.

"What's this stuff going to do to me?"

Mr. Yates did not attempt to protest against the act of violence. But a dark flush spread over his face and he said solemnly:

"It'll take you by the throat and strangle you. It'll send a bullet into your back. It'll throw you under the feet of a mad horse. Or it'll kill you with the horrors, if it feels like it!"

The youngster tossed off his liquor again, coughed, and then shrugged his shoulders.

"I don't understand what you're driving at," he said, "and I don't know that I give a damn! Is there any writing paper in that other room?"

There was still more contention upon the tip of the tongue of Yates, but he controlled himself with an effort, for words flow more willingly from the lips of an old man than water from a rich spring. He merely said: "There's always paper there, and welcome!"

There was no answer to this courtesy. The cowboy turned from the bar and kicked open the door. His chair screeched as he drew it up to a table, and after that there was silence from the second room, and silence at the bar, also. The five farmers and cowhands smoked their pipes or cigarettes and watched the thoughtful cloud upon the brow of their host.

"And who is he?" asked one at length.

"Him? Didn't you have a fair look at him?"

"It's Cliff Main," said another. "I knew him over in the Ridoso Valley a few years back, and I'm sure it's him."

"Yes," nodded Yates, "it's the same man."

But one of the others said suddenly: "Why, partner, that's the name of Harry Main's brother!"

Again the saloon keeper nodded.

"It's him," he confessed.

This was followed by a deeper and longer silence, and more than one apprehensive glance was cast at the door of the second room. A weather-beaten farm hand approached the bar and leaned against it.

"Tell me," he murmured, "is he like Harry?" And he hooked a thumb over his shoulder.

"You can see for yourself," said Yates solemnly. But he added, forced on by a keen sense of fairness: "No, he ain't a killer, you might say. He's gone straight enough. But still he ain't any lamb!"

The farmer shuddered a little.

"What's his game here?" he asked.

"It's that girl up the valley...her that young Royal is after."

"Which Royal?"

"I mean Christopher."

"It's the Lassiter girl that Chris Royal goes with, ain't it?"

"That's the one. They say that Main seen her at a dance down in Phoenix last year, and it addled his head a good deal. So I guess that's why he's here."

"That would be a thing!" said the farmer. "A Lassiter to look at a Main, eh?"

"Well, I've seen stranger things happen," said Yates. "A pretty girl takes to a strong man, and a strong man takes to a pretty girl. Goodness and badness ain't considered much, and neither is the poor old family tree. But that ain't the point. Georgie Lassiter, she's got one strong man already, and that had ought to be enough! I guess that no woman can ask for more than a Royal, eh?"

He leaned on the edge of the bar.

"I guess that no woman could ask for more than that," he echoed himself, and he shook his head slowly from side to side and laughed softly.

The others nodded in understanding, as though they were all familiar with the qualities of the family which had given its name to the valley and to the town.

In the meantime, the storm had been rising and quickening like the pulse of a sick man's heart, and now the wind broke with hysterical wailing around the saloon. The windows and the doors rattled furiously. The very roofs seemed about to be unsettled, and a contrary gust came down the chimney and knocked a puff of smoke through every crack of the stove.

"What a night!" breathed Yates.

"I'll take another whisky!" said one.

"And me!" said another. "We'll set 'em up all around. I say that I don't mind a night like this when you can sit warm around a fire with something to keep your heart up. But I could tell you about a night that was a twin brother to this, except that it was in February with ice in the wind. I was back up in Montana, that winter, riding range for the...."

The door quivered and then jerked open, and the wind, like an entering flood of water, made every man cringe in his place.

With that burst of the storm came a big young man who thrust the door shut behind him with a strong hand and then leaned against the bar, stamping the water out of his soaked riding boots and shaking the rain out of his hat, He was neither beaten nor even embittered by the force of the wind and the rain. It had merely brought a rosy glow into his face and dimmed the brightness of his eyes a bit with moisture.

"Well, Chris Royal," said the bar-keeper. "What're you having?"

"Nothing," said he. "I'm bound home, you see, and mother doesn't like me to have liquor on my breath. I stopped and put my mare in your shed for a feed, and a bit of rest. She was fagged by bucking this wind all the way up the valley."

He broke off to speak to the other men in the room and, as he completed that little ceremony and had asked after their welfare, you might have put him down as the son of a great landed proprietor on whose estates all of these men were living; so that their welfare, in a way, was his. However, that was not the case, but the Royals had been so long in the valley, had given it its name and had dominated all affairs in it, that they were placed in a truly patriarchal position. There were no political parties in Royal County or in Royal Valley, for instance. There were only the Royal partisans and their opponents. And the opponents were sure to be merely a scattering and spiteful handful. In other ways, too, the family dominated the region.

"It's a sort of queer name...Royal," someone had said to a man from the valley, and the answer had been instant: "That's because you ain't seen them. They're all fit to be kings!"

"But look here, Christopher," said Yates. "D'you know that if you don't drink you're missing one of the best things in life?"

"I take a drink now and then," said Christopher. "I like it as well as most, I suppose. But it bothers mother to have me do it. So I don't when I'm going toward her, you see."

"Ah, well," said Mr. Yates, holding up a bottle toward the light. "Here's something twenty-five years old that I was going to offer you a sip of, but Heaven knows that I'd make trouble between no boy and his mother. She's a grand lady, Christopher, and amazing how well she carries her years, ain't it?"

"Years?" said Christopher. "Years?"

"Well, she's getting on, ain't she?"

Christopher Royal looked rather blankly at his host.

"I never thought of that," he said. "She isn't really old, you know."

"No, not old! Not old!" said Yates, smiling. "But when we have white hair...."

"Her silver hair," said Christopher, "is beautiful. It's always been silver, you know. As far as I can remember."

"I can remember farther back than that, though," smiled the saloon keeper.

"I can remember when she first came to Royal Valley. It was a dark, mean day, and she come in a covered carriage, all made snug. But I had a glimpse of her through the carriage window and saw her face all pink and white and her yellow hair like a pool of sunshine in the shadows of the carriage."

Christopher shook his head.

"I can hardly think that my mother was ever like that," he said, smiling in rather a bewildered way. "But you mustn't call her old!"

"Why, Chris, at sixty you can't exactly call her young, can you?"

"Sixty?" exclaimed Christopher. He began to think back.

"I'm twenty-five, Duncan is twenty-eight, Edgerton is thirty-one, and Samson is thirty-five. By heavens, you're right, and she's sixty years old. I should never have guessed that. One doesn't connect years and time with her."

He added with a smile to Yates: "And you're one of the unchangeables, too. You've never been any different, have you? Not in my lifetime!"

"Well, lad, well!" smiled Yates. "I do well enough. I just shrink and shrivel a bit as time goes on. I get a little whiter and a little drier, and there's less hair for me to bother about combing, from year to year. But I don't change much. Neither does the old place."

"You've put a new wing on the shed, though."

"You noticed that, eh?"

"Yes. Who did you have to do the work?"

"I had the slaves of Adam," said Mr. Yates, and he held out his two hands with a chuckle.

"You did it all yourself?" Christopher whistled. "You're a rare old one!" said he. "If there were more like you, there'd be no room for the youngsters in the world. You'd take our work away from us."

A door crashed just behind him.

"Are you Chris Royal?" asked a voice, and he turned about and looked into the dark eyes of Cliff Main.

"I'm Christopher Royal," he admitted.

The other stepped up and faced him at the bar.

"I started to find you today," said he. "Then the rain dropped on me and I put in here. I want to have a talk with you, Royal."

"A talk? Where?"

"Well, there's an empty room back here. We might go there!"

II
"The Locked Room"

Christopher regarded the newcomer rather dubiously for a moment, but then he nodded and followed him into the other apartment. The door closed behind Main, and the lock grated as it was turned.

"Hello!" said the saloon keeper, starting around from behind the bar. "I don't like that!"

"What're you going to do, Yates?" asked one of the farm hands, catching his sleeve as he passed.

"I'm going to have that door open!"

"Now, don't you do it. You know Main. Don't take more'n a little thing like that to send Harry Main crazy. And his brother looks like the same kind of gunpowder."

Yates paused, biting his lip with anxiety.

"Besides, there ain't gunna be no trouble," said one of the others. "It ain't as though Duncan or Edgerton or Samson Royal was in there. Christopher, he's softer than the rest. He's easier and quieter. He's more like a girl, you'd say, compared to his older brothers! He can get on with anybody. I never heard of Chris having an enemy."

"And that's all gospel," said Yates, going back behind the bar. But he paused, now and again, and shook his head. "I don't like that locked door," he sighed. "I remember once that me and my wife had a bad quarrel. And it started with me locking the door...." He broke off with a laugh. "And when I wanted to open that door, I'd lost the key!"

There was general mirth at this, until a sudden uproar of the wind, and its loud whistling beneath the door, caused the human voices to fall away. The wind itself dropped to a murmur, shortly afterward, and every one in the barroom could hear the voice of Christopher Royal, saying sharply, "I tell you, man, that I don't want any trouble with you! I swear that I've never done you any harm!"

The wind began again, and all the six in the barroom looked mutely at one another, with great eyes.

"It's the whisky," said Yates suddenly. "I might of knowed it. I told him when he was pouring it down that way. I've seen it happen before. And I tell you that door'll never be unlocked until there's been hell to pay inside!"

He rushed out from behind the bar and tore at the knob.

"Open the door!" he yelled.

There was a sudden sound of thunderous scuffling within, and then a heavy body crashed against the door. Yates, terribly frightened, shrank away.

"Why don't you do something?" he wailed. "Ain't they in there killing each other? Ain't there five of you, big and strong and young, to stop 'em? Why do you stay here with your hands hangin'?"

They looked at one another, these five. Surely they were as strong and as brave as most men, but the sound and the thought of the battle which was raging beyond that door baffled and overawed them. They could not move to help. Perhaps in another instant they would have recovered their courage and been able to act, but the whole duration of the scuffle within the other room lasted only a single moment. It ended with the sound of a revolver shot.

Then the key grated in the lock.

"May Heaven forgive me!" said old Yates. "But I'm gunna die with poor young Chris or revenge him!"

And he picked up a shotgun from behind the bar and laid it level with the opening door, his old face white and tense with savage energy.

The door swung wide — and Christopher Royal stepped out, while a gasp of wonder and relief came from the others in the place. For their sense of suspense had been as great as if they had been forced to stand by while a man was caged with a tiger. And now the man came forth alive!

In the hand of Christopher there was hanging a big Colt, with a thin wisp of smoke still clinging to its muzzle like a ghost.

"He's dead, I think," said Christopher, and he leaned against the bar. "I wish that some of you would go and see!"

They poured into the writing room. It was half a wreck. One could see that two very strong men had wrestled here, and whatever they touched had given way.

And Cliff Main lay in the corner on his back with a smudge of blood across his face. There was no reason for a second glance. He had been shot fairly through the brain.

When they came back into the barroom, Yates hastily filled a glass with whisky and in silence placed it beside the youngster. He gripped it eagerly — and then pushed it away.

"She wouldn't like it," he explained.

He raised his head and, seeming to discover the gun in his hand, or to remember it for the first time, he threw it on the bar and shuddered violently. He was very white, with a look of sickness in his face, but he was extremely steady and quiet.

He said: "Is your telephone working in spite of the storm, Yates?"

"It's working, Chris."

"Then I want you to ring up the sheriff and tell him what's happened out here."

"I'll do that."

"There's nothing to be done for...him, I suppose?"

"For Main? No, he's dead, Chris."

"I thought so. But what did you say the name was?"

"Cliff Main...Harry Main's brother."

"Harry Main's brother!"

He took the glass of whisky which was standing on the bar. He tossed it off, and then without another word he strode away into the night.

"Look at him," said Yates, addressing the door through which his guest had just disappeared. "Look at him! And you call him soft! I tell you, even Harry Main wouldn't get any better than his brother, if he should come along to even things up. There's something in the Royal blood, and it can't be beat and it can't be downed! Did you notice him when he came out from that room? Sick looking, because it had been a dirty job and a dirty sight at the finish. But like a rock, eh?''

He rubbed his hands together. "As for the killing of Cliff Main,'' he added with a sudden sternness, "you was all here to witness how Main carried on from first to last, wasn't you?''

"We seen it all,'' said one of the farmers. "They'll never lay a hand on Chris for this. It's only Harry Main that he's got to think about! And I thank Heaven that I ain't in the boots of Chris!''

III
"Dark Thoughts"

The wind had changed, so that as Christopher Royal rode up the valley the rain was volleyed at him from the side, stinging his face until he was forced to cant his head against it. It was an automatic movement. The howling of the wind and crashing of the rain which had seemed terrible enough to him before were now as nothing, for there was a war in his spirit which quite overwhelmed all mere disturbances of nature.

He had killed a man! To Christopher the miracle was that in the crisis, when his back was against the wall, his skill with a gun, built up by many a long year of practice, by many a strenuous hunting season, had not deserted him. But when the need came, mechanically the weapon had glided into his hand and he had shot swift and true. So swiftly and truly, indeed, that Cliff Main had not been able to complete his own draw before the pellet of lead had crashed through his brain.

But suppose that he had known that the name of the man was Main? Suppose that he had known that this was none other than a brother to the famous fighting man, Harry Main? What then?

It made convulsive shudders run through the body of Christopher, and in the blackness of the night, with the rush of the storm about him, he told himself again the secret which no one other than the Almighty and his own soul had ever been cognizant of before: he was a coward!

How then could he have come to the age of twenty-five years without having that weakness publicly exposed by the rough men of Royal Valley, where he had spent his life?

The answer was, simply, that his family were all above the shadow of reproach. They had filled the mountains with their deeds for many a year, and this present brood seemed to have improved upon the old stock rather than fallen away from the good tradition. If there were a riding or a hunting or a shooting contest, one could be sure that one of the Royals would be the winner. And when it came to fighting — why, who was apt to forget that the scars on the face of Samson Royal had been received in hand-to-hand battle with a grizzly? And who could fail to know that Edgerton Royal had ridden single-handed into Pinkneyville, when he was deputy sheriff, and come out again herding two prisoners before him — prisoners he had taken away from beneath the eyes of a hundred of their friends? As for Peter Royal, he had proved that he was worthy of spurs on that dire night when the three Mexicans cornered him, and only a year before Duncan Royal had shot out an argument with two men on the Chimney Trail.

So they were all proven, and there had remained only the youngest of the brood, Christopher, to make his name. Yet it had hardly needed making. Men took it for granted that one Royal was about as good as another. There might be little differences, but the world generally agreed that all were lions — pick which you would!

And they looked alike, for one thing. That is to say, the smallest of them all, Samson, was a full two inches above six feet, and the tallest of them, Duncan, towered a palm's breadth above his older brother. They had all the same sort of shoulders, filling a door as they went through it. And concerning their might of hand, wonderful and beautiful fables filled the land. How Samson had twisted the iron bar in the blacksmith shop in Royal town — behold, it still hangs against the wall, for proof! And how Edgerton could take two packs of playing cards and tear them across. And how Christopher himself had lifted the entire bulk of a horse!

Such stories filled the mountains with echoes. And since not one of the band had ever been found weak in any manner of physical or nervous test, it was taken for granted that all were of the same true, pure steel.

But one person in all the world knew the facts. He knew that Duncan and Edgerton and Samson and Peter were all undoubted heroes with hearts even stronger than their hands. But he knew also that there was one fatally weak link in the chain of brotherhood. That was himself. For Christopher, during years and years, had felt a weakness in his spirit, and he had waited for the dreaded moment when he should be tested. Or could it be that the family name and fame would shield him effectually all his life?

In his school days he had not so much as guessed at it. No matter how mighty had been the tradition which his brothers had left behind them in the little white schoolhouse by the river, he had not been overawed. The height of Duncan's jump, and the width of Peter's leap, and the speed of Samson on foot, and the weight of Edgerton's fist had all become proverbial in the school. But young Christopher bided his time and surpassed them, one by one. He was just as strong as they, and in addition he was a little more supple, a little more graceful, a little more brilliantly swift and sure of hand. And other graces had been lavished upon him, as though Nature, who had framed his brothers on so magnificent a scale, had been merely practicing for the moment when she was to create Christopher. So she had made the others big and glorious. But she gave to

Christopher the gift of beauty, also. The others were dark. She made him fair. There was a touch of gloom about the others, as there is apt to be with big men, but Christopher she made joyous from the beginning. So that, altogether, if the citizens of Royal Valley had been asked to select one of the family as the representative of all that was best and finest in them, they would have picked Christopher with almost one voice. There were a few, of course, who were not impressed by his gentleness.

But in this lavishness of hers, Nature had forgotten the prime and essential gift. She had left out the vital spark of courage. And though no man knew it except Christopher himself, he had passed through many a dreadful moment when he stood face to face with his secret.

Now the very secrecy which enveloped the fault was threatened. For, as certainly as lightning strikes, Harry Main was sure to come to avenge the death of his brother. And when Harry Main came, what would Christopher do?

In his desperation, he vowed that he would go out to meet the destroyer and in some hidden place, with no man to see, he would fight and die. Yet, in his heart of hearts, he constantly knew that he would not be able to meet the great test. When Harry Main approached the valley, Christopher would slink away — and never again dare to show his face among his kin. Somewhere far off he would have to find a new place in the world, a new name, and there live out his wretched destiny.

And when he thought of these things, it was typical of Christopher that he did not think of the faces of his four strong brothers, hard with scorn and contempt, but the picture that rose before him was of two women. One was his mother, and the other was the lovely Georgia Lassiter, whose head was always carried so jauntily high.

And he was sure that the reason she loved him so passionately was not so much for himself, his mind and his spirit, as because of an ideal of manhood which she had conceived and which she had grafted upon Christopher. She loved, not him, but her idea of him. And if once she guessed at such a dreadful taint as cowardice, all her love would be replaced by a fiery disgust.

And his mother? When Christopher thought of her, his heart bowed almost to the mud of the road. What she would think and do and say was beyond him, for he knew the sternness which underlay her motherhood, and he knew the iron of her pride in her family.

He reached the turning from the main road and saw before him the avenue of poplars, their heads shaken and bent beneath the fierce hand of the wind. Down the gravel drive he galloped the tired mare and so wound into view of the Royal House itself, with its lofty front and its romantic wooden battlements. From the top of the neighboring hills the naked eye could see Royal House like a great natural landmark of the valley, and from directly beneath it looked rather like a great palace than the residence of a rich rancher.

Behind its wide-flung arms were the sheds, the barns, and the maze of the corrals where the weaker cattle were sheltered and fed through the severer winters; there were the quarters for the hired men, also; and day and night, for all these years, there had never been a moment when smoke did not rise from some chimney in that group of buildings.

Christopher, looking at it all, and thinking of what it meant, felt again what he had often felt in his childhood — that big and strong as all his brothers were, his father who had built these things must have been even to them as a giant to pygmies. And his mother had been the proper wife of such a man. Still she ruled the establishment with a power as firm as it was mild, and even her eldest son dreaded her quiet voice more than the booming of a cannon.

Christopher had been a little different. He had been the baby of the family. He had been the petted one. For having raised so many sons so well, even such a woman as Marcia Royal could afford to relax a little and favor her youngest child.

He thought of this bitterly now. For if he had passed through the same stern school as the others, might he not have developed, like them, the same iron core to his spirit? Might he not have grown, like them, into a hero of heart and hand also?

He gave the mare to a stable boy. Then he turned to the house, and as he walked he wondered how he should tell the story. And what would the others say? He decided that he would say nothing for the time being. So he went into the living room and found them all, except Samson, gathered in easy-chairs near the fire on the open hearth.

He changed his clothes, and when he came down again he found that his mother had a cup of hot coffee waiting for him. She stood behind his chair, with her hands on his shoulders, while he drank it.

She spoke quietly: "Christopher, dear, you shouldn't have come out on such a night. You know that!"

"I tried to telephone from Wooley's, but the line was down in the wind, I think. I was afraid you'd worry if you didn't hear from me. So I came on out."

"And why not telephone from Yates's place? And stay there the rest of the night?"

He did not have a chance to answer, for just then Samson came in and fixed his dark eyes instantly and firmly upon the face of his youngest brother, so that Christopher understood that Samson knew all that had happened.

IV

"No Assistance"

There was something so unusual about Samson's air that the others noticed it instantly. For that matter, the oldest brother of the Royal family was always so direct, so fiercely sincere, that it was not usually difficult to understand what was going on in his mind.

He came across the room after a moment and stared down at Christopher, who stirred uneasily beneath that glance. Afterward, Samson went before the fire and stood with his back to it, until steam began to rise from his wet clothes.

"Now what is it, Sammie?" asked his mother.

Samson was the only member of the family that dared disregard for an instant a direct remark from his mother. In place of answering, he suddenly put back his head and shook with silent laughter.

"Samson!" cried Mrs. Royal.

At this, he came to himself with a start.

"What on earth is the matter with you?"

"Nothing, mother."

"My dear, you must tell me at once. You make me nervous."

Samson allowed a broad smile to spread over his face, while he stared straight across the room directly at Christopher.

"Look there!" he commanded.

"There is Christopher, of course," said the mother. "You are really rude, Samson. Now, what about Christopher?"

"I don't know what you mean. What should there be about him?"

"Don't beat about the bush, Samson!"

He sobered down at that, but still there was a suppressed exultation in his eyes and in his voice.

"You haven't heard. He wouldn't say anything about it. He doesn't want to shock you!" And the laughter broke out again, not mirthful, but savage. "I'll tell you what," said Samson, "this old Christopher of ours, whom we've always thought so gentle, and all that, he's a lion under the fleece! I've always guessed it. And tonight he's proven it!"

Mrs. Royal turned on her youngest son.

"Christopher, what have you done?"

Christopher stirred in his chair and tried to answer, but he could only shake his head and murmur, "I can't talk about it!"

"It was too much," said Samson, with a grim satisfaction. "Nasty business. He doesn't want to talk about it. Doesn't want to at all! Well, I'll tell you what happened! I came up the road to Yates's Saloon and got there just after Chris left. I heard what had happened, and I saw!"

"What was it, Sammie, in the name of Heaven!"

"Why, I'll tell you what it was! I found there the proof that Chris is your real son, mother!"

"Have you doubted that? Did you think he was a foundling?" asked Mrs. Royal, looking fondly at her youngest son.

Samson went over to her and dropped his big hands on her shoulders.

"You understand, mother, that it was always easy to see that Chris was like you in one way...like the gentler side of you...but we didn't think that he had your iron."

"Am I iron, Sammie dear?"

"You may smile at me, Mother, but you can't fool me. Yes, you are iron, in the time when iron is needed. And if you hadn't been a woman, you would have made as hard a man as ever stepped!"

"That needs some explaining, foolish boy."

"Well, we all remember the time that the Crogan dog went mad, and tried to get at us, and how you stood it off with your walking stick!"

"That was a horrible day!" she said.

"No, you liked it! I'll never forget how your eyes shone as you stood up to that wild, foaming beast!"

"Tush, Sammie. But I want to hear about Christopher."

"Well, about darling Christopher!" murmured Samson, and he turned his powerful, homely face toward Christopher. "I'll tell you. But watch him squirm! Watch him wriggle while I talk!"

"Don't be too ridiculous, Samson. Just tell me the facts!"

"There were several facts. To begin with, Chris was at the Yates place this evening. And so were several others. And one of them was young Main."

There was a sudden stiffening in the attitudes of all of the family.

"You mean Harry Main's younger brother?" asked Duncan, the giant.

"Yes."

"A ruffian, like his brother Harry!" exclaimed Mrs. Royal.

"Look at Mother's eyes shine," nodded Samson. "She's gentle...no iron about her." He stopped to laugh with a savage satisfaction again.

"Samson!" cried Christopher hoarsely. "I don't want to hear any more of this!"

"You can't help it, Chris. You simply can't help hearing it."

"I can, though, and I shall!"

And Christopher strode hurriedly from the room.

"Now will you tell us before we all go mad?" said Mrs. Royal.

"It was like this: Cliff Main had come to the place of Yates, poured down some stiff whiskies, and then gone into the next room to write a letter. Then Chris came in. He wouldn't drink, not when he was riding home to his mother."

He paused and grinned.

"My darling Christopher!" smiled Mrs. Royal.

"He's a darling," nodded Samson. "A perfect lamb! Wait until you hear the end of this yarn, though."

"I want to hear it, if you'll only get on!"

"Main come out of the other room and found Christopher...."

Here the door opened suddenly, and caused every one to start. It was Christopher coming back — a pale and shaken Christopher.

"Samson," he said, "I want you to stop making such nonsense over what happened!"

"Well?"

"I'll tell them myself exactly what happened. Since you have to know the truth about the miserable affair."

"Go on, old man! Of course we have to know!"

"Cliff Main made me leave the barroom with him. We went into that other little room. The moment we were alone, he grew insulting. And after a time, when he saw that I wanted to be friendly, and keep out of trouble, he grew overbearing...horribly so! And finally he said that he happened to be interested in Georgia Lassiter, and that that was reason enough for me to stop paying attention to her!"

There was a stifled exclamation from Mrs. Royal. Christopher, his eyes closed, rested a hand against the wall.

He said slowly, "I couldn't quite stand for that, you know. And I had to tell him that the thing would not do."

"And then?"

Christopher did not speak for a moment. He was recalling that moment over again — the sinking of his heart, and the sickness of his spirit, and the manner in which he had felt that he was slipping into a sea of darkness. Another instant and he would have begged for mercy. Another instant and he would have tried to flee from the room. But that instant was not given him by the brutal Main. There had been a flash of a hand toward a gun. And he instinctively had moved to make his own draw — and made it first!

"And then," said Christopher faintly, "he started for his gun. And I had to start for mine...." He paused, breathing hard. "The bullet passed through his brain." Christopher sank down in a chair. He was overcome by horror.

His mother was suddenly beside him, her arm around him.

"Chris, my dear boy! I know! No matter what a brute he was, he was a human being. But now that you've done this thing, there'll never be any need for you to do another. You detest bloodshed, and having proved that you're a man who cannot be tampered with safely, the others will be sure to leave you alone! Dear boy, how my heart aches!"

He did not answer. He could not look at her. She thought his horror was because he had had to take a life. But it was not. It was horror at the knowledge of how close he had been to a nervous collapse, to a complete hysteria of cowardice.

"But you're wrong, Mother," said Edgerton Royal, the logician of the family. "You're quite wrong. Before the week's out there'll be another gun fight on the hands of Chris!"

"What do you mean?"

"Think for yourself. Will Harry Main allow the man who killed his brother to get on without another fight?"

"Harry Main! That murderer! That gunfighter! No, you will all band together and prevent him! You'll all meet him and crush him!" cried Mrs. Royal.

"Wait!" said Peter Royal, for he was the judge of the family. "Wait, mother, and tell me if you yourself would allow other people to fight your battles if you were a man?"

She hesitated. Christopher, his face buried in his hands, waited breathlessly. Then he heard her saying slowly, "No, I couldn't. And not a one of you will be different. Not a one of you will want to help poor Chris, though every one of you would die to avenge him! But oh…what a dreadful trial for my poor Chris! Such a man as Harry Main!"

Samson was speaking, Samson the mighty, the ugly of face, the steely-hearted. "Chris'll beat him! Let these gentle fellows get the taste of blood and they're worse than the worst of the gunfighters that are born hard and mean. I'm a prophet. You wait and see what happens. For a million I wouldn't be in the boots of that fellow Harry Main!"

Harry Main? To Christopher, it was as though he had been thinking about a great tiger, rather than a man. Harry Main? He would as soon stand up to a thunderbolt as to that destroyer! What was Cliff Main compared to such a devil of a man?

He waited. A pause of solemnity had come in the talk of the room. And in that solemnity he knew that every one of the stern and strong brothers was resolving that the battle must be fought out man to man.

So his last hope was thrown away!

V
"Words for the Weak"

Sleep came to him that night as a most unexpected guest. And the morning dawned and found him twelve hours nearer, not to death, but to his humiliation. For all thought of standing for the trial of courage against Harry Main had left him. But, knowing that in the crisis he would not be present, he was able to put on a smile when he went down to breakfast. The others greeted him with a forced cheerfulness which made him feel that they already thought him as good as dead. Only his mother did not smile, but sat very sternly erect, her eyes looking far away. What schemes might be passing through that formidable brain of hers, equal to any man's?

After breakfast, Peter called him to one side.

"Here's that Winchester of mine that you've always liked, Chris," he said. "I want you to have it."

And Peter hurried away, leaving Christopher more thoughtful than ever. For his brother Peter was a great hunter and this was his favorite rifle, of which he had often said that the gun had a will and a way of its own in shooting straight to the mark. Such a gift meant a great deal. It was more than a rifle. It was as though Peter had parted from some of the strength of his very soul.

And, to be sure, Harry Main was as apt to fight with a rifle as with a revolver. Various stories of his prowess passed through the mind of Christopher. He remembered that old tale of how the four Brownell brothers had gone on the trail of Harry Main and shot him from behind, and how he had dragged himself from his fallen horse to a nest of rocks and bandaged his wound, and fought them off through all of a hot, windless day among the mountains. Three of the Brownell boys he killed outright. And Jack Brownell, with a bullet through his shoulder, rode fifteen miles to get to a doctor. As for Harry Main, he had needed no doctor, but cured his own hurts.

That was one eloquent testimonial to the skill of Harry with a rifle. And Christopher's face contorted a little in unwilling sympathy as he thought of the injured man dragging himself about among the rocks and firing at some momentarily exposed bit of an enemy among the adjacent rocks.

However, though rifles were a possibility, revolvers were far more likely. And as for the examples of the hardihood of Main with a Colt, there were a dozen to select from, each well-nigh as incredible as the other. Perhaps none was quite so startling as that tale of how, when he was little more than a boy, he had followed three Mexican cattle thieves who had raided his father's little ranch — followed them over a thousand miles, until the trail crossed the Rio Grande, and on the other side of that famous river had encountered them in broad daylight, unexpectedly, at a bend of the road. All three had opened fire. But Harry escaped without so much as a wound, laid the three dead with three bullets, and then turned and began the long march back toward the ranch, driving the lean cattle ahead of him.

That had been revolver work, and upon a revolver it was most likely that Harry would depend now. So Christopher took a pair of Colts and a loaded ammunition belt. He went back behind the house to a quiet little dell where the poplars walked in their slender beauty along the banks of a winding stream. It was an unforgettable spot, in the mind of Christopher, because at this place he had first told Georgia Lassiter that he loved her, and she had said so frankly and joyously that she had always loved him.

It gave him seclusion, now. With his heavy knife he sliced a blaze on the faces of six posts and then, at twenty paces' distance, he walked rapidly past those posts and put a shot in each.

He examined them afterward. A bullet had cut through the heart of each white spot except for one, where the pellet had torn through the margin of the blaze. But even so, it would have touched the heart, had that post been a man!

He was infinitely pleased with this exhibition of skill. Not that it determined him any the more strongly to remain and wait for the coming of Harry Main into the valley, but because he had worked for so many years to make himself expert with weapons that there was a meager satisfaction in seeing to what a point his skill had attained.

He went on to other little bits of marksmanship. He would select a tree, mark it with a blaze, and then turn his back upon it, close his eyes, and whirling rapidly around, look and fire all in an instant. It was terribly trying work. He missed the blaze three times out of four, but still he always managed at least to strike the tree trunk.

Then he had another little exercise of skill which he often worked at. If you knock a man down with your first bullet, he may still shoot and kill you while he lies bleeding and sprawling on the ground. So he marked trees with a double blaze, one head-high and one against the roots, and he began to fire his shots in pairs, and the sap oozed from the wounds which he made in the tender saplings.

He changed from that to picking up bits of wood, or stones, and tossing them high in the air then whipping out a revolver and firing at the flying target. Once in three times he hit with his first shot. And half of the remainder he managed to smash with a second shot. But one in three fell to the ground untouched. However, such shooting could never be made perfect. And it was a wonderful test and training for speed and accuracy of hand and eye combined.

Three times in succession he tossed high into the air a stone no larger than his palm in size, and three times in succession he blew it into a puff of powder with a well-planted bullet. As the last bit of sandstone dissolved in the sunshine into a glimmering mist, there was a little burst of hand-clapping from the side of the meadow, and Georgia Lassiter rode out to him on the little white-stockinged chestnut which he had given to her the year before.

She was the last person in the world he wanted to see. All the rest he could give up, and endure their loss — even his mother. But Georgia was different.

She swung down from the saddle and into his arms, and she stood there holding him close and straining back her head a little from him to look up into his face.

"You'll beat even Harry Main!" she declared. "You can't fail! It really isn't in a Royal to fail, Christopher!"

"Mother has told you, then?" asked Christopher gloomily.

"Your mother didn't need to tell me, because every one in the valley is talking about nothing else, and last night the telephones were simply humming with the news. And every one says the same thing, Chris...that you'll beat him! Because an honest man is stronger than any scoundrel and thief!"

"Is Harry Main a thief?" he asked rather blankly.

"He is! He is!" cried Georgia, who never failed to defend her opinions with vehemence. "A man who picks pockets is a thief when he only takes away a watch or a wallet. Then what about a villain who uses his greater training and cleverness to steal the lives of other men? Isn't he a thief...a murdering thief?"

"He always uses fair fight, Georgia!"

"I know, and there's something grand and terrible about Harry Main. But still...when I stood there and watched you practicing, Christopher, I couldn't see how any man in the world could safely face you!"

"There's a difference between target practice and practice at a living target, you know."

"You seem so pale and gloomy, dear!"

He looked vaguely at her, like a child, hardly seeing her, and yet keenly aware of details, such as the depth of tan in the hollow of her throat, and the trembling in the wind of the cornflower at her breast.

"I'm not very cheerful," he told her anxiously. And he waited, to see if that would make her guess anything. She was merely a little irritated.

"There's Lurcher, too," said she, "looking as if you'd just beaten him!"

Lurcher was a melancholy crossbred hound, a very ugly beast which had strayed down the road to the Royal ranch and there stayed, adopting Christopher as his particular sovereign deity. But he would never follow Christopher farther than the limits of the ranch, which he seemed to know by a peculiar instinct. Even when there was a hunt, he would not follow a trail beyond the borders of the Royal estate.

For Lurcher had passed through many a dreadful trial, it seemed, in his earlier life, and he was fixed in his determination to remain as much as possible on the soil where he had found freedom from persecution. Now he skulked in from the edge of the meadow and lay down in the shadow of his master, raising his mournful eyes toward the girl.

"I never beat Lurcher," explained Christopher, a little hurt by her tone.

"I wish that you would," said she in one of her petulant moods. "It might do him good. It would stop him from thinking so much about his troubles by giving him something to worry about."

"He's not a bad dog," said Christopher. "He does things, you know!"

He drew his hunting knife and threw it dexterously so that it stuck in a poplar trunk thirty feet away. "Get it, Lurcher!" And the hound trotted obediently over, worked the blade from the trunk and came back wagging his tail with joy, to lay the knife at his master's feet and then raise his sorrowful eyes in worship toward the face of Christopher.

"Without cutting himself!" cried Georgia.

"You see, Georgia, he's not such a bad dog."

"But he's a coward, Chris. And I never could understand how a Royal could endure any cowardly creature near!"

This was pressing him very close, and he winced from the thought. "He's not cruel or treacherous or unkind or bullying or underhanded or disloyal, Georgia," he argued. "You have to admit that that's a good deal to say for any character!"

"Is it?" She shrugged her shoulders and then burst out: "I'll tell you, Chris, it really doesn't amount to anything. What's the good of friendship that doesn't dare to fight for the sake of its friend? What's the good of love that won't die for the thing that's loved? Can you answer me that?"

VI
"A Woman of Steel"

He went back to the house with Georgia at his side, sitting lightly in her saddle.

"All the rest seem to think that it's the same as sure death to have Harry Main go on the trail of a man, but I don't feel that way," said Georgia Lassiter. "I know that courage and the right have a force in the world. I thank Heaven for that faith! And...I want to have our engagement announced tomorrow...before anything can happen to you!"

He caught at the bridle of her horse, but she reined the chestnut dexterously out of his reach.

"Georgia! Georgia! Do you mean that?"

"Why, of course I mean that, silly!"

"And then...suppose that something happens...?"

"Something may happen to you, but that won't kill my love for you, dear. You don't suppose that because a bit of a bullet might strike you down, Chris, it would strike down my love also? No, I laugh at such an idea. I've no fear of myself! And once I've let the world know that I love Christopher Royal and intend to marry him, I'll never change my mind. Nothing can change it! And I tell you, Chris, that I'd be as true to your ghost as to yourself!"

She said it with a fiery enthusiasm, her nostrils dilating a little. And he thought that there was something rather more knightly than womanly in her bearing. It seemed odd to Christopher that his mother and this girl, both so deeply in his life, should have such a strength between them. And he such a weakness!

"Georgia!" he breathed. "I wish...I wish...."

"What do you wish?"

"I wish that there didn't have to be any change, but that the two of us could just go on like this forever...no tomorrow...no yesterday...."

"You'd get hungry after a while," observed Georgia.

"That's the way that the gods live," said Christopher. "Always in the present, with no sorrow for what has been and no dread of what is to come."

"Chris, you're talking like a pagan priest!"

"To be like this, Georgia dear, with you on your horse, within the sweep of my arm, and I walking here beside you, and the good rich yellow sunshine pouring down on us both, and the face of that river always silver ahead of us...don't laugh, if you please!"

"I won't laugh. You frighten me when you talk like that!"

"Frighten you? You?"

"Do you think that I can never be frightened?"

"Yes, I've always thought that."

"I'll tell you what, Chris. If something happens...oh, why should I beat about the bush? I mean...suppose that Harry Main actually kills you, I'll have to go the rest of my life like this...I mean, with my back turned on what's around me, and always looking away on the times when you and I were together and alone. There aren't many of those times. I suppose that I'll begin to wonder why I didn't spend every moment with you while I had the chance, and why I didn't beg you to marry me quickly, and why I didn't have a baby to keep after you! And...I'm getting so sorry for myself that I'll be crying in another minute!"

Christopher could not answer, for such a coldness of dread and of sorrow had grown up in him that he felt the very nerves of his knees unstrung, and a horrible weakness of spirit passing over him.

"Georgia, you'd better go on home."

"No, I want to talk to your mother first."

"There's no good in that. You understand? I don't want to talk about Harry Main. I don't want to think about him...until I have to!"

She swung the chestnut closer and dropped her arm over his shoulders.

"I know," she said. "That's the right way...not to worry about the game until it has to be played. But Heaven won't dare to let Harry Main win!"

He looked up to answer her. She kissed him, and then galloped the chestnut away. He watched her across the fields. Lurcher, who had followed the galloping pony to the first fence, stood up with a forefoot resting on the lower rail and looked after her with a low whining which was the nearest approach to a voice of any kind that people had ever heard him use.

And there was something wonderfully touching, to Christopher, in the dumb excitement and grief of the dog. He called Lurcher back to him, and went on into the house where he found the letter that laid the last stone in the wall of his misfortune.

It came from Harry Main, and it said simply:

They've brought me news about how Cliff died. I'm coming down into your valley as soon as I can. That ought to be by about Thursday. I suppose that you'll want to meet me somewhere around Royal Town. Wherever you say will suit me fine. I'm coming to Yates's Saloon to talk to old Yates. And you could leave a message with him for me.

Yours very truly,

Harry Main

It was all so very quietly written, and so rather gentle, in a way, that Christopher could hardly believe that the quiet words which he had been reading could have flowed from the pen of the man whose terrible guns had brought him such a crimson fame throughout the land.

But, after all, Christopher knew perfectly well that the loud-mouthed and cursing heroes are of a very inferior breed compared with the silent and work-manlike gunfighters who build their fame by actions rather than by boasts.

He read and re-read that letter, and then he showed it to his mother. She read it with care, as though it were a much longer document.

"I'm sorry," said Mrs. Royal. "Because I'd hoped that you would not be destroying such a thorough man as this letter seems to be from. I'd hoped that you would simply be facing a vagabond and a bullying scoundrel. But it seems that Harry Main is not that sort. It's a very good letter, Chris. Don't you think so, dear?"

He could nod in answer to this.

"One feels so much assured strength and self-reliance in it," she went on. "And no cursing, and no boasting, and no threatening. In fact, it's just the sort of a letter that I would hope to see *you* write, Chris, if you were in a similar position!"

He said, "If one of my brothers were killed, would you want me to ride down to murder the murderer, Mother?"

For he was curious, and listened to her with a sort of detached interest, although he knew her answer beforehand.

"No," said Mrs. Royal, "I shouldn't expect you to do anything like that... not trail until your older brothers had ridden out first, I mean to say!" She added this as a sort of afterthought.

"But suppose that they all went down, one after the other...?"

"Oh, of course you would go! Why do you ask such a foolish question?"

"Because in some parts of the country they think that the law should be left to handle such work as this."

"In some parts of the land," she replied, "the law is a grown-up force, but it's not grown-up out here. It's simply a child. And one poor sheriff has less chance of keeping order among the wild men of these mountains than a single little boat would have of policing the seven seas. So that's why there's a different code. And there has to be! Manhood is the mainly important thing! Just sheer manhood. That's what we have to worship out here!"

He could see that there was no use trying to persuade her into another viewpoint, for she had lived so long in this land and had grown so inured to its strange ways that she could not feel or think in any fashion other than this.

She believed in the lynch law for cow and horse thieves, for instance, and there was on record a case when she masked herself and rode with the mob to see justice done.

And yet there was very little of the iron to be seen in her face. She was rather a small woman, delicately made, and her hand was smaller, indeed, than the hand of Georgia Lassiter. Her carriage was as daintily erect as Georgia's, too, and her laughter had almost as young a ring in it. Youth might wear a different face in Mrs. Royal, but its heart was not greatly altered.

"There are still forty or fifty years for growing old," she loved to say, "and I'll never use them all."

"What do you mean?" some one would always ask her.

"One of these bucking horses will finish me one of these days. Or else, one of our enemies will creep up and shoot me. I only hope that it's not in the back! I only hope that I can see my death coming straight before me. I don't think that I'll flinch!"

That was not an affectation, but the actual state of her mind and of her desires. She had lived like a lady all her life. But she wanted to die with her boots on, like a man.

"I don't know that my granddaughters will have much use for me," she also used to say, "but I want all my grandsons to be able to look up to my memory!"

Which was the reason why Christopher, hearing her speak in this fashion, could not help wishing that some of the "manhood" which she worshipped, and which she also possessed in such a degree, could be stolen away and placed in his own heart. But he saw that for the first time in his life he would be able to draw no comfort from her. For the way she saw the matter was far closer to the manner in which Harry Main was seeing it than it was to the viewpoint of her own son.

He went up to his room and sat there in a brooding silence. He could see that there was no cause for changing his earlier decision. And if he could manage to slip away from the house that very night, he had better do so, because there were only two days left before the announced date of the arrival of Harry Main, and before that time he must be far, far away, leaving a small track to be followed, as followed he must be!

VII
"Flight"

He made himself quite jolly through that evening, because he knew that he was making his last impression save one upon his family. And in the course of the evening Peter Royal could not help breaking out:

"I wish that I had your fine nerve, Chris! To stand up to the music like this while every minute is bringing that devil closer and closer!"

Christopher, when he was alone in his room, brooded over this, sitting by the window and looking into the dark, deep face of night that lay outside. He was called down to the telephone, then, and Georgia's voice came sweetly to him.

"I had to speak to you again today, Chris. I've had a dreadful feeling all the time, as though you were slipping away from me. No, it's not prophetic. It's only fear! It's only fear, Chris! But oh, I wish the thing were over with!"

He said good night to her hastily, for the sound of her voice had sent a thrilling weakness through all of his veins, and he felt that he had hardly the strength to get back up the stairs to his room.

He turned out the lights and lay down to rest a little, if he could, but the blackness swirled above him and stifled him like the beating of wings of enormous moths. Time dragged on miserably until at length the house grew quieter, then silence, and he knew that he alone was awake — or should be awake! He made up his pack for the trip. He made it small, consisting of the barest essentials, so that it could be done into a tight roll inside his slicker. He had in mind the horse he would take. It was the flea-bitten roan which Samson had given him as a birthday present the year before. The gelding would never tire at his work, wherever it led.

When he had completed the preparations, he remembered that he had forgotten Peter's rifle. That was just the last thing in the world that he wished to leave behind him, so he reached into the closet to find it. Pulling it out, the old bamboo fishing rod swayed out and tapped its slender stem against his forehead. He stood for a moment in the darkness, gripping it, and remembering with a sudden rush a thousand things out of his boyhood, when he had first learned to use that rod. He saw again the windings of the creeks, and the creaming surfaces of the little rapids, and the broad, brown faces of the pools, where the fish would be lurking beneath the fallen logs along the banks. He saw himself once more trudging home with the rod on his shoulder and the dangling fish snapping their lank tails at the dust, and he heard his voice raised with the voices of his companions, proclaiming lustily what manner of men they should be when they grew up. Ah, there would be no cowardice in them surely!

He remembered the day that a wave of scorn ran over the boys in the school when they heard how a forgotten outlaw had walked into a bank in broad daylight, and had held up the cashier and three or four others, made them open the safe, and shovel the contents into a sack, which he then carried away with him, mounted his horse, and cantered cheerfully and unharmed away from the city. Ah, how the schoolboys had raged when they heard of it! Had only a few of them been in that town of cravens, they would have upheld the law in a more fitting manner! But they had not been there, and little Christopher Royal, lying awake in his excitement at night, had dreamed long and wildly of what things he should accomplish when he grew older.

He thought of this as his hand closed around the narrow shaft of the fishing rod, and then he turned sadly away and closed the door. For he felt gloomily that he had shut away one part of himself in that closet, and all his hopes of what he might be were confined with the old toys in the dark of the closet.

Then he hurried from the room, opening the door with care, lest some squeaking of the hinges might betray him. But as he stepped out, he tripped and stumbled heavily over a form which lay in the hall just outside his door. It was Lurcher, who now came cringing to him and licked his hand by way of apology.

He cursed the dog in a whisper, for the noise he had made might have caught the attention of his mother, who was a very light sleeper. But after listening a moment and finding all silent in the house, he went softly down the stairs to the lower floor. The side door creaked badly, so he did not attempt that, but spent a moment sliding the bolts of the front door gently back and then turned the big key slowly, without making the slightest whisper of sound.

After that, he slung his pack over his shoulder and turned for a last look at the old house. As he did so, he saw a glimmering form on the lowest landing of the stairs. And then he made out his mother's face as she watched him.

It was characteristic of her that she had not cried out to him. But there could be no doubt that she understood. The pack at his back and the rifle in his hand, and the hour of the night, could mean only one thing. So he stood confounded before her, and she came finally down to him.

She said: "Then we were all wrong, Christopher! After all, you couldn't stand it?"

"No, after all, I couldn't stand it!"

She sat down and drew her white dressing gown closer around her, because the night air was chill and though, she did not speak, her eyes never moved from his face, and he knew that her stern heart was breaking.

"Will you say something, Mother?" he begged.

"What can I say, Christopher? I know that your own heart has said all of these things to you before me."

He nodded, dumb with shame and remorse.

"What are your plans?"

"To go somewhere far off. I don't know where. And take a new name and try for a new life."

She shook her head.

"Some one from this part of the country would be sure to find you and tell what you had done."

"I suppose that there's a chance of that."

"And then?"

"Then I'd have to move on again."

"Oh, Christopher, a man can die only once!"

He bowed his head.

"And if you stayed, and if you fought, Heaven wouldn't let you lose! It couldn't! And you've already won once!"

He could not lift his head to answer. He began to tremble from head to foot.

"And Georgia?" she asked suddenly.

He did raise his head then.

"I've thought of Georgia every minute!"

"Why, if that thought doesn't stop you, then I suppose that I've no influence whatever. And still I can't help talking. I wish...oh, I wish that I could disguise myself and pass for you. How gladly I'd take a gun and face him! Oh, how gladly, Christopher, if that would save you!''

He felt the lash and winced.

''Christopher, you've already met one of them and beaten him! Do you think of that?''

''I didn't know who he was,'' said Christopher, ''not till afterward. And even before a stranger that I didn't know, I was in a blue funk. And when Samson and the rest hear what I've done....'' He struck his hand across his face with a groan. And then he looked out at her and found her watching him with a cold eye of agony.

''It's the fear of death?'' she asked him. ''It's not knowing what will happen after death?''

''No, it's not death. I don't think that's what tears me in two. But there's a dread feeling in standing up to a man who actually wants your life, and seeing his eyes turn to fire, and a grin like a beast on his mouth. It's seeing a man turn into a beast, and then being filled with a horror of the thing that he's become. And...oh, what's the use of trying to explain? Because it's cowardice, and I know it, but you don't. You've never really felt such a thing, and you never will!''

''When I was a little child,'' said she, ''I was afraid of the dark!''

''I don't believe that, hardly. But at any rate, you beat it!''

''I went up to the top room in the tank house and locked the door just at dusk and threw the key out the window. And there I stayed till the morning. It was very hard. But before daylight came, I was no longer afraid of the dark!''

''How old were you when you did that, mother?''

''I was seven, I think, or six.''

He sighed and shook his head at her.

''I have to go now,'' he said nervously.

''I won't try to persuade you, Christopher. I won't tell you what it means to me, or how big things are made to look small by facing them. I'll say good-bye to you, if I have to.''

He took her in his arms and kissed her forehead.

''I'll tell you this...that every day I'll pray for more strength and, when I find strength, I'm going to come back to Royal Valley and find Harry Main....'' His voice trailed away. For she was nodding and trying pitifully to smile as though she believed the lie. He could not endure the strain for another moment and, whirling away from her, he caught up his pack and rifle and ran through the door.

Her voice stopped him.

''What are your plans?''

He turned, glad that he had the darkness of the night to cover his face.

''Christopher, only tell me where you're going, so that I'll know how to pray for you, and where to turn my face toward you!''

"I'm going up to the woods beyond Emmett's. You remember that little cabin where we camped one summer six years ago?"

"I'll think of you there, dear!"

"Aw, Mother, forgive me if you can!"

And he turned and ran blindly through the night.

VIII
"Bitter Thoughts"

The greater excitement began very early in the morning when Peter went into Christopher's room and found matters in disorder there, and Christopher gone. He went hastily down. Everywhere he hunted for Christopher, and everywhere Christopher was not to be seen. And then it was found that the strong, flea-bitten roan was missing also. That explained matters clearly enough.

Christopher had fled! So Peter went bounding into the house and, as a matter of course, went straight to the head of the family...his eldest brother, Samson. To that dark and somber man he told the terrible news, and Samson listened with a look of agony in his eye.

"It's the waiting," said Samson. "There was never a son of our father that could be a coward. But it was the waiting that killed him! But, Peter...what will happen to Mother when she finds out?"

"She mustn't find out. It would be the death of her."

"How can we keep it from her? Won't she miss Chris in five minutes? Doesn't she really love him more than she loves all the rest of us put together?"

They stared at each other, unable to find a solution to this dreadful problem. And, in due course, the rest of the brothers were gathered in a solemn conclave, where each had a different opinion.

Duncan was for rushing off single-handed, meeting with the famous Harry Main, and destroying him in order that the shame of Christopher Royal should not be noised abroad.

"You'd never have a chance against Main," said Samson bitterly. "None of us would. And Chris would have simply died if he'd met him, because the fellow is a devil. The only language he understands, really, is the chattering of a fanned Colt. But what's there in death compared with the shame? No, I won't let you throw yourself away, Duncan. But what's to be done with Mother?"

"Go straight to her, Samson, and tell her the truth. That's the only way."

"Go straight to her? I'd a lot rather go tell her that Chris is dead!"

"It's your business to talk to her. You're the oldest. And besides, do you think we could pull the wool over her eyes for ten minutes? She sees through me as though I were made of plate glass, and I think that I'm as politic as the rest of you."

That advice of Peter's was considered, though bitter, a wise pill to swallow, and therefore Samson Royal went straight to his mother and found her already down in the garden, working with her own trowel, with her usual energy. He helped her to her feet." Mother," he said, forgetting the speech which he had tried to prepare on the way, "Mother, I'm sorry to say that Christopher seems to have left...."

She waved the trowel at him.

"Of course he has," said Mrs. Royal.

Samson stared. "Of course?" he echoed, completely at sea.

"Dear Sammie," said his mother, "can't you understand that Christopher won't fight with Harry Main right here in my home? But he's gone off to meet him!"

"Gone to meet him!" exclaimed Samson. "Without saying good-bye to any of us?"

"Of course! Of course! Samson, you can see that he wouldn't want to trouble the rest of you and say good-bye in a melancholy way when he goes out to die?"

"But it doesn't seem like Christopher's way of doing things," said Samson.

"Do you really believe that you understand him?"

Samson frowned in thought. "No," he said slowly, at last, "I suppose that I forgot that he's his mother's son, after all."

And he went back to tell the new idea to his brothers. They accepted this interpretation without any hesitation, for they were accustomed to taking the word of Mrs. Royal as the truth. And they went out to their work without further question.

The morning mail brought further news to Mrs. Royal. It was a brief note from Harry Main addressed to Christopher, and she opened it without hesitation.

"Dear Royal," ran the note, "I'm going to be at Yates's place this evening. Will that do for you? I'll expect to hear from you there."

And while she sat in a gloomy quandary over this note, there was a call from Georgia Lassiter on the telephone.

"Mrs. Royal, we've heard very, very odd news...that Christopher has left the valley just as Harry Main came into it!"

And ah, how cold was the voice of Georgia! What wonder? For she had been raised in a family which was full of legends of war, and three quarters of her uncles and cousins had died fighting for the lost cause of the Confederacy.

"He's simply made a meeting place with Harry Main outside the valley," said Mrs. Royal. "You couldn't expect him to want to shed blood on my doorstep, Georgia dear!"

There was a little silence, and then a voice broken with mingled grief and joy came ringing back: "Ah, why didn't I think of that? But I've been wondering and terribly worried. Because I was afraid...afraid...oh, well, that's all gone! I'll never doubt again!"

Mrs. Royal, left to herself, turned the problem for the thousandth time in her mind. Something led her up the stairs, and into the attic to those old boxes where the worn clothes of the family had been stored for years — not that there was ever much chance that they would be needed, but because Mrs. Royal was a woman of system and thrift. And, moreover, whenever she thought of giving the clothes away, something always held her back.

She opened the box where Christopher's things had been deposited. And it seemed to her, as she lifted them out and looked them over, that it was not a mere collection of clothes smelling of moth balls, but Christopher himself, resurrected and lying there preserved in her memory. For she could remember with an odd and unhappy distinctness how he looked in this blue sailor suit, that last day that his father saw him on this earth. What were the thoughts of that stern spirit now, as he looked down from the kingdom above and peered into the heart of the craven?

And here was the first pair of long trousers, which had made Christopher so inordinately proud. She could remember with what care he had always hitched them up at the knees before he sat down.

None of her other sons had been able to appreciate the graces of society as Christopher had done. Not one of them had ever been so close to her. There had always been a feminine delicacy in the instincts of this lad which enabled him to look into her mind and know what she felt before she could express herself in words. And when she looked forward to old age, it was always with the thought of Christopher as a son and as a friend to lean upon. The rest of the world was a dim thing in prospect, but Christopher's gentle and wise heart was a vision of sunshine.

But now he was gone. He was already worse than dead! And she wished with a stern bitterness that she could have closed the book of her thoughts when he was in his second-and-twentieth year, say, the most admired and loved man that had ever ridden a horse down Royal Valley. Then there would have been in her heart, to the end of her days, a fixed worship of this gentle boy, a fixed belief in the great man that he might have become. But now he was gone, and her heart was filled with grief.

She closed the box and hurried from the dimness of the attic, with the ghosts of her sad thoughts about her. In the brighter sunshine of her own room, new courage and a new idea came to her. Death itself, for Christopher, seemed to her no tragedy now. It was only the desire to let him die bravely, or at least where no third person might see his cowardice.

She caught up a pen and paper and wrote hurriedly upon it:

Dear Main:

I am waiting for you at the little cabin in the hollow above Emmett's. Come when you can.

Christopher Royal

Then she doubted. For it might very well be that Main would question the genuineness of this handwriting.

She hunted through her desk until she found a letter from Christopher. Then, with a resolute hand, she rewrote her note, making the letters as bold and firm and sweeping as the hand of Christopher himself. She addressed the note in the same manner.

Then she called Wong, the cook. He was the only person in the household so stupid that he would not think this a most suspicious affair. To him she entrusted the note with a word to drive down the valley as fast as he could and leave the letter at the saloon of Yates.

And presently she heard the wheels of the buggy grinding down the gravel of the driveway. And she knew that Wong was gone, and that she had set in motion the wheels of death that must overtake her son before another twenty-four hours had spun away.

And in the meantime, she was to wait, striving to close her eyes against the passing of time, and praying every moment, with all her heart, that Christopher would find in his soul enough courage to let him meet death as a man should meet it.

She went down to her garden. There she could leave behind her most surely the thoughts of her boy.

"Where is Lurcher?" she asked of Granger, the gardener. "He's always basking there on the terrace at this time of the morning."

"Lurcher's gone," said the gardener. "I called him for his breakfast, and he didn't come in. I whistled and hollered for him. You know that he never leaves the ranch. And so I'm afraid that something must of happened to him here!"

But Mrs. Royal's breath caught as she heard. For could it be that the strange dog had indeed left the place and followed her boy, with an animal's strange instinct for an approaching death?

IX
"The Phantom"

When Christopher stumbled away from the house toward the corrals, you may be sure that half his mind was behind him in the house with his mother. But instinctively he found the saddle shed, his saddle, bridle and rope, and dragged them out into the corral. He had hardly emerged before a dozen sleek-coated horses started to their feet in a corner of the enclosure, ready to bolt from threatened danger, but they were already too late to flee. He could pick out the roan by the size and the ugliness of his head, and the snaky loop of rope darted through the air and settled true to its aim. The rest of the saddle band fled, and he went on methodically with the saddling of the roan, glad that this work had not caused enough disturbance to waken the cowpunchers in the bunkhouse.

When he was saddled, at last, he swung into the saddle, and the big gelding, having his head, thrust it well out and down and proceeded to unlimber himself with a little artistic pitching. Christopher let him have his way, because he rather enjoyed anything in the way of excitement that would take his mind from his wretched self.

That struggle did not last long. The bone-breaking grip of his knees and the iron of his hand upon the reins soon assured the roan that fighting was no use. He stopped, and shook his head, as though partly bewildered. And at that moment he received a cruel prick with the spurs and his head was quickly straightened at the fence.

Ears flattened, eyes trailing fire, mouth agape under the pull of the bits, he bolted straight at the loftiest part of the fence, and Christopher let him go. And as he rode, he wondered grimly to himself what other man in Royal Valley would have put an untried mount at such an obstacle? Aye, but courage across fences was not what was needed in his life. Courage to face a fighting man was the thing!

The fence rose sheer before him, then the roan pitched into the air. His two trailing hind hoofs clicked sharply against the upper bar, and then they were away across the field beyond.

He gave the big horse his head for two miles up the valley and by the time they had come to Fisher's Well, where the road forked toward Emmett's on the right and toward Cluster Cañon on the left, the roan had had enough of such high life. He came back to a moderate canter and then to a soft, sweeping trot that brushed the miles away behind him with a wolfish ease.

There was a miserable satisfaction in the heart of big Christopher as he considered the action and the breathing of his mount. A few days on the road, and the roan would be in such condition that Harry Main, desperate rider and expert trailer as he was famed to be, would have much to do to keep up with such a pace as the fugitive could set.

But then, even Harry Main could not fathom, surely, the problem that now lay before him. And unless Christopher had a mind reader working against him, he was confident that he could lie in secure hiding among the tall, dark woods above Emmett's.

After that, he would wait a number of days until it was certain that Harry Main was away from the trail, and then he would ride down to a new country, and far off where the name of Royal had never been heard and his race of tall brothers had never been seen.

He turned the roan onto the right hand road and turned to look back down the valley, perhaps for his last look at it. He could see the lofty roof of the Royal House looming above the distant trees, and nearer at hand a shadow slipped from one bush to another, across the road.

"Coyote!" murmured Christopher, and turned his face forward again.

When he was climbing the divide, leading toward the upper ranges of the hills, he glanced back down the winding trail again. There was not much light. There were clouds enough to kill the stars, and behind the high-blown mist the moon sailed in a pale-gray canoe. But still there was enough light to show him once more a shadow skulking from bush to bush behind him.

He drew rein at that, and instinctively reached for his rifle — for since when had coyotes begun to trail lone riders? And the creature behind him was not half large enough for a wolf!

After a moment, hearing nothing but the hiss of the wind through the willow by the creek, and seeing nothing but the hurried bobbing of the heads of the trees, he turned his face forward along the trail again.

Yet it worried him. For though wolves and bears were apt to trail men, all other animals were either unable to keep up with the pace of a horse or else were too thoroughly afraid of the lords of creation to come near for any length of time. And so this small thing remained a mystery to him that troubled his mind as he toiled up the slopes, with the good horse bowing his head to the work.

He reached Emmett's in the gray of the coming dawn, and passed it, keeping well within the forest, so that only now and then could he see the lights of the little village twinkling dim and cold through the mist which lay pooled in the hollow. Beyond Emmett's he rode up to the dell where that deserted cabin stood in which they had passed the vacation those years before. He could see to the right the hilltop from which he had sighted the big grizzly in the valley beyond — that grizzly which he had trailed for three days and nights before he caught up with it and finished its marauding life with a well-placed bullet.

Now it was his turn to be hunted! He dismounted and, throwing the reins, he entered the cabin. It was far gone with moldering time, now. Those years before it had been small and simple enough, but now it was a complete wreck, and a board of the flooring crunched away to rotten pulp under the weight of his stride as he entered. It was so damp, so dark, so utterly dismal, that he was half inclined to spend the night beneath the dank and dripping trees rather than in this place, and yet when he thought of the matter, he could see that the more hopelessly ruined the shack was, the more perfect would be his security in it.

So he entered with a shudder and, lighting a match, looked around him. He noted the table, leaning to the floor in a corner of the room, and the fallen branch of a great tree, blown down in a storm, which had crunched its way through the rotten roof and showed its ragged butt as though even now ready to fall farther.

Yes, the cabin was a complete wreck. But now he felt that he was satisfied. It was safe — safe from all men, and therefore it was dearer to him than any palace of a king.

As he crossed the old, brush-grown clearing again, the wind slashed and tugged at his slicker, and the rain cuffed his face with cold fingers, but in the dripping forest he busied himself cutting a number of tender fir branches, till he had gathered a great armful.

These he carried back to the cabin, beat the water out of them thoroughly, and then built them into the foundation of a bed in the cabin. He laid down his meager blanket roll over them, and then he looked about to take care of the horse.

By this time the roan had cooled off so much that there was no danger of chilling him by removing the saddle, and now he remembered the little natural meadow higher up on the creek, surrounded by trees so tall and thick that it was amply fenced in against all manner of bitter weather.

To this place he led the gelding. The grass was tall, and matted with the remains of old crops around its roots. The dense trees shut out the cutting edges of the wind, and yonder was the leaning rock, which stood out so far from the side of the mountain that it made a natural shelter against the rain, unless it was blowing from the east.

What better place could a hardy cow horse have asked — one that had fought its way through half a dozen of the range winters? He hobbled the roan here, and left it contentedly cropping the grass beneath the shelter of the hanging rock.

Then he turned back toward the cabin and, passing through the trees, he was sure that in the freshening daylight a small animal darted from one tree to another.

He could not be certain that he had actually seen any shape, however, and since the light had not strengthened to such a point that he could effectually study a trail, he marched on to the cabin, kicked off his boots, and lay down with a grunt upon the damp bed.

He was very tired. Body and soul had been worn by the trials through which he had been passing and by the long ride he had made. And so sleep dropped in a sudden wave over him and had almost swallowed his senses when he awakened again with a start and sat up, a cold sweat on his forehead, for it seemed to him that something had been watching him from the entrance to the cabin.

Yet it could not be! He gritted his teeth as he clutched his rifle and started to his feet. If there were the dread of man in him, at least there was no dread of any other beast, and he would be able to prove that he dared as much as in the hunt as any human in the world.

So he leaped to the door but, when he glanced toward the clearing through the growing glow of the dawn light, it seemed to him that he saw a subtly moving form melt like a shadow among shadows into the margin of the wood. He jerked the rifle to his shoulder and fired point-blank. The range was very short, his hand was never steadier, and he was confident that he must have nailed the fugitive with the bullet.

He was so very confident, indeed, that he did not even go out to look for the dead, but turned back to the cabin and to his bed, where he stretched himself and allowed himself to drop securely toward slumber until.... He sat up again, this time with a racing heart, and as he sat up he made sure, from the corner of his eye, that a fugitive form was leaping through the doorway into the day outside.

He had only a glimpse, but his hand moved lightning fast to snatch a revolver and fire. There was no sound to answer the shot. He rushed to the door, and once more all that he saw was the dark and ominous face of the forest rising tall and deathly silent before him.

He sprinted around the shack, thinking that the creature must have dodged out of sight by that route, but still there was no sign of it high or low. And, as he leaned his broad shoulders against the wall of the shack, the dreadful thought came to Christopher that it was no animal of flesh and blood at all, but a phantom sent to cross his way with a foreboding of doom.

X
"An Ancient Creed"

He had no need of sleep after that. There was no trace of the white mist which had obscured the hollows and tangled among the forest trees as he was climbing the trail. All was bright sunshine — far brighter than the lowlands could ever know.

So he began to cut for sign through the woods. But though he thought that he found traces, here and there, so thick was the carpeting of pine needles which lay everywhere beneath the trees that he could not make sure of anything that he saw by way of foot impression upon the soil.

And where the pine needles did not lie, grew rank, tall grass, with the matted dead remains of other seasons entangled about the roots to such a degree that the tread of a horse upon it could hardly have been distinguished from the step of a bear, for it curled upward again the moment the pressure of the step was removed

Then, as he came to a pause, he heard the sudden howl of a wolf not a hundred yards away — a cry that went thronging through the trees and seemed to well up to his ears from every side. He made no effort to trace the beast by the cry, for the grim surety came to him that tracing would do no good. Twice he had tried the nature of this phantom with good powder and lead, and twice the thing had escaped from him unscathed.

Perhaps it would have seemed a small affair to some, but to Christopher, whose nerves were already on edge and whose whole spiritual stamina had been broken down by shame and grief and self-disgust, this was enough to carry away the last of his resolution and he determined upon leaving the cabin behind Emmett's as soon as possible and hunting out another hiding place deeper in the mountains — some place, for instance, where the cheerless woods would not be standing so perilously close to him.

He went to the roan at once, saddled it, rolled his blankets, and started forging through the pass which opened above him. It was a cheerful cañon, after the depression of the hollow, and he enjoyed the keen morning sun which smote between his shoulder blades. It was just such a day as leads to the dispelling of all foolish illusions.

So he followed the dim trail along the edge of a creek, until the way turned into a shallow ford. He was in no hurry, and therefore he dismounted and examined the bottom of the ford, to make sure that it was safe for the roan. The rocks at the bottom seemed firm and secure enough, and he led the gelding across. On the farther side, he paused to mount once more, and doing so, he scanned the valley up which he had just been riding.

It was very open and clear. There was hardly a stone big enough for a prairie dog to have hidden behind, and there was not the slightest sign of the ghost wolf which had haunted him before. He nodded to himself with satisfaction, and had turned to put his foot in the stirrup when he found himself looking straight into a pair of eyes — human eyes that watched him from close by.

It was an Indian, so old that his wasted body could have illustrated the legend of Tithoonus, and clad in such tatters that his half-naked body and his clothes, and even the homely fishing rod which he held, melted into the patchwork of the valley side, with its bronzed rocks and spotted shrubs. And yet Christopher was a little startled that he could have been so close to a man without noticing the existence of the other. That was before he studied the eyes of this stranger, and saw that they were vacant with age. There was no more life in this withered creature than in a dying tree, say, or some blind growth that floats in the depths of the sea, untouched by the sun.

Said Christopher: "Do you have luck here, my father? Do the fish take the bait?"

The ancient Indian looked at him without interest and then, lifting his head, he glanced at the pale blue of the mountain sky. When he spoke, it was with a voice wonderfully deep and hoarse, and with a humming indistinctness of sound, so that it passed away into the noise of the brook and was almost lost there.

"The Great Spirit sends the fish and the fisher," said he. "Sometimes the fish are taken, and sometimes the fisher!"

Christopher, staring at him, was sure that he was in contact with something other than an ordinary Indian. Here was a man of such age that he must have ridden his ponies and taken scalps long before the repeating rifle had been dreamed of. Even the revolver was still an unheralded invention in the days of the youth of this chief. How much had been seen by the old man. Half the continent had first been explored, and then fought for, and conquered, and peopled during the span of his existence.

"However," said Christopher, falling in with the old fellow's own phraseology, "the Great Spirit has favored men a little more than He has favored fish, you must admit."

"How?" asked the Indian gravely.

"He has given us brains."

"To walk on the dry land, but the fish lives in water. Can we follow him there?"

"He has only a thin stream or a little muddy pool for his life."

"His rivers lead down to the ocean, my son."

Christopher stared. It was very odd to find so much mental agility in so dead a body as that which sat before him.

"However," said Christopher, "he has given us a soul, you know."

"Look!" said the chief, and he scooped up some sand in his claw-like hand. "How many grains of sand are here? But if all of them were the souls of men, only one of them all would come to the life of the Sky People and stand before the face of the Great Spirit, and ride His horses there and take scalps, and live in happiness."

"Only one?" asked Christopher, enchanted by this voice from the past and this prophet of a dead creed. "But what of all the rest?"

"Some," said the chief, "will die having done no great deed. For many men grow old and they have done nothing greater than to skin a buffalo or to make an arrow."

He let most of the sand sift away from his bony fingers.

"And there are a few," said he, "who have fought like men and been strong and true, but in the last moment they turned coward before their enemies, and the enemies have taken them and split their heads with axes, and taken off their scalps and left their souls to blow up and down the earth forever like that leaf, never resting."

Christopher turned and regarded the little spinning, twisting, drifting leaf with curiosity. The thought sent a thrill of coldness through him.

"But suppose," said he, "that these men have fought bravely and been overcome in battle by numbers, but not with fear?"

"That cannot be," said the chief. "For the brave men cannot die in battle. It is only chance that kills them...and that is the Great Spirit leaning from the sky to take them because he has watched them too long and wished to have them close to Him!"

"Then only cowards die?" asked Christopher, smiling a little.

"Only the cowards," nodded the Indian. "All these people have souls so that they may suffer. They see death always before them. It is curled up like a rattlesnake among the rocks. It stands in the darkness of the tepee and watches them like a hawk. It whistles for them in the wind. It beats on them in the hail and rain. It strikes for them in thunderstrokes. So that the cowards are always dying."

"But some men are brave until they come to their death battle!"

"Yes," nodded the chief, "some are brave in little dangers, but their souls turn to water when they see great odds before them. But it is always the thing we fear that kills us, otherwise nothing can take us from the earth except the hand of the Great Spirit!"

"Come, come!" said Christopher, "you will not treat all of your friends and family so harshly, because I can guess that a great many of them died in battle."

"Ah," said the Indian gravely. "All of my people and the families of my brothers have died in battle. They were all cowards."

"Are you still sure of that?"

"Oh, yes."

"Then I must say that the Great Spirit is a spendthrift, to throw away so many good people and let their souls blow up and down the world!"

"I shall tell you about the Great Spirit," said the old man, perfectly calm and speaking from a great height of dignity. "He is like you and me. We have known many people. We have seen ten thousand faces, but we have only one friend. And so it is with the Great Spirit. He has seen ten million souls turn to powder and blow away in the wind, and only one is left, but that one is a bright soul and worth all the rest, and so the Great Spirit, when He has made sure that the one soul really shines, snatches it greedily up to Him in the sky and there they live happily together!"

As he spoke he had shaken out the rest of the sand grains and now he held up between his thumb and his forefinger only a single little fragment of quartz, transparent, and with a gleaming thread of gold in it, so that it poured forth a stream of sparkles in the keen morning light.

Christopher could not help being moved by such imagery.

He said, "But consider yourself, father. Certainly no enemy has ever taken your scalp...."

The other nodded at once, unoffended.

"And yet the Great Spirit has allowed me to grow old and thin as a blade of dried grass? That is true. But it is because He could not be sure. Sometimes I seemed to shine, and then sometimes I seemed very dark and dull. He watched me in battle, and He saw me ride through the ranks of the Sioux as though they were the standing brush in the field. He saw me make their heads fall, as a little boy with a stick makes the heads of the tall cornflowers bend. He saw me take many scalps and count many coups, and often His heart grew hot with joy and He stretched his hand down from Heaven so close that I could feel his fingers in the wind, tugging at my hair. But always He drew his hands back again and waited, and watched, for He could not be sure!"

"Hello!" murmured Christopher. "How could He have doubted?"

"With men, He knew I was brave. But...listen!"

He held up a cautionary finger, and up the valley floated the echoing, dismal call of a wolf.

XI
"Watched"

Christopher, remembering his phantom in the hollow, shuddered a little. He could not help it!

"It is always there," said the old man, leaning his head to listen as though to hear a terribly familiar music. "It is always somewhere between me and the edge of the sky. Sometimes it is so far away that I do not hear it. Sometimes it holds its voice and crawls up to watch me, but it is always there."

He nodded his head with a religious conviction.

"But what is it, father?" asked Christopher, beginning to feel his flesh creep.

"It is the werewolf," said the old Indian, "that has kept me away from the Great Spirit for all these years."

"A werewolf!" exclaimed Christopher.

"There are two kinds of werewolves," said the chief, holding up two fingers of his hand. "The first are the ones which have been men and become wolves. They are only terrible for a short time and then they become stupid. Then there are others. They are the wolves which cannot become men until they have killed the warrior which has been marked out for them."

He closed his eyes, and then added: "When I was a little boy, I frightened the horse of Black Antelope, the medicine man, and he got a fall when the horse bucked. I was very happy. I danced and yelled with pleasure to see him in the dirt. But then I heard him shouting out of the dust cloud: 'The werewolf is waiting to take you! May he take you soon!'

"I saw that he had known this for a long time. But the knowledge had been forced from his lips by his passion. Then I could remember, young as I was, that often I had seen wolves skulking near me. Fear jumped in my throat. You are a young man and a big man. Have you ever been afraid?"

He leaned forward a little and a cruel flame appeared in his eyes as he scanned the face of Christopher. Then he leaned back, nodding.

"You will understand," said he, "what I am saying."

And a little chill passed through Christopher as he saw that his secret was plain before this terrible old wizard of the mountains.

"When I knew that it was a werewolf that was waiting for me," said the Indian, "I did not fear men. If the Great Spirit had meant a werewolf to inherit my soul, then I could not die until that one wolf reached me, if it were able. And therefore I laughed at men. In battle I knew that their bullets could not touch me. I went into the fights singing my songs, and the Sioux became women before me. They turned their backs upon me, and I shot my arrows between their shoulder blades. I became a great man in my tribe. But I never hunted at night, and after dark I stayed in my tepee, until one cold winter night a wolf put its head through the flap of my tepee and snarled at me.

"The next day, I saddled my best pony and fled to the south and left my squaws and my children behind me, for I felt that the time had almost come, and that the wolf was about to take me. He was a brown wolf, young and strong.

"If I had stayed, the wolf would not have dared to face me. I should have rushed out into the night and fought with it, though I carried nothing but a knife. But I was afraid, and the moment that fear lays a whip on our backs we cannot stop running. So I have been fleeing all the days of my life, and the wolf follows me. I saw him only so long ago as the waning of the old moon when it was like the paring of a fingernail in the sky. He is a gray wolf now. His back is arched and his belly is tucked up with age. One of his fangs is broken. With the other he still hopes to cut my throat. But some day I shall hear him and leave my fire and go out in the darkness and call to him, with my knife in my hand. I shall fight him and kill him and, when he is dead, the Great Spirit who has waited and watched so long for me will snatch me up in His fingers and make me happy forever."

The Indian ended his tale in a raised voice with a glitter in his eyes, but at that moment the wolf call boomed with a melancholy note up the pass, and the eyes of the chief were instantly struck blank. The fishing rod trembled in his hand.

When Christopher had given the old fellow half the tobacco in his pouch, he rode up the trail again, but he was a very thoughtful man. Of course the whole matter was plain to him, and he could see how the momentary malice of the old medicine man, Black Antelope, had poisoned all the following years of this man's life. Yet he could not smile at the superstition. He had lost the callused hardness of self-assurance, and into his opened soul strange thoughts dropped, like those falling stars which show the blackness of the heavens.

When he reached the ridge of the divide, he looked across a far prospect with the mountain crests tossed up as rough and crowded as storm waves on a sea. After all, why should he flee into this unknown region? For if there were indeed anything supernatural following him, it was better to face it in a place he knew.

Suddenly he turned and rode down the trail up which he had just passed. Not that I would have you think that he took as true all that the Indian had told him, or any of it, for that matter. But no matter how sophisticated we may become, superstitions will leave a trace and a taint within our souls. So it was with Christopher, and he was like the man who sees the moon over his left shoulder, and scorns the superstition of bad luck, but cannot keep a chill from passing down his blood.

Whatever it was that had haunted him, he was sure that it had been a living creature of flesh and blood. He was sure, and yet a coldness was spreading through body and soul. And it happened that just now, halting the roan for breath, he looked back and saw, or thought he saw, a shadow behind the shadow of a bush. He took quick aim, fired, and then spurred the roan furiously back to the spot.

There was nothing there. He dismounted and examined the ground. It was a soft sand which would have registered the impression even of a falling leaf, and yet there was not a trace upon it. And he stood up and mounted again with a prickling sense of dread coursing up and down his back.

Yet there had been, he felt, an infinite amount of truth in what the Old Indian had told him. The fears that we flee from are those which will eventually master us. Those which we face shrink away from us in turn and become as nothing.

So he went straight back to the deserted and moldering cabin in the hollow, which he had left so gladly that morning. You will say that he should have carried his philosophy a stage further and gone back to his home to outface his first impelling terror — the dread of Harry Main and his guns. But to tell the truth, his mind did not dwell upon Harry Main. This other uncanny fear had overmastered him, and its problem, to be scorned and mocked by his consciousness, continually lurked in the back of his brain.

When he got to the cabin, it was midafternoon. A rabbit had lifted its head above a rock a quarter of a mile above the edge of the pines of the hollow, and he tried his Colt with a snap shot.

When he rode to the rock, he found the rabbit's body secure enough, the brains dashed out by the bullet. No, his hand had not lost its cunning or its surety.

He cleaned the rabbit on the spot and carried it on toward the cabin for his dinner. But as he went the darkness of his brain increased. He had fired at the rabbit with no more skill and surety than at the ghost thing which had been hunting him in a wolfish shape, and yet the other had twice escaped.

The moment he entered the dark circle of the pines, he regretted his return to the spot, for the stretching shadows that covered him darkened his spirit more than his eyes. He cooked the rabbit and ate it, but it was with a forced appetite, and he went about his preparations for the night mechanically. His heart was not in them. He had to urge himself forward continually with the remembered words of the old chief.

He decided, as the evening began, that he would try his nerves in the forest itself while the darkness gathered, and so he sat down beneath the trees and lighted his pipe. It suddenly occurred to him that the glowing light in the bowl of the pipe would be like a guiding lantern to direct any danger toward him, and to blind his eyes against all drifting shadows — such as the form of an old gray wolf, its back arched with age, and its belly gaunt, and with one broken fang, and the other capable of splitting open the throat of a man.

Now he wished mightily that he had continued on his way through the unknown mountains to the north and the east, but he would not saddle the roan for a night journey. It was not because he pitied the weariness of the horse, but because he dreaded the trip through the solemn woods worse than death.

He left the trees at last, and went into the cabin. He found that he was crossing the clearing with a slinking gait and with his head down and, though he forced himself to walk erect, his heart he could not lift.

So he came to the cabin and laid down his blanket roll there. Outside the wind was rising and, across the moon, volleys of high-blown clouds swept and crossed the threshold of the cabin with waves of light and shadow.

The whole world had become an eerie place, indeed, and a setting in which all that was wild and strange might happen. And then he thought of the old Indian, and his lifetime passed in the midst of just such dread as this reënforced by a superstition which turned fear into a thing as concrete as a pointed gun.

What unbelievable force of nerve and courage had maintained the old man so long — living as he did, in the lonely middle of the mountains, waiting for death in a strange form? He pulled the pile of branches that supported his bedding to a corner of the cabin from which he could watch the door. There was a window, also, from which he could be spied upon, but a ragged fragment of a board was nailed across it and no wolf could jump through.

He smiled at his own conceit, but you may be sure there was no mirth in his smile.

XII
"Only a Man"

It seems most strange that Christopher Royal should have been brought to such a nervous state because a lurking shadow had crossed his path a few times. But undoubtedly he was unstrung chiefly by his interview with the old Indian whom he had met that day fishing at the side of the brook.

However that may be, he had almost reached the point of hysteria, listening to imaginary sounds and watching the alternate dimming and brightening of the moonlight on the floor. And then came a thing that blinded him with fear.

Beyond the door, in the clearing, he heard the unmistakable though soft crackle of a twig beneath an approaching, stealthy foot! All of this time he had been telling himself with a breathless insistence that there was nothing at all in his dread beyond a sort of fear of the dark, and that when the morning came he would simply mount the roan and ride away from this wretched nightmare in spite of the advice of the crazed Indian.

And now came the positive proof that there *was* a living creature in the clearing — a creature that guessed his presence in the cabin; for otherwise why should the cabin have been stalked with such care?

Too paralyzed even to think of clutching the Colt at his hip, Christopher stood up against the wall opposite the door just in time to see a shadow cross the dim moonlight that passed the threshold of his door. It was not like the shadow of a wolf. Christopher suddenly glanced up and found himself peering into the face of Harry Main!

He had never seen that famous man in the flesh before, but he could have recognized him even by dimmer light than this as the brother of Cliff Main, whom he had killed by luck rather than by valor. In the hand of Harry Main the revolver was quickly steadied on its target.

"It's all right, kid," said Harry Main. "I'm here to finish you off, but there ain't any need for me to rush around about it. I understand everything. You lost your nerve waiting for me, and you come up here in a blue funk. I understand all of that, and I'm gunna wait till you've had a chance to get hold of yourself before I tackle you with a gun. You can depend on that, because I keep my promises."

And he dropped his revolver back into the holster. An instant later he was startled with a thrill of cold fear, for he had seen Christopher standing against the wall, a very picture of abject, helpless, frozen terror only a moment before, and now he heard Christopher break out into a wild and ringing laughter while he cried: "Are you the wolf? You?"

"Am I the wolf? I?" asked Harry Main, retreating toward the doorway behind him. "What in the name of Heaven do you mean? Are you crazy, Royal?"

And perhaps no man in the world ever looked closer to insanity than did Christopher at that moment. For his life, which had come to a stop, was beginning again, and as it began, a flare of warmth and fiery self-confidence flamed in his eyes and dilated his nostrils and made his breast heave.

Under the dreadful shadow of an unearthly fear, he had quite forgotten that it was the original dread of Harry Main that had forced him from his home and into the mountains. He had quite forgotten that, and there remained before him only the overpowering horror of a supernatural enemy.

To such an extent was this true that as he had been standing against the wall he had been saying to himself, quoting the Indian: "A werewolf is one of two kinds — either a man turning into a wolf, or a wolf turning into a man."

And to be sure, if one looked closely at the handsome dark features of Harry Main, one could not help finding something decidedly wolfish in his appearance. There was a smallness and a brightness in the eyes, which were moreover set abnormally close together, that gave his face a touch of animal cunning. And the bulge of his jaw muscles added a rather brutal strength to the lower part of his face. He looked as brown, too, as a creature capable of living without any covering other than its own pelt.

But Christopher was not ready at that moment to mark small differences and peculiarities. What mattered to him was that he had been more than half expecting the dreadful apparition of a wolf or a wolf-man in the doorway. And instead, here was a man — a mere being of flesh and blood like himself. And that was why Christopher laughed — laughed at the sight of that famous and dreadful Harry Main! He laughed out of pure relief and excess of thankfulness and joy that, after all, he was to be tested by something less than supernatural power.

Now, when this flood of relief had coursed through the veins of Christopher and when the laughter had burst from his lips, he could not help crying out: "By eternal Heaven, it's only Harry Main!"

Harry Main had been fairly certain that this fellow was insane, the moment before. But he rather doubted it now after facing Christopher for a moment, and he began to wish that he had kept his Colt in his hand.

"Only Harry Main!"

A very singular remark, surely, concerning the most terrible of all those practiced gunfighters who rode the mountain desert. It literally took the blood from the heart of the man of might and threw it all into his face.

"And what more do you want to have on your hands than Harry Main?" he exclaimed.

"What more? Why," cried Christopher, "if there were half a dozen of you, I should still laugh at you, Main! I should still laugh at you!"

Harry Main listened and positively gaped with childish wonder, and with horror also, for he could not feel that this was stage playing. There was a ring of such tremendous sincerity and honesty about the words of Christopher that a more skeptical man than Harry Main would have been convinced.

Said Main: "I'm about to finish you off, Royal. I dunno that it's any pleasure to me to have to kill you, but you took that out of my hands and left me no choice in it. You murdered poor Cliff...."

"That was a perfectly fair fight," declared Christopher.

"Fair?" cried Main, his hot temper rising. "Why everybody knows that Cliff was only a kid!"

"He was two years older than I," answered Christopher.

The heat of Harry Main increased. For, having found no ready answer, he was naturally all the more enraged, and he exclaimed: "You ain't gunna be allowed to sneak out of that blood this way, Chris Royal!"

"Sneak out? Sneak out?" said Christopher. "Why, man, I'll tell you an honest fact — I was never so glad of anything as I am of the sight of you tonight!"

"The hell you are!" growled the gunfighter, and he stared more closely at Christopher Royal.

But it was true. Yes, it was very true. He would have been the worst sort of a blind man not to see that Christopher meant all that he said and had not the slightest fear of his famous antagonist.

"Oh, yes," said Christopher, "but since you seem a decent fellow, Harry, I rather hate to have to send you after your brother!"

"D'you hate to do that?" snarled Main. "Why, I'm ready to tear your heart out, if you got the guts to stand up to me!"

Another cross passed like a shadow over the face of Christopher. And then he shrugged his shoulders, as though to get rid of the idea.

"Well?" asked Main sharply.

"I'm thinking of the long stretch after I've dropped you, Harry, as drop you I surely shall. And besides, I'm wondering if we wouldn't both be happier if we had sunlight instead of moonshine for our work."

"Moonlight is good enough," declared Main.

Christopher nodded.

"You're getting nervous, I see," said he very kindly. "And if that's the case, why, we'll have it out now, man, of course. I suppose that you might become rather a nervous wreck if you had to wait until the morning."

"To the devil with your coolness!" cried Harry Main. "Me turn into a nervous wreck? I ain't got a nerve in my body and, when it comes the time for the guns to work, I'm gunna show you I mean what I say!"

"You shoot very well, I hear," said Christopher.

"That's best told," said Harry Main darkly, "by them that ain't no longer got a voice in this here world!"

"By the dead, you mean?" interpreted Christopher, nodding. "You've killed a great many people. I've heard that you've killed all of fourteen men, Main?"

"Up to tonight, and not counting the greasers, yes. And you'll be the fifteenth white man."

"I shall?"

Christopher looked at Harry Main and then smiled brightly and carelessly, as though to announce that he did not care to argue such an absurd suggestion. And a little mist of perspiration — a cold sweat — came out upon the forehead of Harry Main.

"All right," said Christopher, "if you're not afraid to wait until the morning...."

"Do you think that you can bluff me out? I'll have your nerves all frazzled out if you wait that long in the same house with me."

"Will you?" murmured Christopher, stretching his arms out luxuriously. "Well, you watch me."

And he threw himself down on the bed, took a turn in the blanket, and was almost instantly asleep, leaving Harry Main standing by the door, with the killing power still gathered in his face, and a strangely empty and foolish feeling in his heart.

XIII
"Ready"

It must be admitted that it was a most peculiar situation for Harry Main. He had most certainly prophesied to himself that Christopher Royal, in spite of the shooting of Cliff, had turned yellow when he started up toward the higher mountains and, with that sense of surety supporting him, Harry Main had proceeded with a sort of contemptuous carelessness on the trail of revenge. He had never started out on a manhunt without feeling that he was superior in his skill with guns to any other man on the range.

And now this surety had been snatched out of his hands. He sat down and watched the pale, slow hand of the moonlight stretch across the floor and find the hand and then the face of Christopher. He stood up and leaned over the sleeper, and saw that he was smiling as in the midst of a happy dream.

No wonder that Main scratched his unshaven chin in great anger and perturbation. Such coolness was absolutely inexplicable to him, because it never occurred to him that Christopher had been existing in this cabin under the shadow of a fear so much more awful than that of any human being that it made even the hostile presence of Harry Main not a terror but an actual comfort. And having no key to the situation, Harry Main began to feel that, so far from having reached a craven fugitive, he had come up with the bravest man he had ever known.

But to have fallen asleep in the presence of the gunfighter — the great and celebrated Harry Main — that surely was a thing not to be believed. But sleeping — yes, and snoring — that lad most certainly was. Why then had Christopher left the valley? Simply because he wished to take the ugliness of battle away from the vicinity of his home? It had seemed a most hollow sham and pretext to Harry Main, at the first, but now he began to believe that there must be something to it.

He began to regard Christopher Royal more closely, and there was much about him that deserved the narrowest scrutiny. He watched the heaving of the high-arched chest while the young fellow slept, and he regarded the wide and smooth slope of the shoulders, and the strength of the jaw and, above all, the long-fingered hands. Men said that there was both infinite might and great speed in those hands, and Harry Main, who was an expert in such affairs, could well believe it. The weight of a Colt, for instance, would be no greater than that of a feather to the power of this man, and the round wrist and the tapering fingers promised the most flashing and dazzling speed of execution.

Now it seemed to Harry Main, at about this time, that the hours of the night were marching along with a very painfully slow step, and that the morning lingered with disgusting persistence beneath the edge of the eastern sky.

He himself tried to lie down and to rest but, when he had stretched himself out in a resolute composure and closed his eyes, it always seemed to Harry Main that his terrible young companion was slowly opening his eyes, and then peering sidewise, and then sitting up and reaching for a gun.... At that point of his imaginings, Harry Main would be snatched out of semi-slumber, and sit up with a jerk, only to find Christopher Royal sleeping most peacefully.

Two or three times this was repeated, and at last Main abandoned all attempts at resting. He stood by the door, or he walked up and down outside it, watching a pale mist that had boiled across the face of the moon and that was now gathering under the heads of the great forest trees. Frequently, however, he had to drag himself away from his thoughts and peer through the open door at young Christopher.

And rage began to grow up in the breast of Harry Main. For he felt that by a low trickery Christopher Royal was enjoying a heartening and strengthening rest, whereas he, Harry Main, who had entered that house with the drop on the man he wanted and who had surrendered that advantage willingly because he did not choose to murder but preferred to fight — he, Harry Main, walked up and down through the night fog and wondered what the devil had ever entangled poor Cliff with this cold-nerved devil of a boy!

But why not end the matter, now that there was no eye to watch? Main strode through the door with the Colt ready in his hand. But when he leaned over the sleeper his finger withdrew its weight from the trigger. Once before, and long ago, just such a crime as this had attracted Harry Main, and on that occasion he had not resisted temptation. But he had long since vowed that he would never have another such stain upon his conscience.

So he went back to the door, stealthily, without making a sound, as he thought. And then, turning around, he found the eyes of the supposed sleeper fixed steadily upon him.

It was far from a pleasant experience for Main. And then Christopher sat up and yawned in his face.

"It was better not to do that," he nodded. "I see that you're all shot to pieces, Main. And look here...if you want to postpone this business until the nerves have had a chance to settle down again, of course I'm agreeable to that. I don't want to hurry you ahead, you understand!"

"Hurry me ahead? Hurry me ahead?" snarled Main. "Why, if the daylight would only come, I'd polish you off in half a second."

"Polish me off?" smiled Christopher, standing up and stretching forth his arms. "Well, man, the day has begun."

"What!"

"It's a thick mist. We often have 'em in this hollow. And that's what blankets the sun away. But...look here. It's seven o'clock. And let me know, old fellow, if you want to fight now, or after breakfast?"

There was such a world of good humor in his voice that Harry Main felt his heart shrink into a cold, small knot.

"Now," said Main steadily. "You can bring in the gun work now, and I'll be contented. But damn me if I'll wait for another five minutes to play the nurse to you!"

"Nurse?" laughed Christopher Royal. "Well, well, the odd thing about it all, from my viewpoint, is that when I left the valley I was actually afraid of you, old fellow. Frightened to death of you. And now, as a matter of fact, I'm almost sorry that I shall have to turn loose a gun upon you!"

Harry Main lowered his head a little for the purpose of scowling out beneath his gathered brows at the other, when he suddenly realized that no facial expressions were apt to daunt the very composed self-sufficiency of this young man.

He could not help saying suddenly: "Royal, when you left the valley, it wasn't to meet me up here. I dunno why you sent me the letter. But I know that you never intended to meet me here!"

"What letter?" asked Christopher.

"What letter? Why, the one where you told me that you'd be waiting for me in this cabin...the one that the Chink brought down to Yates's place for me."

It took the breath of Christopher to hear this. Certainly he had dispatched no such letter, and there was no one in the world who knew where he intended to hide himself with the exception of his mother. But could she have done such a thing, and betrayed him to his enemy? Then, in a blinding flash, he understood everything, and the prayer which she must have breathed to have her son dead rather than shamed — her blind hope, too, that when the crisis came he might find a mysterious strength to meet the emergency. And he had done so. For whether he could master Harry Main or not he could not tell, but master himself he certainly had!

So he looked up again to Main and said gently: "You've guessed the facts. I was afraid of you when I left."

"Then what happened?"

"Something that you wouldn't understand. There's no use in trying to talk about it or to explain."

"I'd like to judge that for myself!"

"I'll tell you this," said Christopher suddenly. "After what has happened to me up here, I feel as though there's no real harm that can be done by a bullet."

"All right," said Harry Main. "I guess that's beyond me."

"And there," said Christopher, "is a bit of blue sky for you. It's broad enough day, and I suppose that we have to go through with this thing."

"We do," said the gunfighter solemnly.

"Notwithstanding that I wasn't at fault with your brother?"

"You?"

"I give you my word of honor, Main, that I tried to back out of the fight. I didn't want his blood on my hands. I didn't want to fight with anybody, as a matter of fact."

Harry Main listened with a thoughtful frown, and again he felt the transparent honesty of this youth and felt a shudder go through him.

"That ain't what matters," he said at last. "The only fact that counts is that you stood up to poor Cliff and killed him, and now everybody expects me to stand up to you and kill you...or to do my best. And that's what I'm here for!"

"I understand," nodded Christopher. "Your reputation for being invincible is worth more to you than your life. You've got to risk that to protect your good fame. Well...there's nothing that I can say to that!"

"No," declared Harry Main, "there ain't anything you can say. But are you ready?"

"Ready," said Christopher, and they walked out of the little cabin side by side.

"It ain't much better than moonshine, though," said Main, regarding the fog which hung in dense clouds through the trees. "We'll have to stand close to each other with our guns, old-timer."

"Yes, that seems logical."

"But, by Heaven, kid, you're the coolest hand that I ever had to shoot at. We'll take ten paces."

"All right. Which way?"

"Stand here. I'll measure off the distance."

He stalked ten strides away, halted, and spun about toward Christopher.

"Are you ready, Royal?"

"Ready!"

XIV
"Beyond Fear"

No matter what doubts had been passing through the mind of Harry Main during the long hours of the night, they deemed to disappear, now that he faced his foe in the open, and it seemed to Christopher that the very body of the other man swelled with passion. A gathering battle fury glittered in the eyes of the gun-fighter. He was like a bull terrier, which seems to have a ten-fold power poured into it by the mere chance to bare his teeth at an enemy.

As for Christopher, he felt no passion, and certainly least of all did he feel fear. The fury which was rising in the other would have appalled him beyond words only the day before, as he well knew. But now he was possessed of a perfect calm, a cool indifference and, though he stood on the ground at point-blank range from this proved man slayer, he had the attitude of one who looks on a strange scene from a great distance.

And, instead of fear, out of that calmness a great sense of superior might flowed through him. He looked at the terrible Harry Main and looked down on him. He remembered what the Indian had said, and of how as a young brave he had careened through the ranks of the enemy laughing at their bullets, because he was conscious of a stranger and more deadly fate than mere bullets or arrows could deal out to him.

So it was with Christopher Royal, and as he stared at Harry Main he could not help wondering where that other and haunting shadow might be, and was it not ever present, watching the man who had been marked down for it? And the instant that Harry Main was gone, would not that devilish film of a creature be at his heels once more?

"Harry," he called.

"Go for your gun!" said the other, trembling with a dreadful eagerness. "Go for your gun, kid. I give you the first chance!"

Like a wrestler offering his hand openly to a weaker foe. But Christopher merely smiled.

"Go for your gun!" yelled the gunfighter again.

"I want to ask you for the last time," said Christopher, "to think the thing over, will you? I don't fear you, Main. But there's no reason I should try to kill you, and there's no reason why you should kill me. Do you think that you will ever be taunted for not having butchered me? No, people know you too well and your record is too long."

"My record is a fighting man's record," said the killer, growing momentarily more savage. "I'm no damn chattering jay...like you. I've give you warning, Royal!"

"I've heard your warning, and I take it," said Christopher, "but I won't go for my gun first."

"What?"

"I mean what I say. Make the first move if you will. I'll never shoot except in self-defense, man!"

"By Heaven!" cried the other, "your blood is on your own head, for being a fool. I offer you the free chance. There ain't nobody here to report it on you."

"Except one's conscience," said Christopher, "and that's enough!"

A wolf howled up the valley, and a sudden shudder went through the body of Christopher. It seemed that the other noted it, for he said instantly:

"That varmint is going to yell again in a minute. He's got something cornered! He'll yell again and, when he yells, that'll be the signal for us, Royal. You agree?"

"Yes," said Christopher, feeling that there was a sort of hidden fate in this arrangement, "I agree to that. He'll howl a death yell for one of us!"

"Exactly. Afterwards, kid, I'll treat you fine. I'll see that you don't lie here and rot in the middle of the woods. I'll cart your body down into the valley where somebody can find you on the road and let your folks know."

"Thank you," said Christopher.

He looked a trifle away. He raised his head boldly, and looked up to the smoke-white mist, now riven away in the heart of the sky so that dim, delightful blue shone through.

"Are you prayin', kid?" asked the gunfighter savagely.

"No, no," said Christopher. "I'm only pitying you, Main!"

And he said it so impulsively and so gently that Harry Main started convulsively. He had been in a hundred battles but never before had he seen a man in the presence of death conduct himself in such a manner as this. He was amazed, and the awe took possession of the very nerves of his fingers and made them half numb. He rubbed the knuckles of his right hand swiftly into the palm of his left — swiftly, for at any moment the fatal cry of the wolf might ring up the hollow.

"And if the bad luck should come to you, Harry," said Christopher Royal, "where shall I take you, and where shall I send your last message?"

"Cut out all this fool's talk!" snarled the other. "I don't want to hear no more of it!"

"What, man? Is there no one to whom you want to send your last thoughts? Is there no kindness for any one?"

"I've seen the world for what it is," said the other grimly, "half sneaking, and half lying, and all hypocritical. There ain't nobody that likes nobody else, except for what they can get out of him. Folks have knowed me and they've used me. I've knowed them and I've used them. And when the finish comes, I thank Heaven that there ain't nobody that can say that he's trimmed me worse than I've trimmed him. Because where the score was ag'in me, I've used a gun and settled it that way."

"Heaven forgive your unhappy soul," said Christopher.

"You talk partly like a fool, and partly like a sky pilot!" sneered Harry Main, gripping at the butt of his revolver. "I'm going to wipe out that smile of yours with a .45 slug of lead, in half a minute."

Christopher looked up once more to the blue heart of the heavens, where the fog was still rapidly thinning, and through that remaining film of cloud he could see the splendors of the sun flooding across the upper sky.

And at that moment, while his glance was still high, the booming note of the wolf's cry pounded up the valley, mixed with its own flying echoes.

Harry Main, the instant that he heard, bounded to the side and tore out his Colt as he sprang. It was an old trick of his in which he trusted implicitly, for it had won many a battle for him. But Christopher, seeing the move, had no doubts. His own weapon glided smoothly into his touch. At the hip he spun it up. From the hip he fired, and he saw Harry Main fire his own weapon into the ground, and then lunge downward, very much as though he had intentionally fired downward at an invisible enemy, and then fallen down to grapple with it hand to hand.

Christopher did not need to go forward to investigate. He knew just where his own bullet had struck home, and he raised his head in an odd quiet of the soul, and saw that the last wisps of the upper mist had been cleared away and, in a deep well of blue, shot through with golden sun, the heavens opened above him as though for the free reception of a winged spirit.

Then he went to poor Harry Main and turned the body on its back. He had been shot straight through the heart. The top buttonhole of the open coat had been the target of Christopher, and right through that slim target the bullet had torn its way.

He closed the eyes of Harry Main. And while he was on his knees, performing that last rite, a chilly sense of being watched from behind made him leap to his feet.

He looked behind him into the underbrush beneath the woods, for from that direction he knew the eyes had been upon him, The thing was back once more to hound him!

There had been no joy in him for the victory. There had been no exultation. It was merely the assurance which came at the heels of his conscious superiority. There had been no chance for poor Main from the first instant that they faced one another in the cabin.

But Harry Main was forgotten. All that was remembered was the dreadful unseen thing which moved so noiselessly around him. What was it?

When he had gained control of himself once more, he went to the roan and found him down-headed, dull-eyed, with his lower lip hanging and a tremor in his legs. He had a wisp of green grass hanging from his lips, and when he was led to the water he refused to drink.

Christopher, with a terrible sinking of the heart, felt that he understood what had happened. The gelding, too, had seen more than the eye of a brute could understand, and had felt more than an animal heart could stand.

He rubbed the strong animal down and swung into the saddle. And the gelding, taking more heart with his first steps along the trail, was soon going ahead at a good gait, and lifting his head more as he warmed up.

Straight down the hollow rode Christopher, for the first thing to do was to take the word of what had just taken place to the people below. He must send for the dead body, and then he must carry word of what he had done to his mother. And how could he face her, or she him, since he knew that she had sent Harry Main to face him in this hiding place?

However, all of that was very far away and of little importance, and what really mattered was simply that he get out of these tall, dark woods as fast as he could.

He rode with a terrible conviction that he would never pass through those woods alive. Now he was in the grip of whatever power it was that hounded him. The old Indian, it was true, had kept the foe at bay for three-quarters of a long lifetime, but that old Indian had a power of will such as Christopher felt that he could never aspire toward.

His head was never still as he went through the shadows. But he could see nothing except soft shiftings of shadows, which well might be the quiet passing of some pursuer. On the other hand, it might be the mere effect of the shifting lights which passed down through the wind-stirred trees. And as for hearing anything, every slight murmur was lost in the continual patter of dropping water, for the fog had left the branches and the twigs covered with dim, silver drops.

So he crossed the little dark-hearted brook and, turning the next winding of the narrow forest trail, he came on a sight that stopped his heart. For in the middle of the way, flat on his back, his arms thrown crosswise, and his dead eyes fixed sightlessly upon the trees above him, lay the Indian.

XV
"Back to the Valley"

Christopher dismounted instantly and ran to the spot. And as he leaned over the dead man, he groaned with veritable horror. For the throat of the Indian had been torn across — and not by any knife. It had been ripped open — just as by the fang of a wolf!

So the long trail of the old hero had come to an end. And how long before Christopher's end should come, also? He felt that his knees were turned to lead. He staggered back to the roan, and was coming toward him with outstretched hands when something in his way of approach startled that most patient of horses. He tossed his head and with a sudden frightened snort he fled on down the trail.

Christopher, left alone, called after him until the wailing notes of his own voice frightened him. Then he went on in the same direction, but every step he took was one of agony. He gave up all control and dashed madly forward, blind with terror. And then, behind him, he was sure that he heard the breathing of a pursuer. So he whirled with a gasp of terror, and flung his back against a tree. Just behind him the fleeting shadow darted out of view behind a tree. And his pounding heart turned to ice!

For he felt, now, that his death was to follow that of the Indian. Destiny was thick around him. And to make all sure, presently he heard a faint whine, and it drew before his imagination the dreadful picture of an old wolf, gray with years, his back arched and his belly gaunt, and his grinning mouth showing only a single fang for murder.

And then it seemed to him that he saw something drift noiselessly into the midst of a small bush. Yet he was almost sure that the glitter of eyes shone out at him. Instinctively, without aiming, he jerked up the muzzle of his gun and fired.

There was a yelp of fear and pain, and then out of the covert, straight toward him, wriggling on his belly with fear and with pain, came the familiar form of Lurcher!

Christopher, watching him and sick with wonder and relief and pity, suddenly understood all that had happened. Lurcher, the silent hunter who never left the Royal ranch, had indeed left it this time, because in his dog's heart he had known that some great trial lay before his master. He had trailed the big rider, but from a guilty distance, and when he tried to come closer, at last, he had been received with a bullet that must have missed him narrowly. And again as he strove to crawl in out of the cold of the night to his master — to his master and away from the wolfish voices in the woods — poor Lurcher had been fired at point-blank'. It was most miraculous that he had not been killed.

This was the hunting ghost, then, which had filled Christopher Royal with such supernatural dread that even terrible Harry Main meant nothing to him. He dropped on his knees and Lurcher, moaning with joy and terror and pain combined, stood up and staggered into his master's arms.

Tears poured into the eyes of Christopher. He dashed them away. But still his lips were trembling with pity as he worked over the hurt dog. Off went his coat. His shirt was ripped to shreds. He cleansed the wound of the bullet which had passed through the breast, close to one shoulder, and out the side of the hound through a gaping wound. Then he stopped the flow of the wound with dust — and with his prayers. For he felt that this poor trembling, heartbroken, spiritless creature had been the strange instrument through which his own soul had been saved from much, much worse than death, and he worked for Lurcher with a passionate intensity.

He saw the great eyes grow dim. He took his pocket flask of whisky and forced a bit down the throat of the weakening dog. And then — the bleeding stopped as if by a miracle. A sheer miracle, indeed, Christopher always considered it. After that he made the bandage, tenderly but firmly; and last of all, he took his coat, and using it as a litter, he carried Lurcher out of the woods.

He had thought that he was deep in the heart of the forest, but now he found that the crisis had come upon him when he was on the verge of the trees. Clean, sweet sunshine beat upon him as he issued from the damp and the shadows, and he saw the familiar beauty of Royal Valley spread out beneath him. Just below there was the Kendrick house, with a banner of smoke hanging white above it, and he thought that he had never before seen a picture of such beautiful quiet as this which was before him. Indeed, it appeared to Christopher as though he had never beheld it before — or as though he had always been living in a dream until this time.

Lurcher was rapidly dying in his arms. Twice he stopped, as he was hurrying down the hill, and laid the hound upon the ground for the sake of letting him recuperate. Twice, under his hand and his voice, the dog opened his eyes and smiled vaguely at him, as only the eyes of a dog can do. And then he hurried on once more, never daring to break into a run for fear lest the jarring would prove instantly fatal to Lurcher. He reached the front gate of the Kendrick yard and kicked it open with such a crash that pretty Mary Kendrick came running out onto the verandah.

She screamed loudly at the sight of him.

"Oh, Chris, Chris!" she cried. "Harry Main has killed you and you've come here to die!"

"Don't talk foolishness," said he. "I'm not hurt. It's only blood from this dog...the finest dog in the world. Where's there a bed for him?"

"Bed? Chris! For a dog!"

"Yes, yes, yes! I mean what I say. Where's there a bed for him? I'll pay for it! He's got to lie soft and be contented."

In the little side room off the verandah there was a fine old couch where Lurcher was laid down to bleed and die.

"Now get Doctor Hutchison on the telephone and tell him to come over here as fast as he can gallop his horse, Mary!"

"But Chris! The dog is shot right through the body! He can't live! And do you know that Harry Main is looking for you and threatening...."

"Harry Main will never threaten any one again. Get the doctor, I say! And tell him that there's a thousand-dollar case here for him...a thousand dollars if he saves the life of a dog!"

She gave one more frightened glance at him to make sure that he was not mad, but her brains were still addled when she reached the telephone. And presently she was calling across the wire:

"Mrs. Hutchison! Mrs. Hutchison! This is Mary Kendrick. And Christopher Royal isn't dead. He's here. But maybe he's dying. I don't know. And Harry Main shot his dog. And then Christopher fought with him with his bare hands and killed him. And isn't it terrible? I think I'm going to faint. And Christopher is quite mad. And he says that he'll pay your husband a thousand dollars for saving the life of the dog...."

At this point in the recital, there was an interruption made by Mrs. Hutchison smashing the receiver into the hook. There is a time for politeness. It is not, however, when there is an opportunity to win a thousand dollars.

She bounded to the back porch. Her voice, wire drawn and piercing as a knife, stabbed the air.

"Hank! Ha-a-a-n-nk! Hurry! Hurry! Hurry!"

And Hank hurried. When he got to the Kendrick place, his horse was staggering and Hutchison himself was pale with expectancy and terrible hope. He had never seen a thousand dollars gathered together in all his life. And here was his great chance. For the word of a Royal was a great deal better than a gold bond for any amount within thinking distance.

So old Doctor Hutchison reached the house of the Kendricks and rushed into it, not even as much as waiting to rap at the front door. He found himself in a house of terrible turmoil and confusion, in which the domestics and the family hurried here and there on urgent errands. And then he was shown into a small room where Christopher Royal, his big body half-naked to the waist and his clothes streaked and spotted with crimson, was on his knees beside a couch, and lying partly on the couch and partly on the arms of his master was an old hound, whose glazing eyes were fixed upon the eyes of Christopher as though in them he saw his only stars of hope.

The long arm of Christopher reached out and jerked the doctor also upon his knees.

Forget it's a dog, Hank," said Christopher. "Think it is a human being. And I can tell you that he has meant more than any human being in my life. No matter what you can do for him, you get five hundred. And if you save him…a thousand! You hear?"

"My Heaven, yes!" said the doctor. "Don't I, though?"

And that was the beginning of the strangest scene that had ever been witnessed in Royal Valley, for day and night the two men would not leave the side of the dying dog! Christopher because, whenever he moved, there was a moan from Lurcher; and the doctor because his skilled attention was bringing Lurcher alive through each succeeding hour when it seemed as though death must take him at the next moment.

The doctor had a growing reward dangling before his eyes and, when Christopher saw that the old skilled veterinary was actually accomplishing some results, his delight knew no bounds, and he could not contain himself. On successive days he raised the proffered sum to fifteen hundred and then to two thousand dollars.

And so it was that Royal Valley came to hear of the "Two-Thousand-Dollar Dog."

XVI
"A Queer Dog!"

All of this time, it must be remembered that Royal Valley had other things to consider. When the party went up into the hollow, according to the directions of Christopher, to find the body of the famous Harry Main by the cabin near Emmett's, they also found on the way that there was a dead Indian lying along the trail in the forest.

They buried him at the side of the trail and put up a little mound of stones to mark the spot. Then they went on and forgot all that they had seen of him when they saw Main indeed lying with a bullet through his heart. They carried Harry Main down into the valley and laid him out in state in the church, where he was viewed by literally thousands.

Cliff Main had lain there before, and now the more famous and more deadly brother lay there also. Men came who had felt his bullets in their body. And others came who had heard the hiss of them going by. And still others there were who had merely been witnesses.

All of these followed the body to the grave, almost with the air of mourners, and afterward they rehearsed again the wild and grand feats which they had seen this man perform. And by hundreds and hundreds those who had never been sufficiently blessed to see the great Main in action drank in these words of the wise.

Royal Valley was particularly glad to hear all that magnified the greatness of Harry Main, just as the Jews of another day were glad to magnify the greatness of Goliath, they having their own David. That David was acting very oddly now, but given such a bit of freakishness as this frantic struggle to save the life of a mere cur was forgiven.

"You can't expect a gent like Christopher Royal to act like common folks. Everything about him is big...and different!" they said affectionately.

He had explicitly denied the story which described him as rushing bare-handed upon terrible Harry Main and killing him by sheer might of hand and frightful heroism in the face of odds. For that matter, there was the unbruised body of Harry Main, with the bullet through his heart, to deny the tale most effectually. But that was not enough. For men will believe what they want to believe, and the most catching story is always the most lasting one. Christopher was made into a prodigious hero, and all the while he was by the bed of a sick dog too busy to pay attention to his fame.

Mrs. Royal started the instant that she heard where he was, but she was passed on the road by Georgia Lassiter on a flying horse, and with a pale, lovely face.

Poor Georgia! She got to the Kendricks' house and entered only to find her lover too deeply engrossed in his labors as a nurse to pay the slightest attention to her. She turned crimson — and then she fell to work to help.

And after her came Mrs. Royal, to whom her son merely extended a stained hand and said: "I understand everything. And it's all right, Lurcher and you saved me."

Mrs. Royal did not quite understand. But she was a patient woman, and she could wait for explanations. Just what Lurcher had done she could not dream.

And how could any mother be expected to understand how a common, spiritless hound could have been magnified into a danger so terrible that the mere encounter with a celebrated gunman was as nothing to her son?

But on the fifth day the crisis came. And the doctor, rising to shaking knees, motioned Christopher away from the bed. Unshaven, hollow and black about the eyes, with sunken cheeks and parched lips, they stared down at the sleeping dog, and saw Lurcher quiver and jerk and whine in his sleep.

"He's gunna win through!" said the doctor. "He's sleeping sound and fine now. He'll be a better dog when he wakes up! But always lame in that off shoulder. Mind you, he's sure to be lame in that shoulder."

"Confound it, man," said Christopher Royal, "you've done the greatest thing in the world. I'll never forget it!"

And they rested their arms on one another's shoulders and wavered a little with weariness and gladness as they looked down upon their accomplished work.

Then Christopher could sleep in turn and, when he awakened, he found Georgia sitting on the floor beside him. For he would lie on the floor in the same room with the dog.

"Hush!" she was saying. "Hush!" And as he stared up into her face, she added, "There are no such things as werewolves, dear Chris!"

"No such things!" he breathed, and gripping her hand, he fell asleep again.

You may say, if you will, that this is only a history of how a dog found a man, but as a matter of fact it is a narrative of how a man found himself. The Royal blood had been reclaimed for Christopher, and it was never to be lost again.

Only once he tried to tell the story of the facts to Georgia. But he failed dismally, because after he had finished she merely looked with a smile at him and said: "Oh, of course, Chris, you want to tell me that you're not a hero at all. But that's always the way with the really brave men. They always think that the things they do are accidents. And of course what you say about yourself is right. And of course what every one else in the valley says about you is all wrong. You silly dear."

I think that even Georgia, though she was as large-hearted as the day, grew a little jealous of Lurcher before the end, but the old hound had secured a lasting place in the household and could not be removed to his death's day.

And it was a common sight, in Royal Town, to see an old, gray-tinged, lean-ribbed hound trailing along behind the tall, graceful figure that Christopher Royal remained throughout his life.

"A queer dog for such a handsome man to own!" strangers would say.

And the answer was as ready as "a borrower's cap."

"Looks like a common dog, don't it? But everybody in these parts can tell you that two thousand dollars was spent on the same hound, sir!"

And such a remark was sure to silence all objections because, as the saying has it, "You have to pay for class."

Christopher had paid. And not in cash only! For to the end of his life, while all the rest of his hair was black, there was a decided sprinkling of gray about the temples, and one deep crease drawn down the very center of his forehead.

The werewolf had put its mark upon him.

B.M. BOWER

BERTHA MUZZY BOWER (1871–1940) was born the ninth of ten children in Cleveland, Minnesota. She was educated for a time in public schools but at home as well (her mother was a former schoolteacher). Bower's father was no less a strong influence: he taught her music, how to fish, shoot, and draw blueprints. "From 'Paradise Lost' to SHE in one evening was quite a jump for a kid," Bower later recalled about books her father recommended to her, "but he encouraged me to make it." When Bower was sixteen, the Muzzy family moved to the Big Sandy district in Montana where Bertha spent many hours roaming the ranges and visiting with cowboys. Her first professional employment was as a schoolteacher herself, an experience she later used as background for her novel, THE NORTH WIND DO BLOW (Little, Brown, 1937).

The first of her three marriages was to Clayton J. Bower in 1890 and it would be under his surname that she would write for her entire career. Bower herself claimed that she first began writing Western fiction in 1903. It was apparently a slow beginning, but by 1904 her stories were selling well and the appearance of "Chip of the Flying U" in Street & Smith's *The Popular Magazine* led Bower to sign her first multi-story contract with this publisher to secure her income in what was an effort to escape the circumstances of her failing marriage. The two older children from her marriage to Bower she sent to live with their grandparents in the State of Washington while she went with her youngest son, Roy, to live in Great Falls. Bertrand W. Sinclair, with whom she had become friends and who had helped her with technical aspects of ranch life, was also in Great Falls. Bower's divorce from her first husband became final in March, 1905, and she and Sinclair were married in August of that year. A daughter, Della Frances Sinclair, who would become Bower's literary executor, was born in 1907 in the midst of a blizzard. Della was named for the Little Doctor in CHIP OF THE FLYING U, albeit she would later change the spelling of her name to Dele.

Bower's marriage to Sinclair also proved a failure. Her growing literary reputation and her greater financial success, when compared to Sinclair's, caused endless friction. They were divorced in 1912. This second divorce placed even greater physical and emotional stress on Bower. She developed heart trouble and even suffered a nervous breakdown. Notwithstanding, with Roy and Dele now living with her, a twice-divorced woman and single mother at forty, Bower signed a contract with Little, Brown, and went on to produce two books a year for almost the next thirty years. Her serials continued to be featured in Street & Smith magazines and she developed a relationship with film production companies where she authored several scenarios, including work in the Tom Mix unit at Selig.

Bower's tumultuous life is seldom reflected in the Western fiction she wrote, although the physical abuse endured in her first marriage and the drinking problems both husbands had during their marriages to her are only thinly disguised in what remains one of her finest novels, LONESOME LAND (Little, Brown, 1912).

Toward the end of the decade, Bower became re-acquainted with Robert Ellsworth Cowan, a cowboy-bartender as Sinclair had been who worked in the Big Sandy area. They were married in 1920. Although this marriage lasted until 1939, for the last years the couple did not live together. Bower was troubled by Cowan's insistence that he was the prototype for Chip Bennett. To "console Bud for not being 'the original Chip,'" Bower once confessed in a letter, she used him as the basis for the hero of COW COUNTRY (Little, Brown, 1921), Bud Birnie (Cowan was familiarly known as "Bud"). The serial version of this story appeared in *The Popular Magazine* the same year they were married. Yet as late as 1933 Bower had to confess that Bud still "never seems to remember that he's the feller in COW COUNTRY." Bower insisted that "Chip is no one I ever knew. In looks he resembled somewhat a bronc rider I knew there [in Montana], who has since became a well-known author. I speak of Bertrand W. Sinclair.... That keen sarcasm somewhat resembles Sinclair as he was at the time; also the trick of tearing off his cigarette papers. There the resemblance ceases." Since Bower did not meet Charles M. Russell until after the Chip serial had been published when she moved to Great Falls, Chip, the cowboy artist, could not have been (as has often been supposed) a reference to Russell (although he did the illustrations for the first book edition published by Dillingham in 1906). The name itself was inspired by Bertha's brother, Newton Muzzy, who loved eating Saratoga potato chips. As for the Flying U, Bower admitted that "there is no original Flying U ranch such as I described in all my stories. I wish there were. I've been homesick (if I may use the word) to have my stories become real. Those boys as characters are very real to me, and I hope to my readers. But as living persons — well, they are composites of all cowpunchers, I suppose." However, this disclaimer cannot be applied to Dry Lake in the Flying U stories. It is an honest representation of the Big Sandy area as Bower knew it.

Insofar as CHIP OF THE FLYING U's narrative structure is that of a ranch romance, Bower did owe a heavy debt to Owen Wister's THE VIRGINIAN. However, unlike Wister, Bower considered the West the norm and throughout her fiction continued to poke fun at Easterners and Eastern values. Indeed, quite often the major plot contrivance in a Bower novel is the arrival of an Easterner in the West who must either adapt to the Western way of doing things or return to the East an acknowledged failure.

Harry E. Maule, editor of *West* magazine and *Short Stories* for Doubleday, Doran & Company, persuaded Bower to write new stories about Chip Bennett set prior to his marriage to the Little Doctor. THE WHOOP-UP TRAIL (Little, Brown, 1933), serialized in *Short Stories,* recounts the arrival of Claude "Chip" Bennett in Montana from Colorado and his hiring on at the Flying U while searching for his older brother, Wane. When the short novel "Chip Rides Alone" appeared in *West* (12/33), Maule announced in the "Come and Get It" section that "this novel is the first of a series of Chip of the Flying U novels [to be featured in *West*], and the next will appear as soon as we can get it. B.M. Bower is hard at work on it now." A box on the front pages of "Chip and the Wild Bunch" in *West* (3/34) announced: "B.M. Bower scores in this novel another triumph in a long list of meaty stories of the real West, stories with something more to them than blazing guns and death and destruction, stories whose convincingly human characters play naturally dramatic parts against the rugged background of the northern cattle lands, stories whose events and settings spring less from imagination than from actual experience. These new novels of Chip of the Flying U are written about the author's own country and own people." "Chip Rides Alone" and "Chip and the Wild Bunch" were compiled and integrated to form THE FLYING U STRIKES (Little, Brown, 1934), a story in which Chip goes up against Butch Lewiston, a villain based on the historical bandit, Butch Cassidy. TROUBLE RIDES THE WIND (Little, Brown, 1935) deals with Chip's efforts to defend the good name of the Flying U ranch. This saga, spread over many years, with some novels such as RODEO (Little, Brown, 1929) showing Chip and Della's son almost having reached his majority, and others set before the first serial to feature Chip, are now being reprinted in keeping with their internal chronology by Chivers Press in their Gunsmoke hard cover Western series, beginning with THE WHOOP-UP TRAIL.

Two of Bower's strongest novels that do not concern Chip or the Flying U and which are similar in that the focus is on the personal quests of their heroes to return stolen property to its rightful owners are VAN PATTEN (Little, Brown, 1926) and THE SWALLOWFORK BULLS (Little, Brown, 1929). THE SWALLOWFORK BULLS is also notable for some of Bower's best descriptions of the savagery of Western winters and the difficulties of travel under such conditions.

Another novel equally worthy of mention is THE HAUNTED HILLS (Little, Brown, 1934).

In it, the hero, first viewing the heroine, reflects: "He had read so many Western stories that he had become imbued with the idea that all range-bred girls are entrancingly lovely — romantic heroines waiting to be discovered by the hero of the story. At first glance this girl was not true to type — granting that the story girls are typical. Her hair was a sunburned brown, with neither luster nor sheen; the desert wind saw to that. It seemed abundant enough for any heroine, however, and all native to her own head. She wore it braided and hanging down her back, with the end of the braid falling loosely into two end-roughened curls. There was no ribbon bow, but a twist or two of what looked suspiciously like common grocery twine. No heroine in any story that Shelton had ever read used grocery twine to tie her hair. She wore an old felt hat that looked as though it had seen hard usage and a faded calico shirtwaist with a skirt of brown denim. Her face was sunburned with a tendency toward freckles across her nose, and her hands were brown and rough.''

Five years before Bower had a story published in *Adventure,* she wrote a letter to the editor, published in ''The Camp-Fire'' (12/10/24), in which she took umbrage with a reader who claimed that frontier women were drab and forlorn. ''The women, you must remember,'' she wrote, ''were the mothers and the wives and the sisters of the men. There were hundreds of them, and I never met one of the colorless, forlorn type. All the pioneer women I ever knew were past middle age — by the time I was old enough to take notice — and they were alert, vibrant with interest in all that went on around them; ready to talk your head off, usually, and never happier than when they could talk and talk of past adventures and paint in all the dramatic high lights. If they were weazened and forlorn, hopeless, drab things in their youth, in heaven's name what happened to perk them up so amazingly in their old age?'' She added, ''I can personally vouch for the fact that pioneering was — and still is — about ninety percent monotonous isolation to ten percent thrill. It is scarcely fair to turn the picture upside down and present the public with ninety percent thrill and ten percent normal, everyday living.''

Bower was herself very much a pioneer since she was the first woman to gain an international reputation and devoted following as an author of Western stories. Others came along in close proximity, Eli(za) Colter, Cherry Wilson, Willa Cather in her way for several of her books, and the tradition has expanded ever since, from Dorothy M. Johnson to Ann Ahlswede, from Janice Holt Giles to Jeanne Williams, from Cynthia Haseloff to Gretel Ehrlich. But B.M. Bower was there first, and she did it on her own.

Bertha and Bud Cowan settled in Depoe Bay, Oregon, in 1930 due to Bud's distaste for city living and his asthma. Bower's son, Roy, who was an artist by avocation by 1933 was also living in Depoe Bay. Bill Sinclair had moved to British Columbia and quit writing to make a living as a deep-sea fisherman. Roy, in his own way, took to the sea and tried being a salmon troller; and it was at sea that Roy died. There is a bronze plaque still near Depoe Bay harbor commemorating the rescue mission which cost Roy Bower his life. It proved a final, terrible, devastating blow for Bower in a life which had held, for all her financial success, so much personal sorrow. Dele and her daughter, Sara Katherine, moved in with Bertha who now turned her attention to trying to salvage much of her early fiction which, published under the Copyright Act of 1870, would pass into the Public Domain forty-two years after first publication.

B.M. Bower died in Los Angeles on July 23, 1940. The year before CHIP OF THE FLYING U (Universal, 1939) had been released with Johnny Mack Brown in the title role, following an eminent line of screen Chip Bennetts, of whom Tom Mix had been the first and perhaps Hoot Gibson the most memorable. Indeed, the photoplay edition of CHIP OF THE FLYING U reprinted by Grosset & Dunlap in 1925 to coincide with the release of the Hoot Gibson Special based on this novel with stills from the film used to illustrate the text may be even more satisfying to the bibliophile than a copy of the Dillingham first edition.

Bower published a brace of Chip Bennett stories in *Argosy* in 1933: "Law of the Flying U" (9/16/33) and "Bad Penny" (12/2/33). "Bad Penny" was reprinted in *Zane Grey's Western Magazine* (1/49) and was accorded the distinction of being "A Zane Grey Western Award Story" which meant it was included in the anthology of ZANE GREY WESTERN AWARD STORIES (Dell, 1951) edited by Don Ward, who was also editor of the magazine. There is much of the flavor and ambiance of Bower's Western fiction in this vignette and, while occasionally humorous, it embodies Bower's human values which were also those of the men and women about whom she wrote. What in Owen Wister was made to seem alien and eccentric here is accepted as a preferable way of life.

BAD PENNY
1933

The Flying U beef herd toiled up the last heartbreaking hill and crawled slowly out upon the bench. Under the low-hanging dust cloud which trailed far out behind, nothing much could be seen of the herd save the big, swaying bodies and the rhythmically swinging heads of the leaders. Stolid as they looked, steadily as they plodded forward under the eagle eye of the point man, the steers were tired. Dust clogged blinking eyelashes, dust was in their nostrils, dust lay deep along their backs. The boys on left flank rode with neckerchiefs pulled up over their noses, yet they were not the most unfortunate riders on the drive, for the fitful gusts of wind lifted the gray cloud occasionally and gave them a few clean breaths.

Back on the drag where the dust was thickest, the man they called Penny choked, gasped, and spat viciously at the hindmost steer. He pulled off a glove and rubbed his aching, bloodshot eyes with bare fingertips, swearing a monotonous litany meanwhile, praying to be delivered from his present miseries and from any and all forms of cowpunching. Let him once live through this damnable day and he promised — nay, swore by all the gods he could name — that he'd chase himself into town and buy himself a barrel of whisky and a barrel of beer and camp between the two of them until he had washed the dust out of his system.

Shorty, who was wagon boss during beef roundup for Jim Whitmore and had stopped half a mile back to gossip with a rancher out hunting his horses, galloped up in time to hear this last picturesque conception of a heaven on earth.

"Make it two barrels while you're about it," he advised unsympathetically. "You'll get 'em just as easy as you will a bottle." He laughed at his own humor — a thing Penny hated in any man — and rode on up to the point where he could help swing the herd down off the bench to the level creek bottom which was their present objective.

Penny renewed his cussing and his coughing and looked across at Chip Bennett, who was helping to push the tired drag along.

"You hear what that damn son-of-a-gun told me?" he called out. And when Chip nodded with the brief grin which he frequently gave a man instead of words, Penny swung closer. "You know what he done to me, don't yuh? Put me on day herd outa my turn...and don't ever think I don't see why he done it. So's

I wouldn't get a chance to ride into town tonight. Gone temperance on me, the damn double-crosser. You heard him make that crack about me not gettin' a bottle uh beer, even? Runnin' a wagon has sure went to Shorty's head!"

"I don't think it's that altogether." Chip tried to soothe him. "You want to remember...."

Penny cut in on the sentence. "Remember what happened last time we shipped, I suppose. Well, that ain't got nothin' to do with this time. I ain't planning to get owl-eyed this time and raise hell like I done before. I swore off three weeks ago, and Shorty knows it. I ain't had a drop fer three weeks."

Chip wheeled his horse to haze a laggard steer into line, and so hid his grin. Penny's swearing off liquor three weeks ago was a joke with the Flying U outfit. The pledge had followed a spree which no one would soon forget. For Penny had not only shot up the new little cow town of Dry Lake and stood guard in the street afterward watching for someone to show his nose outside — to be scared out of his senses by Penny's reckless shooting and his blood-curdling war whoops — but he had been hauled to camp in the bed wagon next day, hog-tied to prevent his throwing himself out and maybe breaking his neck.

It was after he had recovered that he swore he never would touch another drop of anything stronger than Patsy's coffee. Those who had known him longest laughed the loudest at that vow, and Shorty was one of them; though he, being lord of the roundup, had to preserve discipline and do his laughing in secret.

"It sure is tough back here," Chip conceded when the cattle were once more strung out and the two rode alongside again. "Cheer up, Penny. It'll be all the same a hundred years from now." And he added, when he saw signs of another outbreak in the grimed face of Penny, "Anyway, we'll all be in town tomorrow."

"If not before," Penny said darkly. "T'morra don't help me none right now." He whacked a dusty red steer into line with his quirt. "What grinds me is to have Shorty take the stand he does; slappin' me on herd outa my turn, like as if he was scared I might break out agin.... Why, blast his lousy hide, I ain't got any idee of goin' in to town before t'morra when we load out. Er I didn't have," he amended querulously. "Not till he went to work and shoved me on herd, just to keep me outa sight of the damn burg as long as he could." He stood in the saddle to ease the cramp in his legs. "Why, hell! If I wanted to go get me a snootful, it'd take more'n that to stop me!"

Still standing in the stirrups, he gazed longingly ahead over the rippling sea of dusty, marching cattle and swore again because the dust shut out the town from his straining sight. Miles away though it was, from this high benchland it would be clearly visible under normal conditions. The men on point could see the little huddle of black dots alongside the pencil line of railroad, he knew that.

"You know damn well, Chip," he complained, settling down off-center in the saddle so that one foot swung free, "that ain't no way to treat a man that's reformed and swore off drinkin'."

"Well, you don't have to stay back here on the drag eating dust," Chip pointed out. "Why don't you get up front a while? You can probably see town if you ride point a while, Penny. And another thing; you don't want to take this day-herding too personal. With Jack sick, somebody had to go on outa turn."

"Sick nothin'!" Penny snorted. "I know when a man's playin' off. Jack shore ain't foolin' me a damn bit. And anyway, Shorty didn't have to go and pick on me."

Chip gave up the argument and swung back to bring up a straggler. Today they were not grazing the herd along as was their custom. The midsummer dry spell had made many a water hole no more than a wallow of caked mud, and most of the little creeks were bone dry. This was in a sense a forced drive, the day herders pushing the herd twice the usual distance ahead so that they would camp that night on the only creek for miles that had water running in it. That it lay within easy riding distance of town was what worried Penny.

Privately Chip thought Shorty had shown darned good sense in putting Penny on day herd. He'd have to stand guard that night — probably the middle guard, if he were taking Jack Bates's place — and that would keep him out of temptation, at least until after the cattle were loaded, when a little backsliding wouldn't matter so much. Whereas, had he been left to his regular routine, Penny would be lying around camp right now wishing he dared sneak off to town. He would have the short guard at the tail end of the afternoon, and at dusk he would have been relieved from duty until morning. With town so close it was easy to guess what Penny would have done with those night hours.

As it was, Penny would have no idle time save the two or three hours of lying around camp after the herd had been thrown on water. Then he'd have to sleep until he was called for middle guard. In the morning the whole outfit would be called out, and they'd be hard at it till the last steer was prodded into the last car and the door slid shut and locked. Then there would be more than Penny racing down to where they could wash the dust from their throats. No, Jack did get sick right at the exact time when it would keep Penny from getting drunk when he was most needed. A put-up job, most likely. Shorty wasn't so slow after all.

"We'll be down off the bench and on water in another hour," Chip yelled cheeringly when he came within shouting distance of Penny again.

Penny had turned sullen and he made no reply to that. He rode with both hands clasped upon the saddle horn, one foot swinging free of its stirrup, and a cigarette waggling in the corner of his mouth. His hat was pulled low over his smarting eyes, squinted half shut against the smothering dust that made his face as gray as his hat.

Not once during the remainder of the drive did he open his lips except when he coughed and spat out dust or when he swore briefly at a laggard steer. And Chip, being the tactful young man he was, let him alone to nurse his grudge. He did not sympathize with it, however, for Chip was still filled with a boyish enthusiasm for the picturesque quality of the drive. Even the discomfort of riding on the drag, with twelve hundred beef cattle kicking dust into his face, could not make him feel himself the martyr which Penny did.

For that reason and the fact that he never had felt the drunkard's torment of thirst, Chip certainly failed to grasp the full extent of Penny's resentment. He thought it was pretty cute of Shorty to fix it so Penny couldn't get to town ahead of the herd. He had simply saved Penny from making seventeen kinds of a fool of himself and maybe kept him from losing his job as well. Let him sulk if he wanted to. He'd see the point when it was all over with and they were headed back onto the range again after another herd.

So they rode in the heat and the dust, each thinking his own thoughts. The herd plodded on in the scorching, windless heat, stepping more briskly as they neared the edge of the bench.

Bellowing thirstily, the cattle poured down the long, steep slope to the sluggish creek at the mouth of the narrow coulee. As the drag dipped down from the level, even Penny could see the long, level valley beyond and the little huddle of houses squatting against the farther hill. Two hundred yards up the creek and inside the coulee, the tents of the Flying U showed their familiar, homey blotches of gray-white against the brown grass. Behind them a line of green willows showed where the creek snaked away up the coulee. Never twice in the same setting, flitting like huge birds over the range to alight where water and feed were best, those two tents were home to the Flying U boys — a welcome sight when a long day's work was done.

Chip's eyes brightened at the sight, and he cleared his throat of the last clinging particles of dust. With a whoop he hailed the two men ambling out from camp to relieve them. Others would follow — were following even as he looked — to take charge of the tired, thirsty cattle already blotting the creek altogether from sight where they crowded to drink. Cal Emmett and Slim rode straight on to meet Chip and Penny.

"Gosh, ain't it hot!" Cal greeted them, voicing an obvious fact as is the way of men who have nothing important to say. "Weather breeder, if yuh ask me."

"Well, if it holds off till we get these cattle in the cars it can rain all it damn pleases," Chip replied carelessly. "I want to get caught up on my sleep, anyway."

"Don't you ever think it'll hold off! Bet you'll be huntin' buttons on your slicker tonight." Cal grinned. "Sure glad I don't have to stand guard t'night!"

"By golly that's right," Slim agreed. "If it don't cut loose an' rain t'night I miss my guess."

Penny scowled at him, grunted, and rode on past. "Let 'er rain and be damned to it!" he muttered as he pricked his horse into a lope. But Chip had also put his horse into a gallop and failed to hear anything Penny might say.

At the rope corral as they rode up, Shorty was speaking to someone over across the remuda, judging from the pitch of his voice.

"No sir! The man that rides to town before this beef is loaded can take his bed along with him. The cars'll be spotted sometime tonight, ready for us to start loadin' whenever we're ready tomorrow. I shore as hell ain't goin' to stop and round up a bunch of drunken punchers before I start workin' the herd in the morning."

Penny muttered an unprintable sentence as he dismounted and began loosening the latigo, and Chip gave him a quick questioning glance as he stepped down from his saddle close by. He glanced at Shorty, let his eyes go questing for the man he had been speaking to, and returned his glance to Penny.

"That's him every time, hittin' yuh over another man's back," Penny grumbled, and shot an angry, sidelong glance at the wagon boss. "If he's got anything to say to me, why don't he spit it out to my face?"

"Ah, he wasn't talking to you," Chip protested, biting the words off short as Shorty turned and walked toward them.

The wagon boss gave them a sharp glance as he passed, almost as if he had overheard them. But he did not say anything and Penny did not look up.

Though other men chatted around him, Penny ate his supper in silence, scowling over his plate. Afterward he lay in the shade of the bed tent and smoked moodily until it was time to catch his night horse. No one paid any attention to him, for tempers were quite likely to be short at the end of a beef roundup, when sleep was broken with night-guarding a herd as temperamental as rival prima donnas are said to be, and almost as valuable. If a man went into the sulks it was just as well to let him alone while the mood lasted. Which did not mean, however, that no one knew the state of mind he was in.

By the set of his head and the stiffness of his neck while he saddled his horse Penny proclaimed to his world that he was plenty mad. He looped up the long free end of the latigo, unhooked the stirrup from the horn, and let it drop with a snap that sent his horse ducking sidewise. He jerked him to a snorting stand, fixing a stern and warning eye upon him, hesitated just a second or two, and instead of tying him to the wagon as he should have done he jerked down his hat for swift riding, thrust his toe in the stirrup, and mounted.

"Here! Where you think you're goin'?" Shorty called out in surprise, leaping up from the ground.

"Goin' after my mail! Be right back," Penny grinned impudently over his shoulder as he wheeled his horse toward the open land. He was off, galloping down the coulee before Shorty could get the slack out of his jaw.

"His mail! Hell!" Shorty spluttered angrily, glaring after the spurts of dust Penny left behind him. "He ain't had a letter in all the two years I've knowed him." He stood irresolute, plainly tempted to give chase. Then he relaxed with a snort. "Think I'll hog-tie him and haul him out in the wagon again and sober him up?" he said disgustedly. "I'll fire the son-of-a-gun...."

Then he remembered that he was no longer just one of the Happy Family, free to speak his mind, but a full-fledged roundup foreman who had the dignity of his position to maintain. He stalked off to the cook tent and unrolled his bed, knowing full well that Penny would be howling drunk before midnight, and that by morning he would be unable to sit in the saddle — to say nothing of reading brands and helping work the herd and weed out strays before loading the cattle. The Flying U was already working shorthanded. He'd just have to consider himself shy another man, which went against the grain. Penny sober was a top hand — and, darn the luck, Shorty liked him.

He spread his blankets and started to get ready to crawl in, then decided that the air was too sultry inside and dragged his bed out under the mess wagon. Other men were deserting their canvas shelter in spite of the threatening clouds. For even at dusk the air was stifling. If it busted loose and rained they could move inside, but they'd be darned if they were going to suffocate in the meantime.

"Saddle yourselves a night horse before you turn in, boys." Shorty made a sudden decision as a whiff of cool air struck his face. "We can't take any chances at this stage of the game." And he went off to practice what he preached.

It was a sensible precaution, for if the storm did strike before morning there was no telling how bad it might be nor how the herd would take it. Shorty had seen beef herds stampede in a thunderstorm and he hoped never to see another one — certainly not while he was responsible for the safety of the cattle. So, having done what he could to prepare for an emergency, Shorty crawled into his blankets and was snoring inside five minutes. And presently the dim bulks on the ground near by were likewise sleeping with the deep, unheeding slumber of work-weary men untroubled by conscience or care.

Down beyond the coulee mouth the night guard rode slowly 'round and 'round the sleeping herd. By sound they rode mostly, and by that unerring instinct which comes of long habit and the intimate knowledge it brings. As the sullen clouds crept closer it was so dark they could not see one another as they met and passed on. But the droning lullaby tones of their voices met and blended for a minute or so in pleasant companionship and understanding. Then the voices would draw apart and recede into the suffocating blackness. The whisper of saddle leather, the mouthing of a bit, the faint rattle of bridle chains grew faint and finally were lost until, minutes later, the meeting came again.

Chip was young, and his imagination never slept. He liked the velvet blackness, the brooding mystery that descended upon the land with the dusk. Even the frogs over in the creek did their croaking tonight with bashful hesitation, as if they, too, felt the silence weigh upon them and only croaked because the habit was too strong for them. Chip thought of this breathless night as a curtained dome where some gigantic goddess walked and trailed her velvet robes, treading softly with her finger on her lips. Which only proves how young and imaginative he could be on night guard.

Away across the herd came the plaintive notes of a melancholy song which Weary Willie seemed to favor lately, for no good reason save that it had many verses and a tune that lent itself to melodious crooning. Chip hushed his own low singing to listen. In that breathless air, across twelve hundred sleeping steers, the words came clear.

> "Oh, bury me not on the lone prairee
> Where the wild coyotes will howl o'er me,
> Where the rattlesnakes hiss and the wind blows free —
> Oh-h, bury me not on the lone prairee."

Chip wondered who had written those words, anyway. Not a real cowboy, he'd bank on that. They'd sing it, of course, with that same wailing chorus plaintively making its sickish plea between the verses. But he didn't believe any real cowpuncher ever felt that way, when you came right down to it.

When a cowboy's light went out — according to the opinion of all the fellows he had ever heard discoursing on the subject — he didn't give a damn where they laid his carcass. They were quite likely to say, with unpleasant bluntness, "Just drag me off where I won't stink." But when they stood guard, like Weary tonight, nine times in ten they'd sing that maudlin old song. And though Chip would never admit it, over there in the dark the words lost their sickish sentimentality and seemed to carry a pulsing tremor of feeling.

> "Oh bury me where a mother's prayer
> And a sister's tears may linger there!
> Where my friends may come and weep o'er me —
> Oh, bury me not on the lone prairee!"

In daylight Chip would have hooted at the lugubrious tones with which Weary Willie sang those words, but now he did not even smile to himself. The night like that and with sheet lightning playing along the sky line with the vague and distant mutter of thunder miles away, death and the tears and prayers of loved ones did not seem so incongruous.

> "Oh, bury me not — but his voice failed there,
> And they gave no heed to his dying prayer.
> In a narrow grave just six by three-e,
> They-y buried him there on the lone prairee — "

The singer was riding toward him, the soft thud of his horse's feet and the faint saddle sounds once more audible. A steer close to Chip blew a snorting breath, grunted and got to his feet, his horns rattling against the horns of his nearest neighbor. Chip forgot Weary and his song and began a soothing melody of his own. Another steer got up, and another. Black as it was, he sensed their uneasy, listening attitudes.

It couldn't have been Weary who wakened them. Weary had circled the herd many times with his melancholy ditty, his presence carrying reassurance. Chip dared not quicken his pace, dared not call a warning. Instead he began singing in his clear young tenor, hoping to override whatever fear was creeping on among the cattle.

> "Come, love, come, the boat lies low —
> The moon shines bright on the old bayou — "

Almost overhead the clouds brightened with the sudden flare of lightning, but the rumble that followed was slow and deep and need not have been disquieting to animals that had grown up in the land of sudden storms.

> "Come, love, come, oh come along with me,
> I'll take you down-n to Tenn — "

Off in the night there came the drumming of hoofs — some strange horseman coming at a swift gallop straight toward the herd. A chill prickled up Chip's neck. Slowly, carefully as a mother tiptoeing away from her sleeping baby, he reined aside and walked his horse out to meet and warn the approaching rider.

"Slow down!" he called cautiously when another lightning flare revealed the rider. "You'll be on top of the herd in another minute, you damn fool!"

A shrill, reckless yell from just ahead answered him: "*Ayee-ee*...Yipee! Them's the babies I'm a-lookin' for! Gotta stand guard! *Whee-ee*! Bossies, here's yer...what the hell?"

With an indescribable sound of clashing horns and great bodies moving in unison, the herd was up and away like flushed quail. There was no more warning than that first great swoosh of sound. Here and there steers bawled throatily — caught in the act of getting to their feet. Now they were battered back to earth as the herd lunged over them. For the cattle had taken fright on the outer fringe nearest camp and the open valley, and were stampeding across their own bed ground toward the bench.

The night was no longer silent under a velvety blackness. It was a roaring tumult of sound, the never-to-be-forgotten clamor of a stampede in full flight. Weary Willie, by God's mercy out of their path as he swung round the side toward the valley, yelled to Chip above the uproar.

"What started 'em? Y'all right, Chip?"

And Penny with a pint or more of whisky inside him and two quart flasks in his pockets, answered with another yell, "I did! Jus' sayin' hello...the damn things've fergot me a'ready!" He gave a whoop and emptied his six-shooter into the air as he galloped.

"Go it like hell!" he jeered, racing jubilantly after them. "Git a move on! *You* don't need no sleep, anyhow! What you want's...ex-ercise! Dammit, ex-ercise, you rippety-rip...." Cursing, laughing, shooting, he rode like a wild man, urging them on up and over the hill.

Up in camp Shorty lifted his head as the distant yelling came faint on the still air. Then came the shots and the vibrant roar of the stampede, but that was when Shorty had already jumped to his feet.

"Pile out!" he yelled. "The cattle's running!"

Five words only, but they brought every man in camp out of his blankets, and grabbing for his clothes. Not much behind Shorty's hurried dressing they jerked on their boots, stamping their feet in on their way to their horses. They untied their mounts by the sense of touch alone, felt for stirrups in the inky blackness between lightning flashes, mounted and were off, streaming down the coulee at a dead run. Even Patsy the cook was up and dressed and standing outside listening and swearing and trying to guess which way the cattle were running. Patsy had been almost caught in a stampede once when a herd had run past camp, and since then he took no chance if he could help himself.

To have a beef herd stampede in the night is a catastrophe at any time. To have it happen on the last night before they are crowded into cars and sent lurching away to market is next to the worst luck that can happen to range men at shipping-time. The ultimate disaster, of course, would be to have the herd wiped out entirely.

Shorty looked at the clouds, quiet yet as approaching storms go, and wondered what had started the cattle. The shooting, he guessed, had been done in the hope of turning the herd. Then, above the fast decreasing rumble of the stampede he heard a shrill yell he knew of old.

"Penny, by thunder!" He dug his heels into the flanks of his horse and swore aloud in his wrath. Certain broken phrases whipped backward on the wind he made in his headlong flight. "If I ever git my hands on the...." And again: "A man like him had oughta be strung up by the heels!...any damn fool that will go yellin' and shootin' into a beef herd bedded down...."

Shorty was not even aware that he was speaking. His horse stumbled over a loose rock, recovered himself with a lurch, and went pounding on across the creek and up the steep slope to the bench beyond. The horse knew and followed the sounds without a touch on the reins, would follow until he dropped or overtook the herd.

Around and behind him the riders were tearing along, their horses grunting as they took the steep hill in rabbit jumps. Good thing the cattle headed along the back trail, Shorty thought as his horse strained up the last bitter climb and lengthened his stride on the level. That hill would slow the herd down, maybe. Give the boys a chance to turn them. But with that drunken maniac still whooping up ahead, the prospect didn't look very bright.

On the left flank of the herd the night guards were racing, yelling, and shooting to turn the cattle. But they could not cover the unmistakable bellowing chant of Penny riding behind and to the right of the maddened herd and undoing the work of the left-flank boys. Shorty was so incensed that he actually turned that way with the full intention of overtaking Penny and shooting him off his horse. It seemed the only way to silence him. He didn't want to kill the cussed lunatic, but if he had to do it to shut him up no jury of range men would call it murder.

The storm clouds, too, were moving overhead, the lightning playing behind the tumbling thunderheads and turning them a golden yellow, with an occasional sword thrust of vivid flame. But still the rain did not come down upon the thirsty land. The bulk of the storm, as Shorty saw with one quick backward glance, was swinging around to throw itself bodily against the rugged steeps of the mountains beyond.

Out upon the level, as the lightning brightened for an instant the whole landscape, they saw the herd a black blotch in the distance. With the cattle they glimpsed the night herders riding alongside the left flank, swinging the galloping herd more and more to the right. Of Penny they saw nothing. There was no more shooting, no more yelling.

"He's cooled down mighty sudden," Shorty gritted unforgivingly. "But that won't do him a damn bit of good when I get my hands on him. I'll sure as hell make him wish his mother'd been a man. He's through with this outfit, the rippety-rip...."

Away on the ragged fringe of the herd rode Chip and two other herders, with voice and swinging loops forcing the leaders around until they were running back the way they had come. As the bulk of the herd followed blindly where the others led, they too changed the course of their flight. In ten minutes or less the entire herd ran in a huge circle that slowed to a trot, to a walk. "Milling," the cowboys called that uneasy circling 'round and 'round.

Within a mile or so the stampede was stopped, and except for one top hand forever disgraced and banished from the Flying U — and from the range, wherever the story seeped out — and a few broken-legged steers that would have to be shot, no harm had been done. The herd, at least, was intact. They had lost weight. Shorty would delay the shipping as long as he could hold the cars, to bring the cattle up to the best condition he could. A day, if maybe — he'd ride in and see how much time he could have. Bad enough, but it could have been worse.

He rode over to where the lightning showed him Chip and Weary, meeting and halting a minute to compare notes and breathe their winded mounts.

"Good work, boys. Where's that — ?" With as many unprintable epithets as he could string together he named the name of Penny.

"Search me, Shorty," Chip replied with a note of excitement still in his voice. "We dropped him right after we got out on the bench. He'd of had us clear down to the Missouri if he hadn't quit trying to shoot the tails off the drag. He's drunk as forty dollars."

"He'll be sober when I git through with him," Shorty promised darkly. "Bed the cattle right here if they'll settle down. Storm's goin' 'round us, I guess.

You boys stand another hour and come on in. Have to double the guard from now till mornin'.''

"Hell, listen to that wind!" Cal Emmett called out as he rode up. Men drew rein and turned in their saddles to look and listen. The clouds were thinning, drifting off to the north where the lightning jagged through the dark, but a great roaring came out of the nearer distance.

"That ain't wind," Shorty contradicted, and swung his horse around to stare at the inky blackness, until now utterly disregarded, in the east. "It's comin' from off that way." And suddenly he jumped his horse into a run toward the valley. "My God, it's water!" he yelled as he rode, and all save the night guard, doubled now to six, followed him top speed.

At the brink of the steep hillside they pulled up short and looked below. With that tremendous roaring in their ears they scarcely needed the flickering light of the distant storm or the feeble moon struggling through the clouds overhead. They could not see much, but they saw quite enough and they could guess the rest.

Down below, where the creek had meandered languidly through the willows, there was a solid, swirling wall of water. Down the coulee it pushed its resistless way, and they heard it go ravening out across the valley. The horses snorted and tried to bolt, though up there on the bench's rim they were safe. But where the herd had bedded for the night, down there beside the creek, there pushed a raging flood. Where the night hawk had taken the remuda none of them knew. Out into the valley, probably. If he heard and heeded he could run his horses to safety on high ground.

But the camp — "Patsy's caught!" yelled Shorty, and reined his horse up along the hillside. They raced up the coulee side to where they could look down upon the camp — or where the camp had stood. A smooth brown plane of water flowed swiftly there, the willow tops trailing on the surface like the hair of drowned women.

No one mentioned Patsy again. Without a word they turned and rode back to the cattle. There was nothing else that they could do until daylight.

By sunrise the flood waters had passed on, and they rode down to search for the body of their cook and to retrieve what they could of the camp outfit. They passed the wagons, overturned and carried down to the mouth of the coulee where both had lodged in the bedraggled willows.

"We'll get them later on," said Shorty, and rode on. Without putting into words the thought in the minds of them all, they knew that Patsy came first.

He did. Waddling down the muddy flat with a lantern long burned dry, he met them with his bad news.

"Poys! Der vagon iss over!" he shouted excitedly as they rode up.

"Over where, Patsy?" Shorty asked gravely with a relieved twinkle in his eye.

"On his pack, you tamn fool!" snorted Patsy. "Der vater iss take him to hell and der stove mit. I cooks no preakfast, py tamn!"

They crowded around him, plying him with questions. Patsy, it appeared, had lighted the lantern and listened with both ears, ready to run if the cattle came up the coulee. The rush of water he had mistaken for the stampede coming, and he had run clumsily to the nearest coulee wall and climbed as high as he could. He had seen the wagons lifted and rolled over and carried off down the coulee. The demolition of the tents had not impressed him half so much, nor the loss of all their beds and gear.

There was nothing to do there, then. They rode back down the coulee hunting their belongings. One man was sent to town for grub and a borrowed outfit to cook it on, together with dishes and such. Hungry as when they had left the bench, the relief rode back to the herd.

Free for the moment, Chip started up the hill alone. "Where yuh goin'?" Shorty yelled after him irritably, his nerves worn ragged with the night's mishaps.

"Going to find Penny," Chip yelled back. "You've cussed him and called him everything you could lay your tongue to...but it never seemed to occur to you that Penny saved the cattle...and a lot of your necks, too. What if you'd been asleep when that cloudburst....?"

"Aw, don't be so damn mouthy!" Shorty cut him off. "I'll tend to Penny's case."

"Well, time you were doing it, then," snapped Chip, just as if Shorty were still one of the boys with no authority whatever. "Me, I don't like the way he choked off his yelling so sudden, last night. I was on guard or I'd have looked for him then. The rest of you don't seem to give a damn."

"Now that'll be enough outa you," growled Shorty. "I guess I'm still boss around here." He spurred his horse up the hill and disappeared over the top.

And Chip, with Weary Willie at his heels as usual, followed him grinning a little to himself.

"Mamma! You want to get yourself canned?" Weary protested as their horses climbed. "Shorty's went through a lot, remember."

"Well, he ain't through yet," replied Chip, grinning. "He'll go through a change of heart, if I ain't mistaken." And he added cryptically. "He's going to find Penny." And when Weary looked at him questioningly, he only shook his head. "I got there first, as it happens. On my way down. You wait."

So Shorty found Penny. He was lying almost as he fell when his horse stepped in a hole last night. Where the horse was now a systematic search might reveal; certainly he was nowhere in sight. A faint aroma of whisky still lingered around the prone figure, but there were no bottles. Chip had seen to that.

Penny had a broken collarbone and an ear half torn off and one twisted ankle, but he was conscious and he managed to suppress a groan when Shorty piled off and knelt beside him.

"Yuh hurt, Penny?" A foolish question, but one invariably asked at such moments.

Penny bit back another groan. "The herd...did I git here...in time? Did I save...the cattle?" he murmured weakly, just as Chip had told him he must do.

"The cattle? Yeah, they're all right. Safe as hell, Penny. How...."

"Then...I got here...in time," muttered Penny, and went limp in his foreman's arms.

"And I was goin' to fire the son-of-a-gun!" said Shorty brokenly, looking up blur-eyed into Chip's face as he and Weary rode up.

ERNEST HAYCOX

ERNEST HAYCOX (1899–1950) was born in Portland, Oregon. He spent a rather unhappy boyhood in logging camps, shingle mills, on ranches, and in small towns in Oregon. He served with the National Guard on the Mexican border in 1916 and went to France for fourteen months with the American Expeditionary Force during the Great War. Following the Armistice, he attended Reed College and was graduated from the University of Oregon in 1923 with a Bachelor's degree. While still an undergraduate, Haycox started writing fiction, using an abandoned chicken coop for his office where he literally papered three walls with rejection slips before his stories began to sell. His first sale was "The Trap Lifters" to Street & Smith's *Sea Stories* (10/22). However, it was first in 1924, after having made a study of the history of the Revolutionary War, that Haycox came to concentrate exclusively on the Western and frontier story.

What certainly made the essential difference in Haycox's life was his leaving Oregon after graduation and a short stint as a reporter for *The Oregonian* in Portland (which allowed him to amass $400 to make the trip) and his going to New York to call on F.E. Blackwell, editor of *Western Story Magazine*. He met Jill Marie Chord in the club car on the train. She was from Baker, Oregon, on her way to New York to study commercial art. They were married in 1925 and went back to Portland where Haycox lived for the rest of his life. The year and a half Haycox resided in New York he always called his "starvation stretch." He had twelve stories published in *Western Story Magazine* in 1924, one a month that he pounded out on his typewriter in his room in Greenwich Village. Haycox told fellow author, Robert Ormond Case, that after he had sold three stories to *Western Story Magazine* Blackwell asked him to come again to his office. Blackwell never raised his voice, even at the climax of what he was saying, but instead would hitch his chair closer to his listener and hunch over and whisper. "Haycox," he began at this second meeting, "I've bought three of your short stories, and I think we're running into plot trouble." It was at this point that Blackwell hitched his chair closer. "In your first story, Haycox, you had two men and one woman. In your second story there were two women and one man. In your third you have one man and one woman. My God, Haycox — " (now whispering) — "*where do we go from here?*"

That kind of question from an editor was an aggravation and, back in Oregon, Haycox never again felt the need to be physically close to any of the editors who published his stories, although he corresponded extensively with them. Haycox loved working outdoors and working with his hands. In 1939 he began making improvements to a monstrous Southern Colonial-style home of some thirty rooms in the hills above Portland. He couldn't stop. Spacious lawns and gardens followed, a 400-square-foot chicken house on concrete footings, as well as a tool house and a pump house. On the generous lot he also developed a vegetable garden and planted an orchard that occupied an entire acre. He worked nights and weekends on these projects and this is what he knew and loved best, having ultimately no interest in horses or cattle ranches or guns of any kind. His writing he did during the day in an office in downtown Portland where he came and went just as if it were to a regular office job. William Mac-Leod Raine did much the same thing in Denver, Colorado, and perhaps that is why both authors wrote as much and as consistently as they did. Haycox was so steeped in Western history he could not sit through a Western film without feeling compelled to complain about inaccuracies. When he made an error, such as placing the beginning of the sagebrush a hundred miles too far east in Nebraska, his serious readers in Nebraska saw to it that he heard about it.

"It seemed reasonable," Haycox once told his son, "...that a fellow who writes about the West ought to be able to live in it." For Haycox the West symbolized not only a way of life, but a spiritual freedom, an antidote to disillusionment, no matter how fraught with hardship it might be. His relationship with Jill Marie deepened and matured his innate romanticism and, although he might scarcely have thought it possible for a woman to function at her best *without* a man, similarly he did not think it was possible for a man to function at his best without a woman. I have observed nothing in over half a century of living to contradict him.

When he was feeling his way as an author of the Western story, he wrote of what he knew, and most of his early fiction is set in Oregon, including the series of inter-related stories dealing with Burnt Creek set in eastern Oregon. Harry E. Maule who edited *West, The Frontier* (later *Frontier Stories*), and *Short Stories* for Doubleday, Page & Company welcomed Haycox, encouraged him to experiment, to set stories in various locales and time-frames. Maule serialized Haycox's first novels and Doubleday, Doran & Company, as this publisher became in 1928, published the hard cover book editions. There is a prototypical plot that Haycox worked out for his serials while writing for Maule and it was ideally embodied in a four-part serial titled "Fighting Man" in *West* (3/5/30, 3/19/30, 4/2/30, 4/16/30) and much later reprinted in paperback as ON THE PROD (Popular Library, 1957). This was a title Charles N. Heckelmann of Popular Library appended to it and its original title has now been restored for its first hard cover publication in FIGHTING MAN (London: Hale, 1994). It was in his serials subsequently for *Collier's* and book publication by Little, Brown that Haycox produced many of his finest novels, including those I have enjoyed most and read many times, SUNDOWN JIM (Little, Brown, 1938), SADDLE AND RIDE (Little, Brown, 1940), and RIM OF THE DESERT (Little, Brown, 1941). Haycox's novels are now being reprinted by Chivers Press in its hard cover Gunsmoke series, beginning with RETURN OF A FIGHTER in 1994 and SUNDOWN JIM in early 1995. With THE BORDER TRUMPET (Little, Brown, 1939) Haycox's serials became even more tied to historical events in frontier history and this tendency on his part culminated in BUGLES IN THE AFTERNOON (Little, Brown, 1944) which deals with the Custer defeat at the Little Big Horn.

It would take too much space for me to detail the degree to which Haycox was the doyen of the Western story for an entire generation of American writers of the West. Suffice it to say, that no one before him and no one after him had this kind of impact on how the Western story was told for an entire generation. Wayne D. Overholser (who also wrote as Joseph Wayne), Norman A. Fox, L.P. Holmes (who also wrote as Matt Stuart), Will Cook (who also wrote as James Keene and Wade Everett), Tom W. Blackburn, Frank Bonham, Harry Sinclair Drago (who also wrote as Bliss Lomax and Will Ermine), Charles N. Heckelmann, Barry Cord, Peter Dawson, Luke Short, Bill Gulick, Louis Trimble, E.E. Halleran, Allan Vaughan Elston, Frank O'Rourke, Noel M. Loomis, Roe Richmond, Elmer Kelton, Wayne C. Lee, Les Savage, Jr., fellow Oregon writers Robert Ormond Case, Dwight Bennett Newton, Thomas Thompson, Giff Cheshire (who also wrote as Chad Merriman and Ford Pendleton), and John Cunningham and the list could go on and on — *all* wrote novels embodying the Haycox prototypical plot. Indeed, even Nelson C. Nye did on one occasion: SALT RIVER RANNY (Macmillan, 1942). Is it any wonder when Nye and Thompson brought all these writers together in forming the Western Writers of America they at first wanted to name what became the Gold Spur Award an "Erny?" It is also for this reason that I am inclined to say that with Ernest Haycox the Western story in the 20th Century truly entered its Golden Age.

Yet, as fine a novelist as Haycox was, and as influential, he was an even better short-story writer. In his short stories he experimented more than in his serials; he introduced a wide variety of very real and sympathetic characters for intense vignettes from frontier life; he recreated a number of unusual, but historically quite accurate, situations; and he probed the inner workings of both the economic and social structures of the frontier communities he depicted. His U.S. Cavalry stories are as fine as any by James Warner Bellah and more balanced in their historical perspective. His first-person narratives of a youth growing up in New Hope, Nebraska, are reminiscent of Ernest Hemingway's Nick Adams stories and without Hemingway's bravura and posturing. Haycox short story collections have appeared and been reprinted and will soon be appearing again in mammoth bargain-book hard covers while audio versions of some of his finest short stories are being published by Durkin Hayes.

In his last years, Haycox made another change in the direction of his work. LONG STORM (Little, Brown, 1946) with its indeterminate ending and doubt-ridden characters was the *first* Haycox novel not to be serialized in any magazine. He outlined what would be a series of inter-related long historical novels which would survey the years of Oregon's frontier heritage. He signed a contract with Little, Brown to do these books and he and Jill Marie abandoned the great house on the hill for a more modest residence. Sadly, Haycox was prevented from finishing what would surely have been his *magnum opus,* although the first volume was published posthumously, THE EARTHBREAKERS (Little, Brown, 1952). In 1950 he was diagnosed with inoperable intestinal carcinoma and died twelve days after celebrating his fifty-first birthday.

"Blizzard" first appeared in *Collier's* (2/25/39). No one could surpass Haycox at evoking the bitter cold of Western winters, as early as "The Snowbird" in *Western Story Magazine* (10/11/24) — Haycox's answer, incidentally, to Blackwell's question of *"where do we go from here?"* — and as late as "Deep in this Land" in *Playboy* (1/90), in the closing pages of RIM OF THE DESERT, and above all in this story. Haycox almost always has an involving story to tell, one in which there is also something else not so readily definable that raises it above its time, an image perhaps, a turn of phrase, or even a sensation, the smell of dust after rain or the solitude of an Arizona night. He was fond of saying that writing was 95% hard work, which modestly permitted him to neglect the most vital requisite and one that he had in abundance: talent.

BLIZZARD
1939

There was no sun and no wind, but it was the kind of morning that bit into a man's bones, with a steel-colored haze lying in the south and an extreme silence covering the land. When Bill Post knocked the ice from the water bucket and washpan this sound rattled all around the Circle Dot yard; the air, he thought, was pretty thin. It was a comfort to enter the kitchen's warm smell of coffee and flapjack batter and frying bacon and sit against the table lamp's yellow light. Yet even inside the house that pervading thinness and silence were noticeable.

"Storm coming up," he said.

There were four here — Post, the cook, and two winter riders. Post said to his riders: "Still a small jag of beef in the timber. Better go up and get it out of there before snow hits."

The telephone sounded two long and two short rings for Bryce Blackerbee's ranch at Towson Crossing. This was pretty early for the phone; usually the operator in Custer didn't go on until eight. A little while later the three long bells for Dentler's store, at the edge of the badlands, grated through the house.

It kept up like this: Somebody called the Arrowhead ranch; then it was Beldings. The signals were all familiar to him and he would have listened in had he been curious, as was customary for people to do; but he knew the meaning of most of these calls. The promise of bad weather had gotten everybody busy, for a heavy storm would send down the lines by night and snow in the whole country. In a little while he heard his own ring; Bois McLean's voice alternately scratched and blasted and whispered its way across twenty-five miles of desert.

"Bill, you smell snow?"

"Sure," said Post. "I'm just startin' out to ride the drift fence."

"All right. Tom Nelson's covering it from my side. Didn't see you at the dance last night. Hell of a swell time. I guess everybody's home now. Should be, anyway, with this breeze coming along. You seen Ray Kennedy? He's supposed to be on his way here."

There were listeners on the line and now Pack Duster, at Topance Lake, broke in: "He passed here half an hour ago, Bois, packin' a headache big enough for a horse."

"And probably still thirsty," said Bois McLean. "I'll call Blackerbee's and head him off. Nobody's got any business crossin' the desert today."

Bill Post hung up at once, hearing the phone ring for Diamond-and-a-Half; everybody was trying to get everybody else and the operator at Custer wouldn't have much luck leaving the switchboard for breakfast. Post put on a long pair of wool socks, stored another pair in his pocket in case of wet feet and struggled into his sheepskin. Against possible weather he took his full-length blue army overcoat, chucked his hands into fleece gauntlets and crossed the yard to saddle a horse. Southward the loose steel coloring was more distinct and the air here was as thin as he had ever felt it to be. He cinched up the saddle and warmed the metal bit in his gloves a moment before slipping on the bridle.

"A little stick of candy, my friend," he murmured to the horse. "Come on now, sweetheart, open up those liver lips, or I'll bat down your ears."

The horse had a knot in its back and as soon as Post hit the saddle it proceeded to unravel the knot, head down and pitching over the frozen ground with a heavy grunt at each jump, the exhalations of its breathing lying like steam in the air. It was a way of getting warm for horse and rider. Post let it finish out the pitching and left the yard at a run. But he soon pulled around and returned to the house, going in to get his gun. He hadn't worn it for months and it was more or less a matter of instinct that made him take it now.

Forty miles eastward the Kettle Hills stood in low outline; behind Post, in the west, were the ragged heights of the Silver Lode. Between these two mountain chains lay the trough of the desert and up this trough the storm now made its way. A quarter-hour from the house, trotting straight over the flats, Post realized the storm would hit him broadside before he finished riding the drift fence. There was a change in the air; it was a variation of temperature that registered on his skin; it was a slow haze dropping out of the sky. This was morning, but southward the sky slowly filled with a blurring shadow.

The drift fence was a small dark line in the north, running straight over the desert to keep cattle from traveling toward the northern end of the desert. In time of blizzard it was a trap. Cattle drifting with the wind, reached it and piled against it and died there. Out in the middle reaches of the desert hulked the low shadow of Hub Weston's deserted log hut and lean-to. Bill Post aimed at it and at the scatter of beef south of it. Far over on the Kettle Hills side he thought he saw a rider's shape, but could not be sure; elsewhere — and he scanned the desert carefully to be certain of this — there were no travelers.

When he came up to the cattle he saw they were uneasy; they were winding around, heads southward, and they had quit feeding and were slowly bunching together; the instinct of danger made them do this. Woolly darkness moved toward him as he rode the edges of the small herd and put it in motion, driving it slantwise toward the Silver Lode side of the range. Back of him now the shape of the faraway rider became distinct for a moment and afterward sank into the strange-forming mist. It would be Bois McLean's rider, he decided.

He had moved the cattle perhaps a mile when a forerunning notice of the storm hit him in the shape of a half gust of dry wind that plucked up the loose soil and broken sage stems and made small clouds of dust all over the desert, like gray steam springing from the earth. He took off his hat, pulled out the chin strap, and thus anchored his headgear; and turned the direction of the beef a little to correct its inclination to give with the wind.

When the edge of the storm struck him, it was like a solid object; he felt the pony give with it and saw the cattle swing. He went around the lee edge of the herd, singing out as he rode, at once realizing that the wind was taking his words and throwing them away. There had been, all this while, the distant glimmer of his ranch lights; suddenly those lights vanished and it was dark.

He had his quick thoughts and made his quick decision. It was eight miles to the ranch, and only three back to Hub Weston's log hut. He knew then that his particular problem had changed, becoming a matter of safety for himself rather than of driving the cattle. Swinging about, he headed east for the log hut whose shape had died to the dimmest and grayest shadow in this pulsing dark. He put his horse to a run.

He had covered perhaps half the distance to the log hut more or less blind; now he saw it through the snow flurry considerably south of where he thought it to be, showing hint how much the pony had drifted. Making a point on the hut, he trotted ahead; in the back of his mind was a shadow of worry over the lone rider he had seen eastward.

Wind and snow grew greater and the shape of the hut faded behind the increasing screen of snow; he knew then that this would be a tough day and a tough night. The cattle had figured it out quicker than he had; it was just one of those faint warnings that animals get sooner than men. This snow had a cut to it and the increased chill of the wind was almost like the sensation of extreme heat on his cheekbones. There was, so far, no depth of snow on the ground. The wind swept it up in great ragged sprays and threw it forward; the wind boiled like water and whirled together great white columns of snow and then broke those columns apart, this thick mass driving across Bill Post. He had lost sight of the hut again and turned his horse to compensate for the force of the wind.

When next he saw the hut — and he saw it as a fugitive and bodiless shadow — it was almost directly south of him. He had, he discovered, missed it and would have gone by had it not been for the temporary pocket of visibility in the storm. Hauling around, he ran at it and lifted its shape out of the dizzy weave of the blizzard; coming hard by the hut, he followed its wall closely, reached a small outhouse, and sighted the lean-to farther on. The lean-to's closed side was on the windward side, making shelter. He left the horse here, walking toward the outhouse again. From this distance the hut was barely visible, though only fifty feet away; the snow kept driving in, denser and denser. In another hour, he realized, a man wouldn't be able to see his hand before him, and this thought turned him back to the hut.

When he closed the door the partial silence was a tremendous letdown, so steady had been the drive of wind against his eardrums. A rat scurried over the dirt floor and vanished in a crack; the place was clammy cold and held the rank odor of a passing skunk. This hut was a kind of emergency station for traveling riders and had a tin stove, a bunk and a table, a coffeepot and an old skillet, and usually the tag end of a few dry groceries cached in a big lard can.

Post lighted the lantern he found on the table, built a fire from the half-burned chunks of a fencepost, and put his back to the growing heat, realizing he was here for the duration of a storm, which might last a day or a week. His ears burned a little. Taking up the coffeepot, he opened the door — bracing it with his shoulder to keep it from blowing back on its hinges — scooped the pot full of snow and returned it to the stove; when the snow had melted he threw in a small fistful of coffee from a half-filled can on the table.

He had placed the coffeepot on the stove and was in the act of bending to collect the fragments of an old newspaper when he heard through the slap and rush and increasing snore of the blizzard a faint, wind-thinned sound — the sound of someone calling from a distance.

He turned to the door, opening and sliding through and closing it behind him. Wind nailed him to the door; it choked him and made him drop his head to get his breath. The hard snow rattled against the side of the hut like the strike of hard-driven grains of wheat. All he saw before him was a woolly, streaming wall of snow, solid and whitely opaque. At this stage of intensity a man could buck into the teeth of it for a little while before wearing himself out; in another hour or less it would be a force no man could face. He drew in his breath and let out a long yell, and afterward felt faintly embarrassed for having done so silly a thing; in this weather his voice had about as much effect as a lighted match. He reached inside his coat — the wind whipping it away from his legs when he unbuttoned it — and got his gun and fired twice. The two reports were thinned and smothered and carried away the moment they left the muzzle.

For one moment a crosswise current of wind broke the steady northerly sweep of the blizzard, whirling the snow upward from the immediate earth and giving Post a fragmentary view of the roundabout prairie. The shape of horse and rider stood out there, about a hundred yards off, the rider crouched low, the horse turned away. Immediately Bill Post yelled again and fired the gun. The shape on the horse roused and swung around and then the snow closed in and Post no longer saw it.

Post had to brace himself against the wind and he had to put a hand over his nose to breathe. After a half minute of waiting he fired once more; he kept this up at spaced intervals until the hammer fell on an empty shell, and got inside the hut to reload, and went out again. There was no blur in the white smother, no materializing shape; visibility was cut down to a mere arm's length, no more. Probably this was Tom Nelson, Bois McLean's line rider. Nelson was an old hand, smart enough to know what the blizzard was doing to him and smart enough to try to figure a way of reaching the hut. But this was bad. If Nelson missed the hut he was a gone coon.

Post sent out his gunshots at longer intervals. The bitter cold got at his feet; he kicked them against the ground. The ice-hard snow blasted against the exposed areas of his face like driven sand. Between periods of firing he shouted, more or less to keep active than for any other reason. It was tough to stand here with a man out there within hailing distance but he knew that if he stepped a yard away from the hut he would be blind and lost, as good as a thousand miles from shelter. When the snow lifted the next time, for one brief interval, he saw nothing of the rider. Nelson had missed the cabin and had drifted on.

He sent one more shot into the wild-racing smother. He had taken part of a step away from the wall of the hut and suddenly the wind got treacherously behind him, catching him off guard and throwing him out from the wall. It had that tremendous force. He tried to dig his heels into the hard ground. Wheeling like a vane in the wind, he saw the hut fade from sight and short fright hit him in the pit of the stomach and he fell flat on the ground, anchoring himself. He could not see the hut but he kept his eyes pinned to the one spot where he knew it must be and crawled forward, never daring to let his eyes drop. When the wall materialized he stood up and seized the latch of the door. He had his taste of that howling emptiness then; and mentally said good-bye to Tom Nelson.

He had lifted the door latch to go inside when he heard a voice again. It was straight upwind from him and broke against him and fled by, one clear high call of distress. It was clearer and nearer than before and, suddenly, turned back to face the weather, he knew something he had not known before: it was a woman. The voice was high and sharp — and within short yards of the hut.

Post fired at the sky and whipped into the hut. He seized his rope from the table, ran out and tied one end to the door latch; and with this as an anchor, he walked into the blizzard, paying out the rope. When he reached the end of the rope he stood momentarily still, stretching it as tight as he could in the hope that if the woman missed the house her horse might hit the rope and stop.

He waited long enough to know that she wasn't on this side; the wind was driving her on at another angle, or else she had done the fatal thing of dismounting. Still hanging to the rope he walked forward, the arc of the rope carrying him partly around the hut. There was nothing here. Returning to the hut he untied the rope from the door latch, crawled around the hut with his hands pressed against its wall and made another tie at the back door, searching the area as thoroughly as he could. He fired a shot and walked unexpectedly into the side of the outhouse; he struck his head against it before he saw it. Here he tied the free end of the rope, walked back along it to the hut and untied that end, and marched into the smother, making a complete circle of the outhouse with the rope as his only security. He used his gun again and caught a faint, a thin, a quick-dying fragment of a cry.

Post dragged the rope's end into the blankness again and stumbled against the hut wall. He tied the rope here and went inside, wrestling with the door. The storm died out of his ears and for a little while he could hear nothing at all; the wind had tightened his face so that when he moved his lips the surrounding skin seemed to crack. He took off his gloves and scrubbed his cheekbones, standing against the heat of the stove with his head down and his mind alive. Apparently she had sighted and overshot the hut, and had sighted it again, or had heard his gun. She had made a second effort. That would be about all in the teeth of this steadily increasing blizzard; horseflesh wouldn't stand up against another try.

Nor would this girl. Nobody could keep clearheaded out there very long. So she'd just go along with the push of the storm, and end up against the drift fence. There wasn't much chance for her after that unless she knew the country mighty well and could figure out where the drift fence led; even so it was a small chance. By the time she got to the drift fence she wouldn't have much strength left and fear would do the rest. The edge of this weather cut through anything. Well, he thought carefully, she really had no chance at all.

He took his knife and caught up a chunk of the fence post and shaved out a double handful of sticks. The coffeepot had begun to boil. He took a drink of it, scalded his tongue, and set the pot aside as he meanwhile dropped a handful of coffee beans into his pocket. Now he blew out the lamp, unscrewed its top and spilled part of the kerosene over the kindling he had made. He wrapped the kindling in a piece of old paper and jammed this small bundle into his pocket. Taking the coffeepot, he started to leave the hut, but one more thought turned him back. Screwing the lamp together, he lighted it and got another piece of paper from the floor and searched out the stub of an old tally pencil from his pocket. He stood over the table a little while, figuring the thing through in his head and at last writing this enigmatic phrase on the paper: "Drift fence — girl — Bill Post." By the time the blizzard died out, there would be ten feet of snow banked against the drift fence and it was better than an even chance both of them might be underneath. It was just a thought in case a search party later came over the desert; it might save the search party some trouble.

He blew out the lamp, still paused by the table thoughtfully, listening to the stiff whining of the blizzard around the corners of the log hut. It was a scream, an actual yell. Back of this sound was a deeper one — an immense, overpowering drone. At this moment it seemed as though all the wind in the world rushed over this desert, drowning it in fury. Bill Post lifted his shoulders and settled them — shrugging these thoughts away. He left the hut and had to brace his feet to haul the door shut. He untied the rope and followed it to the outhouse, made another tie at the back side of the outhouse and thus guided himself into weather as thick as a solid stream of oatmeal, as thick, as stinging, as suffocating. At the end of the rope he saw nothing and worked the ground slowly back and forth.

When the gray column of a lean-to post came before him he saw how badly he had drifted in the space of a fifty-foot walk. He tied the rope end to the post, left the coffeepot here and followed the rope back to the outhouse; freeing it, he pulled himself to the lean-to again, rolled up the rope and attached it to the saddle. The coffee in the pot had cooled down; now he took a long drink, emptied the pot and tied it to a saddle thong. After that he climbed to the saddle.

The lean-to's covered side broke the sweep of the wind and for a short while he sat in this dark cell of shelter scooped from the heart of a blank bitter world. The corner posts of the lean-to were well buried in the ground but the blizzard, racing up a hundred miles of open desert, hit the lean-to with tremendous impact, bending the boards, shaking the posts.

As soon as he left the lean-to the wind hit him in the back like the end of a plank. He had expected it and had braced himself; nevertheless it was worse than he had imagined. He had to grab the horn and bend down to take some of that pressure from his frame. The horse felt it, moving at a driven, running walk. The force of the blizzard boosted him head on toward the drift fence three miles north; he had no worry about riding past it, since the fence was fifteen miles long, yet he did have a problem in guessing the course of the girl once she reached the fence. Now and then he inclined the pony toward the right in order to hit the fence well eastward, in order to intercept her if she had turned that way. As soon as he released the pressure of the reins the pony straightened again, refusing to quarter the wind.

The way it was now he could hear nothing save that steady, high-above roar and whistle and scream of the wind. It was a sound a man could not describe — like an avalanche coming down a mountain, like the trembling rush of millions of gallons of water through a tunnel, like almost anything the imagination might catch up. At times during this unrelenting howl something happened to the wind above him, as though crosscurrents hit each other, and at those times it seemed that thunder burst on top of his skull. He could make out the notch of his horse's head, this silhouette growing ragged because of the forming ice on his eyebrows; a steady, painful cold ate its way through his coat and came up his legs. The heavier snow had begun to stick to the ground; he could not see it but he felt it rise around him when quick explosions of wind raked it up and threw it at him, slapping the sleety sheets against him like the stinging, salt-sharp spray of breakers. Far distant in his mind was a casual, colorless thought: "Be a damned good man if you make this."

He hit the fence long before he figured. He didn't see it, but the horse nosed into the wire and wheeled and stopped dead and for a moment it was pretty tough to have the feeling that the pony had given up. To the right lay maybe fifteen miles of fence, to the left less than six or seven, this western end breaking into the badlands. If the girl had reached the fence and had turned east, she might have passed him; otherwise she was somewhere down the western line. This was his way of looking at it. It was a gamble when he turned west following the fence. He could not afford the time spent in tracking eastward.

The wind drove at his flank; it pushed the pony into the fence, time and again, Post's legs now and then striking the top strand of wire. Each time Post hauled the pony away it drifted back; broadside, this way, the traveling was tougher. Perhaps two miles down the line he rammed a cow; it stood motionless, rump to the wind and as he bent over he saw the hard crust of sleet on its back. From this point on he began to pass cattle singly and in clusters. He had it figured out he was four miles along the fence when he came to what seemed the main bulk of the herd he had started off the desert at the beginning of the blizzard; they were in a motionless, tight bunch — the sight of them a vague blur. He went around there, passed a cow down on its knees, and faced the opaque screen of weather again; but here he was arrested by the tag end of a memory and wheeled and backtracked. In that blur of cattle there had been something standing above the dark line of their backs.

When he reached the edge of the herd he put his horse through, the cattle stupidly giving to the pressure, and he was directly beside the girl before he saw her. Her horse was trapped here and she was bent over, as if trying to sleep. She didn't see him or hear him and he had to reach over and pull at her arm. Her face, even at arm's length, was a small white blur in the gray. He saw her lips move but couldn't hear her speak. He caught her reins and worked his way out of the herd, but he stopped when he observed the way she held both mittened hands to the saddle horn. The cold had gotten at her.

He bent over and shouted: "Hold tight," and dismounted. His feet hurt when his weight went on them; his legs felt a little strange. Hanging to the reins he had some difficulty fishing out his gun. He walked over to the nearest cow and shot it point-blank through the head and gave it a push so that it fell with its belly to leeward of the wind. He had to remove his glove to get at his knife, and the sharp sting of the weather on it warned him that the contrasting dullness of his feet was a bad sign. Kneeling in the snow, still hanging to the reins of the horse, he slashed open the cow's belly; and got up again and handed his reins to the girl to hold. Back on his knees, he scooped out the dead animal's entrails, cutting recklessly. A little blood flowed and was frozen; the warmth of the cow's belly was very rank. He turned to the girl and pulled her from the horse, shouting in her ear: "Crawl in."

She went in feet first. He slashed the back quarters, giving her a little more room. She got part of her shoulders in, and lay this way, with the raw edges of the cow's belly half sheltering her. The heavy awning of ice on his brows blurred his view of her face; he knocked the ice away, bending down until her eyes were a foot away. It was the schoolteacher from Beldings, a girl who knew the country as well as he did. Looking up at him, she suddenly smiled.

He bent back, thoroughly astonished at that smile. He had caught her in time, for the cold had got at her, numbing her and making her a little light-headed. He stood up, steadily kicking his feet against the crust of snow. There was a deepening drift against the fence; the cattle were blurred all around him and would be dead by morning. He held the reins of the two horses, cool enough to measure his own resources. Maybe they could get out of this, maybe they couldn't. It was perhaps three miles to the end of the fence and a little more to the line cabin at the entrance to the badlands, hard by the fence. From the fence to the badlands was blind going, though it would not be hard to strike Donner gulch which intercepted the fence. If the snow had not drifted too deep in the gulch and if they could make these last three miles — it might be done.

He had given her ten minutes; it was a break, maybe taking the chill from her, but this was the end of it. The blizzard battered at him and when he crouched down to call her he felt the oncreep of slowness, in muscles and thinking. He helped her up; he stood by her horse, bracing her as she crawled to the side-saddle. He yelled: "All right?"

The wind tore her answer away. For a moment he debated switching his overcoat to her, regretfully decided against it. It was just one of those choices a fellow had to make; he needed the coat to live. If he didn't live, she would be dead that much sooner. When he took three tries to get into the saddle he knew then it would be a close call. He held the reins of her horse and thus with the girl beside him, he set off broadside to the full slash and venom of the blizzard at a run. Neither horse wanted to move this fast. He had to kick his own pony to it, and he had to yank at the girl's horse; there was no other way. He no longer trusted his senses completely, as to direction or as to the passage of time; because of this he now and then let the wind take them into the fence that he might be sure they still had it by them. Even so, he misjudged his distance. Coming out of the last run, he drifted with the wind and found no fence. They had ridden past it.

He stopped in the streaked, solid, stinging race of snow; he bent near the girl, shouting: "All right?" He didn't hear her answer. He was more and more suspicious of himself and took time to tie her reins about his wrist, and went on. There was a limit to all this and the limit grew nearer. They had no longer any kind of guide in this howling blast, and his head was a little bit light. Somewhere in front lay the gulch; somewhere, within a mile, lay the line cabin at the head of the gulch.

He said to himself: "I'm gettin' soft. Be careful now," and he repeated certain instructions to himself, so that they would be deep-fixed in his nerves should his head betray him: "When we get to the gulch, we turn left. We turn left." Momentarily he seemed to be afloat in this overwhelming wind. They were drifting north with it; at times he checked his pony around but always the wind carried them. He felt the horse stumble and sink and he thought he was falling, yet when the wind's force no longer pressed like a pitchfork against his ribs and when he heard it howling more distinctly overhead, he realized they had dropped into the gulch. He said doggedly aloud: "We turn left," and made the conscious swing with his arms and legs.

The horse didn't turn; it kept going straight. He didn't try a second time, realizing the pony had probably made the turn out of instinct. Somewhat later he realized the pony had stopped, and shock revived him when he realized he had been sitting dumbly in the saddle for several moments, staring at the dim wall of the line cabin. Both horses had their heads at it.

When he slid down he held to his stirrup a moment, taking no chances with the kind of dreams a man got in this coldness. He steadied himself by the head of the horse, seeking the line cabin's door and pushing it open; turning back, he pulled the girl from the off side of her horse and propped himself against her weight. He pushed her through the door and shut it and halted in the cabin's darkness, still holding her. He said distinctly: "All right?"

"Yes," she said.

He got his gloves off, slapping his hands violently together. "There's a lantern here, I remember. My matches are in my right-hand pants pocket." He had to remind himself of these things as he jerked the front of his big coat open by force. He had been so fearful of losing this girl in the storm that some of that fear still remained, even in the small room. He said, "Stay right there," and stepped across the unnatural stillness. He came up against the stove and scratched a match across its surface; the glare showed him the lantern, but it took him three matches to get the light going.

She hadn't moved from the wall. He said: "Kick your feet against the floor until you feel something." He pinched his own legs, and caught a delayed sense of pain. He opened the stove and shoved in the nest of kindling he had soaked with kerosene; when he bent behind the stove to catch up the wood in the box, he was careful to bend from the hips instead of the knees. He was still anxious, still suspicious of his luck until he saw the kindling catch the light and begin to burn. When he turned around he found her standing in the middle of the room. She had a long riding coat on, with a kind of cowled top that came over her head; all he saw was the white round surface of her face and the sparkle of the lantern's light against her eyes.

He said: "Don't sit down and don't get near the fire." He dredged the coffee beans out of his pocket, spilling them on the table, and got his knife; he walked around the room, feeling the stinging nerves in his legs and the odd kinking of muscles and the good sensation of weight on them. He faced the door, pretty reluctant to go out. But he went out, cut the coffeepot from the saddle thong and scooped it full of snow, and brought it back to the stove. She had dropped to the room's single chair; he walked over and pulled her up. He shook her by the shoulders until he saw her face change. He put his fingers against her cheeks and deliberately squeezed in. Her head jerked back; he saw the resentment in her eyes. He said: "Just wanted to make sure."

"I'm a little tired," she murmured, and sat down again.

He put the coffeepot on the stove and scooped in the beans. Going back to the girl, he saw her eyes lift and almost beg him to let her be still; but he pulled her from the chair, hooked her arm into his arm and walked her along the far wall of the room, back and forth. When he hit the floor with his boots he felt the shock of it in his heels; needlelike currents ran strongly up his legs and his cheeks were burning. The coffee had begun to boil when he let the girl go.

"Sure you're all right? No dead places?"

"I'm all right."

He faced the door, dead-beat, yet knowing he had another chore to do. He went out, closing the door behind, and unsaddled the horses, throwing this gear and the saddle blankets inside the hut. He took off the bridles and watched the horses move into the riot and whirl of snow. There would be a kind of shelter for them under the cut bank. He reëntered the cabin.

She stood by the stove, holding an empty can she had found in the cabin. She stood there, waiting for him, with her eyes holding to him as he crossed the room, with her body caught in thorough stillness. When he was quite near she turned to fill the can from the coffeepot, and held it out to him. It was the way she held it — upward in both her hands — and the way her eyes — black as night — rose and remained on him, that hit him solidly under the heart.

He said, "Go ahead and drink it."

"No," she said in a soft, indrawn voice. "You're first." The blackness of her eyes seemed to break, and a light showed through; and then the blackness returned. "Do you know what I mean? This is as near as I can say it."

The coffee was rank; it was hot and took the chill out of him. It made him cheerful and sound again, the old vigor running smooth and strong through him. Looking back over the past hours, he found it a little difficult to remember how tough it had been.

He gave her the can, watching her refill it and stand by the stove, warming her hands and slowly sipping the coffee. She had removed her coat and he saw that she was a tall round-armed girl and that her lips were long and red by the lantern's yellow light. She closed her eyes when she drank; her hair was heavy; it was a brilliant dark shade.

He said: "How'd you get out in this?"

"I went to the dance last night. It didn't look bad early this morning when I set out. It caught me halfway. I heard your shots from Hub Weston's hut. I went around it twice. Then I just said, 'So long,' and drifted."

"Well," he said, "it's the long way home."

She came by him, taking one of the blankets. There was an upper and lower bunk in this small room. He watched her settle into the lower bunk and curl up like a small child and spread the blanket over her. He went back to the stove, slowly soaking in the heat; he bent his head over it, closely thinking of all this — of how it had been, and of her. It was pretty hard to talk about. Probably neither of them would ever say anything more about it, but the memory was there and it would stick. Suddenly he removed his heavy coat and carried it to the bunk. He laid it over her and took her hand as it came out to catch his heavy fingers. The wind had loosened her hair; it lay around her head, softening her face, and she was smiling and her black eyes held him completely.

"The long way home," she murmured. Standing there, holding her hand, he watched her features sweeten and soften, until she was asleep, with a half-smile remaining on her lips.

PART THREE

STORYTELLERS OF
THE GOLDEN AGE

PETER DAWSON

JONATHAN HURFF GLIDDEN was born in 1907 in Kewanee, Illinois. Eighteen months later Jon's younger brother, Frederick Dilley Glidden, was born. The brothers — almost black Irish twins, as the expression went — grew up in Kewanee and were very close. Their father, who worked as the treasurer of the Kewanee Boiler Company, died of coronary thrombosis while on a fishing trip in 1921. He was little more than forty years of age. Their mother lived to a ripe age, dying in 1973, two years before her younger son and twenty-three years after her elder son.

Both of the Glidden brothers entered the University of Illinois at Urbana. Jon remained until he was graduated in 1929 with a Bachelor's degree in English literature. Fred transferred to the University of Missouri at Columbia where he was graduated with a Bachelor's degree in journalism. While Fred ventured to Canada where he trapped furs and took a number of odd jobs, Jon in the meantime married Dorothy Steele whom he had met while at the university and secured a good job with Cities Service Oil Company, selling gas conversion burners. He was based in Lexington, Kentucky. Fred, something of a fiddlefoot, had come somehow to work as an archeologist's assistant outside Santa Fe, New Mexico, and had married Florence Elder of Grand Junction, Colorado. Fred had tried various newspaper jobs, but none had panned out for him. He started writing Western fiction for the magazine market and was making a living at it when he wrote to Jon, urging him to come for a visit. Jon and Moe, as Jon called his wife, visited Santa Fe and Fred launched a major campaign to convince Jon he should be an author of Western fiction. Jon's argument that Fred was the journalism major fell on deaf ears. Butch, as Fred called his wife, was writing, too. Her first story, titled "The Chute to Love," had been sold to *Rangeland Romances* for $50. Fred wrote as Luke Short, Butch as Vic Elder. Jon agreed to give writing a try.

Setting up a table and typewriter in the basement of the Lexington home, after eight hours of sales work Jon would write. He sent his stories to Fred who would return them with suggestions. Finally upon reading Jon's story, "Gunsmoke Pledge," Fred thought it good enough to send to his agent. The agent sold it to *Complete Stories* for $135. The name the agent, Marguerite E. Harper, chose for Jon was Peter Dawson and he would write under this name for the rest of his natural life, predominately Western fiction, but some detective and aviation stories as well, and a number of magazine serials later published as Western novels.

Moe figured it would require $200 a month for them to live if Jon was only to write and she was supportive of him in the effort. What he wrote was readily sold and soon he was earning more than the minimum Moe had set. By 1937, they had moved to New Mexico and bought an 18th-Century hacienda across the road from Fred and Butch in Pojoaque. In his Western fiction, Jon followed a very different course from the one Fred pursued. Fred preferred serials. Jon worked at the shorter forms, in part because the short story and short novel allowed him to depart from the obligatory structure in most serials of a hero, heroine, and villain, with the story ending in a romance. In "Owlhoot Reckoning" in *Western Story Magazine* (8/20/38), the protagonist is forty-three years old and has spent his last fifteen years in Yuma State Prison. He has a limp in his right leg (other authors might have a character who limps but would not, as Jon, bother to tell the reader which leg was affected), a slight stoop to his shoulders, and an ugly, shiny scar on his right cheek dating back eight years to a prison riot. This character, Trent Stone, could never be a Luke Short hero, a man usually in his twenties.

Although he became a master of the short story form (the one film based on his work so far is an adaptation of a short story), Jon also wrote many excellent short novels. One of them — which he titled "One Man Hold-Out" and which was retitled "A Gun-Champion for Hell's Half-Acre" when it appeared in *Complete Western Book Magazine* (7/39) — concerns Ed January who refuses to sell his land as part of a sheep-ranching scheme. Bill Atwood, an old prospector killed on Ed's land while Ed is away, inspires Ed to reflect: "'The good ones always seem to go first. I hope it was clean and quick. That's the way he'd want to go.'" From this and numerous similar remarks throughout Jon's Western fiction, I surmise that the death of his father had a greater emotional impact on him than it did on Fred. This short novel, possessed of complex plotting, deft movement, fine characterizations, with a mystery that is illumined through delayed revelation, augmented by adept dialogue, is indicative this early of Jon's basic approach to his fiction. He worked at it, writing and rewriting, polishing, improving a scene with small but telling refinements. Jon also insisted on working at his own pace, which tended to infuriate Marguerite Harper, while Fred worked comparatively fast, completing a 60,000-word serial in as little as six weeks.

Jon was still writing for the magazine market, producing such fine short novels as "Ghost Brand of the Wishbones" which appeared as the "novel" in *Western Novel and Short Stories* (6/40) under the title "Half-Owner of Hell's Last Herd," when Street & Smith and Dodd, Mead announced a $2,000 prize for a first Western book-length novel. Fred had written serials for *Western Story*

Magazine and *Argosy* but he had graduated by the late 1930s to writing for *Collier's*. With Fred urging Jon to try it, and Harper doing the same (largely because Street & Smith wanted someone who wrote "just like Luke Short"), Jon did. The result was THE CRIMSON HORSESHOE (Dodd, Mead, 1941) which won the prize and was run serially in *Western Story Magazine*. Even though Jon would follow this novel with a highly successful and distinguished group of Western novels, he also continued to write short stories and short novels.

It was a good way of life. Up and at work by 7:30AM, working five hours, then breaking to polish well into the afternoon until Moe would come in softly and offer him a sandwich. The Second World War changed that. Fred was often in Hollywood and then in 1943 worked briefly in Washington, D.C., for the Office of Strategic Services. Jon entered the U.S. Army Air Force and attended Officer Candidate School in Miami in 1942. He was sent to London with the U.S. Strategic and Tactical Air Force. Jon was stationed in France, near Versailles, at the time of the occupation of Germany and was about to be deployed to the Pacific theater when Japan capitulated.

As Fred aged, he grew increasingly bored with writing Western fiction. His Golden Age was from 1938 to 1949. After that, he published less and less and virtually all of it is inferior to his earlier work. It was quite the opposite for Jon. He returned to Pojoaque and to writing, providing fiction for the magazine market as well as novels published by Dodd, Mead. RENEGADE CANYON (Dodd, Mead, 1949) was the first of four Peter Dawson novels serialized by *The Saturday Evening Post*.

In 1950 Jon was asked to return to service, this time as Assistant to Chief of Station in Germany. It was during this two-year tour of duty that he began experiencing severe angina pains. In fact, his stay in Germany was shortened by six months due to medical problems. He suffered his first heart attack while attending his twenty-five year reunion at the University of Illinois. He was living in New Mexico and writing, having just completed his serial, "Treachery at Rock Point," for the *Post,* when he went on a fishing trip to the Wagon Wheel Ranch near Creede, Colorado. It was while on this trip, much as had happened to his father, that Jon suffered his final heart attack.

Peter Dawson emerged in a period during which quite a number of outstanding authors wrote Western fiction and he still came to be recognized as a highly gifted and original talent. The more historical research he would do, the more he enjoyed what he wrote, and that sense of discovery and enjoyment continues to enhance the vast body of his work, a substantial achievement for any writer to have accomplished in a career that lasted only a little over two decades. Jon Glidden's Western stories remain remarkable for their precision, suspense, and the complexity of their narrative structures. Moreover, to the extent that a distinction can be made between plot and story, they are engaging for the interaction between various characters and the perceptive use of group psychology within frontier communities. Presently many of his finest novels, GUNSMOKE GRAZE (Dodd, Mead, 1942), HIGH COUNTRY (Dodd, Mead, 1947), and DEAD MAN PASS (Dodd, Mead, 1954), among them, are being reprinted in hard cover editions by Chivers Press in its Gunsmoke series.

"Retirement Day" was sent to Marguerite Harper on February 11, 1939. She was apparently not too fond of its off-trail plot, but it was sold for $45 on October 30, 1941 to the recently launched *Western Tales* from Popular Publications where it appeared in the February, 1942 issue. After the war, Jon would continue to do some of his best work for this magazine which, after this issue, changed its name to *Fifteen Western Tales* and, alone of Popular Publications' Western pulp magazines, emerged in late 1954 as a slick, bed-sheet size magazine. "Retirement Day" embodies several of the concerns and preoccupations Jon Glidden brought to the Western story, not the least of these being that a culture may be judged by the manner in which it treats its older members.

RETIREMENT DAY
1942

Slim, the apron, poured out a double shot of rye whiskey and told old Joe Miles, "This is on the house, Joe. For old time's sake."

The half dozen men at the bar heard Slim and tried not to look at Joe, making small talk among themselves and not doing very well at it.

When old Joe said, "So long, boys. See you...well, see you one of these days," they bid him good-bye with a forced cheerfulness and were relieved when the swing-doors up front hid his stooped slat of a figure.

"To hell with the railroad!" Slim grunted, rinsing Joe's glass and toweling it viciously. "To hell with all these new-fangled ideas! There's probably the last time we'll ever lay eyes on that old jasper. He's still a good man and they're kickin' him out."

"He's sixty-seven," someone ventured.

"He's as old as he thinks he is," Slim glowered at the speaker. "And until they gave him the sack, he was younger'n me or you. Listen here, brother...," Slim leaned across the bar and wagged a forefinger in the man's face, not caring that his customer was a comparative newcomer and didn't know Joe Miles as well as he did the rest, "I've seen that old fool work three nights runnin' without sleep, freightin' food in here from the rail-head through a blizzard you'd be scared to stick your nose out into. I've seen him take a three-team stage over a washed-out hill trail you'd balk at walkin' a mule across. Don't tell me Joe's no good any more. When his old heart stops pumping, when they've throwed six feet of dirt on him, then he'll be ready to retire."

A stillness settled over the near-empty saloon. No one had a word to say. It was, in a way, the most fitting tribute paid Joe Miles that day.

Going along the street toward the stage station, old Joe hunched up his narrow shoulders and tilted his head down, so that the rain didn't hit his face but instead trickled down off the limp brim of his wide Stetson. He felt tired today, utterly weary for the first time in his keen memory. Maybe he was getting too old, like they said. He let himself get only so far along that line of thinking before he grumbled a ripe oath and hurried on.

He turned in off the walk at the office of the Blue Star Stage Lines, a weathered frame shack at the front of a huge hump-roofed barn. The man behind the wicket looked up from under his green eye-shade as Joe came in and said in an embarrassed attempt at joking, "It'd spoil things if you had good weather for your last run, eh?"

The oldster snorted, shook the rain from his coat. "What're they doin' with you, Len?"

"Makin' me bookkeeper down at Sands. I go down Tuesday, by train."

"Reckon I ought to ride the blamed thing myself just to see what it's like," old Joe said, smiling wryly, his lips a thin line below his cornsilk longhorn. "Maybe I ought to ask the railroad for a job, seein' as how they done me right plumb out of this one."

The door opened and a tall rangy man strode in, shaking the rain off his slicker. This was Ray Dineen, thirty and married. For ten years he had ridden shotgun alongside old Joe on the stage run out of this mining camp to Sands, the town on the plain, where the Blue Star had its division office, halfway along its main line.

Ray was making this last trip down with old Joe today, riding shotgun on the bank's regular week-end payroll shipment. Rumor had it that the money chest would contain an additional fourteen thousand in gold for the railroad crew working out of Sands. There wasn't going to be any fuss taking it through, since the rail officials weren't anxious to attract attention. Starting next week, the new spur would be finished and they would be sending trains through here and down to Sands and this short branch of the Blue Star Lines would be a thing of the past.

Ray Dineen said, "Hi yuh, Joe," and his face was serious. He had something to say and didn't know how to say it. Finally he blurted out, "I did every damn thing I could, Joe. Saw that young pup, Ted Baker, the new superintendent. What a boss! My age, and he's orderin' around men old enough to be his father." He shook his head soberly. "It's no use, Joe. Baker claims you're too old. He brought up that business about our gettin' drunk down in Vegas last December, too. Said I was lucky to be stayin' on after what happened."

Old Joe nodded. "Maybe we did raise too much sand that night. But we got here on time, didn't we, drunk or sober? And we didn't kill no horses or wreck no equipment." He shrugged, as though dismissing the thought. "What have they lined up for you, Ray?"

A little of his inward pride couldn't help but show in Ray Dineen's eyes. "They're giving me a try at the ribbons."

Old Joe's eyes lighted up. He smacked a fist into an open palm. "Drivin'? The main line! Ray, there's big pay, a future. I'll give you ten years before they make you division superintendent."

Ray shook his head. "But that's the job they should be givin' you. Hell, you deserve it. I don't."

"Don't go soft-hearted for me," Joe said. "I got plans for the future. Besides, I got a notion I ought to retire, live on my savin's."

"What savings? You borrowed twenty from me last pay-day." Ray Dineen's square face took on a bull-dog look. But then he saw the pointlessness of the argument, swore, and said, "Let's get her rolling. They're waitin' out there on the walk by the bank. They'll be sore if we don't hurry."

Five minutes later, slicker on, his Stetson pulled down hard on his ears, old Joe wheeled the Concord down off the barn ramp and led his two half-wild teams of Morgans down-street under tight rein. No passengers were along this trip. Lately the load had been mostly freight, as today. Ray Dineen sat beside Joe, a double-barreled Greener cradled across his knees. As the Concord pulled in at the edge of the walk by the bank, where four guards waited with a brass-bound money-chest, the rain was coming down in a relentless spray whipped by the wind. The street was a sea of mud, fetlock deep to the horses; the town had a bedraggled, sodden look about it.

"Sling her up here where we can keep an eye on 'er," Joe shouted to the guards, pitching his voice to carry above the drone of rain on a nearby tin roof. He and Ray reached down, got a hold on one of the chest's leather handles, and heaved it to the boot beneath them.

While Ray lashed it in place with a length of half-inch rope, Joe called, "O' course we'll make it," in answer to a question Len Rivers, president of the bank, shouted from the doorway.

The teams slogged into the pull a moment later, and the Concord rolled out from the walk and down the street, past the stores and the awninged walks, past the few brick and frame houses and the many tar paper shacks along the cañon slopes, and finally out past the shaft houses of the Dolly Madison and Wee Willie mines.

Then the town lay behind and the stage was rolling along a winding trail through the high pines and scrubby cedars. Old Joe hadn't paid the town much attention purposely, for he hated good-byes and knew he might never again see the place he'd called home for thirty-four years. He'd live down in Sands from now on, get a cheap room and be handy for a job if any came along. The railroad was hiring men at pick and shovel work along the new right of way. Maybe they'd take him on.

"What did Rivers say?" Ray Dineen shouted above the downpour and the rattle of doubletree-chains and the creaking of harness.

"Asked me if I thought we could get across Graveyard Wash," old Joe growled. "As though I hadn't been drivin' this road long enough to know!"

Ray frowned. "I wondered about that myself. Sue and the kids are ahead somewhere in the wagon. They want to get to Sands before dark."

"They'll make it," old Joe said, expertly concealing the instant's tightening of worry inside him. Sue Dineen and Ray's kids, Ellen and young Tommy, heading down out of the mountains in a storm like this? Sue with a wagon-load of goods, furniture, bedding, all their worldly possessions. And she a frail woman at that, barely able to manage a team!

He was blaming Ray when he remembered that at one o'clock, two hours ago, the sun had been shining on a balmy summer afternoon. This had been one of those freak summer storms, with the clouds piling up behind the peaks for the last two days and spilling their rain when they rolled on over the mountains to hit the cold up-drafts on this side. It would be a good long rain if old Joe's weather eye was cocked right.

Joe decided not to worry. Sue had good enough sense not to head across Graveyard Wash if there was any water running. It was different with an old hand like him. He'd cheated the Graveyard more times than he could count on his gnarled fingers and crooked toes. He'd learned to gauge the water that foamed along the bed of that hundred-yard-wide wash that ran a torrent each time it even sprinkled in the hills. He'd taken his stage across many a time with half a day's traffic of riders and wagons and rigs held up on the road on each side, all afraid to tackle the surging flood of water. Once he'd caught hell for it from the superintendent when the water boiled in over the floor below and soiled the dress of a woman passenger.

Four miles down-cañon old Joe hit the first wash-out in the trail, with a fifty-foot drop to the cañon floor on one side and a sheer climbing wall on the other. The Concord swayed dangerously, but was righted with perfect precision as Joe flicked one on-wheeler's rump with his whip and made the animal lunge into the pull. As the right rear wheel hit solid ground again and jarred the vehicle clear to the throughbraces, Ray Dineen suddenly groaned and doubled up with pain. He straightened a second later, but not before old Joe had shot him a glance to see his rugged face white and lined in agony.

Old Joe tightened the ribbons and drove home the brake. "Bouncin' too much, Ray?" he called.

Ray shook his head. "Gut ache. It must be something...." A griping pain took him and he broke off his words and doubled over once more. His hand went to his side, below his belt. Then he caught himself and straightened up, taking his hand away. "Go on. I'll be all right in a minute or two."

"We'll stop at Ford's," Joe said. He knew the signs, had seen men taken with appendicitis before. He was wondering how long it would take John Ford to hitch his team to his buckboard and get Ray back to town. One thing they could all be thankful for was young Doc Slade, the sawbones who'd come in last year and started healing people instead of feeding them those sugar pills old Doc Wheelwright had left in his office when he died.

They drove in at Ford's, a thirty-acre ranch in a clearing along the cañon, a quarter hour later. By that time the pain had hit Ray once again and then eased off.

Ray was stubborn and wanted to go on.

"What'll Sue and the kids do without me?" he kept insisting.

"I'll look after Sue," old Joe said. He met John Ford halfway between the yard fence and the house, explaining what he wanted.

"Sure, I'll take him in, right away," Ford agreed. Joe turned and started back toward the Concord, but Ford reached out and took a hold on his arm, saying in a lower voice, "But there's something you ought to know before you go on, Joe. Chet Richter and Barney Ryan went past here about an hour ago, headed out to the road."

"What have them two tramps got to do with this? I tell you Ray's sick, John. You hurry and get that team harnessed." He started out across the yard again.

"Listen, you bull-headed old fool!" Ford called. "Think a minute. I said Chet Richter and Barney Ryan. You're carryin' the railroad's gold, ain't you?"

"And I'll be carryin' you out to that wagon-shed unless you get a sudden move on!"

"Chet and Barney were fired last Tuesday for tryin' to lead the crew out on strike. They've been tryin' to work off their grudge against Paul Duval all week. Don't that mean nothin' to you?"

It did. Old Joe finally got it. What Ford could have said in as few words was that Chet Richter and Barney Ryan were a couple of hard cases, that they'd been fired for making trouble for Paul Duval, boss of the section gang working the railroad right of way below town, and that it wasn't out of the realm of possibility to suppose that they'd try and hold up the stage on the road and get even with Duval and the owners.

Old Joe faced John Ford with an angry light blazing in his watery blue eyes. He was worried, tired, and his patience was worn thin. "John, you ain't never got over shootin' that rustler twenty years ago. These ain't the old days. If Chet and Barney laid so much as a finger on that money-chest they'd have every railroad detective this side of Kansas City out after 'em. Now get that rig ready and get Ray to town to Doc Slade. And if Ray don't get there in time, you're answerin' to me...plenty!"

Old Joe felt lost and worried five minutes later, as John Ford, Ray beside him, drove his buckboard out of sight up-cañon, around a turning in the trail. He climbed up onto the seat and kicked off the brake. He cut the lead team across the ears with his whip, sorry the moment he'd done it. He had never abused his animals.

He settled to the long grind, and the rain turned into a downpour lashed by a cold wind, whipping up a spray off the rocks and trees that made it hard to see the road ahead. It was as miserable a drive as Joe could remember. He was cold to the bone and, in his sodden discomfort, without Ray's company, he was once more an old man, lonely, without hope, finished.

He had a few regrets, not many. Of course he should have saved his money through the years, put enough aside so that he could spend these last empty years in some degree of comfort, resting. Probably he should have married

Martha Drew forty years ago, instead of being afraid to ask her and letting her wait so long she'd finally gone away with Spence Amsden.

But he admitted grudgingly that his good times and his throwing away his money had made up for most of the things he lacked now. When a man couldn't any longer work, he ought to crawl into a hole and pull it in after him.

He thought of John Ford, and of Chet Richter and Barney Ryan. He reached down and took the old Greener from the hangers under the seat and broke open the weapon, seeing that the buck-shot loads were fresh. Then he laughed.

"That's one thing you never was, Joe Miles...spooky!" he growled as he hung the shotgun under the seat again.

He hadn't thought much about the payroll but, now that he remembered it, he was thinking of the old days when the town up above was booming, when every gold stage carried gun-guards inside and out, and even then sometimes didn't get through with their precious freight. That was forty years ago, when the scum of humanity had flocked into these hills with the gold fever, when he'd worn a six-gun, the same as he'd worn his boots, and used it often.

But today wasn't forty years ago. The formality of sending a guard along with each payroll shipment was merely a habit of Len Rivers's, who was of the old school, Joe's school, that had lived the hard way. In case of real trouble, a driver was expected to hand over what was in the boot and let the insurance detectives take care of running down the thieves. Chet Richter and Barney Ryan! Two undersized, lazy tramps who couldn't give a real man a workout either with guns or fists. Men didn't know how to use guns any more, not the way they had forty years ago.

This country was settled, civilized; the stages were giving way to the railroads. Joe Miles and his generation were giving way to men like Ray Dineen and Ted Baker, the new Blue Star superintendent, men who would bring in new and better equipment, run it faster and longer and make more money, advancing ahead of the railroads and maybe in the end going over to the railroads themselves. In this sober moment, old Joe saw that his going was symbolic of a dying age, and in his loneliness he was a little proud of his past, glad he wasn't beginning in this new era of change.

The cañon walls fell away and the trail cut in through the low foothills, and in the next two hours old Joe crossed three washes running water, one badly. The rain still held to a steady downpour. He heard the far-off roar of Graveyard Wash from a half mile's distance, and gauged its sound. It was running high; two more hours, he judged, would find it impassable.

His first sight of the wide wash brought a dry chuckle out of his flat chest. Muddy water boiled bank to bank across its hundred-yard width. Already there was better than a foot and a half of water, with three-foot waves churning up over the bars and the sand riffles. There was some driftwood, small seedling trees and bushes that had probably fallen in with caved cutbanks. Soon there would be larger trees. In fact, there was one down already, barely in sight upstream, a half-foot-thick cottonwood, branches sheered off along its straight trunk, its huge bole of spreading roots turning slowly in cartwheel fashion as it rolled lazily with the force of the current.

He drove as far as the down-grade cutting in the high bank, a pleasing excitement running along his nerves, making him forget how he'd felt back a ways. This was what his life had been, a series of small adventures testing his ingenuity and toughness. Like this, getting two teams and a heavy stage across a roaring torrent. Few men could do it without letting an animal go down or bogging in quicksand. He could; he was still tough enough to do it right.

He pulled in the teams, letting his eye run over harness, the lashings on the boot; he tested the brake, spotted the line of the road opposite and lifted the reins to send his Morgans into the down-grade.

He heard the cry then, faint yet unmistakable.

"Ray! Ray!"

It was muted by the roar of the water, yet there was an emergency to the voice that brought him to his feet, looking downstream. Then it came again from downstream, "Ray!" and he was gripped in a paralysis of stark, sudden fear.

It was Sue Dineen's voice.

His bleak old eyes whipped over the angry waters. What he saw made him lift his whip. Twenty rods below, within a quarter of that distance of a sage -studded narrow strip of land still above water toward the far bank, he saw the wagon and the horse and Sue and the kids.

The wagon was bottom-side up, the wheels half out of water. Sue clung to the hub of the near front wheel, only her head and shoulders showing and the water foaming about her shoulders, pressing her in against the wheel. She was caught there; otherwise she'd be with the kids, who were standing above her on the overturned bed of wagon, only to their knees in water. One horse was down, drowned, his four stiff legs sticking out of the water. The weight of the carcass must have been dragging at the harness for, as Joe took that one fleeting look, he saw the remaining animal lunge and try to break loose.

With the horse's lunge, Sue screamed. Joe heard it plainly and laid his whip to his teams. As the Concord lurched ahead, tilted into the down-grade, a distant explosion sounded out from behind. Joe looked back there. A hundred yards back along the trail he saw two riders coming in fast toward him. The one he recognized as Chet Richter aimed a six-gun and fired at him as he watched.

The Concord lurched badly, righted itself, and the Morgans shied down off the bank and into knee-deep water. Old Joe laid on his whip, forgetting that to trot a horse in fast water is unsafe. The off-wheeler stumbled, went to his knees and was up again. Joe held the horses to a walk, his eye on the wagon downstream. It might have been his imagination, but he thought that Sue was already lower in the water than when he'd first seen her.

All at once, fifty yards out, the right front wheel went down. Too late, old Joe remembered that there was quicksand out here. He whipped the teams and they were pulling clear of the sand when suddenly a bronc went down. An instant later the report of a shot cut into the steady roar of the rushing water. Joe looked back to see Chet Richter and Barney Ryan about to head their horses into the water after him. Barney had shot the horse.

The Concord's front wheel sank lower into the quicksand. Then, lazily almost, the stage went over on its side. Joe jumped, landed on the back of the animal alongside the downed bronc, and with his clasp-knife he cut the wounded, kicking horse from the tangle of harness. He slid off the back of the animal, stood on the long tongue of the coach. Then, the water boiling about his legs and threatening to drag him off his slender perch, he unhitched the lead team from all but their singletree.

The last thing he did before leaving the over-turned Concord was to edge back and cut the lashings from the front boot. He worked feverishly while he watched Barney Ryan and Chet Richter wade their ponies on through the water toward him, Richter brandishing his pistol and calling something unintelligible above the roar of the water. The chest slid out from the ropes, stuck on a metal brace. Old Joe kicked it viciously and it finally slid into the water with a sucking splash to sink out of sight.

He shook his fist at Ryan and Richter, twenty yards away now and coming fast. Then he freed the one remaining wheel bronc with a few deft slashes of his knife and threw himself on the back of one of the leaders. He drove them away from the stage, clear of the tongue, and cut obliquely out at a walk toward the over-turned wagon.

He was almost even with it; every muscle in him strained to use the ribbons as a whip; yet he knew it meant disaster and a quick death if the horse he rode lost his footing on the shifting sandy bottom. He looked back once to see Chet Richter sitting his pony alongside the stage, holding Ryan's. Ryan was aboard the Concord, kicking in a window, probably in search of the money-chest. Old Joe laughed harshly at the thought of how futile their search would be.

Working in toward the wagon now, he called encouragingly, "Steady, Sue! I'm comin'."

Then he happened to look upstream. There, less than forty yards away, rolling relentlessly down in line with the wagon, turned the huge bole of the uprooted cottonwood, enough weight in rock and soil in its roots to crush the wagon like matchwood.

"Ray!" Sue called. Then she saw who it was. "Joe! Hurry!" Her voice jerked him out of his momentary paralysis.

Tom, Ray's ten-year-old boy, was holding onto his sister, Ellen. His straight yellow hair, like his Dad's, was plastered down across his forehead. He was crying, calling out in a choking voice to his mother, trying to reach down to take her hand.

The water was up to Sue Dineen's neck, occasionally boiling up over her head so that her call to Joe as he drove the horses alongside was a gasp. "Joe, I'm caught. My legs are under the wagon. Take the children, Joe. Please! Get them away before it's too late."

Joe slid off the back of the horse, holding the reins tight. "Hold on a minute longer," he called. He darted a glance at the oncoming cottonwood. It was closer, but rolling out of line. There would be time enough now. The water sweeping up his thighs, he waded over and took Ellen under one arm, Tom under the other.

Tom fought, screaming, "Don't leave Mother!" until Joe said, "We'll get her out. Now you act like a man, Tom." He carried the children back to the horses, and lifted them onto the back of the nearest. "Hold on tight to the belly-band," he shouted, and clamped their hands to the leather. Then he left them for the wagon again.

He was working with an intent coolness now, not wasting a move. He caught up the one rein of the frantic bay horse still hitched to the wagon. Somehow he backed the animal and then headed him downstream. He gathered the one rein and all at once lashed out fiercely, yelling his lungs out in a high-pitched sharp yell. The horse, frightened into violent action, lunged against the harness. Joe whipped the animal unmercifully. The wagon slid, turned on its side, and then rolled on downstream as though its weight was no more than a packing box's.

Sue tried to stand, couldn't, and went under. Joe was swept off his knees as he lunged to stop her from being dragged on with the current. He went under, then, miraculously, caught a hold on her skirt and held it.

He struggled to his feet, picked the girl up and carried her to the horses. She was a dead weight in his arms, limp, but somehow Joe managed to throw her over the back of the horse alongside her children. He slapped her face hard. She stirred and her eyes opened.

He yelled, "Plenty of time now, Sue. Grab a hold and I'll climb on with the kids." She heard him, pulled herself onto the Morgan's back and took a hold on the heavy collar, a wave of thankfulness flooding her eyes as she saw that her children were there beside her.

Joe worked on around her horse and in alongside the other. On the way, he saw the cottonwood, its huge bole towering twice as high as his head, ten feet to one side. He was relieved that it had finally rolled out of line with them.

All at once the lower roots tilted crazily. They must have struck a boulder, for the weight of the bole fell outward and whipped the trailing stem of the tree out of the water. It rose from the current in a blinding sheet of spray. The Morgan shied. Old Joe, a weak hold on the harness-strap, was dragged off his feet.

The horse lunged, Joe's boots came down into the surging water, and his hold broke. He fell face down into the muddy roiling water, his last glance toward the Morgans showing them lunging into a run. Then he was under, rolling over and over along the gravelly bottom. His lungs fought for air, but he held his breath. Then he managed to strike out with hands and knees and slow the force of his rolling weight. The next time he turned over, he was facing squarely downstream, with the current at his back. He struggled to his feet, his head above water and his lungs dragging in pure cold air. He got one full breath before the water swept his legs from beneath him and he was down again.

This time he was under longer, fighting, trying to remember what little he knew of swimming. Once more his head was above water; once more his lungs gasped for air. He struggled to his knees, to his feet. He spread his legs far apart, bracing himself against the mighty suck of the water. He looked downstream. The rolling bole of the cottonwood, trailing its slender trunk, was now nothing but a shadow in the blur of rain, fast disappearing. The horses were out of sight.

He screamed time and again, "Sue! Sue, answer me! Tommy! Ellen!" but his voice was only a feeble croak in the rush of water and the torrent of the storm.

The strength left his legs and he knew he was going down again, and this time he didn't care. He was too tired to care. He looked dully downstream once more. Coming toward him, dragging the broken front axle and one wheel of the wagon, was the remaining horse of Ray Dineen's team of bays. The horse was plunging wildly, crazed with fear, straight up the stream.

Joe struggled five steps and caught the one trailing rein as the horse lunged by. He held on, dragged hand over hand up the rein until he was alongside the animal. Then, in a last desperate effort, holding to the harness collar, he pulled the horse's head in toward the far bank, his legs dragging along the wash's rocky bottom. The bay stepped on him, tried to kick him, but he was lucky enough to keep his body out of line with the slashing hoofs.

Five minutes later the bay was standing head down on the stream bank, and old Joe was lying on his back in the sand, arms aching.

When he could move, he started walking downstream, looking for some sign of Sue and the children. All he could remember was the plunging horses; the children couldn't have held on. He walked back and forth until dark, and all he found was the blue sweater Ellen had been wearing, caught on the branch of a dead willow two miles below the road. He gave up then, knowing the answer.

He walked back as far as the road and sat on the bank, looking out at the rushing waters through the darkness. There was four feet of water running now, nothing showing of the Concord but one rear wheel idly turning in the current. The rain had stopped. Later, the sky cleared and the stars came out. He walked a half mile looking for Ray Dineen's bay horse and finally caught him. He found signs along the road that told him Chet Richter and Barney Ryan had ridden back into the hills. He gave them little thought, thinking mostly of Sue and those two kids of Ray's.

At midnight, when he judged he could get the horse across the wash in the receding water, he began to think seriously of what to do. The first thing was to get to Ray, to break the news as gently as he could. He'd tell him how Sue had fought to save the youngsters and then how he'd fought to save them all. He had waited here because the nearest ranch in toward the hills was eight miles away and he was afraid the tired bay couldn't carry him that far. But if he could get the gelding across the wash, there was a homesteader, Caylor, who had a place within a mile.

He cut the one long rein and made two shorter ones of it, fastening them to the bay's bit. He finally climbed onto the bay and headed him into the water, deeper than any he'd ever put a horse into; but he made it.

Caylor's place a mile down the trail was deserted. The corral was empty; the wagon Joe had often seen in the barn-lot on his way past was gone. So was the homesteader's team. But there was a saddle in the barn, and Joe took the hull and threw it on the bay. He was worried about the tired horse being able to carry him the four miles in to Sands.

The bay horse walked most of the four miles, and during that long hour and a half the ghosts of Sue and Ellen and Tommy Dineen rode with Joe. When he saw the winking lights along the town's street, he felt his first reluctance to face what lay ahead. He'd have to make a report to the sheriff; there would be questions, maybe accusations. He'd have to get the superintendent, young Ted Baker, out of bed and report the loss of four horses and all his equipment.

Of course they'd find the money-chest; the damned money-grubbers would dredge the bed of the wash for ten miles for their payroll.

But that wouldn't bring back Sue and Ellen and Tommy Dineen.

He was a quarter way along the street when he noticed the scattered crowd along the walk far ahead in front of the lights of the Blue Star stage station. It was late for such a crowd; but then a fight or a noisy drunk or maybe a man hurt could attract these countless loafers who never seemed to sleep.

From far out of the distance came the wailing long note of a locomotive's whistle. Old Joe read a personal insult into the sound. But for the locomotives and the twin ribbons of steel cutting across the plain, he'd still have his job, have it until he died, and Sue and the kids wouldn't have been on their way down today.

He was even with the first stores along the street and riding down toward the group in front of the Blue Star when someone on the walk shouted suddenly, "Look! It's Joe Miles! Either him or his ghost!"

Men stepped down off the walk, looked his way. Then another man shouted, "It ain't no ghost!" and started running toward him. Half a dozen more followed. The swing-doors of a saloon across the street burst outward and a line of men filed out. More came from a saloon further along and joined the quickly gathering crowd in the street. Someone shouted, "Get him and bring him over here!"

Old Joe didn't know what was happening. He tried to turn the bay, but he wasn't fast enough. Hands reached up and pulled him out of the saddle. He was hoisted to two pairs of shoulders, even though he struck out feebly to shake loose the holds on his legs.

Men crowded those who were carrying him. A few hats went into the air and the shouts grew frenzied. They carried Joe across to the Blue Star stage station. All he knew was that these men were cheering, that they weren't mad. Abruptly he was lowered and pushed up onto the walk to face young Ted Baker, the new Blue Star superintendent, who stood in the office doorway.

Baker held up a hand to command silence. He was smiling as the shouts died away and a stillness settled back along the crowd. Old Joe shook loose a man who was holding him and waited, an ugly twist to his wrinkled face.

"Well, Joe, we hardly know what to say," Ted Baker began.

"You could start by tellin' me what the hell all this ruckus is about," said Joe. "I don't feel like jokin'. Something's happened. If you've planned this as a send-off, you young squirt, you can lay off and listen to some bad news.

"This afternoon I hit Graveyard to find a woman and two kids drownin', Ray Dineen's kids. Tryin' to get 'em out, I lost your outfit, horses and all. And I lost Sue and the kids, too. Now the whole pack of you clear out and let me...."

"Joe," Baker cut in. "Joe, Sue and the children are across at the hotel, in bed. Alive! Safe! Larry Caylor brought them in, in his wagon. They thought you'd drowned. We all thought you'd drowned. The sheriff has a posse rounded up, ready to start looking for your body at sunup."

Old Joe Miles stood there a good five seconds, while the expectant hush held the crowd. Tears came to his eyes, streamed down his grizzled cheeks. Then, before any of them could reach out to catch him, his knees buckled and he fell full length on the walk in a dead faint.

Ted Baker was more worried than anyone else. For a half hour he paced the hallway before the hotel room where they had carried old Joe. The doctor was in there with Joe, trying to bring him around. The medico was an ornery old devil who insisted on having the room cleared before he went to work.

Finally the door opened.

"What about it?" Ted Baker asked quickly. "Will he live?"

"Live!" the medico snorted. "There's nothin' wrong with that old cuss. A little tuckered out, maybe, and bruised a bit. He'll be fit as a fiddle in the mornin'."

Baker took the chair alongside as Joe sat up. Baker pushed him down again, said, "Take it easy, Joe."

Neither of them said anything for a couple of minutes. Then Baker began, "Sue Dineen told me everything that happened. She thought you'd drowned under that tree. She told me about Chet Richter and Barney Ryan. They were shooting at you, weren't they? They tried to take that payroll, didn't they?"

Joe nodded. "I reckon. But your money's safe in the wash. I wasn't thinkin' much about Barney and Chet. It was the girl, and them kids. I can't see yet how they got away safe."

Baker shook his head, his glance touched with admiration. "Because of you, Joe," — Baker had never before condescended to talk to his driver in this familiar off-hand way. Joe hardly knew what to make of it — "There'll be a reward out for saving that payroll, Joe. It'll amount to maybe five or seven hundred dollars. There's another thing I'd like to talk over."

"Shoot," old Joe said, hoping young Baker wasn't going to go sentimental over his thanks or make more excuses about letting him go.

"It's this, Joe. We've tried Ed Salzman for a year as superintendent on the southern division. He isn't working out well. I've done some thinking. We can run this efficiency and this new system into the ground. What we need is to keep the best of the old-timers, men who can pull us out of a tight spot when we get in one, like the one today. This superintendent's job is mostly inside work, nothing like you're used to. But I was wondering if we could make you decide to stay on a few more years and take it?"

Old Joe swallowed once, trying to clear his throat so he could say yes. Baker understood. He got up out of his chair and went to the door. "I suppose you'll want Ray Dineen for one of your drivers, won't you?"

Joe thought of something, sat up suddenly. "I forgot to tell you about Ray," he said. "This afternoon he...."

"I know," Baker cut in. "A man just rode in with a note from Doc Slade to Ray's wife. Ray had his appendix out this afternoon. He's in fine shape." He looked at his watch. "Get some sleep and I'll see you in the morning, Joe. We'll whip this line into shape and make it pay."

Old Joe couldn't get to sleep for better than an hour. It didn't worry him much. He had always insisted that a man who slept too much was old or soft, and he wasn't either of these.

T.T. FLYNN

THEODORE THOMAS FLYNN, JR. (1902–1979) was born in Indianapolis, Indiana. He was graduated from Indianapolis Technical High School, but decided against entering college. Instead, he enlisted in the merchant marine where he worked initially as a stoker in coal-burning ships and then as a ship's carpenter. Quitting the sea, Flynn and a friend on a lark paddled a canoe along the Ohio River and then down the Mississippi to New Orleans. What changed his life was meeting a woman named Gertrude, familiarly known as Molly, and marrying her, probably in 1924. Flynn was always ruthlessly secretive about his life. He went to work for the railroad, first as a brakeman, and then got a job in a roundhouse. It was at this time that he first began to write fiction. When Flynn was fired from his roundhouse job for writing on company time, he was convinced one could not write part-time. It had to be a full-time vocation, or none at all. In early 1925 Flynn became a client of literary agent Marguerite E. Harper. With the story "A Matter of Judgment" in *Adventure* (10/30/25) Harper began getting Flynn published in the higher paying pulp magazines.

Living in Hyattsville, Maryland, with Molly, Flynn continued to work capably and quickly at stories with a variety of settings. Because Molly suffered from tuberculosis, Flynn moved with her to New Mexico since the climate there was reputed to be salutary for lung ailments. Molly suffered terribly before she died. A perceptive reader could deduce that Flynn had witnessed her passing since his descriptions ever after of deaths in his fiction could only have been written by a man with first-hand knowledge. There are no grimaces or grins on his corpses, only the frozen vacancy, the terrible silence, the pallor as the blood vanishes from the surface of the skin.

Now that Flynn was settled in Santa Fe, he bought himself a large Chrysler Airstream trailer with which he traveled extensively. A New Mexican woman of Spanish, Apache, and German descent helped bring Flynn through his grief and depression after Molly's death. They married in 1930 and their daughter, Mary Cecilia but known as Cela, was born in 1932. The marriage, however, did not work out and Flynn always blamed himself when he spoke to Cela about it. Flynn was married for the last time to Helen Brown, a woman twelve years his junior whom he met on a trip to New Orleans. With Helen he had two sons, Thomas, later a physician, and Richard, later an Episcopal minister.

Following this marriage, Flynn gave up permanent living quarters and just traveled with Helen and the trailer — at any rate until young Tom was born. Part of the year the Flynns parked the trailer near Fred Glidden's home in Pojoaque and would visit with Fred and his brother, Jon, who lived across the road. Flynn had been such a staple at *Dime Detective* and *Detective Fiction Weekly,* editor Rogers Terrill, in launching *Dime Western,* had wanted a Western story from Flynn and Harper agreed to ask him to write one. The next year, when *Star Western* began publication in the wake of the earlier magazine's success, Flynn was again among the inaugural contributors. It is to Ted Flynn's early fiction in these magazines that we owe the paradigm of a Western story in which the protagonist is seen to endure the tribulations of Job, where the losses pile up and the odds become more and more heavily stacked against him. It fit the bleakness of the Depression years and it certainly influenced the fiction written later by the two Gliddens.

After dozens of Western stories in *Dime Western, Star Western,* and in other pulp magazines, Flynn began contributing regularly to Street & Smith's *Western Story Magazine* in 1938. In fact, in the period between 1932 and 1952 Flynn contributed over 100 Western novelettes and short stories to the magazine market, although he did not abandon other kinds of fiction, especially detective and crime stories. Subsequently, Flynn also wrote five Western novels published in paperback Dell First Editions, the best known being THE MAN FROM LARAMIE in 1954 which ran first serially in *The Saturday Evening Post* and was filmed under this title by Columbia Pictures in 1955. It is now available in a hard cover reprint edition from Chivers in the Gunsmoke series.

In the years following 1960, Flynn's obsession with the race track and his following the horses from track to track increasingly consumed all of his time. His final novel, and in some ways one of his very best, NIGHT OF THE COMANCHE MOON, remained in manuscript until it was published as a Five Star Western in September, 1995.

In January, 1978, Flynn and Helen moved to Baton Rouge. His son, Tom, recalled that his father's "last years were spent...traveling back and forth to the racetracks...and trying to get me to 'invest' in his handicapping scheme. He was a very bitter man during the last twenty years of his life, and totally consumed with the racetrack to the point that I avoided visiting when he came home." Flynn had developed arrhythmia of the heart. Today this condition can be corrected by a lithium implant in the heart that maintains a constant heart beat even when the electrical impulse from the brain to do so is interrupted. One night, at dinner with Tom Flynn and his wife, Linda, a cardiac nurse, I suggested that had Ted been a little more fortunate he might still be living by virtue of such an implant. "But," Tom said pointedly, "I doubt he would have wanted one."

As T.T. Flynn continued to fashion his Western stories over a span of thirty years, they became increasingly a comedy of manners, in which the first step in any direction can often lead to ever deepening complications. He also became increasingly concerned with the emotional and psychological dimensions of his characters and, already by the late 1930s, his preoccupation with mortality had become transfused with an examination of dysfunctional families and relationships. Mike Tilden, Rogers Terrill's successor as editor of *Dime Western,* after reading "What Color Is Heaven?" insisted that Ted alter the ending. He himself changed the title to "Those Fighting Gringo Devils" when it appeared in the May, 1942, issue. Now, with its ending restored, the interrogative title Flynn gave this story, with its reference to storming the heavens with an eternal question verily out of the Gospel of Saint Matthew, shimmers again with all the passionate wondering and intimations of the deeper reality which he had intended to suggest by means of it. His daughter, Cela, perhaps put it best when she reflected on the last visit her father paid her shortly before his own death. Ted spoke to her about his beloved Molly. "She died in his arms," Cela recalled. "He never stopped loving her.... He talked a lot about her, and brought out her picture in the leather case, which I had seen numerous times in the past. Why I was named after her. Why I meant so much to him. He said then he would be with his love soon."

"WHAT COLOR IS HEAVEN?"
1943

I
"Home-Coming"

When the stage guard opened fire at the piled and tumbled rocks off-side the road, Rick Candleman had the quick feeling that once more the Iron Hat range held bad luck for him. Eight years had passed since that night he had tangled with Rufus Madden and then had lathered a horse away from the Iron Hat country.

And the news that Rufus Madden hadn't died after all caught up with Rick in the Argentine. He had stayed on down there under the Southern Cross. Now he was visiting home again — and, before the stage got him to Laguna, trouble was breaking in his face. The stage guard's roaring shotgun was the signal.

Rifles among the rocks answered the guard's gun. A bullet dropped one of the four stage horses. The tangled mêlée in the harness brought the stage to a swerving, reeling stop. The girl sitting opposite Rick exclaimed under her breath. Through the dust swirling around the stage they could hear the driver swearing as he fought the reins.

The other two passengers were men. The wizened, nattily dressed little man at the girl's side was a drummer for the hardware trade. Beside Rick was a blocky, broad-shouldered cowman with a black mustache and black, challenging brows. And as the stage stopped, the cowman reached under his coat.

"Better not, friend!" Rick warned. "They mean business! We got a lady here!"

The cowman blurted, "Don't sit there an' be yellow! Grab a gun!"

"Haven't got a gun. You'll have it all to swing...and get us shot up, too, if you play it like this!"

The wizened drummer sat with open mouth. The cowman glared at Rick. The girl eyed him with an intent, tense look.

She wasn't afraid, Rick decided. He might have expected it from the hot red glint of her hair, and from the provocation in her look when the cowman had climbed on the stage at Mission Wells and ogled her.

And now, while the stage still rocked and the driver fought the plunging horses, the guard's body rolled off the top, struck the road hard and stayed where it landed.

"One dead already!" Rick said curtly.

The cowman half rose to his feet, looked out at the body. The fight went out of him and he sat back heavily.

"Couple of rifles lined on us over there in the rocks," Rick said, looking out. "Only one man showing himself. You wouldn't have had a chance!"

"Plenty of chance if I'd half a man to help me!" the big fellow snapped under his breath.

One outlaw was running out from the rocks to the stage. He carried a six-shooter and wore a shapeless yellow slicker in the blistering midday heat. An old black hat was pulled low over a bandanna mask. He knew what he was about.

"Toss down that Laguna bank box!" he called to the driver as he came down through the big rocks.

The driver's voice cut back through the settling dust. "Ain't no bank box for you this trip!"

"One started from the railroad! It better hit the ground fast or the boys'll open up! Half a minute's all you get!"

"That's half a minute too long, damn you! Ain't no box here for a pack of low-down thieves an' killers!"

Rick had noticed the driver as the stage loaded at Mission Wells. A lean, dried-out old fellow with a huge drooping mustache, the driver was the type to take a stubborn stand and hold to it.

The little dudish drummer shrank back in the seat. "They'll k-kill him, won't they? They'll kill all of us if they start shooting?"

"Likely," Rick agreed.

The gunman outside the stage spoke venomously behind the bandanna. "Time's almost up!" He had no interest in the passengers.

The drummer whimpered: "Ought to be something we c'n do!"

"Not much," Rick told him. "That dead horse has got us hog-tied."

The cowman snorted.

The red-headed girl said suddenly: "They'll kill that driver if he stays stubborn!"

"Maybe not," Rick answered without much conviction.

"Of course they will! And maybe us, too!" She was off the seat as she spoke. "I'll stop it! If he won't tell them about that box, I will!"

Rick caught her arm as she opened the door. But she jerked away and stepped quickly out into the open. Rick followed her out irritably. This was a hair-trigger business. She could make it worse with a word.

"They put an old carpetbag on top that was heavy enough to have gold inside!" she called rapidly to the gunman. She stepped away from the stage, pointing to the top. "It's that green bag, between the two leather cases!"

The six-shooter threatened Rick to a stop. But the gunman chuckled behind his bandanna to the girl. "If every stage carried something purty an' helpful like you, lady, it'd make this business a cinch!" Then the venomous threat snapped in his voice again as he addressed the driver. "Throw off that carpetbag!"

Dust spurted as the carpetbag landed heavily a foot from the dead man.

The gunman kicked the bag, nodded satisfaction. "You saved the stubborn old coot's skin," he told the girl. "Set over there on a rock while he cuts that dead horse loose an' rolls on."

She started to obey, then stopped at Rick's cold voice. "The lady's riding the stage with us."

"She *was,* you mean. Git back in there. The lady's stayin' here."

Rick hesitated, shrugged, climbed back into the stage and slammed the door. And without sitting down he snapped under his breath to the blocky cowman: "Gimme that gun!"

Startled, the man reached under his coat without asking a question. Rick caught the gun from his hand, turned quickly in the cramped space between the seats. His shoulder drove the stage door open, and he plunged out to what was probably the end of Rick Candleman.

Two rifles, maybe more, were lined on the stage. But Rick was counting on one slight advantage as he catapulted back into the open. None of the outlaws was expecting a play like this.

The gunman in the slicker had half-turned to look at the girl. Rick was on the ground, crouching, dodging, before a rifle up the long, boulder-strewn slope fired to bring him down.

The bullet missed, screamed off the rim of the back wheel; and the gunman, not half a dozen steps away, whirled for trouble.

By then Rick was where he wanted to be. The slicker-clad figure was shielding him somewhat from the rifles. And he had hit the ground with six-gun cocked and ready. He fired first, two shots almost as one. He hit the man's gun arm, shattering it.

Rick heard the girl cry out as he plunged forward. He knew her fear and it couldn't be helped. Better to frighten her a little now, better to put her in some danger than to let the stage roll on and leave her here.

The man in the slicker had dropped his gun. He was hurt and rattled. He turned to run, inviting a shot in the back. Rick held back the shot, caught him, grabbed the slicker collar and yanked him to a stop.

"Tell 'em to hold those rifles!" Rick panted, gouging the gun muzzle into the man's back and holding him close for a shield.

The rifles stayed silent and the man in the slicker bawled, "He's got a gun in my back! Hold it, boys!"

Rick backed his prisoner toward the stage and called to the driver. "Cut that dead horse out of the harness!"

The girl had not moved. Rick blurted at her. "Climb in the coach! You're all right now!"

But he wasn't so sure she was all right. A rifle bullet could drop the prisoner and Rick Candleman, too. The gunners hidden up there in the rocks might think the Laguna bank shipment was worth losing one man. But the guns were silent as Rick backed to the stagecoach.

The girl came to his side.

"Get in!" Rick snapped at her.

Standing at the stage step, she said a queer thing. "You look like a Candleman. You're Rick Candleman, aren't you?"

"Yes," Rick answered, wondering why she hadn't asked the question before. He was struck again by her coolness, her self-possession. And then the last thing he expected to happen caught him off-guard and stunned him.

The red-headed girl spoke in husky warning and put a gun muzzle in his back. "I'll stay here! Drop your gun and the stage can go on!"

She had gotten out of the stage with a woman's leather hand-purse which must have held a small gun. And because he had looked into her face and eyes and judged her, Rick did not doubt her warning.

An instant later he was blindly angry at the fool figure he'd cut. She had intended all along to stay here with the outlaws. She'd known there would be a hold-up. And because she was pretty as a red-headed jungle cat and probably twice as merciless, Rick did not try to argue.

"I'll drop nothing!" he said savagely. "Pull that damned trigger and I'll still have time to get this curly wolf in front of me!"

"He should be killed anyway for letting you cripple him," she answered with a lack of emotion that made Rick's nerves crawl. And she spoke past Rick's shoulder in the same unmoved tone. "Get up in the rocks, Slim."

Blood was dripping off Slim's wrist and hand. Sweat stood out on his neck. But more than pain and sweat from the hot slicker inspired his hoarse reply. "He'll shoot if I try it!"

"So?" the girl said, and suddenly she was speaking in Spanish like a native. "Does it matter who shoots you now? Quick, before I do myself!"

The man took a hesitating step away from Rick's gun. Nothing happened, and he took a longer step. Then, with blood dripping off his fingers, he began to run up the rocky slope as if death already were at his heels.

And Rick, with the strange prescience that greater dangers than his gun threatened the fellow, let him go.

"You see," the girl said behind his shoulder, "now there is nothing left. Must I shoot you?"

Rick shrugged and tossed the gun down beside the green carpetbag and the dead man.

The old stage driver had been using a pocket knife with furious haste on the harness of the dead horse. The knife was still in his hand as he turned back toward his stage seat, saw the outlaw running and Rick tossing down his gun.

"What'n hell?" the old man gasped.

"Take a look," Rick said with ironical bitterness. "And then get your stage out of here fast...if you can."

"But...but the lady! What's she...?"

"She ain't a lady!" Rick rasped.

He heard the girl chuckle under her breath and he held that against her, too. He was angry as only a strong man can be angry and she was laughing at him.

"You heard *Señor* Candleman," she told the driver.

The old man gave Rick a startled look. "Candleman?" He spat. His big mustache was quivering as he looked at the rocks where the gunmen were hidden and then back at them. "I've done heard plenty," he said, and he spat again and added: "An' seen more!"

He climbed on the stage.

"*Adios,*" the girl said to Rick; and she was laughing again as she finished in Spanish: "It's better you return to the Rio Tigre quickly."

"What the devil do you know about the Rio Tigre?" Rick snapped back in Spanish.

She had stepped away from his back. When he turned she was beyond reach, showing white teeth in a smile he would never like. The short-barreled gun she carried waved him to the stage step.

The driver had the reins and the whip. Rifles were waiting up there in the rocks. Rick glared at her and swung into the stage.

The long-lashed whip cracked like a pistol shot. The driver yanked the three remaining horses wide around the dead animal, swung the stage back into the road beyond, and they rolled toward Laguna.

Rick's hands were unsteady as he rolled and lighted a cigarette. Anger still ran hot and wild through his nerves. He paid no attention to the furtive, half-fearful looks the little drummer was giving him.

She had known his name — and that, perhaps, wasn't so puzzling, for he had the Candlemans' rangy build, high cheekbones, black hair and dark eyes that old Ross Candleman had given to his three sons.

But she couldn't have guessed about the Rio Tigre ranch, down there in the deep pampas of the Argentine. She had to know Candleman business to know that name. And once more Rick had the uneasy feeling that the Iron Hat range held bad luck for him.

II
"End of the Murder Trail"

Laguna had not changed in eight years. The same dun-colored hills and distant mountains brooded under the hot blue sky. The stamp of the border country was in the low, thick-walled adobe houses, hugging the earth that had spawned them.

It was Saturday, and wagons and horses were thick at the hitchracks. The same saloons were doing the same brisk business that Rick remembered out of past Saturdays. The three-horse stage pulled up in front of the hotel and Rick looked for familiar faces in the crowd that quickly gathered.

The stage driver piled down, shouting: "Hold-up got the bank shipment! Might be a chance to git it back if a posse starts quick! Where's Dud Sloane?"

Rick saw the angular, familiar face of a young man about his own age and pushed through the crowd.

"Pat, you crop-eared maverick!"

It took an instant for a broad grin of recognition to flash on Pat Cody's face. His hand grabbed Rick's hand.

"I been lookin' for you, Rick! Your brother Dan told me he'd written you to come home."

For the third time Rick had that sharp uneasy sense of trouble waiting here for him. It wiped most of the smile off his face.

"I didn't get the letter, Pat. Must have left before it got there. Is Dan in town?"

"Haven't seen him."

"Why'd he want me to come home?"

"Figured he needed you, I guess."

"Trouble?"

"Always a little trouble one way or another, ain't there?" Pat Cody evaded. "Who jumped the stage?"

"Strangers...and a girl who rode from Mission Wells."

"*Girl?*" Pat said in amazement.

"A red-head. Pretty...and a hell-cat behind it. I've never seen one like her, and I've run across some wild ones since I left."

"A red-head?" Pat Cody repeated. He looked startled. His voice sharpened. "Didja see the men?"

"No."

Pat looked quickly around, as if scenting danger or trying to take in quickly what was happening.

The crowd had grown. The sheriff had arrived, star pinned on his scuffed leather vest, worry on his broad face as he talked with the old stage driver, the little drummer, and the blocky cowman. And so quiet had the crowd gone around the spot that Rick heard the cowman's rasping words.

"She asked if he wasn't Rick Candleman an' he allowed he was. So what does he do but throw down my gun an' let the feller lope away. An' then he jabbered Mex with her an' climbed back in the stage! I dunno what the name Candleman means around here, but I got my ideas after what I seen...."

Pat Cody's hand closed on Rick's arm, his voice low and urgent.

"Rick, I was headin' out to the ranch. Got a little spread of my own now, a swell wife an' a couple of kids. Come along an' stay with us tonight."

"Right now," said Rick grimly, "I'll drop my loop around that lying loud-mouth talking to the sheriff!"

"Don't!" Pat pleaded. "There comes Rufus Madden on that horse!"

"Dan wrote me the old trouble I had with Rufe was crossed off by the law."

"What of it, Rick? Rufe's as ornery as he ever was. He's got a hand in the bank now, since his old man got heart trouble three-four years ago. Come on."

But Rick shook off Pat's restraining hand and pushed through the crowd.

Rufe Madden had dismounted behind the stage and shouldered to the sheriff. Rick reached them as Rufe was speaking angrily.

"There was twelve thousand dollars in the shipment! Maybe more! Sloane, why the devil don't you get after it?"

Rick stopped beside them, and it seemed to him the years rolled away. He felt the inner bristle that always had been there when he was around Rufe Madden since they were kids, meeting at the same little school house with Rufe's younger sister, Jean.

And yet it was like meeting a stranger, too. Rufe had grown heavier; and it all was bad meat, soft and puffy. Rufe's loose mouth had taken on a thick, vindictive set.

Dusty black pants were outside Rufe's boots; his dusty hat was pushed back on his curly black hair. His look slid off Rick and he jerked back with startled recognition. "What the devil are you doing here?" Rufe burst out.

Rick spoke to the sheriff. "I'm Rick Candleman. You've just heard one kind of talk about what happened out there on the road. Now I'll give you my say."

Sloane, the sheriff, had silver at his temples and his broad, slack, lazy face was beginning to look harassed.

"Tell it quick," he said without enthusiasm. "I got to get down the road after that money."

The sheriff's eyes were on Rufe Madden as he said it. He listened to Rick's terse story as if his mind were already on other things.

Rufe Madden conferred hurriedly in undertones with other men as Rick faced the sheriff and, as Rick finished, Rufe's harsh accusation cut in.

"I just heard how Rick Candleman tied in with that hold-up! He's a damn thief and a killer, Sloane, like all the rest of his name! Why the devil don't you lock him up and get going?"

Rick thought as he turned that he might have known something like this would happen. He should have stayed clear from the Iron Hat country. He should never have come back.

Then his hard fist smashed Rufe Madden's thick, vindictive mouth. And the fierce satisfaction that flooded him as Rufe went down was tempered by the knowledge that the years had closed up and again he had trouble on the Iron Hat range. Trouble once more with the Maddens. Wasted now were the memories of Jean Madden that had finally brought him back.

Rufe bounced up bellowing from a bloody mouth. Rick knocked him down again. This time Rufe stayed in the dust and the crowd surged back as Rufe snatched under his coat.

Rick wasn't armed, and Rufe could see it. But that didn't matter to Rufe Madden. It was as if that furious night eight years back were repeating itself, action by action. Rick could have told them all what Rufe would try to do and, because he knew, Rick moved fast and mercilessly.

A jump brought his sharp-heeled boot and full weight down with paralyzing force on Rufe's elbow. Rufe yelled with pain and Rick caught the arm, heaved and slammed the heavy figure over on the ground.

Fury out of the past and of the present kept Rick from stopping there. Rufe's hat had fallen off. Rick grabbed the black curly hair and drove Rufe's puffy face hard into the dust again and again. He would have stopped after a moment and taken Rufe's gun away and let him up. But men caught him and hustled him back, holding his arms.

The red-faced sheriff jumped in front of Rick as Rufe Madden scrambled up. Rufe's face was smeared with blood and dirt and his eyes were half-blinded by dust as he pawed under his coat.

"Don't try it, Rufe!" the sheriff yelled. "I'll have to lock you up, too! A mess like this ain't gettin' the bank's money back! Grab Rufe, men! He don't know what he's doin'!"

Rick smiled crookedly. Rufe knew exactly what he was doing. Nothing the matter with Rufe's calculating mind, ever. But then, even Rufe Madden couldn't shoot a man who was shielded by the sheriff and held by other men.

Rufe pulled out a handkerchief instead of the gun and wiped eyes and face. A smile forced out on his bloody lips, already beginning to puff. He peered at Rick, then without a word he turned back to his horse, mounted, angled down the street and across to the bank, still wiping at his face.

"We'll settle all this after I git back!" the sheriff told Rick angrily. "Come along now...I'm gonna lock you up!"

Part of the crowd followed them to the jail. From a cell Rick heard the posse collecting out in front, heard the drum-beat of departing horses.

Rick rolled a cigarette, sucked in the smoke, and smiled crookedly at his bruised knuckles. All the trouble he could handle. The Maddens wouldn't let it rest at this. If there was any way of pinning that stage hold-up on him, they'd see that it was done.

Rick's smile left when he got to that point. His mind switched hard to the hold-up and the red-headed girl.

She'd known too much about him. The stage driver's manner had been peculiar when he heard the name Candleman. And Pat Cody's manner and words hadn't been any more reassuring. Rick looked up as a man stepped into the cells. It was Pat Cody, keys in hand, a grin on his angular face.

"Might as well move out while everybody's busy," Pat said as he unlocked the cell door.

"How come?" Rick demanded as he emerged.

"I deputied around for old man Sloane. He's a forgetful cuss," Pat said. "Likely to leave his keys anywhere. He hides an extra set in the bottom drawer of his desk, just in case. Thinks he's the only one that knows about it. He'll figure you found a mouse hole an' crawled through, an'll get drunk trying to puzzle it out. I got a horse for you out back with mine. We'll ride to my place, over on the north fork of the Sugarleaf, across the hills from your land."

No one noticed them as they kept off the main street, rode out of town, and put the horses into a lope.

"Let's have it," Rick said soberly. "What's wrong?"

"I figured you knew."

"Those two brothers of mine never were much on writing letters. If there was trouble, they'd be the last ones to bother me with it."

"Dan bothered you this time, Rick...only you didn't get it. I might as well tell you what everyone knows. Joe's gone bad. The Maddens claimed they caught him rustling. There was some shooting. Joe killed a man in the posse that tried to round him up and skipped across the Border."

Rick's low whistle was amazed. "Joe rustling? He's only a kid!"

"He growed up while you were gone," Pat said dryly. "Dan says Joe told him he wasn't rustling. But it was too late then to matter. Joe threw in with a hard bunch of Border jumpers. Made no bones about it when he met the men across the line that he knew. They hole up over there under the wing of a half-breed named Sebastian Obrion, who cuts some ice as a politico in the Domingo section. And they raise plenty of hell on this side. Half the dirt that's done along this stretch of the Border can be laid to the bunch."

"And Dan couldn't straighten Joe out?"

"Dan's had his hands full with his own troubles," Pat said bluntly. "Word's been around for some time that Dan must have a tie-in with the Obrion riders. Don't matter that he's lost cattle like everyone else. Folks have got the idea those Border jumpers are always welcome at Dan's place and Dan cuts in on some of their pickings."

"Anybody who knew Dan would know it was a dirty lie!"

"A man gets to believing things he hears when he's being thieved out himself, Rick."

"It's because of Joe!"

"Sure...but there it is. A man got a black eye just working for Dan. Three of his hands quit before he wrote you. Left him with old Cady Sowers. Dan'll be glad to see you, Rick."

Rick said slowly, "Not after the extra dust I've kicked up in coming here. Last letter I had from Dan almost a year ago didn't mention a thing." Rick rolled a cigarette and kept his eyes on it as he said casually: "Dan's letter said Jean Madden busted up with a fellow she was going to marry. She made the jump since?"

"Nope. It was Curt Hanna. Likely looking fellow who bought out the Cross Bit spread after you left. Hanna's done well. He's a friend of Rufe Madden's and has bought into the bank. It looked like a good match. Nobody ever heard that Jean and Hanna had trouble. Surprised everyone when Jean busted it off at the last minute and never said why. She and Curt Hanna still seem to be friends, too. Just one of those things, I guess."

"That red-headed girl in the stagecoach meant something to you," Rick said abruptly.

"And to everybody else who heard a red-head had a hand in the business and faded off with the men," Pat admitted. "This Sebastian Obrion is a red-head and so is his sister, Maisa. Their father was a red-headed Irishman named O'Brien. They Mexed up the name and dug in over there. Talk has it that Obrion's red-headed sister and Joe are next thing to married...if they ain't married. Anyway, Joe's crazy about her...and if the devil had red hair and skirts, he'd probably be her."

Rick nodded and rode in silence, thinking how bad it was. And when they crossed the deep, dry gash of the Arroyo Hondo, Rick nodded toward the brush covered hills rising west of them.

"I'll cut off this way to the home place. I want to see Dan."

Pat nodded in understanding. "Dan'll feel the same way. I haven't seen him in better'n a week, but I guess he's waitin' for you. If there's anything I can do, ride over and name it."

That next hour's ride was the hardest Rick had ever made. There wasn't much left to think about. Joe, the slim straight kid brother with blue eyes and friendly grin, had taken his way and would have to cut his own tally.

Dan, the older, was messed up and tangled up. He might have a plan, but probably he didn't. Rick himself couldn't have arrived in worse circumstances. They both were tarred with the same black outlaw stick that Joe had brought home to the Candlemans.

Rick's throat tightened a little when he passed the home fences and swung over to a solitary cow and read the familiar CA brand on hip and shoulder. He rode faster toward the meeting with Dan. And when he reached the trickle of water in Gunshot Creek, Rick pulled up short, staring.

Gunshot Creek's sands were white and dry as usual. On the other side, upstream, the tall cottonwoods thrust into the late sunlight as Rick had remembered through the years.

The old thick-walled adobe house was there, too. But it was different. Windows and doors were gaping. Faint blue curls of smoke drifted lazily from where the roof should be. Buzzards were wheeling in the blue sky and the challenging nicker of a horse at the back corner of the house was the only life Rick could make out as he slashed his own horse into a gallop.

The creek bed hid him for a moment and, when he rode up under the cottonwoods, the strange horse and a rider were poised to leave. The man had jerked a rifle from the saddle scabbard and held it ready.

The place had been burned out. And the wheeling buzzards signaled death.

"What happened here?" Rick called roughly, and a second later saw the rider was a girl. Then he recognized the girl and a stifled gladness held him wordless as he rode to her.

"Rick!"

He nodded, seeing her for an instant in short dresses at school, and later slim and eager in the year they had drawn close before he went away. She was older now, lovelier in her mid twenties, and uneasily he noticed that her eyes were tearful.

"Dan said you were coming, Rick!"

"Where's Dan?"

"There!" Jean said huskily, pointing to the back of the house. "And Cady Sowers, too. Inside. I...I had to make sure before I left. Oh, Rick!"

III
"Breed of the Dark Trails"

The air reeked of charred wood and dying fire as Rick saw Dan Candleman lying in the back doorway. Sowers, inside the building, had not been so fortunate.

The heavy log *vigas* of the burning building had crashed in on Sowers. His body was half-buried in the roof wreckage. But Sowers had been dead from a head wound before the roof fell. Haystacks, the old bunkhouse, saddle shed and store house, all had been burned.

Jean was with the two horses, wiping her eyes, when Rick came back to her with a stony face.

"Any idea what happened, Jean?"

She shook her head. "I rode over to ask Dan again when you were coming. Rick...Dan didn't expect anything like this! He was worried, but not about *this!*"

Bitterly Rick told her: "Dan never could figure that men can be as dirty as they are." And with the same bitterness: "I tangled with Rufe again as soon as I got in Laguna."

"Was it necessary?"

"Maybe not. I could have agreed with Rufe." He told her what had happened. "Jean, you know Candlemans and Maddens never got along. I didn't help my family any when I tangled with Rufe eight years ago and rode away from here."

"Rufe said the trouble was over me, Rick. I've always felt I was to blame."

Rick shrugged. "If it hadn't been you, it would have been something else. Joe hit the Candlemans harder when he went bad. This stage hold-up today makes it worse. Joe might have been back there in the rocks himself, sighting a gun on the stage. Chances were he was, if that red-head was his girl. Maybe that's why I didn't get shot when I jumped out and took a hand."

Jean stayed pale and silent, and Rick turned to the ruin behind them. "The Candlemans didn't do *this*. It was done before the stage hold-up. Dan and the old man in there couldn't have had much chance. Neither one has got a gun that I can see. They weren't looking for trouble. Dan opened the door and got shot down like a dog. And then Sowers got it and the place was fired over their bodies. It was murder, Jean...murder, to get the last Candleman out of the way around here! Who'd do that?"

Jean was pale. "I don't know, Rick."

He seemed to have forgotten her for the moment. "I didn't see much beef inside Dan's fences. Looks like the place is cleaned out. Joe wouldn't have done that to his brother. I wonder who knew I was coming home."

"I don't know," Jean said huskily. But her pallor was intense; something like fright was in her look.

Rick eyed her without comment. It was impossible to guess what was in his mind. "It's late. Better start home," he said.

"I...I can ride to Laguna and let them know."

"Laguna didn't help Dan while he was alive," Rick answered her shortly. "I'll do what's needed here...alone."

Jean rode away without looking back.

Rick finished by firelight. The graves were under the cottonwoods beside the creek. No coffins, no shrouds. He'd been lucky to find an unburned shovel. Dan would stay here as he had lived, the last Candleman on the place. But not the last Candleman.

It was late when he reached Pat Cody's. Barking dogs brought Pat out.

"Trouble, Rick?" Pat guessed.

"A little." Rick got stiffly out of the saddle and tersely told his story. "Everybody around here knew I was coming back," he guessed.

"Dan told me he'd written you to come. Said he'd told Jean Madden, too. That's all I know of."

"That's good enough. Got a fresh horse, a rifle, and a gun?"

"Sleep on it, tonight," Pat urged. "If the men who killed Dan are around these parts, you'll be jumping right under their sights. The law's after you anyway. They'll have you where they want you."

"I'm riding south after Joe," Rick said.

"I'll get your outfit," Pat yielded. And when the fresh horse was saddled, sandwiches stuffed in the saddle pockets, rifle in the saddle boot, belt gun and cartridges strapped on Rick, they had a final smoke out under the stars.

"I hate to see you riding for trouble, Rick."

"I ran away once," Rick said slowly. "I thought I was staying down there in the Argentine because I was making money and liking it. But mostly I guess I was staying away from trouble. I knew if I came back there'd be Candlemans tangling with Maddens again. It's been that way ever since Ross Candleman and Cory Madden settled in these parts and had their trouble over water rights in the year of the big drive."

"I know," Pat agreed. "But it don't have to keep up."

"I'll see you before I start back south," Rick said.

Two days later he was in the Domingo country south of the Border. From a cactus-studded rise he saw, far off, the blood-red sheen of the setting sun on water that would be the Laguna Domingo. The blot of low adobe houses and trees on the west shore of the lagoon was Domingo, crossroads for open and furtive trails a hundred miles in any direction.

He had been there once as a boy, with his father. He had thought Domingo pretty then, the three-sided little plaza opening on the placid lagoon; the sandy winding streets vanishing back among the low sprawling adobe houses and corrals. But big Ross Candleman had carefully barred the door of the low patio room behind a *cantina* where they had spent the night. And had slept with loaded gun under his pillow.

Years afterward Rick remembered the noisy music, loud talk, yells and singing of the night. Gunshots, too, and in the middle of the night a man's cry outside their door. In the morning he had seen drying blood on the patio flagstones, and understood with hot excitement that death had stopped outside their door in the night. Now once more in the town, Rick again had the feeling of death as he stepped inside the *cantina* where he had slept as a boy.

Massive ceiling beams were dark with age. Dull brass lamps threw heat into the smoky reek. Mexicans and *Americanos* were in the place. Girls from both sides of the Border. A drunken *peon* in rags snored in a dark corner. Men were arguing at the end of the bar. A few couples were dancing. Later there would probably be more dancers and the night would be wilder.

Men looked him over as he drank at the bar. Strangers were under suspicion in a town like this until their business was known.

A Mexican barman with drooping black mustache and beady eyes shook his head when Rick asked where Joe would be. And a man who had stepped in at Rick's shoulder said: "You looking for Joe Candleman, too, stranger?"

The speaker was as tall as Rick, broader and a few years older. He was American, dressed in dusty gray broadcloth, a silver-mounted gun visible under his coat. Teeth flashed in his heavy handsome face and his eyes crinkled.

"I'm Pete Jones."

"I'm Pete Smith," Rick said briefly.

"Drink?"

"Another'll hold down the first one," Rick grinned.

They were smiling as they drank. Jones looked like a prosperous cattleman. "They say Joe Candleman ought to be back tonight sometime. He'll stop in here."

"Who says so?"

"Sebastian Obrion, his brother-in-law." Jones twisted his glass between strong white fingers and grinned, but his eyes were thoughtful. "You remind me some of Joe Candleman. Same build...something about your faces. Joe Candleman's a great boy."

"I haven't seen him lately," Rick said briefly. "Maybe you can tell me where his brother-in-law lives."

"Right now," said Jones, "he's back there at the corner table."

"Thanks," said Rick. "Thanks for the drink, too." He wondered as he left the bar how crooked the American was. He looked like a prosperous cattleman who had crossed the Border to turn a shady deal in beef.

Then the man at the corner table took all Rick's attention. He was built in the shoulders like a bull. The hat pushed back on his head showed challenging red hair. Seeing the brother, you would know the girl who had ridden in the Laguna stage.

"I'm Joe Candleman's brother," Rick said bluntly. "Where's Joe?"

Obrion drained his beer glass. He could pass for either American or Mexican. But his smile was Latin.

"So? Dan Candleman?"

"I'm Rick Candleman."

"Ah...the one from South America?" Obrion stood up, chuckling as he dropped a heavy arm on Rick's shoulder.

"José is a brother to me. *Señor* Rick, you are of the family. Command me."

South of the equator you lived with such courtesy. Rick stayed blunt. "Where's Joe?"

"*¿Quien sabe?*" Obrion said expansively. "He will be here."

"A sign on the back bar says they've got rooms here. I'll put up my horse and catch some rest," Rick decided.

Sebastian Obrion rapped on the table with an empty beer bottle. The man who hurried to them was short, bloated, and swarthy.

"A room, hot water and a razor; anything my friend wants. And his horse will be put in my corral," Obrion ordered expansively.

It was done so hurriedly that a stranger could not doubt Obrion's power in these parts. In a patio room Rick washed, shaved in hot water brought in a bucket, and dropped on the bed and closed his eyes for half an hour.

He felt better when he got up. He dressed, blew out the lamp, and stepped out to see about Joe. Furtive movement in the darkness at the left of the door made him lunge suddenly that way.

He caught an arm — and, because he remembered this patio from past years, Rick was fast and rough in grabbing the stranger's throat and slamming him against the wall. The match he thumbed into flame showed a dapper little Mexican with fear-popping eyes and purpling face.

"Crawled out of a rat-hole to snoop on me, eh?" Rick snapped in Spanish.

"*Madre mi,* I was but find my room!"

"You found it! *¡Vamos!*" Rick sent the man stumbling across the dark patio.

A low-vaulted passage led to a door in the end of the big barroom where music and noise were louder now. Rick was halfway through the doorway when he caught sight of the red-headed girl of the Laguna stage — Joe's wife.

He had expected to meet her here, had guessed Joe had been with her across the Border. And Joe's wife here in the *cantina* was not what stopped Rick in mid-stride. Sebastian Obrion's sister was the type who would go where she pleased in Domingo. No, it was the sight of Jean Madden at the same table, smiling at the man who called himself Jones, that wrung a stifled oath from Rick.

He could see Jean had ridden hard and long. She looked tired. She must have started south quickly after leaving Dan's body and the smoldering ranch house. Her friendliness with the lot of them at the table turned Rick cold and bleak.

But Joe wasn't there. While Rick looked over the crowd for him, the dapper little Mexican Rick had shoved into the dark wall sidled to Sebastian Obrion's ear with a message.

Obrion had put a watch on Joe's brother and was getting his report. Rick turned back to his room, got his rifle, locked the door, and tossed the key out in the dark patio.

Years ago there had been another vaulted passage at the back of the patio and a barred door leading outside. The door was still there.

He had gone with his horse to Obrion's corral. He went back there now. The two *peones* in charge squatted beside a tiny fire at one corner of the shed.

The men showed no surprise. Strangers evidently came and went from Sebastian Obrion's corral at all hours of the day and night. And because Obrion's orders had covered everything he might want, Rick tried for a fresh horse.

"*Si, señor,*" he was told readily.

The fire flared as the other man dropped on a twist of hay. Rick peered at the uneasy horses. "That big bay ought to do."

"Another one, *señor.* That is the horse of Don José Candleman."

"So, he's back, is he?"

"Don José is in the bed with a lame foot, *señor.*"

"Where's his house?"

"Where but the house of Don Sebastian?"

"I'll take that black horse," Rick said quickly and, when he rode from the corral, he had directions for finding Obrion's house.

A block beyond the plaza, facing the downslope to the lagoon, Obrion's house looked big and massive, for all of being one story high. Iron bars covered the windows. The single narrow entrance through a roofed passage to the patio was closed by an iron grillwork gate.

The gate was locked. But a shadowy, blanket-wrapped figure rose up from the passage floor.

"I will see Don José," Rick said in Spanish, and it hardly seemed he could be talking about his kid brother.

"Don José is asleep, *señor*"

"Wake him up."

"Don José will not see anyone," was the surly answer.

Rick grabbed through the gate bars, got the blanket, the shoulder under it, yanked the figure close against the gate. His gun jabbing through the bars stopped a warning cry.

"Open up!" Rick said viciously.

The place was bigger than he had suspected. There was a back wing and a back patio; and in a corner of that back wing the gateman knocked on the door of a lighted room. A lusty bellow of Spanish answered.

Rick pushed the gateman into the room and followed.

Joe Candleman was in a chair by a table with his bandaged left foot propped on another chair. Joe had been oiling a gold-mounted six-gun. He stared and lurched up with a delighted yell.

"Rick! My God, what're *you* doing here?"

It was hard to find the kid brother in this tall, muscular young fellow with a lean, reckless face. Joe was a man now. But he was more. Joe was hard. Even while he laughed delightedly and pumped Rick's hand, his eyes were gray and slatey and there were lines on Joe's face that should not be there at his age.

"Can this *pelado* speak English?" Rick asked.

"Only a few words," Joe said. "What's the idea of bringing him in here this way?"

"He tried to keep me out. Said you weren't seeing anybody. Your brother-in-law told me over at the *cantina* that you were out of town. He got me a room at the *cantina,* and then put a man watching me."

"So?" said Joe. He was smiling as he took a limping step, slapped the *peon,* and demanded why the house was barred against this visitor. He had to slap the man again before he got the whimpered answer that Don Sebastian's orders had been followed.

Joe cursed him, shoved him to a corner, and sat down. "I don't know what this means, Rick. I'll find out when Sebastian comes in. Horse pitched me off the other day and sprained my ankle."

"He should have broken your neck," Rick said in a level voice.

Joe went sulky as he looked up. "Never mind saying it. This is the way it turned out. It's my hard luck and my business."

It was like speaking to a stranger. Joe's gray eyes were slate-hard now. But Rick was hard, too. "It's my business when I find the name Candleman means something low-down and no-good. It was Dan's business, too."

"Dan gets along."

"He will now," Rick agreed. "He's dead...murdered. And the house burned down over him. I buried Dan myself before I started south."

Joe's mouth opened. He suddenly looked older, stricken. "Tell me about it," he said thickly.

Rick told him with cold, edged words

The handsome recklessness was gone from Joe's face as he stood up. He talked jerkily as he limped around the room.

"Last time I saw Dan was a couple of months ago. He was worried about money to make a payment to the Laguna bank. But he wouldn't take my money. Said it was blood money."

"Wasn't it?"

"Hell, don't rub it in, Rick! I told Dan the Laguna bank wasn't any better. A man named Curt Hanna who bought into the bank after you left had been working with Sebastian Obrion since before I had my trouble and jumped the Border. Sebastian got drunk and let it out just before I saw Dan. That's how Sebastian always has luck when he sends men across the Border."

"That's all I need," Rick said. "It was worth riding here to get it. Dan was the kind to threaten this Curt Hanna and the bank that he was going to make trouble. I guess that's when he wrote me to come help."

"Funny, ain't it?" Joe said grinning crookedly. "Me an outlaw here across the Border...and the Madden bank back there in Laguna riding high and holy?"

"Funny," Rick agreed. "The Maddens got as low-down as you made the Candlemans...only they stayed smarter. Good-bye, Joe."

Joe had tied a rope-soled sandal on his bad foot, had put on gunbelt and coat. Now he caught a sombrero off a wall peg.

"Let's go, Rick."

Behind Rick in the doorway a woman said: "*Querido mi,* where do you go?"

Joe's red-headed wife had returned in riding clothes. A braided quirt still dangled from her wrist. She was, Rick thought, something half-wild and dangerously lovely as she smiled at Joe.

"Rick says he met you on the stage," Joe said. "We're riding, Maisa."

She was not surprised at Rick's presence. Obrion had evidently told her he was here in Domingo. But she begged Joe quickly. "I'm just back...and you're leaving me?"

"I told you to let that stage alone, Maisa."

"But it was fun. Please, Josito...don't leave me tonight."

Joe answered her deliberately. "Maisa, you're like fire in the night near gunpowder...pretty as hell, but a man never knows what'll happen. I'm tired of wondering and not liking most of the things that happen. I hate to say it in front of my own brother...but, when they cut hang ropes for all of us, they'll need one for you, too. Now go to bed or figure out some dirt with your brother. I'm riding with Rick."

The wild, stormy side of her blazed at him then. "Joe, you fool! You can't go with him! Suppose your brother Dan is dead? You can't help him! You belong here with us! You've got to take what happens along with all of us!"

Joe took a step and caught her wrist. "What do you know about Dan? Did you and Slim and the boys kill Dan while you were over there taking that stage?"

"No, Joe! I didn't know about it until I got back! Sebastian told...."

She stopped abruptly, frightened by the look on Joe's face.

IV
"Last of the Fighting Candlemans"

Only that look on Joe's face kept Rick quiet, coldly waiting for what Joe would do. And Joe, even a stranger could have seen, was meeting his own hell as he looked at his red-headed wife. The hell wrenched out in Joe's voice.

"So Sebastian had my brother killed?"

She was suddenly like a lovely trapped cat, too frightened now to flare and fight with her temper and willfulness. Joe was not hurting her arm, but a low moan of denial came from her.

"Not Sebastian, Joe! He didn't have anything to do with it. But he knows about it. Just today he knows, I think. And he's angry. He told me that your brother Dan was going to make trouble for Curt Hanna and his partner in Laguna. Dan warned Hanna there would be trouble. Curt Hanna's here in Domingo now."

"Why?" Joe asked through tight lips.

"For his share of the bank's money we brought back. Sebastian is with him at the *cantina!*"

Rick spoke to her quietly. "Curt Hanna is the big fellow who was talking to Jean Madden at your table?"

"Jean Madden?" Joe blurted.

And Maisa said: "We found her on the trail with a lame horse She was riding here to meet her brother."

"Why does she have to meet her brother here across the Border?"

Rick answered Joe's question with rough bitterness that had seethed since his sight of Jean at the *cantina* table.

"She followed Rufe here to warn him trouble's coming fast about Dan. She's a Madden. I used to think different...but there it is. Rufe must have started this way after I tangled with him in Laguna."

Joe glared at his wife. "Is Rufe Madden here too?"

She swallowed, nodded. "He came in the *cantina* just before I left."

Joe let go of her wrist. His voice was deadly. "Maisa, you got into my blood like a fever I couldn't shake off. I stood a lot. This is the end. Don't leave this room or let Gregorio out until I tell you to!"

"Joe, don't go! You'll get into trouble!"

"You heard me," Joe said, turning to the door.

Rick wouldn't have believed until this moment that tears would ever soften terror in her eyes as they did now.

"Josito!" she pleaded. "Sebastian needs those men from the Laguna bank! You know Sebastian. He thinks only of himself!"

"I know Sebastian," Joe said, and hobbled out behind Rick.

"Robbing that Laguna stage was kinda snapping at the hand that fed him, wasn't it?" Rick said.

"Not the way the Laguna bank is run," Joe grunted. "They'll claim they lost twice as much as Maisa and the boys got. It'll cover a lot that's already been taken out of the bank. Hanna'll get some gold from this end, too, as his cut. Everybody wins but the other stockholders in the bank. That's the way Hanna and Rufe Madden do business."

They fell into silence as they crossed the dark back patio. And the silence was a bond from the past....

In the front patio Rick's hand dropped to his gun as they unexpectedly met Sebastian Obrion hurrying back toward Joe's room.

"José?" Obrion called, stopping.

"It's Joe tonight," was the short answer. "Joe Candleman and Rick Candleman. What the devil's the idea of having Rick kept out of the house?"

"So?" Obrion said. He chuckled. "Have you seen Maisa?"

"Yes."

"Then you know my friend Hanna is here from Laguna. And he's angry, Joe, because your brother Dan promised him trouble for the bank. *Dios*...what can I do? I told Hanna you were out of Domingo. It is better that you don't go to the *cantina* now, eh?"

"Sebastian, you're damned careful of me all of a sudden," Joe snapped.

Sebastian Obrion chuckled. "Okay, Joe. You're going to the *cantina*, no? But I told you."

"Yeah," Joe said. "I'll remember it. Is the Madden girl there with her brother and Hanna?"

"So now you ask me," Obrion said, shrugging his big shoulders. "At the *cantina*, Joe, if you got to know."

"Fine," Joe said. "Come along."

"Later. First I will see Maisa."

"I told you not to make a mistake about me tonight," Joe said in sudden warning. "Watch him, Rick, while I see why there's a light in that room over there where guests are always put."

"*Por Dios,* Joe!"

But Joe had already faded across the dark patio, limping toward a thin thread of light at a curtained window.

Obrion swore angrily under his breath. "I wash my hands of it. Good night."

"Hold it," Risk said, hand on his gun. "Joe knows what he's doing."

The door opened to Joe's knock, letting out yellow light. The murmur of voices came to them. Obrion again swore angrily.

Then the door closed. Joe started limping back to them. And Sebastian Obrion gave a shrill piercing whistle and jumped back.

Rick drew fast. He could have shot the man. But he was not here to kill Sebastian Obrion in his own house. The black shadows to the front of the patio swallowed Obrion's plunging form.

"Who whistled?" Joe called.

"Obrion. He's running out the front!"

Joe cursed. "I knew he was pulling a ranny on us! Come on!"

They bolted through the passage together, Joe moving as quickly as he could, his face taut in a grimace. But when they got outside, a running horse was fading off into the night, and Rick's horse was gone.

"We need horses first!" Joe panted. "This place is full of gunnies who cut wood when Obrion yells whittle. Let's get to the corral. Sebastian was lying, Rick. Jean Madden was in that room. He knew she was there all the time. Keep your gun handy!"

And as they moved side by side through the night, Rick held his pace in rein with Joe's. His brother muttered: "No use wondering who Sebastian's siding with! I could have told you. He's for anything that makes him money!"

Joe was gasping for breath from the strain as they ran down the alley that sided the Obrion pole corral. The tiny fire was burning at the corner of the saddle shed. The two *peon* hostlers were squatting beside it, smoking, as Rick emerged from the shadows, Joe directly behind him.

"Two horses saddled quick!" Joe called in Spanish. "My El Rey and another."

One of the hostlers threw an armful of hay on the fire as Joe started clumsily toward the saddle shed. And as the flaming hay blazed light over the corral, Rick yelled: "Down, Joe!"

Rick's gun fired at the corner of the saddle shed where a man had appeared with a rifle sighted at Joe. The licking flame above the dry hay made the target clear. The rifle bullet tore into Joe as Rick's gun fired.

The men dodged back into the shed. And Joe went spinning, staggering off to the right, hit badly, helpless, without even a chance to draw his own gun as he plunged to the ground.

Rick felt a cold shock in his left leg, heard the rifle shot back across the corral. His first hunch on the Laguna stage had been right. The Iron Hat range was poison for him. First, Dan dead in the burned ranch house. Then Jean Madden to mock the memories that had brought him on the long journey back. Then Joe, outlawed and gone bad. And when he had Joe back at his side, as a brother once more for a night, this ambush had dropped Joe with a treacherous shot. And here death was spitting across the corral at him.

But he could still move, still keep his feet — and Rick ran, now limping himself, to the fire. He heard a second rifle shot behind him. It missed him or hit Joe, crawling torturously on the ground. Rick ran through the fire, kicking hard, scattering blazing hay and wood embers in a shower of sparks, flame, and smoke. And in the flare of light it made, Rick dived to the ground at the end of the saddle shed.

The *peones* had vanished. Frightened horses were whinnying and raising dust as they bolted around the corral. And the scattered fire died to a duller glow.

The long gun's thin report came again across the corral. The bullet screamed away into the night. And from behind the gun a voice shouted: "He's there at the end of the shed, Curt! I hit him! Go out an' get him!"

But Curt Hanna was swearing, groaning inside the adobe end wall of the shed, and he did not answer. Another rifle bullet drove dirt particles from the adobe wall into Rick's face.

"Curt, are you gonna get him?"

Rick answered with bitter fury out of the past years. "Try it yourself, Rufe! Or aren't you man enough?"

"I'm man enough!" Rufe's shout came back through the rising dust that was hampering his shooting. "I was man enough to get that damn brother Dan of yours! You'll be the last one, Rick Candleman! We got Dan first before you could get back. And soon as I found out you'd skipped jail, I started across the Border to catch you with Joe, if Hanna hadn't killed Joe first as he started out to do. I knew you'd head this way to hook up with him. We're sending the last of the Candlemans to hell tonight! And Sebastian Obrion's bringing his men to help. Come out and get it before some of Obrion's men drag you out!"

Dust was drifting thicker over the dying fire glow as Rick came out, his hands reaching for the top pole of the corral. He went over fast, falling on the dirt outside, and there was no shot from Rufe Madden's gun. The milling horses, the dust, the dying fire light might have kept Rufe from seeing him.

Half a dozen freight wagons stood outside the back of the corral. When Rick passed them and turned the next corner of the corral, he heard the obscene taunts of Rufe Madden ahead. He saw Rufe's dark bulk crouching, sighting a rifle through the corral poles.

"Come get the last Candleman, Rufe!"

Rufe Madden whirled, snatching the rifle back from the corral bars. It was too dark to see Rufe's thick, vindictive face, but he was caught by surprise. His hasty shot missed.

Rick ran at him, shooting. The first one missed. Rufe had time to lever in another cartridge and start to snap-shoot. He never pulled the trigger. Rick's lead smashed him on down to the ground.

Rick stopped for an instant to make sure it was done, and kept going to the corral gate which he jerked wide. Joe was flat on the ground in that dangerous mill of frightened horses.

A running figure reached the gate as Rick started in. He almost drove a bullet before he recognized Maisa Candleman.

"Where's Joe?" she cried at him. "I heard shooting!"

"Joe's down here under the horses!" Rick snarled at her. "Rufe Madden did it...but your damn brother's in on it! Going to wipe out all the Candlemans tonight. Get outa here before I forget you're a woman!"

But she darted into the corral. Rick followed her. And the nearest horses instantly found the open gate and led out a thundering, frightened stampede.

A gun blasted loudly in the middle of the corral and, when Rick plunged through the settling dust, he found Joe sprawled on his face, six-gun still in his hand. Beyond Joe, near a smoldering brand from the fire, lay big handsome Curt Hanna with his face to the stars and the ugly smashed hole of a .45 bullet in his right cheek. Joe had done that and collapsed again.

And when Rick turned back, he found Maisa Candleman down in the dirt and dust, holding Joe's head, crooning and crying to him.

"Joe, speak to me! My dear! My dearest *querido!* My big, brave *niño!* Joe, if you die, your Maisa dies too!"

"You're wastin' your breath!" Rick said harshly. "Here comes your brother and a bunch of his hard cases to finish it off! Get outa the way. Lemme drag Joe in the shed and make a fight of it!"

Maisa gave him no answer. He might not have been there as she caught the big .45 from Joe's hand and whirled up, facing the corral. Some light still came from the last embers of the fire. Enough to show the wild frantic passion on the red-headed girl's features as she stood over Joe and faced the gate with the gun cocked.

Rick had heard the shouts of running men, had guessed correctly. Sebastian Obrion had gone to the plaza for help. Now Rick knew what was coming; his crawling nerves cried to get under cover in the saddle shed. And yet he could not leave Joe out here in the open with his wife. Rick crouched, gun ready, waiting for the shot that would start the end of the Candlemans.

But the shadowy forms that ran to the outside of the corral stopped there uncertainly as they saw the girl facing them. Then Sebastian Obrion's angry shout came from among them.

"Come out, Maisa! Get back to the house!"

"Not until he's dead," she cried wildly back at her brother. "And when he dies, then I come to kill you, Sebastian! I swear it on our mother's grave! Tonight I promise you, Sebastian Obrion, I kill you for this thing you have done to my Joe! Shoot me now! If he dies, then I die, too, anyway! And now I shoot the first one who comes near my Joe!"

In the silence that followed, a rough amazed comment from one of the gunmen burst out: "Does she *mean* it? Sebastian, she's yore sister! It's up to you!"

Sebastian Obrion's reply through the corral bars was injured. "Maisa, this is not my work! Hanna and Madden came here to do this!"

She cried back: "What do I care about them now? They're dead! You are the one who can hurt Joe! Come here, Sebastian, like a man, and face me over my Joe!"

"I don't think I can do that now," Sebastian Obrion refused out of the night. "But if Madden and Hanna are dead, Maisa, what have I to do with this? I didn't come across the Border to kill your Joe."

"You lie, Sebastian!"

"I swear it," said Sebastian reasonably. "If Hanna and Madden are dead, what do we gain by hurting my sister? Put up the gun so we can help Joe."

"I think he means it," Rick said.

"Where there is no money to make, he means it!" she choked, and lowered the gun and dropped to her knees beside Joe again.

Joe was stirring, speaking Rick's name painfully. Rick went to a knee quickly. Joe's dirt-crusted face worked in a painful grin.

"I heard most of it, Rick. Ain't she somethin' to love? I told her she was in my blood like fever, an' she was, an' always will be!"

"I don't blame you, kid," Rick said with a lump in his throat. "How bad you shot?"

"Can't tell. It's up under my shoulder. Kinda numbs me but there ain't any blood in my mouth yet. Rick, listening to Maisa made me think of something I almost forgot, the way things happened so quick. That Jean Madden was all tore up about you when I talked to her in the doorway. She came across the Border lookin' for you. Said Pat Cody told her you was headin' this way. Her brother Rufe had come home, questioned her sharp about you, and saddled for a trip. She figured Rufe was coming after you an' she out-rode him to get here ahead of him and warn you he was coming. Said she told Maisa and the others she was lookin' for Rufe, so they wouldn't stop her getting to you when you showed up. Rick, she was near crying for worry about you."

"Joe," said Rick in a shaking voice, "you aren't lying to me?"

"Would I lie, Rick, when I'm this close to Heaven and with Maisa to think about for myself?" Joe denied weakly. "Seems like you ought to do something about Jean Madden, Rick."

"I came back from the Argentine to do it," Rick confessed. "Joe, they're going to take you to the house. I'll see you there."

Joe was grinning knowingly as Rick stood up and Obrion's men swarmed around the spot. They were used to bullet wounds. They'd take care of Joe as well as anyone.

But Rick turned back, pushed through the men and knelt again by Joe.

"Joe, I'm going back to the Argentine quick now. There's plenty of place for you and your wife down there...and nobody worries about what's happened in the past up in this part of the world. It'll be a home and a chance again."

Joe was still smiling faintly up at the dark sky, his face pale in the moonlight, when Rick suddenly realized that he and Maisa were alone, and turned blindly away. Maisa let out a scream and yanked Joe's body to her.

Rick rose then and passed silently among the Mexicans who had gathered around Joe in the corral, not seeing them. He vanished in the shadows of the night, but he had been walking in the direction of the room Obrion reserved for guests.

WALTER VAN TILBURG CLARK

WALTER VAN TILBURG CLARK (1909–1971) was born in East Orland, Maine, and in 1917 moved with his family to Nevada, the state which served as the setting for most of his subsequent fiction. He was graduated with a Bachelor's degree from the University of Nevada in 1931 and went on for a Master's degree in English, writing a thesis on the Tristram legend. He published a volume of poetry, TEN WOMEN IN GALE'S HOUSE AND SHORTER POEMS (Christopher Publishing House, 1932), and then accepted a teaching apprenticeship at the University of Vermont. While there he earned a second Master's degree, writing a thesis on Robinson Jeffers. Clark had personally met Jeffers at his Thor House on the California coast and was as impressed with the man himself and his way of life as with his poetry.

According to Max Westbrook in his biographical and critical study, WALTER VAN TILBURG CLARK (Twayne Publishers, 1969), the two most significant influences on Clark's creative writing were Jeffers and C.G. Jung. Clark's first Western novel was THE OX-BOW INCIDENT (Random House, 1940). It won him an immediate place in American letters. On the surface, this novel would seem to be concerned with the notion of frontier justice. It tells of three men encountered on the trail by a vigilante group and hanged as cattle rustlers only for them ultimately to be proven innocent. Westbrook's reading of this story, however, proceeds on a deeper level. "The subject of THE OX-BOW INCIDENT," he wrote, "...is not a plea for legal procedure. The subject is man's mutilation of himself, man's sometimes trivial, sometimes large failures to get beyond the narrow images of his own ego. The tragedy of THE OX-BOW INCIDENT is that most of us, including the man of sensitivity and the man of reason, are alienated from the saving grace of archetypal reality. Our lives, then, though not without possibility, are often stories of a cruel and irrevocable mistake."

The terrain, thus, is again familiar, encountered in one aspect or another in "The Last Thunder Song," "The Desert Crucible," and "Werewolf." Yet, none of the authors of these stories approached the Western story with quite Clark's profound erudition in addition to the stress he placed on human psychology, the psychology of the personal unconscious, the collective unconscious, and group psychology. In its way, THE OX-BOW INCIDENT proved as shattering and powerful an influence on the way the Western story would be written as in their way Owen Wister's THE VIRGINIAN, T.T. Flynn's early fiction for *Dime Western* and *Star Western,* or Ernest Haycox's serials for *Collier's* had also in their ways. T.V. Olsen openly admitted his debt to Clark's novel and the new dimension it opened for the way the Western story could be written. Les Savage, Jr., in his Western fiction also focused on the psychological dimension in ways that were far less apparent in the work of Western writers before Clark. Indeed, to a degree, it might be said that not a Western story written with a serious intent after 1940 is totally lacking in this heightened awareness of the psychological dimension of character. There are even intimations of it in the stories I have included by Peter Dawson and T.T. Flynn.

Because of the commercial success of his first novel and its sale to motion pictures, with William Wellman directing the screen version, Clark hoped that he could henceforth concentrate on writing fiction and leave his teaching career behind him. He published a number of short stories while he worked diligently on his very long and not very successful THE CITY OF TREMBLING LEAVES (Random House, 1945). It is an initiation story in which setting and a sense of the land are negligible. This painful failure prompted Clark to seek his roots in the West. In 1946 he went to live in Taos, New Mexico, and returned to Nevada toward the end of the decade. THE TRACK OF THE CAT (Random House, 1949), the distillation of this effort at spiritual renascence, is a story that demonstrates why two hunters are killed pursuing a panther, symbolizing the principle of evil in the world, because they do not understand it, and why two hunters who do understand it are able to slay the beast. Herman Melville's MOBY-DICK was very obviously the paradigm Clark had in mind, but the primal inspiration evident in THE OX-BOW INCIDENT is lacking in its immediacy and the later novel is ultimately only epigonal. It was, however, also sold for a motion picture adaptation and, upon release, became just a hunting adventure film.

Clark next published a collection of his short stories titled THE WATCHFUL GODS AND OTHER STORIES (Random House, 1950). Unfortunately, having been so gracious toward his first book, the critics became increasingly harsh in their appraisals of each book Clark published after it. In an essay titled "The Western Writer and the Eastern Establishment" in *Western American Literature* (Winter, 67) the late Vardis Fisher observed, "I read recently a surmise that Walter Clark, a fine artist, gave up writing because of the unfairness of some of his critics. If true, what a pity that he paid any attention to them!" This may well have been the reason Clark did quit writing. He returned to teaching, at the university level, and left behind only the fragments of an unfinished novel when he died. However, this notwithstanding, THE OX-BOW INCIDENT assures him always of a pivotal rôle in having charted the course of the Western story in the new direction it would take in the 1940s and 1950s.

"The Wind and the Snow of Winter" is a short story from THE WATCH-FUL GODS AND OTHER STORIES. It is one of the few stories Clark wrote that has much of the power and depth of his first novel. And the land *is* a character. Indeed, here as too seldom elsewhere, Clark was able to combine a vivid description of physical topography and characterization of a human personality with an eerie sense of metaphysical shadows and meanings less decipherable but somehow more potent as they are also in the best works by Zane Grey and Max Brand.

THE WIND AND THE SNOW OF WINTER
1944

It was near sunset when Mike Braneen came onto the last pitch of the old wagon road which had led into Gold Rock from the east since the Comstock days. The road was just two ruts in the hard earth, with sagebrush growing between them, and was full of steep pitches and sharp turns. From the summit it descended even more steeply into Gold Rock in a series of short switchbacks down the slope of the cañon. There was a paved highway on the other side of the pass now, but Mike never used that. Cars coming from behind made him uneasy, so that he couldn't follow his own thoughts long, but had to keep turning around every few minutes, to see that his burro, Annie, was staying out on the shoulder of the road, where she would be safe. Mike didn't like cars anyway, and on the old road he could forget about them, and feel more like himself. He could forget about Annie too, except when the light, quick tapping of her hoofs behind him stopped. Even then he didn't really break his thoughts. It was more as if the tapping were another sound from his own inner machinery and, when it stopped, he stopped too, and turned around to see what she was doing. When he began to walk ahead again at the same slow, unvarying pace, his arms scarcely swinging at all, his body bent a little forward from the waist, he would not be aware that there had been any interruption of the memory or the story that was going on in his head. Mike did not like to have his stories interrupted except by an idea of his own, something to do with prospecting, or the arrival of his story at an actual memory which warmed him to closer recollection or led into a new and more attractive story.

An intense, golden light, almost liquid, fanned out from the peaks above him and reached eastward under the gray sky, and the snow which occasionally swarmed across this light was fine and dry. Such little squalls had been going on all day, and still there was nothing like real snow down, but only a fine powder which the wind swept along until it caught under the brush, leaving the ground bare. Yet Mike Braneen was not deceived. This was not just a flurrying day; it was the beginning of winter. If not tonight, then tomorrow, or the next day, the snow would begin which shut off the mountains, so that a man might as well be on a great plain for all he could see, perhaps even the snow which blinded a man at once and blanketed the desert in an hour. Fifty-two years in this country had made Mike Braneen sure about such things, although he didn't give much thought to them, but only to what he had to do because of them. Three nights before, he had been awakened by a change in the wind. It was no longer a wind born in the near mountains, cold with night and altitude, but a wind from far places, full of a damp chill which got through his blankets and into his bones. The stars had still been clear and close above the dark humps of the mountains, and overhead the constellations had moved slowly in full panoply, unbroken by any invisible lower darkness; yet he had lain there half awake for a few minutes, hearing the new wind beat the brush around him, hearing Annie stirring restlessly and thumping in her hobble. He had thought drowsily. Smells like winter this time, and then, it's held off a long time this year, pretty near the end of December. Then he had gone back to sleep, mildly happy because the change meant he would be going back to Gold Rock. Gold Rock was the other half of Mike Braneen's life. When the smell of winter came, he always started back for Gold Rock. From March or April until the smell of winter, he wandered slowly about among the mountains, anywhere between the White Pines and the Virginias, with only his burro for company. Then there would come the change, and they would head back for Gold Rock.

Mike had traveled with a good many burros during that time, eighteen or twenty, he thought, although he was not sure. He could not remember them all, but only those he had had first, when he was a young man and always thought most about seeing women when he got back to Gold Rock, or those with something queer about them, like Baldy, who'd had a great, pale patch, like a bald spot, on one side of his belly, or those who'd had something queer happen to them, like Maria. He could remember just how it had been that night. He could remember it as if it were last night. It had been in Hamilton. He had felt unhappy, because he could remember Hamilton when the whole hollow was full of people and buildings, and everything was new and active. He had gone to sleep in the hollow shell of the Wells Fargo Building, hearing an old iron shutter banging against the wall in the wind. In the morning, Maria had been gone. He had followed the scuffing track she made on account of her loose hobble, and it had led far up the old snow-gullied road to Treasure Hill, and then ended at one of the black shafts that opened like mouths right at the edge of the road. A man remembered a thing like that. There weren't many burros that foolish. But burros with nothing particular about them were hard to remember especially those he'd had in the last twenty years or so, when he had gradually stopped feeling so personal about them, and had begun to call all the jennies Annie and all the burros Jack.

The clicking of the little hoofs behind him stopped, and Mike stopped too, and turned around. Annie was pulling at a line of yellow grass along the edge of the road.

"Come on, Maria," Mike said patiently. The burro at once stopped pulling at the dead grass and came on up towards him, her small black nose working, the ends of the grass standing out on each side of it like whiskers. Mike began to climb again, ahead of her.

It was a long time since he had been caught by a winter, too. He could not remember how long. All the beginnings ran together in his mind, as if they were all the beginning of one winter so far back that he had almost forgotten it. He could still remember clearly, though, the winter he had stayed out on purpose, clear into January. He had been a young man then, thirty-five or forty or forty-five, somewhere in there. He would have to stop and try to bring back a whole string of memories about what had happened just before, in order to remember just how old he had been, and it wasn't worth the trouble. Besides, sometimes even that system didn't work. It would lead him into an old camp where he had been a number of times, and the dates would get mixed up. It was impossible to remember any other way; because all his comings and goings had been so much alike. He had been young, anyhow, and not much afraid of anything except running out of water in the wrong place; not even afraid of the winter. He had stayed out because he'd thought he had a good thing, and he had wanted to prove it. He could remember how it felt to be out in the clear winter weather on the mountains; the piñon trees and the junipers weighted down with feathery snow, and making sharp, blue shadows on the white slopes. The hills had made blue shadows on one another too, and in the still air his pick had made the beginning of a sound like a bell's. He knew he had been young, because he could remember taking a day off now and then, just to go tramping around those hills, up and down the white and through the blue shadows, on a kind of holiday. He had pretended to his common sense that he was seriously prospecting, and had carried his hammer, and even his drill along, but he had really just been gallivanting, playing colt. Maybe he had been even younger than thirty-five, though he could still be stirred a little, for that matter, by the memory of the kind of weather which had sent him gallivanting. High-blue weather, he called it. There were two kinds of high-blue weather, besides the winter kind, which didn't set him off very often, spring and fall. In the spring it would have a soft, puffy wind and soft, puffy white clouds which made separate shadows that traveled silently across hills that looked soft too. In the fall it would be still, and there would be no clouds at all in the blue, but there would be something in the golden air and the soft, steady sunlight on the mountains that made a man as uneasy as the spring blowing, though in a different way, more sad and not so excited. In the spring high-blue, a man had been likely to think about women he had slept with, or wanted to sleep with, or imaginary women made up with the help of newspaper pictures of actresses or young society matrons, or of the old oil paintings in the Lucky Boy Saloon, which showed pale, almost naked women against dark, sumptuous backgrounds — women with long hair or braided hair, calm, virtuous faces, small hands and feet, and ponderous limbs, breasts, and buttocks. In the fall high-blue, though it had been much longer since he had seen a woman, or heard a woman's voice, he was more likely to think about old friends, men, or places he had heard about, or places he hadn't seen for a long time. He himself thought most often about Goldfield the way he had last seen it in the summer in 1912. That was as far south as Mike had ever been in Nevada. Since then he had never been south of Tonopah. When the high-blue weather was past, though, and the season worked toward winter, he began to think about Gold Rock. There were only three or four winters out of the fifty-two when he hadn't gone home to Gold Rock, to his old room at Mrs. Wright's, up on Fourth Street, and to his meals in the dining room at the International House, and to the Lucky Boy, where he could talk to Tom Connover and his other friends, and play cards, or have a drink to hold in his hand while he sat and remembered.

This journey had seemed a little different from most, though. It had started the same as usual, but as he had come across the two vast valleys, and through the pass in the low range between them, he hadn't felt quite the same. He'd felt younger and more awake, it seemed to him, and yet, in a way, older too, suddenly older. He had been sure that there was plenty of time, and yet he had been a little afraid of getting caught in the storm. He had kept looking ahead to see if the mountains on the horizon were still clearly outlined, or if they had been cut off by a lowering of the clouds. He had thought more than once, how bad it would be to get caught out there when the real snow began, and he had been disturbed by the first flakes. It had seemed hard to him to have to walk so far, too. He had kept thinking about distance. Also the snowy cold had searched out the regions of his body where old injuries had healed. He had taken off his left mitten a good many times, to blow on the fingers which had been frosted the year he was sixty-three, so that now it didn't take much cold to turn them white and stiffen them. The queer tingling, partly like an itch and partly like a pain, in the patch on his back that had been burned in that old powder blast, was sharper than he could remember its having been before. The rheumatism in his joints, which was so old a companion that it usually made him feel no more than tight-knit and stiff, and the place where his leg had been broken and torn when that ladder broke in '97 ached, and had a pulse he could count. All this made him believe that he was walking more slowly than usual, although nothing, probably not even a deliberate attempt, could actually have changed his pace. Sometimes he even thought, with a moment of fear, that he was getting tired.

On the other hand, he felt unusually clear and strong in his mind. He remembered things with a clarity which was like living them again — nearly all of them events from many years back, from the time when he had been really active and fearless and every burro had had its own name. Some of these events, like the night he had spent in Eureka with the little, brown-haired whore, a night in the fall in 1888 or '89, somewhere in there, he had not once thought of for years. Now he could remember even her name. Armandy she had called herself: a funny name. They all picked names for their business, of course, romantic names like Cecily or Rosamunde or Belle or Claire, or hard names like Diamond Gert or Horseshoe Sal, or names that were pinned on them, like Indian Kate or Roman Mary, but Armandy was different.

He could remember Armandy as if he were with her now, not the way she had behaved in bed; he couldn't remember anything particular about that. In fact, he couldn't be sure that he remembered anything particular about that at all. There were others he could remember more clearly for the way they had behaved in bed, women he had been with more often. He had been with Armandy only that one night. He remembered little things about being with her, things that made it seem good to think of being with her again. Armandy had a room upstairs in a hotel. They could hear a piano playing in a club across the street. He could hear the tune, and it was one he knew, although he didn't know its name. It was a gay tune that went on and on the same, but still it sounded sad when you heard it through the hotel window, with the lights from the bars and hotels shining on the street, and the people coming and going through the lights, and then, beyond the lights, the darkness where the mountains were. Armandy wore a white silk dress with a high waist and a locket on a gold chain. The dress made her look very brown and like a young girl. She used a white powder on her face, that smelled like violets, but this could not hide her brownness. The locket was heart-shaped, and it opened to show a cameo of a man's hand holding a woman's hand very gently, just their fingers laid out long together, and the thumbs holding the way they were sometimes on tombstones. There were two little gold initials on each hand, but Armandy would never tell what they stood for, or even if the locket was really her own. He stood in the window, looking down at the club from which the piano music was coming, and Armandy stood beside him, with her shoulders against his arm, and a glass of wine in her hand. He could see the toe of her white satin slipper showing from under the edge of her skirt. Her big hat, loaded with black and white plumes, lay on the dresser behind him. His own leather coat, with the sheepskin lining, lay across the foot of the bed. It was a big bed, with a knobby brass foot and head. There was one oil lamp burning in the chandelier in the middle room. Armandy was soft-spoken, gentle, and a little fearful, always looking at him to see what he was thinking. He stood with his arms folded. His arms felt big and strong upon his heavily muscled chest. He stood there, pretending to be in no hurry, but really thinking eagerly about what he would do with Armandy, who had something about her which tempted him to be cruel. He stood there, with his chin down into his heavy dark beard, and watched a man come riding down the middle of the street from the west. The horse was a fine black, which lifted its head and feet with pride. The man sat very straight, with a high rein, and something about his clothes and hat made him appear to be in uniform, although it wasn't a uniform he was wearing. The man also saluted friends upon the sidewalks like an officer, bending his head just slightly, and touching his hat instead of lifting it. Mike Braneen asked Armandy who the man was, and then felt angry because she could tell him, and because he was an important man who owned a mine that was in bonanza. He mocked the airs with which the man rode, and his princely greetings. He mocked the man cleverly, and Armandy laughed and repeated what he said, and made him drink a little of her wine as a reward. Mike had been drinking whisky, and he did not like wine anyway, but this was not the moment in which to refuse such an invitation.

Old Mike remembered all this, which had been completely forgotten for years. He could not remember what he and Armandy had said, but he remembered everything else, and he felt very lonesome for Armandy, and for the room with the red, figured carpet and the brass chandelier with oil lamps in it, and the open window with the long tune coming up through it, and the young summer night outside on the mountains. This loneliness was so much more intense than his familiar loneliness that it made him feel very young. Memories like this had come up again and again during these three days. It was like beginning life over again. It had tricked him into thinking, more than once, next summer I'll make the strike, and this time I'll put it into something safe for the rest of my life, and stop this fool wandering around while I've still got some time left — a way of thinking which he had really stopped a long time before.

It was getting darker rapidly in the pass. When a gust of wind brought the snow against Mike's face so hard that he noticed the flakes felt larger, he looked up. The light was still there, although the fire was dying out of it, and the snow swarmed across it more thickly. Mike remembered God. He did not think anything exact. He did not think about his own relationship to God. He merely felt the idea as a comforting presence. He'd always had a feeling about God whenever he looked at a sunset, especially a sunset which came through under a stormy sky. It had been the strongest feeling left in him until these memories like the one about Armandy had begun. Even in this last pass, his strange fear of the storm had come on him again a couple of times, but now that he had looked at the light and thought of God, it was gone. In a few minutes he would come to the summit and look down into his lighted city. He felt happily hurried by this anticipation.

He would take the burro down and stable her in John Hammersmith's shed, where he always kept her. He would spread fresh straw for her, and see that the shed was tight against the wind and snow, and get a measure of grain for her from John. Then he would go up to Mrs. Wright's house at the top of Fourth Street, and leave his things in the same room he always had, the one in front, which looked down over the roofs and chimneys of his city, and across at the east wall of the cañon, from which the sun rose late. He would trim his beard with Mrs. Wright's shears, and shave the upper part of his cheeks. He would bathe out of the blue bowl and pitcher, and wipe himself with the towel with yellow flowers on it, and dress in the good dark suit and the good black shoes with the gleaming box toes, and the good black hat which he had left in the chest in his room. In this way he would perform the ceremony which ended the life of the desert and began the life of Gold Rock. Then he would go down to the International House, and greet Arthur Morris in the gleaming bar, and go into the dining room and eat the best supper they had, with fresh meat and vegetables, and new-made pie, and two cups of hot clear coffee. He would be served by the plump blonde waitress who always joked with him, and gave him many little extra things with his first supper, including the drink which Arthur Morris always sent in from the bar.

At this point Mike Braneen stumbled in his mind, and his anticipation wavered. He could not be sure that the plump blonde waitress would serve him. For a moment he saw her in a long skirt, and the dining room of the International House, behind her, had potted palms standing in the corners, and was full of the laughter and loud, manly talk of many customers who wore high vests and mustaches and beards. These men leaned back from tables covered with empty dishes. They patted their tight vests and lighted expensive cigars. He knew all their faces. If he were to walk down the aisle between the tables on his side, they would all speak to him. But he also seemed to remember the dining room with only a few tables, with oilcloth on them instead of linen, and with moody young men sitting at them in their work clothes — strangers who worked for the highway department, or were just passing through, or talked mining in terms which he did not understand or which made him angry.

No, it would not be the plump blonde waitress. He did not know who it would be. It didn't matter. After supper he would go up Cañon Street under the arcade to the Lucky Boy Saloon, and there it would be the same as ever. There would be the laurel wreaths on the frosted glass panels of the doors, and the old sign upon the window, the sign that was older than Tom Connover, almost as old as Mike Braneen himself. He would open the door and see the bottles and the white women in the paintings, and the card table in the back corner and the big stove and the chairs along the wall. Tom would look around from his place behind the bar.

"Well, now," he would roar, "look who's here, boys. Now will you believe it's winter?" he would roar at them.

Some of them would be the younger men, of course, and there might even be a few strangers, but this would only add to the dignity of his reception, and there would also be his friends. There would be Henry Bray with the gray walrus mustache, and Mark Wilton and Pat Gallagher. They would all welcome him loudly.

"Mike, how are you anyway?" Tom would roar, leaning across the bar to shake hands with his big, heavy, soft hand with the diamond ring on it. "And what'll it be, Mike? The same?" he'd ask, as if Mike had been in there no longer ago than the night before.

Mike would play that game too. "The same," he would say.

Then he would really be back in Gold Rock: never mind the plump blonde waitress.

Mike came to the summit of the old road and stopped and looked down. For a moment he felt lost again, as he had when he'd thought about the plump blonde waitress. He had expected Cañon Street to look much brighter. He had expected a lot of orange windows close together on the other side of the cañon. Instead there were only a few scattered lights across the darkness, and they were white. They made no communal glow upon the steep slope, but gave out only single, white needles of light, which pierced the darkness secretly and lonesomely, as if nothing could ever pass from one house to another over there. Cañon Street was very dark, too. There it went, the street he loved, steeply down into the bottom of the cañon, and down its length there were only the few street lights, more than a block apart, swinging in the wind and darting about that cold, small light. The snow whirled and swooped under the nearest street light below.

"You are getting to be an old fool," Mike Braneen said out loud to himself, and felt better. This was the way Gold Rock was now, of course, and he loved it all the better. It was a place that grew old with a man, that was going to die sometime, too. There could be an understanding with it.

He worked his way slowly down into Cañon Street, with Annie slipping and checking behind him. Slowly, with the blown snow behind them, they came to the first built-in block, and passed the first dim light showing through a smudged window under the arcade. They passed the dark places after it, and the second light. Then Mike Braneen stopped in the middle of the street, and Annie stopped beside him, pulling her rump in and turning her head away from the snow. A highway truck, coming down from the head of the cañon, had to get way over into the wrong side of the street to pass them. The driver leaned out as he went by, and yelled, "Pull over, Pop. You're in town now."

Mike Braneen didn't hear him. He was staring at the Lucky Boy. The Lucky Boy was dark, and there were boards nailed across the big window that had shown the sign. At last Mike went over onto the board walk to look more closely. Annie followed him, but stopped at the edge of the walk and scratched her neck against a post of the arcade. There was the other sign, hanging crossways under the arcade, and even in that gloom Mike could see that it said Lucky Boy and had a Jack of Diamonds painted on it. There was no mistake. The Lucky Boy sign, and others like it under the arcade, creaked and rattled in the wind.

There were footsteps coming along the boards. The boards sounded hollow, and sometimes one of them rattled. Mike Braneen looked down slowly from the sign and peered at the approaching figure. It was a man wearing a sheepskin coat with the collar turned up round his head. He was walking quickly, like a man who knew where he was going, and why, and where he had been. Mike almost let him pass. Then he spoke.

"Say, fella...?"

He even reached out a hand as if to catch hold of the man's sleeve, though he didn't touch it. The man stopped, and asked impatiently, "Yeah?" and Mike let the hand down again slowly.

"Well, what is it?" the man asked.

"I don't want anything." Mike said. "I got plenty."

"O.K., O.K.," the man said. "What's the matter?"

Mike moved his hand towards the Lucky Boy. "It's closed," he said.

"I see it is, Dad," the man said. He laughed a little. He didn't seem to be in quite so much of a hurry now.

"How long has it been closed?" Mike asked.

"Since about June, I guess," the man said. "Old Tom Connover, the guy that ran it, died last June."

Mike waited for a moment. "Tom died?" he asked.

"Yup. I guess he'd just kept it open out of love of the place anyway. There hasn't been any real business for years. Nobody cared to keep it open after him."

The man started to move on, but then he waited, peering, trying to see Mike better.

"This June?" Mike asked finally.

"Yup. This last June."

"Oh," Mike said. Then he just stood there. He wasn't thinking anything. There didn't seem to be anything to think.

"You knew him?" the man asked.

"Thirty years," Mike said. "No, more'n that," he said, and started to figure out how long he had known Tom Connover but lost it, and said, as if it would do just as well, "He was a lot younger than I am, though."

"Hey," said the man, coming closer, and peering again. "You're Mike Braneen, aren't you?"

"Yes," Mike said.

"Gee, I didn't recognize you at first. I'm sorry."

"That's all right," Mike said. He didn't know who the man was, or what he was sorry about.

He turned his head slowly, and looked out into the street. The snow was coming down heavily now. The street was all white. He saw Annie with her head and shoulders in under the arcade, but the snow settling on her rump.

"Well, I guess I'd better get Molly under cover," he said. He moved toward the burro a step, but then halted.

"Say, fella...?"

The man had started on, but he turned back. He had to wait for Mike to speak.

"I guess this about Tom mixed me up."

"Sure," the man said. "It's tough, an old friend like that."

"Where do I turn to get to Mrs. Wright's place?"

"Mrs. Wright?"

"Mrs. William Wright," Mike said. "Her husband used to be a foreman in the Aztec. Got killed in the fire."

"Oh," the man said. He didn't say anything more, but just stood there, looking at the shadowy bulk of old Mike.

"She's not dead, too, is she?" Mike asked slowly.

"Yeah, I'm afraid she is, Mr. Braneen," the man said. "Look," he said more cheerfully. "It's Mrs. Branley's house you want right now, isn't it? Place where you stayed last winter?"

Finally Mike said, "Yeah, I guess it is."

"I'm going up that way. I'll walk up with you," the man said.

After they had started, Mike thought that he ought to take the burro down to John Hammersmith's first, but he was afraid to ask about it. They walked on down Cañon Street, with Annie walking along beside them in the gutter. At the first side street they turned right and began to climb the steep hill toward another of the little street lights dancing over a crossing. There was no sidewalk here, and Annie followed right at their heels. That one street light was the only light showing up ahead.

When they were halfway up to the light, Mike asked, "She die this summer, too?"

The man turned his body half around, so that he could hear inside his collar. "What?"

"Did she die this summer, too?"

"Who?"

"Mrs. Wright," Mike said.

The man looked at him, trying to see his face as they came up towards the light. Then he turned back again, and his voice was muffled by the collar.

"No, she died quite a while ago, Mr. Braneen."

"Oh," Mike said finally.

They came up onto the crossing under the light, and the snow-laden wind whirled around them again. They passed under the light, and their three lengthening shadows before them were obscured by the innumerable tiny shadows of the flakes.

DOROTHY M. JOHNSON

DOROTHY MARIE JOHNSON (1905–1984) was born in McGregor, Iowa, and grew up in Whitefish, Montana. She was graduated with a Bachelor's degree from the University of Montana at Missoula. She worked variously as a stenographer before venturing to New York City in 1935 where she found employment, first with the Gregg Publishing Company until 1944, then with Farrell Publishing Corporation until 1950. It was while doing editorial work at these magazine and book publishing companies that she herself began writing in earnest (she had had only one short story published before leaving Whitefish). Her first book, BEULAH BUNNY TELLS ALL (Morrow, 1942), is a collection of short stories about a fictitious schoolteacher previously published in *The Saturday Evening Post*.

It was also during this period that she began reading extensively about the Plains Indians and visited the museums in the area which specialized in their artifacts and cultures. It was as a result of this activity that she began to create her first Indian stories, selling them principally to *Argosy, Collier's, The Saturday Evening Post,* and *Cosmopolitan*. When queried as to the reason her work had gone so thoroughly in this direction, her truthful answer was that she was homesick for Montana. She returned to Whitefish on a vacation in 1950. When she was offered the position of news editor for the Whitefish *Pilot,* a weekly newspaper, she flew back to New York and stayed there only long enough to resign from her job at Farrell Publishing and to pack up her things. In 1953 she moved to Missoula to work as the secretary-manager of the Montana Press Association and the next year was also appointed an assistant professor of journalism at her former *alma mater*.

Bill Gulick, a frequent contributor of Western stories to many of the same magazines for which she wrote, once said of Johnson, "She was not a woman who needed to be liberated by legislation; she was born liberated, and never changed." She had nothing but contempt for political correctness in the Western story, or anywhere else. In a letter to the editor of *The Missoulian* protesting the newspaper's clumsy attempt to avoid "sexism" in its Help Wanted columns, she wrote: "The city of Missoula advertised for applications for the position of Ward 5 'alderperson.' This nicety makes me gag. There is nothing wrong with the last syllable of 'alderman' except to persons who just can't get their minds off sex. Sometimes I worry about the *huperson* race. (Signed) Dorothy M Johnson, a *woperson*."

Among the hundreds of Western writers with whom I have spoken and corresponded over the years, Dorothy M. Johnson was always the most crisply accurate in her assessments and the most poignantly amusing. Accuracy, in fact, even got into an obituary notice following her death from Parkinson's disease. Benjamin Capps, in his *memoria* for Johnson in *The Roundup* (1/85), cited Dorothy Powers's tribute to her friend in the Spokane *Spokesman-Review*. Johnson had insisted that the inscription on her headstone contain a single word: "Paid." Johnson had told Powers, "God and I know what that means, and nobody else needs to know." Powers's conclusion was "that Dorothy Johnson meant she had done her best to live a life that left nothing owing the world for her time and space in it. Even in death she was — as always — accurate. But she was much too modest. That marker should really read: 'Accounts Receivable.' For this world is greatly in *her* debt — for laughter and literacy and love of life."

"A Man Called Horse" was first published in *Collier's* (1/7/50). It incorporates a theme common in Johnson's Western stories whereby men and women grow as human beings through humiliation rather than by conquest. The story was included in Johnson's first collection of her short Western fiction, INDIAN COUNTRY (Ballantine, 1953), dating from that early period during which Ian and Betty Ballantine published their Western story titles simultaneously in both hard cover and paperback editions. Jack Schaefer contributed a Foreword in which he observed that Johnson was "one of the few writers whose authenticity, integrity, sheer vigor and excitement were helping to build a body of true literature about the American West." Her second story collection, published as an original paperback by Ballantine in 1958, was titled THE HANGING TREE. This appeared for the first time in hard covers in the reprint edition from Gregg Press in 1980.

Controversy never accorded the story began with the appearance of the motion picture version, A MAN CALLED HORSE (National General, 1970). "Rather than a tale of Indian life," Dan Georgakas wrote in "They Have Not Spoken: American Indians in Film" in *Film Quarterly* (Spring, 1972), A MAN CALLED HORSE "is thus really about a white nobleman proving his superiority in the wilds. Almost every detail of Indian life is incorrect. An angry Sioux writing to the *Village Voice* complained...that the Sioux never abandoned widows, orphans, and old people to starve and freeze as shown in the film." This posture concerning Sioux attitudes is also the one promulgated by Black Elk as recorded by John G. Neihardt:

I could see that the Wasichus [white people] did not care for each other the way our people did.... They would take everything from each other if they could, and so there were some who had more of everything than they could use, while crowds of people had nothing at all and maybe were starving. They had forgotten that the earth was their mother.

Whatever else he may have been, Black Elk was neither an historian nor an anthropologist. "Some old people, unwanted or without relatives, had no place to go," Royal B. Hassrick noted in THE SIOUX (University of Oklahoma Press, 1964). "These were forced to live alone at the edge of the encampment. Here they were given food and supplies by the generous young men who thereby gained prestige...but at best theirs was a tragic lot, too often filled with insecurity and despair." The same was true also for the Crow Indians, in history as in Dorothy M. Johnson's story. And, in the event, Johnson cannot be held accountable for any foolishness produced by Hollywood. Once, when I commented to her on how poor a film I thought A MAN CALLED HORSE to be, she responded with asperity, "If you think that one's bad, wait until you see TRIUMPHS OF A MAN CALLED HORSE [HBO, 1983]!" I did. It was the second sequel, and she was right.

There are two principal ways to end a captivity story: a captive may somehow secure freedom, or remain with the captors. "There was only one group lower in status than the women; that was the slave or captive group," Mildred P. Mayhall recorded in THE KIOWAS (University of Oklahoma Press, 1971). "This group held an impermanent status, for captives, showing fortitude and bravery, could be accepted into the tribe, usually by adoption into a family. For a girl, also, marriage with an important man might change captive status. Many captives did not desire to return to their own people." Perhaps the most telling difference between now and the 19th-Century American West is that there were *once* alternatives to the invaders' culture.

A MAN CALLED HORSE
1949

He was a young man of good family, as the phrase went in the New England of a hundred-odd years ago, and the reasons for his bitter discontent were unclear, even to himself. He grew up in the gracious old Boston home under his grandmother's care, for his mother had died in giving him birth; and all his life he had known every comfort and privilege his father's wealth could provide.

But still there was the discontent, which puzzled him because he could not even define it. He wanted to live among his equals — people who were no better than he and no worse either. That was as close as he could come to describing the source of his unhappiness in Boston and his restless desire to go somewhere else.

In the year 1845, he left home and went out West, far beyond the country's creeping frontier, where he hoped to find his equals. He had the idea that in Indian country, where there was danger, all white men were kings, and he wanted to be one of them. But he found, in the West as in Boston, that the men he respected were still his superiors, even if they could not read, and those he did not respect weren't worth talking to.

He did have money, however, and he could hire the men he respected. He hired four of them, to cook and hunt and guide and be his companions, but he found them not friendly.

They were apart from him and he was still alone. He still brooded about his status in the world, longing for his equals.

On a day in June, he learned what it was to have no status at all. He became a captive of a small raiding party of Crow Indians.

He heard gunfire and the brief shouts of his companions around the bend of the creek just before they died, but he never saw their bodies. He had no chance to fight, because he was naked and unarmed, bathing in the creek, when a Crow warrior seized and held him.

His captor let him go at last, let him run. Then the lot of them rode him down for sport, striking him with their coup sticks. They carried the dripping scalps of his companions, and one had skinned off Baptiste's black beard as well, for a trophy.

They took him along in a matter-of-fact way, as they took the captured horses. He was unshod and naked as the horses were, and like them he had a rawhide thong around his neck. So long as he didn't fall down, the Crows ignored him.

On the second day they gave him his breeches. His feet were too swollen for his boots, but one of the Indians threw him a pair of moccasins that had belonged to the half-breed, Henri, who was dead back at the creek. The captive wore the moccasins gratefully. The third day they let him ride one of the spare horses so the party could move faster, and on that day they came in sight of their camp.

He thought of trying to escape, hoping he might be killed in flight rather than by slow torture in the camp, but he never had a chance to try. They were more familiar with escape than he was and, knowing what to expect, they forestalled it. The only other time he had tried to escape from anyone, he had succeeded. When he had left his home in Boston, his father had raged and his grandmother had cried, but they could not talk him out of his intention.

The men of the Crow raiding party didn't bother with talk.

Before riding into camp they stopped and dressed in their regalia, and in parts of their victims' clothing; they painted their faces black. Then, leading the white man by the rawhide around his neck as though he were a horse, they rode down toward the tepee circle, shouting and singing, brandishing their weapons. He was unconscious when they got there; he fell and was dragged.

He lay dazed and battered near a tepee while the noisy, busy life of the camp swarmed around him and Indians came to stare. Thirst consumed him and, when it rained, he lapped rain water from the ground like a dog. A scrawny, shrieking, eternally busy old woman with ragged graying hair threw a chunk of meat on the grass, and he fought the dogs for it.

When his head cleared, he was angry, although anger was an emotion he knew he could not afford.

It was better when I was a horse, he thought — when they led me by the rawhide around my neck. I won't be a dog, no matter what!

The hag gave him stinking, rancid grease and let him figure out what it was for. He applied it gingerly to his bruised and sun-seared body.

Now, he thought, I smell like the rest of them.

While he was healing, he considered coldly the advantages of being a horse. A man would be humiliated, and sooner or later he would strike back and that would be the end of him. But a horse had only to be docile. Very well, he would learn to do without pride.

He understood that he was the property of the screaming old woman, a fine gift from her son, one that she liked to show off. She did more yelling at him than at anyone else, probably to impress the neighbors so they would not forget what a great and generous man her son was. She was bossy and proud, a dreadful bag of skin and bones, and she was a devilish hard worker.

The white man, who now thought of himself as a horse, forgot sometimes to worry about his danger. He kept making mental notes of things to tell his own people in Boston about this hideous adventure. He would go back a hero, and he would say, "Grandmother, let me fetch your shawl. I've been accustomed to doing little errands for another lady about your age."

Two girls lived in the tepee with the old hag and her warrior son. One of them, the white man concluded, was his captor's wife and the other was his little sister. The daughter-in-law was smug and spoiled. Being beloved, she did not have to be useful. The younger girl had bright, wandering eyes. Often enough they wandered to the white man who was pretending to be a horse.

The two girls worked when the old woman put them at it, but they were always running off to do something they enjoyed more. There were games and noisy contests, and there was much laughter. But not for the white man. He was finding out what loneliness could be.

That was a rich summer on the plains, with plenty of buffalo for meat and clothing and the making of tepees. The Crows were wealthy in horses, prosperous and contented. If their men had not been so avid for glory, the white man thought, there would have been a lot more of them. But they went out of their way to court death and, when one of them met it, the whole camp mourned extravagantly and cried to their God for vengeance.

The captive was a horse all summer, a docile bearer of burdens, careful and patient. He kept reminding himself that he had to be better-natured than other horses, because he could not lash out with hoofs or teeth. Helping the old woman load up the horses for travel, he yanked at a pack and said, "Whoa, brother. It goes easier when you don't fight."

The horse gave him a big-eyed stare as if it understood his language — a comforting thought, because nobody else did. But even among the horses he felt unequal. They were able to look out for themselves if they escaped. He would simply starve. He was envious still, even among the horses.

Humbly he fetched and carried. Sometimes he even offered to help, but he had not the skill for the endless work of the women, and he was not trusted to hunt with the men, the providers.

When the camp moved, he carried a pack trudging with the women. Even the dogs worked then, pulling small burdens on travois of sticks.

The Indian who had captured him lived like a lord, as he had a right to do. He hunted with his peers, attended long ceremonial meetings with much chanting and dancing, and lounged in the shade with his smug bride. He had only two responsibilities: to kill buffalo and to gain glory. The white man was so far beneath him in status that the Indian did not even think of envy.

One day several things happened that made the captive think he might sometime become a man again. That was the day when he began to understand their language. For four months he had heard it, day and night, the joy and the mourning, the ritual chanting and sung prayers, the squabbles and the deliberations. None of it meant anything to him at all.

But on that important day in early fall the two young women set out for the river, and one of them called over her shoulder to the old woman. The white man was startled. She had said she was going to bathe. His understanding was so sudden that he felt as if his ears had come unstopped. Listening to the racket of the camp, he heard fragments of meaning instead of gabble.

On that same important day the old woman brought a pair of new moccasins out of the tepee and tossed them on the ground before him. He could not believe she would do anything for him because of kindness, but giving him moccasins was one way of looking after her property.

In thanking her, he dared greatly. He picked a little handful of fading fall flowers and took them to her as she squatted in front of her tepee, scraping a buffalo hide with a tool made from a piece of iron tied to a bone. Her hands were hideous — most of the fingers had the first joint missing. He bowed solemnly and offered the flowers.

She glared at him from beneath the short, ragged tangle of her hair. She stared at the flowers, knocked them out of his hand and went running to the next tepee, squalling the story. He heard her and the other women screaming with laughter.

The white man squared his shoulders and walked boldly over to watch three small boys shooting arrows at a target. He said in English, "Show me how to do that, will you?"

They frowned, but he held out his hand as if there could be no doubt. One of them gave him a bow and one arrow, and they snickered when he missed.

The people were easily amused, except when they were angry. They were amused, at him, playing with the little boys. A few days later he asked the hag, with gestures, for a bow that her son had just discarded, a man-size bow of horn. He scavenged for old arrows. The old woman cackled at his marksmanship and called her neighbors to enjoy the fun.

When he could understand words, he could identify his people by their names. The old woman was Greasy Hand, and her daughter was Pretty Calf. The other young woman's name was not clear to him, for the words were not in his vocabulary. The man who had captured him was Yellow Robe.

Once he could understand, he could begin to talk a little, and then he was less lonely. Nobody had been able to see any reason for talking to him, since he would not understand anyway. He asked the old woman, "What is my name?" Until he knew it, he was incomplete. She shrugged to let him know he had none.

He told her in the Crow language, "My name is Horse." He repeated it, and she nodded. After that they called him Horse when they called him anything. Nobody cared except the white man himself.

They trusted him enough to let him stray out of camp, so that he might have got away and, by unimaginable good luck, might have reached a trading post or a fort, but winter was too close. He did not dare leave without a horse; he needed clothing and a better hunting weapon than he had, and more certain skill in using it. He did not dare steal, for then they would surely have pursued him, and just as certainly they would have caught him. Remembering the warmth of the home that was waiting in Boston, he settled down for the winter.

On a cold night he crept into the tepee after the others had gone to bed. Even a horse might try to find shelter from the wind. The old woman grumbled, but without conviction. She did not put him out.

They tolerated him, back in the shadows, so long as he did not get in the way.

He began to understand how the family that owned him differed from the others. Fate had been cruel to them. In a short, sharp argument among the old women, one of them derided Greasy Hand by sneering, "You have no relatives!" and Greasy Hand raved for minutes of the deeds of her father and uncles and brothers. And she had had four sons, she reminded her detractor — who answered with scorn, "Where are they?"

Later the white man found her moaning and whimpering to herself, rocking back and forth on her haunches, staring at her mutilated hands. By that time he understood. A mourner often chopped off a finger joint. Old Greasy Hand had mourned often. For the first time he felt a twinge of pity, but he put it aside as another emotion, like anger, that he could not afford. He thought: What tales I will tell when I get home!

He wrinkled his nose in disdain. The camp stank of animals and meat and rancid grease. He looked down at his naked, shivering legs and was startled, remembering that he was still only a horse.

He could not trust the old woman. She fed him only because a starved slave would die and not be worth boasting about. Just how fitful her temper was he saw on the day when she got tired of stumbling over one of the hundred dogs that infested the camp. This was one of her own dogs, a large, strong one that pulled a baggage travois when the tribe moved camp.

Countless times he had seen her kick at the beast as it lay sleeping in front of the tepee, in her way. The dog always moved, with a yelp, but it always got in the way again. One day she gave the dog its usual kick and then stood scolding at it while the animal rolled its eyes sleepily. The old woman suddenly picked up her ax and cut the dog's head off with one blow. Looking well satisfied with herself, she beckoned her slave to remove the body.

It could have been me, he thought, if I were a dog. But I'm a horse.

His hope of life lay with the girl, Pretty Calf. He set about courting her, realizing how desperately poor he was both in property and honor. He owned no horse, no weapon but the old bow and the battered arrows. He had nothing to give away, and he needed gifts, because he did not dare seduce the girl.

One of the customs of courtship involved sending a gift of horses to a girl's older brother and bestowing much buffalo meat upon her mother. The white man could not wait for some far-off time when he might have either horses or meat to give away. And his courtship had to be secret. It was not for him to stroll past the groups of watchful girls, blowing a flute made of an eagle's wing bone, as the flirtatious young bucks did.

He could not ride past Pretty Calf's tepee, painted and bedizened; he had no horse, no finery.

Back home, he remembered, I could marry just about any girl I'd want to. But he wasted little time thinking about that. A future was something to be earned.

The most he dared do was wink at Pretty Calf now and then, or state his admiration while she giggled and hid her face. The least he dared do to win his bride was to elope with her, but he had to give her a horse to put the seal of tribal approval on that. And he had no horse until he killed a man to get one....

His opportunity came in early spring. He was casually accepted by that time. He did not belong, but he was amusing to the Crows, like a strange pet, or they would not have fed him through the winter.

His chance came when he was hunting small game with three young boys who were his guards as well as his scornful companions. Rabbits and birds were of no account in a camp well fed on buffalo meat, but they made good targets.

His party walked far that day. All of them at once saw the two horses in a sheltered coulee. The boys and the man crawled forward on their bellies, and then they saw an Indian who lay on the ground, moaning, a lone traveler. From the way the boys inched forward, Horse knew the man was fair prey — a member of some enemy tribe.

This is the way the captive white man acquired wealth and honor to win a bride and save his life: He shot an arrow into the sick man, a split second ahead of one of his small companions, and dashed forward to strike the still-groaning man with his bow, to count first coup. Then he seized the hobbled horses.

By the time he had the horses secure, and with them his hope for freedom, the boys had followed, counting coup with gestures and shrieks they had practiced since boyhood, and one of them had the scalp. The white man was grimly amused to see the boy double up with sudden nausea when he had the thing in his hand....

There was a hubbub in the camp when they rode in that evening, two of them on each horse. The captive was noticed. Indians who had ignored him as a slave stared at the brave man who had struck first coup and had stolen horses.

The hubbub lasted all night, as fathers boasted loudly of their young sons' exploits. The white man was called upon to settle an argument between two fierce boys as to which of them had struck second coup and which must be satisfied with third. After much talk that went over his head, he solemnly pointed at the nearest boy. He didn't know which boy it was and didn't care, but the boy did.

The white man had watched warriors in their triumph. He knew what to do. Modesty about achievements had no place among the Crow people. When a man did something big, he told about it.

The white man smeared his face with grease and charcoal. He walked inside the tepee circle, chanting and singing. He used his own language.

"You heathens, you savages," he shouted. "I'm going to get out of here someday! I am going to get away!" The Crow people listened respectfully. In the Crow tongue he shouted, "Horse! I am Horse!" and they nodded.

He had a right to boast, and he had two horses. Before dawn, the white man and his bride were sheltered beyond a far hill, and he was telling her, "I love you, little lady. I love you."

She looked at him with her great dark eyes, and he thought she understood his English words — or as much as she needed to understand.

"You are my treasure," he said, "more precious than jewels, better than fine gold. I am going to call you Freedom."

When they returned to camp two days later, he was bold but worried. His ace, he suspected, might not be high enough in the game he was playing without being sure of the rules. But it served.

Old Greasy Hand raged — but not at him. She complained loudly that her daughter had let herself go too cheap. But the marriage was as good as any Crow marriage. He had paid a horse.

He learned the language faster after that, from Pretty Calf, whom he sometimes called Freedom. He learned that his attentive, adoring bride was fourteen years old.

One thing he had not guessed was the difference that being Pretty Calf's husband would make in his relationship to her mother and brother. He had hoped only to make his position a little safer, but he had not expected to be treated with dignity. Greasy Hand no longer spoke to him at all. When the white man spoke to her, his bride murmured in dismay, explaining at great length that he must never do that. There could be no conversation between a man and his mother-in-law. He could not even mention a word that was part of her name.

Having improved his status so magnificently, he felt no need for hurry in getting away. Now that he had a woman, he had as good a chance to be rich as any man. Pretty Calf waited on him; she seldom ran off to play games with other young girls, but took pride in learning from her mother the many women's skills of tanning hides and making clothing and preparing food.

He was no more a horse but a kind of man, a half-Indian, still poor and unskilled but laden with honors, clinging to the buckskin fringes of Crow society.

Escape could wait until he could manage it in comfort, with fit clothing and a good horse, with hunting weapons. Escape could wait until the camp moved near some trading post. He did not plan how he would get home. He dreamed of being there all at once, and of telling stories nobody would believe. There was no hurry.

Pretty Calf delighted in educating him. He began to understand tribal arrangements, customs and why things were as they were. They were that way because they had always been so. His young wife giggled when she told him, in his ignorance, things she had always known. But she did not laugh when her brother's wife was taken by another warrior. She explained that solemnly with words and signs.

Yellow Robe belonged to a society called the Big Dogs. The wife stealer, Cut Neck, belonged to the Foxes. They were fellow tribesmen; they hunted together and fought side by side, but men of one society could take away wives from the other society if they wished, subject to certain limitations.

When Cut Neck rode up to the tepee, laughing and singing, and called to Yellow Robe's wife, "Come out! Come out!" she did as ordered, looking smug as usual, meek and entirely willing. Thereafter she rode beside him in ceremonial processions and carried his coup stick, while his other wife pretended not to care.

"But why?" the white man demanded of his wife, his Freedom. "Why did our brother let his woman go? He sits and smokes and does not speak."

Pretty Calf was shocked at the suggestion. Her brother could not possibly reclaim his woman, she explained. He could not even let her come back if she wanted to — and she probably would want to when Cut Neck tired of her. Yellow Robe could not even admit that his heart was sick. That was the way things were. Deviation meant dishonor.

The woman could have hidden from Cut Neck, she said. She could even have refused to go with him if she had been *ba-wurokee* — a really virtuous woman. But she had been his woman before, for a little while on a berrying expedition, and he had a right to claim her.

There was no sense in it, the white man insisted. He glared at his young wife. "If you go, I will bring you back!" he promised.

She laughed and buried her head against his shoulder. "I will not have to go," she said. "Horse is my first man. There is no hole in my moccasin."

He stroked her hair and said, *"Ba-wurokee."*

With great daring, she murmured, *"Hayha,"* and when he did not answer, because he did not know what she meant, she drew away, hurt. "A woman calls her man that if she thinks he will not leave her. Am I wrong?"

The white man held her closer and lied, "Pretty Calf is not wrong. Horse will not leave her. Horse will not take another woman, either." No, he certainly would not. Parting from this one was going to be harder than getting her had been. *"Hayha,"* he murmured. "Freedom."

His conscience irked him, but not very much. Pretty Calf could get another man easily enough when he was gone, and a better provider. His hunting skill was improving, but he was still awkward.

There was no hurry about leaving. He was used to most of the Crow ways and could stand the rest. He was becoming prosperous. He owned five horses. His place in the life of the tribe was secure, such as it was. Three or four young women, including the one who had belonged to Yellow Robe, made advances to him. Pretty Calf took pride in the fact that her man was so attractive.

By the time he had what he needed for a secret journey, the grass grew yellow on the plains and the long cold was close. He was enslaved by the girl he called Freedom and, before the winter ended, by the knowledge that she was carrying his child....

The Big Dog society held a long ceremony in the spring. The white man strolled with his woman along the creek bank, thinking: When I get home I will tell them about the chants and the drumming. Sometime. Sometime.

Pretty Calf would not go to bed when they went back to the tepee.

"Wait and find out about my brother," she urged. "Something may happen."

So far as Horse could figure out, the Big Dogs were having some kind of election. He pampered his wife by staying up with her by the fire. Even the old woman, who was a great one for getting sleep when she was not working, prowled around restlessly.

The white man was yawning by the time the noise of the ceremony died down. When Yellow Robe strode in, garish and heathen in his paint and feathers and furs, the women cried out. There was conversation, too fast for Horse to follow, and the old woman wailed once, but her son silenced her with a gruff command.

When the white man went to sleep, he thought his wife was weeping beside him.

The next morning she explained.

"He wears the bearskin belt. Now he can never retreat in battle. He will always be in danger. He will die."

Maybe he wouldn't, the white man tried to convince her. Pretty Calf recalled that some few men had been honored by the bearskin belt, vowed to the highest daring, and had not died. If they lived through the summer, then they were free of it.

"My brother wants to die," she mourned. "His heart is bitter."

Yellow Robe lived through half a dozen clashes with small parties of raiders from hostile tribes. His honors were many. He captured horses in an enemy camp, led two successful raids, counted first coup and snatched a gun from the hand of an enemy tribesman. He wore wolf tails on his moccasins and ermine skins on his shirt, and he fringed his leggings with scalps in token of his glory.

When his mother ventured to suggest, as she did many times, "My son should take a new wife, I need another woman to help me," he ignored her. He spent much time in prayer, alone in the hills or in conference with a medicine man. He fasted and made vows and kept them. And before he could be free of the heavy honor of the bearskin belt, he went on his last raid.

The warriors were returning from the north just as the white man and two other hunters approached from the south, with buffalo and elk meat dripping from the bloody hides tied on their restive ponies. One of the hunters grunted, and they stopped to watch a rider on the hill north of the tepee circle.

The rider dismounted, held up a blanket and dropped it. He repeated the gesture.

The hunters murmured dismay. "Two! Two men dead!" They rode fast into the camp, where there was already wailing.

A messenger came down from the war party on the hill. The rest of the party delayed to paint their faces for mourning and for victory. One of the two dead men was Yellow Robe. They had put his body in a cave and walled it in with rocks. The other man died later, and his body was in a tree.

There was blood on the ground before the tepee to which Yellow Robe would return no more. His mother, with her hair chopped short, sat in the doorway, rocking back and forth on her haunches, wailing her heartbreak. She cradled one mutilated hand in the other. She had cut off another finger joint.

Pretty Calf had cut off chunks of her long hair and was crying as she gashed her arms with a knife. The white man tried to take the knife away, but she protested so piteously that he let her do as she wished. He was sickened with the lot of them.

Savages! he thought. Now I will go back! I'll go hunting alone, and I'll keep on going.

But he did not go just yet, because he was the only hunter in the lodge of the two grieving women, one of them old and the other pregnant with his child.

In their mourning, they made him a pauper again. Everything that meant comfort, wealth, and safety they sacrificed to the spirits because of the death of Yellow Robe. The tepee, made of seventeen fine buffalo hides, the furs that should have kept them warm, the white deerskin dress, trimmed with elk teeth, that Pretty Calf loved so well, even their tools and Yellow Robe's weapons — everything but his sacred medicine objects — they left there on the prairie, and the whole camp moved away. Two of his best horses were killed as a sacrifice, and the women gave away the rest.

They had no shelter. They would have no tepee of their own for two months at least of mourning, and then the women would have to tan hides to make it. Meanwhile they could live in temporary huts made of willows, covered with skins given them in pity by their friends. They could have lived with relatives, but Yellow Robe's women had no relatives.

The white man had not realized until then how terrible a thing it was for a Crow to have no kinfolk. No wonder old Greasy Hand had only stumps for fingers. She had mourned, from one year to the next, for everyone she had ever loved. She had no one left but her daughter, Pretty Calf.

Horse was furious at their foolishness. It had been bad enough for him, a captive, to be naked as a horse and poor as a slave, but that was because his captors had stripped him. These women had voluntarily given up everything they needed.

He was too angry at them to sleep in the willow hut. He lay under a sheltering tree. And on the third night of the mourning he made his plans. He had a knife and a bow. He would go after meat, taking two horses. And he would not come back. There were, he realized, many things he was not going to tell when he got back home.

In the willow hut, Pretty Calf cried out. He heard rustling there, and the old woman's querulous voice.

Some twenty hours later his son was born, two months early, in the tepee of a skilled medicine woman. The child was born without breath, and the mother died before the sun went down.

The white man was too shocked to think whether he should mourn, or how he should mourn. The old woman screamed until she was voiceless. Piteously she approached him, bent and trembling, blind with grief. She held out her knife and he took it.

She spread out her hands and shook her head. If she cut off any more finger joints, she could no more work. She could not afford any more lasting signs of grief.

The white man said, "All right! All right!" between his teeth. He hacked his arms with the knife and stood watching the blood run down. It was little enough to do for Pretty Calf, for little Freedom.

Now there is nothing to keep me, he realized. When I get home, I must not let them see the scars.

He looked at Greasy Hand, hideous in her grief-burdened age, and thought: I really am free now! When a wife dies, her husband has no more duty toward her family. Pretty Calf had told him so, long ago, when he wondered why a certain man moved out of one tepee and into another.

The old woman, of course, would be a scavenger. There was one other with the tribe, an ancient crone who had no relatives, toward whom no one felt any responsibility. She lived on food thrown away by the more fortunate. She slept in shelters that she built with her own knotted hands. She plodded wearily at the end of the procession when the camp moved. When she stumbled, nobody cared. When she died, nobody would miss her.

Tomorrow morning, the white man decided, I will go.

His mother-in-law's sunken mouth quivered. She said one word, questioningly. She said, "*Eero-oshay?*" She said, "Son?"

Blinking, he remembered. When a wife died, her husband was free. But her mother, who had ignored him with dignity, might if she wished ask him to stay. She invited him by calling him Son, and he accepted by answering Mother.

Greasy Hand stood before him, bowed with years, withered with unceasing labor, loveless and childless, scarred with grief. But with all her burdens, she still loved life enough to beg it from him, the only person she had any right to ask. She was stripping herself of all she had left, her pride.

He looked eastward across the prairie. Two thousand miles away was home. The old woman would not live forever. He could afford to wait, for he was young. He could afford to be magnanimous, for he knew he was a man. He gave her the answer. "*Eegya,*" he said. "Mother."

He went home three years later. He explained no more than to say, "I lived with Crows for a while. It was some time before I could leave. They called me Horse."

He did not find it necessary either to apologize or to boast, because he was the equal of any man on earth.

LES SAVAGE JR.

LESLIE HUNTER SAVAGE JR. (1922–1958) was born in Alhambra, California. When he was graduated from Hollywood High School in 1940, it had already long been his intention to pursue a career in art. This changed once he enrolled at Los Angeles City College and started writing fiction. His first professional effort was a story he titled "Bullets and Bullwhips." He sent it off to Street & Smith's *Western Story Magazine* and was delighted when it was accepted and he was praised by the magazine's current editor, John Burr.

There are perhaps two ways to view Savage's first Western story which was subsequently reprinted in *The Pulp Vault* #9 (10/91). In the light of the tremendously high quality of the stories he would be writing not even half a decade hence, it seems a minor effort. Yet that would be to take the story on terms other than its own. While it is true that in "A Colt for Captain Bullwhip" in *Frontier Stories* (Summer, 49) Savage would make gripping and astonishingly dramatic use of a bullwhip fight between two bullwhackers and even more so in his posthumously restored novel, FIRE DANCE AT SPIDER ROCK (Five Star, 1996), already in 1942 he had researched bullwhip techniques sufficiently to impress any reader. Moreover, even this early — at the very beginning, in fact — he created a protagonist who was "off-trail," so much so that when he is first encountered he has just come off a three-year drunk, a spiritually defeated man who is scarcely handsome and clean-cut in the way expected at the time of a Western hero.

Savage had written and had published two stories in *Star Western*, one in *10 Story Western,* and one in *Frontier Stories* when he became a client of the August Lenniger Literary Agency. The first story Savage submitted to the Lenniger Agency was sold in April, 1943, to Fiction House and appeared as "Gunsmoke Ghost" in *Lariat Story Magazine* (11/43). His stories would appear elsewhere but much of the best of what he wrote in the 1940s was showcased in Fiction House magazines. Savage was the first author to receive star treatment there since Walt Coburn in the 1920s, even to having his photograph reproduced in issues of the magazines carrying his stories and his name was always emblazoned on the covers. It was in these stories that Savage developed his formidable backgrounds: the era of the fur trade, Santa Fe in the period the Mexican War and before, and overland freighting prior to the Civil War. Whereas, following the Wister tradition, most Western stories for decades had been set in the years after the Civil War, from virtually the beginning Savage harked back to earlier periods and he could invariably be relied on to tell a riveting story, highly atmospheric, assiduously accurate as to period, with characters vividly evoked. He came to have an intimate grasp of the terrain wherever he set a story, a vital familiarity with the characteristics of flora amid changing seasons as well as the ways of horses, mules, women and men on the frontier. He did this in an entirely natural and graceful manner, displaying only covertly specialized learning in a dozen disciplines from mining, geology, and period furniture to manner of dress, anthropology, and firearms. He might have been a poet because of the striking images he could conjure. Take this example from his last novel, TABLE ROCK (Walker, 1993), in which he conveys zoological information by means of poetic imagery: "He knew those of the marten, the paws printed faithfully in pairs, each oblique to the other, like delicate embroidery in the snow."

Malcolm Reiss, general manager at Fiction House, was Savage's first mentor and he repeatedly encouraged him to experiment with his stories. This appealed to Savage's already keenly volatile imagination so that he would alter traditional patterns of the Western story, even iconoclastically, and upon occasion produce a story without any romantic interest whatsoever. Conversely, another ultimately frustrating tendency which Reiss permitted and New York book editors later would not was Savage's realism in presenting romances on the frontier between his protagonists and females who were mixed-bloods, full-blood Indians, Mexicans, or in one instance — in "The Lone Star Camel Corps" in *Frontier Stories* (Summer, 45) a Syrian woman and in another, NORTH TO KANSAS (a novel he was forced to abort in 1955 but which will eventually be published as he wrote it), a black slave woman.

Don Ward, who edited *Zane Grey's Western Magazine*, was Savage's next mentor. Most of Savage's early novels were condensed for single installment serial publication in this magazine because Ward was convinced of the integrity and power of Savage's fiction. This was fortunate for Savage because this magazine paid 4¢ a word which is more than any of the other pulp magazines did at the time.

In the late 1940s Savage's life underwent significant changes. He published his first novel, TREASURE OF THE BRASADA (Simon and Schuster, 1947), and the next year he married Marian Roberta Funck. Marian brought to this marriage her young son, John, whom Les called Butch and he later adopted him. He dedicated LAND OF THE LAWLESS (Doubleday, 1951): "To Butch, My Son, and I could search the world and never find a better one."

To say more about how Savage was forced to conform to political correctness by book publishers in the 1950s would take us too far afield. Suffice it to say that this situation, forty years later, is now being corrected beginning with TABLE ROCK, THE TIGER'S SPAWN (Chivers, 1994), THE TRAIL (Chivers, 1994), and even the story which follows.

While working on BEYOND WIND RIVER (Doubleday, 1958), Savage was more aware than ever that he was dying. He dedicated this book: "To Dr. Wendell Keate — Who Kept the Machine Running." He died on May 26, 1958, only a few days before his tenth wedding anniversary, from a heart attack brought on by a combination of his hereditary diabetes and elevated cholesterol.

Les loved the Western story. In his own time, as his agent and editors were only too cognizant, he was wont to wander off trail, but that was because the impulse was ever within him to propel the Western story unrelentingly in the direction of greater and greater realism and historical accuracy. Elmer Kelton, T.V. Olsen, Frank Roderus, Cynthia Haseloff, and Douglas C. Jones are only a few of those who took up this cause where Savage left off, so that today it is possible to publish Savage's stories and novels as he wrote them. Much as Stephen Crane before him (and whom he replaces in this second edition), while Savage continued to write, the shadow of his imminent demise grew longer and longer across his young life and he knew that, if he was going to do it at all, he would have to do it quickly. He did it well, better than most who have written Western and frontier fiction, ever. And so now, with his novels and stories being restored to what he had intended them to be, his achievement irradiated by his profoundly sensitive imagination will be with us always, as he had wanted it to be, as he had so rushed against time and mortality that it might be.

It was in 1948 that Savage began making his initial forays into the psychological Western in ways previously attempted by only a few, preëminently Max Brand and Walter Van Tilburg Clark. It was with these stories that Savage would have a great impact on other Western writers just starting out. "The Shadow in Renegade Basin," which harks back to the spiritual terrain of Greek drama, was submitted by August Lenniger to Fiction House under the title "Bushbuster" — which Savage's agent felt seemed more "Western" or, at least, more traditional than certainly was the story. Malcolm Reiss bought the novelette on May 4, 1948; but, once having it, he didn't know what to do with it. An author of Western fiction himself in the early 1930s, Reiss rewrote the ending to give it a ranch romance conclusion and finally published it in the Summer, 1950 issue of *Frontier Stories* under the title "Tombstones for Gringos." The themes of incest and fratricide were also modified. Yet, once they were, the Æeschylian notion of evil being visited upon generation after generation of a once great house was lost. It may also be worth noting, in regard to this tale, that one of the legends spun in Classical Antiquity about Teiresias, the blind seer who figures so prominently in Sophocles's Theban cycle of plays about Œdipus, is that his blindness was a punishment meted out to him by the goddess Artemis for his once having looked upon her naked body while she was bathing.

THE SHADOW IN RENEGADE BASIN
1950

I

It was just one of the many mountains forming the Patagonias, a few miles north of the Mexican border, but something made it stand out from the other peaks — some singular, almost human quality of brooding, dominating malignancy. Its dome rose toward the sky, like a bare, scarred skull, and a line of stunted timber grew in a strange, scowling line across its brow. Some mineral in the land caused its shadow, settling across the basin, to have the deep, mordant tint of wet blood.

Colin Shane had halted his Studebaker wagon at the crest of Papago Divide to stare at the mountain, his deep-socketed eyes luminous with the growing spell of it. "Almost gives you the creeps, doesn't it?" he told his brother.

Farris Shane stirred on the wagon seat beside him, chuckling deep in his chest. "You got too much of Ma's old Irish in you, Colin. All full of lepre-chauns and fairies."

"I heard a miner talking about it in Tombstone," said Colin. "El Renegado he called it. Some kind of legend connected with the mountain. When he heard we were planning to prove up on a homestead in Renegade Basin, he got a funny look on his face, and started this story. That was when you came in with word that Ma was worse. I wish we'd stayed to hear the story, now, somehow."

His face, turned somberly toward the south again, was not made for much humor, some Celtic ancestry lending the gaunt, bony structure of cheek and brow a countenance as dour and brooding as the mountain. His body was neatly coupled for such a long man, negligible through belly and hips, the only broad thing being his shoulders.

His younger brother beside him was in complete opposition, a short, heavy-chested replica of their father, with all the Red Irish of the man in his flaming hair and blue eyes. His thighs were so burly with bulging muscle they had split his jeans out along the seams, and his red flannel shirt was rolled to the elbows over heavy forearms, covered with hair as gold and curly as cured mesquite grass.

"You don't stop mooning, we'll never make the river by nightfall," he grinned.

Colin tried to shrug off his sense of oppression, turning to peer through the pucker of the Osnaberg sheeting covering the wagon. "You all right, Ma?"

Laura Shane's pain-wracked body stirred feebly beneath the blankets, within the stifling wagon. "Drive on, son. I'm still kickin'."

As Colin turned back, shaking the reins, a dim shout came from somewhere down the road. The tired horses drew them toward the sounds till the wagon rounded a turn in the road, and the words were intelligible.

"Ay, you *rumbero*, you are killing my birds. Nacho, *por Dios*, I have not revealed a thing. I am only a poor *pajarero*...."

The horses came down off the grade and around a big rock, and Colin could see the two struggling men, among the bizarre, ridged shapes of tall saguaro. There were half a dozen bright-colored birds fluttering and squawking around in the air, scattering their feathers over the two men fighting in the sand, and half a dozen *amole* cages lying on the ground, some with their spindled doors torn open, three or four still holding shrieking parrots.

One of the men was a swarthy, thick-waisted Mexican in a fancy *charro* jacket and gleaming *taja* leggings. His immense sombrero had been torn off, and his long, black hair swung in greasy length down over his vivid, savage face, as he held the other man pushed down to his knees in the sand, beating at him — a greasy, fat little man with a pock-marked face and a red bulb for a nose, squirming and struggling to dodge the brutal blows.

"Let the little guy go, you big tub o' lard," shouted Farris, jumping off the wagon before it had stopped.

The squawking birds and rain of sand kicked up by the struggling men had excited the horses, and Colin was still fighting to halt them when Farris reached the Mexicans. He caught the bigger one by an arm, swinging him around to sink a vicious right fist in that thick waist. Colin had never seen a man before that whom Farris could not down with such a blow, but the Mexican only grunted harshly, taking a step backward and bringing both arms up to cover himself. Farris looked surprised, then plunged on in.

Colin had the horses halted by now, and jumped off the seat. The Mexican had already blocked Farris's first blow with his left arm, and was putting his own fist in under it. Farris staggered back, and the Mexican followed, hitting him again. This stiffened Farris. His face was white and working and his whole body was lifted upward in a perfect, unprotected setup for the Mexican, as he brought his third blow in, low to the belly.

"Meddling little *gringo*," he snarled, as he struck. Farris jackknifed at the waist over that fist. The Mexican stepped back and allowed him to fall.

At the same time Colin had reached them, charging in with all the long, close-coupled whiplash of him. He had seen how little effect his brother's blows had on the man and knew, if Farris could not do it that way, he couldn't, so he threw himself bodily at the Mexican's knees.

Legs pinned together by Colin's long arms, the man went over backwards, striking the ground heavily. Colin fought up across him to grab that long, greasy black hair, beating his head against the ground. They were in among the squawking, squalling birds now, with the fat little Mexican jumping around them and clapping his hands together.

"Ay, ay, that's it, beat the black Indian to a pulp! *¡Que barbaridad!* If anyone deserves this, it is Nacho. What a bull you are, *señor....*"

It was like trying to stun a rock. Nacho's face was twisted with the pain of the blows, but he still reached up with scarred, thick hands, pawing for Colin. Colin tried to avoid them, sparring from side to side and beating that head again and again into the ground. Then one set of fingers caught on his arm, closed on it. He shouted aloud with the crushing pain. The other fist groped inexorably for his free hand, caught it, pulled him in. He squirmed spasmodically in the grip, appalled by the strength of the man beneath him. Like a bear, Nacho hugged him in, till his whole consciousness was popping and spinning in crushed pain.

"Hang on a minute, Colin, boy," he heard from somewhere behind him.

Colin opened his mouth as wide as he could, sunk his teeth into the nose beneath him. There was a deafening howl of pain, a spasm of wild thrashing. He hung on desperately. Neither would Nacho loosen his bear hug. He settled back, breathing through his mouth in a guttural, savage way, and began applying pressure once more.

Colin thought his lungs would burst. Ribs began to snap and crack. A terrible, maddening suffocation gripped him. Then he heard the sound. A dull, solid, whacking sound. Once. Twice. Three times. Suddenly the arms fell limply from around him. He lay a long time, sprawled across the body, gasping like a fish cast upon the land. Finally he lifted his head to see Farris standing weakly above them, leaning on the spare wagon tongue he had unleashed from beneath the Studebaker.

"Couldn't do much more," he panted. "My guts are all stove in. Never saw a man with that kind of punch."

Colin got to his feet, slowly. The little Mexican was scrambling around among the cages, righting them and slipping the raucous birds back into them, a comical, pathetic little figure in an archaic, hooded cloak and red Turkish trousers that ballooned out around the ankles.

"Come here, Pepita," he called to one of the birds perched on a saguaro. "Come little one, back to your cage. He is a macaw, *señores,* from the land of the white Indians, in Darien. And Roblero there...come, Roblero, your castle awaits...Roblero is a white-necked raven. He even talks. Say something, Roblero."

"*Que un rumbero,*" squawked the raven.

"We know all your birds now," said Colin. "How about you?"

"Ah," the little man cackled, turning toward them with a sly, upraised finger. "I am Pajarero. It means bird-catcher, *señores*. You must have seen us in Tintown. The place is made up of bird-catchers. Would you like to buy this tanager? Only three pesos. A rare bird, *señores*."

"As rare as this one on the ground?" said Farris, turning his pale eyes to Nacho, who was beginning to regain consciousness now.

The sly humor left Pajarero as his eyes dropped to Nacho. He made the sign of a cross before himself as Nacho rolled over, lifting himself painfully to his hands and knees. Shaking his head, he looked up at Colin, and the intent was plain in his smoldering eyes.

"Do anything more and I'll clout you again!" growled Farris, moving in with the wagon tongue.

Nacho rose to his feet. His hand opened and closed above the butt of his holstered gun, but Farris could have struck him again before he got it free.

"There are many more days left in the year, *señores*," he said at last and turned to walk out among the saguaros. Colin expected him to get out of range of that wagon tongue and then turn back, going for his gun. He took a breath that swelled his flat belly against the barrel of his own gun, stuck naked through his belt, just behind the buckle, and waited that way, to pull at it if Nacho turned. But the man disappeared among the tall, haunted cactus without wheeling back.

"You had better leave the basin before another of those days comes," said Pajarero, at last. "I have heard him say that to seven men. They are all dead now."

"We don't scare that easy," said Colin. "We aim to prove up on some government land here. We couldn't go on if we wanted. We're out of money and Ma's too sick. I don't even think the horses could pull another mile."

"Homesteading...here?" said Pajarero, in an awed voice.

"What's wrong with here?" asked Farris.

"You have not heard about...El Renegado?"

"The mountain?" Colin asked him. "What about it?"

"Ooh...," the man pouted his lips, pulling his fat head into his shoulders, "perhaps I had better not tell you."

Farris shifted his weight, with that wagon tongue. "Perhaps you had. I'm tired of all this mystery."

"Very well, *señor*, very well," said the man, hastily. The pout faded from him as he turned toward the mountain. "Do you see how empty the valley is? Not a house, not a man. The richest basin in this area, more water, more grass, more everything than you could find within a hundred miles. Open to homesteading many months now. Yet not a house, not a man."

"Yes?" said Farris, cynically.

"It is said," murmured Parjarero, turning back to him, "that anyone who settles in the shadow of El Renegado is doomed."

II

The two brothers made camp that evening in the rich river bottom. Colin cut willow shoots for his mother's bed, laying them herring-bone to make a light, springy mattress. Farris found fresh meat in a mule deer back in the hills, and they had that and sourdough for supper. The Mexican bird-catcher had come with them, and ate sparingly as his feathered charges, for all his corpulence, regaling them with fabulous stories of his wanderings in search of birds. Farris's cynicism had kept him from elaborating upon what he had said about the mountain, and it was not until after supper that it was again brought to Colin's attention. Laura Shane did it. She had eaten little and was feverish and, as Colin sat by her bed, she caught at his wrist with one veined, bony hand.

"I heard what that Mexican said this afternoon," she moaned. "He was right, Colin. Don't settle here. The land is cursed. I can feel it."

"Don't let your Irish blood get the best of you, Ma," soothed Farris. "The land's no more cursed than we are, just because we've been plagued with a little bad luck these last years."

"You're the practical one, Farris," muttered their mother. "Too much like your father. If you can't put your hands to a thing, it don't exist. It does for Colin. He knows what I mean. Don't stop here, Colin...."

"We've got to, Ma," Colin told her. "It's our last chance. You know that...."

He had meant to say more but it would not come. There was a figure in the firelight to stop him. He did not know exactly how she had gotten there. A woman. The dark, haunted face of a woman, tawny, dusky flesh and great black eyes that reflected the firelight opaquely. It was hard to separate her black hair from the night behind her. There was a jet rosary at the swell of her breast, immense black pearls and silver bracelets on her slender wrists.

Pajarero had risen from the fire, staring at her with wide, liquid eyes, gripped in some strange enchantment. Colin felt the same way, unable to speak. It had always been Farris who had been easy with the women anyway, grinning confidently, now, and wrapping his tongue around the blarney.

"Well, an angel stepped right out of heaven; how can the basin be cursed when they grow such beautiful flowers here, a little bit o' colleen wrapped up in Spanish lace and called *señorita*. We're the Shanes. I'm Farris, my brother Colin, and our mother, Laura."

"I am Christina Velasco," the woman murmured, her English accented just enough to give her husky voice a tenuous, piquant appeal. "My hacienda is on the other side of the basin. I heard your mother was ill. I wondered if I could help."

"With the gratitude of Erin to greet you," smiled Farris, holding out his hand. Colin could see the little lights kindling in his eyes, as they played over her body. She allowed the redhead to guide her over the rough, matted ground toward Laura Shane, but halted momentarily before Colin.

"You have not spoken," she said.

"When my boy has anything worth saying," Laura Shane said, from her sickbed, "he'll speak."

Christina Velasco inclined her head to one side in a thoughtful, studying way, smiling faintly at Colin. Then she moved on, passing Pajarero. He had been staring at her all the while with those shining eyes and faintly parted lips. She nodded at him in a gracious, dimly condescending way as she passed. A shudder seemed to travel through his whole body.

"*Señorita,*" he whispered, dropping to his knees and reaching out one hand, as if to grasp the hem of her skirt and kiss it. But she pulled it up at that instant to avoid a hummock of dirty grass, and he drew his hand back sharply, a strange, apologetic line rounding his shoulders.

The woman knelt beside Laura Shane and spoke on a sharp, disgusted little exhalation. "You are letting her drink this water? How stupid. That's the first thing you should have stopped. Even boiling it does not help the newcomer to the valley. There is some wine in my *carroza.* Please get it for me?"

The tilt of her head indicated the road, and Colin started off through the willows. He found the *carroza* to be an old Spanish coach, parked alongside the road. A man rose from where he had been squatting against the high back wheel, smoking a cigarette. He looked Indian, with a round, enigmatic face and sullen eyes, his smooth wrists tinkling with turquoise and silver jewelry.

"*Señorita* Velasco sent me to get some wine," Colin said.

The man nodded, opened the door, bent inside to get a clay jar. He handed it to Colin without speaking, and squatted back against the wheel, staring at Colin with unwinking eyes. Colin wended his way back through the matted undergrowth of these rich bottomlands to their camp. Christina was still kneeling beside his mother, washing her face now and murmuring Spanish in an unintelligible, soothing way.

"She's so feverish," she told Colin, reverting to English.

"You don't need to talk Yankee if you don't want," Colin told her in Spanish. "We were raised on the Texas border before we hit for Missouri."

She looked up in surprise, then asked him, "Have you anything for her?"

"The doc in Tombstone gave us some Dover's powder."

The woman made a disgusted sound, picking up her skirts as she rose, and headed for the undergrowth. Colin followed her in puzzlement. He found Pajarero at his heels, staring after the woman with that dog-like devotion. She called for a torch, and Farris thrust a length of sappy wood into the fire, bringing the light to her. In a few moments she had collected what looked like a bunch of common weeds, carrying them back to the fire in her skirts.

In amazement, Colin watched her slender, aristocratic hands go about the work with such skill. She labored for hours with his mother, feeding her the romero tea, performing the mysterious, amazing healing arts of these Border people, learned slowly, painfully, through the long centuries when there was no doctor within a thousand miles. They were all dozing about the fire when Laura finally became quieter, drifting off into a troubled sleep. Christina rose from her side, waking Colin with the movement. He got up unsteadily, gazing at his mother.

"That's the first real sleep she's had in weeks," he said.

"It is well," said Christina. "She will feel more like traveling in the morning. You must bring her to my hacienda for a few days before you leave the valley."

"We aren't leaving the valley," Colin told her.

She whirled on him, a strange, wild look obliterating the almost Oriental calm of her face for a moment, then disappearing as violently as it had come, wiped away by some inward effort of her own. "You can't stay," she said intensely.

"You're not talking about the mountain?" he asked.

"How can you think of staying, if you know?"

"I don't know," he said. "Pajarero started to tell us, but he closed up tight when Farris scoffed at him. What is it?"

She stared up at his eyes in a fixed, fascinated way, held by the rapport the sincerity of his voice brought. She started to smile; then it faded before a puzzled frown drew her brows together. She began, haltingly at first, her voice gaining conviction at the quiet attention on his face.

"When Don Juan Oñate first made his conquest of this country," she said, "he established a *presidio* in this basin, with a priest for the mission, and a company of Spanish soldiers and their families. Commanding them was a young captain who fell in love with an Indian girl belonging to the tribe in the Patagonias. These Indians were so war-like that the priest had only converted a few of them, who were working in the mission as neophytes. The others planned to wipe out the *presidio*. Through his contact with the woman, the captain knew this, and could have saved his comrades. But he betrayed them, running off to the mountain with the woman. He was called El Renegado, and the mountain came to be named after him.

"The attack came near evening, when the shadow of the mountain touched the *presidio*. It was the changing of the guards, and with help from the neophytes inside, the Indians overwhelmed the garrison and wiped them out, women and children and all. The priest was mortally wounded but, before he died, he declared the ground touched by the shadow of the mountain to be cursed by the death of so many innocents. The basin is so shaped that all of it, during the course of the day, is touched by that shadow, and there is not one person to try and settle here who has not been blighted by that curse."

"Why are you here, then?" he asked.

She turned sharply away from him, as if to hide the subtle alterations hardening her face. "Because I am," she answered, finally, and then lifted her chin toward the east, dawn light making a cameo of her face. "The sun will be up in a few minutes. If you will wake your mother, I will go and prepare the coach for her. It will be more comfortable to her than that wagon."

He walked over to kneel by his mother, taking her shoulder gently. It felt cold. He shook her lightly. Her body reacted with the lifeless motion of a rag doll. He bent down to stare at her face. There was no sign of breathing. He gazed for a long, blank moment at her closed eyes, conscious of Farris's rising from the fire, to come over by him.

"I guess you won't have to get the coach ready," he told Christina, at last. "Mother's dead."

At that moment, the sun lifted its first brazen rays above the undulating silhouette of the mountains to the east. But its brightness did not seem to touch them, here. Colin realized why, at last. The bulk of the sun lay behind the ugly, brooding peak of El Renegado, throwing its shadow across the valley, to shroud their whole camp.

III

There was not much will for living left in either of the brothers for several weeks after their mother's death. They buried her on a hill above the camp they had made in the bottoms, and remained there, hunting and fishing for the food they needed. It was Farris who seemed to recover first, finally coming up with the suggestion that they build a house. This hard work helped to take their minds off their mother's death.

After they had built a three-room adobe and some corrals, they made a trip north, over Papago Gap, trading some of their meager household goods from Missouri for onions and chile from the Mexican *pajareros* in Tintown. And farther north, among the Papagos and Pimas, they found one butcher knife was worth a wagon load of melons and squash and Indian corn for seed crops. They got half a dozen peach and apricot trees to transplant about their house, and the fruit was beginning to ripen by June. And then it was that evening when Colin stood out among those trees, enjoying a cooling breeze after the heat of the late spring day, seeking satisfaction in what they had built here.

He did not find as much as he sought. He wondered if his mother's death was still too recent. Or was it something else? Farris came up behind him, smoking his pipe.

"You got Tina on your mind?" he asked.

"What makes you say that?" smiled Colin.

"You're looking off toward her place."

"Seems to me you're the one who should have her on your mind," Colin told him. "You've gone to see her every Saturday we've been here."

"You might as well have come along," chuckled Farris. "Seems all we talked about was you. Makes me jealous, she's so interested. Wanted to know why you didn't call. I told her you was shy with women."

"What did she say?"

"She said she didn't think that was true...you just moved a little slower than me, and didn't say anything until you could really mean it."

"I should think so," said Colin, with one of his rare, fleeting smiles. "With all your blarney." He sobered. "I guess I was thinking about her, in a way, Farris. We've got the house to a place where it needs a woman."

"The same thought's been in my mind," Farris murmured.

Colin turned to look at his brother in some surprise, and Farris chuckled, poking the pipe at him. "We aren't going to be in competition, are we, Colin?"

For a moment, Colin wanted to answer it with a grin, but he could not. When it finally came, it was forced. "What chance would I stand, against a lady's man such as yourself...?"

He stopped speaking to stare out at something beyond. The earth beneath him seemed to be trembling. Then there was the sound. A great, growing sound.

"Earthquake?" asked Farris, stiffening.

"Stampede!" cried Colin, with the first bawl of cattle reaching him. "Those blackhorns up the valley. Get your horse, Farris! If they come through our fields, we'll lose everything."

Their stock was fat, now, from the rich graze of the valley, moving restlessly in the pack pole pen behind their corral. Colin hooked a bridle from the top pole and swung the gate open, jamming it in the first mouth he found, swinging aboard without waiting for a saddle. It was one of the bays they had used in the wagon team, a good enough horse for this short run.

Colin raced out through their new orchard and across the alfalfa on this side of the river. On the opposite bank he could see them, now, a milling, bawling herd of blackhorns, trampling through the Indian corn just thrusting its tender green shoots from the soil.

"Keep them on that side or they'll ruin our alfalfa, too," shouted Farris, coming up from behind Colin on another animal, and both of them plunged into the ford toward the cattle. It did not look like a stampede to Colin. The cattle were headed in no definite direction as yet. They seemed to have milled in the cornfields, and now were being shoved unwillingly into the river by some unseen pressure.

Before the brothers were halfway across the broad, shallow ford, however, the leaders of the herd were plunging into the water. More and more cattle followed, and their direction was becoming more definite. Colin started shouting hoarsely in an effort to turn them back. The leaders spooked at his loud voice and oncoming horse, trying to turn aside, but there were too many behind them.

The true charge began with a burst, as the whole front rank seemed to break into a deliberate charge at Colin, bawling and screaming in the stupid, bovine frenzy that would carry them blindly forward when the primeval fright of the stampede finally reached them.

"Get out of the way, Colin!" yelled Farris, from behind. "You can't stop them now. They'll run you down...."

Colin only half-heard him, urging his own spooked mount on ahead, in a deep, black anger that so many months' work could be wiped out in a few minutes. He was into the leaders, then, still screaming at them in an effort to start a mill. But their impetus carried his horse back on its haunches. The beast tried to turn and run with them. It stumbled on the rough bottom, and began lunging from side to side, squealing, losing its head entirely. Colin realized he would go down in another moment.

Halfway between the bank and the herd, Farris had started to turn his horse aside. When he saw what had happened to Colin, he wheeled the animal around and raced straight for the herd.

"Get back, you fool," Colin screamed at him. "You'll only get killed too!"

But Farris plunged right on toward him. Colin had managed to rein his horse around in the direction of the cattle, but he was pinched in between two of the leaders, now, and the animal had not yet found its footing. He felt it stumble again, heavily, and knew, with the knowledge born of a lifetime on horseback, that this time it was going down for good. Farris must have seen it too, for just as he reached the head of the herd, he wheeled his horse broadside, shouting at Colin to jump for it.

A dozen feet separated them. Colin lunged upward on his foundering, falling horse, got purchase enough with one heel on its off-flank to kick away, and jumped. He struck the side of a steer, caromed off, hit shallow water with both flailing feet. He ran three stumbling steps before the impetus of his jump robbed him of balance completely. The tail of Farris's horse was before his eyes as he went over. Blindly he clawed at it. He heard Farris shout, and felt the animal lunge forward under a kidney kick. It almost tore the tail from his hands, his arms from their sockets. He had a dim, vivid sense of little, bloodshot eyes and waving, tossing horns and churning legs, and realized Farris was running down the front ranks of the herd in a diagonal line, attempting to get out to the side before his own horse was caught up in them. The ford fell into deeper water, and then the tail was torn from Colin's hands as the horse stumbled and lost its feet, too.

He went under in a plummeting force, striking bottom, kicking off. He came to the surface, gasping for air, getting water instead, doubling over in a paroxysm of coughing that would have put him under again. He was too dizzy and disorganized to find control. But as he went down, panic paralyzing him, he felt a hand on his hair. He fought wildly, losing all sense in the terrible, primal fear of being drowned. There was a cracking blow against his jaw, and he seemed to sink into the delicious coolness of the deepest water....

His next sensation was of gritty sand, and a muttering, a distant sound. He opened his eyes, tasting silt, coughing up a quart of water, before he saw Farris hunkered above him. He lay back, swearing at his brother affectionately.

"Damn fool. I ought to pin your ears back. You could have gotten killed."

"You *would* have," grinned Farris. "It makes us even for the time you pulled Nacho off me."

"Let's not start keeping score," said Colin, sitting up. "I couldn't count high enough for the tight spots you've pulled me out of."

He stopped talking to stare after that muttering, dying sound of stampeding cattle running across the valley. Before his eyes lay the trampled, ruined alfalfa fields, the little grove of transplanted trees uprooted and mangled, the ocotillo corrals wrecked beyond repair and all the animals in them stampeded off with the beef. Then, somehow, his attention was not on that. It was beyond, climbing the steep, scowling slope of that scar of timber forming a frowning brow, and above, to the somber, brooding dome of El Renegado, dominating the valley, and the night, with its malignancy.

IV

There was nothing they could do that night but try and get some sleep. The house was still intact, though one wall had been knocked in. When Colin awoke the next morning, Farris was not there. The redhead's guns were not in evidence either, and Colin decided he had gone hunting.

He spent the morning searching the river bottom for their horses. He found the bay he had ridden, up on the bank where it had dragged itself to die, with both front legs broken, and shot the hapless beast to put it out of its misery. Near noon he found the one Farris had forked, three miles downstream where it had been swept by the river. It was calmly cropping gramma, and sound enough to ride.

Colin returned to find Farris still gone. He put a saddle on the horse and started tracking his brother. He found fresh sign leading out across the river into the hills behind them. Within these foothills he came across other sign mixed with Farris's footprints, the mark of hoofs, shod and unshod. He lost them in the general trampling the herd had made here, and was still trying to unravel it all when he sighted Farris hiking back down a rocky slope toward him. His face was so covered with alkali it looked like a death mask, and even this could not hide the strange expression of it. He did not seem to see Colin till he was close, and only then did he make an effort to change the look.

"What is it?" said Colin.

"Nothing. Been hunting. Nothing up there."

"Horses mixed in with those cattle tracks," said Colin. "A shod one in with the unshod. What is it, Farris? Why won't you tell me?"

"There's nothing to tell," the redhead's voice was lifted shrilly. "Now let's get back."

Colin reined the horse around to block his brother's move to leave, one leg coming against the thick, sweating chest of him. He bent forward to peer at Farris. "You went up to the woman's place last Saturday."

"What makes you say that?" said Farris angrily.

"You don't get that slicked up to irrigate our corn."

"All right," said Farris. "So I went up to the woman's place. What's that got to do with it?"

"That's what I'd like to know," said Colin. "What's that got to do with this?"

The redhead's alkali-whitened face lifted in a sharp, strained way, and that same expression flitted through his eyes. "Listen, Colin," he said, tightly. "Quit swinging this horse around and let me by, will you? I been on a long hike and I'm tired and my temper won't stand all this blather."

"Tell me what you found and I'll let you past."

"Nothing, damn you, I told you...."

"It's got something to do with her. You're shielding her!"

"The hell I am. You know...." Farris halted himself with an effort so great it twisted his face. He stood there for a space that had no measure, chest rising and falling against Colin's leg, dampening it with sweat. Finally, Farris reached up to fold his fingers around the stirrup leather, speaking in a grating restraint. "Listen, Colin, you and I have had our spats in the past, but this is different. I don't want to fight with you this way so soon after mother's death. Or any other time, for that matter. Leave the woman out of it, will you?"

Colin had quieted, for this moment, too, and the rapport they had known before was between them. He stared deeply into Farris's pale, blue eyes. "You really got a case on Tina, haven't you?"

"Colin," said Farris. "I think I'd kill the man who tampered with her...in any way."

Colin drew a deep breath. "Then I won't ask you what you found up there, Farris. Let go and I'll find out for myself."

"No." A tortured look passed through the redhead's face. "Please, Colin, there's nothing up there...."

"Then why are you so bent on my not seeing it?" said Colin. "Let go, Farris."

"No."

"Farris...," there was a deadly, final quality to the tone of Colin's voice, startling after their rising shouts, "I'll ask you once more. Let me go."

"Only if you turn around and come home with me."

Colin snapped his foot from the stirrup, shoved it against Farris's chest with the leg jackknifed, straightened that long, lashing leg with a vicious force.

Farris went over backward with a shout, hand torn loose of the stirrup leather. Colin slipped his foot back into the oxbow and booted the animal forward. He heard Farris call his name, but did not turn around, and then he was over the crest and into the next shallow valley.

Each great, ruddy rock clung hatefully to its rough slope, scowling down upon Colin like some crouching, mordant demon. The scar of timber forming its brow was shadowed darkly, ominously, with no sign of life breaking the spell. Above timberline, the bald, lithic head thrust the seamed, scarred planes of its skull ominously toward the sky, like Lucifer defying Saint Michael and all the angels.

Irish inheritance of a deep mysticism gave Colin an acute sensitivity to such influences, and he pushed forward without trying to laugh away the real, tangible sense of awe, almost of fear, the mountain engendered in him. He did not try to cross its crest, but pushed inward on the mountains behind by rounding its slope beneath the timber. Following Farris's tracks, he at last realized he was on some kind of trail leading through endless tiers of varicolored rocks. They blocked off sight of the valley behind him, now. The air up here was stifling. His clothes were drenched with sweat. It seemed difficult to breathe, somehow. He kept glancing up at the mountain, as if seeking the cause in its malignancy. Then it spoke to him.

"*¿Que paso?*" it said, in a voice like the rustle of quaking aspens.

Colin halted his horse, shivering with the shock of it. He keened his head up toward the sound. It was not the mountain. It was a man, sitting on a rock above the narrow trail, grinning down on him.

Colin did not think he had ever seen such an age. The man's face was no more than a skull with parchment for skin, stretched so tightly the bones appeared ready to come through. The eyes stared, huge and feverish, from the gaunt coign of their sockets. The flesh of the hands was wrinkled and seamed, burned the color of ancient mahogany by the countless years of this land's sunshine, and the fingers shook with palsy on the butt plate of the ancient rifle that looked like a matchlock Colin's father had hung above the mantle in Missouri.

"You are one of Captain Velasco's men?" asked the ancient, in a strange, stilted Castilian. "Is he coming today?"

"I'm Colin Shane," Colin told him in Spanish. "Who are you?"

"Shane?" The man bent forward in senile belligerence, repeating the name in a shrill, suspicious way. "Shane? Shane? No one by that name with the captain. I've been waiting a long time. They say Don Oñate will be here soon. Did you see the inventory Captain Velasco made of his clothing? A true *conquistadore*. They say he has garters with points of gold lace in colors to match each costume. And doublets of royal lion skin. Do you believe that? Six pairs of Rouën linen shirts. Why should a man have that many? He can only wear one shirt at a time. Shane." He seemed to snap back with a jolt. "Shane?" He bent forward again. "Are you one of the Indians?"

"I come from the valley," said Colin, staring at the old man, trying to find mockery in him. There was a weird, sardonic light to those old eyes, a secretive leer on his lips. Or had the sun done this? Then he made out what it was beside the old man. An ancient, rusted Spanish helmet, and a cuirass of tarnished metal, backed with rotting leather that was still damp with sweat.

There was something dream-like about it — the strange costume, the archaic dialect, talk of men so long dead — but the harsh reality of it was brought home to Colin by the lighted match in the man's hand. His own response came automatically, a sudden move to rein the horse away, halted by the flick of the old man's hand toward the touch hole. Colin stared down the immense bore of that ancient gun, unwilling to believe that it could still fire, yet held stony by the possibility of it. The old man bent toward him, cackling.

"I told him no more would come up from the valley. Fray Escobar's curse is useless. We're still alive, aren't we? And you die. One by one, you die. Even the Don himself will not escape alive. Velasco is master here. El Renegado is king."

"Don't bring that match any closer, you fool," said Colin, trying to keep his voice level. "I'm not with Oñate. I'm an Irishman. Shane. Does that sound Spanish? I'm not your enemy...."

"That's what the last one told me and I let him by. He said he was an Indian bird-catcher from Tintown. Captain Velasco was in a great rage. He followed him out and killed him. He would have killed me if I wasn't such a faithful friend. Oh, no. Not this time. I'll kill you this time."

That ghastly cackle rang against the rocks. Colin stared at the lowering match, filled with an awesome helplessness. He gathered himself for a last, desperate effort, meaning to wheel his horse and drop off the side at the same time. The tension filled him till he thought he would burst, and the match reached the touch hole.

"Stop it, *Cabo!*"

It was a clear, cutting voice, from above in the rocks. The old man jerked the match away with a surprised moan. Powder in the touch hole hissed, went out. Colin stared at the gun, trembling all over and, for the first time, he felt the clammy sweat sticking his shirt to him. Finally he found himself staring upward. Christina Velasco sat a black horse with four white stockings on a huge rock fifty feet above them. She was moving it now, bringing it carefully, delicately down some narrow trail Colin could not see. Colin had not seen a woman in pants too often. They were *charro,* of red suede, tight fitting as another layer of skin, and he could not help staring. She had a *charro* jacket, too, with gold frogs embroidered across the lapels against which her breasts surged. There was a strange, dark look to her face, almost an anger, as she reached their level. Colin could not tell if it was directed at him or the old man.

"*Cabo,*" she said. "Go back, now."

"But Captain Velasco told me to...."

"I told you to go back," she said, sharply. "You're relieved."

"It's about time," muttered the old man, gathering up his armor. "Seems like I've been out here for years."

"You have, you old fool," muttered Tina, too low for his ears. She waited till he had hobbled on up the trail and out of sight among the rocks, then turned to Colin. He was watching her with a strange mixture of suspicion, and something else he could not define.

"*Cabo*," he said. "Corporal?"

"The sun of this country can addle the brain, Colin," she said. "He is only a crazy old man who thinks he is back in the 16th Century with Don Juan Oñate."

"And Captain Velasco?" said Colin.

She shrugged. "All right."

"You didn't tell me you were descended from him."

"Just because my name is the same?"

"Are you?"

"All right," she said, in a sudden anger. "So I am descended. And so I didn't tell you. It isn't something one goes around bragging about. He was a traitor, a murderer, a renegade, and all his descendants...."

She cut off sharply, and his black brows raised, as he asked her, "All his descendants what?"

"Nothing," she said, shaking her head sharply. "This is no place to talk. My hacienda is lonely. Will you join me in afternoon chocolate?"

They turned their horses down the slope, and she did not speak again till they were out of the rocks and into timber once more. Then he found her eyes on him, studying his face.

"What were you doing up there?" she asked.

"A herd of cattle stampeded across our land last night," he told her. "Ruined most of our crops for this year. We found some horse tracks mixed in with the cattle sign this morning. Farris found something up here but he wouldn't tell me what."

Perhaps it was the expression in his eyes looking at her, for she lifted her body in the saddle. "So you think I've taken to stampeding cattle now?"

"I didn't say that."

"You might as well."

"All right," he said. "What *are* you doing up here?"

"I...I...." she broke off, biting her lips, eyes dropping. She shrugged. "You wouldn't believe me anyway."

"Yes, I would, Tina," he said. "Tell me one straight thing and I'll believe you."

Those big eyes raised again, gratefully. "I can see the mountain from my hacienda. I saw you come up here and thought you might run into The Corporal.

He's old and he's crazy, but he can be dangerous. I didn't want you hurt, Colin.''

He inclined his head. "I'm sorry. I guess I should be thankful instead of suspicious. My apologies."

"That makes me feel much better," she smiled, and drew her horse over to lean towards him. "Now, if you will wipe that scowl off your face and come down to the house, perhaps you and I together can clear up just how you feel about me."

V

It had once been a magnificent, extensive hacienda, with a high adobe wall surrounding an acre of buildings and corrals, but much of the wall was fallen in, now, and all but one of the patios was overgrown with yucca and gramma. They rode through a great gate into this one garden, where a stream gurgled through a little red-roofed well and peach trees dropped their delicate bloom across the sun-baked tile topping the wall. The Indian Colin had found by the coach that first night appeared through a spindled door, taking their horses.

Smiling, the woman whipped dust from her *charro* pants with a quirt, and turned to walk toward a cane chair by a long table. Colin started to follow her, and it was then they saw the man.

He had been standing in the deep shade of the wall, smoking a cigarette, and Colin had the sense of eyes being on them all the time, in that sly malevolence.

"Nacho!" The woman's voice held whispered shock.

He smiled, pinching out the cigarette and dropping it to grind the butt into the earth with his heel. With a thumb, he pushed the brim of his sombrero upward till the hat was tilted back on his head at a rakish angle. Then he hooked his hands in the heavy gunbelt at his waist, and moved toward them in an unhurried, swaggering way, the chains on his great Mexican cartwheel spurs tinkling softly with each step.

"You consort with the *gringo* now," he told the woman.

"In my house, Americans are no more *gringos* than Mexicans are greasers," she said.

"Your house?" Nacho asked, brows raising in that mocking smile. Only then did he condescend to move his eyes to Colin. "Is this the day, *señor?*"

Remembering what the man had said that first time, Colin lowered his head a little. "Any day you want."

"I'm glad you leave the choice to me," smiled the man. "You will not wait long, *señor*." He turned to the woman. "I want to speak with you."

"You would ask me to leave my guest?"

"Not asking you, telling you."

"Whatever you want to say can be said right here," she told him.

Those spur chains tinkled again. His movement forward was so fast Colin could not follow it till the man had grasped Tina by the wrist. She tried to pull away. Colin saw Nacho's knuckles go white. Tina's face contorted with the pain of the squeezing grip. She lifted the quirt to lash it across Nacho's face. He shouted with the stinging pain, and it allowed her to tear loose, stumbling backward across the garden. Tears squeezed from his squinting eyes as Nacho started after her. At the same moment, the Indian appeared once more through the spindled gate. He stopped, however, just within, making no move to stop Nacho. Colin spoke, then.

"Nacho."

Again, the utter, deadly quiet of his voice had a startling effect after all the violence and noise. It stopped both Nacho and the woman. Nacho turned back his way. Colin was standing perfectly straight, with no inclination of body or arm to advertise his intent, yet Nacho's eyes flickered momentarily across the stag butt of the big Paterson he had thrust through his belt just behind the buckle.

"*¿Si, señor?*" Nacho said, in that mocking tone.

"Get out of this garden," said Colin.

"Now, *señor?*" asked Nacho.

"I won't ask you again," said Colin.

"You won't have to," said Nacho. His draw was as blinding as the rest of his movements. He halted it so abruptly his whole body shuddered. His gun was only halfway out of his holster, and he held it there with a tense, bent arm, staring in unveiled surprise at the Paterson filling Colin's hand, pointed at the middle of his belly.

The Indian had started some overt move, too, over there by the spindled gate, and half stopped it as quickly as Nacho, with sight of Colin's weapon. Tina let out a small, moaning sound. Nacho allowed his gun to slip back in its holster, raising his eyes to Colin.

"Get out and on your horse," said Colin. "I'll be watching you out of sight. And I'll have this in my hand all the way."

"There are still enough days left in the year, *señor,*" said Nacho, softly. He met Colin's gaze for a moment longer, his own eyes showing no particular defeat, smoldering with the banked coals of that subterranean hate. Then he turned, chains tinkling as he walked to the *zaguan*. He moved through the large gate and disappeared for a moment. They could hear the creak of saddle leather. Then he appeared again, spurring his horse cruelly into a headlong run. Colin inclined his head at the Indian.

"How about you?"

"That's all, Ichahi," said the woman. The Indian let those enigmatic eyes pass over Colin as he turned to go. Tina's glance followed Colin's movement as he thrust the Paterson back into his belt. Then she raised her eyes to his face, a new measure of him in their depths.

"I would not have taken you for a gunfighter," she said.

"I'm not," said Colin. "Dad always said a man had no right to use tools unless he could use them well."

A mingling of emotions brought a subtle, indefinable change to her face, and then left it with only a strange, withdrawn calculation. She walked over to sit on the long, comfortable bench beneath a peach tree. She toyed idly with a ring on her middle finger, pouting a little. Feeling awkward, standing in the middle of the garden, he finally joined her. His attention was caught by the ring's strange design.

"Looks like some kind of Mexican brand," he said.

She held it up for his inspection. "It is called a *rubrica*. In the old days, the Moors wore rings with designs on them...their initials, or something signifying their house ...and, instead of signing their name, stamped this in hot wax on the paper, forming sort of a seal. The Moors carried it into Spain in their conquest. The design in this ring has been handed down through our family for generations."

"You're full of stories."

"You don't have to restrain yourself so nobly. You've been looking at me that way ever since *Cabo* mentioned Captain Velasco, up there on the mountain."

"I don't deny it. When you first told me the legend of El Renegado, you were very careful not to name the captain who betrayed his people. How are you descended from him?"

"There are many versions of the legend of El Renegado," she said. "One of them is a belief, as persistent as it is false, that the descendants of Captain Velasco are back in the Patagonias somewhere, a race, a people to themselves, really. Not true half-breeds, because the mating of Velasco and the Indian girl was so many centuries before, that the division of blood has almost been lost. They are supposed to be renegades, as he was, bandits, murderers, veritable ogres, capable of appalling atrocities, holding the simpletons of Tintown and the other settlements outside the basin in constant fear. You know how a thing like that can grow through the centuries. Every deed of violence within a thousand miles is attributed to this band."

"And there's no truth in it?"

"I am the only descendant of Velasco," she said. "He did have children, but they drifted down off the mountains into this basin years ago, adopting the customs and language of the Spaniards who had come into New Mexico by then. One of them did such service to the Spanish Crown that he was pardoned for his ancestor's crime, and granted the land this hacienda occupies."

He studied her face, finding logic in those curiously haunted eyes. He leaned toward her, a vagrant smile catching at his mouth for the first time.

"Will you forgive my suspicions?"

"I'm used to them. It is the usual reaction to the name, Velasco. I didn't realize how bad it really was till father died. It left me completely alone here."

She sat, staring moodily at the flagstones, and he had to say something, anything. "How did he die?"

For a moment, he thought a cloud had passed before the sun. The shadow crossing her face was that palpable. Then, instinctively, he glanced toward El Renegado.

"You aren't thinking of the...the...."

"The curse?" she finished, head lifting in some sharp defiance. "You sound like your brother. I thought you were different. I thought you were sensitive to those things. Do you know how old I am? Twenty-five. Do you know how many days I've heard laughter in this house? Not one. In all my life, not one!"

She was standing now, staring at the wall, fists clenched at her sides, giving vent to some violent release that had been gathering force for a long time. "Do you know how much pain and tragedy and death I've seen? A grandfather paralyzed when he fell from his horse, sitting for ten years like a stone statue faced toward the mountain. A grandmother burned to death in the stables. A mother killed when she was thrown downstairs by her husband in a drunken rage. A son killing him for it. A lifetime of loneliness because my name is Velasco. Not a man in the towns around here who has had the courage to look at me, for fear of the curse. How can I help but think of that curse, when I say anything, do anything, remember anything?"

He saw she was on the verge of crying and got to his feet sharply, catching her. She turned to him with a hunger which surprised him, molding her body into the circle of his arms, and then he was answering the hunger, pulling her against him with a savage passion he had not known himself capable of, cupping a hand under her chin to lift her face. His lips were still on hers when he heard someone call her name.

"Tina? Tina?"

The voice was unmistakable. It caused him something close to pain to pull his mouth away and turn toward the sound. All the romance of Erin had always given Farris Shane his way with women, and it was so typical of him to make a flourish of it that way, ignoring the half-open gate in the *zaguan* to come vaulting over the top of the adobe wall itself, from the back of his horse outside. Mouth still open from calling her name, he had already seen them before he landed.

His knees bent with the weight of his body striking the ground, then straightened, and he was staring at them with eyes already blackened by storm.

"Colin?" he said, in a small, unbelieving way. "Colin," he repeated, his voice now hoarse, angry.

"Farris," cried Colin, releasing the woman abruptly. "Don't be a fool."

"I *have been* a fool," said Farris, his tone so thick with anger he could hardly speak. "It was you. Behind my back. Knowing how I felt about her, and meeting her like this."

"Farris...."

"I told you, Colin, how it would be."

The rest of it was lost as he rushed Colin in that blind, roaring rage. Colin tried to wheel aside, but Farris spun him against the wall. He caught Colin there, doubling him over with a vicious punch to the groin. Gripped in the nauseating pain of it, Colin would have fallen to the ground except for Farris there in front of him, pinning him against the wall.

Dimly, somewhere down in the pain-filled recesses of him, he realized that if Farris hit him once more he would be through. With Farris's body against him, holding him up, he felt the surge of muscle, shifting away from his own left side, that told him of his brother's right arm brought back for a second blow.

His long legs found purchase, and he shoved with all the strength of them, just as Farris struck. Tripping backward, Farris's blow lost all its force, falling weakly against Colin's shoulder. Colin kept shoving, his arms wound about the man's waist. Farris came up against something with a tumbling crash of wood and stone. He seemed to surge upward in Colin's arms, as if something had lifted his feet off the ground. Then all the tension left Farris's body. He fell backward. There was another sharp crack, something sickening this time.

It must have been Farris's head striking that oaken bench, for he lay sprawled on his back just beside it, darkening the flagstones with his blood. Colin swayed above him, staring at the growing red stain. Then, face twisting, he dropped to his knees beside his brother.

"Farris?" he said, in a weak, husky voice. There was no answer. "Farris?" Lifting the head up. "Farris?" Seeing the eyes roll open, white and sightless and dead.

"I'll...I'll get some water," whispered Tina, standing above them.

Colin dropped his brother's head back. "He doesn't need any water," he told her, in a voice that did not belong to him. For a moment, he thought the blood had spread across all the patio floor, to darken it that way. Then he felt the chill of the garden, and turned his face upward. The woman was looking in that direction, too, an ominous fulfillment torturing her face. The sun was setting behind the Patagonias, and the shadow of El Renegado lay black as Farris's blood across the whole garden.

VI

Consciousness of a great heat came to Colin. He tried to open his eyes. There was blinding brightness. He realized he was on his back, and rolled over. The grit of earth scraped his belly. He got to his hands and knees, opening his eyes again. He saw that there was barren land about him — great, ruddy rocks and steep, sandy barrancas. He had a dim, whirling memory. Farris was in it somehow. He sat down, holding his head in his hands, trying to think.

It returned then, like a blow, memory of the fight in the garden. Farris dead? He raised his head, unable to believe it. He was a murderer, then. Of his own brother.

In this torture, he stared around him, trying to make out where he was. There seemed to be mountains all about him, stark, barren, unworldly. He thought, for a moment, of a dream. But it was too real for that. More memory came, filtering in painfully, dim and tantalizing. He could almost see the man stumbling out through that *zaguan,* eyes blank and staring in the madness of realizing what he had done. Was it him? He had wandered, then. He had run from the scene of his crime and wandered to this spot, too crazed with grief and guilt to have any lucid memory of it.

He looked at his shirt. It was in tatters. How long had he been wandering? He felt his beard. It was a rough stubble an inch long. It had been days. He tried to rise, fell back. On his second attempt he made it.

Now he knew a burning thirst, and began walking, aimlessly, hands outstretched, unable to see half the time that the sun was so bright. He stumbled and fell many times. The one thought in his mind was water. Then something else began replacing that. He felt his arms twitch, as if tensing to strike something. His lips moved in someone's name. He saw a face before him, and saw himself hitting at it. Farris. Farris, on the ground before him, with the blood darkening the flagstones. A scream of anguish escaped him and he dug his fists into his eyes to escape the vision, running from it, running with small, animal sobbing sounds, stumbling and falling again, losing sanity before the persistent, maddening memory that blended with reality until he could not tell them apart.

He ran on down the sandy, desolate slope, a tattered, babbling figure, sinking finally into the same apathetic state which had led him wandering so long with no memory of it.

When he became lucid again, the heat was gone, the burning thirst. He knew a great sense of coolness. Above him was a ceiling, laced with the herringbone pattern of the willow shoots they laid beneath the foot of earth forming the roofs of their adobe houses. Under these stretched the *viga* poles that were the rafters, forming dim, smoke-blackened lines from wall to wall. Then it was the face, the greasy, bland, grinning face, and the man squatting back on his heels.

"Pajarero."

"*Si,*" smiled the bird-catcher. "I found you wandering the Patagonias. *Loco* in the head. Ay. Does it torture one so, to kill his own brother?"

Colin's face twisted. "You know?"

"The whole basin knows," said Pajarero. "You and he fought in the woman's garden and he died in the shadow of El Renegado." He seemed to be looking beyond Colin. "Did you ever wonder why it was you who lived, and not he?"

Colin tried to sit up. "How do you mean?"

"He was the one who scoffed at Renegado. Sometimes the unbelievers are punished in strange ways for their heresy."

Colin's efforts to rise brought a chorus of squawks from the birds in the cages around the room. The bird-catcher rose from his hunkers and fluttered around from one to another, calming them.

"Quiet, Pepita. *Caramba*. Are you old women, that you screech at a mouse? Silence, Garcia. That does not befit a gentleman."

Finally he had them quieted down, and he shuffled over to a pot of stew simmering over one of the pot-fires on the adobe hearth, ladling out a bowl for Colin, muttering into his fat jowls. Colin sat amid the fetid sheepskin pallets, gulping the stew ravenously, following it with a dozen cold tortillas piled on a plate.

"We're in Tintown?" he asked Pajarero, at last.

"In the Patagonias," said the man.

"I thought you lived in Tintown."

"I live wherever my travels take me," said the man, grumpily.

Colin studied the man. "Why did you take me in, Pajarero?"

Something withdrew in that round, greasy face. "You would have died out there. You had the fever. This is your first clear head in three days. I been nursing you like a baby."

Colin moved again, feeling the weakness in him. Even talk cost him an effort. But he had to know. "Why, though, Pajarero?" he insisted. "You know how I stand with Nacho. I think he's quite capable of killing you for taking me in this way. Don't you?"

The man squinted, as if in pain at the name, and Colin had it. "Maybe because I saved you from him that first time?" he asked.

"Well, well," muttered Pajarero, "so I am not so noble, so I had a reason for taking you in. Maybe you are the only one in the valley who has opposed Nacho and lived. I heard about that business with the guns. Poom!" He made a gesture of drawing a gun, index finger pointed. "So fast nobody saw it come out. So fast Nacho started first and still didn't have anything free in time."

"And you're hiding from him?" said Colin. The man made vague, shrugging movements with his shoulders and arms, pouting and muttering incoherently, moving over to pour coffee he had put on to boil "Why?" asked Colin. "Why was he trying to kill you that first day?"

"How would I know?" said Pajarero, turning away.

"Does he run a gang back here in the Patagonias?"

"I don't know *nada* about nothing."

"You mean you're afraid to tell. How is Tina mixed up in it? What is Nacho to her?"

"*Dios*," exploded the man, waving his hand so violently he spilled the coffee. "Haven't I saved your life? Is that not enough? What do you want? The history of the New World? Drink your coffee and be thankful I have found it in my groveling little soul to do this much. Now, rest a while. I have to go and get water from the *tinaja*."

A *tinaja* was a natural rock sink in which rain water collected during the wet season. Colin expected the man back in a few moments, but time stretched out to an hour, two hours. He was stirring feebly within the stifling hovel, worried about the bird-catcher, when the man's grimy, weary face poked through the low door.

"*Agua,*" he grinned. "Enough to last a couple of days if we do not wash."

"Don't mean to tell me it's that far away," muttered Colin.

"Over two mountains," chuckled Pajarero.

"You really are holed in," said Colin.

"*El Diablo* himself could not find us," smiled the man, secretively. "The Patagonias themselves are so inaccessible that no more than a dozen men have penetrated them in the last century, and this is the most inaccessible spot in all the Patagonias."

Colin knew it was useless to ask the man again why he was so afraid of Nacho. He settled down to recovering, dozing most of that first day, moving about some the second. He began to brood soon, about Farris, sinking into a black, ugly mood that lasted for hours.

"But it was not your fault," Pajarero pleaded with him, over and over. "You did not mean to kill him. You were only defending yourself. It was an accident, *amigo,* that bench."

When that failed, the man would try to amuse him by babbling about his experiences in Yucatan, or Darien, or some other forgotten section of Mexico, hunting birds. It helped, somehow. There was a naïve simplicity to Pajarero, for all his travels, all his strange, exotic knowledge, that lifted Colin out of his depression. But there was always something behind the talk — in those quiet, expressive eyes of Pajarero's, in the way he watched Colin sometimes — a sense of pendant waiting. Colin had regained most of his strength by the third time Pajarero had to go for water. After the man had left, Colin went outside the door, hunkering down against the wall, squinting against the haze of heat the sun brought.

It was just a little one-room adobe *jacal,* walls crumbling with age, a corral of cottonwood poles behind, holding Pajarero's jackass and a couple of mangy horses. On every side, the mountains lifted their jagged, barren steeps to the sky, utterly devoid of vegetation. A buzzard circled high above. The silence had a palpable pressure. Shadows lengthened slowly, crawling like black fingers across the rocks to touch Colin. They brought him a sudden chill. He stirred, realizing how long Pajarero had been gone.

He went inside, lying on the fetid sheepskins. He must have dozed, for when he awoke, it was night. A loafer wolf filled the darkness with its mourning. Colin moved restlessly about the building, looking off in the direction Pajarero always took.

When the moon began to rise, shedding a pale, unworldly light over the peaks, he went inside, pawing through the sheepskins till he found where Pajarero had put his Paterson. He shoved the gun in behind his belt buckle and went to get one of the horses. There was an ancient Mexican tree-saddle on the top pole of the corral. With this on the beast, he set off up the trail he had watched the bird-catcher take.

It was so rocky the hoofs left no mark, and he soon lost his way. He was on the point of turning back when he realized the horse was tugging at the reins, trying to face the other way. A thirsty animal had some sense of water many miles away, and he gave the animal its head. The horse went at a deliberate walk, as true as if it had traveled the trail all its life, carrying him across one of the knife-like peaks and into another valley. The wolf was still howling off in the distance somewhere, when the other sound joined it. A faint mewing, like a sick cat.

He saw it, finally. Pajarero had been tied to a jumping cholla. Some of the longer spines had thrust clear through his body at the sides and other narrower portions. His shirt front was rusty with blood. There were the charred coals of a fire at one side, with several half-burnt stalks of Spanish dagger. Jumping off his horse and going to his knees beside the man, Colin saw what they had been used for. Pajarero's eyes had been burned out.

"*Agua,*" whispered the fat, little Mexican, moving his head from side to side. "*Ruego de alma mia, señor,* I can hear you...help me...." He broke off, chest lifting with his sharp breath. "Nacho?"

"No, Pajarero," said Colin, gently. "It's Colin. Take it easy and I'll have you off this."

"No, no," bleated the man, like a weak child. "I die soon. Do not cause me more pain."

Colin settled back to his heels, holding the man. "Why did Nacho do this?"

"He wanted me to tell where you were." He made a ghastly attempt at a smile. "I'm proud of myself, *señor.* When you go through Tintown, do me the favor of telling the other bird-catchers that Nacho is not so terrible. He could not even make Pajarero talk."

"This wasn't why he was trying to kill you that first time."

"I suppose not."

"Can't you tell me now, Pajarero? Who is Nacho?"

"There are some things even the wind dare not whisper, *señor.*"

"You're protecting Tina. It has something to do with her."

"Does it, *señor?*"

"Why did you stay in the basin, knowing Nacho would kill you?"

"I have traveled two continents in the quest of rare birds," said the man, weakly. "There was one rarest, most beautiful of all...which I desired more than any other in the world. But I am only a fat, stupid little Pajarero, a comical clown of a bird-catcher and it was denied me. All I could do was flutter about inside its cage."

Colin's throat twitched as he realized who Pajarero meant. He remembered the dog-like devotion in the man's eyes that first time they had seen Tina, remembered how Pajarero had tried to kiss the hem of her skirt, on his knees. At the time, it had been almost amusing to him. The full pathos of it struck him now.

"Ay," said Pajarero, at his silence. "You see, now. And if I had it to do over again, it would be no different. For but one more look at her, I would take ten times this torture. They kept trying to get you to go, didn't they?"

"Tina?"

"She. Your mother. Even I told you how foolish you were to stay, once. And yet, you stayed. You had seen her, too. We are not very different underneath, *señor*. Your plumage may be more brilliant, but inside it is the same. I would ask you as a dying favor, to leave now. But I know how useless that would be. You will stay and be killed, because you have seen her. Renegado is fulfilled in strange ways."

He leaned back against the cactus, greasy face contorting in some last spasm of pain. Then he sank down, and the shallow breathing stopped. Staring down at the round, fat face, Colin felt a tear begin rolling down his cheek. He was crying. The pain of his anguish was the more intense because he could make no sound.

Later, he untied the man and gathered rocks for a cairn, piling them over his body. Then he gathered up the gum-pitched *morrales* Pajarero had been carrying the water in, slinging them over the withers of his horse, and set off on the trail. The rock and talus had given way to parched earth, here, which recorded the prints of four horses faithfully. By the moonlight, it was not too hard to follow.

VII

The mountains seemed to rise and fall about Colin, before him, behind him, like a gigantic sea, as he traversed peak after peak, valley after valley. He came to vegetation, ocotillo spreading from an arroyo like a fountain of gold, candlewood spouting a torch of flame from its spidery wands. And then, ahead, El Renegado, appearing suddenly behind a nearer range, like a great, somber skull, thrusting up out of its cerements.

The awe it brought struck Colin so forcibly he felt a vague nausea. It caused him great effort to push on, keeping his attention on those tracks. He knew he was nearing the basin now, and wondered if they were seeking him at his house.

He plunged through creosote, yellow with flower, into a steep arroyo, still on the trail, finding it again as it came from the creosote into the sandy wash. Then the walls of the arroyo echoed and reverberated to crazy, cackling laughter, and that voice filled with the archaic accent of Castilian.

"Here is an *Indio, Capitan*. I have an *Indio, Capitan*...."

Recognizing the voice, Colin pulled up his jaded horse, staring about him. A gun crashed, and his horse leaped into the air with a scream. Colin threw himself off the thrashing animal before it went down, pulling his gun as he fell.

He struck heavily, rolling through deep sand to come against mesquite with a loud crackle. Stunned, he crawled into the bushes.

He could hear horses galloping back down the arroyo, now. Three riders burst around its winding curve into the broadening wash, with Nacho in the lead, spurring his horse, brutally. Colin raised to his knees in the bushes, holding his gun out till he had it point blank on the man's body, and fired. Nacho shouted in pain, pitching upward and backward off his animal, with arms spread eagled to the sky.

Colin saw the other two men wheel in the saddle toward him, trying to pull their horses up and fire all at once. It was too fast and too confused to be sure of hitting the men now, and Colin lowered his gun to shoot their horses out from under them, one after the other. The first animal went down by the front, tumbling its rider over the head, and the second veered off sideways suddenly, crashing into the rocky slope of the arroyo, and wiping his man out of the saddle. He flopped down to the bottom of that slope like a doll with all the sand gone, and lay moveless there. Further back, in the broader bottom of the arroyo, the other man lay on his back, calling softly in pain.

"Nacho...Nacho...come get me, damn you. My leg's broke, my leg's broke...."

This had all taken no more than a minute, but as Colin's attention was swept back to the spot where he had shot Nacho, he could not see the man. Blood stained the sand and made an unmistakable trail into the creosote on the other side of the arroyo. Colin searched those bushes for some sign of movement, unwilling to move, with The Corporal still somewhere up above him.

One of the horses he had shot lay kicking and writhing in the sand, and the other had fallen to its side, in death. Farther up the arroyo, where Colin had first entered it, was Nacho's horse. Nacho rode with split reins, and they had dropped to the earth. He must have been trained for ground-hitching, as most Mexican animals were, for he had spooked that far from the excitement, and then halted, fiddling around nervously.

Colin wanted that horse the worst way, with his own animal down. He decided at last that he had to find The Corporal before he could expose himself, and turned to worm his way through the cover of rocks and bushes up his side of the arroyo, seeking the spot from which the crazy old man had shot his horse.

"Nacho," called the man, from down at the bottom. "Come and get me, damn you, come and get me, my leg's broke, I say."

Almost at the lip of the arroyo, Colin heard a dim, muttering sound. He wormed through mesquite toward it. Through this brush, finally, he made out The Corporal crouched down over that ancient matchlock, fumbling with the pan. Colin must have made some rustle in the mesquite, for the old man's head jerked up. Colin felt his gun move abruptly to cover The Corporal. The man leered blankly at him.

"Have you got a match, comrade?" he said. "The Indians are down in the valley and I'm out of matches."

"You damn old fool," muttered Colin. He still kept his gun on the man, knowing a frustrating indecision. Before it left him, there was some movement down in the arroyo to attract his attention. It was in the creosote, up at the end where Nacho's horse had halted. The animal began fiddling again down there, ears pricked. Colin could not help raise up as he saw a man pull himself out of the creosote, clutching at a stirrup. The horse tried to dance away, but the man caught a leather, hauling himself erect.

It was Nacho. He must have crawled through the brush from where he had fallen to get his horse, knowing that Colin was looking for him. Colin started moving, trying to find a position that would clear the man for his gun. But Nacho was mounting on the opposite side of his horse. In desperation, Colin aimed at the animal.

"Watch out, *Capitan*," screamed The Corporal, from behind Colin. "The *bribón* is going to shoot you...."

Colin half-turned in time to see the old man jumping at him, that gun clubbed. He ducked under it, throwing The Corporal over his shoulder. Nacho was racing down the arroyo now. Colin snapped a shot at him, but he was going too fast, and too far away.

Colin wheeled to where The Corporal's horse stood, a mangy crow-bait with trailing reins. The animal did not even shy when he ran up on it. He had to boot it unmercifully to get any movement. He passed The Corporal, trying to climb back up the slope from where Colin had thrown him, and then he slid the horse down the bank into the arroyo. Pushing the horse, he reached the end of this to run out into a series of benches with Nacho in sight, crossing them.

Colin knew there was no use trying to catch Nacho, on this old nag, but he felt no desire to. It was a certainty in him, where the man was going, and he figured Nacho would be more sure to keep in that direction if he thought he was not followed. Colin allowed his horse to slow down, until Nacho ran out of sight into the timber at the footslopes of El Renegado.

With the mountain there, Colin knew where he was, now, and he took a southwesterly direction, not even bothering to follow Nacho's trail directly. El Renegado brooded over him the whole distance, some malignant portent in its air of patient, sinister waiting. He was tense in the saddle, with its spell, when he came out into the flats of the basin. The Velasco hacienda was ahead of him. He approached it through the cottonwoods growing in the river bottom. This cover brought him right up against the high adobe wall surrounding the place. Down this wall about fifty feet was a broad *zaguan,* the logical gate to use for anyone coming from the direction Colin had. And before it, on the ground, even at this distance, he saw the bloodstains.

Thought of Farris was in his mind, as he lifted himself to a standing position in the saddle, against the wall, grasping the tiles on top and hoisting his body over. A weeping willow dropped its foliage over the wall here, and in this momentary screen he reloaded his gun from the handful of shells he always carried in his pocket.

After this was done, he found himself unwilling to move. He was torn between a deep reluctance to find Nacho with Tina, and a bitter desire to finish this up, for Pajarero, for Farris, for his mother.

He forced himself from the screen of willow, dropping off the wall. There was a row of sheds ahead of him, filled with the muted stamp and snort of horses, and he realized he was in the back end of a stable yard. He moved through the reek of rotten hay and droppings, around the end of this row of adobe stalls. This brought him to the main yard, into which the *zaguan* opened. It was lit by flaring torches, and Nacho's horse stood hipshot and blowing next to a half-open door.

Colin stepped to the door, listened a moment. There were muffled voices from far within. Carefully, he pushed the portal open. He was staring down a long hall, lined with the niches in which they placed their carved wooden saints. Blood stains made a trail down the floor to another door at the end, partly ajar. Colin made his way to this. The voices seemed to lift away from him now. He saw beyond the second door a great room, lit by a dozen candles, filling the candelabra of beaten silver on a great oak table. The light drank in mauve *savanarillas* hanging on the walls, seemed to catch up the faded red of a Chimayo blanket draped across the adobe *banco* that ran all the way around the room to form a foot-high bench molded in against the wall.

At the far side of the room, a stairway rose, railed in wrought iron, tarnished and rusted with age. Finally he could wait no longer. He pushed the door open with a boot. Nothing happened. He stepped into the room, ducking over back of the table. Still nothing. He darted for the wall by the stairway. He was almost to the corner, where it would afford him cover from the steps higher up, when a shot rocked the room.

It caught him across the side of his thigh, filling him with the hot, inchoate sense of a burning, lashing blow, twisting him halfway around. His run carried him up against the wall at that corner, however, half-falling across the adobe *banco.* With this for support, he bent forward and sent a shot up the dark stairwell.

There was the scream of a ricochet, a sharp, withdrawing movement up there. He took that indication of retreat to jump onto the stairs, firing upward again, seeing the dim shape above. There was one answering shot, ripping adobe off in pale flakes from the wall at the side of his head. He fired a third time with the body full in his sights.

"¡*Por Dios!*" screamed Nacho, pain rending his voice. Then there was a heavy, thumping, sliding sound, as of someone dragging themselves down a wall. Colin's leg would bear his weight no longer, and he went down on the stairs before he reached the top. Lying there, with light from below still strong enough to see, he made out that the bullet had struck the great outer muscle of his thigh, going down in a long, deep flesh wound to come out at his knee on the same side.

"Nacho?" called a woman's voice, from up there. "Nacho, please...."

It was Tina, her voice driving Colin to crawl on up the stairs. His head came over the top step, and he could see down another long hall. Light from its end was blocked off by the woman's body. He saw a low niche in the wall above him, and reached up to clutch at its edge, pulling down the wooden *santo* it contained as he struggled up. Tina reached him then, trying to keep him from going on.

"Colin, please, you can't do it, please!"

"Maybe you didn't see what he did to Pajarero," said Colin, twisting inexorably around her.

Tina's struggles to hold him became more violent. "Pajarero? I can't help it, you mustn't, not Nacho...."

"If I had more guts, it would be you, too," he said, tearing loose. He almost fell, then put himself into a headlong run that carried him in a stumbling, hurtling passage down the hall. He came to the head of the stairs giving off light from below, and saw Nacho on the landing, halfway down. The man turned, raising his gun. But Colin had his held level, waist high, and all he had to do was pull the trigger. It made a deafening crash. Nacho was punched heavily back against the wall. Then he pitched forward, rolling down the stairs to the bottom. Colin went down after him to make sure.

Nacho's dead right hand was thrust outward, a ring on the curling fourth finger. Colin stared at the design on it, the Velasco *rubrica*. The rustle of skirts brought his head around. Tina was staring at the ring with wide, tortured eyes.

"Are you satisfied now?" she asked.

He looked up at her with frowning eyes. "He's a Velasco?"

"My brother."

"And I thought," muttered Colin, staring blankly at Nacho. "I thought...."

"You thought he was my lover?" she finished, when he would not go on.

Colin nodded dully. "You mentioned your father throwing your mother downstairs in a drunken rage, and a son killing him for it."

"That was Nacho," she said. "It changed him somehow. We tried not to blame him for killing father. It was such a terrible thing father had done. But it twisted Nacho. He had been such a good boy before. He turned into something wild, like an animal, running off into the Patagonias and gathering that bunch of filthy, crazy *bribónes* around him, like The Corporal, taking advantage of the Renegado legend about the descendants of Velasco being back in there, just to maraud the countryside. And then he would come back for a little time, and be the boy he had been, giving me the company and companionship I craved so here, and I would know the hope that he was changing. That's why I wanted you to leave. He was still my brother. Can you understand the position I was in? I knew that one of you would kill the other if you stayed. From the first, it was obvious. He was my brother *and* my lover. Isn't that a happy choice? And now...now?" She sank to her knees beside Nacho, the tears running silently down her face. "Now one of you has killed the other."

"No wonder Pajarero wouldn't tell me your connection with Nacho," murmured Colin. "And it was you who stampeded those cattle and Farris found you up on Renegado that day?"

"Yes," she nodded, dully. "Ichahi and I did it. Do you blame me?" He was silent so long she raised her head, meeting his eyes, seeing what was in them. "I didn't know Farris was coming that day, though, Colin. I didn't plan *that*. You can't believe I did."

In a sudden, impulsive way, unable to put his answer into words, he reached out for her, lifting her to her feet, encircling her with his arms. For a long time they stood that close, finding comfort in the nearness, until he finally sensed the subtle tension flowing into her body. He felt as if something had touched him from behind, and realized they were no longer standing in the dawn sunlight. A shadow had dropped across them. They both turned as one, staring at the mountain, forming its somber, brooding silhouette against the morning sunrise. Tina made a small, tortured sound.

"You've got to get that out of your system," he said. "Nacho was causing everything as much as the mountain."

"Did he cause your mother's death?" she said. "Or Farris's?"

He felt something within him contract at the thought of Farris, and could not help its showing on his face, that dark, mystic sensitivity to the spell of the mountain.

"You'll take me away from here, Colin? You won't try to stay here any longer? You feel it as deeply as I do?"

"Where I am going, Tina, you cannot come."

"But where are you going?" she asked, arching away from him in sudden defiance.

"If you will show me where Farris's body is buried, I shall move him, so he can rest beside our mother's grave."

"And then?" she asked.

"Then," he said sadly, but with a dim light of hope in his eyes, "then I will begin all over again. I told you the night our mother died, Tina. *We* aren't leaving the valley." With the chill of that shadow in his very bones, tears now again in his eyes, he repeated the words slowly. "No, Tina. Where I am going, you cannot come."

PART FOUR

VISIONS OF DREAMS AND DANCING

LOUIS L'AMOUR

LOUIS DEARBORN LAMOORE (1908–1988) was born in Jamestown, North Dakota. He left home at fifteen and subsequently held a wide variety of jobs although he worked mostly as a merchant seaman. From his earliest youth, L'Amour had a love of verse. His first published work was a poem, "The Chap Worth While," appearing when he was eighteen years old in his former hometown's newspaper, the *Jamestown Sun*. It is the only poem from his early years that he left out of SMOKE FROM THIS ALTAR which appeared in 1939 from Lusk Publishers in Oklahoma City, a book which L'Amour published himself; however, this poem is reproduced in THE LOUIS L'AMOUR COMPANION (Andrews and McMeel, 1992) edited by Robert Weinberg. L'Amour wrote poems and articles for a number of small circulation arts magazines all through the early 1930s and, after hundreds of rejection slips, finally had his first story accepted, "Anything for a Pal" in *True Gang Life* (10/35). He returned in 1938 to live with his family where they had settled in Choctaw, Oklahoma, determined to make writing his career. He wrote a fight story bought by Standard Magazines that year and became acquainted with editor Leo Margulies who was to play an important rôle later in L'Amour's life. "The Town No Guns Could Tame" in *New Western* (3/40) was his first published Western story.

During the Second World War L'Amour was drafted and ultimately served with the U.S. Army Transportation Corps in Europe. However, in the two years before he was shipped out, he managed to write a great many adventure stories for Standard Magazines. The first story he published in 1946, the year of his discharge, was a Western, "Law of the Desert Born" in *Dime Western* (4/46). A call to Leo Margulies resulted in L'Amour's agreeing to write Western stories for the various Western pulp magazines published by Standard Magazines, a third of which appeared under the byline Jim Mayo, the name of a character in L'Amour's earlier adventure fiction. The proposal for L'Amour to write new Hopalong Cassidy novels came from Margulies who wanted to launch *Hopalong Cassidy's Western Magazine* to take advantage of the popularity William Boyd's old films and new television series were enjoying with a new generation. Doubleday & Company agreed to publish the pulp novelettes in hard cover books. L'Amour was paid $500 a story, no royalties, and he was assigned the house name Tex Burns. L'Amour read Clarence E. Mulford's books about the

Bar-20 and based his Hopalong Cassidy on Mulford's original creation. Only two issues of the magazine appeared before it ceased publication. Doubleday felt that the Hopalong character had to appear exactly as William Boyd did in the films and on television and thus even the first two novels had to be revamped to meet with this requirement prior to publication in book form.

L'Amour's first Western novel under his own byline was WESTWARD THE TIDE (World's Work, 1950). It was rejected by every American publisher to which it was submitted. World's Work paid a flat £75 without royalties for British Empire rights in perpetuity. L'Amour sold his first Western short story to a slick magazine a year later, "The Gift of Cochise" in *Collier's* (7/5/52). Robert Fellows and John Wayne purchased screen rights to this story from L'Amour for $4,000 and James Edward Grant, one of Wayne's favorite screenwriters, developed a script from it, changing L'Amour's Ches Lane to Hondo Lane. L'Amour retained the right to novelize Grant's screenplay, which differs substantially from his short story, and he was able to get an endorsement from Wayne to be used as a blurb, stating that HONDO was the finest Western Wayne had ever read. HONDO (Fawcett Gold Medal, 1953) by Louis L'Amour was released on the same day as the film, HONDO (Warner, 1953), with a first printing of 320,000 copies.

With SHOWDOWN AT YELLOW BUTTE (Ace, 1953) by Jim Mayo, L'Amour began a series of short Western novels for Don Wollheim that could be doubled with other short novels by other authors in Ace Publishing's paperback two-fers. Advances on these were $800 and usually the author never earned any royalties. HELLER WITH A GUN (Fawcett Gold Medal, 1955) was the first of a series of original Westerns L'Amour had agreed to write under his own name following the success for Fawcett of HONDO. L'Amour wanted even this early to have his Western novels published in hard cover editions. He expanded "Guns of the Timberland" by Jim Mayo in *West* (9/50) for GUNS OF THE TIMBERLANDS (Jason Press, 1955), a hard cover Western for which he was paid an advance of $250. Another novel for Jason Press followed and then SILVER CANYON (Avalon Books, 1956) for Thomas Bouregy & Company. These were basically lending library publishers and the books seldom earned much money above the small advances paid.

The great turn in L'Amour's fortunes came about because of problems Saul David was having with his original paperback Westerns program at Bantam Books. Fred Glidden had been signed to a contract to produce two original paperback Luke Short Western novels a year for an advance of $15,000 each. It was a long-term contract but, in the first ten years of it, Fred only wrote six novels. Literary agent Marguerite Harper then persuaded Bantam that Fred's brother, Jon, could help fulfill the contract and Jon was signed for eight Peter Dawson Western novels. When Jon died suddenly before completing even one book for Bantam, Harper managed to engage a ghost writer at the Disney stu-

dios to write these eight "Peter Dawson" novels, beginning with THE SAV-
AGES (Bantam, 1959). They proved inferior to anything Jon had ever written
and what sales they had seemed to be due only to the Peter Dawson name.

Saul David wanted to know from L'Amour if *he* could deliver two Western
novels a year. L'Amour said he could, and he did. In fact, by 1962 this number
was increased to three original paperback novels a year. The first L'Amour
novel to appear under the Bantam contract was RADIGAN (Bantam, 1958). It
seemed to me after I read all of the Western stories L'Amour ever wrote in preparation for my essay, "Louis L'Amour's Western Fiction" in A VARIABLE
HARVEST (McFarland, 1990), that by the time L'Amour wrote "Riders of the
Dawn" in *Giant Western* (6/51), the short novel he later expanded to form SIL-
VER CANYON, that he had almost burned out on the Western story, and this
was years before his fame, wealth, and tremendous sales figures. He had developed seven basic plot situations in his pulp Western stories and he used them
over and over again in writing his original paperback Westerns. FLINT (Bantam, 1960), considered by many to be one of L'Amour's better efforts, is basically a reprise of the range war plot which, of the seven, is the one L'Amour
used most often. L'Amour's hero, Flint, knows about a hideout in the badlands
(where, depending on the story, something is hidden: cattle, horses, outlaws,
etc.). Even certain episodes within his basic plots are repeated again and again.
Flint scales a sharp V in a canyon wall to escape a tight spot as Jim Gatlin had
before him in L'Amour's "The Black Rock Coffin Makers" in *.44* Western
(2/50) and many a L'Amour hero would again.

Basic to this range war plot is the villain's means for crowding out the other
ranchers in a district. He brings in a giant herd that requires all the available
grass and forces all the smaller ranchers out of business. It was this same strategy Bantam used in marketing L'Amour. *All* of his Western titles were continuously kept in print. Independent distributors were required to buy titles in lots of
10,000 copies if they wanted access to other Bantam titles at significantly dis-
counted prices. In time L'Amour's paperbacks forced almost every one else off
the racks in the Western sections. L'Amour himself comprised the other half of
this successful strategy. He dressed up in cowboy outfits, traveled about the
country in a motor home visiting with independent distributors, taking them to
dinner and charming them, making them personal friends. He promoted himself at every available opportunity. L'Amour insisted that he was telling the stories of the people who had made America a great nation and he appealed to pa-
triotism as much as to commercialism in his rhetoric.

His fiction suffered, of course, stories written hurriedly and submitted in
their first draft and published as he wrote them. A character would have a rifle
in his hand, a model not yet invented in the period in which the story was set,
and when he crossed a street the rifle would vanish without explanation. A
scene would begin in a saloon and suddenly the setting would be a hotel dining

room. Characters would die once and, a few pages later, die again. An old man for most of a story would turn out to be in his twenties.

Once when we were talking and Louis had showed me his topographical maps and his library of thousands of volumes which he claimed he used for research, he asserted that, if he claimed there was a rock in a road at a certain point in a story, his readers knew that if they went to that spot they would find the rock just as he described it. I told him that might be so but I personally was troubled by the many inconsistencies in his stories. Take LAST STAND AT PAPAGO WELLS (Fawcett Gold Medal, 1957). Five characters are killed during an Indian raid. One of the surviving characters emerges from seclusion after the attack and counts *six* corpses.

"I'll have to go back and count them again," L'Amour said, and smiled. "But, you know, I don't think the people who read my books would really care."

All of this notwithstanding, there are many fine, and some spectacular, moments in Louis L'Amour's Western fiction. I think he was at his best in the shorter forms, especially his magazine stories, and the two best stories he ever wrote appeared in the 1950s, "The Gift of Cochise" early in the decade and "War Party" in *The Saturday Evening Post* (6/59). The latter was later expanded by L'Amour to serve as the opening chapters for BENDIGO SHAFTER (Dutton, 1979). That book is so poorly structured that Harold Kuebler, senior editor at Doubleday & Company to whom it was first offered, said he would not publish it unless L'Amour undertook extensive revisions. This L'Amour refused to do and, eventually, Bantam started a hard cover publishing program to accommodate him when no other hard cover publisher proved willing to accept his books as he wrote them. Yet "War Party," reprinted here as it first appeared, possesses several of the characteristics in purest form which I suspect, no matter how diluted they ultimately would become, account in largest measure for the loyal following Louis L'Amour won from his readers: the young male narrator who is in the process of growing into manhood and who is evaluating other human beings and his own experiences; a resourceful frontier woman who has beauty as well as fortitude; a strong male character who is single and hence marriageable; and the powerful, romantic, strangely compelling vision of the American West which invests L'Amour's Western fiction and makes it such a delightful escape from the cares of a later time — in this author's words from this story, that "big country needing big men and women to live in it" and where there was no place for "the frightened or the mean."

WAR PARTY
1959

We buried Pa on a sidehill out west of camp, buried him high up so his ghost could look down the trail he'd planned to travel.

We piled the grave high with rocks because of the coyotes, and we dug the grave deep, and some of it I dug myself, and Mr. Sampson helped, and some others.

Folks in the wagon train figured Ma would turn back, but they hadn't known Ma so long as I had. Once she set her mind to something she wasn't about to quit.

She was a young woman and pretty, but there was strength in her. She was a lone woman with two children, but she was of no mind to turn back. She'd come through the Little Crow massacre in Minnesota and she knew what trouble was. Yet it was like her that she put it up to me.

"Bud," she said, when we were alone, "we can turn back, but we've nobody there who cares about us, and it's of you and Jeanie that I'm thinking. If we go west you will have to be the man of the house, and you'll have to work hard to make up for Pa."

"We'll go west," I said. A boy those days took it for granted that he had work to do, and the men couldn't do it all. No boy ever thought of himself as only twelve or thirteen or whatever he was, being anxious to prove himself and take a man's place and responsibilities.

Ryerson and his wife were going back. She was a complaining woman and he was a man who was always ailing when there was work to be done. Four or five wagons were turning back, folks with their tails betwixt their legs running for the shelter of towns where their own littleness wouldn't stand out so plain.

When a body crossed the Mississippi and left the settlements behind, something happened to him. The world seemed to bust wide open, and suddenly the horizons spread out and a man wasn't cramped any more. The pinched-up villages and the narrowness of towns, all that was gone. The horizons simply exploded and rolled back into the enormous distance, with nothing around but prairie and sky.

Some folks couldn't stand it. They'd cringe into themselves and start hunting excuses to go back where they came from. This was a big country needing big men and women to live in it, and there was no place out here for the frightened or the mean.

The prairie and sky had a way of trimming folks down to size, or changing them to giants to whom nothing seemed impossible. Men who had cut a wide swath back in the States found themselves nothing out here. They were folks who were used to doing a lot of talking who suddenly found that no one was listening any more, and things that seemed mighty important back home, like family and money, they amounted to nothing alongside character and courage.

There was John Sampson from our town. He was a man used to being told to do things, used to looking up to wealth and power, but when he crossed the Mississippi he began to lift his head and look around. He squared his shoulders, put more crack to his whip and began to make his own tracks in the land.

Pa was always strong, an independent man given to reading at night from one of the four or five books we had, to speaking up on matters of principle and to straight shooting with a rifle. Pa had fought the Comanche and lived with the Sioux, but he wasn't strong enough to last more than two days with a Kiowa arrow through his lung. But he died knowing Ma had stood by the rear wheel and shot the Kiowa whose arrow was in him.

Right then I knew that neither Indians nor country was going to get the better of Ma. Shooting that Kiowa was the first time Ma had shot anything but some chicken-killing varmint — which she'd done time to time when Pa was away from home.

Only Ma wouldn't let Jeanie and me call it home. "We came here from Illinois," she said, "but we're going home now."

"But Ma," I protested, "I thought home was where we came from?"

"Home is where we're going now," Ma said, "and we'll know it when we find it. Now that Pa is gone we'll have to build that home ourselves."

She had a way of saying "home" so it sounded like a rare and wonderful place and kept Jeanie and me looking always at the horizon, just knowing it was over there, waiting for us to see it. She had given us the dream, and even Jeanie, who was only six, she had it too.

She might tell us that home was where we were going, but I knew home was where Ma was, a warm and friendly place with biscuits on the table and fresh-made butter. We wouldn't have a real home until Ma was there and we had a fire going. Only I'd build the fire.

Mr. Buchanan, who was captain of the wagon train, came to us with Tryon Burt, who was guide. "We'll help you," Mr. Buchanan said. "I know you'll be wanting to go back, and...."

"But we are not going back." Ma smiled at them. "And don't be afraid we'll be a burden. I know you have troubles of your own, and we will manage very well."

Mr. Buchanan looked uncomfortable, like he was trying to think of the right thing to say. "Now, see here," he protested, "we started this trip with a rule. There has to be a man with every wagon."

Ma put her hand on my shoulder. "I have my man. Bud is almost thirteen and accepts responsibility. I could ask for no better man."

Ryerson came up. He was thin, stooped in the shoulder, and whenever he looked at Ma there was a greasy look to his eyes that I didn't like. He was a man who looked dirty even when he'd just washed in the creek. "You come along with me, ma'am," he said. "I'll take good care of you."

"Mr. Ryerson" — Ma looked him right in the eye — "you have a wife who can use better care than she's getting, and I have my son."

"He's nothin' but a boy."

"You are turning back, are you not? My son is going on. I believe that should indicate who is more the man. It is neither size nor age that makes a man, Mr. Ryerson, but something he has inside. My son has it."

Ryerson might have said something unpleasant only Tryon Burt was standing there wishing he would, so he just looked ugly and hustled off.

"I'd like to say you could come," Mr. Buchanan said, "but the boy couldn't stand up to a man's work."

Ma smiled at him, chin up, the way she had. "I do not believe in gambling, Mr. Buchanan, but I'll wager a good Ballard rifle there isn't a man in camp who could follow a child all day, running when it runs, squatting when it squats, bending when it bends and wrestling when it wrestles and not be played out long before the child is."

"You may be right, ma'am, but a rule is a rule."

"We are in Indian country, Mr. Buchanan. If you are killed a week from now, I suppose your wife must return to the States?"

"That's different! Nobody could turn back from there!"

"Then," Ma said sweetly, "it seems a rule is only a rule within certain limits, and if I recall correctly no such limit was designated in the articles of travel. Whatever limits there were, Mr. Buchanan, must have been passed sometime before the Indian attack that killed my husband."

"I can drive the wagon, and so can Ma," I said. "For the past two days I've been driving, and nobody said anything until Pa died."

Mr. Buchanan didn't know what to say, but a body could see he didn't like it. Nor did he like a woman who talked up to him the way Ma did.

Tryon Burt spoke up. "Let the boy drive. I've watched this youngster, and he'll do. He has better judgment than most men in the outfit, and he stands up to his work. If need be, I'll help."

Mr. Buchanan turned around and walked off with his back stiff the way it is when he's mad. Ma looked at Burt, and she said, "Thank you, Mr. Burt. That was nice of you."

Try Burt, he got all red around the gills and took off like somebody had put a burr under his saddle.

Come morning our wagon was the second one ready to take its place in line, with both horses saddled and tied behind the wagon, and me standing beside the off ox.

Any direction a man wanted to look there was nothing but grass and sky, only sometimes there'd be a buffalo wallow or a gopher hole. We made eleven miles the first day after Pa was buried, sixteen the next, then nineteen, thirteen, and twenty-one. At no time did the country change. On the sixth day after Pa died I killed a buffalo.

It was a young bull, but a big one, and I spotted him coming up out of a draw and was off my horse and bellied down in the grass before Try Burt realized there was game in sight. That bull came up from the draw and stopped there, staring at the wagon train, which was a half-mile off. Setting a sight behind his left shoulder I took a long breath, took in the trigger slack, then squeezed off my shot so gentle-like the gun jumped in my hands before I was ready for it.

The bull took a step back like something had surprised him, and I jacked another shell into the chamber and was sighting on him again when he went down on his knees and rolled over on his side.

"You got him, Bud!" Burt was more excited than me. "That was shootin'!"

Try got down and showed me how to skin the bull, and lent me a hand. Then we cut out a lot of fresh meat and toted it back to the wagons.

Ma was at the fire when we came up, a wisp of brown hair alongside her cheek and her face flushed from the heat of the fire, looking as pretty as a bay pony.

"Bud killed his first buffalo," Burt told her, looking at Ma like he could eat her with a spoon.

"Why, Bud! That's wonderful!" Her eyes started to dance with a kind of mischief in them, and she said, "Bud, why don't you take a piece of that meat along to Mr. Buchanan and the others?"

With Burt to help, we cut the meat into eighteen pieces and distributed it around the wagons. It wasn't much, but it was the first fresh meat in a couple of weeks.

John Sampson squeezed my shoulder and said, "Seems to me you and your Ma are folks to travel with. This outfit needs some hunters."

Each night I staked out that buffalo hide, and each day I worked at curing it before rolling it up to pack on the wagon. Believe you me, I was some proud of that buffalo hide. Biggest thing I'd shot until then was a cottontail rabbit back in Illinois, where we lived when I was born. Try Burt told folks about that shot. "Two hundred yards," he'd say, "right through the heart."

Only it wasn't more than a hundred and fifty yards the way I figured, and Pa used to make me pace off distances, so I'd learn to judge right. But I was nobody to argue with Try Burt telling a story — besides, two hundred yards makes an awful lot better sound than one hundred and fifty.

After supper the menfolks would gather to talk plans. The season was late, and we weren't making the time we ought if we hoped to beat the snow through the passes of the Sierras. When they talked I was there because I was the man of my wagon, but nobody paid me no mind. Mr. Buchanan, he acted like he didn't see me, but John Sampson would and Try Burt always smiled at me.

Several spoke up for turning back, but Mr. Buchanan said he knew of an outfit that made it through later than this. One thing was sure. Our wagon wasn't turning back. Like Ma said, home was somewhere ahead of us, and back in the States we'd have no money and nobody to turn to, nor any relatives, anywhere. It was the three of us.

"We're going on," I said at one of these talks. "We don't figure to turn back for anything."

Webb gave me a glance full of contempt. "You'll go where the rest of us go. You an' your Ma would play hob gettin' by on your own."

Next day it rained, dawn to dark it fairly poured, and we were lucky to make six miles. Day after that, with the wagon wheels sinking into the prairie and the rain still falling, we camped just two miles from where we started in the morning.

Nobody talked much around the fires, and what was said was apt to be short and irritable. Most of these folks had put all they owned into the outfits they had, and if they turned back now they'd have nothing to live on and nothing left to make a fresh start. Except a few like Mr. Buchanan, who was well off.

"It doesn't have to be California," Ma said once. "What most of us want is land, not gold."

"This here is Indian country," John Sampson said, "and a sight too open for me. I'd like a valley in the hills, with running water close by."

"There will be valleys and meadows," Ma replied, stirring the stew she was making, "and tall trees near running streams, and tall grass growing in the meadows, and there will be game in the forest and on the grassy plains, and places for homes."

"And where will we find all that?" Webb's tone was slighting.

"West," Ma said, "over against the mountains."

"I suppose you've been there?" Webb scoffed.

"No, Mr. Webb, I haven't been there, but I've been told of it. The land is there, and we will have some of it, my children and I, and we will stay through the winter, and in the spring we will plant our crops."

"Easy to say."

"This is Sioux country to the north," Burt said. "We'll be lucky to get through without a fight. There was a war party of thirty or thirty-five passed this way a couple of days ago."

"Sioux?"

"Uh-huh...no women or children along, and I found some war paint rubbed off on the brush."

"Maybe," Mr. Buchanan suggested, "we'd better turn south a mite."

"It is late in the season," Ma replied, "and the straightest way is the best way now."

"No use to worry," White interrupted; "those Indians went on by. They won't likely know we're around."

"They were riding southeast," Ma said, "and their home is in the north, so when they return they'll be riding northwest. There is no way they can miss our trail."

"Then we'd best turn back," White said.

"Don't look like we'd make it this year, anyway," a woman said; "the season is late."

That started the argument, and some were for turning back and some wanted to push on, and finally White said we should push on, but travel fast.

"Fast?" Webb asked disparagingly. "An Indian can ride in one day the distance we'd travel in four."

That started the wrangling again and Ma continued with her cooking. Sitting there watching her I figured I never did see anybody so graceful or quick on her feet as Ma, and when we used to walk in the woods back home I never knew her to stumble or step on a fallen twig or branch.

The group broke up and returned to their own fires with nothing settled, only there at the end Mr. Buchanan looked to Burt. "Do you know the Sioux?"

"Only the Utes and Shoshonis, and I spent a winter on the Snake with the Nez Perces one time. But I've had no truck with the Sioux. Only they tell me they're bad medicine. Fightin' men from way back and they don't cotton to white folks in their country. If we run into Sioux, we're in trouble."

After Mr. Buchanan had gone Tryon Burt accepted a plate and cup from Ma and settled down to eating. After a while he looked up at her and said, "Beggin' your pardon, ma'am, but it struck me you knew a sight about trackin' for an Eastern woman. You'd spotted those Sioux your own self, an' you figured it right that they'd pick up our trail on the way back."

She smiled at him. "It was simply an observation, Mr. Burt. I would believe anyone would notice it. I simply put it into words."

Burt went on eating, but he was mighty thoughtful, and it didn't seem to me he was satisfied with Ma's answer. Ma said finally, "It seems to be raining west of here. Isn't it likely to be snowing in the mountains?"

Burt looked up uneasily. "Not necessarily so, ma'am. It could be raining here and not snowing there, but I'd say there was a chance of snow." He got up and came around the fire to the coffeepot. "What are you gettin' at, ma'am?"

"Some of them are ready to turn back or change their plans. What will you do then?"

He frowned, placing his cup on the grass and starting to fill his pipe. "No idea...might head south for Santa Fe. Why do you ask?"

"Because we're going on," Ma said. "We're going to the mountains, and I am hoping some of the others decide to come with us."

"You'd go alone?" He was amazed.

"If necessary."

We started on at daybreak, but folks were more scary than before, and they kept looking at the great distances stretching away on either side, and muttering. There was an autumn coolness in the air, and we were still short of South Pass by several days with the memory of the Donner party being talked up around us.

There was another kind of talk in the wagons, and some of it I heard. The nightly gatherings around Ma's fire had started talk, and some of it pointed to Tryon Burt, and some were saying other things.

We made seventeen miles that day, and at night Mr. Buchanan didn't come to our fire; and when White stopped by, his wife came and got him. Ma looked at her and smiled, and Mrs. White sniffed and went away beside her husband.

"Mr. Burt" — Ma wasn't one to beat around a bush — "is there talk about me?"

Try Burt got red around the ears and he opened his mouth, but couldn't find the words he wanted. "Maybe...well, maybe I shouldn't eat here all the time. Only...well, ma'am, you're the best cook in camp."

Ma smiled at him. "I hope that isn't the only reason you come to see us, Mr. Burt."

He got redder than ever then and gulped his coffee and took off in a hurry.

Time to time the men had stopped by to help a little, but next morning nobody came by. We got lined out about as soon as ever, and Ma said to me as we sat on the wagon seat, "Pay no attention, Bud. You've no call to take up anything if you don't notice it. There will always be folks who will talk, and the better you do in the world the more bad things they will say of you. Back there in the settlement you remember how the dogs used to run out and bark at our wagons?"

"Yes, Ma."

"Did the wagons stop?"

"No, Ma."

"Remember that, son. The dogs bark, but the wagons go on their way, and if you're going some place you haven't time to bother with barking dogs."

We made eighteen miles that day, and the grass was better, but there was a rumble of distant thunder, whimpering and muttering off in the cañons, promising rain.

Webb stopped by, dropped an armful of wood beside the fire, then started off.

"Thank you, Mr. Webb," Ma said, "but aren't you afraid you'll be talked about?"

He looked angry and started to reply something angry, and then he grinned and said, "I reckon I'd be flattered, Mrs. Miles."

Ma said, "No matter what is decided by the rest of them, Mr. Webb, we are going on, but there is no need to go to California for what we want."

Webb took out his pipe and tamped it. He had a dark, devil's face on him with eyebrows like you see on pictures of the devil. I was afraid of Mr. Webb.

"We want land," Ma said, "and there is land around us. In the mountains ahead there will be streams and forests, there will be fish and game, logs for houses and meadows for grazing."

Mr. Buchanan had joined us. "That's fool talk," he declared. "What could anyone do in these hills? You'd be cut off from the world. Left out of it."

"A man wouldn't be so crowded as in California," John Sampson remarked. "I've seen so many go that I've been wondering what they all do there."

"For a woman," Webb replied, ignoring the others, "you've a head on you, ma'am."

"What about the Sioux?" Mr. Buchanan asked dryly.

"We'd not be encroaching on their land. They live to the north," Ma said. She gestured toward the mountains. "There is land to be had just a few days further on, and that is where our wagon will stop."

A few days! Everybody looked at everybody else. Not months, but days only. Those who stopped then would have enough of their supplies left to help them through the winter, and with what game they could kill — and time for cutting wood and even building cabins before the cold set in.

Oh, there was an argument, such argument as you've never heard, and the upshot of it was that all agreed it was fool talk and the thing to do was keep going. And there was talk I overheard about Ma being no better than she should be, and why was that guide always hanging around her? And all those men? No decent woman — I hurried away.

At break of day our wagons rolled down a long valley with a small stream alongside the trail, and the Indians came over the ridge to the south of us and started our way — tall, fine-looking men with feathers in their hair.

There was barely time for a circle, but I was riding off in front with Tryon Burt, and he said, "A man can always try to talk first, and Injuns like a palaver. You get back to the wagons."

Only I rode along beside him, my rifle over my saddle and ready to hand. My mouth was dry and my heart was beating so's I thought Try could hear it, I was that scared. But behind us the wagons were making their circle, and every second was important.

Their chief was a big man with splendid muscles, and there was a scalp not many days old hanging from his lance. It looked like Ryerson's hair, but Ryerson's wagons should have been miles away to the east by now.

Burt tried them in Shoshoni, but it was the language of their enemies and they merely stared at him, understanding well enough, but of no mind to talk. One young buck kept staring at Burt with a taunt in his eye, daring Burt to make a move; then suddenly the chief spoke, and they all turned their eyes toward the wagons.

There was a rider coming, and it was a woman. It was Ma.

She rode right up beside us, and when she drew up she started to talk, and she was speaking their language. She was talking Sioux. We both knew what it was because those Indians sat up and paid attention. Suddenly she directed a question at the chief.

"Red Horse," he said, in English.

Ma shifted to English. "My husband was blood brother to Gall, the greatest warrior of the Sioux nation. It was my husband who found Gall dying in the brush with a bayonet wound in his chest, who took Gall to his home and treated the wound until it was well."

"Your husband was a medicine-man?" Red Horse asked.

"My husband was a warrior," Ma replied proudly, "but he made war only against strong men, not women or children or the wounded."

She put her hand on my shoulder. "This is my son. As my husband was blood brother to Gall, his son is by blood brotherhood the son of Gall, also."

Red Horse stared at Ma for a long time, and I was getting even more scared. I could feel a drop of sweat start at my collar and crawl slowly down my spine. Red Horse looked at me. "Is this one a fit son for Gall?"

"He is a fit son. He has killed his first buffalo."

Red Horse turned his mount and spoke to the others. One of the young braves shouted angrily at him, and Red Horse replied sharply. Reluctantly, the warriors trailed off after their chief.

"Ma'am," Burt said, "you just about saved our bacon. They were just spoilin' for a fight."

"We should be moving," Ma said.

Mr. Buchanan was waiting for us. "What happened out there? I tried to keep her back, but she's a difficult woman."

"She's worth any three men in the outfit," Burt replied.

That day we made eighteen miles, and by the time the wagons circled there was talk. The fact that Ma had saved them was less important now than other things. It didn't seem right that a decent woman could talk Sioux or mix in the affairs of men.

Nobody came to our fire, but while picketing the saddle horses I heard someone say, "Must be part Injun. Else why would they pay attention to a woman?"

"Maybe she's part Injun and leadin' us into a trap."

"Hadn't been for her," Burt said, "you'd all be dead now."

"How do you know what she said to 'em? Who savvies that lingo?"

"I never did trust that woman," Mrs. White said; "too high and mighty. Nor that husband of hers, either, comes to that. Kept to himself too much."

The air was cool after a brief shower when we started in the morning, and no Indians in sight. All day long we moved over grass made fresh by new rain, and all the ridges were pineclad now, and the growth along the streams heavier. Short of sundown I killed an antelope with a running shot, dropped him mighty neat and looked up to see an Indian watching from a hill. At the distance I couldn't tell, but it could have been Red Horse.

Time to time I'd passed along the train, but nobody waved or said anything. Webb watched me go by, his face stolid as one of the Sioux, yet I could see there was a deal of talk going on.

"Why are they mad at us?" I asked Burt.

"Folks hate something they don't understand, or anything seems different. Your ma goes her own way, speaks her mind, and of an evening she doesn't set by and gossip."

He topped out on a rise and drew up to study the country, and me beside him. "You got to figure most of these folks come from small towns where they never knew much aside from their families, their gossip and their church. It doesn't seem right to them that a decent woman would find time to learn Sioux."

Burt studied the country. "Time was, any stranger was an enemy, and if anybody came around who wasn't one of yours, you killed him. I've seen wolves jump on a wolf that was white or different somehow…seems like folks and animals fear anything that's unusual."

We circled, and I staked out my horses and took the oxen to the herd. By the time Ma had her grub-box lid down, I was fixing at a fire when here come Mr. Buchanan, Mr. and Mrs. White and some other folks, including that Webb.

"Ma'am" — Mr. Buchanan was mighty abrupt — "we figure we ought to know what you said to those Sioux. We want to know why they turned off just because you went out there."

"Does it matter?"

Mr. Buchanan's face stiffened up. "We think it does. There's some think you might be an Indian your own self."

"And if I am?" Ma was amused. "Just what is it you have in mind, Mr. Buchanan?"

"We don't want no Injuns in this outfit!" Mr. White shouted.

"How does it come you can talk that language?" Mrs. White demanded. "Even Tryon Burt can't talk it."

"I figure maybe you want us to keep goin' because there's a trap up ahead!" White declared.

I never realized folks could be so mean, but there they were facing Ma like they hated her, like those witch-hunters Ma told me about back in Salem. It didn't seem right that Ma, who they didn't like, had saved them from an Indian attack, and the fact that she talked Sioux like any Indian bothered them.

"As it happens," Ma said, "I am not an Indian, although I should not be ashamed of it if I were. They have many admirable qualities. However, you need worry yourselves no longer, as we part company in the morning. I have no desire to travel further with you...*gentlemen.*"

Mr. Buchanan's face got all angry, and he started up to say something mean. Nobody was about to speak rough to Ma with me standing by, so I just picked up that ol' rifle and jacked a shell into the chamber. "Mr. Buchanan, this here's my Ma, and she's a lady, so you just be careful what words you use."

"Put down that rifle, you young fool!" he shouted at me.

"Mr. Buchanan, I may be little and may be a fool, but this here rifle doesn't care who pulls its trigger."

He looked like he was going to have a stroke, but he just turned sharp around and walked away, all stiff in the back.

"Ma'am," Webb said, "you've no cause to like me much, but you've shown more brains than that passel o' fools. If you'll be so kind, me and my boy would like to trail along with you."

"I like a man who speaks his mind, Mr. Webb. I would consider it an honor to have your company."

Tryon Burt looked quizzically at Ma. "Why, now, seems to me this is a time for a man to make up his mind, and I'd like to be included along with Webb."

"Mr. Burt," Ma said, "for your own information, I grew up among Sioux children in Minnesota. They were my playmates."

Come daylight our wagon pulled off to one side, pointing northwest at the mountains, and Mr. Buchanan led off to the west. Webb followed Ma's wagon, and I sat watching Mr. Buchanan's eyes get angrier as John Sampson, Neely Stuart, the two Shafter wagons and Tom Croft all fell in behind us.

Tryon Burt had been talking to Mr. Buchanan, but he left off and trotted his horse over to where I sat my horse. Mr. Buchanan looked mighty sullen when he saw half his wagon train gone and with it a lot of his importance as captain.

Two days and nearly forty miles further and we topped out on a rise and paused to let the oxen take a blow. A long valley lay across our route, with tall grass wet with rain, and a flat bench on the mountainside seen through a gray veil of a light shower falling. There was that bench, with the white trunks of aspen on the mountainside beyond it looking like ranks of slim soldiers guarding the bench against the storms.

"Ma," I said.

"All right, Bud," she said quietly, "we've come home."

And I started up the oxen and drove down into the valley where I was to become a man.

WILL HENRY

HENRY WILSON ALLEN (1912–1991) was born in Kansas City, Missouri. After attending Kansas City Junior College for two years, he drifted west, working at odd jobs until he ended up in Los Angeles. He worked for a newspaper for a time and then found employment in 1935 with a company manufacturing animated films. Two years later Allen was hired by M-G-M as a junior writer in their short subjects department. It was first in midlife that Allen decided to try his hand at the Western story. NO SURVIVORS (Random House, 1950) was his first Western novel. It was published under the byline Will Henry because Allen did not want anyone in the film industry to know he was writing novels (something he later dismissed as a wrong-headed notion). While numerous authors of Western fiction before Allen had provided sympathetic and intelligent portrayals of Indian characters, Allen from the start set out to characterize Indians in such as way as to make their viewpoints and perspectives an integral part of the story he had to tell.

Allen's second novel was RED BLIZZARD (Simon and Schuster, 1951). Harry E. Maule, who had become Western fiction editor at Random House in 1940, rejected it. When another publisher accepted it, Allen's agent, August Lenniger, had Allen adopt a different pseudonym, reserving Will Henry for novels published by Random House. The second byline was Clay Fisher. It is probable that what Maule detected in RED BLIZZARD was Allen's tendency to impose an often superfluous historical framework upon what remained in essence a traditional Western plot. However, in view of Maule's rejection of this second novel, Allen's reaction — only natural under the circumstances — was to believe that he was able to write two totally different kinds of Western stories without himself being certain as to just how and why one was distinct from the other. Every time Maule rejected a novel, it became a Clay Fisher. In the event, there is really no difference between a Will Henry and a Clay Fisher novel except as an indication of the whimsies of Harry E. Maule's personal taste. Allen's next Will Henry novel was TO FOLLOW A FLAG (Random House, 1953) and this story is as much a straight action narrative as the next Clay Fisher title, SANTA FE PASSAGE (Houghton Mifflin, 1952).

Frequently, Allen could be intimidated by historical sources. He might add merely a dramatized floss to an historical account, such as his reworking of

James D. Horan's version of Jesse James in DESPERATE MEN (Bonanza Books, 1949) in the Will Henry novel, DEATH OF A LEGEND (Random House, 1954). In RECKONING AT YANKEE FLAT (Random House, 1958) by Will Henry, Allen provided a fictional account of the Henry Plummer gang. Since Professor Thomas J. Dimsdale wrote THE VIGILANTES OF MONTANA (1866), this story has intrigued novelists. Allen may have been more meticulous than many of his precursors in depicting the actual historical events, but he could not succeed in bringing Plummer himself to life, relying instead on quotations from people who had known or seen the man. Yet, curiously, in the much later SUMMER OF THE GUN (Lippincott, 1978), with no historical context to intimidate him, Allen was able to create a truly vivid character in the gang leader, Fragg, whose fictional personality is much closer to that of the historical Henry Plummer than the ambiguous shadow in RECKONING AT YANKEE FLAT. Of all his attempts at straight fictional biography, perhaps only I, TOM HORN (Lippincott, 1975) can be judged a complete success. Indeed, it is more than that. It is a masterpiece, perhaps most fully realized not in the motion picture based upon it with Steve McQueen in the title role but in the full-length audio version from Recorded Books, Inc., as read by Frank Muller.

In general many of Allen's best novels deal with the failure of the frontier experience, the greed, the rape of the land, the apparent genocide, novels which end tragically because, in the history of the American West and given the premises built into these plots, such an outcome is inevitable. In this group belong two of the novels for which Allen won Golden Spur Awards: FROM WHERE THE SUN NOW STANDS (Random House, 1960) and CHIRICAHUA (Lippincott, 1972). Also worthy of inclusion are THE LAST WARPATH (Random House, 1966), an inter-connected series of tales about the Cheyenne Indians (illustrating how Allen was basically a short story writer whose novels are often a patch-work of novelette-length sequences fused together but able easily to stand alone), and MAHEO'S CHILDREN (Chilton, 1968), a story of Preacher Nehemiah Bleek and his Indian orphans set against the background of the Sand Creek massacre. THE GATES OF THE MOUNTAINS (Random House, 1963) is a highly romantic retelling of the Lewis and Clark expedition and is clearly not in quite the same class as these others, despite its having also won a Spur. The shortcomings in this last title, however, apply to an extent even to Allen's best novels where the use of historical sources tends usually to be somewhat improvisational. MAHEO'S CHILDREN, in fact, was first intended as a straight historical narrative to be published under the byline Henry W. Allen and Allen submitted it to Don Ward, at the time an editor at Hastings House, a publisher of Western history books. Ward sent a section of the manuscript to Mari Sandoz (who herself published several not altogether reliable historical accounts with this same publisher) and her reactions were contained in a letter dated July 26, 1964 to Don Ward, reprinted in LETTERS OF MARI SANDOZ (University of

Nebraska Press, 1992) edited by Helen Winter Stauffer. "The foreword or introductory bit tells one right off that the author knows nothing of the Cheyenne religion," Sandoz commented. "...All Allen offers here is the usual uninformed white man idea of sun, rain, and earth gods. Living up on the Tongue [River] even a few days should have taught him better about the Cheyennes. If not, Allen can read, can't he?" The books Sandoz cited, however, are by George Bird Grinnell with their openly favorable view of the Cheyennes and biased portrait of the Pawnees. Obviously, Allen once more felt intimidated by historical sources and, therefore, turned this attempt at straight history into a fictional account intended now for a young adult audience. But he did get two books out of it, MAHEO'S CHILDREN and THE DAY FORT LARKING FELL (Chilton, 1968).

The appeal of Allen's historical Western fiction to some critics has been his political and social perspectives. Betty Rosenberg in her Introduction to the Gregg Press' library reprint edition of FROM WHERE THE SUN NOW STANDS in 1978 wrote: "The information...for realistic and honest novelization of the Indian wars was available. Lacking was a novel-reading audience willing to accept tragedy in place of romance. Such an acceptance would force the reader to recognize that Indian cultures and ways of life are sophisticated realities and their destruction wanton evil; that the invaders' Manifest Destiny was a blatant hypocrisy, an excuse to cover the theft of land and commercial exploitation; that missionary activities were a tool of subjugation; that the imposition of an Anglo culture upon the Indians was an unwelcome curse." The subject of this novel is the war against the Nez Perce Indians in 1877 and their subsequent defeat. These Indians did have a long tradition of peace and friendliness with the whites and in their terrible passage from Idaho through Montana to reach Canada, in which attempt they failed, they did not harm a single white woman or child because, in the words of the Nez Perce first-person narrator of the novel, "we had lived too long as brothers of the white man. Even in our last hours, we could not kill and mutilate his loved ones." As the 1960s progressed, such a sympathetic posture would become politically correct in viewing *all* of the Indian nations and tribes which, in its way, overlooked what made the Nez Perce stand out as victims and made this episode in their relations with Anglo-American culture such a poignant tragedy. For all of that, in Will Henry's MacKENNA'S GOLD (Random House, 1963), Allen characterized the frontier buffalo soldiers as having "the hot blood of their savage African ancestors running wild in them" — an image right out of James Warner Bellah's SERGEANT RUTLEDGE (Bantam, 1960).

Possibly David Remley in his essay, "Sacajawea of Myth and History" in WOMEN AND WESTERN AMERICAN LITERATURE (Whitson Publishing, 1982) edited by Helen Winter Stauffer and Susan J. Rosowski, in his critique of THE GATES OF THE MOUNTAINS came closest to a balanced view of Allen's historical fiction. He found this book "full of the opposites of moral vision built into the Judeo-Christian heritage — the beautiful, the ugly, the saved, the damned; the free, the slave, the good, the bad. Will Henry's is a split vision which tells us much about ourselves but probably has little, if anything, to do with who the American Indian — and Sacajawea — really is, or was. Probably too the love La Charrette thinks Sacajawea feels for him and Clark 'or any white man' — not passion for one but brotherly love for all — is, in part, Will Henry's own need for reconciliation projected upon her. It is a need for forgiveness — for release from old guilt — sensitive whites seem driven to ask of the American Indian and of the whole vast brooding continent itself." Doubtless, such a critique can be seen to apply no less to subsequent, and even more neurotic and subjectively agogic, attempts at dealing with the American Indian by writers in the post-Will Henry tradition such as Richard S. Wheeler and Win Blevins.

After SUMMER OF THE GUN, Allen found it impossible to write another novel, although he was urged to do so by editors. After 1980 his memory began increasingly to fail so that by 1990 he would confess that he could no longer keep together the threads of any story. He stopped typing and his last letters were hand-written. In the years of our friendship, we must have exchanged 200,000 words with each other. I shall always miss his spiritual companionship. He was a good friend.

"I am but a solitary horseman of the plains, born a century too late and far away," Allen once wrote about himself. He felt out of joint with his time and what alone may ultimately unify his work is the vividness of his imagination, the tremendous emotion with which he invested his characters and fashioned his Western stories. At his best, he could weave an almost incomparable spell that can involve a reader deeply in his narratives, informed always by his profound empathy with so many of the casualties of the historical process. The story which follows first appeared in the Will Henry collection, SONS OF THE WESTERN FRONTIER (Chilton, 1966).

THE TALLEST INDIAN IN TOLTEPEC
1966

Where the wagon road from the small town of Toltepec, in the state of Chihuahua, came up to the Rio Grande, the fording place was known as the old Apache Crossing. This was because the Indians used it in their shadowy traffic in and out of Texas from Old Mexico. It was not a place of good name, and only those traveled it who, for reasons of their own, did not care to go over the river at the new Upper Crossing.

This fact of border life was well understood by Colonel Fulgencio Ortega. He had not forgotten the Indian back door to El Paso on the American side. That is why he had taken personal charge of the guard post of his troops at this point.

A very crafty man, Colonel Ortega.

And efficient.

It was not for nothing that the *descamisados,* the starving shirtless poor, called him the Executioner of Camargo. Chihuahua had no more distinguished son, nor another son half so well known in the ranks of the irregular *rurales,* which was to say the stinking buzzards of the border.

Now, with his men, a score of brutes so removed from decency and discipline that only their upright postures stamped them as human beings, he lounged about the ashes of the supper fire. Some of the bestial soldiers bickered over the cleaning of the mess kits. Others sat hunched about a serape spread on the ground, belching and complaining of the foulness of their luck with the cards and with the kernels of shelled corn which passed for money among them. The heat of the evening was stifling. Even with the sun now down at last beyond the Rio, it was still difficult to breathe with comfort. The horseflies from the nearby picket line still buzzed and bit like rabid foxes. It was a most unpromising situation. In all of the long daylight they had wasted at the ford, no fish had come to their net, no traveler from Toltepec had sought to pass the crude barricade flung across the wagon road.

"*¡Válgame!*" announced Ortega. "God's name, but this is slow work, eh, Chivo?"

The name meant "goat" in Spanish, and the bearded lieutenant who responded to it seemed well described.

"True, *jefe.*" He nodded. "But one learns patience in your service. Also hunger. Hiding. Sand fleas. Body lice. How to use corn for money. How to live on water with no tequila in it. Many things, Excellence."

Ortega smiled and struck him across the face with the butt of his riding quirt. The blow opened the man's face and brought the bright blood spurting.

"Also manners," said the Colonel quietly.

Chivo spat into the dirt. "*Sí,*" he said, "also manners."

Presently, the man on duty at the barricade called to his leader that someone was coming on the road.

"By what manner?" asked Ortega, not moving to rise.

"A burro cart."

"How many do you see?"

"Two. A man and a boy. Hauling firewood, I think."

"*¡Pah!* Let them go by."

"We do not search the cart, *jefe?*"

"For what? Firewood?"

"No, *jefe,* for *him;* these are Indians who come."

Instantly, Ortega was on his feet. He was at the barricade the next moment, Chivo and the others crowding behind. All watched in silence the approach of the small burro cart. Had they begun to pant or growl it would have seemed natural, so like a half circle of wolves they appeared.

On the driver's seat of the cart, Díaz grew pale and spoke guardedly to his small son.

"Chamaco," he said, "these are evil men who await us. Something bad may happen. Slip away in the brush if there is any opportunity. These are the enemies of our leader."

"You know them, Papa, these enemies of our *Presidente?*"

"I know the one with the whip. It is Ortega."

"The Executioner?" The boy whispered the dread name, and Juliano Díaz, slowing the plodding team of burros, answered without moving his head or taking his eyes from the soldiers at the barricade.

"Yes, my son. It is him, the Killer of Camargo. As you value your life, do not speak the name of *El Indio* except to curse it. These men seek his life."

El Indio was the name of love which the shirtless ones had given the revolutionary President whom they had brought to power with their blood, but who now fought desperately for the life of his new government and for the freedoms which he sought to bring to the *descamisados* of all Mexico, be they Indians, such as himself and Juliano and Chamaco Díaz, or of the Spanish blood, or of any blood whatever. To the small boy, Chamaco, *El Indio* was like Christ, only more real. He had never seen either one, but he knew he would die for his *Presidente* and was not so sure about the Savior.

He nodded, now, in response to his father's warning, brave as any ten-year-old boy might be in facing the Executioner of Camargo.

As for Ortega, perhaps the sinister appellation was only a product of ignorance and rebelliousness on the parts of the incredibly poor Indians of the Motherland. He understood this for himself, it was certain. But being a soldier was hard work, and the people never comprehended the necessity for the precautions of military control. This did not mean that one of the Spanish blood could not be gracious and kind within the limitations of his stern duty. The Colonel waved his whip pleasantly enough toward the burro cart.

"Good evening, citizen," he greeted Díaz. "You are surprised to see us here, no doubt. But the delay will be slight. Please to get down from the cart."

"*¿Qué pasa,* Excellence? What is the matter?" In his fear, Díaz did not obey the request to step down but sat numbly on the seat.

"Ah, you know me!" Ortega was pleased. "Well, it has been my work to get acquainted among the people of *El Indio.* Did you hear my order?"

"What?" said Díaz. "I forget. What did you say, Colonel?"

Ortega moved as a coiled snake might move. He struck out with his whip, its thong wrapping the thin neck of Juliano Díaz. With a violent heave, the guerrilla leader threw the small man from the cart onto the ground, the noose of the whip nearly cracking his vertebrae.

"I said to get down, *Indio,*" he smiled. "You do not listen too well. What is the matter? Do you not trust your Mexican brothers?"

Díaz was small in body only. In heart he was a mountain.

"You are no brothers of mine!" he cried. "I am an Indian!"

"Precisely," answered Ortega, helping him up from the dirt of the roadway. "And so is he whom we seek."

Díaz stood proudly, stepping back and away from the kind hands of Colonel Fulgencio Ortega. He made no reply, now, but the boy on the seat of the burro cart leaped down and answered for him.

"What!" he exclaimed, unable to accept the fact anyone would truly seek to do ill to the beloved *Presidente.* "Is it true then that you would harm our dear...?" Too late, he remembered his father's warning and cut off his words. Ortega liked boys, however, and made allowances for their innocence.

"Calm yourself, little rooster," he said kindly. "I said nothing of harming *El Indio.* Indeed, I said nothing of your great *Presidente* in any way. Now how is it you would have the idea that it is him we look for, eh?"

All of Mexico knew the answer to the question. For weeks the outlands had thrilled to the whisper that *El Indio* would make a journey to the United States to find gold and the hand of friendship from the other great *Presidente,* Abraham Lincoln. It was understood such a journey would be in secret to avoid the forces of the enemy en route. But from Oaxaca to the Texas border the *descamisados* were alerted to be on the watch for "the Little Indian" and to stand at all times ready to help forward the fortunes of his journey.

Chamaco Díaz hesitated, not knowing what to say.

His father, brave Juliano, broke into the growing stillness to advise him in this direction.

"Say nothing, my son," he said quietly, and stood a little taller as he said it. Chamaco nodded. He, too, straightened and stood tall beside his father.

They would talk no more, and Ortega understood this.

"My children," he said, "you have failed to comprehend. We do not seek to harm the *Presidente,* only to detain him."

If standing tall, Chamaco was still but a small boy. He had not learned the art of dishonesty.

"Why do you stop us, then, Colonel?" he demanded. "We are only poor wood gatherers from Toltepec, going to El Paso."

"Just exactly my problem," explained Ortega, with a flourish of the whip. "You see, *pobrecito,* it is my order that every Indian going across the border must be measured against that line which you will see drawn on the dead oak tree." He pointed to the sunblasted spar with the whip. "Do you see the line on the tree?"

"Yes, Colonel."

"Well, it is drawn five feet from the ground, *chico.* That is just about the tallness of your great *Presidente,* not being too precise. Now the problem is that I, myself, am not familiar with this great man. I would not know him if I saw him. But we have his height reported to us, and I have devised this method of...shall we say?...ruling out the chance that *El Indio* shall get over the river into the United States and complete his journey."

"Colonel," broke in Juliano Díaz, going pale despite his great courage, "what is it you are saying?"

Ortega shrugged good-naturedly.

"Only that if you are an Indian not known to me, or to my men, and if your height is the same as that of *El Indio,* and if I detain you, then I have prevented a possible escape of your great *Presidente,* eh?"

"You mean that you think I, Juliano Díaz of Toltepec, am...?" He could not finish the thought, so absurd was it to his simple mind. Could this rebel colonel truly believe such a thing? That he, Díaz, was the leader, the great *El Indio?* Díaz gave his first hint of a relieved look. It may even have been the trace of a smile. There was, after all, and even with the sore neck from the whip, something ironic about the idea. "Please, Excellence," Díaz concluded, forcing the small smile to widen for the sake of Chamaco's courage, "take me to the tree and put me against the mark, that my son and I may go on to El Paso. I have not been well, and we need the *pesos* from this wood to buy medicine in Texas."

"Chivo," snapped Ortega, no longer smiling, "measure this Indian!"

Chivo seized Díaz and dragged him to the tree. Pushing him against its scarred trunk, he peered at the line.

"He comes exactly to it, *jefe.* Just the right size."

"Very well. Detain him."

The matter was finished for Colonel Ortega. He turned back to the fire. He did not look around at the pistol shot which blew out the brains of Juliano Díaz. To a scrofulous sergeant, even with the startled, sobbing cry of Chamaco Díaz rising behind him, he merely nodded irritably. "Coffee, Portales. Santa Maria, but it is hot! Curse this river country."

What would have been the fate of Chamaco, the son, no man may say. Chivo was hauling him to the fire by the nape of his neck, pistol poised to finish him as well, with the Colonel's permission. Also, no man may say if Ortega would have granted the favor. For in the instant of death's hovering, a thunder of hoofs arose on the American side of the river and a rider, tall sombrero proclaiming his Mexican identity, dashed his lathered mount across the ford and to a sliding stop by the fire of the Executioner of Camargo.

"Colonel!" he cried. "I come from El Paso! Great news is there. *El Indio* is in the town. He has already been to see the American *Presidente* and is on his way back to Mexico!"

Ortega stepped back as though cut in the face with his own whip. The wolf pack of his men drew in upon him. Chivo, in his astonishment that *El Indio* had gotten out of Mexico and was ready to come back into it, dropped his rough hands from Chamaco Díaz. It was all the signal from above that the quick-witted Indian youth needed. In one scuttling dive he had reached the crowding growth of river brush and disappeared, faithful, belatedly, to his dead father's instruction.

Chivo, pistol still smoking, led the yelping rush of the guerrilla band after the boy. Ortega cursed on his men, raging about himself with the lashing whip.

"Kill him, you fools!" he screamed. "He must not get over the river. Shoot! Shoot! Stomp him out and shoot him. He must not warn the Americans that we know they have *El Indio!* After him, after him, you idiots!"

Deep in the brush, Chamaco wriggled and squirmed and raced for his life. The rifle bullets of the renegades cut the limbs about him. The cruel thorns of the mesquite and catclaw and black chaparral ripped his flesh. He could hear the soldiers panting and cursing within a stone's toss of his heels. He cried for his dead father as he ran, but he ran! If God would help him, he would reach the other side of the river and *El Indio*.

As the desperate vow formed in his mind, he saw ahead a clearing in the tangled growth. Beyond it, the waters of the Rio Grande flowed silver-red in the sunset dusk.

Riding through the twilight toward El Paso, the thoughts of Charlie Shonto were scarcely designed to change the sunburned leather mold of his features — not, at least, for the happier.

A job was a job, he supposed, but it seemed to him that all the while the work got harder and the pay less.

Who the hell was he, Charlie Shonto? And what the devil was the Texas Express Company? And why should the two names cause him pain, now, as he clucked to his weary buckskin and said softly, aloud, "Slope along, little horse, there's good grass and water awaiting."

Well, there was an affinity betwixt the likes of Charlie Shonto and the Texas Express Company, even if it hurt. The latter outfit was a jerkwater stage line that had gotten itself about as rump-sprung as a general freight and passenger operation might manage to do and still harness four sound horses, and Shonto was a "special agent" for the stage company. But Charlie Shonto did not let the fancy title fool him. There was a shorter term, and a deal more accurate, for the kind of work he did for Texas Express. If a man said it with the proper curl of lip, it came out something awfully close to "hired gun."

Shonto didn't care for the label. He didn't especially relish, either, the risks involved in wearing it. But a "riding gun," be he on the driver's box with an L.C. Smith or Parker on his lap, or in the saddle with a Winchester booted under his knee, made good money for the better jobs. The better jobs, of course, were those in which the survival odds were backed down to something like, or less than, even money. So it was no surprise to Shonto to be sent for by Texas Express for a "special assignment." The surprise might lie in the assignment, itself, but the sun-tanned rider doubted it. It could be assumed that when Texas Express sent for Charlie Shonto, the "opportunity for advancement" was one already turned down by the Rangers and the U.S. Army, not to mention Wells Fargo, Overland Mail, or any of the big staging outfits.

Shonto clucked again to the *bayo coyote,* the line-backed buckskin dun, that he rode.

"Just around the bend, Butterball." He grinned dustily. "Billets for you and bullets for me."

Butterball, a gaunt panther of a horse which appeared wicked and rank enough to eat rocks without spitting out the seeds, rolled an evil eye back at his master and flagged the ragged pennant of his left ear. If he had intended further comment than this one look of tough disgust, the urge was short-circuited.

Scarcely had the comment about "bullets" left Shonto's lips than a respectable, if well-spent, hail of them began to fall around him in the thicket. Next instant, the sounds of the rifle shots were following the leaden advance guard in scattered volleys.

Instinctively, he ticked Butterball with the spurs, and the bony gelding sprinted like a quarter-mile racer for the near bend ahead. When he brought Shonto around that bend, the latter hauled him up sharply. Across the Rio Grande a tattered company of Mexican irregulars were target-practicing at a dark, bobbing object in midstream. Shonto's immediate reaction was one of relief that the riflemen had not been firing at him. The next thought was a natural curiosity as to what they had been firing at. It was then the third message reached his tired mind, and his mouth went hard. That was a little kid swimming for the American side out there.

The night was well down. In the Texas Express office in El Paso, three men waited. The drawn shade, trimmed lamp, the tense glances at the wall clock ticking beyond the way-bill desk, all spoke louder than the silence.

"I wish Shonto would get here," complained the express agent, Deems. "It ain't like him to be late. Maybe Ortega crossed over the river under dark and blind-sided him."

The second man, heavy-set, dressed in eastern clothing, calm and a little cold, shook his head.

"Shonto isn't the type to be blind-sided, Deems. You forget he's worked for me before. I didn't exactly pull his name out of a hat."

Deems stiffened. "That don't mean Ortega didn't pull it out of a sombrero!"

Sheriff Nocero Casey, last of the trio, nodded.

"Deems is right, Mr. Halloran. I don't care for Charlie being late either. It ain't like him. If Ortega did hear we had sent for Charlie Shonto...." He broke off, scowling.

Halloran took him up quickly. "It's not Shonto being late that is really bothering you, is it? I counted on you, Sheriff. I didn't dare import a bunch of U.S. marshals. I hope you're not getting cold feet."

"No, sir. It's common sense I'm suffering from. This job is way out of my bailiwick. The government ought to send troops or something to see it through. It's too big."

Again Halloran shook his head. "The U.S. government can't set one toe across that river, Sheriff. You know that. It's the law. That's why we've brought in your 'special agent.' Mr. Shonto is a man who understands the law. He appreciates its niceties, its challenges."

"Yeah, I've often wondered about that," said the sheriff. "But I won't argue it."

"Ah, good. You see, there is no law which says Texas Express cannot ship a consignment such as our invaluable Item Thirteen into Toltepec. It will be done every day now that the new Mexican Central line has reached that city."

Agent Deems interrupted this optimism with a groan.

"Good Lord, Mr. Halloran, what's the use of talking about what we can ship when that cussed Mexican Central Railroad starts running regular between Toltepec and Mexico City? They ain't even run one work engine over that new line that I know of. Them blamed ties that are laid into Toltepec are still oozing greenwood sap!"

Halloran's heavy jaw took a defiant set.

"Are your feet feeling the chill, also, Deems? I thought we had the plan agreed to. Where's the hitch?"

Agent Deems stared at his questioner as if the latter had taken leave of whatever few senses government secret service operatives were granted in the beginning.

"Where's the hitch, you say? Oh, hardly anywhere at all, Mr. Halloran. You're only asking us to deliver this precious Item Thirteen of yours to railhead in Toltepec, Mexico, fifty miles across the river, tonight, with no one wise, whatever, right square through Colonel Fulgencio Ortega's northern half of the loyalist guerrilla army, guaranteeing to get our 'shipment' on the train at Toltepec safe and sound in wind and limb and then to come back a-grinning and a-shrugging and a-saying, 'Why, shucks, it wasn't nothing. It's done every day.' Mister, you ain't just plain crazy, you're extra fancy nuts."

"As bad as all that, eh?"

"Fair near," put in Sheriff Casey. "We don't know if that Mexican train will be in Toltepec. We don't even know if those wild-eyed coffee beans even got a train. All we know is that you government men tell us they got the train, and that it'll be in Toltepec if we get this Item Thirteen there. Now that's a heck of an 'if.' "

Halloran was careful. He knew that only these local people — Texans familiar with every coyote track and kit-fox trail leading into Chihuahua — could bring off the delivery of Item Thirteen. Nothing must go wrong now.

"If we took Item Thirteen five thousand miles, Sheriff, surely Texas Express ought to be able to forward shipment the remaining fifty miles to Toltepec."

"Huh!" said Deems Harter. "You got one whack of a lot more faith in Texas Express than we have. In fact, about forty-nine miles more. As agent, I'll guarantee to get your precious shipment exactly one mile. That's from here to the Rio Grande. Past that, I wouldn't give you a nickel for your chances of making that train in Toltepec. *If* there's a train in Toltepec."

Halloran shook his head, unmoved.

"I'm not exactly thinking of my faith in terms of Texas Express, Harter. It's Charlie Shonto we're all gambling on."

"Yeah," said Harter acridly. "And right now Charlie Shonto looks like a mighty poor gamble."

"Well, anyways," broke in Sheriff Nocero Casey, who had drifted to the front window for another look up the street, "a mighty wet one. Yonder comes our special delivery man, and it looks to me as though he's already been across the river. He's still dripping."

Halloran and Harter joined him in peering from behind the drawn shade. It was the express agent who recovered first.

"Good Lord!" he gasped. "What's that he's toting behind him?"

Sheriff Nocero Casey squinted carefully.

"Well," he said, "the bright lights of El Paso ain't precisely the best to make bets by, but if I had to take a scattergun guess at this distance and in the dark, I'd say it was a sopping-wet and some-undersized Chihuahua Indian boy."

In the shaded office of the Texas Express Company, the silence had returned again. First greetings were over. Shonto and Halloran had briefly touched upon their past experiences during the war between the States, and the time had very quickly run down to that place where everyone pauses, knowing that the next words are the ones that the money is being paid for. Sheriff Casey, Agent Harter, Shonto, even little Chamaco Díaz, all were watching P. J. Halloran.

"Now, Charlie," said the latter, at last, "we haven't sent for you to review the squeaks you've been in before." He let the small grimace which may or may not have been a smile pass over his rough features. "But I did feel that some slight mention of our past associations might prepare you for the present proposal."

"What you're saying, Mr. Halloran, is that you figure your Irish blarney is going to soften up my good sense." Shonto's own grin was a bit difficult to classify. It was hard as flint and yet warmed too, somehow, by a good nature or at least a wry appreciation of life as it actually worked out in the living. "But you're wasting your talents," he concluded. "I've had a couple of birthdays since I was crossing the Confederate lines for you, and now I don't sign up just for a pat on the back from my fellow countrymen. I've learned since the war that a man can't buy a bag of Bull Durham with a government citation. Not that I regret my time in the 'silent service,' mind you. But a fellow just doesn't like to be a hog about the hero business. Especially when he did his great deeds for the North, then went back to earning his keep in the South. If you spend your time in Texas, Mr. Halloran, you don't strain yourself reminding the local folks that you took your war pay in Union greenbacks."

Halloran nodded quickly.

"Don't be a fool, Charlie," he said. "Harter, here, and Sheriff Casey were carefully sounded out before we ever mentioned your name. They are not still afire with the Lost Cause. We can forget your war work."

"I'm glad you told me, Mr. Halloran. Somehow, I still remember it every so often. Matter of fact, I still occasionally wake up in a cold sweat. Now I can put all that behind me. Isn't it wonderful?"

"Shonto" — Halloran's hard face had turned cold again — "come over here to the window. I want to show you something." He took a pair of binoculars from Harter's desk, and Shonto followed him to the drawn shade. There, Halloran gave the glasses to him and said quietly, "Look yonder on the balcony of the Franklin House. Tell me what you see. Describe it exactly."

From the other's tone, Shonto knew the talk had gotten to the money point. He took the glasses and focused them on the hotel's second-story *galería,* the railed porch so common to the southwestern architecture of the times. As the view came into sharp detail, he frowned uneasily.

"All right," he began, low voiced. "I see a man. He's short, maybe not much over five feet. He stands straight as a yardstick. Stocky build. Big in the chest. Dark as hell in the skin, near as I can say in the lamplight from the room windows behind him. He's dressed in a black Eastern suit that don't fit him, and same goes for a white iron collar and necktie. Black hat, no creases, wore square like a sombrero. Long black hair, bobbed off like it was done with horse shears." He paused, squinting more narrowly through the binoculars. "Why," he added softly, "that's a blasted Indian dressed up in white man's clothes!"

"That," said P. J. Halloran, just as softly, "is exactly what it is." They turned from the window. "Up there on that balcony," Halloran continued, "is the most important man, next to Lincoln, in North America. I can't reveal his identity, and you will have to know him as Item Thirteen, until you have him safely on that waiting train at Toltepec."

"What train at Toltepec?" Shonto frowned. "Since when have they built the Mexican Central· on into that two-burro burg?"

"Since today, we hope," said Halloran. "The idea was that, precisely as you, no one knew the railroad had been laid on into Toltepec. Those last few thousand yards of track were to be spiked down today. The gamble is that not even Ortega and the *rurales* would hear about it in time. Or, hearing of it, not realize a train was waiting to be run over it."

"That's what I'd call house odds, Mr. Halloran. This Item Thirteen must be one heck of a table-stakes man."

"He's one heck of a man," answered the government operative. "Anyway, Charlie, the train is supposed to be waiting at midnight in Toltepec. If we can get Item Thirteen there, the train can get on down past Camargo by daybreak and out of Ortega's reach...if the train's waiting in Toltepec."

"Longest two-letter word in the world," said Shonto. "Go ahead, drop the other boot."

"Well, we know that powerful enemies lie between El Paso and Toltepec. There's no point explaining to you the type of enemy I mean. I believe you're familiar enough with Colonel Ortega and his loyal militia."

"Yes, just about familiar enough. In case you're still wondering how Chamaco and I got ourselves doused in the Rio, it was meeting Ortega's loyal army, or as big a part of it as I came prepared to handle. I'd say there was twenty of them. They were pot-shooting at the kid swimming the river. He got away from them while they were murdering his father. Butterball got excited at the rifle fire and ran away with me: bolted right into the river. Next thing I knew, I was in as bad shape as the kid and, long as I figured two could ride as cheap as one, I scooped him up and we made it back to the American side by way of hanging onto Butterball's tail and holding long breaths under water on the way. I have got to get me another horse. In my business, you can't be fooling around with jumpy crowbaits like that."

"When you decide what you want for Butterball," put in Sheriff Nocero Casey, "let me know. I've been looking for just such a *loco* horse."

"Charlie," broke in Halloran, "are you interested or not? We've got to move soon."

Shonto nodded speculatively, a man not to be rushed.

"Depends. You haven't dropped that other boot yet."

"All right." Halloran spoke quickly now. "The small man in the black suit carries a letter of credit...a U.S. letter of credit...for an enormous amount of money. Some say as high as fifty million dollars. That's fifty million U.S., not Mexican. It's to bail out his revolution down there." Halloran gestured toward the Rio Grande and Mexico. "I don't need to tell you, Charlie, what men like Ortega will do to prevent that letter from getting to Mexico City. The money means the rebels are through...loyalists, they call themselves...and that the revolution will succeed and will stay in power. As you have already learned when your horse ran away with you, Colonel Ortega has been assigned the job of sealing off the border in Chihuahua State. Now, it becomes your job to unseal that border."

Charlie Shonto's grin was dry as dust.

"Shucks, nothing to that...nothing that I couldn't do with ten or twelve companies of Rangers and a regiment of regular cavalry."

"Don't joke, Charlie." Halloran pulled out an official document and handed it to Shonto. "Here are my orders. You don't need to read them. But check that final postscript at the bottom of the page against the signature beneath the Great Seal of this country you and I fought for, when he asked us to."

Shonto glanced down the page, reading aloud slowly. "'Any man who may aid the bearer of these orders in the business to hand will know that the gratitude of his government and my own personal indebtedness shall be his and shall not be forgotten. [Signed] A. Lincoln.' Well now," he said, handing back the document as gingerly as though it were the original of the Declaration of Independence. "Why didn't you say so, Mr. Halloran?"

"Like you" — Halloran smiled, and this time there was no doubt it was a smile — "I always save my best shot for the last target. What do you say, Charlie?"

"I say, let's go. For *him* I'd wrestle a bear, blindfolded. Who all's in it?"

"Just you, Charlie. I've brought our man this far. Sheriff Casey and Agent Harter have handled him here in town. But from here to Toltepec, he's your cargo...*if* you'll accept him."

Shonto winced perceptibly.

"There's that word again. You got anything extra to go with it this time?"

Halloran picked up a rolled map from Harter's desk.

"Only this chart of the area between here and Toltepec supplied by the Mexican Government. You know this ground as well as any man on this side of the Rio Grande. Take a look at this layout of it and tell us if you spot any way at all of getting past Ortega's patrols, into Toltepec."

He spread the map on the desk. Harter turned up the wick, and the four men bent over the wrinkled parchment. Behind them, the little Indian, Chamaco Díaz, had been forgotten. He stood silently in the shadows, wondering at the talk of these Americans. Chamaco had been to school some small time in El Paso and knew enough English to follow the conversation in the rough. Lonely and sorrowful as he was, he knew who that other little Indian in the black suit was, and his heart swelled with love and pride for these American men, that they would talk of risking their lives that *El Indio* might live and might reach Mexico City with the United States money which would save the *Presidente*'s brave government of the *descamisados* and *pobrecitos* such as his father, Juliano Díaz, who had given their lives to establish it. Now, Chamaco watched the four big Americans bent over the map of Toltepec — his part of the beloved Motherland — and he waited with held breath what the verdict of the one tall man with the dried leather face would be.

For his part, the latter was having considerable last doubts. The map wasn't showing him anything he didn't already know. Presently, he glanced up at Halloran.

"There's no help here," he said. "I was hoping to see an old Apache route I've heard stories of. But this map shows nothing that wouldn't get me and the little man in the black suit stood up against the same tree that Chamaco's daddy was stood up against. Ortega knows all these trails."

"There's nothing, then? No way at all?"

"Yes, there's that Apache brush track. It was never found by the Rangers, but they know it exists. They've run the Chihuahua Apaches right to the river, time and again, then seen them vanish like smoke into midnight air. If we knew where that trail went over the Rio, we might have a coyote's chance of sneaking past Ortega's assassins." Shonto shook his head. "But there isn't a white man alive who knows that Apache track...."

His words trailed off helplessly, and the four men straightened with that weary stiffness which foretells defeat. But into their glum silence a small voice, and forgotten, penetrated thinly.

"*Señores,* I am not a white man."

Shonto and his companions wheeled about. Chamaco moved out of the shadows into the lamplight.

"I am an Indian," he said, "and I know where the old trail runs."

The four men exchanged startled looks and, in their momentary inability to speak, Chamaco thought that he detected reproof for his temerity in coming forward in the company of such powerful friends of Mexico. He bowed with apologetic humility and stepped back into the shadows.

"But of course," he said, small-voiced, "you would not trust to follow an Indian. Excuse me, *señores*."

Shonto moved to his side. He put his hand to the thin shoulder. Telling the boy to follow him, he led the way to the office window. He held back the drawn shade while Chamaco, obeying him, peered down the street at the Franklin House.

"Boy," he said, "do you know who that small man is standing up there on the hotel balcony?"

Chamaco's eyes glowed with the fire of his pride.

"Yes, *patrón!*" he cried excitedly. "It is *him!* Who else could stand and look so sad and grand across the river?"

Shonto nodded. "You think *he* would trust an Indian boy?"

Chamaco drew himself up to his full four feet and perhaps five inches. In his reply was all the dignity of the poor.

"*Patrón,*" he said, "he once *was* an Indian boy!"

Charlie Shonto nodded again. He tightened the arm about the boy's shoulders and turned to face the others.

"Don't know about you," he said to them, "but I've just hired me an Indian guide to Toltepec."

The men at the desk said nothing, and again Chamaco misinterpreted their hesitation.

"*Patrón,*" he said to Charlie Shonto, "do *you* know who it is up there standing on the *galería* looking so sad toward Mexico?"

"I could take an uneducated guess," answered Shonto, "but I won't. You see, Chamaco, I'm not supposed to know. He's just a job to me. It doesn't matter who he is."

The Indian boy was astounded. It passed his limited comprehensions.

"And you would risk your life for a stranger to you?" he asked, unbelievingly. "For an Indian in a rumpled white man's suit? A small funny-looking man with a foreign hat and long hair and a dark skin the same as mine? You would do this, *patrón,* and for nothing?"

Shonto grinned and patted him on the head.

"Well, hardly for nothing, boy."

"For what, then, *patrón?*"

"Money, boy. *Pesos. Muchos pesos.*"

"And only for that, *patrón?*"

At the persistence, Shonto's cynical grin faded. He made a small, deprecatory gesture. It was for Chamaco alone; he had forgotten the others.

"Let's just say that I was watching your face when you looked up at that hotel balcony a minute ago. All right, *amigo?*"

The dark eyes of Chamaco Díaz lit up like altar candles.

"*Patrón,*" he said, "you should have been an Indian; you have eyes in your heart!"

Shonto grinned ruefully. "Something tells me, boy, that before we get our cargo past Ortega tonight we'll be wishing I had those eyes in the back of my head."

Chamaco reached up and took the gunman's big hand. He patted it reassuringly. "*Patrón*" — he smiled back — "do not be afraid. If we die, we die in a good and just cause. We lose only our two small lives. Him, up there on the *galería,* he has in his hands the lives of all of the poor people of Mexico. Is that not a very fair exchange, our lives for all of those others, and for his?"

Shonto glanced at the other men. "Well, Chamaco," he said, "that's one way of looking at it. Excuse us, gentlemen; we've got a train to catch in Toltepec."

He took the boy's hand in his and they went out into the street. Halloran moved to follow them. At the door he halted a moment, shaking his head as he looked back at the express agent and the sheriff.

"Do you know what we've just done?" he said. "We've just bet fifty million dollars and the future of Mexico on a Chihuahua Indian kid not one of us ever laid eyes on prior to twenty minutes ago. I need a drink!"

The coach bounced and swayed through the night. Its side lamps, almost never lit, were now sputtering and smoking. They seemed to declare that this particular old Concord wanted to be certain her passage toward the lower ford would be noted from the far side — and followed.

The idea was valid.

The lower crossing, the old Apache route, was the way in which a mind of no great deception might seek to elude examination by the *rurales* at the upper, or main, crossing. The driver of the old Texas Express vehicle, a canvas-topped Celerity model made for desert speed, held the unalterable belief that the Mexican mind was so devious as to be very nearly simple. It twisted around so many times in its tracks, trying to be clever, that in the end it usually wound up coming right back where it started.

The driver was banking on this trait. He was depending on Colonel Fulgencio Ortega to think that, when the planted rumor from El Paso reached him by avenue of his kinsmen in that city, he would say, "Aha! This stupid *American* stage-line company thinks that if they announce they will try to cross with *El Indio* at the old lower ford, that I shall at once conclude they really mean to cross at the new upper ford, and that I shall then be waiting for them at the new upper ford and they can cross in safety at the lower place. What fools! I shall quite naturally watch both crossings, and this they realize full well. What they are trying to do is see that I, personally, am not at the lower ford. They think that if they can contest the crossing with my men...without me...it will be a far easier matter. Well, now! *¡Ai, Chihuahua!* Let them come. Let them find out who will be waiting for their disreputable stagecoach and its mysterious passenger at the old lower ford! Hah! Why will they attempt to match wits with the Executioner of Camargo?''

Of course, if Colonel Ortega did not reason thus, the driver of the coach would have made a grievous error, for the entire plan depended on meeting the Executioner.

The driver, a weather-beaten, leathery fellow, wrapped the lines of the four-horse hitch a bit tighter. He spoke to his leaders and his wheelers, tickling the ears of the former and the haunches of the latter with the tip of his fifteen-foot coaching whip.

"Coo-ee, boys!" he called to the horses. "Just so, just so." Leaning over the box, he spoke to the muffled, dark-faced passenger — the only passenger — in the rocking stage. "*Señor,* it is all well with you in there?" He used the Spanish tongue, but no reply came in kind from the interior. Indeed, no reply came in any tongue.

A very brave fellow, thought the driver. His kind were not many in the land below the Rio or any land.

"You are a very small boy," said the somber-looking little man. "How is it that you are so brave?"

"Please, *Presidente.* I beg of you not to say more, just now. We are very near to the place, and there is great danger." Chamaco spoke with awed diffidence.

"I am not afraid, boy." *El Indio* patted him on the shoulder. "Do I not have a good Indian guide?"

"*Presidente,* please, say no more. You don't know Colonel Ortega."

"I have dealt with his kind. I know him, all right. They are all alike. Cowards. Jackals. Don't be afraid, boy. What did you say your name was?"

Chamaco told him, and the small man nodded.

"A good Indian name. It means what it says. How much farther now, boy, before we cross the river?"

They were moving on foot through a tunneled avenue in the river's brushy scrub of willow and rushes. It was the sort of thoroughfare frequented by the creatures of the night. None but very small men — or boys — might have used it at all, and then only very small Indian men or boys. If the Rangers had wanted to know one reason, just one, why the Apaches raiding up from Chihuahua had been able to disappear before their eyes on the American side of the Rio, it would have been that they were seeking some "hole" in the brush which would accommodate an ordinary mortal, not a Chihuahua Indian. But Chamaco Díaz was not alone a small Indian boy; he was a patriot.

"*Presidente,*" he now pleaded, "will you not be quiet? *Por favor,* Excellence! We are coming to it this moment."

The small man in the black suit smiled.

"You dare to address me in this abrupt manner!" he said. "You, an Indian boy? A shirtless waif of the Border? A brush rat of the river bottom? *¡Ai!*"

"*Presidente,*" said the boy, "I will ask it one more time. I know that you do not fear the Executioner. I know that I am only a *pobrecito,* a *reducido,* a nothing. But in my heart you live with the Lord Jesus. I will die for you, *Presidente,* as I would for Him, even sooner. But I have sworn to guide you across the river and to the rendezvous. I have sworn to get you to Toltepec by midnight this night. Therefore, why should we die, when you must live for the people of our suffering land? I am taking you to Toltepec, *Presidente.* And if you continue to speak along the way, I will die for nothing and Mexico will never get the money you bear and she will not be saved. But mostly, *Presidente,* you will be dead. I cannot bear that. You are the life of all of us."

They had stopped moving. *El Indio,* in a streak of moonlight penetrating the arched limbs above them, could see the tears coursing down the dark cheeks of Chamaco Díaz. He reached quickly with his fingers and brushed away the tears.

"An Indian does not weep," he told the boy sternly. "Go ahead, now. I shall be still."

Chamaco swallowed hard. He dashed his own hand quickly at the offending eyes. His voice was vibrant with pride.

"It was the brush, *Presidente,* the small limbs snapping back and stinging me across the face. You know how it is."

El Indio nodded once more.

"Of course, boy. I have been in the brush many times. Go ahead, show the way. I have been an old woman, talking too much. We are both Indians, eh? Lead on."

Straight as a rifle barrel, Chamaco Díaz stood before him a moment. Then, ducking down again, he scuttled on ahead. *El Indio* watched him go. Just before he bent to follow, he glanced up at the patch of moonlight. The beams struck his own dark face. They glistened on something which seemed to be moist and moving upon his own coffee-colored features. But then of course in moonlight the illusions are many, and the lunar eye is not to be trusted. Had he not just said, himself, that Indians did not weep?

The coach of the Texas Express Company splashed over the old Apache Crossing and came to a halt before the flaring bonfire and wooden barricade across the Toltepec road. "*¿Que pasa?*" the tall driver called down to the leering brigand who commanded the guard. "What is the matter? Why do you stop me?"

"*De nada.* It is nothing." Lieutenant Chivo smiled. "A small matter which will take but a moment. I hope you have a moment. *Yes? Very well. Colonel,*" he called to the squat officer drinking coffee by the fireside, "the stage for Toltepec has arrived on time."

The Colonel put down his tin cup and picked up a long quirt Uncoiling the whip, he arose and came over to the barricade. He stood looking up at the coachman. After a moment, he nodded pleasantly enough and spoke in a friendly manner.

"Please to get down," he said.

"Sorry, I can't do it," replied the driver. "Company rules, Colonel. You understand."

"Of course," said the guerrilla chief easily. "Without rules nothing is accomplished. I'm a great believer in discipline. Did I introduce myself? Colonel Fulgencio Ortega, of Camargo. Now do you care to get down?"

"*The* Colonel Ortega?" said the American driver, impressed. "*Jefe,* this a great honor. And these are your famed *rurales?*" He pointed with unqualified admiration to the surly pack stalking up, now, to stand behind the colonel and his lieutenant. "My, but they are a fine-looking troop. Real fighters, one can see that. But then, why not? On the side of justice all men fight well, eh, Colonel?"

Ortega ignored the compliments.

"Did you hear what I said?" he asked. "I wish you to get down. I do not believe I have met your passenger, and I think you should introduce me to him. My men will hold your horses."

His men were already holding the horses, as the driver was keenly aware. Also, he did not miss the fact the soldiers were holding something else for him: their rifles — pointed squarely at him. But he was the steady sort, or perhaps merely stupid.

"Passenger?" he said. "I carry no passenger, Colonel. Just some freight for Toltepec."

Ortega stepped back. He looked again into the coach.

"Freight, eh?" he mused. "Strange wrappings you have put around your cargo, *cochero.* A black suit. Black hat with round Indian crown worn squarely on the head. And see how your freight sits on the seat of the coach, just as if it were alive and had two arms and two legs and might speak if spoken to. That is, if fear has not sealed its cowardly Indian tongue!" His voice was suddenly wicked with hatred, all the smile and the pretense of easiness gone out of it — and out of him. "Chivo!" he snapped. "Please to open the door of this coach and help *El Presidente* to dismount!"

The stage driver straightened on the box.

"*El Presidente?*" he said to Ortega. "Whatever in the world are you talking about, *jefe?*"

"We shall see in a moment." Ortega nodded, in control of himself once more. "Hurry, Chivo. This *cochero* does not understand the importance of his passenger. Nor is it apparent to him that jokes about 'freight' which walks and talks like an Indian are not laughed at in Chihuahua just now. *¡Adelante!* Get that coach door opened, you fool!"

Chivo, grinning as only a dog wolf about to soil the signpost of his rival may grin, threw open the door of the Concord and seized the lone passenger by the arm. With a foul-mouthed oath, he pulled the small figure from the coach and hurled it viciously to the ground.

His surprise was understandable.

It is not the usual thing for a victim's arm to come off at the shoulder and remain in the offending hand of its assaulter while the remainder of the torso goes flying off through the night. Neither was it the usual thing for the poor devil's head to snap off and go rolling away like a melon when the body thudded to earth.

"*¡Santisima!*" cried one of the brute soldiers of the guard. "You have ruined him, you dumb animal!"

But Lieutenant Chivo did not hear the remark, and Colonel Ortega, if he heard it, did not agree with the sentiment, except perhaps as to Chivo's intelligence. For what the guerrilla lieutenant had pulled from the Texas Express Company's Toltepec stage was quite clearly a dressmaker's dummy, clothed to resemble a very short and large-chested Mexican Indian man who always sat straight on his seat and wore his black hat squarely on his head.

Moreover, Colonel Fulgencio Ortega was given no real time in which to comment upon his soldier's awed remark or his lieutenant's amazed reaction to the arm in his hand and the head rolling free upon the firelit banks of the Rio Grande. For in the small moment of stricken dumbness which had invaded all of them when *El Presidente*'s body had come apart in mid-air, the American driver of the Toltepec stage had wrapped the lines of his four-horse hitch, stepped to the ground in one giant stride from the precarious box of the old Concord, and all in the same motion slid out a long-barreled Colt revolver and buried its iron snout in the belly of the Executioner of Camargo.

"*Jefe,*" he announced quietly. "if you make one false movement, your bowels will be blown out all over this river bank," and this statement Colonel Fulgencio Ortega had no difficulty whatever in comprehending.

"Chivo!" he cried out. "In the name of Maria, hold the men. Let no one touch trigger!"

"Yes, Chivo." The leather-faced American "*cochero*" nodded, spinning Ortega around so that the muzzle of the Colt was in his spine. "And so that you do not in greed seek to replace your beloved *jefe* in command of the *rurales* of Camargo…that is to say, that you do not in this moment of seeming opportunity make some move deliberately to get me to shoot him…permit me to introduce myself."

"Ah?" queried Chivo, who truly had not yet thought of this obvious course of treachery to his leader. "And to what point would this be, *cochero?* Do you think that I am in fear of stagecoach drivers?"

The tall driver shrugged.

"Well, I think you ought to have the same break I give any other man I'm paid to get past."

There was something in the way that he spoke the one word "paid" which penetrated Chivo's wily mind. He hesitated, but two of the soldiers did not. Thinking that they stood well enough behind their companions to be safe, they moved a little aside from the pack to get a line of fire at the big American. The instant they were clear of their friends, however, flame burst from behind the back of Colonel Ortega — one lancing flash, then another — and the two soldiers were down and dying in the same blending roar of pistol shots.

"Shonto," said the stage driver to Chivo, the smoking muzzle of the Colt again in Ortega's spine. "Over there across the river, they call me Shonto."

"*¡Madre Maria!*" breathed Chivo, dropping his rifle, unbidden, into the dirt of the wagon road. "Carlos Shonto? *Por Dios, pistolero,* why didn't you say so?"

"I just did." Charlie Shonto nodded. "Now you better say something. Quick."

Chivo shrugged in that all-meaning way of his kind.

"What remains to die for?" he inquired. "You do not have *El Indio* in the stage. You have fooled us with the dummy on the ground over there. Somewhere, *El Presidente* is no doubt riding through the night. But it is not upon the stage for Toltepec. Another of our guards will get him. For us, the work of the day is over. Command me."

Shonto then ordered all the soldiers to drop their rifles and cartridge bandoleers. All knives, pistols, axes went into the common pile. This arsenal was then loaded into the stage along with Colonel Fulgencio Ortega, bound hand and foot by his faithful followers. The work went forward under Chivo's expert direction, the spirit of the *rurales* now totally flagged. With their chances of snaring *El Indio* had gone their interest in being heroes. Like soldiers everywhere, they were of no great menace in themselves. Deprived of leadership, they were just so many surly dogs quarreling among themselves. Shonto had gambled on this, and gambled exceedingly well.

Yet, as in every risk, there lurks the element of the unknown, the thing that cannot be depended upon except in the name of "luck." Shonto's luck ran out with the command he now issued to the scarfaced Chivo.

"All right, Lieutenant," he said. "Up you go. You'll be the *cochero* now. I'll ride shotgun. You savvy '*la escopeta?*' " With the question, he reached for the double-barreled Parker laid across the driver's box, and Chivo nodded hastily. He "savvied" shotguns very well. One did not argue with them at close range, not ever. But Shonto had made his basic mistake some time ago, when he had put the thought of succeeding to Ortega's place of power in Camargo in the mind of the brutal lieutenant. Such towering aspirations had never flooded his dark brain. True, he would have seen Ortega killed in a moment, should that suit his purpose. This much was exactly what Shonto had guessed. What the wary gunman had not foreseen, however, was that, until he, Shonto, had mentioned the matter, Chivo had never really thought about the possibility of promoting himself over his Colonel.

Now the prospect inflamed his jackal's mind.

"Whatever you say, *jefe,*" he told Shonto, fanging a smirk which the latter hardly supposed was a grin of good nature. "You see, I climb to the seat gladly. I take the lines and am ready to drive for you. Come on. Let's go."

Shonto started to swing up after him. For one moment both hands were occupied. It was in that moment that the boot of Lieutenant Chivo drove into his face. Shonto fell backward, landing hard. The shotgun was still in his grasp but was useless from that angle. Above him, Chivo was shouting the horses into motion. The coach lurched forward. Shonto made it to his feet in time to leap for the trunk straps in the rear. He caught one of them, held on, and dragged behind the moving stage for fifty feet. He still had the shotgun in his right hand.

The soldiers, sensing his helplessness, ran toward him. They seized clubs and picked up rocks on the run. Chivo, in response to their yells, slowed the stage, thinking to allow them to beat and stone the dragging American.

Shonto held onto the trunk strap. When the snarling soldiers were near, he raised the shotgun and fired it with one hand into their faces. The first barrel and the second blasted as one. The soldiers fell away, three to stagger and fall mortally wounded, two others clutching at their shredded faces, screaming in the agony of the immediate torture and the knowledge, even in their terrible pain, that they would never use their eyes again.

Chivo, on the driver's box, turned in time to see Shonto haul himself up over the rear of the Concord. He had no weapon, now, but neither did the *rurale* lieutenant.

Chivo knew the one way open to him and took it. Over the side he went, rolling to the ground and free of the speeding wheels, the excited teams running wild the moment he flung away the lines. Shonto, weaving precariously, made it to the driver's box and threw himself down between the straining horses to recover the lines.

His luck now returned. He was able to gather up the lines and return to the box, the coach under control and still upright on the wagon road to Toltepec.

But now he knew the wolf pack behind him had a leader again. He could guess how long it would take Chivo to mount the survivors and take up the pursuit.

"Coo-ee, coo-ee," he called to the snorting team. "Steady down, you beauties. You've not begun your night's work yet. Save that pep and vim for the last lap!"

Where he had said he would be waiting beside the wagon road to Toltepec with *El Presidente,* there Chamaco Díaz waited when, half an hour's loping run from the Rio, Shonto pulled up his panting horses and hailed the underbrush. The Indian boy had guided his charge without fail and on foot through the night and between the prowling soldiers of Colonel Ortega's four miles south of the river. The ancient and secret Apache escape route from Texas, which the two had traveled to reach their rendezvous with Charlie Shonto and the stage for Toltepec, lay still unknown behind them. Shonto did not ask Chamaco where it ran, and the boy did not tell him. He was an Indian, even now, and Charlie Shonto was a white man.

Swiftly, then, the last part of the plan was put into operation. The four horses were unhooked from the coach. Four saddles and bridles were brought from the coach trunk, and the mounts were readied. Colonel Ortega was removed from the stage and hung over the saddle of one mount in the manner of a sack of grain. Shonto tied his hands to his feet under the horse's belly, halfway hoping the ropes would not hold. Where the rutted track of the road bent to go past the rendezvous, an eighty-foot bluff rose above the Chihuahua plain. Over this drop, Shonto and his two Indian friends now tossed the Concord's load of fire-arms. There was no time for more effective disposal. Mounting up, the party set out, away from the road, Chamaco leading, Shonto bringing up the rear with the pack horse of the Executioner of Camargo. The goat path along which the small Indian boy took them disappeared into the desert brush within a pistol shot from the wagon road. Shonto had no more idea where the trail led than did Ortega or *El Presidente.* No options remained in any event. Behind them, along the road from the river, they heard now the shouts of men of Mexican tongue and the hammer of horses' hoofs in considerable number. In a pause to listen, they all recognized the high yelping tones of Lieutenant Chivo, discovering the abandoned stage and guessing, amid a goat's beard of rotten curses, the manner of flight of his enemies. And more: from Chivo's murderous bleats, they made out that he had with him another patrol of Ortega's *rurales,* evidently encoun-tered along the way. These new soldiers, whatever their number, would be armed and were clearly being commanded by the colonel's good lieutenant. All might still have been well — yes, surely would have been so — considering the depth of the brushland and the blindness of its cover. But in the press of time and because he had not thought ahead to the complication of Chivo's picking up more arms en route, Shonto had not taken the precaution he ordinarily would have of gagging the captive colonel.

He thought of it, now, as Ortega's galling shout echoed down the slope they were climbing.

"*¡Aquí, aquí, muchachos!* I am here! I am here!"

His head was hanging on that side of the horse nearest Shonto. The shout for help was cut off by the toe of the gunman's boot knocking out four front teeth and knocking out, too, the owner of the teeth. But the price of poker had just gone up, regardless.

"Chamaco," he said, "we have one chance: to split up."

"Never, *patrón*."

"Listen, kid" — Shonto's voice went hard as quartz — "you do what I tell you. I'm running this show."

"No, my American friend, you are not." The denial did not come from the boy but from the small man in the black suit. "It is I who must say what will be. And I say we stay together. You are not with Spaniards, my friend. You are not with traitors who call themselves Mexicans. You are with Indians. Lead on, boy."

Shonto knew he was helpless. He knew, as well, that they were helpless, that it would be but a matter of minutes before the *rurales* would come up to them, blind brush or not. They were so close behind that they could follow by ear the sounds of the stagecoach horses breaking through the brush. The rifle firing would commence any moment, and a bullet, unaimed except by the noise of their ponies crashing ahead, would soon enough find all and each of them. There was no other end within reason.

Yet Chamaco Díaz was no victim of such knowledge. He had been supported by his *Presidente,* had heard him with his own ears say, "You are with Indians." What was not possible in the service of such a man?

"*Patrón!*" he now called to Shonto, voice high and sharp with excitement. "There is a way. Follow me, and don't worry about making noise. The Rangers from your Texas side of the river did not always obey the law!"

Their horses were plowing on up the slope now, and true to Shonto's fear the guerrillas were beginning to fire blindly at the sound of their progress. The bullets hissed and sung about them. But the boy's shout had intrigued Charlie Shonto.

"What's that?" he yelled back.

"The Rangers of Texas," answered the boy, laughing for the first time in Shonto's memory of him. "Many times they would run the Apaches right on across the river, *patrón*. Then the Apaches had to have a way on this side to 'lose' them. I know the way, *patrón*. Ride hard and jump your horse when I demand it."

Shonto wanted to know more about that "jump" business, but the guerrillas were too close now. All he could do was bend low in the saddle and hope the bullet with his name on it went astray. It did. They came to Chamaco's "jumping place" without a wound. The place itself was a declivity in the trail — dug by hand and centuries gone — where no rider, not knowing that it waited beyond the steeply descending hairpin turn which hid it from above, could ever lift his mount over it in time. The animal's momentum, coming down the roof-steep pitch of the decline, would have to carry it and its rider into the "Ranger trap." And this is the way that it worked with the eager *rurales* of Chivo. All of the horses of Chamaco's party, even the pack horse with Colonel Ortega's unconscious form, cleared the break in the trail, leaping it like deer because spurred to the effort by their desperate riders. But the mounts of the guerrillas, scrambling around the hairpin, snorting furiously under the urging of their savage masters — the scent of the kill hot in the nostrils now, so close were they — had no chance to see or to lift themselves and their riders over the yawning pit. Into the waiting blackness of the man-made chasm the first dozen horses and soldiers went screaming and kicking. Another dozen soldiers and their mounts piled up in the trail above and did not plunge into the abyss with the others. But neither did they seem to retain their previous eagerness for the blood of *El Presidente* and the elevation of Lieutenant Chivo to the rank of Executioner of Camargo.

As for Chivo, himself, Shonto never knew if he was among the first group of riders, or the second. All that he did know was that, following the first spate of screamings from the fallen, he did not hear again the harsh yelping voice of the bearded lieutenant.

"*¡Madre!* Chamaco," he said to the Indian boy, in the first moment of stillness following the piteous cries from above, "what is in that Apache trench up there?"

"Tiger's teeth," said the youth, "their points burned to hardness of iron, their butts set in the cracks of the mother rock. I don't wonder at the screams, *patrón*. I've looked down in that hole."

"*¡Santísima!*" breathed Shonto. "A staked pit!"

"For a pack of animals, the death of a pack of animals." The Oaxacan accents of *El Presidente* seemed sad. "Let us go on and catch that train in Toltepec. There is so much work to do in Mexico. The people cry out to me, and there is little time, so little time, for me to answer them."

Shonto did not answer, feeling the moment belonged to another. Chamaco understood the courtesy.

"Yes, *Presidente,*" he said softly. "Please to follow your humble servant."

At once the small man in the black suit spurred his horse up beside that of the Chihuahua Indian boy.

"You are no one's humble servant," he said sternly. "Remember that always. You are a citizen of Mexico, a free man, humble to no one. If you believe in a god, you can thank him for that. If you believe in a man, you can thank a man."

"Yes, *Presidente,* I thank you *and* God."

"In that order, eh, boy?" A trace of warm amusement crossed the dark Indian features. "But you are wrong about the man, *muchacho*. It is another *Presidente* whom I charge you to remember. See that you don't forget his name, citizen; you owe it your life. Burn it in your mind, if you are a true Mexican: Abraham Lincoln."

It was all downhill from there. Some minutes short of midnight, Shonto rode into Toltepec with his charges. By a quarter past the hour, "Item Thirteen" was aboard the waiting train. Steam being up and the dawn all too near, the parting was abrupt. Camargo must be run past in the dark. Also, for the benefit of good health, those who must remain behind when the train pulled out would do well to be drawing in American air come sunrise of that risky day. *El Presidente,* surrounded by his faithful guard aboard the train, was virtually "taken away" from Shonto and Chamaco. So, as well, was the one-time Executioner of Camargo. In a last-second view, *El Presidente* seemed to spy the tall American and the tiny Indian boy sitting their horses in the lamplight spilling from his car's window. Shonto and Chamaco thought they saw him wave to them, and they returned the wave, each with his own thoughts. If the Texas gunman saw the bright tears streaming down the dark cheeks of Chamaco Díaz, he said nothing of the matter, then or later. Each man was permitted his own manner of farewell. But when the train had pulled away from Toltepec — before, even, its smoke had trailed into the Chihuahua night behind it — Charlie Shonto knew all he ever cared to know of the ending of the story. His big hand reached through the dark to touch the knee of his companion.

"Come along, Chamaco," he said. "We had better make long tracks. It's forty-nine miles to the river."

The boy nodded obediently, saying nothing. They turned their horses and sent them into a weary lope.

As they rode, Shonto's rawhide features softened. He was watching the proud set of the thin figure riding by his side. He was aware, surely, that the small Indian man in the ill-fitting black suit had been Benito Juárez, the liberator of Mexico, his people's Abraham Lincoln. But that part of it did not impress the big gunman unduly. For Charlie Shonto, the biggest Indian that he saw that night was always a little Chihuahua boy who barely reached to his gunbelt. History would not record, Shonto suspected, the secret fact that Juárez had been spirited to the Capitol in Washington, D.C. History would never record, he knew certainly, the added fact of the strange manner in which the legendary *El Indio* had been returned safely to his native land. But Charlie Shonto and Texas Express would know the way that it was done, and so would the tallest Indian in all of Toltepec!

When he thought of that, somehow even Charlie Shonto felt better. As the shadows of the Toltepec hills closed behind them, he was sitting as straight in the saddle as Chamaco Díaz.

But of course not as tall.

ELMER KELTON

ELMER KELTON (1926–) was born on a ranch in Andrews County, Texas, and spent his youth and early manhood associating with cowboys and Western old-timers around the Midland-Odessa ranching country of West Texas. Kelton's great-grandfather, in his words, "came out into West Texas about 1875 with a wagon and a string of horses, started a big family and died young, leaving four boys to break broncs, punch cattle, and make a living as best they could, supporting their mother and two baby sisters."

Following graduation from high school, Kelton entered the University of Texas but his further education was interrupted by the Second World War in which he served with the U.S. Army Infantry in the European theater. Upon his discharge, he resumed his education at the University of Texas at Austin and was graduated in 1948 with a Bachelor's degree in journalism. From 1948 to 1963 he worked as a livestock journalist reporting for the *San Angelo Standard-Times* and, subsequently, spent twenty-two years as associate editor of *Livestock Weekly*. He had always wanted to write fiction, in particular the Western story, studying the Western fiction of Ernest Haycox, Luke Short, S. Omar Barker, Walt Coburn, and others. It was during his last semester at the university that he sold his first Western story, "There's Always Another Chance," to *Ranch Romances* (1st April 48). Some of Kelton's early fiction from this period has been collected in THERE'S ALWAYS ANOTHER CHANCE AND OTHER STORIES (Fort Concho Museum Press, 1986). HOT IRON (Ballantine, 1955), a story set in Texas dealing with the cattle business (something in which even at this time Kelton was well versed), marked his debut as a novelist. BUFFALO WAGONS (Ballantine, 1956) followed, a story about hide hunters in the Comanche territory in the early 1870s, and it won him the first of six Golden Spur awards from the Western Writers of America. Perhaps ironically, Kelton's reworking of this novel as the much-expanded SLAUGHTER (Doubleday, 1992) earned him his fifth Golden Spur.

As he matured as a novelist, Kelton came increasingly to be concerned with history and at the same time his fiction changed in tone and substance. "As a fiction writer," Kelton remarked once in an address to the Texas Folklore Society, "I have always tried to use fiction to illuminate history, to illuminate truth, at least as I see the history and truth. A fiction writer can often fire a reader's interest enough to make him want to dig into the true story and make him search out the real history to find out for himself what happened."

Kelton was not afraid to experiment and to expand the horizons of the Western story. THE DAY THE COWBOYS QUIT (Doubleday, 1971) is centered on a little-known episode in the range history of Texas when the cowboys defied great landowners and cattle kings. However, as fine as this and other of Kelton's novels are, I believe his THE TIME IT NEVER RAINED (Doubleday, 1973) is one of the dozen or so best novels written by an American in the 20th Century. It is set in Texas in the 1950s during a seven-year drought. Charlie Flagg, the protagonist, is an aged man possessed of the qualities most admired by Kelton in human beings: determination, integrity, and endurance. Above all, the land itself is a character in this novel, the land around Rio Seco and nearly all the attitudes and the behavior of the various characters are in some way responses to the land. Charlie Flagg can only persist, cling to the land, and hope to try again. He refuses to beg from the federal government; he asks only to live by his own lights and to be left alone. The old Comanche buried on top of Warrior Hill becomes a symbol for Charlie and for the strength of character invested in him. "'I'd be a lot more satisfied if Uncle Sam didn't hire so many left-handed nephews to run everybody's business,'" is how Charlie puts it. A significant enemy to human survival in THE TIME IT NEVER RAINED, and one more irrefragable than any stereotyped Western villain, is the federal government and its utter inability with its many wasteful and ineffectual programs to address real human needs outside of a narrowly political context that tends only to promote self-serving and unsympathetic bureaucratic posturing.

Kelton's sixth Golden Spur came for his essay, "Politically Correct or Historically Correct?" It appeared in *The Roundup* (9–10/93), the house organ of the Western Writers of America, and it is an apt critique of the writings of politically correct eco-extremists, most of whom "live in urban areas which they and their neighbors have forever blighted" and who "couldn't tell sideoats grama from burro grass." Not only is historical accuracy not on the side of their fanatical devotion to a revisionist presentism, but "they are judging past generations in the light of a current generation's attitudes. They are rewriting 19th-Century history to fit a 1990s political and social agenda. I can't help wondering how future generations are going to regard all this someday when they face the payday for our penchant for spending money we don't have and leaving the note hanging over our grandchildren's heads." Looking back to the time of his own great-grandfather on the frontier, Kelton could only conclude: "I recognize that he was a product of *his* time, as we are a product of *our* time. If we were placed in his time I doubt that we would have done any better. We might very possibly not have done nearly so well."

Elmer Kelton's Western fiction is not character-driven, as is that of T.V. Olsen or Max Brand, to name only two authors in whose work this quality is preëminent, but it is concerned with character, in both the narrow sense and the general sense. His men and women are sensitively drawn people of integrity who suffer hardships in building their homes and working the land, who find the wages of changing times relentless, and whose struggles are of more than passing interest for their own lives and to future generations. Knowing full well — as that past-master, William MacLeod Raine, and numerous other authors of the Western story were aware before him — that these qualities in a story are not likely to attract accolades from the critical establishment, Kelton once observed how "for many critics a writer is important only when he savages his subject matter. If he writes with understanding and hope, with respect and love, he is considered trivial." Yet, because this is precisely what Elmer Kelton has attempted in his work, his appeal as his subject matter are likely to outlive the time in which his work was created, just as his contributions to the Western story have continually revitalized and enriched it.

When I was preparing the first edition of this anthology, I had read all of the short stories Kelton had written over the years, mostly for magazines, and found none that seemed to me the equal of his best novels. Therefore I suggested that I adapt an episode from THE WOLF AND THE BUFFALO (Doubleday, 1980) which had then only recently been published. The humility of the man was such that he honestly wanted to know what I thought of that book, was it really good? My answer is still yes, it is; and it remains in many ways the Western novel of his perpetuation as an artist, a celebration of the American spirit, chastened by the land, instilled by the Great Mystery with a profound reverence. It also records human suffering, and human defeat, and spiritual despair.

"Desert Command" was the title I chose for my selection from that novel. It was later anthologized in THE HORSE SOLDIERS (Fawcett Gold Medal, 1987) edited by Bill Pronzini and Martin H. Greenberg and yet again in THE MAMMOTH BOOK OF THE WESTERN (Carroll and Graf, 1991) edited by Joe E. Lewis. The episode deals with a troop of buffalo soldiers lost in the wastes of the Southwestern desert. It is a theme with which Kelton dealt earlier in "Apache Patrol" in *Ranch Romances* (2nd March 52) but not quite so well as here. The last line in this novel reads: "Old Rangers and old warriors would often smoke together and share memories of an open-plains era lost to them all." It has not been completely lost. Elmer Kelton is among those who have brought it to life again in his fine and memorable Western stories.

DESERT COMMAND
1980

The captain went through the motions of setting up a guard mount, but it was a futile effort. Most of these suffering men could do little to defend themselves should the Indians choose this time to attack. Gideon's vision was so blurred that he could not have drawn a bead. Sergeant Nettles could no longer control his limp. He kept his eyes on the captain and contrived not to move more than necessary when the captain looked in his direction.

Gideon asked, "Sergeant, why don't you take your rest?"

Nettles's eyes flashed in anger. "You tryin' to tell me what to do, Private Ledbetter?"

"No, sir. Just come to me that you had a hard day."

"We all had a hard day. Mine ain't been worse than nobody else's."

"You've rode back and forth, walked back and forth, seein' after the men. You gone twice as far as most of us. You rest, why don't you? Tell me what you want done and I'll do it."

"I want you to leave me alone. Ain't nothin' wrong with me that ain't wrong with everybody here."

"The rest of them got no arrow wound that ain't ever healed up."

The anger in Nettles's eyes turned to sharp concern. "It's all right, and I don't want you talkin' about it." He glanced quickly toward the captain and showed relief to find Hollander's attention focused elsewhere.

Gideon said accusingly, "You been hidin' it from him."

He could not remember that he had ever seen Nettles show fear of anything. But the sergeant was fearful now. He gripped Gideon's arm. "Don't you be tellin' him. Don't be tellin' nobody. Without the Army, what could I be? Where could I go?"

"Lots of things. Lots of places."

"You know better than that. In the Army I'm a sergeant, a *top* sergeant. I'm somebody, and I can *do* somethin'. Anywhere else, I'm just another nigger."

"Captain'll see for hisself sooner or later."

"Not as long as I can move. Now you git to your own business."

Sometime during the early part of the evening Gideon heard horses walking. He pushed up from the ground, listening, hoping it was Jimbo and the canteen carriers coming back. He was momentarily disoriented — dizzy — but he realized the sound was from the wrong direction to be Jimbo. It was coming from along the column's backtrail, to the west. He thought about Indians, but they wouldn't make that much noise. The clinking and clanking meant cavalry horses.

Captain Hollander figured it out ahead of Gideon. He walked to the edge of camp and did his best to shout. "Waters! Sergeant Waters! Up here!" His voice was weak and broke once.

The horses seemed to stop for a moment. The men — one of them, at least — had heard the captain. Hollander shouted again, his voice hoarser now. After a moment, the horses were moving again. The captain grunted in satisfaction. His good feeling was soon spoiled, for the horses kept walking, right on by the knoll.

"Waters!" Hollander tried again. Gideon took up the shout, and so did several others. The riders continued to move, passing the hill and going on eastward. The captain clenched his fists in anger.

Gideon volunteered, "I'll go, sir. I'll fetch them back." Hollander only grunted, but Gideon took that for approval. He started down the hill, his legs heavy. He shouted every so often for Waters, but he heard no reply. When he stopped to listen he could tell that the horses were getting farther from him. He tried to run but could not bring his legs to move that rapidly. He stumbled over the crown of some dried-up bunchgrass and sprawled on his belly. He invested a strong effort into getting on his feet.

Behind him Hollander called, "Come back, Ledbetter. Let them go."

He wavered on the point of insubordination but found he could barely hear the horses any more. He had no chance to catch them. Wearily he turned and began the struggle back up the hill. It must have taken him an hour to reach the huddled company and fall to the ground.

Hollander stood over him, against the starlight. "You tried."

When he had the breath, Gideon said, "They just never did hear me."

"They heard you. Waters simply did not choose to stop. He's saving himself, or trying to."

A question burned in his mind, and he came near asking it aloud. *Are we going to save ourselves?* His throat was too dry to bring it out.

Nettles came over after a while to see if he was all right.

Gideon demanded, "What was the matter with Sergeant Waters? I know he heard me. I never figured him to panic out of his head."

"I seen him when the men commenced to groan. It was the groanin' done it. You ever wonder why he drank so much? It was to drive the groanin' sounds out of his mind."

"I don't understand."

"Old days, Waters was a slave catcher. It was him that kept the hounds, and him the white folks give the whip to when he caught a runaway. He didn't have no choice — they'd of took the whip to *him* if he hadn't done it. Now and again they made him keep whippen' a man till the life and the soul was beat out of him. I reckon them dead people been comin' after Waters ever since, in his mind."

The night breeze turned mercifully cool, but it held no hint of moisture. Gideon woodenly stood his guard duty, knowing he would be helpless if anything challenged him. He heard men groaning. The sound made his skin crawl. He could imagine how it had been with Waters. Across the camp someone babbled crazily, hallucinating. Gideon lapsed into sleep of sorts, or unconsciousness. When he awoke, color brightened the east. His head felt as if someone were pounding it with a hammer. His tongue was dry and swollen, his mouth like leather.

Sergeant Nettles lay on his blanket, his eyes open. Gideon crawled to him on hands and knees. He knew what he wanted to say, but his tongue betrayed him. He brought out only a jumble of sounds. He worked at it a long time before he summoned up a little saliva and forced his tongue to more or less his bidding. "You all right sir?" he asked.

Nettles nodded and pushed himself slowly from the ground. At the edge of camp, Captain Hollander was moving about, the first man on his feet.

Little effort was made toward fixing breakfast. The men could not eat. They could not swallow without water. The captain started trying to pack the mules. The regular packer had fallen behind yesterday with Waters. Gideon began to help. It was almost more than he could do to lift a pack to the level of a mule's back. Had the mules been fidgety, he could not have managed. But they were too miserable to move around.

He could see a little better this morning, for the rest, and his legs moved easier than last night, but the gain was of only minor degree. A stir among the buffalo hunters attracted his attention. He became conscious that many of their horses and pack mules were gone. They had strayed off during the night, or perhaps Indians had stolen into the edge of camp and quietly made away with them. The hunters staggered around uncertainly, accusing one another mostly by gesture, for they were as hard put as the troopers to convert gestures into understandable words. In a little while hunters and soldiers started a ragged march down the gentle slope and left the round hill behind them.

Grasping at hope wherever he could find it, Gideon told himself that perhaps Jimbo and the others had stopped at darkness for fear of losing the trail, and by now they were on the move again, coming to the rescue.

The morning sun was soon punishingly hot. Miles went by slowly and painfully, and Jimbo did not come. Far up into the morning, after a couple of troopers had slumped to the ground, Hollander called for a rest stop. They had moved into a sandy stretch of ground with low-growing stemmy mesquite trees and small oak growth shinto knee-high. Many of the men draped blankets over these plants and crawled under them as far as they could go for partial protection against the punishing sun.

Gideon turned to look for Sergeant Nettles. He found him shakily trying to dismount from his black horse, Napoleon. Gideon reached to help him. He spread a blanket across a bush and pulled the corner of it over Nettles's head.

Young Nash tried to dismount but fell and lay as he had landed. Little Finley sat hunched, crying but not making tears. He tried to talk, but the words were without form.

Hollander was somehow still able to articulate, though he spoke his words slowly and carefully. He said it was his judgment that José had become lost and was not coming back — not today, not ever. The men who had gone on after him with the canteens must be sharing whatever fate had overtaken José.

Thompson argued sternly that somewhere ahead lay Silver Lake, and that it was no doubt José's goal. It couldn't be more than a few more miles — fifteen or twenty at most, he declared.

Hollander shook his head violently, his face flushed. If water were that near, and José had found it, Jimbo and the others would be back by now. The captain pointed southeastward. He still had his compass. Water anywhere else was a guess, and evidently a bad one. But he *knew* there was water in the Double Lakes. It was time to stop gambling and go for the cinch.

Thompson was aghast. "You know how far it is to the Double Lakes? Those darkies of yours — they're almost dead now. They'll never live for another sixty-seventy miles."

"They'll live. They've *got* to live."

Thompson insisted that water lay much closer, to the northeast.

Hollander countered, "You said that yesterday. How far have we come? How many more men can we afford to lose?"

"Go that way," Thompson insisted, pointing his chin across the sandy hills toward Double Lakes, "and you'll lose them all."

"There is water at Double Lakes. There is only death out here in these sands. Will you go with us?"

Thompson turned and studied his hunters. "No, we're trying for Silver Lake. It's there. I know it's there. I beg you, Captain, come on with us."

But Hollander had made up his mind. "I've already gambled and lost. I'll gamble no more on water that may not exist. Best of luck to you, Thompson."

The buffalo hunter saw the futility of further argument. "God go with you, Frank."

Hollander nodded. "May He walk with us all." Anger stood like a wall between the men, but each managed to thrust a hand forward. The two groups parted, the hunters toward the hope of Silver Lake and a short trail, the soldiers toward the certainty of Double Lakes, a long and terrible distance away.

The last time Gideon glimpsed the hunters, fading out of sight far to his left, four were walking, the rest hunched on their horses. Though he had not become personally acquainted and could not have named any except Thompson, he felt an ache of regret, a sense of loss as they disappeared into the shimmering heat.

He had no feeling for time. His legs were deadweights that he dragged along, one step and another and another. His vision blurred again. He trudged with his head down, following the tracks of the men in front of him. He no longer thought ahead, or even thought much at all. He fell into a merciful state of half consciousness, moving his body by reflex and instinct. His tongue had swollen so that it almost filled his mouth, and at times he felt he would choke on it.

He was conscious of hunger but unable to act upon it. He put hardtack into his mouth but could not work up saliva to soften it. It was like dry gravel against his inflexible tongue. He had to dig the pieces out with his finger.

Rarely did the horses or mules urinate but, when they did, someone rushed with a cup. The thought was no longer revolting to Gideon. Captain Hollander passed out brown sugar for the men to stir into the urine and increase its palatability. Some was given back to the horses, which at first refused but later accepted it.

By midafternoon, when the heat was at full fury, a horse staggered and went down. Hollander cut its throat to put it out of its misery. Finley came with his cup and caught the gushing blood and drank it, and others took what they could catch before death overtook the animal and the flow stopped. Some of the men became violently ill; the blood was thick and bitter from the horse's dehydration.

Hollander was compelled to call a halt. Men were strung out for half a mile. Orders meant next to nothing. This was no longer a column of soldiers; it was a loose and straggling collection of half-delirious men struggling for individual survival. Gideon saw Nash fall and wanted to go to help him but for a long time could not move his legs. Only when he saw Sergeant Nettles collapse upon the sun-baked sand did he muster the strength to stagger twenty steps and throw blankets over the men's heads to shield them from the sun. He slumped then, too exhausted to do the same for himself. He lapsed into a dreamlike state and seemed to float away like some bodiless spirit, back to the plantation. He heard the happy voice of Big Ella and the others there, and he splashed barefoot into the cool, flowing river.

The heat abated with sundown, and night brought a coolness which broke Gideon's fever. He roused to the point that he could look about him and see the other men lying in grotesque positions, many groaning, half of them suffering from delirium.

He rallied enough to crawl to Sergeant Nettles. At first he could not tell that the man was breathing. He held his hand just above Nettles's mouth and felt that faint but steady warmth of breath. Probably the sergeant was unconscious. Gideon saw no point in trying to bring him out of it. The Lord was being merciful.

Sometime in the night Captain Hollander started trying to get the men on their feet to use the cooler hours for easier miles. Gideon watched him impassively at first, until the man's strong determination began to reach him. Sergeant Nettles arose and began limping from one man to another. Gideon pushed to his feet and helped.

He heard Hollander say thickly, "Good man, Ledbetter. Get them going."

In the moonlight it was apparent that several horses had wandered away. Judas was gone. Gideon could not bring himself to any emotion over that. Half the men were afoot now, their horses strayed or dead. Many of the pack mules were missing. Nettles asked Gideon to count the men, to be sure they left none behind. He found it difficult to hold the figures in his head. His mind kept drifting to other things, other times, other places far better than this one.

Many blankets and packs were left on the ground as the company moved out. A couple of men dropped their carbines, and Gideon forcibly put them back in their hands. A little later he looked back and saw that one of the men was empty-handed again.

He dreaded sunrise, but it came. He sensed that they had walked or ridden many miles in the cool darkness. The heat was blunted the first couple of hours by a thin cover of dry clouds that held no promise of rain. These burned away, after a time, and the men and horses trudged under the full punishment of an unforgiving July sun.

A transient thought flitted through Gideon's mind. He wondered where the Indians were. It struck him as strange that he had gone so long without the Indians intruding on his consciousness. It occurred to him that it had been most of two days since he had heard them mentioned. Odd, that the mission which had brought the soldiers into this blazing hell had been so completely forgotten in the face of a more elemental challenge, simple survival.

A staggering horse brought the procession to a halt. Without waiting for the captain to give an order, one of the troopers cut the animal's throat, and several fought over the gushing blood. Gideon saw Nettles start toward the men to break up the fight, then go to his knees. Gideon took it upon himself to part the fighters, throwing a couple to the ground with more strength than he had realized he still owned. Little Finley's own horse went down on its rump. Finley stared dumbly, making no effort to join the struggle to capture its blood. He lay down on the short, brittle grass and wept silently, his shoulders shuddering.

Through all of it, Nettles sat helplessly. The spirit was still strong in his black eyes, but the flesh had gone as far as it could. Gideon managed to get the men under some semblance of control, making gruff noises deep in his throat because he could not force his tongue to form clear words. He felt the eyes of Hollander and Nettles upon him. Without being formally bidden to do so, he took command upon himself and motioned and coaxed and bullied most of the men into movement. Lieutenant Judson, weaving a little, got on his droop-headed horse and took the lead.

Soon only five men were left, Gideon and Hollander on their feet, the sun-struck Nash and shattered little Finley lying on the ground, Sergeant Nettles sitting up but unable to keep his legs under him.

By signs more than by words, Nettles conveyed his intention of staying with Nash and Finley until they were able to move. Then he would bring them on, following the company's trail to water. Captain Hollander nodded his assent, though Gideon saw sadness in the man's blue eyes. Hollander took the big black hand in both of his own and squeezed it for a moment, silently saying good-bye to an old friend. Hollander turned away quickly, not looking back. Nettles raised his hand again, and Gideon took it.

The sergeant mumbled, but Gideon made out the words he was trying to say. "Take care of them, soldier."

Gideon tried to assure him he would be back as soon as they found water, but the words would not come. He turned back only once, a hundred yards away, and took a final look at the sergeant, still sitting up, holding the reins of big, black Napoleon. For a moment, in spite of the heat, Gideon felt cold.

The column moved until upwards of midday, when the heat brought more horses to their knees, and more of the men. By this time the company was out of control. Now and then a man in delirium struck out on a tangent of his own, away from the main body. At first Gideon tried to bring them back but soon had to give up, for the effort was a drain on whatever strength he still held in reserve. He stopped thinking ahead but concentrated on bringing one foot in front of the other.

When Lieutenant Judson went down, slipping from the saddle and landing limply in the dry grass, the column stopped. The lieutenant's horse braced its legs and stood trembling. It no longer sweated, though a crust of dried mud clung to its hide. Hollander tried to rouse Judson but could not. Hollander gave a little cry and slumped to the ground, covering his face with his hands. By instinct more than reason, Gideon helped him to a small mesquite and threw a blanket over it to shade him, and to shield the captain's emotions from view of the men. The lieutenant's horse, untethered, began wandering off southward, dragging the reins, drawn by instinct in the direction of Concho. Gideon knew he should make some effort to bring it back, but he lacked the willpower to move. He sat with his legs stretched out before him on the ground and watched the horse stumble away to a slow death somewhere out there on the parched prairie.

After a time, Gideon became aware that the captain was trying to call him. Hollander motioned with his hand. Gideon crawled to the officer on hands and knees.

Hollander extended his silver watch, despair in his sunken eyes. Very slowly, very deliberately, he managed a few dear words. "Wife. Give to my wife and baby."

Gideon reached for the watch until the import of the captain's words penetrated his fevered brain. Hollander was giving up. Gideon looked slowly around him at the men sprawled on the ground, covering their heads with blankets if they still had them, hats if they did not.

If Hollander died, these men would die. Hollander might be no better man than they, but his was the leadership. His was the example they had been conditioned to follow, as they had been conditioned all their lives to follow one white man or another. It came to Gideon that if he accepted the watch, that would release the captain to die in peace.

He felt a flare of deep anger. The captain had no right to die! He had brought these men here; he had to live and take them out. Gideon drew back his hand. Shaking his head, he tried to form words first in his mind, then get them out on his dry, swollen tongue.

"No! You'll live. *You* give it to her."

The captain reached out with both hands, the silver chain dangling. His eyes begged, though his cracked lips formed no discernible words.

Gideon almost gave in to pity, but the anger was still hot in his face. Stubbornly he pulled back. The words came clearly in his mind, though he could not get his tongue to speak them.

You got a baby now, more than likely. You owe that woman, and you owe that baby, and you owe us! You goin' to live if I got to kill you!

Only the anger came out, not the words. But the captain seemed to understand that Gideon refused to release him from his responsibilities. Hollander turned his head away, in the shadow beneath the blanket. He clutched the silver watch against his chest, his shoulders heaving.

In a while he was somehow on his feet again. He motioned for Gideon to help him lift the delirious lieutenant onto the captain's own horse. Gideon tied the young officer in the saddle. Hollander struck out again southeastward, his steps slow and deliberate. He was setting a pace, an example. His shoulders had a determined set. Gideon sensed that the captain would not give up again. He might die, but he would not surrender.

Gideon had trouble distinguishing reality from hallucination. His head roared from fever, and it ached with a steady rhythm like a drumbeat. He imagined he could hear the post band playing a parade-ground march, and he tried in vain to bring his feet into step with it. His vision was distorted, the men stretched out of shape, the prairie rolling in waves. Cajoling, threatening, he got the men to their feet one by one and set them to following the captain. Some moved willingly, some fought him, but by and by he had them all on the move.

Stumbling, bringing up the rear so no one could drop out without his knowledge, Gideon moved in a trance. It occurred to him that a couple of the pack mules had strayed off on their own. Only two were left.

Each time a horse staggered and fell, its throat was cut, and the men caught the blood and gagged it down. The captain's horse gave up after a long time, going to its knees. Gideon struggled to untie the lieutenant but could not bring his unresponsive fingers to the task. He cut the rope and tried to ease the officer to the ground. He lacked the strength to hold him. He and the lieutenant fell together in a heap. Gideon looked up at the horse, afraid it might roll over on them. He dragged himself and the lieutenant away before someone cut the animal's throat.

That was the last of the horses.

He lay struggling for breath; the exertion had been severe. The men were like gaunt scarecrow figures out of a nightmare, their uniforms a dusty gray instead of blue, many hanging in strips and ribbons. The faces were stubbled, the beards matted grotesquely with dust and horses' blood as well as some of their own, for their lips were swollen out of shape and had cracked and bled. They no longer looked like soldiers, they looked like madmen — and Gideon feared he was the maddest of them all.

The packs were untied from the mules, and Lieutenant Judson was lifted aboard one of the last two surviving animals. Again Gideon tried to tie him on, but he could not coordinate his hands and gave up the task. Delirious or not, Judson would have to retain instinct enough to hold himself on the mule.

The ragged column plodded and staggered and crawled until far into the afternoon. Hollander motioned for a rest stop in an open plain that lacked even the low-growing dune mesquites over which a blanket could be stretched for shade. Hardly a blanket was left anyway. The men had dropped them one by one, along with everything else they had carried. Troopers sprawled on the ground, faces down to shield them from the sun. Gideon fell into a state more stupor than sleep. After a time, he felt someone shaking his shoulder. Hollander was motioning for him to get up, and to get the other men up. Gideon went about the task woodenly. He helped Hollander and one of the other troopers lift the lieutenant back onto the mule.

Gideon saw that Hollander was studying the other mule, which had remained riderless. The wish was plain in the officer's eyes, but Gideon saw there a reluctance, too. They were no longer officers and men; they were simply men, all in a desperate situation together. Hollander was uncertain about using the advantage that might save his life.

Gideon felt a sudden temptation to take the mule himself. He had the strength to do it. At this moment, he was probably the strongest man in the column. Nobody — not even Hollander — could stop him if he made up his mind.

The thought became action to the point that he laid his hands on the reins, and on the mule's roached mane. He leaned against the mule, trying to summon strength to pull himself up. But he could not, and he realized slowly that it was more than simply a matter of strength. It was also a matter of will. Sergeant Esau Nettles forcibly pushed himself into Gideon's mind. In Nettles's eyes, such a thing would be a dishonor upon Gideon and upon the company.

Gideon cried out for Nettles to leave him alone, but in his mind he could see the sergeant's angry eyes burning like fire, and their heat seemed to touch him and force him back from the mule.

Gideon motioned for Hollander to take the mule. Somehow his tongue managed the words. "Ride him. Sir."

He had not been willing to give Hollander release to die, but now he offered him release to live. Hollander stared at him with remorseful eyes. With Gideon's help, he got onto the mule's back. He reached down and took up the reins to lead the mule on which the lieutenant had been placed.

A momentary wildness widened Hollander's eyes. The thought behind it was too clear to miss: with these mules the white men could leave the black soldiers behind and save themselves.

Reading that temptation, Gideon stared helplessly, his mouth hanging open. He knew he could not fairly blame Hollander, for he had almost yielded to the same temptation. One pleading word shaped itself into voice. "Captain...."

The wildness passed. Hollander had put aside the thought. He pointed with his chin and motioned for Gideon and the others to follow. They moved off into the dusk, toward a horizon as barren as the one behind them. But the waning of the day's heat brought a rebirth of strength. Gideon kept bringing his legs forward, one short step at a time.

Darkness came. He knew men had dropped out, but he could do nothing any more to help them. He followed the cloudiest notion of time, but somewhere, probably past midnight, he heard a cry from Hollander. Fear clutched at him — fear that Hollander was stricken. Gideon forced his legs to move faster, bringing him up to the mules. He stumbled over an unexpected rut in the prairie, and he went heavily to his hands and knees.

Hollander was making a strange sound — half laugh, half cry. He pointed at the ground. "Trail," he managed. "Trail."

Gideon felt around with his hands in soft sand, trying to find solid ground to help him push back to his feet. Slowly he understood what Hollander was trying to say. He had stumbled into a trail — a rut cut by wagon wheels.

"Shafter," Hollander said plainly. "Shafter's trail."

Shafter. Of course. Colonel Shafter had been all over this country the year before, exploring it in a wetter, more amenable season. These ruts had been cut by his long train of supply wagons.

Lieutenant Judson seemed more dead than alive, responding not at all to Hollander's excitement, or to Gideon's.

Hollander pointed down the trail. "Double Lakes. Come on."

Gideon felt as if he were being stabbed by a thousand sharp needles. Strength pumped into his legs. He struggled to his feet and found voice. "Water, boys. Water, yonderway!"

The men quickened their steps, some laughing madly, some crying without tears. Gideon stood at the trail in the bold moonlight, pointing the troopers after the officers and the mules as they passed him, one by one. When the last had gone — the last one he could see — he turned and followed.

The mules moved out farther and farther ahead of the men afoot, and after a long time Gideon thought he heard them strike a trot. It was probably in his mind, for surely they no longer had that much strength. Unless they had smelled water....

That was it, the mules knew water lay ahead. His legs moved faster, easier, because now they were moving toward life, not death.

It might have been one mile or it might have been five. He had walked in a half-world much of the time and had little conception of anything except his re-vived hope. But suddenly there it was straight in front of him, the broad dust-covered expanse of the dry playa lake, and the moon shining on water that had seeped into the holes the men had dug in another time that seemed as long ago as slavery. The soldiers who had reached there ahead of him lay on their bellies, their heads half buried in the water. Captain Hollander was walking unsteadily around them, using all his strength to pull some men back lest they faint and drown themselves.

"Not too much," he kept saying thickly. "Drink slowly. Drink slowly."

Gideon had no time for reason. He flung himself onto his stomach and dropped his face into the water. The shock was unexpected. He felt his head spinning. He was strangling. Hands grabbed him and dragged him back.

"Easy now. Easy."

He tried to scramble to the water again, even as he choked and gagged, but the hands held him. "Slow, damn it. Slow." The voice was Hollander's.

He lapsed into unconsciousness. It might have lasted a minute, or it could have been much longer. When he came out of it, he was hardly able to raise his head. The terrible thirst returned to him, but this time he realized he had to keep his reason. He pulled himself to the edge of the water and scooped it up in his hands. He realized that if he fell unconscious again it must be on the dry ground, lest he drown before anyone could respond.

The water still had an alkali bite, but that was no longer a detriment. Gideon had never known water so sweet. He rationed himself, drinking a few sips, waiting, then drinking again, always from his cupped hand. He became aware that some men had slid into the water and were splashing around in it with all the joy of unleashed children. That this compromised sanitation never entered his mind; he kept drinking a few swallows at a time. Almost at once, it seemed, his tongue began to shrink. He thought of words, and they began to pass his lips in creditable fashion. "Praise Jesus! Bless the name of Jesus!"

Finally, when he came to a full realization that he would not die, he lay down and wept silently, no tears in his eyes.

There was no guard duty, unless Hollander stood it himself. Occasionally the thirst came upon Gideon with all its furious insistence, and he drank. When finally he came fully awake, the sun was shining warmly in his face. Gradually he heard stirrings, men going to the water or from it. He pushed to his knees, blinking in surprise at a bright sun an hour or more high.

His eyes focused on Captain Hollander, sitting up and staring back. Hollander's face was haggard, his eyes still sunken. But he was an officer again. "Ledbetter, let's see if you can walk."

It took Gideon a minute to get his legs unwound and properly set beneath him. But finally he was standing, swaying. He took a few steps.

"Ledbetter," Hollander said, "I need a noncom. I want you to regard yourself as a corporal."

"And give orders?" Gideon was stunned. "I ain't never led nobody. I been a slave for most of my life."

"So was Sergeant Nettles."

"I sure ain't no Nettles."

"Most of us would still be out there in that hell if it hadn't been for you. Perhaps all of us. Like it or not, you're a corporal." He dismissed further argument. "We left some men behind us. I want you to pick a couple or three of the strongest, fill what canteens we have left and go back. Take a mule." He pointed his chin at Lieutenant Judson. "The lieutenant will ride the other to the base camp and bring up wagons and supplies. I'll send a wagon on after you."

Gideon sought out three men he thought had regained strength enough to walk. Almost everything had been discarded along the way, so they had nothing to eat except a little hardtack. The men drank all the water they could comfortably absorb so they would not have to drain the canteens later. Those would be needed for whatever men they found along the trail. Looping the canteens over the mule, he set out walking, his step improving as he went along. His mind was reasonably clear, and he began mentally upbraiding himself for not counting the men at the lake before he left. He didn't know, really, how many were still out. His memory of yesterday's ordeal was hazy at best. Men had dropped by the wayside — he could remember that — but he could not remember who or how many.

The rescue party came in time to a Mississippian named Kersey, lying in yesterday's blown-out tracks. It took a while to revive him, and then he clutched desperately at the canteen, fighting when anyone tried to pull it away for his own good. Gideon asked if he knew who else might be behind him, but the man could only shake his head. He could not speak.

Gideon left one of his three men with Kersey and set out walking again, northwestward. Before long his legs began to tremble, and he knew he was approaching his limit. He and the other two looked at each other and reached silent agreement. They dropped to rest, the sun hot upon their backs.

By night they had found just one more man. Gideon had managed to shoot a couple of rabbits, and the men shared those, half cooked over a small fire before sundown. They smothered the fire and walked on for a time to get away from the glow, in case it might attract Indians.

All day he had watched the unstable horizon, hoping to see Esau Nettles and Nash and Finley riding toward them. Now and again a distant shape would arise, only to prove itself false as the heat waves shifted and the mirages changed. His hopes ebbed with his strength.

Night gave him time to brood about Jimbo. He could visualize Jimbo and the men who had gone with him, following the trail of the lost guide until one by one they fell. Jimbo would have been the last, Gideon fancied, and he probably had not given up hope until he had made the last step that his legs would take.

More men had dropped out than Gideon had found. The others had probably wandered off in one direction or another. Some might find the lakes for themselves. The others.... He slept fitfully and dreamed a lot, reliving at times his own agony, seeing at others Jimbo or Esau Nettles, dying alone in that great waste of sand and burned short grass.

They moved again in the coolness of dawn, but the men had less of hope now to buoy them along. Though no one spoke his doubts, they were clear in every man's eyes.

The wagon came as Hollander had promised. The other men stayed behind to leave the load light. Gideon got aboard as guide. The driver and his helper had not been on the dry march. They could only follow the tracks, the trail of abandoned equipment, the swelling bodies of horses that had died one by one along the way. Riding silently on the spring seat as the wagon bounced roughly over dry bunchgrass and shinnery, Gideon drew into a shell, steeling himself for what he had become convinced he would find at the end of the trip.

It was as he had expected, almost. They found little Finley first. To Gideon's amazement, he was still alive. He fought like a wildcat for the canteen Gideon held to his ruined lips. Gideon was unable to keep him from drinking too much at first, and for a while he thought Finley might die from overfilling with the alkali-tainted water.

Like a candle flame flickering before it dies, Gideon's hopes revived briefly. Perhaps finding Finley alive was a good omen.

The hopes were soon crushed. They found black Napoleon, dead. As an act of mercy, Nettles had taken off the saddle and bridle and turned the horse loose on the chance it could save itself. The gesture came too late. Soon Gideon found Esau Nettles and the young trooper Nash lying beneath a blanket spread for shade over a patch of shin oak. Even before he lifted the blanket, Gideon knew with a shuddering certainty. They were dead. He dropped in the sand beside them, drew up his knees and covered his face in his arms.

In the wagon he could hear little Finley whimpering, out of his head. Anger struck at Gideon, sharp, painful and futile. For a moment the anger was against

Finley, a liar, a sneak thief, a coward. Why should he live when a man like Esau Nettles had died? For a moment, Gideon's anger turned upon God. Then he realized with dismay that he was railing against the faith drilled into him since boyhood, a faith he had never questioned in his life.

The anger exhausted itself. Only the sorrow remained, deep and wounding.

The trip back to the Double Lakes was slow and silent. Little Finley regained mind enough to be afraid of the two bodies and to move as far from them as possible without climbing out of the wagon. "They're dead," he mumbled once. "Why don't we leave them?"

Gideon chose not to dignify the question by answering it. His contempt for Finley sank deeper into his soul. He made up his mind that he would do whatever he could to force the little man out of this outfit, if not out of the Army. He wanted to blame Finley for Nettles's death, though he knew this was not totally valid. Perhaps Nettles had realized he would never make it to the Double Lakes on that bad hip. Perhaps he had stayed behind with Nash and Finley so someone else later would not have to stay behind with him. The more Gideon pondered that possibility, the more he wanted to believe it; it gave reason to Nettles's death, even nobility.

As the wagon went along, it picked up the men who had stayed behind. Most had walked some distance in the direction of the lakes rather than wait to be hauled all the way. All looked in brooding silence at the blanket-covered bodies. Those exhausted climbed into the wagon beside them. Those who could walk continued to do so. Gideon got down and joined them, for he was feeling stronger. The exertion of walking helped the black mood lift itself from him.

Captain Hollander met the wagon as it pulled up to the edge of the lake. Gideon stared, surprised. The captain had shaved and washed out his uniform. It was wrinkled but passably clean, within the limitations of the gyppy water. Army routine had again prevailed over the challenge of the elements.

Hollander counted the men who walked and who climbed out of the wagon. He asked no unnecessary questions. He seemed to read the answers in Gideon's face. He lifted the blanket and looked at the bodies, his face tightening with a sadness he did not try to put into words. "We had better bury them here. This weather...."

The digging was left to men who had come up from the supply camp, for they had the strength. Hollander had brought no Bible to read from, an oversight some might regard as indicative of the reasons for the company's travail. The captain improvised a long prayer asking God's blessings upon these men, these devoted servants of their country and their Lord, and upon any others like them who had met death alone on that hostile prairie, unseen except by God's own messengers come to lead them to a better land.

Three more men had wandered into camp during Gideon's absence, men who had lost the trail but somehow retained enough sense of direction to find the lakes. Toward dusk Gideon heard a stir and looked where some of the men were pointing, northward. He saw horsemen coming. His first thought was Indians. But soon he could tell these were soldiers. And the man in the lead was unmistakable.

Jimbo!

Jimbo spurred into a long trot, and Gideon strode forward to meet him. Jimbo jumped to the ground, and the two men hugged each other, laughing and crying at the same time.

In camp, when all the howdies were said and the reunions had lost their initial glow, Jimbo explained that the guide, José, had missed the Silver Lake he was trying to find and had come instead, somewhat later than he expected, to a set of springs just off Yellow House Cañon. Jimbo and the soldiers who followed had stayed at the springs long enough to recoup their own strength and that of their horses. Some had remained there with the buffalo hunters who straggled in, but Jimbo and three others had filled canteens and set out along their backtrail to carry water to the column they expected to find somewhere behind them. Hollander's decision to strike out for Double Lakes had thwarted them. They marched much farther than they intended and found no one. Fearing that the rest of the company had died, they had returned heavy-hearted to the springs, rested a while, then set out to find Double Lakes and the base camp below.

Captain Hollander's face twisted in remorse as he listened. The hunters had been right; if he had followed them his troops would have reached water sooner than they did. Perhaps Esau Nettles and Private Nash would not be dead; perhaps others would not still be missing.

Lieutenant Judson tried to reassure him. "You used your best judgment based on the facts at hand, Frank. You knew this water was here. You couldn't know there was water where the hunters wanted to go. They were just guessing. What if they had been wrong? You had the responsibility for all these men. Those hunters could gamble. You could not."

Gideon knew Judson was right, as Hollander had been. But he could see the doubt settling into the captain's eyes. As long as Hollander lived, it would be there, the questions coming upon him suddenly in the darkness of a sleepless night, in the midst of his pondering upon other decisions he would be called upon to make in the future. To the end of his life, Hollander would be haunted by Esau Nettles and the others, and the unanswered question: did it have to be? Gideon looked at him. It was one of the few times in his life he had ever genuinely pitied a white man.

Gideon wrestled awhile with his doubts, then approached the captain hesitantly. "Sir...." He took off his hat and abused it fearfully in his nervous hands. "Sir, you done right. Old Sergeant, he'd of said so hisself, if he could. He'd of said you *always* done right."

Hollander stared at the ground a long time before he looked up at Gideon. "Thank you, Ledbetter. There's not a man I'd rather hear that from than you...and *him*."

Early on the fifth day, having sent out search parties and having given up hope that any stragglers still out would ever turn up alive, Hollander ordered the company to march southward to the supply camp. Water there was better, and timber along the creek would provide shade. The trip was slow and hot and dry, and Gideon found himself skirting along the edge of fear as terrible memories forced themselves upon him.

Late on the afternoon of the sixth day, a column of mounted men and two army ambulances broke through a veil of dust out of the south. A rider loped ahead of the column, pulling up in the edge of camp. He was the civilian scout, Pat Maloney, from the village of Ben Ficklin. He whooped in delight as he saw Captain Hollander and Lieutenant Judson standing beside a wagon.

"Frank Hollander! Dammit, man, we thought you were dead!"

He pumped Hollander's hand excitedly, but that was not enough. The ex-Confederate gripped the Union officer's arms and shook him in a violence of joy. "Tell you the God's truth, Frank, we come to hunt for your body. We thought every man jack of you had died."

His gaze swept the camp. Gideon felt the scout's eyes stop momentarily on him and Jimbo, lighting with pleasure at the sight of them.

Hollander replied gravely, "A few of us *are* dead. The best of us, perhaps."

Maloney looked around a second time, his face going grim as he missed Nettles. "The old sergeant?"

Hollander looked at the ground. "We buried him."

Maloney was silent a moment. "We thought from what we heard that we would have to bury you all!" He explained that Sergeant Waters had somehow made it back to Fort Concho, with two others. They had brought a report that Captain Hollander and all his men had been led astray by Indians on that great hostile plain, that they and all those buffalo hunters were dying from heat and thirst. They were certain, Waters reported, that no one except themselves had survived.

Maloney pointed to the approaching column. "You can imagine how that news tore up the post at Concho."

Apprehension struck Hollander. "My wife...Adeline. She heard that?"

"Everybody heard it."

"She must be half out of her mind. This, and the baby coming.... We'll have to send word back right away."

Maloney smiled. "You know I got me a new baby boy, Frank?"

Hollander seemed not quite to hear him. "That's good, Pat. Glad to hear it." But his mind was clearly elsewhere.

Maloney said, "Who knows? He may grow up to marry that little girl *your* wife had. Join the North and South together again, so to speak."

Hollander's eyes widened. He had heard *that*. "A girl, you say? You've seen it?"

"Went by there last thing before I left the post. She looks like her mother. Damn lucky thing, too, because her papa looks like hell."

The trip back to Fort Concho was made slowly and carefully, for more men were afoot than on horseback, and none had completely regained strength. At times even the civilian Maloney would step down from his horse and walk a while, letting some tired black trooper ride.

Messengers had carried the news of their approach ahead of them, so that most of the people of Saint Angelo were lined up to watch the arrival of men who had come back from the dead. An escort and fresh horses were sent out from the post. Hollander and Judson and Maloney rode at the head of the column. Gideon was behind them, urging the men to sit straight and look like soldiers that Esau Nettles would have wanted to claim.

Ordinarily they would not have ridden down the street, but this was an occasion, and the escort wanted to show them off. Lined along Concho Avenue were civilians of all ages, sizes, and colors, white to brown to black. Most cheered the soldiers as they passed, though Gideon looked into some eyes and found there the same hostility he had always seen. Nothing, not even the ordeal the soldiers had been through, had changed that. Nothing ever would.

Two-thirds of the way down to Oakes Street, a seedy, bearded man leaned against a post that held up the narrow porch of a new but already-dingy little saloon. As Hollander came abreast of him the man shouted, "Say, Captain, why didn't you do us all a favor and leave the rest of them damned niggers out there?"

Hollander stiffened. He turned in the saddle, rage bursting into his face. He freed his right foot from the stirrup and started to dismount. Maloney caught his arm. "Frank, you ain't got your strength back."

Maloney swung slowly and casually to the ground, handed his reins to Gideon and walked up to the man with a dry and dangerous smile set like concrete. He crouched, and when his fist came up it was like a sledge. The man's head snapped back, then his whole body followed. He slid across the little porch, winding up half in and half out of the open front door.

Maloney looked first to one side, then the other, challenging one and all. Nobody took up his challenge. He reached down for the struggling man.

"Here, friend, let me help you up."

When the man was on his feet, Maloney hit him again, knocking him through the door and into the saloon. With a wink, he took his reins from Gideon's hand, swung back into the saddle and gave the silent Hollander a nod.

"You're welcome," he said.

T.V. OLSEN

THEODORE VICTOR OLSEN (1932–1993) was born in Rhinelander, Wisconsin, and continued to live in the area all his life as had Olsens in his family since his paternal grandfather emigrated there from Norway in 1890. Growing up, Olsen felt he labored under a considerable handicap in that he was creative, a loner, and an individualist with a dislike for taking orders. Those were once all excellent reasons to head out into the territories. In Olsen's case, they prompted him to turn his literary attention to the frontier. He discovered Luke Short the year between high school and college. He felt that while Ernest Haycox "was a matchless stylist" that his characters "with their distant, Homeric quality seemed less than human to me. Short's less intrusive prose, his warm treatment of characters as people, his attention to small details in their behavior, made for greater reader involvement...." He discovered Les Savage, Jr., and Elmore Leonard in the pages of *Zane Grey's Western Magazine* and he read Walter Van Tilburg Clark's THE OX-BOW INCIDENT.

Olsen was graduated from Central State College at Stevens Point, later part of the University of Wisconsin system, in 1955 with a Bachelor's degree. He had begun his own Western novel in 1953 and, once he had completed it, he sent it together with a reading fee of $35 to the August Lenniger Literary Agency. He titled it VALLEY OF THE HUNTED. Six months later he heard from John Burr, the last editor of *Western Story* then working for Lenniger, that if he was willing to cut the novel by 15,000 words Doro Stiles, an editor at Ace Books, was interested in purchasing it. The advance was $1,000 and the next year it was published under the title HAVEN OF THE HUNTED (Ace, 1956). This first novel, while indebted somewhat to Luke Short, is perhaps even more indebted to Savage and Clark for the complexity of its psychological motivations and the interactions of its characters.

It was apparently not easy for him to follow this novel with another and so, for the next two years beginning with "Backtrail" in *Ranch Romances* (1st April 56), Olsen turned to the Western short story. His success in the shorter form was at once evident since "Backtrail" was purchased for $3,000 by "Dick Powell's Zane Grey Theatre" and was televised in the spring of 1957 with Powell in the leading role.

By late 1957, Olsen turned again to the novel with a story he titled THE KID

FROM NOWHERE. Some revision was required by Doro Stiles but in the end it was accepted for publication as THE MAN FROM NOWHERE (Ace, 1959). By the time this novel was published, August Lenniger took Olsen on as a personal client. Olsen wrote a new Western titled DAY OF THE VULTURE which Lenniger sold to Fawcett for an advance of $2,000 and it was published as McGIVERN (Fawcett Gold Medal, 1960). HIGH LAWLESS (Fawcett Gold Medal, 1960) followed along with GUNSWIFT (Fawcett Gold Medal, 1960) and RAMROD RIDER (Fawcett Gold Medal, 1961). All had been written in 1960 and, from starting the year almost flat broke, Olsen finished it with a total of $8,000 in advances.

In an article titled "What Do Americans Want in Westerns?" in *The Roundup* (2/62), Olsen entered the controversy then at issue among members of the Western Writers of America between the traditional Western and the off-trail Western. In describing what he felt the proper direction for the Western story, he also summed up the significance of his own tremendous contribution to what would become increasingly the direction of his own fiction: "...a commercial Western fictioneer of today would do well to regard each book as a new creative challenge in development of plot and situation and highly varied characterization, with mature and intelligent concepts of theme and treatment but strive simultaneously to recapitulate more truly the traditional elements that have made the Western beloved of Americans: the historical feel of the place and the people and the times, the sense of freedom, of a wild and wide-open land, sex presented more honestly but still not sensationally, tough-minded men who did what they damned well had to and never mind about Mr. Jones, a swift, close-knit pace carried by lots of fast-moving action, and the decisive triumph of good over evil by a protagonist who can make mistakes and commit an occasional wrong because he is understandably human."

What in effect Olsen was accomplishing at the time in his own Western fiction was to remove the Western story from the idealized models which harked back to Greek drama and the epic poems of Homer and Vergil and to populate his stories with realistic human beings who, notwithstanding, are caught in the same web of moral questions as found in Classical precursors — is this right? is this wrong? how ought one live? what is most important in life? So-called mainstream fiction had long abandoned any pretense it had ever had at addressing such questions but Olsen, with other Western writers of his generation including Elmer Kelton, Brian Garfield, Noel M. Loomis, and Robert MacLeod, was asking them in a stronger voice than ever before, following the trail Les Savage, Jr., had blazed in which the focus increasingly is turned toward psychological motivations directly related to the historical events and circumstances and personalities of the period and place where the story is set.

It would be as Theodore V. Olsen that he would publish what to that point would prove his most successful novel, THE STALKING MOON (Doubleday,

1965). It had occurred to Olsen in a flash of inspiration to combine the notion of a killer stalking a helpless family with a real-life Apache Indian who had had a penchant for killing Mexicans. At the WWA convention in Portland, Oregon, in 1964, Olsen was dismayed to hear from Harold Kuebler of Doubleday that he was thinking of rejecting the novel on the basis of the outline he had been provided. Author and editor thrashed out reservations on the spot and Olsen's proposals for a revision of the plot were accepted at once. Doubleday's marketing department was so impressed with the novel that, rather than issue it in the Double D library line, the decision was made to bring it out in a general trade edition. Several motion picture producing companies expressed an interest in the novel and it was finally sold to National General where it was produced starring Gregory Peck and Eve Marie Saint. In THE STALKING MOON, as so often on the frontier, despite the savagery of the struggle to survive, there does emerge from the long battle a fundamental human decency that extends beyond any thought of racial or cultural or ethnic differences, beyond even any notion of civilization. It is this same theme which preoccupies another of Olsen's finest novels, BLIZZARD PASS (Fawcett, 1968). Yet in this story it is welded to a cognizance that human evil is a reality that must not be denied. Though limited in number, each of the cast of characters in this novel is etched so deeply and developed so poignantly that the narrative has an incredible depth. It has recently been reprinted in a hard cover edition in the Gunsmoke series by Chivers Press.

Beginning with McGIVERN, Olsen's novels have the same sort of visceral, wrenching involvement found in THE STALKING MOON and BLIZZARD PASS. Once past the first chapter, it is nearly impossible to put them down. They are stories that work on two levels: the gnawing question of what will happen next combined with a profound emotional involvement with characters about whom a reader comes to care deeply. The events may be those of an action/adventure narrative but the characters provide such a rich texture to the stories that they carry forward the plot as readily as do the events. Above all, in common with Euripides, the universe of T.V. Olsen's West is one in which reason does not prevail and therefore all that happens is unpredictable, as it is also in life. All that remains to Olsen's battered and struggling protagonists, male and female alike, is their commitment to decency, to loyalty, to friendship, in a word to each other. The losses are great and irretrievable but the ordeals form a school for character that alone becomes decisive in an individual's life even if, as sometimes happens, he loses it.

There are no two characters alike in any Olsen story even if they have undergone similar experiences. Sara Carver in THE STALKING MOON is one kind of American woman who survived Indian captivity. Miss Cresta Lee in ARROW IN THE SUN (Doubleday, 1969) is a wholly different case. She is made of such stern stuff that living with an alcoholic father who abandoned her at eight to an orphanage did not daunt her any more than the two years of captivity she spent with the Cheyenne Indians as the wife of war chief, Spotted Wolf. She may not be a good shot with a pistol or a rifle, but she is clever and determined and manages, finally, to elude her Cheyenne captors. It was Ralph Nelson, director of the film version under the title SOLDIER BLUE (Avco-Embassy, 1970), who decided to append to this story a slaughter of helpless Indian women and children similar to the Sand Creek massacre. Olsen knew his history of the Indian wars too well, and had too much respect for the Indian nations that were once at war with the United States, to depict them repeatedly as helpless victims of a genocidal holocaust which, for the Vietnam War-era political activist, was found embodied in Dee Brown's BURY MY HEART AT WOUNDED KNEE (Holt, Rinehart, 1971), a popular account albeit with an equivalent slant to the kind of history of Rome Spartacus might have written.

For five years Olsen researched and wrote his first major historical novel, THERE WAS A SEASON (Doubleday, 1971), concerned with the young Jefferson Davis during the years 1828–1833 when he was a young Army lieutenant on the Wisconsin frontier and Davis's bittersweet love affair with Sarah Knox Taylor, daughter of Zachary Taylor, later hero of the Mexican War and President of the United States. Ted regarded it as his *magnum opus*. It was finally published in a paperback edition in 1994 by Leisure Books which has been systematically reprinting all of T. V. Olsen's novels.

As he continued to write Western stories, Olsen's horizons continued to broaden. Increasingly his male protagonists and female protagonists could only succeed when they pulled together, varying strengths in the one compensating for weaknesses in the other. He also opened the Western story to spiritual dimensions that have traditionally been shunned. The Navajo shaman, Adakhai, — the character's name was borrowed from Savage's LAND OF THE LAWLESS (Doubleday, 1951) — in THE GOLDEN CHANCE (Fawcett Gold Medal, 1992) is in touch with the spirits who rule the world. In DEADLY PURSUIT (Five Star, 1995) Adakhai is able to conjure visions both from the past and the future. As early as "The Strange Valley" in GREAT GHOST STORIES OF THE OLD WEST (Four Winds, 1968) edited by Betty Baker, Olsen began injecting elements of a metaphysical, meta-temporal, and supernatural nature into his fiction. They are surely to be found in "Jacob's Journal."

Ted Olsen and I were friends for twenty years. It was he who first introduced me to Les Savage, Jr.'s Western fiction. For his last years, I was his agent. In fact, while Les was my first estate client, Ted was my first living client. His sudden and unexpected death from myocardial infarction in 1993 was a devastating blow to me that has yet completely to heal. I found among his papers in the little cottage where he did his writing four unpublished novels in long-hand and four unpublished short stories. So even if death claimed him too early, new Olsen stories will remain forthcoming into the new century. Bill Pronzini had suggested to Ted that there should be another collection of his short fiction. The previous one was WESTWARD THEY RODE (Ace, 1976). It is due to this suggestion that Ted took time between novels to write the story that follows. It was first published posthumously in *Louis L'Amour Western Magazine* (11/94) and will eventually be the title story in an Olsen short Western fiction collection (there are sufficient stories for two more such book-length collections).

"…Olsen is an efficient and compelling storyteller who more often than not uses his skill to touch on serious themes," Joe R. Lansdale concluded in TWENTIETH CENTURY WESTERN WRITERS (St. James, Press, 1991). "…I can not but feel with the right press Olsen could command the position currently enjoyed by the late Louis L'Amour as America's most popular and foremost author of traditional Western novels." Yet, even having said that much, Lansdale may not have gone far enough since "traditional" is not a meaningful adjective when surveying Olsen's contributions to the Western story. He succeeded by going beyond traditional boundaries in almost all that he wrote. In common with such very, very select company as Les Savage, Jr., Bill Gulick, and Lewis B. Patten, Olsen never published a story that is less than very good and most are better than that. Were it not that the Western story has always been classed as category fiction, it would have been possible before this late date to recognize in T.V. Olsen one of the outstanding American literary novelists of the late 20th Century as well as one of the brightest lights in the firmament of the Western story, a man whose modesty and reclusiveness worked at odds, always, with the wide readership his fiction deserved and will continue to deserve far into the future.

JACOB'S JOURNAL
1994

June 8, 1886

    Sarah is dead. I killed her with my own hands and buried her beneath tons of rock. I know she is dead. Yet this forenoon I saw her...alive?

    I do not know. But I saw her as clearly as I see the page on which I indite these words.

    I was crossing from the commandant's office to the agency house — a long-ish walk of perhaps two hundred yards — when I became aware of being watched. Turning my head, I saw her. A woman standing on the prickly pear-and-chaparral-covered rise a little south of the agency house.

    At first I took only passing note, supposing her to be the wife of one of Fort Bloodworth's officers or enlisted men. But something in the way she stood, ab-solutely motionless and watching me, as I believed, arrested my attention. Leaving the well-worn path, I started across the intervening hundred or so yards of nearly barren ground toward her.

    I was quite close before I recognized her but, when I did, recognition came unmistakably. The sunlight lay full on her face and on the brightness of her red-gold hair.

    It was Sarah.

    I stopped, petrified with fear and incomprehension. Either I was experienc-ing an hallucination or I was a victim of some gigantic hoax. But the latter pos-sibility, at least, seemed out of the question. None but I — I was positive — knew the truth behind my wife's sudden disappearance.

    Screwing up my courage, I advanced slowly toward her. I was nearly to the rise when my nerve broke utterly and I shouted her name. Screamed it, more than likely.

    Until that moment she had neither moved nor changed her expression by a hair's breadth. It was as severe and aloof as — damn her soul! — Sarah had so long been toward me.

    Now I saw her smile. A lovely and alluring smile, one such as I had rarely seen on her face during our years together. And while she smiled, she slowly raised an arm and beckoned to me. Then she turned, not hurrying, and walked over the crest of the rise and out of sight.

    When I had scrambled to its top, she was nowhere to be seen. She had van-

ished as if the rocky soil and scant vegetation had swallowed her up. Impossible! When I looked for any tracks which might help solve the riddle, I found nothing, not even the trace of a footprint. Still, the ground was so stony and impervious to ordinary sign that even a skilled tracker might have found nothing. Except....

The fact comes to mind only now. As though, earlier, my mind had rejected the knowing. A hot wind was blowing off the desert, strongly enough to whip particles against my face. The woman on the knoll wore a voluminous dress with a wide skirt, identical to that in which I buried Sarah.

Yet in all the time I saw her, the woman's clothing, the drape of its fabric, was unstirring in the blast of wind. As though the wind could not touch her, could not have its way with her in any particular....

With the last few sentences, the bold sprawl of Jacob Creed's rapid writing turned into a shaky, dashed-off waver. Then the entry suddenly ended.

Major Phineas Casement had been reading slowly aloud from the leatherbound journal he had slipped open at random, pausing often to squint at the words, swearing and muttering. Now he said a disgusted oath, slapped the journal shut, and tossed it on his desk.

"Good God, what a pack of nonsense! Sheer balderdash. The fellow must have been deranged."

"Possibly, sir," said Lieutenant Mayberly. "But every entry he made in that book, if you except this one persistent delusion, has proved out to a detail."

"I'm sure, Mr. Mayberly, I'm sure. That fine probing intellect of yours would do its damnedest to ferret out the whole truth, no matter where it led."

Major Casement reached for the humidor on his desk, extracted a cigar, and offered the humidor to Mayberly with an impatient thrust of his hand. Politely, as Casement had known he would, the lieutenant refused a cigar.

Major Casement pushed his swivel chair back from his desk and rose to his feet, grimacing as the movement peeled his blouse sweatily away from his back and paunch. Arizona Territory — Christ! you'd think that after a dozen years of being stationed at one or another of its raw frontier outposts, a man would be used to the furnace heat of its relentless summers.

He lifted a foot onto the chair, struck a match on the heel of his high cavalry boot, and lighted the cigar, glancing enviously at the younger officer, seated at ease in the room's only other chair.

Mayberly looked as cool as a January thaw. His double-breasted blue miner's blouse and blue trousers, with the yellow cavalry stripe down the outseams, were hardly stained by dust, not at all by sweat. His black, neatly blocked campaign hat rested on the knee of his crossed leg; his dark hair was neatly parted above a sober, cleft-chinned face. The subaltern was only a year out of West Point; Fort Bloodworth was his first assignment. Yet he'd blended into this inhospitable land with the adaptability of a chuckwalla lizard. A leather dispatch case was propped against his chair.

Major Casement swiped a hand over his sweat-dewed, nearly bald head, clamped the cigar between his bulldog jaws, and slowly paced his narrow office, up and down. "The fellow was a heavy drinker, I'm told. How much of that *persistent delusion* of his came out of a bottle?"

"There may or may not be a way of telling, sir." Lieutenant Mayberly leaned forward to take Creed's journal from the desk. He flipped backward through the pages. "In any case, the journal entries which are of main concern to us begin at a much earlier date. May I quote from them?"

Major Casement rolled out an irritable plume of smoke.

It would be his duty to write up a full report on the whole unsavory mess to the Secretary of War and file a duplicate report with the U.S. Department of the Interior, since Jacob Creed had been the agent assigned to one of the hellholes they called their Indian reservations. Before doing so, the major would need as thorough a briefing as possible from his ultracompetent aide, Mayberly, whom he'd ordered to investigate the almost simultaneous deaths of Agent Jacob Creed and Colonel Richard Dandridge, Fort Bloodworth's late commandant. Major Casement had been hastily dispatched here to replace Dandridge, and Mayberly had already given the major a sketchy report on his findings.

"By all means, Mr. Mayberly," Casement said sourly. "The damned fellow's hand is so execrable I could scarcely make out the words. Read it aloud, if you please...."

May 17, 1886

Today, after two months at this God-forgotten post, cautiously trying the tempers of the officers at Fort Bloodworth as well as those of the headmen on the adjacent reservation, I made my approach to Colonel Dandridge. Not only is he in the ideal position to abet my scheme, he possesses the requisite qualities to implement it.

Beneath his façade of an efficient and highly regarded career officer (President Lincoln himself bestowed a Medal of Honor on him during the late conflict), Dandridge is a savagely bitter and disillusioned man. This in consequence of his being several times passed over for advancement to a brigadier generalship, due to favoritism toward officers of far lesser qualification who were, nevertheless, politically well situated....

The echo of taps died away in the gray twilight. Lamps winked out as darkness closed over the parade ground of Fort Bloodworth. From the Chiricahua reservation to the south drifted the lone, keening bark of a camp dog.

Jacob Creed had locked up his sutler's post. Standing on the porch, teetering gently back and forth on his heels, feeling mellow as all hell, he took an embossed whiskey flask from his coat pocket, uncapped it and took a small swig.

Creed was a bearded, thick-set man whose coarsened features and bloodshot eyes showed little of his genteel background. His belly was badly burning from the effects of intermittent drinks he'd consumed during a day of haggling with the Apaches who came to trade at his post. By now the damned siwashes should be aware that no one left Jacob Creed on the short end of a trade. Yet they never ceased trying. Born hoss-traders (as well as hoss-stealers) they were. All the bastards were.

Creed chuckled quietly. He treated himself to another pull at the flask. Things would be different from now on. A hell of a lot different.

As to bartering with him, the Apaches had little choice. Post trader Jacob Creed was also the Indian agent for the San Lazaro Reservation. In addition to his government salary, he received an allowance of federal funds to buy steers from local cattle ranches to furnish the monthly beef ration allotted the reservation Chiricahuas.

Behind the combination trading post and agency headquarters was a cattle corral. An issue chute was set up across the weighing scales adjoining the corral. And the steers were driven through the chute where the head of each family presented his ration ticket, had it stamped, and watched his cattle being weighed.

Colonel Richard Dandridge, as the fort C.O., was required to add his official presence to the weighing-out but, after their conference this morning, that would be a mere formality. Seething with his private bitterness, the aging career officer had been almost eagerly amenable to Creed's proposal.

For the hundredth time, Creed chuckled over the development.

It was simple. So damned simple. From now on he would buy up the poorest of the cull steers the ranches had for less than half the ordinary price, then pocket the balance of allotted moneys. A simple matter, also, to rig the scales so that the sorriest steer would be well within the minimum poundage allowed. One-third of Creed's swindled government funds would keep Colonel Dandridge's bitter-thin mouth silent. And the Apaches, unable to subsist on gaunt, stringy, possibly diseased beef, would be forced to trade at Creed's post for supplies.

Jacob Creed took another mild swig from his flask, capped it, and put it away. He took a step off the porch and damned near fell on his face.

Jesus! Was he that drunk?

Sure he was.

Why had he made the deal with Dandridge? Sold whatever dregs of gentle birthright he could still lay claim to for a mess of conspiratorial pottage?

Then, reflecting on Sarah and the miserable course his life with her had taken, he thought: *Why should I give a solitary shit?*

He straightened upright and lurched homeward along the sandy, thin-worn path to the agency house beyond the fort, considering (as he often did) ways in which he could repay her treatment of him.

Creed grinned crookedly. There was one sure-as-hell way....

Even the most incorruptible man, when all his hopes and ideals have been repeatedly dashed by adverse fortune, may become approachable....

"Damn the fellow's complacency!" Major Casement cut disgustedly into his subordinate's reading. "Did he fancy that *his* reason was any better or different from that of the man he bribed?"

Mayberly raised his brows. "Probably not, sir. I think it was Creed's wry, oblique way of telling himself as much. As I suggested earlier, his difficulty with his wife must have been a powerful goad behind all his actions."

"M'm." Casement rolled the cigar from one side of his mouth to the other. "Powerful enough to drive him to murder. Go on, Mr. Mayberly."

Again the lieutenant flipped back through the pages. "I think, in the light of subsequent developments, that this entry is a revealing one, sir. It was made on the day Creed arrived with his wife on the stage from Silverton to take over duties at the San Lazaro Agency...."

March 12, 1886

The conditions at our new post are not nearly as desolate as we had feared. The reservation itself is situated at a considerable height above the desert lowland to the south, to which much of the reservation land forms a striking contrast. Numerous stands of giant pine lend a cool and indeed attractive aspect to our new home, although they are interspersed with terraced open flats which, I am told, have defied the sorry efforts of my reservation wards to farm them. As if we could, in a brief decade or so, transform a race of nomadic warriors, barely subdued by us, into tillers of the soil!

The agency house itself is a gratifying surprise to us. I do not know what we expected to dwell in — perhaps an oversized hut of baked adobe. However, the agent who preceded me at this post was James Montoya, a man — I was told — of pure Spanish descent and a true aristocrata. *Clearly he chose to build after the fashion of his* hidalgo *forebears and, with all the splendid pine roundabout, found no need to build of stone or mud.*

The squared giant timbers that compose both the inner and outer walls were hand-shaped by adze and drawknife, fitted so beautifully together that one can hardly slide a knife blade between them, and the tiers of logs are fastened at all ends and corners with vertical iron rods. It must have cost him a pretty penny to import the highly skilled labor necessary to put up such an edifice. Most of the furnishings went with Montoya when he departed, but what remains indicates that they were opulent and costly. I was told, however, that his people have money. Of course the raw timber was free for the taking, and the rough labor (Indians and mestizos, no doubt) to cut the trees and trim the logs and transport them to the spot could be hired cheaply.

Salud, Don Jaime: Your family must have been a large one. (As is more often the case than not, of course, with these Papists.) There are no less than a dozen spacious rooms, including six chambers on the second floor, three to a side with a hallway dividing them. Of particular interest are the two wide central balconies with their iron-wrought grillwork railings. Built off the center rooms on either second-story side of the house, one faces north, the other south. Thus, I should imagine, an occupant might enjoy sun or shade on almost any day, according to his preference.

Even Sarah seems delighted with the house and its piney surroundings, and she is particularly taken with those charming balconies. Could this herald a change for the better in the steady dissolution of our married life? One can only hope....

"Obviously it didn't." Major Casement plumped himself back into his chair, folding his hands over his paunch. "Eh?"

"No, sir." Mayberly turned a block of pages, going forward in the journal now. "Here's his entry for June 4th. It reads simply, 'Damn Sarah: Damn her soul to eternal hell: Last night....'"

"That's all?"

Mayberly nodded. "His temper reached such a passion that his pen-nib slashed through the paper at that point, and a scattering of ink blots suggests that he flung the pen down in a rage. Whatever provoked the outburst apparently occurred on the previous day or evening. From the shakiness of the writing, I should say he was barely recovered from a monumental debauch."

Major Casement unlaced his fingers, tapping them on his paunch. "No entry for that date...June 3?"

"None, sir. The journal is full of gaps and omissions...for our purpose, at least. We can only speculate on the missing parts. My inquiries among our own garrison personnel turned up a few things that may help fill in the picture."

"Such as?"

"Well, it seems that Mrs. Creed *did* take a hankering to those second-floor balconies. She loved to sit of an afternoon on the one that faces north...on the side toward the fort."

"Is that where...?"

"Yes, sir. Where Creed fell through the nailed-shut door."

Major Casement frowned. "I haven't paid a lot of notice to the agency house, but I'd assumed that it was a boarded-up window he went through. So there *was* a balcony there?"

"Until Creed had it torn off, sir. Lieutenant Verlain's wife told me that Mrs. Creed preferred the north balcony because it was cool and shaded in the afternoon. She was careful never to expose her creamy complexion, of which she was very proud, to the sun for any great time. In any event she would sit out and read or else let down her hair and brush it, a lengthy ritual." Lieutenant Mayberly cleared his throat. "Seems that some of our chaps at the fort...both officers and enlisted men...would get out field glasses and watch her from the barracks windows. It became a daily piece of business hereabouts."

"Did it now!"

"Sir, there's something mighty provocative in the sight of a beautiful woman brushing out her hair." Mayberly reached in his dispatch case and took out a photograph which he handed across the desk. "That is Mrs. Creed. A picture I found in her husband's effects. Mrs. Verlain verifies it is a recent one. You can't tell from this, of course, but her hair was very long and shining...like a waterfall of reddish gold, Mrs. Verlain put it."

Casement gazed long at the photograph. "A looker, Mr. Mayberly. A looker, all right. Creed had reason to be jealous...if that is why he had the balcony removed."

"That's why, sir. And he had the door that opened out on it nailed shut. For a while after that, Mrs. Verlain claims, Mrs. Creed had recourse to the south balcony, holding a parasol against the scorching sun. But it was awkward and uncomfortable and she soon abandoned the practice...."

Creed sat in the deepening shadows of his sutler's store, drinking and brooding. He was coatless, his single badge of dignity removed, and his shirtsleeves were rolled up. Now and then he hooked his thumb into the ear of a whiskey jug, tilted it on a thick, hairy forearm, put it to his lips and drank deeply, afterward wiping his mouth on the back of his other forearm. He was not drinking idly. He was drinking to get deeply and sullenly drunk.

Damn the woman! He'd never used to drink like this.

Where had it started? When?

Ten years ago and in Washington City, he supposed muddily, if you wanted to go back that long and far. To the beginning of a marriage. It had seemed an ideal match, everyone agreed. He was the young scion of an old New York family and, as the personal secretary of a U. S. senator, privy to secrets at the very pulse of power, destined for great things. She was the Senator's lovely socialite daughter, and they were thrown often and naturally into company.

The engagement had been as brief as propriety allowed, the wedding lavish and festive, and the aftermath stained with acid. Sarah's ideas of Perfect Marriage were gleaned from the purported precepts of HRM Victoria, discreet advice in *Godey's Lady's Book,* and murky tidbits from her mother ("A woman must learn *submission* to her husband, my dear, no matter how demanding he may seem.'') All of this, along with too much festive champagne, had Sarah in a mildly hysterical state by the end of their wedding day. And Creed remembered his nuptial night vividly. The words she had screamed at him: "Oh my God, I never dreamed...*you hairy beast!*"

Words that still cut his memory like blades. Where could a marriage go from there except downhill?

Sarah had soon learned the submission that her mother had recommended. It was all that was required of her and all that she damned well intended to give. Not bad if a man could pleasure himself by embracing a waxen statue, but Creed had found and taken his pleasures elsewhere. Along with a concomitant erosion not only of his married life but of his career in government service.

The pit of his descending fortunes had been reached two years ago, with his appointment as agent to the tiny blister patch of a Jicarillo reservation south of here. Granted, his new assignment to the big San Lazaro reservation was a step back up. But then, once you'd reached the lowest rung on a ladder, where could you go?

You could fall off it on your face, Creed thought with the humor of stark misery, and took another pull at the jug, draining it.

A trapped fly had been buzzing and batting monotonously against the fly-blown window beside his head. Suddenly furious, Creed took a backhand swipe at it with his right hand, shattering the glass.

"Goddammit all to hell!"

He stared at his badly bleeding hand for a half minute, letting out a string of ripe oaths. Then, awkwardly left-handed, he bound the cut up with his handkerchief. It did little to check the bleeding.

He got off the petulant jag-end of his temper by smashing the empty jug on the packed-clay floor. Then he closed up for the night, not bothering to lock the door, and maneuvered foggily across the parade ground. Mulrooney, Troop L's bugler, gave him a bad start by suddenly sounding tattoo just a few yards away. Creed was barely sensible enough to curb his impulse to call the bull-chested Mulrooney a God-dam' bog-trotting mick ————.

He wove his way home along the narrow trail, barged into the agency house, tramped through the front and back parlors and into the kitchen, bawling, *"Sarah!"*

"You needn't shout. But as pixilated as you are, I suppose you wouldn't know the difference."

Creed hauled up in the doorway, glaring at her. Sarah was seated at the small kitchen table, picking at a plate of leftover chicken and biscuits. She gave him a radiant, meaningless smile and nibbled daintily at a biscuit.

"Where's my supper, Goddammit!?"

"You've already drunk it, haven't you?"

Creed started to lurch forward, but the whiskey had caught up to him with a vengeance. He had to grab at the doorjamb for support. "Goddammit...."

"Don't tax your vocabulary, dear. If you have anything to tell me, you might be more at home, not to say lucid, with words of one syllable. Certainly not three."

Oh, Christ! Creed dropped his hot forehead against his bent forearm, braced against the doorjamb. *Ever since he'd had the damned balcony torn off!* Up till then, at least, they had always been tolerably polite, if cool, toward one another. He remembered her outraged cry as Miguel Ortez, the local handyman-of-all-trades whom he'd hired to demolish the balcony, had begun his work.

"Please don't, Jacob! I didn't know those men at the fort were...were spying on me. You can't blame me! Please...I love that balcony!"

Creed had felt a grim satisfaction in ignoring her plea. It was something to have finally broken through her cool and regal façade. All the years of his philandering and her silent knowledge of it had never touched a nerve. At least not so it showed. Now she was wringing her hands, pleading, driven literally to tears. And he'd grinned at her, unspeaking, while they'd listened to the shriek of pulled nails and the wrenching of boards as the destruction went on.

Afterward Sarah had locked herself in her room. Locked her door against him for the first time. Next morning, when he'd come down to breakfast, Sarah was composed and calm-eyed, even humming a little, as she set out a meal for herself alone. When he'd angrily asked where his breakfast was, she'd given him a gentle smile and said nothing as she began to eat.

It was pretty much how things had gone ever since. They never took their meals together. If Sarah chanced to fix more than she felt like eating, she'd leave the remainder on a plate for him. By the time he got home, it would be cold and marbled with grease: a more pointed sign of her contempt than when she left nothing at all for him. Always a meticulous housekeeper, she now abandoned any pretense at housekeeping except for keeping her own bedchamber tidy and washing her own clothes and sheets. Creed abhorred the notion of lowering himself to housework. Although he knew he'd be giving the garrison gossips a field day, he hired Dolores Ortez, Miguel's wife, to clean the place once a week, wash the stacks of dirty dishes, and launder his clothes and bedding.

Creed raised his head and stared at Sarah. She patted her lips with a napkin and rose to her feet. Lamplight ran a silken caress over the red-gold corona of her hair. Smiling faintly, she said: "Do try to be less casual, dear. Your hand is dripping all over the floor."

Somehow it tripped off the last cinch on Creed's temper. In all their years together, however angry and frustrated he'd become, he had never laid a violent hand on her.

Suddenly now, red rage sizzled in his brain. It was uncontrollable. With a throaty growl he surged forward, gripped the edge of the table between them in both hands and flung it aside. It caromed against the wall with a crash of shattering dishes.

As easily as if she'd been expecting this, Sarah slipped around and past him, graceful as a wraith. She paused in the doorway and gave a soft, taunting laugh.

"Temper, Jakey. Is that any way for a petty household tyrant to behave?"

Creed swung wildly around and after her. Sarah glided away, going through the back parlor and up the oak-balustraded staircase.

Creed's vision began to fuzz away as he stumblingly reached the staircase. Then everything tilted crazily in his sight. He wasn't aware of falling, but suddenly his chin crashed against the third rise from the bottom.

Befuddledly he lifted his head, waggling it back and forth, tasting blood. He felt no pain, but knew he had bitten through his tongue. Above him, Sarah stood at the head of the stairs. He had never seen a smile so radiant.

"Sweet dreams, Jacob. You'll have them exactly where you're lying now, I suspect. *Sic semper tyrannis*."

She blew him a kiss and vanished into the upstairs hallway. Creed's head dropped; his chin hit the rise again. The three inside bolts on Sarah's door shot loudly, crisply into place as she secured them. Those were the last sounds Jacob Creed heard before he passed out....

↔

June 7, 1886

I have done the deed.

After several days of mulling over what further indignities I might inflict on that ivory-skinned bitch, I came to the conclusion that there were none. She was now armored in her mind against whatever I might do. There was no recourse left me but the final one. The most final of all.

The longer I mulled on how pleasant it would be to take that cool white throat between my hands, to crush it to jelly between my hands, the more forcefully the idea seized me. Sarah must die. And no way of encompassing her end could be more gratifying.

Yesterday I did not drink at all. I must be as keen and cold as steel to perpetrate the deed. I must make no mistake, leave no sign that might be traced to me. My only fear was that without the crutch of strong drink, my determination might waver at the last moment.

It did not.

I returned home at an early hour to be sure of arriving before she might retire behind the locked door of her chamber. I found her at supper. I throttled her in the midst of one of her tart and supercilious remarks.

God, but it felt wonderful. I could feel the strength coursing through my body into my hands, increasing momentarily, as I watched her face purple into death.

She scratched my hands rather badly, trying to tear them from her throat, but that is a trifle. The marks will soon heal. Let anyone, should I be suspect, prove how I came by them.

Making sure the body will never be found presented no great difficulty. I had already weighed the matter carefully. There was a place ideal for my purpose. Not five hundred yards east of the agency house is a deep arroyo lined with cutbanks of crumbling rock. At one spot was an overhang of massive rubble that, with a little assistance, would collapse in a slide of rocks so heavy that no flash flood would ever undermine them.

Accordingly, well after taps sounded, I left the agency house with the body across my shoulders, clinging to deep shadows against the light of a quarter moon. I laid her out (with hands folded on her bosom; peace be to her shade!) at the bottom of the arroyo beneath the cutbank. Ascending it, I struggled to pry loose a key rock that I was certain, if dislodged, would bring the whole mass of rubble crashing down.

It was quickly done and the evidence of my deed buried forever. The pile of tumbled boulders looks as if it might have been thus for a thousand years....

"The devil," muttered Major Casement. "And the story he gave out was that his wife simply...disappeared?"

"Yes, sir," said Mayberly. "No elaborate cover story. He was supremely confident. What was there that might prove otherwise?"

Casement shook his head slowly. "But to record the act with all incriminating detail in that journal. He *must* have been mad!"

"Well, sir, I've read that a madman may try to collect his scattered thoughts by writing them down. Of course he had the journal well concealed and had no reason to believe anyone would see it while he still lived...in which assumption he was correct. I spent most of a day searching the agency house for clues, for evidence of any sort, before I located this volume. It was in a hidden compartment at the base of an armoire in his room."

"And it enabled you to look for...and find...the remains of Mrs. Creed?"

"Yes, sir. Had only the vague description he gives here to go on. As Creed mentions, there was nothing but tumbled rock to indicate the site, and that could describe almost any spot the length of the arroyo. Which is a quarter mile long, more or less. So I enlisted the aid of our garrison's chief scout, Joe Tana. He is full-blood Pima."

"M'm. One of those fellows could pick up sign on the burned-out lid of hell. Which," the major added sourly, "a good piece of this country comes near to being. Go on."

"Lord knows how Joe Tana found the place, but he did. Then I assigned a half dozen of our troopers to dig through the rubble. After a couple hours of wrestling giant boulders away, they uncovered the body."

"It was identifiable?"

"Just barely, sir. The fall of rock had crushed it beyond facial or physical recognition. And it had been there for well over a month. Only the clothing gave indication of sex." Mayberly paused, looking down at the journal. "The only sure identification was the hair that both her husband's journal and Mrs. Verlain describe so...vividly."

"'Like a waterfall of reddish gold'?"

"Yes, sir. You can't imagine...."

Major Casement grimaced. "Unfortunately, I can. Go on, Mr. Mayberly."

"His entry for the following day records his first seeing the apparition of his wife." Mayberly flipped a few more pages. "Then a week later, this...."

June 15, 1886

Came to an understanding with Colonel Dandridge today. Following Sarah's disappearance, which I duly reported, he ordered patrols out to search for her. When they turned up not a trace, he was inclined to feel that I knew more than I had divulged and bluntly told me so. Wherefore I told him just as bluntly that I have written a full account of our 'arrangement' anent the misappropriated government funds for the Apache beef ration and sent it under seal to my attorney in a city I did not name, with instructions that it be opened in the event of my death. I could as easily add a proviso that if I were to suffer imprisonment or detainment, or be held incommunicado *in any way, it should be opened. In that case I would have nothing to lose. Dandridge...everything....*

Major Casement lifted a quizzical brow. "Was there such a statement?"

Mayberly shrugged. "Apparently Colonel Dandridge believed so, as there's nothing to indicate that he took any action then or later. However, Creed has been dead for weeks, the news widely published, and no attorney, no claimant to his estate, has come forward. I've found no will and no mention of any living relative."

Casement sighed. "Then?"

"All the entries for several weeks thereafter...when he troubled to make them...deal with mundane, everyday matters. As though he had casually laid aside the very memory of his wife. Then...," Mayberly turned a section of pages to another marked place, "we come suddenly to the following...."

July 20, 1886

The gradual cessation of heavy drinking has done wonders for the well-being of my mind and body. Indeed, my sexual vigor is far greater than it has been in years! Not only is this manifest in the state of my flesh, but my attention to comely females has intensified, at times almost to a frenzy I cannot control.

A liaison with one of the women of the fort, the wife or daughter of an officer or enlisted man, even if it could be managed, would be both difficult and dan-

gerous to undertake. It is out of the question. Nor am I inclined, any longer, to cajole and flatter even a willing female. What God-damned bitches women are. I shall never again make the least obeisance to gain the favor of any of them.

Another solution to my need has formed itself in my mind. I have examined it from every side and see no reason why it cannot be accomplished. In fact I shall implement it this very day....

Creed squatted on his hunkers in front of the brush *wickiup* of Sal Juan, a leading headman of the San Lazaro Apaches. Facing him in a similar crouch, Sal Juan was a wolf-gaunt man whose barrel chest strained his calico shirt. His clean shoulder-length hair was streaked with gray, but the lines graven in his mahogany face told more of harsh living than of age.

Sal Juan's eyes were like obsidian chips and they smoldered with hatred. He had reason to hate, as Creed was unconcernedly aware, and he knew that a few short years ago Sal Juan — one of the fiercest of Apache war chiefs — would have killed him without hesitation for what he had just proposed. But Sal Juan's war-trailing days were past. He had surrendered to the *pinda-likoyes,* the white-eyes, so that the pitiful remnant of his half-starved band might be spared a final annihilation.

Presently he lowered his eyes, scooped up a handful of dirt and juggled it in his palm. "What will *Nantan* Creed give to take the daughter of Sal Juan as wife?"

"Horses. Goods." His years on the Jicarillo reservation had given Creed an easy command of the slush-mouthed Apache tongue. "What do you ask?"

Sal Juan raised his hate-filled eyes. "This thing you know as well as I."

"Cattle?"

"Fat cattle. For all the people of the *Be-don-ko-he.* From this time forward we will have fat cattle."

Creed dipped his head solemnly. "Fat cattle for all the people of the Chiricahua from this time forward. It will be as Sal Juan says."

Dandridge wouldn't go for his reneging on their bargain, he knew amusedly. But he wouldn't lift a damned finger to prevent it, either. He couldn't threaten Jacob Creed with anything Creed couldn't turn against him just as effectively. Not while he believed that a certain incriminating statement was in the possession of Creed's attorney.

What attorney? Creed laughed silently at the thought. Sal Juan again bent his head, his face a stone mask. Creed squatted patiently, letting him have all the time he wanted.

Creed shuttled his gaze past the headman to the girl. She was crouched on her heels grinding corn in a stone *metate* and her slim figure was lost in her shapeless camp dress.

But on other visits here he'd seen her moving about at one chore or another, walking graceful as a young willow, the lissome outlines of her body showing through the dress, letting you visualize all her tawny loveliness: gold-skinned, sweet-curving, secret-hollowed. Sweet sixteen and bursting with the just-ripened juices of her youth.

God. Just thinking of her was enough to make his mouth go dry, his hands grow moist. This close, even, seeing her ungracefully squatted at her squaw's work, set up a wild thunder in his blood.

"*Sons-ee-ah-ray* is a good daughter," Sal Juan said presently. "She is strong and works hard. She will breed strong sons."

Creed inclined his chin appreciatively. "This thing I believe."

"A young man called *Gian-nah-tah* has tied his pony before my lodge."

"Has the daughter of Sal Juan taken it to water?"

"Yes. It is her will."

"And Sal Juan's will? How many ponies can the young man give him?"

The headman held up all the fingers of one hand.

Creed spread the fingers of both hands. "I will give Sal Juan this number of ponies."

Supplementing Apache words with an English number, Sal Juan said flatly: "*Nantan* Creed will give seven times that number."

"Three times."

"Six times that number."

"Five times."

"Four."

"No. Five times that number."

Creed nodded. "Five times that number and fat cattle for all the *Be-don-ko-he* from this time forward. It is done?"

Sal Juan was silent. The gift of ponies weighed far less with him, Creed knew, than the welfare of his band. The burden of leadership outweighed even his hatred of Creed. Yet he hesitated.

Creed repeated, "It is done?"

"There is the chief of pony soldiers."

Creed let his beard part in a slow smile. "I tell you what, old man," he said in English. "You just leave *Nantan* Dandridge to me, all right?"

"You, him," Sal Juan said in the same language. "You dogshit. Both you dogshit. I spit on you."

Still smiling, Creed said mildly, "Uh-uh. No you won't. You think your folks have had it bad up till now? You've hardly seen the start of how bad I can make it."

Sal Juan made a fist around the handful of dirt.

Creed said patiently, "It is done?"

The headman did not reply. Something else was troubling him, Creed realized. Giving up a hard-working daughter? Creed doubted it. Sal Juan had his share of women: two wives and a couple more unmarried daughters, neither of them a looker. But Apache standards of beauty were different from whites', and Sal Juan could easily spare one daughter.

"I have wealth," said Creed. "The daughter of Sal Juan will be treated well."

"It is another thing." Abruptly Sal Juan rose to his stocky height. "We will speak with *Skin-ya.*"

Creed got up too, hiding his irritation. *Skin-ya,* that dried-up old buzzard bait! But Apache life was colored with superstitions of every hue. Signs and omens dictated the Apache's choices and actions. Nothing important was undertaken against the wishes of the prevailing spirits. These spoke most trenchantly through the *izze-nantan,* the man of medicine. So *Skin-ya,* the local crucible of mumbo-jumbo, must be consulted.

As he and Sal Juan passed through the village, drowsing in the midday sun, Creed held the girl hungrily in his mind's eye. *Sons-ee-ah-ray.* Morning Star. That's what the name meant and that's what he'd call her. He thought of the consternation he'd cause among the white contingent at the fort by taking a bride so soon after Sarah's disappearance. *A redskin bride!* The thought pleased him so much that he nearly laughed aloud.

As to the promise of a fair cattle issue he'd given Sal Juan, he would keep it for a while. As long as it suited him or as long as it proved convenient. You could never tell. The girl was a good worker; she'd fix his meals and keep that rat's nest of an agency house cleaned up. But she might go all to suet in a few years, the way a lot of these squaws did. In that case....

They found *Skin-ya* seated cross-legged before his *wickiup,* head bent in meditation. Naked save for a breechclout, his wrinkled hide dyed to the neutral color of the arid land which had sustained him for eighty summers or more, he did not look up as the two men hunkered down facing him. He seemed in a trance. At last, slowly, he raised his eyes. They sparkled blackly in his shriveled mummy's face.

"Sal Juan," he husked, "would know the will of the *chedens* in the matter of his daughter's marriage."

Creed stared. "How did you...?"

Sal Juan cut him off with a chopping motion of his hand. "Will *Skin-ya* make the medicine?"

Skin-ya fumbled inside a buckskin bag and took out the accouterments of his craft, spreading them on the ground. A fragment of lightning-riven wood, a root, a stone, a bit of turquoise, a glass bead, and a small square of buckskin painted with cabalistic symbols. He sprinkled them with *hoddentin,* the sacred powder ground from maguey. He sprinkled *hoddentin* on himself, on Creed, on Sal Juan; he scattered *hoddentin* to the four winds.

The ancient shaman sat in silence for a long time, eyes closed. He opened them suddenly, eyeing Creed. "There is a smell of *tats-an* about the *pinda-likove*. Also he walks with a ghost."

Sal Juan said, "What of *Sons-ee-ah-ray?*"

"Would Sal Juan wed his daughter to one who is *tats-an?*"

"I am alive," Creed said harshly.

"Soon you will be *tats-an*. You will not be present."

Jesus. These siwashes had such a damned polite way of saying you'd be dead before long. "*How?*" he spat.

Skin-ya struck his own neck sharply with the edge of his palm and let his head hang grotesquely to one side.

"You lie," Creed said coldly.

"The white-eyes walks with a ghost," *Skin-ya* repeated imperturbably. "The *cheden* of a woman."

He raised a scrawny arm and pointed.

Sarah stood on a barren rise not thirty feet away. Heat danced on the flinty slope and he could see its shimmering waves *through* her body; they made it shimmer and waver too.

She smiled and beckoned to him.

With a hoarse cry he lunged to his feet and stumbled toward the rise and up it. The loose soil cascaded away under his driving feet and sent him plunging on his belly. He lay unmoving and stared. Before his eyes the smiling form grew dim and slowly faded and was gone....

...Sarah. Then I did not imagine the other time. But that was on the day after the night I killed her, well over a month ago. Why has she come back? What does she....

"Balderdash!"

Major Casement's cigar had gone out some time ago. He took the wet stub from his mouth and eyed it distastefully. "You've questioned these Apaches, of course?"

Lieutenant Mayberly nodded soberly. "Sal Juan says he saw nothing. But he believes *Skin-ya* and Creed did."

Casement snorted. "And I suppose the old charlatan *insists* he did?"

"Well...," Mayberly nodded at the photograph of Sarah Creed on the commandant's desk. "I showed that to *Skin-ya* and asked if he had ever seen the woman. He said that was *her*...the ghost that walked with Creed."

"Preposterous! Do *you*...?"

"Sir, I've merely reported what I was able to find out."

"All right...all right!"

"There's a little more. For the next day. His last entry."

"Very well." The major gestured resignedly with his cigar stub. "Get it over with, Mister...."

July 21, 1886
After yesterday's experience in the village, I had no taste for returning home. I dreaded the prospect. What might I now encounter in the very house where I killed her?

I cannot doubt that I actually saw the abomination, for Skin-ya saw it first and directed my attention to it. Badly shaken, I returned to my store and steeped myself to the eyebrows in booze. It gave me the courage to return to the house where, in drunken hallucination, I might easily have seen the apparition again.

But I did not.

I have only the vaguest memory of getting out my journal and recording my second entry of the day, a lengthy and rambling one to be sure. Now, looking back over what I wrote at the time, I have tried to determine how much of it is fact, how much of it fancy.

I can no longer tell. My thoughts are too confounded.

Tonight I must not drink. I must go home cold and clear of head and confront whatever is there, surely and finally. I know something is there. But I must have the truth —

Creed scribbled the last words with an impatient flourish. He was standing at a long counter of his sutler's store, the journal spread open before him. For a moment, pen poised in hand, he glanced over what he had just written. By now it was dark enough so that he had to squint to make it out.

What more was there to say?

Impatiently he thrust the pen back in the inkstand, closed the journal, and thrust it into his coat pocket. Then he skirted the counter and headed for the door, preparatory to locking up.

Creed paused. A sly tongue of thirst licked at his belly.

Liquid courage. Why not? He could use some. He turned quickly back to the counter, reached under it and pulled out a bottle of Old Crow. The best. Saved for a notable occasion. Perhaps now.

No, Goddammit!

Resolutely he stowed the bottle back out of sight. It was a time of reckoning. He had to be certain. No false courage. And no drink-inspired delusions.

Creed locked the door behind him and tramped hurriedly across Fort Bloodworth's parade ground. It was long after tattoo; all lights were out. The path to the agency house was paved by moonglow. Creed kept his head bent, not looking at the dark masses of brush to either side, as though he feared what he might see.

Is it all a damned trick? Couldn't it be a God-damned trick of some kind?

Those God-damned Cheery-cow Apaches hated his guts. They'd like to see him dead, Sal Juan most of all. Suppose that Sal Juan and that shrunken bag of bones, *Skin-ya,* had rigged all this between them. Mesmerized him into thinking he was seeing something that wasn't? Planted a fear in his mind that might trip him to his doom.

That was it, sure. A lot of God-damned hocus-pocus.

The only trouble was, he didn't believe a dust mote of his own rationale....

The house loomed ahead, a flat black oblong against a cobalt sky. Creed's steps slowed. But he had to go in. Had to face whatever was there.

He opened the front door and left it open to the stream of moonlight as he crossed the room to a lowboy where a lamp reposed. He lifted the lamp's chimney, struck a match, shook it free of a sulfurous flare of sparks, and touched it to the wick.

Suddenly the door slammed shut.

Creed started and wheeled around. The tiny spoon of lamp-flame faintly picked out familiar objects of the room. Nothing else.

No wind at all. No draft. Why should the door...?

Now the lamp-flame was guttering in the sudden stir of air from the slamming door. Heart pounding wildly, Creed cupped his hands around it, cherishing the flame. God, if it went out! If he were isolated in total darkness....

The flame held and became steady again. Carefully he replaced the chimney and turned the lamp up high. Carrying it with him, treading with a slow care, he walked from the front parlor to the back one, where the staircase was.

Creed halted at the bottom step. The lower rises were picked out in a waver of shadow and saffron light, but the top of the stairs was lost in darkness. He sleeved away the cold sweat from his forehead. He started up the stairs, making his feet move independently of the congealed fear in his brain and belly.

It is up there. God! It's waiting. I can run from it, but it will still be with me. It will always be with me. I must face it out now, or.... Go on, Goddammit! Don't think about it. Just go on....

He reached the top of the stairs and advanced into the hallway. It smelled musty and unused, like an exhalation from the tomb. He came to the door of his room, a central one whose one window faced south, along with a door that opened on the still-intact south balcony.

Creed opened the door, peered cautiously about, and went in. He set his lamp on the commode and crossed the room to the armoire. Squatting down, he slid back a small panel at its base, exposing the hidden compartment. He took the journal from his pocket, placed it in the compartment and pushed the panel back into place.

"Ja-cob...."

The murmurous whisper froze him where he was, crouched on his heels. Creed did not want to look around. The blood thudded sickly in his temples. And then he looked.

She stood in the open doorway, appearing as real as if she were still flesh. Creamy flesh. Tinted as if the rich blood of life still pulsed beneath it.

The smile formed; the arm raised and beckoned.

Creed let out a mad roar. He surged at her, his hands lifting to grasp and crush. He plunged through her as if she were smoke. Momentum carried him on through the doorway. He crashed against the closed door opposite him.

The door of Sarah's room.

He swung around, wildly. His own doorway was empty now, framed by lamplight and nothing else.

"Ja-cob...."

Where? He froze, straining his ears. No other sound. But he was sure. The cajoling whisper had come from behind Sarah's door.

He wrenched it open and flung it wide, the door banging against the inside wall.

She was in front of him. Smiling still, the arm beckoning. Moonlight from her room's one window, as well as lamplight from his back, picked her out, but more faintly now.

She was transparent. *Again.*

With a howl he dived at her, reaching and closing his hands, seizing hold of nothing at all. And when he wheeled around again, she was gone.

"Jacob. To me. Come."

Sarah's voice. Unmistakably hers. Not ghostly at all. Just words spoken in a calm, quiet tone. Yet firm and commanding.

She was standing close to the window and both her arms were outstretched now. She was not smiling any more. Only positive.

"God damn you to all hell!"

Creed shrieked the words as he dived at her. His hurtling weight smashed against a solid wall. Almost solid.

It yawned open abruptly with a snarl of ripped-out nails, a sound of splintering wood. Jacob Creed plunged on and out into a cool rush of night air, his arms flung wide to embrace nothing.

Falling, he had one last impression: the trailing sound of a woman's laughter....

↔

Lieutenant Mayberly closed the journal and laid it on the commandant's desk beside the photograph of Sarah Creed.

"What happened after he made that last entry, we can only surmise. When he didn't show up at his store the next day, Corporal Higgins of L Troop...

who'd gone to the sutler's to purchase some tobacco...was curious enough to stroll over to the agency house and investigate. What had happened was plain. The door that opened on the north balcony...the door that had been nailed shut after Creed had ordered the balcony torn off....was split nearly in half, dangling from a single hinge. Creed's body was on the ground beneath. Obviously he had smashed through the door...."

"And died of course," Major Casement said irritably, "as that old shaman had divined he would? Eh?"

Mayberly gave a noncommittal nod. "Incidentally, sir, he did. Yes. Of a broken neck."

"Balderdash," the major said wearily. He nudged the journal with his thumb. "For God's sake, Mr. Mayberly, I don't doubt that you've investigated this matter with your usual thoroughness and efficiency. But how in hell can I assemble a report to the department that will make any sense of it all?"

"Sir, I'd simply relate what we've been able to tell for certain. Higgins immediately reported Creed's demise to Colonel Dandridge. I've checked Higgins's story. He says the colonel seemed apathetic, almost indifferent, to the news, and then dismissed Higgins with a disconcerting abruptness. Five minutes later, Sergeant-Major Carmody, at his desk in the outer office, heard a shot. He hurried to the inner office and found the colonel slumped across his desk, his service revolver clenched in his fist. He had shot himself through the head. No doubt because revelation of his complicity with Creed in cheating on the Apache beef issue would have wiped out the last remnant of his career."

"All that is clear enough, Mr. Mayberly," snapped Casement. "What concerns me is this blather about spectral apparitions. I don't see any way to avoid alluding to it if I'm to submit a complete and truthful report on the business." He scowled, tugging at his underlip. "Suppose I can hazard a speculation that Creed was suffering from a massive delusion brought on by feelings of personal guilt or whatever...?"

Mayberly cleared his throat. *As he always did when he found something difficult to communicate,* Casement thought irritably. "Out with it, Mister!" he barked.

"Perhaps you'd better see for yourself, sir." The subaltern cleared his throat again. He nodded at the journal. "It's in there. The last entry."

Casement's patience was worn to an edge. "You said you'd read off the last entry in that damned thing. What...?"

"*Creed's* last entry, sir. But there's another one after it. See for yourself."

Major Casement picked up the journal and flipped impatiently through its pages to the end of Creed's almost indecipherable writing.

He stared at the place.

The short hairs at the back of his neck prickled; his throat felt stuffed with phlegm. He managed to clear it with a couple of mild "harrumphs," trying not to let Mayberly know that he was doing so.

"'Hem. Isn't it possible, Mister, that somebody...for whatever odd reason...added this final entry later on?"

"I doubt it, sir. I found the journal in the base of Creed's armoire, his own place of concealment. The handwriting, as you can see, is crisp and clear, in a backhand script. Quite different from Creed's broad, forward slanting scrawl. Too, as nearly as I can tell, it's a woman's hand."

"Preposterous," the major said in a fading voice.

"One more item, sir...." Mayberly reached in his dispatch case, pulled out a piece of paper and slid it across the desk. "I found this in Mrs. Creed's room. It is a letter she had begun to write to a sister in Boston, but never got to finish."

Mayberly paused, wrinkling his brow. "Don't ask me to explain *this* one, sir. I'm no handwriting expert. But I needn't be one, nor do you, to perceive that the hand which indited this letter and the one which made that final entry in Creed's journal are absolutely identical."

Major Casement stared at the letter. Then his gaze moved with a slow, dreading reluctance, back to the journal spread open on his desk. To its brief and final entry:

Poor Jacob. His fancies overcame him. He fancied that he saw a ghost. Sic semper tyrannis.

CYNTHIA HASELOFF

CYNTHIA HASELOFF (1945–) was born in Vernon (once known as Eagle Flat), Texas. The family story has it that Cynthia's father, stationed in Kansas during part of the Second World War, went AWOL in order to return his pregnant wife to Texas prior to Cynthia's birth rather than allow a Haseloff to be born outside the Lone Star State. Notwithstanding this bit of derring-do, the family did soon move to Cave Springs, Arkansas, where they became Texans in exile. Cynthia was named after Cynthia Ann Parker, perhaps the best-known of the white female Indian captives on the frontier.

As a child, Cynthia suffered from asthma and was often confined to her bed. In the Afterword to her first published novel, RIDE SOUTH! (Bantam, 1980), she recalled that she "really soaked up" the stories and legends about the family and life in Texas that her mother told her. "I even told myself stories at night to put myself to sleep. And I remember vividly the night we all sat up as my father read the whole of a newly arrived biography of Sam Houston." The imaginary West in the form of Western films was a staple of family outings and so became part of the young Haseloff's nurture.

Haseloff was graduated from the University of Arkansas at Fayetteville with a Bachelor's degree in Art and Art History in 1965 and went on there to earn a Master's degree in Rhetoric-Public Address. It was Haseloff's early ambition to be a filmmaker and so she went on to earn a Doctorate degree in Film and Television in 1971 at the University of Missouri at Columbia. Her first novel actually began as a screenplay. Haseloff had made a study of Dorothy M. Johnson's style and went so far as to copy Johnson's captivity story, "Lost Sister" (1956), in long-hand to study her narrative technique. Haseloff decided to turn her screenplay into a novel which she completed in 1974. It was rejected by a number of publishers over the next six years until Haseloff met a vice-president from Bantam Books at a seminar and the executive promised to have someone at Bantam read the manuscript. Bantam accepted the book. However, the publisher felt her gender would have to be disguised and so in that long tradition beginning with B.M. Bower through J.R. Williams, P.A. Bechko, L.J. Washburn, despite having no middle name or initial, she became C.H. Haseloff, according to the back cover blurb "one of today's most striking new Western writers."

A KILLER COMES TO SHILOH (Bantam, 1981), MARAUDER (Bantam, 1982), BADMAN (Bantam, 1983), and DEAD WOMAN'S TRAIL (Bantam, 1984) followed in rather short order. MARAUDER has more recently appeared in a new hard cover edition in the Gunsmoke series from Chivers Press. "If RIDE SOUTH! is a traditional Western novel, Haseloff's approach introduced a female perspective rarely encountered previously in Western fiction by making her protagonist a mother searching for her children out of a sense of love and responsibility rather than out of a desire for revenge or fame," Vicki Piekarski observed in her entry for Haseloff in the second edition of the ENCYCLOPEDIA OF FRONTIER AND WESTERN FICTION (to appear in 1997). "Leah's simple courage and determination to find them, when most others believe them dead, is adeptly juxtaposed against the revenge-seekers, opportunists, and legend-makers who are only interested in self-aggrandizement or self-promotion. In this and subsequent novels, many of Haseloff's characters embody old-fashioned values — honor, duty, courage, and family — that prevailed on the frontier and were instilled in the young Haseloff by her own 'heroes,' her mother and grandmother. Her stories, in a sense, dramatize how these values stand up when challenged by the adversities and cruelties of frontier existence."

The one thing that emerges quite clearly when reading any Haseloff novel is her admiration for the people who lived through the frontier experience. "A love of the Western might just be an inherent tendency, a predisposition like left-handedness or color-blindness," she once remarked. "I guess my writing Westerns can ultimately be attributed to my slow and staggering acceptance of myself, to accepting as worthwhile the things I loved most and had been educated out of. I love the West, perhaps not all of its reality, for much of it was cruel and hard, but certainly its dream and hope and the damned courage of people trying to live within its demands."

For almost a decade after the appearance of DEAD WOMAN'S TRAIL, Haseloff at the behest of Irwyn Applebaum at Bantam tried writing a major historical novel based on the life of Cynthia Ann Parker. In the meantime, her books vanished from the racks and Bantam Books was acquired by a German cartel whose management had little inclination to exploit back list or encourage publication of new Western fiction outside of pulp Western series such as "Rivers West." Starting over at the beginning, something she had done successfully with the first incarnation of RIDE SOUTH!, Haseloff reworked her story into the kind of traditional book-length novel with which she is most comfortable. In this form her sixth Western story, THE CHAINS OF SARAI STONE (Five Star Westerns, 1996), was scheduled for publication and she intends in future novels to carry forward her charting of life on the frontier during the last years on the plains of the wild Comanches.

I do not know if it is something about Arkansas and its close connection in the previous century with the Nations — Judge Parker's court is featured prominently in BAD MAN — or the undying emotional impact of the War between the States — MARAUDER is set in this period — but Arkansas writers such as Douglas C. Jones and Cynthia Haseloff have created new, vivid, and captivating narratives using these periods and themes as well as the time when the Comanches roamed free. In a way they have taken all of us back to reflect poignantly on the unresolved and tragic issues which were at stake in those times and have charted the devastating impact these upheavals from the past have had on the American consciousness *and* our collective unconscious ever since. This same vitality can be witnessed as well in other regions, in the Western stories of Gary D. Svee, Frank Roderus, Stephen Overholser, Tim Champlin, as well as in the works of older masters such as Lauran Paine and Dan Cushman.

It has been a long journey, and a fruitful one, from the earliest intimations and whispers to the point we have reached with this final story. It is taking nothing from Cynthia Haseloff's power and magic as a storyteller to say that without Zane Grey, and Max Brand, and Willa Cather, and Walter Van Tilburg Clark, and Dorothy M. Johnson, and Les Savage, Jr., and T.V. Olsen, and so many more, we could not have attained this plateau where it is become self-evident to all readers that the Western story grew out of the very land which first gave it birth and could not exist without that land, both the physical land where a change in the weather can mean the difference between life and death and that spiritual terrain so unique, the land *just before* the land beyond the sun.

REDEMPTION AT DRY CREEK
1994

"I had a son once," the ragged Preacher said. "But his mother drowned him like a blind pup. Maybe it was because it was my child; or maybe it was because food was already scarce and bad winter was yet comin' on. I do not know why she killed him. I stood there on the river bank and watched her. And I do not know why I did not stop her. Maybe I figured it were hers more than mine; or maybe I figured I done her enough hurt without makin' her drag my child through the rest of her life; or maybe I was just hard as nails and did not give a damn for her or the boy or anything else.

"But I cannot get shut of them...that woman holding that kicking, screaming, living baby under the cold water 'til it was quiet and limp. When she threw him out of the water by his heels like a big fish, I kneeled down and looked at him lying there on the white river rocks, blue as if he'd been painted. A beast has more feeling than I had for that baby.

"I have often looked at the faces of the men I have killed, and I have known I killed them before they could kill me, and that was enough. But I do not know why I let her drown the boy."

"I wasn't going to drown my son," the woman said.

"Reckon not," the Preacher said, sitting beside her. "Ain't no water in a dry creek. You'll have to figure another way."

"I ain't thinkin' on killin' my boy," the woman said. "That ain't my thought."

"Death be here, woman," the Preacher said. "You have some thought a-drawin' it here."

The woman dropped her head and said nothing. The ragged man beside her was right. Her thoughts had been that morning on death, but not to drown the boy. She had seen that morning that there was nothing but the day's worth of food left. After they ate it, there was nothing — nothing but to die.

She had come to the shade tree looking out on the dry creek and sat with the boy, Thom, in her arms. *"Why back in the old country,"* she had said to Thom, *"I done some foolish things, but it were a forgiving land."* She looked at the wet spot near the bank, the last small run of the water still beneath the earth. Her mind went back then to the old country, and she remembered.

"I woke up determined it were Marmie's birthday. I woke up determined to

have her a birthday. I had heard of a birthday lately, just a dab of a article in a yella newspaper about a queen over in England or somewheres a-havin' a birthday, and ever' body a-honoring her and givin' her presents for her birthday. They just picked a day to have her a birthday which weren't her real birthday. Marmie did not know when she was born, though she had all us children wrote down in the Book. And so she never had no party. So I got the idea from that paper you could pick, pick any day you wished, and have a public birthday like that queen.

"There we were alone for the men, and many days from the settlement. And I was determined to give Marmie a birthday. There was Marmie with the ten of us younguns and Selah's nine and five more children with Mary. Marmie made bread every morning in a hollered out log big enough for you to lay down in and stretch out. I's young and feelin' big to do. I figured I'd put the little 'uns to gathering, and I would make Marmie a blackberry cobbler for her birthday. The berries was thick, big as your thumb. Oh, my, Thom, they was pretty and good, too.

"I made up my cobbler and set it on the table, set it in front of Marmie with a bunch of flowers we picked. That was the first time she ever sat first I could remember. And she said she was proud...mighty proud...to have a girl could make up a cobbler so nice and wait on her Ma. The little 'uns couldn't think nothin' 'cept eating so she cut it and took the first bite like I said to be special for her birthday. She chewed that cobbler, and the piece got bigger in her mouth. No happy light came in her eyes. She looked at me so sad. 'Annie, it's salt,' she said.

"I had grabbed up a bag of salt and used it fer sugar. All the pickin' lost. All the wood gatherin' lost. All the rollin' out and mixin' up lost. All the butter and cream and flour lost, too. And the gift plum ruined for one misthought, and Marmie disappointed in me on top. I started to cry, and all the little ones began to cry.

"And, suddenly, Marmie started in a-laughin', laughin' like music, and she hugged me up, and held me, and laughed. 'Why child,' she said, 'you give me the best gift...to be needed. *Old cobbler ain't nothin'.' And she began to throw that cobbler around at the children. They threw it back and at each other. We all had blackberry stains and seeds all over us so we had to go to the spring and wash.*

"Afterwards we all got busy and got more berries, and Marmie made a bigger cobbler, and we ate 'til we hurt. It were a fat country, Thom, the old country, full of green trees and water and berries enough for two big cobblers. Amen."

She had rocked the boy in her arms past noon. He did not fret but lay against her with his black hair stuck to his small round head. She had sometimes fanned the hem of his coarse cotton shirt over his bare legs. The wind had borne against them, stirring the dry leaves the dying tree dropped. Sometimes the sand had cut them when the wind rose hard. The woman had covered the child with her body and had turned her back away from the dry creek and looked at the house.

The house was a ramshackled kind of thing, abandoned before they came. The wind drove against the adobe bricks, dissolving them back into their native earth, carrying them over the land. The boy's father had thrown a *gringo* lean-to of logs against the mud walls. He had dug a root cellar beneath it and had planted a peach orchard in the sandy land. There had been water then.

But the man had seen the dry coming the second year. One morning when the woman got up, he was gone and the horses and the steers. He had taken the gun, too. That had been months back. Annie thought he'd return. By the time she understood he would not, she had a little garden of potatoes and beans and corn besides the peach trees. There was still food in the cellar. She had trapped rabbits that came to the garden, and once she had cut the throat of a thirst-starved deer who had come to the spring. She had dressed it, and there was meat for her and the boy. She had figured to stay 'til she figured out what to do.

The sun took the corn. The peaches never made but knobs. And the potato vines began to die. She had carried water to the vines in the morning and in the evening, and the ground drank the water so that there was barely a shadow where the water had touched it.

The sun had burned hotter and higher 'til the beans rattled in their shells. Annie made a shade over the potato vines where she could. She carried water morning and evening. This was not a country for potatoes, but she knew potatoes, and she strove for them to live because a person could live on potatoes.

The creek began to dry, and the spring became a trickle, and, then, a few drops. There was some to drink, but none for the garden. They ate the dying fish and the beans and the stored food, not all at once, but little by little, the woman eating less and less to feed the child.

Finally, Annie decided to walk with the boy to the town. They started out, climbed the hill behind the house like the man had done. And there they sat down. Annie did not know the way from there. It was a long way, a hundred miles maybe, and they did not know anyone in the town or have any money for food.

She and the boy went back to the house. They gathered berries and any nuts that they had missed along the creek. Coming home with a little firewood and a rabbit, they saw the Indians digging away at the spring, filling their dry gourds by drops, wetting their horses' muzzles. The woman and the boy slept in the brush that night.

When the Indians rode away, they went home and found that the Indians had taken everything that was left, even the coffee and sugar that Annie had hoarded for the company that might one day come. Annie laughed as tears ran down her dry brown cheeks. *"Sure enough,"* she had said, *"her company had been served."*

Annie looked at the ragged man beside her. Beyond him a raven settled onto the creek bank and drank from the spring. There were other ravens walking about in the dry creek. Annie's eyes ran over the evil black birds and the man. He was tall and thin. Coarse, unkempt hair stuck out over his head. A sparse beard covered his sunken cheeks. The coat he wore was black and frayed at collar and cuffs. His elbows poked out at holes in his sleeves. The white shirt beneath his vest was spotted and stained with the red clay of this land. She remembered he'd spoken of killing his child, of killing men, of her thoughts drawing Death to the place.

"Are you Death?" Annie asked.

"Not Death, woman," the Preacher said. "Death is gorged on this land, but I am hungry. Fix me something to eat while I sit here in the shade a spell and think."

"Did them birds come with you?" she asked.

"They did," he said. "They are my friends, and we cannot eat them. They have preserved my life in this lonely land by bringing me carrion morning and evening. I was well until the spring I lived by played out, and the Lord directed me to this place."

"The Lord didn't direct you here if he cared about you," the woman said.

"Hush, woman," the man said. "Get my supper...just a small corn cake."

"There ain't no corn, mister. Not a wormy kernel. We ate them. The only thing left is a couple of dried up potatoes. The boy and I are going to eat them. Then...," Annie looked around at the empty land, no longer even yellow beneath the drought, but sucked dry of all color, "then, I figured, we'd just wait to die."

"I'll take one of the potatoes," the Preacher said.

"I do not think you will," Annie said. "I do not know you, mister. I do not know where you come from or how you got here. And from what I've seen and heard, I do not like you. You have no call on me?"

"I'm the Preacher," the man said.

Annie laughed. "There it is, then, just like Pa said. Where there's a mouthful of food, there'll be a preacher. You're bound to be a Methodist."

"Shut up," the Preacher said. "Make the supper, woman. You'll have your pay."

"Oh, no," Annie said. "I've had my pay of all the preachers they ever was. Preachers pay with worthless script. Preacher prayed for my ma, and she died. Prayed for my little brothers and sisters, and they was took off, too. Prayed my pa would come home. He never did. Finally, when I was left to make my way the best I could, a preacher run me out of town. I been run out of lots of places since, but you ain't runnin' me out of this one. This is where me and my boy and you will die, Preacher."

The Preacher studied the woman's face. His eyes softened. "Fix the supper, woman," he said quietly, looking into her pale eyes. Annie's jaw set and her eyes flared hot hate at the Preacher. "Fix all there is. We'll eat it together."

Annie carried the listless boy back to the house and laid him on the quilt-tossed bed where she could see him if he moved. "Damn," she said reaching into the bin where the potatoes were stored. "Just damn. What are you doin', Annie, feedin' a preacher your last morsel? Pa's rollin' in his grave if he's dead."

Annie found a potato and reached back for the other. Her fingers closed over it. Withdrawing her hand she brushed against another. "Um," she said, "well, there's one apiece. Ain't that nice. Pa's spinnin' for sure me even thinkin' that."

Annie built her little fire thoughtfully, carefully placing each small branch, building the coals on the bed of ashes. "But Ma ain't. Reckon she'd be pleased there was somethin' for the Preacher. There, Preacher, this potato and the good it brings you is for her sake. Even though she was deceived, she believed. It's for her sake not your own I'm givin' it to you. So eat hearty of the miserable thing. It is all you will get from me."

The Preacher came in when the meal was prepared. His face was washed. His hair lay in place. He blessed Annie's food, thanked the Lord for her generosity, knowing Annie did not want to be generous.

"Reckon your God knows that's a lie if he's God," Annie said. "I ain't generous to you, Preacher. I just had a memory of someone. I gave you what you got for *her* sake."

"Yes," the Preacher said. "And why did she give?"

"'Cause she was an ignorant woman who believed in things that can't be."

"Maybe such things can be, *must* be." There was a pause. "I'll take the loft for my sleeping quarters," the Preacher said then. And he climbed the rawhide-tied ladder to the small room.

Annie watched him with her mouth set. "Sure," she said, "you just take whatever you want. Make yourself to home."

"I won't wake you when I get up," the Preacher said. "I'll be out early...visiting with the Lord."

"You just make sure you don't visit my bed on the way out, or I'll kill you dead," said Annie.

The Preacher leaned over and looked down into the lower room. "What is your name, woman?" he asked.

"Annie," she said. "Annie Caudle. My boy is Thom."

The Preacher disappeared. Still sitting at the table, Annie heard him moving things about in the little room. "Well, Thom," she said to the child on the bed, "we got us a boarder."

The next morning, when Annie crawled out of her tumbled bed still clad in her dirty dress, she saw the Preacher sitting beneath the dying tree beside the dry creek. He had taken a chair with him and sat comfortably, one long leg crossed over the other, reading his Bible, looking occasionally toward Heaven. The ravens were perched in the tree above him.

Annie and Thom walked down to get the water that had collected overnight in a pitcher left at the spring. The Preacher never looked at them. His lips moved, but Annie could not hear any words. The boy looked at him while Annie lifted the pitcher and set an empty one in its place.

"Shoot," Annie said, catching the boy's stare, "pray 'til you turn purple." She gave the boy a little water. "Rinse it around your mouth good before you swallow." She watched the boy. He dutifully rinsed before he drank each mouthful she gave him. At last, he looked up into Annie's face. Her eyes softened. "You're a good boy, Thom." She gently touched his head. They walked back to the house with the pitcher.

In the evening the Preacher came in with an armful of small branches. "I gathered these on my walk," he said. "They'll do for the supper fire."

"There ain't nothing to cook," Annie said.

"Look again, Annie," the Preacher said. The woman's lower lip thrust out. "Do it, please, Annie, for Thom's sake."

"You are the cruelest person I ever met, teasing me with the boy's life."

Still looking at the Preacher, Annie reached into the dark dry recesses of the bin. "There...!" she started to say in proof of the emptiness of the bin. But she stopped. "Well, I'll swear." She bent lower, peering into the darkness. When she straightened, she held four good-sized potatoes in her dirty hands.

Annie made their supper on the hearth while the man rocked Thom. After they ate, the Preacher again climbed to the loft. Annie climbed back into the unmade bed and wondered how she had missed the four potatoes until she fell asleep.

The next morning the Preacher was at the dying tree beside the dry creek when Annie and Thom went to get the water. The ravens were gone.

"Where are them old black birds?" Annie asked.

"They are not needed now," the Preacher said. "The Lord has released them."

"The Lord," Annie said. "Most likely they know the water's about gone here. If I's a bird, I'd be gone too. They'll probably come back to pick our bones, though."

"Annie, Annie, what has made you so sour?" asked the Preacher with a smile.

"Preachers," Annie said, and went back to the house.

Each morning the Preacher was at the dying tree beside the dry creek when Annie and Thom went to get the water. Whenever she looked out, he sat with the Book in his lap, tipped back in the chair against the tree. He read and prayed. Each evening he brought a little wood for a fire. And each evening Annie found a few potatoes she'd missed. As the woman and the child began to recover their strength, the strangeness of the day's routine began to gnaw at Annie's mind.

"I know there ain't that many potatoes I missed," Annie said to the boy. She sat in the midst of the tumbled bed which she had long before ceased to make, falling into it in exhaustion and, later, in the stupor of hunger. "I've a mind to tear out them boards and just see what's down there." Annie stood up. "I'll do that. I'll prove to my own mind that there ain't no 'taters. Then I'll talk to that Preacher."

Annie started toward the potato bin. She stopped in the middle of the dirt floor. She turned slowly toward the open door. Beyond it, the Preacher sat under the dying tree beside the dry creek.

"You'll prove it, Annie, old girl," she thought. *"Then where'll the food come from? He's a-gettin' them potatoes somewhere and puttin' 'em in the bin while we sleep. If I make a fuss, he'll have to stop. Then where'll Annie and Thom be?"* Annie was standing in the middle of the floor.

"Come on, Thom. Let's walk out to the old garden and have us a look. Maybe them 'taters did make it. Maybe all that water I carried done some good. If I find he's been diggin' my own potatoes and feedin' 'em to us a few at a time, I'll run his preacher's behind off this place."

Annie and Thom found no signs of digging in the burned-up garden.

That evening the Preacher came again with the firewood. Annie found the potatoes that could not be there, and they all ate their fill.

"Preacher," Annie said, "where do you reckon all them potatoes are comin' from? I mean I might have missed a few, but not all these that's been feedin' us these past days."

The Preacher stood up and walked toward the ladder. "The Lord, Annie," he said, looking back at her.

"The Lord?" Annie said quietly. "And why is He so generous to us, Preacher?"

"Because you have given me a place, Annie," he said.

"I don't believe the Lord puts them potatoes in that bin," Annie said.

"Why not, Annie?" asked the Preacher. "If you plant potatoes and tend potatoes and the year is right, don't you have potatoes in the garden?"

"Why sure I do," Annie said. "I worked it with my own hand."

"Your own hand had not done too well before I came, had it, Annie? But you still have confidence in what you do and what you see, what you wrench out of the earth for yourself. Suffice it for now, God's of a mind to be generous. His way is always yea and amen. His way is always deliverance."

The Preacher went up the ladder and disappeared.

Annie rested her head on the table. *"This's too complicated for me,"* she said to herself. *"Ain't nobody, including the Lord, ever been generous to Annie Caudle."* Annie lay quietly, still thinking. *"Well... Marmie was generous. Better than ever I deserved."*

The next morning when Annie and Thom returned with water to the house, Annie stood in the doorway a long time and watched the Preacher. Later she brought out the bed clothes and shook out the sand and red dust. She turned the mattresses and remade the beds. When the Preacher came with his firewood, the cabin was set in good order. Annie had on a clean apron. She prepared the potatoes, and they all ate 'til they were full.

"You reckon the Lord is so good to you 'cause you let your baby be killed and 'cause you killed all those men, Preacher?" Annie asked. "Or does He just overlook that? Is that why you pace the floor at night? Seein' all them dead faces?"

The Preacher tipped back in his chair, resting his forearm on the table, looking at Annie. "It is the nature of God to be generous, Annie." His eyes were direct and very soft in the firelight.

"Most folks would say you deserve to burn in Hell," Annie said.

"That is fair to say about most folks," the Preacher said. "We are all eager for justice. That is why I killed those men. I figured they *deserved* to die. The better way is to embrace them, consume their hate with love...reconciliation ...redemption."

"Shoot," Annie said. "Sugar candy grows on bushes. You didn't let that baby be killed for justice. You was just plain mean to the core no matter what you tell yourself or how pretty you try to make it out."

The Preacher rubbed his eyes with his thumb and ring finger. "You are right, Annie. I have been thinking on the boy. I had a deep cold place in me. I was mean to the core. I had a curiosity about how mean I could be? I think with the boy I found the limit of the blackness...there was nothing worse...though there were a lot of dead men and ruined women after that."

"And so God fergive you, and you're good all through and through?" Annie said. "God may, but *I* still think you are a sorry thing."

The Preacher smiled. "Good night, Annie."

He went to the loft.

Annie threw herself on the quilt top. "That's what I think. He's a sorry thing. Just got religion. Religion's his disguise. He'll show his spots. A leopard don't change his spots."

Annie went to sleep and dreamed of leopards and spots and the torn and bloody innocent prey they consumed....

Before daylight, she sat up straight up, fully awake. "I reckon we best get out of here 'fore he does show them spots. It just ain't safe here. We're stronger now. Maybe if we walk down the dry creek a ways, we'll get some place, find some help."

Annie got up. "Thom," she said, shaking the boy awake. "There's a piece of moon left. We're going to walk down the dry creek to find us a town where we can live and be safe. Get up, son. There's some potatoes left from supper and water in the jug. Come on, now."

Annie closed the door softly as she and Thom left the shack. She did not hear the Preacher's shout. "Hallelujah! The drought is broken. The rains have started up country. We'll see the manifestation today."

Awake then with his revelation, the Preacher came eagerly down the ladder on his way to the dying tree beside the dry creek. The Preacher passed the beds. The forms of the woman and the child were curled deep in the covers. He smiled. The air was already colder, he thought. He opened the door and stood smelling the light fragrance of distant moisture. The first sparse drops hit the earth kicking up dust, bouncing off the hardness of this land. "Get up, Annie! Get up, young Thom!" he said. "Come, see gentle forgiveness."

He turned into the room. Neither form stirred. He went to Annie's bed and shook her. The piled covers dissolved beneath his hand. "Dear God," the Preacher said.

He ran from the house toward the tree and the creek. Annie's footstep had nearly filled beside the spring. The pitcher lay on its side. Further downstream, he found another track near a small pool in the middle of the dry creek.

The Preacher began to run.

"Annie!" he shouted. "Annie, the rain's up country. Annie, *flood!*"

Even as he ran the noise of the wall of water came to him. The water wall pushed past him as he threw himself onto the bank. He ran along the edge trying to catch the water, losing the race. "Annie," he shouted, but the sound of the water absorbed his words.

Still the Preacher ran. He ran and, at last, he saw a small bit of color — Annie's shawl tangled in a tree. The dry creek tumbled with water and debris from above the homestead. Creek banks of dry sand had collapsed trees weakened by the drought into the boiling waters. The Preacher searched the tumult for the woman and child. "Annie," he shouted. "Annie!"

He reached down to get the shawl and found the woman. The Preacher caught Annie by her shoulders and pulled her from the flood onto the bank. He dragged her away from the edge.

"Thom," she said. "Thom."

The Preacher looked up and began to search the shore for the boy. He ran along the bank looking at the debris, cutting his face and arms on the limbs of the trees that still clung to the high banks. He stopped suddenly. The child was jammed face down in the crotch of a tree. Holding the brittle limbs, the Preacher fell into the flood, racing the raging current for the small body bobbing loose from the tree. He grabbed the boy's ankle. Then, pushing his shoulder against the tree, he lifted Thom from the fork and pulled him to his chest.

"Thom!" the woman shouted. "Preacher, do you have him?"

The Preacher handed her the boy, then used his legs to shove himself off the tree and up onto the clay bank. He rested long enough for air to enter his seared lungs.

Annie held the boy, rocking him gently. "Poor Thom," she said. "So cold."

The Preacher caught her shoulders. "He's blue. Give him to me, Annie." He pushed her gently aside and began to rub the child's arms and legs.

"His breath is gone, Preacher. He ain't breathing," she said. "You took him from me like I knew you would from the beginning!" Annie picked up a rock and struck the Preacher with her weak force on the side of the head. A small trickle of blood appeared.

The Preacher caught her hand and gripped it. "Hold with me, Annie. Hold with me. I ain't your enemy." He jerked her to him and began to pray. "Lord, have You brought further calamity upon this woman with whom I sojourn by slaying her son?"

Then, the Preacher sat over the boy, holding the woman. He seemed to be listening. "No, of course not. By God, he ain't. Get up, Annie. We've a fight to make."

The Preacher stood up. Putting the boy's body over his shoulder, he lifted the woman to her feet.

"He ain't breathing. His breath is gone," she said.

"Don't say nothing now, Annie," the Preacher said quietly. "Now ain't the time."

Inside the shack the Preacher lay the child on the bed. Annie fell beside him and caught him in her arms. "He's blue. He ain't breathing."

The Preacher closed the door. "Get away, Annie. Give me your son."

The Preacher waited.

Annie looked up into his eyes. "He's gone," she said.

The Preacher touched her lips to silence with his fingers and took the boy from her. He held the limp body with one arm as he climbed to the loft.

"Preacher," Annie said to his back, "Preacher, make him live. Oh, dear God, please listen to this man I been so hard on. If he's Your man, I'm sorry for all I said and thought again' him."

The Preacher lay the small lifeless child on the neatly made bed. He stood looking at the boy's face, then sat down beside him. He pulled the cover over the cold body. Finally, he stretched himself on top of the child and held him.

"God," he said. "I ask You this: let this child's spirit come back to him. I ain't willing to let him go."

He held the boy, rubbing his arms. Suddenly anger flashed in the Preacher's black eyes. "Death, you come out of the shadows and show your ugly self and hear me! I recognize your work. You've come again to rob, to kill, and to destroy! But you'll get no help from me this time. I won't let this child go, and you can't take him. I'm telling you that in Jesus's name."

The rain was gentle when the Preacher came down. Annie lay asleep where she had crawled in exhaustion onto the bed. He quietly made a fire and set water on to boil while she slept. He hung the boy's small shirt over a chair back and moved it toward the fire.

"Thom," he said to the boy, standing in his spare shirt with the sleeves rolled up to disclose the child's small hands, "your mother is worn out from all the hard times and the struggle. Why don't you take her a dry blanket and lie down beside her 'til she wakes up?"

The boy pushed his mother's wet hair aside from her forehead and kissed her. "Marmie," he said. "Wake up, Marmie. The Preacher's brought us home safe."

Annie opened her eyes. She caught the boy and pulled him to her. Tears ran down her cheeks as she kissed his eyes and nose and ears and cheeks and mouth.

"I figured you was diggin' up my own potatoes on the sly," Annie said to the Preacher, "and puttin' them in the bin for me to find. I knew you was foolin' me. I knew it, but I wasn't just sure how."

The Preacher smiled. "Annie, Annie. Could it be that God is good, whether a woman plants a patch of potatoes and a man digs them or it comes some other way?"

"I never thought it likely," Annie said. "Pa always said you had to wrestle everything away from the hard-assed old bustard, and then He'd short you. Looked like Pa was right to me after Marmie and the others died."

Annie looked at the boy as she held him unable to let him go. "I been wrong when I thought I was dead sure right before. Why one time I ruined a whole blueberry cobbler taking salt for sugar. It looked just right 'til we bit into it, too. I ain't saying I know what you done here, Preacher. I'm saying, thank you."

"It all begins with that, Annie," the Preacher said. "All belief begins with that...the knowledge that you have a debt to One greater than yourself."

Selected Further Reading

The two principal references sources for authors of Western and Frontier fiction are the second edition of TWENTIETH CENTURY WESTERN WRITERS (St. James Press, 1991) edited by Geoff Sadler and the ENCYCLOPEDIA OF FRONTIER AND WEST-ERN FICTION (McGraw-Hill, 1983) edited by Jon Tuska and Vicki Piekarski. The former is limited only to authors who wrote in the 20th Century and has no illustrations and generally short and not always accurate entries whereas the latter includes authors from the previous century as well as from the 20th Century. The second edition of the ENCY-CLOPEDIA OF FRONTIER AND WESTERN FICTION is currently in preparation and should appear in 1997. Most of the authors included in this second edition are examined in depth in terms of their works and their bibliographies and filmographies (where they exist) are complete, some also having short fiction bibliographies as well. Where little is known of the biography of an author whose work is nonetheless significant, mini-entries in a special section have been included discussing their work. There are also numerous articles including one of considerable length on "Pulp and Slick Western Fiction" and another on "Artists and Illustrators." Illustrations include book jacket covers, pulp magazine covers, stills from motion picture versions, and author portraits.

In the recommendations which follow, titles of novels are to be found under the principal name of an author followed by works under pseudonyms where these apply. Citations are to first editions. Many of these titles have been reprinted or will be reprinted and it is suggested that the interested reader consult the most recent edition of BOOKS IN PRINT. This is a list of personal recommendations. If an author has been omitted, it is simply because for whatever reason I could not cite a novel about which I did not have some reservations, or because space simply did not permit me to cite every author who has written a Western story. No ranking here. These are all good Western stories. It is wrong to ask or expect more, although a particular book might well come to mean more to us as a reader.

Edward Abbey: THE BRAVE COWBOY (Dodd, Mead, 1956), THE MONKEY
    WRENCH GANG (Lippincott, 1975).
Andy Adams: THE LOG OF A COWBOY (Houghton Mifflin, 1903).
Clifton Adams: TRAGG'S CHOICE (Doubleday, 1969), THE LAST DAYS OF WOLF
    GARNETT (Doubleday, 1970);
    as Clay Randall: SIX-GUN BOSS (Random House, 1952).

Ann Ahlswede: DAY OF THE HUNTER (Ballantine, 1960), HUNTING WOLF (Ballantine, 1960), THE SAVAGE LAND (Ballantine, 1962).

Marvin H. Albert: THE LAW AND JAKE WADE (Fawcett Gold Medal, 1957), APACHE RISING (Fawcett Gold Medal, 1957).

George C. Appell: TROUBLE AT TULLY'S RUN (Macmillan, 1958).

Elliott Arnold: BLOOD BROTHER (Duell, Sloan, 1947).

Verne Athanas: ROGUE VALLEY (Simon and Schuster, 1953).

Mary Austin: WESTERN TRAILS: A COLLECTION OF SHORT STORIES (University of Nevada Press, 1987) edited by Melody Graulich.

Todhunter Ballard: INCIDENT AT SUN MOUNTAIN (Houghton Mifflin, 1952), GOLD IN CALIFORNIA (Doubleday, 1965).

S. Omar Barker: LITTLE WORLD APART (Doubleday, 1966).

Jane Barry: A TIME IN THE SUN (Doubleday, 1962).

Rex Beach: THE SPOILERS (Harper, 1906), THE SILVER HORDE (Harper, 1909).

Frederic Bean: TOM SPOON (Walker, 1990).

P.A. Bechko: GUNMAN'S JUSTICE (Doubleday, 1974).

James Warner Bellah: REVEILLE (Fawcett Gold Medal, 1962).

Don Berry: TRASK (Viking, 1960).

Jack M. Bickham: THE WAR ON CHARITY ROSS (Doubleday, 1967), A BOAT NAMED DEATH (Doubleday, 1975).

Archie Binns: THE LAND IS BRIGHT (Scribner's, 1939).

Curtis Bishop: BY WAY OF WYOMING (Macmillan, 1946).

Tom W. Blackburn: RATON PASS (Doubleday, 1950), GOOD DAY TO DIE (McKay, 1967).

Frank Bonham: BOLD PASSAGE (Simon and Schuster, 1950), SNAKETRACK (Simon and Schuster, 1952), THE EYE OF THE HUNTER (Evans, 1989).

Allan R. Bosworth: WHEREVER THE GRASS GROWS (Doubleday, 1941).

Terrill R. Bowers: RIO GRANDE DEATH RIDE (Avalon, 1980).

W. R. Bragg: SAGEBRUSH LAWMAN (Phoenix Press, 1951).

Matt Braun: BLACK FOX (Fawcett Gold Medal, 1972).

Gwen Bristow: JUBILEE TRAIL (Thomas Y. Crowell, 1950).

Sam Brown: THE LONG SEASON (Walker, 1987).

Will C. Brown (pseud. C.S. Boyles, Jr.): THE BORDER JUMPERS (Dutton, 1955), THE NAMELESS BREED (Macmillan, 1960).

Edgar Rice Burroughs: THE WAR CHIEF (McClurg, 1927).

Frank Calkins: THE LONG RIDER'S WINTER (Doubleday, 1983).

Benjamin Capps: SAM CHANCE (Duell, Sloan, 1965); A WOMAN OF THE PEOPLE (Duell, Sloan, 1966).

Robert Ormond Case: WHITE VICTORY (Doubleday, Doran, 1943).

Tim Champlin: SUMMER OF THE SIOUX (Ballantine, 1982), COLT LIGHTNING (Ballantine, 1989).

Giff Cheshire: STARLIGHT BASIN (Random House, 1954);
  as Chad Merriman: NIGHT KILLER (Ballantine, 1960).

Walt Coburn: MAVERICKS (Century, 1929).

Don Coldsmith: TRAIL OF THE SPANISH BIT (Doubleday, 1980).

Eli Colter: THE OUTCAST OF LAZY S (Alfred H. King, 1933).

Will Levington Comfort: APACHE (Dutton, 1931).

Merle Constiner: THE FOURTH GUNMAN (Ace, 1958).

Will Cook: THE WIND RIVER KID (Fawcett Gold Medal, 1958);
  as Frank Peace: THE BRASS BRIGADE (Perma Books, 1956);
  as James Keene: SEVEN FOR VENGEANCE (Random House, 1958);
  as Wade Everett: FORT STARKE (Ballantine, 1959).

John Byrne Cooke: THE SNOWBLIND MOON (Simon and Schuster, 1984).

Dane Coolidge: HORSE-KETCHUM OF DEATH VALLEY (Dutton, 1930); THE FIGHTING DANITES (Dutton, 1934).

Barry Cord (pseud. Peter B. Germano): TRAIL BOSS FROM TEXAS (Phoenix Press, 1948).

Edwin Corle: FIG TREE JOHN (Liveright, 1935).

Jack Cummings: DEAD MAN'S MEDAL (Walker, 1984).

Eugene Cunningham: RIDING GUN (Houghton Mifflin, 1956).

John Cunningham: WARHORSE (Macmillan, 1956).

Peggy Simson Curry: SO FAR FROM SPRING (Viking, 1956).

Dan Cushman: STAY AWAY, JOE (Viking, 1953), THE SILVER MOUNTAIN (Appleton Century Crofts, 1957), VOYAGEURS OF THE MIDNIGHT SUN (Capra Press, 1995).

Don Davis (pseud. Davis Dresser): THE HANGMEN OF SLEEPY VALLEY (Morrow, 1940).

H.L. Davis: HONEY IN THE HORN (Harper, 1935), WINDS OF MORNING (Morrow, 1952).

Ivan Doig: THE McCASKILL FAMILY TRILOGY: ENGLISH CREEK (Atheneum, 1984), DANCING AT THE RASCAL FAIR (Atheneum, 1987), RIDE WITH ME, MARIAH MONTANA (Atheneum, 1990).

Harry Sinclair Drago: SMOKE OF THE .45 (Macaulay, 1923);
  as Will Ermine: PLUNDERED RANGE (Morrow, 1936);
  as Bliss Lomax: PARDNERS OF THE BADLANDS (Doubleday, Doran, 1942).

Hal Dunning: OUTLAW SHERIFF (Chelsea House, 1928).

Robert Easton: THE HAPPY MAN (Viking, 1943).

Gretel Ehrlich: HEART MOUNTAIN (Viking, 1988).

Allan Vaughan Elston: TREASURE COACH FROM DEADWOOD (Lippincott, 1962).

Louise Erdrich: LOVE MEDICINE (Holt, 1984).

Leslie Ernenwein: REBEL YELL (Dutton, 1947).

Loren D. Estleman: ACES AND EIGHTS (Doubleday, 1981).

Max Evans: THE HI LO COUNTRY (Macmillan, 1961); ROUNDERS THREE (Doubleday, 1990) [containing THE ROUNDERS (Macmillan, 1960)].

Hal G. Evarts, Sr.: TUMBLEWEEDS (Little, Brown, 1923).

Cliff Farrell: WEST WITH THE MISSOURI (Random House, 1955).

Harvey Fergusson: THE CONQUEST OF DON PEDRO (Morrow, 1954).

Vardis Fisher: CITY OF ILLUSION (Harper, 1941).

L.L. Foreman: THE RENEGADE (Dutton, 1942).

Bennett Foster: WINTER QUARTERS (Doubleday, Doran, 1942).

Kenneth Fowler: JACKAL'S GOLD (Doubleday, 1980).

Norman A. Fox: ROPE THE WIND (Dodd, Mead, 1958); THE HARD PURSUED (Dodd, Mead, 1960).

Steve Frazee: CRY COYOTE (Macmillan, 1955), BRAGG'S FANCY WOMAN (Ballantine, 1966).

Brian Garfield: VALLEY OF THE SHADOW (Doubleday, 1970).

Janice Holt Giles: THE PLUM THICKET (Houghton Mifflin, 1954), JOHNNY OSAGE (Houghton Mifflin, 1960).

Arthur Henry Gooden: GUNS ON THE HIGH MESA (Houghton Mifflin, 1943).

Ed Gorman: GUILD (Evans, 1987).

Jackson Gregory: THE SILVER STAR (Dodd, Mead, 1931), SUDDEN BILL DORN (Dodd, Mead, 1937).

Fred Grove: NO BUGLES, NO GLORY (Ballantine, 1959).

Frank Gruber: FORT STARVATION (Rinehart, 1953).

Bill Gulick: WHITE MEN, RED MEN, AND MOUNTAIN MEN (Houghton Mifflin, 1955), THEY CAME TO A VALLEY (Doubleday, 1966).

A.B. Guthrie, Jr.: THE BIG SKY (Sloane, 1947), THE WAY WEST (Sloane, 1949).

E.E. Halleran: OUTLAW TRAIL (Macrae Smith, 1949).

Donald Hamilton: SMOKY VALLEY (Dell, 1954).

C. William Harrison: BARBED WIRE KINGDOM (Jason, 1955).

Chales N. Heckelmann: TRUMPETS IN THE DAWN (Doubleday, 1958).

James B. Hendryx: THE STAMPEDERS (Doubleday, 1951).

O. Henry (pseud. William Sydney Porter): HEARTS OF THE WEST (McClure, 1907).

William Heuman: GUNHAND FROM TEXAS (Avon, 1954).

Tony Hillerman: SKINWALKERS (Harper, 1987).

Francis W. Hilton: SKYLINE RIDERS (Kinsey, 1939).

Douglas Hirt: DEVIL'S WIND (Doubleday, 1989).

Lee Hoffman: THE VALDEZ HORSES (Doubleday, 1967).

Ray Hogan: CONGER'S WOMAN (Doubleday, 1973), FORTUNA WEST, LAWMAN (Doubleday, 1983), THE WHIPSAW TRAIL (Doubleday, 1990).

L.P. Holmes: SUMMER RANGE (Doubleday, 1951);
	as Matt Stuart: DUSTY WAGONS (Lippincott, 1949).

Paul Horgan: A DISTANT TRUMPET (Farrar, Straus, 1960).

Robert J. Horton (writing as James Roberts): WHISPERING CAÑON (Chelsea House, 1925).

Emerson Hough: THE COVERED WAGON (Appleton, 1923).

John Jakes: THE BEST WESTERN STORIES OF JOHN JAKES (Ohio University Press, 1991) edited by Bill Pronzini and Martin H. Greenberg.

Will James: SMOKY THE COWHORSE (Scribner, 1926).

Douglas C. Jones: Any (*and* Every) Novel This Author Has Written!

MacKinlay Kantor: WARWHOOP: TWO SHORT NOVELS OF THE FRONTIER (Random House, 1952).

Philip Ketchum: TEXAN ON THE PROD (Popular Library, 1952).

Will C. Knott: KILLER'S CANYON (Doubleday, 1977).

Tom Lea: THE WONDERFUL COUNTRY (Little, Brown, 1952).

Wayne C. Lee: PETTICOAT WAGON TRAIN (Ace, 1978).

Alan LeMay: OLD FATHER OF WATERS (Doubleday, Doran, 1928), WINTER RANGE (Farrar and Rinehart, 1932), THE SEARCHERS (Harper, 1954), THE UN-FORGIVEN (Harper, 1957), BY DIM AND FLARING LAMPS (Harper, 1962).

Elmore Leonard: ESCAPE FROM FIVE SHADOWS (Houghton Mifflin, 1956), LAST STAND AT SABRE RIVER (Dell, 1959).

Dee Linford: MAN WITHOUT A STAR (Morrow, 1952).

Caroline Lockhart: ME SMITH (Lippincott, 1911).

Jack London: THE SON OF THE WOLF: TALES OF THE FAR NORTH (Houghton Mifflin, 1900), THE CALL OF THE WILD (Macmillan, 1903), WHITE FANG (Macmillan, 1906).

Noel M. Loomis: RIM OF THE CAPROCK (Macmillan, 1952), THE TWILIGHTERS (Macmillan, 1955), SHORT CUT TO RED RIVER (Macmillan, 1958).

Milton Lott: THE LAST HUNT (Houghton Mifflin, 1954).

Giles A. Lutz: STAGECOACH TO HELL (Doubleday, 1975).

William Colt MacDonald: POWDER SMOKE (Berkley, 1963).

Robert MacLeod: THE APPALOOSA (Fawcett Gold Medal, 1966), APACHE TEARS (Pocket Books, 1974).

Frederick Manfred: CONQUERING HORSE (McDowell Obolensky, 1959).

E.B. Mann: THE VALLEY OF WANTED MEN (Morrow, 1932).

Chuck Martin: GUNSMOKE BONANZA (Arcadia House, 1953).

John Joseph Mathews: SUNDOWN (Longmans, 1934).

Gary McCarthy: SODBUSTER (Doublday, 1988), BLOOD BROTHERS (Doubleday, 1989), GRINGO AMIGO (Doubleday, 1991).

Dudley Dean McGaughey (writing as Owen Evens): CHAINLINK (Ballatine, 1957); as Lincoln Drew: RIFLE RANCH (Perma Books, 1958).

Larry McMurtry: LONESOME DOVE (Simon and Schuster, 1985).

D'Arcy McNickle: WIND FROM AN ENEMY SKY (Harper, 1978).

N. Scott Momaday: HOUSE MADE OF DAWN (Harper, 1968).

Wright Morris: CEREMONY IN LONE TREE (Atheneum, 1960).

Honoré Willsie Morrow: THE HEART OF THE DESERT (Stokes, 1913), THE EXILE OF THE LARIAT (Stokes, 1923).

Clarence E. Mulford: CORSON OF THE J.C. (Doubleday, Page, 1927), TRAIL DUST (Doubleday, Doran, 1934).

D(wight) B(ennett) Newton: CROOKED RIVER CANYON (Doubleday, 1966), DISASTER CREEK (Doubleday, 1981);

as Ford Logan: FIRE IN THE DESERT (Ballantine, 1954).

Nelson C. Nye: NOT GRASS ALONE (Macmillan, 1961), MULE MAN (Doubleday, 1988);

as Clem Colt: QUICK TRIGGER COUNTRY (Dodd, Mead, 1955).

Frank O'Rourke: THUNDER ON THE BUCKHORN (Random House, 1949), THE LAST CHANCE (Dell, 1956), A MULE FOR THE MARQUESA (Morrow, 1964).

Stephen Overholser: A HANGING IN STILLWATER (Doubleday, 1974), FIELD OF DEATH (Doubleday, 1977).

Wayne D. Overholser: DRAW OF DRAG (Macmillan, 1950), THE VIOLENT LAND (Macmillan, 1954), CAST A LONG SHADOW (Macmillan, 1955);

as Joseph Wayne: LAND OF PROMISES (Doubleday, 1962);

as Lee Leighton: LAW MAN (Ballantine, 1953).

Lauran Paine: TRAIL OF THE SIOUX (Arcadia House, 1956), ADOBE EMPIRE (Chivers North America, 1993);

as Richard Clarke: THE HOMESTEADERS (Walker, 1986).

F.M. Parker: SKINNER (Doubleday, 1981).

Lewis B. Patten: DEATH OF A GUNFIGHTER (Doubleday, 1968), A DEATH IN INDIAN WELLS (Doubleday, 1970), THE ANGRY TOWN OF PAWNEE BLUFFS (Doubleday, 1974), DEATH RIDES A BLACK HORSE (Doubleday, 1978).

Gary Paulsen: MURPHY (Walker, 1987).

Charles Portis: TRUE GRIT (Simon and Schuster, 1968).

John Prescott: ORDEAL (Random House, 1958).

Geo. W. Proctor: WALKS WITHOUT A SOUL (Doubleday, 1990).

Bill Pronzini: STARVATION CAMP (Doubleday, 1984).

William MacLeod Raine: THE SHERIFF'S SON (Houghton Mifflin, 1918), IRONHEART (Houghton Mifflin, 1923), THE DESERT'S PRICE (Doubleday, Page, 1924), THE TRAIL OF DANGER (Houghton Mifflin, 1934).

John Reese: JESUS ON HORSEBACK (Doubleday, 1970).

Eugene Manlove Rhodes: "*Pasó por Aquí*" in ONCE IN THE SADDLE (Houghton Mifflin, 1927), THE TRUSTY KNAVES (Houghton Mifflin, 1933).

Roe Richmond: MOJAVE GUNS (Arcadia House, 1952).

Conrad Richter: EARLY AMERICANA AND OTHER STORIES (Knopf, 1936), THE SEA OF GRASS (Knopf, 1937), THE LADY (Knopf, 1957).

Frank C. Robertson: FIGHTING JACK WARBONNET (Dutton, 1939).

Lucia St. Clair Robson: RIDE THE WIND: THE STORY OF CYNTHIA ANN PARKER AND THE LAST DAYS OF THE COMANCHE (Ballantine, 1982).

Frank Roderus: THE 33 BRAND (Doubleday, 1977), FINDING NEVADA (Doubleday, 1984), THE OUTSIDER (Signet, 1988), MUSTANG WAR (Doubleday, 1991).

Marah Ellis Ryan: TOLD IN THE HILLS (Rand McNally, 1891).

Mari Sandoz: MISS MORISSA, DOCTOR OF THE GOLD TRAIL (McGraw-Hill, 1955).

Jack Schaefer: THE KEAN LAND AND OTHER STORIES (Houghton Mifflin, 1959), MONTE WALSH (Houghton Mifflin, 1963).

James Willard Schultz: RED CROW'S BROTHER (Houghton Mifflin, 1927).

Leslie Scott: BLOOD ON THE RIO GRANDE (Arcadia House, 1959).

John Shelley: GUNPOINT! (Graphic Books, 1956).

Gordon D. Shirreffs: THE UNTAMED BREED (Fawcett Gold Medal, 1981).

Luke Short (pseud. Frederick Dilley Glidden): DEAD FREIGHT FOR PIUTE (Doubleday, Doran, 1940), AND THE WIND BLOWS FREE (Macmillan, 1946), VENGEANCE VALLEY (Houghton Mifflin, 1950).

Leslie Marmon Silko: CEREMONY (Viking, 1977).

Ben Smith: TROUBLE AT BREAKDOWN (Macmillan, 1957).

Charles H. Snow: SIX-GUNS OF SANDOVAL (Macrae Smith, 1935).

Virginia Sorenson: A LITTLE LOWER THAN THE ANGELS (Knopf, 1942), MANY HEAVENS (Harcourt Brace, 1954).

Robert J. Steelman: SURGEON TO THE SIOUX (Doubleday, 1979).

Chuck Stanley: WAGON BOSS (Phoenix Press, 1950).

Wallace Stegner: THE BIG ROCK CANDY MOUNTAIN (Duell, Sloan, 1943).

Gary D. Svee: SPIRIT WOLF (Walker, 1987), SANCTUARY (Walker, 1990).

John Steinbeck: THE RED PONY (Covici, Friede, 1937).

Glendon Swarthout: THE SHOOTIST (Doubleday, 1975).

Thomas Thompson: BRAND OF A MAN (Doubleday, 1958), MOMENT OF GLORY (Doubleday, 1961).

Walker A. Tompkins: FLAMING CANYON (Macrae Smith, 1948).

Louis Trimble: CROSSFIRE (Avalon Books, 1953).

William O. Turner: PLACE OF THE TRAP (Doubleday, 1970).

W.C. Tuttle: WANDERING DOGIES (Houghton Mifflin, 1938).

William E. Vance: DEATH STALKS THE CHEYENNE TRAIL (Doubleday, 1980).

Anne Lee Waldo: SACAJAWEA (Avon, 1979).

Mildred Walker: WINTER WHEAT (Harcourt Brace, 1944).

Brad Ward (pseud: Samuel A. Peeples): FRONTIER STREET (Macmillan, 1958).

L.J. Washburn: EPITAPH (Evans, 1988).

Frank Waters: THE MAN WHO KILLED THE DEER (Farrar and Rinehart, 1942).

James Welch: WINTER IN THE BLOOD (Harper, 1974).

Jessamyn West: THE MASSACRE AT FALL CREEK (Harcourt Brace, 1975), THE COLLECTED STORIES OF JESSAMYN WEST (Harcourt Brace, 1986).

Richard S. Wheeler: WINTER GRASS (Evans, 1983), FOOL'S COACH (Evans, 1989).

Stewart Edward White: ARIZONA NIGHTS (McClure, 1907).

Harry Whittington: VENGEANCE IS THE SPUR (Abelard Schuman, 1960).

Jeanne Williams: NO ROOF BUT HEAVEN (St. Martin's Press, 1990), THE LONG-EST ROAD (St. Martin's Press, 1993).

John Williams: BUTCHER'S CROSSING (Macmillan, 1960).

Cherry Wilson: EMPTY SADDLES (Chelsea House, 1929).

G. Clifton Wisler: MY BROTHER, THE WIND (Doubleday, 1979).

Clem Yore: TRIGGER SLIM (Macaulay, 1934).

Carter Travis Young (pseud. Louis Charbonneau): WINTER OF THE COUP (Doubleday, 1972).

Gordon Young: DAYS OF '49 (Doran, 1925).